Robert Silverberg was born in New York and now lives in the San Francisco Bay area. He is one of the most respected and widely read authors of fantasy and science fiction alive today, having won four Hugo Awards and five Nebula Awards, and he has been President of the Science Fiction Writers of America. His most celebrated and popular previous novels are also in the Majipoor Cycle (*Lord Valentine's Castle*, *Valentine Pontifex*, *Majipoor Chronicles* and *The Mountains of Majipoor*).

D1440032

# ROBERT SILVERBERG

# SORCERERS OF MAJIPOOR

PAN BOOKS

First published in Great Britain 1997 by Macmillan

This edition published 1997 by Pan Books
an imprint of Macmillan Publishers Ltd
25 Eccleston Place, London SW1W 9NF
and Basingstoke

Associated companies throughout the world

ISBN 0 330 34269 X

3 5 7 9 8 6 4 2

A CIP catalogue record for this book is available from
the British Library

Phototypeset by Intype London Ltd
Printed and bound in Great Britain by
Mackays of Chatham plc, Chatham, Kent

Once again, for Ralph

Ne plus ultra
Sine qua non

. . . the hour when safety leaves the throne of kings, the hour when dynasties change.

—Lord Dunsany
The Sword of Welleran

ONE

# THE BOOK OF
# THE GAMES

# 1

There had been omens all year, a rain of blood over Ni-moya and sleek hailstones shaped like tears falling on three of the cities of Castle Mount and then a true nightmare vision, a giant four-legged black beast with fiery ruby eyes and a single spiraling horn in its forehead, swimming through the air above the port city of Alaisor at twilight. That was a beast of a sort never before seen on Majipoor, not anywhere in the land and certainly not in the sky. And now, in his virtually inaccessible bedchamber at the deepest level of the Labyrinth, the aged Pontifex Prankipin lay dying at last, surrounded by the corps of mages and wizards and thaumaturges that had been the comfort of the old man's later years.

Throughout the world it was a time of tension and apprehension. Who could tell what transformations and hazards the death of the Pontifex might bring? Things had been stable for so long: four full decades, and then some, since there had been a change of ruler on Majipoor.

As soon as the word of the Pontifex's illness had first gone forth, the lords and princes and dukes of Majipoor began to gather at the vast underground capital for the double event— the sad passing of an illustrious emperor and the joyous commencement of a new and glorious reign. Now they waited with increasing and barely concealed restlessness for the thing that everyone knew must shortly come.

But the weeks went by and still the old Pontifex clung to

life, dying by the tiniest of increments, losing ground slowly and with the most extreme reluctance. The imperial doctors had long since acknowledged the hopelessness of his case. Nor were the imperial sorcerers and mages able to make any use of their arts to save him. Indeed, they had foretold the inevitability of his death many months ago, though not to him. They waited too, as all Majipoor waited, for their prophecy to be confirmed.

Prince Korsibar, the splendid and universally admired son of the Coronal Lord Confalume, was the first of the great ones to arrive at the Pontifical capital. Korsibar had been hunting in the bleak deserts just to the south of the Labyrinth when the news came to him that the Pontifex did not have long to live. At his side was his sister, the dark-eyed and lovely Lady Thismet, and an assemblage of his usual princely hunting-companions; and then, a few days after, had come the Grand Admiral of the kingdom, Prince Gonivaul, and the Coronal's cousin Duke Oljebbin of Stoienzar, whose rank was that of High Counsellor, and not far behind them the fabulously wealthy Prince Serithorn of Samivole, who claimed descent from no less than four different Coronals of antiquity.

The vigorous, dynamic young Prince Prestimion of Muldemar—he who was generally expected to be chosen as Majipoor's new Coronal once Lord Confalume succeeded Prankipin as Pontifex—had arrived also, traveling down from his home within the Coronal's castle atop great Castle Mount, in Serithorn's party. With Prestimion were his three inseparable companions—the hulking wintry-souled Gialaurys and the deceptively exquisite Septach Melayn and slippery little Duke Svor. Other high potentates turned up before long: Dantirya Sambail, the brusque and formidable Procurator of Ni-moya, and jolly Kanteverel of Bailemoona, and the hierarch Marcatain, personal representative of the Lady of the Isle of Sleep. Then Lord Confalume himself made his appearance: the great

4

Coronal. Some said he was the greatest in Majipoor's long history. For decades he had presided in happy collaboration with the senior monarch Prankipin over a period of unparalleled worldwide prosperity.

So all was in place for the proclamation of succession. And the arrival of Lord Confalume at the Labyrinth surely meant that the end must be near for Prankipin; but the event that everyone was expecting did not come, and did not come, and went on not coming, day after day, week after week.

Of all the restless princes, it was Korsibar, the Coronal's robust and energetic son, who appeared to be taking the delay most badly. He was a man of the outdoors, famous as a huntsman: a long-limbed, broad-shouldered man whose lean hard-cheeked face was tanned almost black from a lifetime spent under the full blaze of the sun. This dreary sojourn in the immense subterranean cavern that was the Labyrinth was maddening to him.

Korsibar had just spent close to a year planning and equipping an ambitious hunting expedition through the southern arc of the continent of Alhanroel. That was something he had dreamed of for much of his life: a far-ranging enterprise that would have covered thousands of miles and allowed him to fill the trophy room that he kept for himself at Lord Confalume's Castle with a grand display of new and marvelous beasts. But after only ten days in the field he had had to abort the project and hurry here, to the somber and musty place that was the Labyrinth, that sunless, joyless, hidden realm deep beneath the skin of the planet.

Where, apparently, he would be compelled, for his father's sake and the sake of his own conspicuous station, to pace and fidget idly in that many-leveled infinity of endlessly spiraling passageways for weeks or even months. Not daring to leave, interminably awaiting the hour when the old Pontifex breathed his last breath and Lord Confalume succeeded to the imperial throne.

Meanwhile other men less nobly born were free to range the hunting-grounds far above his head to their heart's content. Korsibar was reaching the point of not being able to bear it any longer. He dreamed of the hunt; he dreamed of looking upward into the bright clear sky, and feeling cool, sweet northerly breezes against his cheek. As his idle days and nights in the Labyrinth stretched on and on, the force of the impatience within him was building toward an explosion.

"The waiting, that's the filthy worst of it," Korsibar said, looking around at the group assembled in the big onyx-roofed antechamber of the Hall of Judgment. That antechamber, three levels up from the imperial chambers themselves, had become a regular place of assembly for the visiting lordlings. "The everlasting waiting! Gods! When will he die? Let it happen, since there's no preventing it! Let it happen, and let us be done with it."

"Everything will come in the fullness of time," said Duke Oljebbin of Stoienzar in rotund and pious tones.

"How much longer must we sit here?" Korsibar rejoined angrily. "The whole world is thrown into a paralysis by this business as it is." The morning's bulletin on the state of the Pontifex's health had just been posted. No change during the night; his majesty's condition remained grave but he continued to hold his own. Korsibar pounded his balled fist into the palm of his hand. "We wait, and we wait, and we wait. And wait some more, and nothing happens. Did we all come here too soon?"

"The considered opinion of the doctors was that his majesty did not have long to live," said the elegant Septach Melayn. He was Prestimion's closest friend, a tall and slender man of foppish manner but fearsome skill with weapons. "Therefore it was only reasonable for us to come here when we did, and—"

A stupendous belch and then a mighty booming laugh erupted from the huge and heavyset Farholt, a rough uproarious man of Prince Korsibar's entourage who traced his lineage back to the Coronal Lord Guadeloom of distant ancient days. "The opinion of the doctors? The opinion of the doctors, you say? God's bones, what are doctors except false sorcerers whose spells don't work right?"

"And the spells of true sorcerers do, is that what you would claim?" asked Septach Melayn, drawling his words in his laziest, most mocking way. He eyed the massive Farholt with unconcealed distaste. "Answer me this, good friend Farholt: someone has put a rapier through the fleshy part of your arm in a tournament, let us say, and you lie bleeding on the field, watching your blood flow from you in bright wondrous spurts. Would you rather have a sorcerer run out to mutter incantations over you, or a good surgeon to stitch up your wound?"

"When has anyone ever put a rapier through my arm, or any other part of my body?" Farholt demanded, glaring sullenly.

"Ah, but you quite overlook my point, don't you, my dear friend?"

"Do you mean the point of your rapier or the point of your question?" said quick-witted little Duke Svor, that sly, mercurial man, who for a long while had been a companion to Prince Korsibar but now was reckoned among Prestimion's most cherished comrades.

There was a brief flurry of brittle laughter. But Korsibar, with a furious roll of his eyes, threw his arms upward in disgust. "An end to all this idle chatter, now and forever! Don't you see what foolishness it is to be passing our days like this? Wasting our time in this dank airless prison of a city, when we could be up above, living as we were meant to live—"

"Soon. Soon," Duke Oljebbin of Stoienzar said, raising his hand in a soothing gesture. He was older than the others by twenty years, with a thick shock of snowy hair and deep lines in his cheeks to show for those years; he spoke with the calmness of maturity. "This can't go on much longer now."

"A week? A month? A year?" Korsibar asked hotly.

"A pillow over the old man's face and it would all be done with this very morning," Farholt muttered.

That provoked laughter again, of a coarser kind this time, but also stares of amazement, most notably from Korsibar, and even a gasp or two at the big man's bluntness.

Duke Svor said, with a chilly little smile that briefly bared his small wedge-shaped front teeth, "Crude, Farholt, much too crude. A subtler thing to do, if he continues to linger, would be to suborn one of the Pontifex's own necromancers: twenty royals would buy a few quick incantations and conjurations that would send the old man finally on his way."

"What's that, Svor?" said a new and instantly recognizable voice from the vestibule, resonant and rich. "Speaking treason, are we, now?"

It was the Coronal Lord Confalume, entering the room on the arm of Prince Prestimion. The two of them looked for all the world as if they had already succeeded to their new ranks and now, with Confalume as Pontifex and Prestimion as Coronal, had been merrily reshaping the world to their own liking over breakfast. All eyes turned toward them.

"I beg your pardon, lordship," said Svor smoothly, swinging about to face the Coronal. He executed a graceful if abrupt bow and a quick flourish of the starburst gesture of respect. "It was only a foolish jest. Nor do I believe that Farholt was

8

serious a moment ago, either, when he advocated smothering the Pontifex with his own pillow."

"And were you, Farholt?" the Coronal asked the big man. His tone was light but not without menace.

Farholt was not known for the quickness of his mind; and while he was still struggling to frame his reply Korsibar said, "Nothing serious has been said in this room for weeks, father. What is serious is the endless delay in this matter. Which is greatly straining our nerves."

"And mine as well, Korsibar. We must all be patient a little longer. But perhaps a medicine for your impatience—a better one than Svor's or Farholt's—is at hand." The Coronal smiled. Easily he moved to the center of the room, taking up a position beneath a scarlet silken canopy that bore the intricately repetitive Pontifical emblem in a tracery of golden filigree and black diamonds.

Confalume was a man of no more than middle height, but sturdily built, deep-chested and thick-thighed, true father to his stalwart son. From him there emanated the serene radiance of one who has long been at home in his own grandeur. This was Lord Confalume's forty-third year as Coronal, a record matched by very few. Yet he still seemed to be in the fullness of his strength. Even now his eyes were bright and his high sweep of chestnut hair was only just starting to turn gray.

To the collar of the Coronal's soft green jersey a little astrological amulet of the sort known as a rohilla was fastened, delicate strands of blue gold wrapped in an elaborate pattern around a nugget of jade. He touched it now, the quickest of little pats and then another, as though to draw strength from it. And others in the room touched amulets of their own in response, perhaps without conscious thought. In recent years Lord Confalume, taking his cue from the ever more occult-minded Pontifex, had come to show increasing sympathy for the curious new esoteric philosophies that now were so widely embraced on all levels of Majipoori society; and the rest of the court had thoughtfully followed suit, all but a stubbornly skeptical few.

The Coronal seemed to be giving his intimate attention to everyone in the room at once as he spoke: "Prestimion has come to me this morning with a suggestion that has much merit, I think. He is aware, as are we all, of the strain that this period of enforced idleness is causing. And so Prince Prestimion proposes that instead of our waiting for his majesty's death to initiate the traditional funeral games, we set about holding the first round of competition immediately. It will be a way of passing the time."

From Farholt came a grunting sound of surprise mixed with an undertone of approbation. But the others, even Korsibar, were silent for a moment.

Then Duke Svor asked very quietly, "Would such a thing be proper, my lord?"

"On grounds of precedent?"

"On grounds of taste," said Svor.

The Coronal regarded Svor with undiminished amiability. "And are we not the world's arbiters of taste, Svor?"

There was a stirring now in the little group of Prince Korsibar's close friends and hunting companions. Mandrykarn of Stee whispered something to Count Venta of Haplior, and Venta drew Korsibar aside and spoke briefly to him. The prince appeared troubled and surprised by what Venta had to say.

Then Korsibar looked up and said abruptly, "May I speak, father?" Uneasiness was evident on his long strong-featured face, which was tightened and twisted by a heavy scowl; he tugged at the ends of his thick black mustache, he wrapped one powerful hand over the back of his neck and squeezed. "I see it in the same way as Svor: the thing seems improper.

To launch into the funeral games before the Pontifex is even in his grave—"

"I find nothing wrong with that, cousin," offered Duke Oljebbin. "So long as we save the parades and the feasting and the other such celebrations for afterward, what does it matter if we get the contests under way now? Prankipin's finished: that's undeniable, is it not? The imperial sorcerers have cast their runes and tell us the Pontifex is soon to die. His doctors predict the same thing."

"With, let us hope, more substantial evidence than the sorcerers," put in Septach Melayn, who was notorious for his scorn of magics of all sorts even in this most superstitious of ages.

Korsibar made an irritable brushing gesture in the air as though Septach Melayn were no more than a buzzing gnat. "You all know that no one is more eager than I am to end this time of grinding inaction. But—" He halted a moment, frowning deeply and letting his nostrils flare, as if finding the right words involved him in a terrible struggle. Glancing quickly as if for support toward Mandrykarn and Venta, Korsibar said at last, "I beg the great Duke Oljebbin's pardon if I offend him by disagreeing. But there are proprieties, father. There are issues of appropriate conduct here. And—yes, by the Divine, Svor is right!—issues of taste."

"You astonish me, Korsibar," Lord Confalume said. "I thought you of all people would leap at the idea. But instead—this unexpected fastidiousness of yours—"

"What, Korsibar, fastidious?" came a raucous blustery voice from the entrance to the chamber. "Yes, and water is dry, and fire is cool, and sweet is sour. Korsibar! Fastidious! Two words I'd never have thought to hear yoked in a single sentence."

It was Dantirya Sambail, the abrasive and ferocious prince who held the title of Procurator of Ni-moya. Into the ante-chamber now he strode, hard-soled boots clacking against the black marble of the floor, and instantly he was the center of all attention.

The Procurator, offering no gesture of homage to Lord Confalume, fixed his eyes steadily on those of the Coronal and said, "What is it that we are discussing, pray tell, that has brought forth this implausible linkage of opposing concepts?"

"What has happened," Lord Confalume replied, matching Dantirya Sambail's choleric loudness with his own sweetest and most pleasant tone, "is that your kinsman of Muldemar has suggested the immediate inception of the funeral games, because we are all becalmed here unhappily as Prankipin keeps his grasp on life. My son appears to oppose the idea."

"Ah," said Dantirya Sambail, in seeming fascination. And then again, after a moment: "Ah!"

The Procurator had taken up his characteristic spread-legged stance, squarely facing Lord Confalume beneath the central canopy. He was an imposingly sizable man of about fifty, who might have been the tallest in the room had his stubby legs not been so oddly disproportionate to his long, thick torso; as it was, he was second here only to Farholt in bulk, a commanding figure.

But a repellent one. Dantirya Sambail was strikingly, almost magnificently, ugly. His head was a huge glossy dome thickly furred with coarse orange hair; his skin was pale and flecked with a myriad flaming freckles; his nose was bulbous, his mouth wide and savagely downturned, his cheeks fleshy and drooping, his chin strongly jutting. Yet out of this violent and disagreeable face stared incongruously sensitive and tender violet-gray eyes, the eyes of a poet, the eyes of a lover. He was Prestimion's third cousin twice removed, on his mother's side, and by virtue of his authority over the far-off continent of Zimroel was subordinate only to the Pontifex and Coronal among the high ones of Majipoor. The Coronal was known

12

to detest him. Many people did. But he was too powerful to ignore.

"And why, I wonder, does the good Korsibar object to beginning the games?" Dantirya Sambail asked the Coronal. "I would think he'd be more eager than any man here to get them under way." A lively glint of mischief flickered suddenly across those beguilingly poetic eyes. "Can the problem be simply that the idea came from Prince Prestimion, perhaps?"

Even Lord Confalume was startled into silence by the audacity of that remark.

There had lately sprung up a certain unvoiced tension, to be sure, between Korsibar and Prestimion. Here was Korsibar on the one hand, the Coronal's only son and a man of lordly grace in his own right, respected and even beloved throughout the land, but he was barred by age-old custom from succeeding his father on the throne; and here on the other was Prestimion, far less grand by birth and much less imposing in his person, who in all probability would be the outgoing Coronal's choice as his successor. There were those who privately regretted the constitutional necessities that would block Korsibar from taking possession of the Coronal's seat when shortly it became vacant. No one spoke openly of that, though: no one. Especially not in the presence of Korsibar, and Prestimion, and Lord Confalume himself.

Prestimion, who had remained silent since his entry into the room, now said mildly, "If I may speak, my lord?"

Confalume, in what was very nearly an absent-minded way, granted permission with a wave of his left hand.

The prince was a compact, trimly built man of surprisingly small stature but extraordinary physical strength. His hair was of a golden tone but without much sheen, and he wore it cut short, an unfashionable style in these years. His eyes were of unusual keenness and intensity, light greenish-blue in color and set perhaps a shade too close together; his face was pale and narrow, his lips thin.

It was easy to overlook Prestimion in any gathering of the princes of Castle Mount because of his unprepossessing size; but what he lacked in height he made up for in agility, muscular power, innate shrewdness, and energy. In Prestimion's childhood and even in young manhood no one would have predicted any sort of distinction of rank for him; but gradually, in recent years, he had moved to a position of preeminence at the court of the Coronal. By now he was widely recognized throughout the precincts of the Castle as the Coronal-designate, though only unofficially, for it would not have been appropriate for Lord Confalume to make that choice formally known while the old Pontifex was still alive.

Coolly the prince acknowledged the Coronal's permission to speak. The undiplomatic and indeed flagrantly provocative words of his kinsman of Ni-moya did not appear to have ruffled Prestimion in any way. But then, he rarely appeared to be ruffled by anything. He gave the impression always of being governed by premeditation, a man who took no action without much thought and calculation. Even Prestimion's most impulsive moments—and there were many of them—often somehow aroused the suspicion in those who did not entirely admire him that they had been planned.

He offered a calm smile to Korsibar and another to the Procurator, and said, addressing his words to nobody in particular, "What is it, after all, that we commemorate in the games that we traditionally hold upon the death of a Pontifex? The end of a great monarch's life, yes, to be sure. But also the commencement of a new reign, the advancement of a distinguished Coronal to the even higher authority of the Pontificate, the selection of a promising prince of the realm as the world's Coronal Lord. One cycle closes, another begins. Therefore the games should have a double purpose: to welcome the new monarchs of the world to their seats, yes, but also to celebrate the life of the one who is leaving us. And so I feel that it is right and proper and natural to embark on the games while Prankipin still lives. By doing so we create a bridge between the old reign and the new one."

He ceased to speak, and the room was utterly still.

Then the quiet was broken by the sharp sound of Dantirya Sambail's loudly clapping hands.

"Bravo, cousin Muldemar! Bravo! Brilliantly argued! My vote is for the games, at once! And what does the fastidious Korsibar have to say?"

Korsibar, his dark eyes smouldering with only partly suppressed rage, glowered at the Procurator.

"I would be pleased to start the games this very afternoon, if that be the sense of the group," he said tautly. "I never voiced any objection to that. I simply raised the question of propriety. Of unseemly haste, shall we say?"

"And that question has been prettily disposed of by Prince Prestimion," said Duke Oljebbin of Stoienzar. "So be it. I move the question, my lord. I further suggest that we announce the games to the citizens of the Labyrinth not as funeral games but merely as games held in honor of our beloved Pontifex."

"Agreed," Korsibar said.

"Do I hear opposition?" Lord Confalume asked. "No. Good. So be it. Make your preparations, gentlemen, for what we will call the Pontifical Games. The ancient and traditional Pontifical Games. By the Divine, who'll know there's never been such a thing before? It's forty years and some since last a Pontifex has died, and who will remember how these matters are supposed to go, and of those who remember, who will dare speak out, eh?" The Coronal smiled broadly, letting his gaze rest on each member of the company in turn; only when he came to Dantirya Sambail did it seem as if the warmth of

15

his smile cooled somewhat. Then he made as though to leave; but, pausing at the place where the room gave way to the vestibule he looked back at his son and said, "Korsibar, attend me in my suite in ten minutes, if you please."

# 2

Reports of the Pontifex's critical condition had traveled all up and down the immensity of Majipoor, from city to city and shore to shore—from the Fifty Cities of Castle Mount throughout all of far-spreading Alhanroel, and across the Inner Sea to the Isle of Sleep from which the beloved Lady sent forth her soothing dreams, and farther west to the giant cities of the younger and wilder continent Zimroel, and downward into the torrid zone and the hot dry wastelands of the southern continent, Suvrael. *The Pontifex is dying! The Pontifex is dying!* And there was scarcely anyone, among all of Majipoor's innumerable billions of people, who did not in some way feel uneasiness over the consequences of his death. For there was hardly anyone alive who was able to remember a time when Prankipin had not occupied one or the other of Majipoor's two thrones; and who knew what would life be without him?

Indeed fear was general in the land: fear of the dismantling of hierarchies, the disruption of order, the unleashing of chaos. It was so long since a change in the government had occurred that the people had forgotten how strong the bonds of tradition can be. Anything seemed possible once the old emperor was gone; they feared the worst, some dire transformation of the world that would engulf land and sea and farthest heaven.

An abundance of sorcerers and mages stood ready on all sides to guide them in this difficult moment. The time of the

17

Pontifex Prankipin was a time when sorcery had flourished and proliferated luxuriantly on Majipoor.

No one could have expected, when the strapping young Duke Prankipin of Halanx became Coronal long ago, that ultimately he would cause the world to be inundated by a flood of wizardry and magic. The occult arts had always been a significant element in the life of Majipoor, most notably in the area of the interpretation of dreams. But until Prankipin's time it was only the lower levels of society that had embraced such arcane disciplines as lay beyond simple dream-speaking: that huge population of fishermen and weavers and gatherers of wood, of dyers and chariot-makers and potters and smiths, of sausage-sellers and barbers and slaughterers and acrobats and jugglers and boatmen and peddlers of dried sea-dragon meat, that formed the broad base of the giant planet's bustling economy.

Curious cults had always thrived among such people—strange beliefs, often savage and violent, in powers and forces beyond the comprehension of ordinary mortals. The believers in these things had their prophets and their shamans, yes, and their amulets and their talismans, and their feasts and rituals and processions; and those who dwelled in the loftier regions of Majipoori life, the merchants and manufacturers and the members of the aristocracy above them, saw no serious harm in any of that. Perhaps, they said, there might even be some value in it for the poor folk who had faith in such things. On the other hand, very few of those more prosperous people tended to dabble themselves in what they regarded as the fantasies and superstitions of the lower classes.

But the Coronal Lord Prankipin's enlightened trade policies had led Majipoor into a splendid golden age of economic expansion that brought widespread abundance of wealth at every level of society; and with increasing affluence often comes increased insecurity and fear of losing what one has attained. Such feelings frequently breed a longing for supernatural protection. The new wealth also brought an increase in self-indulgence, a hatred of boredom and a willingness, even an eagerness, to experiment with novel and remarkable things.

What had come to Majipoor also, with the access of this new prosperity, was not only greater credulity but also a certain measure of greed, dishonesty, sloth, cruelty, debauchery, a love of wild excess and luxury, and other such vices for which the big planet had not been particularly known before. These things too created changes in Majipoori society.

So a fascination with the occult spread upward in Lord Prankipin's time to the propertied classes, fostered by the multitudes of non-human Vroon and Su-Suheris folk—both of them peoples much given to the practice of the mantic and prognostic arts—who arrived on Majipoor at this time. And through the devices and cunning of these sorcerers people who were already eager for miracles were made to see not only the shape of things to come, but also a great host of wonders, gorgons and cockatrices, salamanders and winged serpents, feathered basilisks that spit hissing flame: and they were allowed to look through chasms of dark smoke and doors of white fire into universes beyond the universe, and the domains of all manner of gods and demigods and demons. Or so it seemed, to those who had faith in the evidence of what was before their eyes, though there were those skeptics that said it was all a fraud and a snare and a delusion. But the number of those sour cold-eyed onlookers grew ever fewer all the time.

Amulets and talismans were worn everywhere, and the scent of incense was ubiquitous in the land, and brisk trade was done in ointments with which to anoint doorposts and thresholds against the forces of evil. Also it became the fashion among certain of the newly rich to consult soothsayers concerning matters of business and investment, and then the more respectable of the new cults and mysteries received the approbation also of the educated and nobly born. The women of the aristocracy and soon afterward the men as well began to hire personal astrologers and seers; and ultimately Lord Prankipin himself gave his formal blessing to many of these exotic predilections by devoting more and more of his time to the company of mages, diviners, thaumaturges, and the like. His court came to have a full complement of sorcerers and wizards, whose wisdom was regularly employed in the course of governmental business.

By the time Lord Prankipin had moved on to the Labyrinth to assume the duties of Pontifex and Confalume succeeded him as Coronal, these policies were too deeply entrenched for anyone, even the new Coronal, to speak out against them. Whether the new Lord Confalume maintained the occult disciplines in their supremacy at first out of inner conviction or mere shrewd tolerance of the status quo was something that he had never revealed even to his closest advisers; but as the years passed he became as wholehearted an advocate of the wizardly philosophies as ever Prankipin had been. With Pontifex and Coronal united on this point, sorcery was a universal practice on Majipoor now.

And so, in this uncertain time, a good many practitioners of dark arts that once might have been deemed curious and strange indeed were available to offer strange and curious consolations to the millions—the billions—of frightened citizens whose souls were uneasy over what might be about to happen.


In Sisivondal, the busy mercantile center through which all the overland caravans of western Alhanroel passed on their way to the wealthy cities of Castle Mount, the Mystery of the

Beholders was the rite by which the people hoped to hold back the dread demons that might burst loose at the hour of the Pontifex's death.

No visitors came to Sisivondal for its beauty or its elegance. It was set in the midst of a bare featureless plain. One could set out from it and travel a thousand miles in any direction and see nothing but dry dusty flat lands. It was a flat dull city in the midst of a flat dull region, and its only distinction was that it was a place where a dozen major highways met.

Like the spokes of a giant wheel were the wide roads that crossed those dreary plains to intersect here, one coming in from the major port of Alaisor to the west, three running down from the north, three from the south, and no less than five connecting Sisivondal with mighty Castle Mount off in the distant east. The boulevards and avenues of Sisivondal were laid out as concentric circles that allowed easy connection from any of the incoming highways to any other. All along the streets that ran between the circular avenues were rows of flat-roofed nine-storied warehouses, each very much like its neighbor, in which goods destined for transshipment to other zones of the continent could temporarily be stored.

It was an uninteresting but necessary place, and its appearance was in keeping with its function. Located as it was in a district of Alhanroel where little rain fell except for a couple of months in the winter, Sisivondal did without the grand and lavish ornamental gardens that were a distinctive mark of nearly all the cities of Majipoor. The monotony of its broad bare streets, dry and dusty under the constant golden-green eye of the sun, was relieved here and there only by plantings of rugged undemanding shrubs and trees, usually arrayed in long regular rows along the curbsides: squat thick-trunked camaganda palms with drooping grayish-purple fronds, and somber lumma-lumma bushes that looked like boulders with leaves and grew so slowly they might just as well have been carved

21

from stone, and spiky garavedas that flowered only once every hundred years, each one sending up a single ominous black spike three times the height of a man.

No, not a pretty city. But here the cult of the Beholders had taken root, and the Beholders, when they held the Procession of their Mysteries, did indeed bring for a brief time an unfamiliar beauty to the drab streets of Sisivondal.

They came forth now, dancing and singing and chanting as they marched past the long stolid rows of identical warehouses that lined Grand Alaisor Avenue. At the head of the procession ran scores of young women in immaculate white garments who strewed the ground with the bright crimson-and-gold petals of halatinga blossoms that had been brought in at monumental expense from Castle Mount, and young men with sparkling mirrors sewn to their jerkins danced after them, sprinkling the streets with balsams and unguents. Next came the massed ranks of sturdy chanters, accompanied by the shrill cries of pipes and flutes as they bellowed over and over, "Make way for the holy things! Make way! Make way!"

Now, marching by herself, there advanced the terrifying figure of a giantess in red boots with soles a foot thick, carrying an enormous two-headed wooden staff that she gripped with both her hands and raised again and again above her head. To her huge shoulders a pair of powerful dark wings was strapped, which fluttered slowly in time to the pounding rhythms of two masked drummers who followed her at a respectful distance. Behind this group came initiates of the cult, walking six abreast, their faces hidden by loose black veils. Their heads had been shaven closely and waxed, those of men and women both, so that the tops of their skulls rose above the swirling veils like domes of polished marble.

Those in the forefront of this group bore the seven artifacts that the Beholders held to be among their most sacred possessions, things which they displayed only at occasions of the highest gravity. One held aloft an elaborately carved stone lamp of curious design, from which a fearsome roaring yellow-tipped flame spurted far into the sky; the next, a palm branch interwoven with strands of gold in the form of a coiling serpent with gaping jaws; the one beyond that, the giant image of a disembodied human hand with the middle finger bent backward in an impossible and menacing way; then a fourth with a silver urn in the shape of a woman's breast, from which he poured an inexhaustible stream of steaming, fragrant golden milk into the streets, and a fifth with a huge fan made of wood, which he swept from side to side in a manner that caused onlookers at the edge of the throng to leap back in fright. A sixth bore the effigy of a plump little pink-fleshed deity whose face had no features, and a seventh came staggering along under the weight of a monstrous male genital organ carved from a long curving slab of purple wood.

"Behold and worship!" the marchers cried.

And from the onlookers came an answering cry: "We behold! We behold!"

More dancers followed—frenzied ones, now, in a delirious, ecstatic furor, leaping crazily from one side of the street to another as though tongues of flame were bursting from the pavement all about them, and uttering brief wordless cries like the yippings of demented beasts. They moved on, giving way to a pair of grim towering Skandars who carried slung between them on a stout wooden pole the Ark of the Mysteries, said to contain the most potent and holy objects of the cult, though these would not be revealed to anyone until the final hours of the world.

And then, at last, borne on a resplendent gleaming cart of ebony inlaid with silver, came the terrifying figure of the high priest, the masked Messenger of the Mysteries. He was a slim naked man of phenomenal height whose rippling body was painted black down one side and gold down the other; he wore over his head the carved visage of a furious-looking yellow-eyed hound with fierce elongated muzzle and long narrow ears standing stiffly erect; and he held in one hand a narrow staff around which golden serpents with swollen necks and red staring eyes were entwined, and in the other a leather whip.

Screams of joy went up from those who lined the path of the procession as he went by, nodding his blessings to the multitudes at every step and occasionally flicking his whip at them. And they fell in behind him, hundreds of them, thousands, the ordinary citizens of Sisivondal, sober, hardworking citizens, now ecstatic, sobbing, laughing eerily, prancing wildly, flinging high their arms, throwing back their heads as they begged the empty vault of the sky for some sign that mercy would be forthcoming. Spittle flecked their faces. Their eyes rolled in their heads, and on some only the whites could be seen. "Spare us!" they cried. "Spare us!" But what it was from which they wanted to be spared, or from whom they expected their salvation to come, very few in that jostling throng that lined Grand Alaisor Avenue would have been able to say, or perhaps none at all.


On that same day in the wind-swept hilltop city of Sefarad on the western coast of Alhanroel a little group of mages clad in saffron-colored chasubles, surplices of bright purple silk, and yellow shoes led the way to the sharp ridge known as Lord Zalimox's Chair, overlooking the roughly tossing waters of the Inner Sea. They were five men and three women of the human kind, stately and tall, with a look of nobility and grandeur about them. Their faces were dabbed with spots of blue powder and their eyesockets were painted a brilliant scarlet, and they carried long white staffs fashioned from sea-dragon ribs carved along every inch of their length with mysterious runic figures in what was said to be the script of the Elder Gods.

A long, winding procession of the citizens of Sefarad followed after them, murmuring prayers to those unknown ancient deities. As they moved steadily forward to the sea they made the sign of the sea-dragon over and over again with their hands, fingers simulating the beating of the voluminous leathery wings, wrists curving to imitate the swooping of the mighty necks.

Many of those who followed the mages to Lord Zalimox's Chair were Liimen, the humblest folk of the town, slender rough-skinned people with dark flat faces much wider than they were high, out of which three circular eyes stared like glowing coals. These simple fishermen and farmers and street-sweepers and sausage-vendors had for many centuries looked toward the huge winged dragons of Majipoor's seas as semi-divine beings. For them the dragons occupied a station midway between the mortal people of Majipoor and the gods who once had ruled this giant planet and had unaccountably departed long ago; and they felt that those gods would one day return to take possession of what was rightfully theirs. Now, in clustering groups of fifty or a hundred, the Liimen of Sefarad hastened to the edge of the sea to beg their vanished gods to hasten their return.

But they were far from alone today. Word had gone about that a herd of sea-dragons would be coming close to shore here this day. That was startling in itself, for the dragons in their long maritime migrations were never a common sight along this coast of Alhanroel; and the notion that this visitation might be a miraculous one, that the immense beasts might somehow have the ability to establish contact with those mysterious ancient gods of which the Liimen had long babbled, had spread like fire in dry brush through every race of the city. Humans, Hjorts, Ghayrogs, and even a handful of Vroons and Su-Suheris, were also to be found in the band of pilgrims that came scrambling up the rocky road to the beach.

And shapes were visible today, far out to sea, that might have been the shapes of dragons, unless they were something else. "I see them!" one pilgrim cried to the next in surprise and delight. "A miracle! The dragons are here!" And perhaps they were. Humped gray forms like bulky barrels floating in the sea? Dark wide-spreading wings? Yes, dragons. Maybe so. Or maybe just illusions, born of the glinting and flashing of sunlight against the churning tops of the waves.

"I see them, I see them!" the pilgrims continued to cry, shouting it until their voices grew hoarse and ragged, each one spurring his neighbor on toward desperate certainty.

And at the very summit of the rock known as Lord Zalimox's Chair the mages in their saffron chasubles and surplices of bright silk lifted their staffs of smooth white bone one by one and held them toward the sea and in tones of the greatest solemnity called out words in a language that no one understood:

*"Maazmoorn . . . Seizimoor . . . Sheitoon . . . Sepp!"*

From the congregation at the water's edge resounded the answering cry:

*"Maazmoorn . . . Seizimoor . . . Sheitoon . . . Sepp!"*

And from the sea came, as ever, the rhythmic murmuring boom of the surf, saying things that the assembled worshippers were free to interpret in whatever way they wished.


In wondrous Dulorn, the shining diamond-bright city of crystalline stone that the reptilian-looking Ghayrogs had built in western Zimroel, the amusements and entertainments of the Perpetual Circus had temporarily been put aside in this troubled hour, so that the huge circular building that housed the Circus could be employed for holier matters.

All the buildings of Dulorn were airy sparkling things of fantasy, but for this one. The white mineral out of which the Ghayrogs had constructed Dulorn was a dazzling light calcite of high refractiveness. They had employed it with surpassing ingenuity in fashioning slender lofty towers of fanciful form, richly ornamented with faceted sides and flying buttresses, with leaping minarets and dizzying diagonal embrasures, everything bright as if lit by sheets of lightning in the midday sun.

But the building of the Perpetual Circus, at the eastern edge of town, was a simple and unadorned circular drum, ninety feet high and in diameter of such an amplitude that it could easily contain an audience of hundreds of thousands. Here, because the snaky-haired forked-tongued Ghayrogs slept only a few months out of the year and were voraciously eager for diversion the rest of the time, theatrical performances of all sorts were held—jugglers, acrobats, teams of clowns, trained-animal shows, prestidigitators, levitators, gobblers of live animals, anything at all that someone might deem amusing, a dozen or more acts at once on the huge stage—continuously, every hour of the day and every day of the year.

Now all that had, however, been put aside in favor of a circus of a different sort. In this city of unique and striking loveliness deformity had lately come to be looked upon as sacred, and monsters of all sorts were brought forth into the arena from every part of Majipoor so that they could be worshipped and implored to intercede with the dark powers that threatened the world.

So here, strutting about like demigods, were pygmies and giants, pinheads and human skeletons, hunchbacks and gnomes, all manner of genetic detritus, the sad prodigies of a hundred kinds of miserable unfortunate births. Every nightmare distortion was on show here, monsters of unthinkable sorts, things so bizarre that no one would ever have dared to dream them: humans, Ghayrogs, Skandars, Hjorts, no species being spared, all packed one up against another. Here were two Ghayrogs whose bodies were joined at the back from shoulder to buttock, but one inverted in regard to the other, heads and feet in opposite ways; here was a woman whose boneless arms writhed like serpents, and a man whose fiery-hued head bore a ravenous orange bird-bill that was curved like the beak of a milufta but even more savagely sharp. A man who was broader-bodied than he was tall, with arms like flimsy little flippers—a quartet of gaunt Liimen who were linked one to the next by a long ropy black umbilicus—a man with one giant eye in the center of his forehead; another with only a single leg like a pedestal proceeding from both his hips—another with feet at the ends of his arms, and hands sprouting from his ankles—All this was displayed in turn to every sector of the immense auditorium, for the entire stage floated in a pool of quicksilver and turned slowly on hidden bearings, making a complete revolution in not much more than an hour. During regular performances of the Circus, those sitting in the circular tiers that rose in sloping circles to the roof of the building had only to sit where they were, and it all would come to them.

But this was not a performance. It was a sacrament. Therefore the audience was allowed to come down out of the stands and mingle on the stage, as never was permitted ordinarily. A corps of Skandar wardens maintained order, keeping the swarming mass of worshippers filing from the seats in a single line with stinging blows of long batons, and prodding them swiftly onward from the stage once they had received the blessing for which they had come. Slowly, patiently, the members of the audience shuffled forward, knelt before this grotesque creature or that one, solemnly touched its knee or its toe or the hem of its robe, and then moved on.

In five locations only, equidistantly arranged around the

great stage to form the points of a giant star, were there any open spaces in this multitude of monstrosities and their adorers. These five open places on the stage had been left clear for the holiest beings of all, the androgynes—those who combined in themselves the attributes of both male and female, and who thus represented the unity and harmony of the cosmos, which was the commodity that everyone on Majipoor most fervently wished to preserve.

No one knew the origin of the androgynes. Some said that they were from Triggoin, that half-mythical city in the northern reaches of Alhanroel where only wizards lived. Some had heard that they came from Til-omon or Narabal or Nimoya or some other city of Zimroel, and some that they were from Natu Gorvinu in remotest Suvrael, while others claimed they were native to one of the grand cities of Castle Mount itself; but though there was no agreement over where it was they had come into the world, it was universally believed that they had been born at a single birthing to a witch-woman who had engendered them herself, entirely unaided, simply through the casting of powerful spells.

They were frail, pallid little creatures, these androgynes. But though they were no taller than children, their bodies were mature. Three had the gentle faces of women and distinct womanly bosoms, though small ones, but the well-developed genitalia of men below. The other two had the wiry, muscular upper bodies of men, with broad shoulders and flat, hard chests, but their hips were wide-flaring female ones, their buttocks and thighs were full and plump, and at the joining of their legs they showed no trace of the male organs of generation.

Naked, impassive, they displayed themselves all day long and all night too at the five points of the imaginary star that linked them on the stage, protected from the eagerly reaching arms of the gaping multitudes by circular boundary-lines of cool red sorceryflame that no one dared to cross, and by platoons of dour-faced baton-wielding Skandars as well, just in case.

The androgynes stood staring at the crowds that passed before them in a distant, uncaring way, silent and aloof, like visitors from some other plane of existence. And throughout the long hours of the day and the night, the fearful people of Dulorn filed ceaselessly by thousands and hundreds of thousands through the drum-shaped building of the Perpetual Circus, paying homage to the sacred monsters and reaching their hands out imploringly to the uncaring androgynes and crying out their prayer in staccato shrieks sharp enough to pierce the sky, and the message that they repeated was the same one going up to the heavens from the marchers in the streets of Sisivondal: "Spare us . . . Spare us . . ."

Far to the south, half a vast continent away in the humid city of Narabal on Zimroel, where winter was unknown and vegetation grew with violent abandon in the cloak of soft, dense, sultry air, the cult of flagellanti held sway. Men in white robes crisscrossed by broad yellow stripes ran through the streets in maniacal bounding leaps, brandishing swords and maces and knives. From time to time they would halt and throw their heads forward until their long hair covered their faces, and dance first on one foot and then the other while wildly rotating their necks, and bite themselves savagely on their forearms with no show of distress, as though they were unaware of pain. Then, eyes wild with glee, they slashed their own flesh with their knives, or presented their bared backs to women who rushed upon them bearing whips made of thokka vines strung with the knucklebones of blaves. Blood flowed freely in the streets, mixing with the rain of Narabal's fine, steady downpours and carried away with it in the cobblestone gutters. "Yamaghai! Yamagha!" they shouted, over and over. Nobody knew what those words meant, but they were deemed to be words of notable power, for one was immune to the pain of the knives and the whips so long as one shouted them. "Yamaghai! Yamagha! Yamaghai! Yamagha!"

It was the blood of bull-bidlaks with which they hoped to purify themselves in great glistening Ni-moya, grandest of the cities of the western continent, seven thousand miles to the east of the crystalline city of Dulorn. By hundreds they crowded into newly built underground sanctums, huddling shoulder to shoulder beneath the slitted gratings that covered these dank musty chambers and looking upward toward the mages in ornate ritual vestments and golden helmets topped with quivering crests of red feathers who stood chanting in the street above them. And the slow heavy-thighed bidlaks were led forth over the grates; and the long knives flashed; and the blood came running down in bright rivulets upon the worshippers below, who crowded forward, shoving one another roughly aside as they strived to receive it on their upturned faces and tongues, to catch it in their hands and smear it over their eyes, to drench their clothing in it. With grunting cries of ferocious joy they received the bloody sacrament and were dizzied and inflamed by it; and then they moved along, some dancing, some merely lurching, and others took their places, and new bidlaks were led into position on the grates above.

In golden Sippulgar on the sunny Stoien coast of Alhanroel on the other side of the world it was Time, the remorseless winged serpent that flies ever onward, whose face was the face of a ravening, all-devouring jakkabole, to whom the people turned as suppliants. Weeping, praying, chanting, they drew his image through the streets on a wheeled platform made of freshly tanned volevant skin stretched over a framework of bright green gabela-wood, accompanied by a thunder of kettledrums and an ear-splitting clash of cymbals and the screeching of hoarse-throated horns. And behind those privileged ones who drew the platform of the god came the other good citizens of golden Sippulgar stripped to loincloths and sandals, their sweating bodies bright with gaudy streaks of paint and their faces turned rigidly toward the sky.

In Banglecode, high up on Castle Mount, it was the fancied disappearance of the moons, and especially the Great Moon, that was the thing most deeply dreaded. Few nights went by when someone did not reach the conclusion that the light of the moons was waning, and rush wild-eyed out into the streets to howl forth his contagious terror. But there were archimages in Banglecode who specialized in the encouragement of the moons. When the people began to weep and gibber over the vanishing of the moons, these mages came forth and made a clattering with brass instruments, they blew loud blasts on trumpets, they clapped cymbals together and waved holy staffs on high. "Sing!" they cried, and the people sang, and gradually—gradually, gradually—the moons seemed to regain the brightness that they had earlier lost, and the crowds went, still weeping but grateful now for their deliverance, to their homes. And the next night it would all be the same way again.

"What a troubled time this is, this time of mysteries and wonders," said Kunigarda, the Lady of the Isle of Sleep; and the hierarch Thabin Emilda, the closest of the Lady's associates at Inner Temple, simply sighed and nodded, for they had had this conversation often enough before in recent days.

It was the task of the Lady of the Isle of Sleep to bring comfort and wisdom to the minds of sleeping millions each night, and in these times she was striving with all her formidable energies to restore peace to the world. From the ancient mechanisms installed in the great stone chambers of her isle the sweet sendings of the Lady and her many acolytes went forth, urging calm, patience, confidence. There was no reason for alarm, they told the world. Pontifexes had died before, on Majipoor. Prankipin had earned his rest. The Coronal Lord Confalume was prepared to assume his new tasks; there would be another Coronal in his place, as capable as Confalume had been; everything would go on harmoniously as it had before, and would forever, world without end.

So the Lady Kunigarda knew, and so she sought nightly to announce. But all her striving was futile, for she herself was a living reminder of the changes that were coming, and the dreams she sent produced as much anxiety as anything else, simply because she was a presence in them.

Her own term as Lady of the Isle was reaching its inevitable end as the Pontifex's life ebbed. By long tradition the mother of the Coronal, or else his closest living female relative, held the Ladyship. So it was that the mother of Lord Confalume had come to the Isle upon his accession; but Prankipin had ruled as Pontifex so long that Lord Confalume's mother had died in office, and the Ladyship had passed to Kunigarda, the Coronal's older sister. Kunigarda had held the post for twenty years, now. But soon she must give way to the Princess Therissa, mother of the new Lord Prestimion, and instruct her in the secret of the mechanisms of the Isle, and then take up residence herself on the Terrace of Shadows where the former Ladies went to live; everyone knew that; and that was one more cause for insecurity and apprehension in the world.

"One thing is sure, that peace and truth will prevail," said the Lady to the hierarch Thabin Emilda. "The old emperor will die, and the new Coronal will come, and the new Lady as well; and perhaps there will be difficulties, but in time all will be well. I believe that, Thabin Emilda, with all my soul."

"And I also, Lady," said Thabin Emilda. But once more she sighed, and turned away so that the Lady would not see the sorrow and doubt in her eyes.


So there was no contending against the tide of magic and fear. In a thousand cities furious confident mages came forth, saying, "This is the way of salvation, these are the spells that will restore the world," and the people, doleful and frightened and hungry for salvation, said, "Yes, yes, show us the way." In each city the observances were different, and yet in essence everything was the same everywhere, processions and wild dances, shrieking flutes, roaring trumpets. Omens and prodigies. A brisk trade in talismans, some of them loathsome and disgusting. Blood and wine freely flowing and often mixing. Incense; abominations; the droning chants of the masters of the Mysteries; the propitiation of demons and the adoration of gods. Flashing knives and whips whistling through the air. New strangenesses every day. Thus it was, in this feverish epoch of new beliefs, that the myriad citizens of the huge planet awaited the end of the time of Prankipin Pontifex and the Coronal Lord Confalume, and the coming of the time of Confalume Pontifex and the Coronal Lord Prestimion.

# 3

The chambers where the Coronal had his lodgings at those times when it was necessary for him to visit the capital city of the Pontificate were located on the deepest level of the Labyrinth's imperial sector, halfway around the perimeter of the city from the secluded bedroom where Pontifex Prankipin lay dying. As Prince Korsibar advanced along the winding corridor leading to his father's rooms, a tall, angular figure stepped smoothly from the shadows to his left and said, "If you would, prince, a moment's word."

Korsibar recognized the speaker as the aloof and frosty Sanibak-Thastimoon, a man of the Su-Suheris race whom he had taken into his innermost circle of courtiers: his personal magus, his caster of runes and explicator of destinies.

"The Coronal is expecting me," said Korsibar.

"I understand that, sir. A moment is all I ask."

"Well—"

"To your possible great advantage."

"A moment, then, Sanibak-Thastimoon. Only a moment. Where?"

The Su-Suheris gestured toward a darkened room within a half-ajar doorway on the other side of the corridor. Korsibar nodded and followed him. It turned out to be a storeroom of some sort, low-ceilinged and cramped and musty, cluttered with tools and cleaning implements.

"In a service closet, Sanibak-Thastimoon?"

"It is a convenient place," the Su-Suheris said. He shut the door. A dim glowlight was the only illumination. Korsibar valued Sanibak-Thastimoon's counsel, but he had never been at such near quarters with the Su-Suheris before, and he felt a quiver of discomfort verging on mistrust. Sanibak-Thastimoon's slender, two-headed figure loomed above him by some seven inches, an uncommon thing for the long-legged prince to experience. A crisp, dry aroma came from the sorcerer, as of fallen leaves burning on a hot autumn day, not an unpleasant odor but one that at this close range was oppressively intense.

The Su-Suheris folk were relative newcomers to Majipoor. Most of them had come as a result of policies established sixty years or so back, early in Prankipin's time as Coronal, that had encouraged a period of renewed migration of non-human peoples to the giant world. They were a smooth, hairless race, slim and tapering in form. From their tubular bodies rose foot-long columnar necks that divided in a forking way, each of the two branches culminating in a narrow, spindle-shaped head. Korsibar doubted that he would ever be fully comfortable with the strangeness of their appearance. But in these times it was folly not to have a reliable necromancer or two on one's staff, and it was commonplace knowledge that the Su-Suheris had a full measure of skill in the oracular arts, necromancy and divination, among other things.

"Well?" Korsibar asked.

Usually it was the left-hand head that spoke, except when the Su-Suheris was delivering prophecies. In that case he employed the cold, precise voice that emerged from the right-hand one. But this time both heads spoke at once, smoothly coordinated but in tones separated by half an octave. "Troubling news has been brought to your father's attention concerning you, sir."

"Am I in danger? And if I am, why does the news come to his attention before it reaches mine, Sanibak-Thastimoon?"

"There is no danger to you, excellence. If you take care not to arouse anxieties in your father's breast."

"Anxieties of what sort? Explain yourself," said Korsibar curtly.

"Do you recall that I cast a horoscope for you, sir, some months back, that indicated that greatness awaits you in days to come? 'You will shake the world, Prince Korsibar,' is what I told you then. You remember this?"

"Of course. Who'd forget a prophecy like that?"

"The same prediction now has been made for you by one of your father's oracles. In the very same words, which is a powerful confirmation: 'He will shake the world.' Which has left the Coronal exceedingly troubled. His lordship is contemplating his withdrawal from the active world; he would not look kindly on any shaking of it at this time.—This has come to me by trustworthy sources within your father's own circle, sir."

Korsibar sought to meet the sorcerer's gaze; but it was an infuriating business, not knowing which pair of icy emerald-hued eyes to look at. And having to look so far upward, besides. Tautly he said, "I fail to see what there might be to trouble him, in a prophecy like that. I mean him no mischief: he knows that. How could I? He is my father; he is my king. And if by my shaking the world it's meant that I'll do great things some day, then he should rejoice. I've done nothing but hunt and ride and eat and drink and gamble all my life, but now, apparently, I'm about to achieve something important, is that what your horoscope says? Well, then, three cheers for me! I'll lead a sailing expedition from one shore of the Great Sea to the other; or I'll go out into the desert and discover the lost buried treasure of the Shapeshifters; or maybe I'll—Well, who knows? Not I. Something big, whatever it is. Lord Confalume ought to be very pleased."

"What he is afraid of, I suspect, is that you will do

something rash and foolish, your excellence, that will bring much harm to the world."

"Does he?"

"So I am assured, yes."

"And does he regard me, then, as such a reckless child?"

"He places much faith in oracles."

"Well, and so do we all. 'He will shake the world.' Fine. What's there in that that needs to be interpreted so darkly? The world can be shaken in good ways as well as bad, you know. I'm no earthquake, Sanibak-Thastimoon, that will bring my father's castle tumbling down the side of the Mount, am I? Or are you hiding something from me of which even I myself am unaware?"

"I want only to warn you, sir, that his lordship is apprehensive concerning you and your intentions, and may ask you bothersome difficult questions, and that when you go before him now it would be best if you took care to give him no occasion whatsoever for suspicion."

"Suspicion of *what*?" cried Korsibar, in some vexation, now. "I *have* no intentions! I'm a simple honorable man, Sanibak-Thastimoon! My conscience is clear!"

But the Su-Suheris had nothing more to say. He shrugged, which for him was a gesture that amounted to drawing his long forked neck halfway down into his chest and hooking his six-fingered hands inward on his wrists. The four green eyes became implacably opaque; the lipless, harsh-angled mouth-slits offered no further response. So there was no use pursuing the issue.

*You will shake the world.*

What could that mean? Korsibar had never wanted to shake anything. All his life he had desired only simple straightforward things: to rove the Fifty Cities of Castle Mount in quest of this pleasure and that one, and to go forth along the remote wilderness trails in quest of the fierce beasts he loved to hunt, and to play at quoits and chariot-racing, and to spend the long nights at the Castle itself drinking and carousing with his comrades. What more could there be for him in life? He was a prince of royal blood, yes, but the irony of his lineage was that he could never be more than he already was, for no Coronal's son had ever been permitted to follow him to the Coronal's throne.

By ancient tradition the junior monarchy was an adoptive one; always had been, always would be. Lord Confalume, when he finally became Pontifex a week or three hence, would officially designate Prestimion of Muldemar as his son and heir, and Korsibar, the true flesh-and-blood son, would be relegated to some grand and airy estate high up on the Mount. There he would spend the rest of his years as he had spent the first two decades of them, living a comfortable idle existence among the other pensioned-off princes of the realm. That was his destiny. Everyone knew that. He had been aware of it himself ever since his boyhood, ever since he could understand that his father was a king. Why had Sanibak-Thastimoon chosen to trouble him now with this oracular nonsense about shaking the world? Why, for that matter, had the chilly-spirited, austere sorcerer been urging him so strongly of late to rise above his pleasant life of luxury and idleness and seek some higher fulfillment? Surely Sanibak-Thastimoon understood the impossibility of that.

*You will shake the world.* Indeed.

Impatiently Korsibar gestured to Sanibak-Thastimoon to stand aside, and went out into the hall.

The immense outer door of the Coronal's suite, all agleam with dazzling golden inlays of the starburst emblem and with his father's LCC monogram—which would have to be changed soon enough to Prestimion's LPC—confronted him.

Three prodigious swaggering Skandars in the green-and-gold uniform of the Coronal's royal guard stood before it.

Korsibar craned his neck to look up at the shaggy four-armed beings, nearly half again as tall even as he, and said, "The Coronal has asked me to come to him."

At the Castle, sometimes, the guardians of the Coronal's office would make him wait like any young knight-initiate, Coronal's son though he might be, because his lordship was busy with his ministers of state, or his intimate counsellors, or perhaps some visiting regional administrators. The son of the Coronal had no formal rank of his own, and those others took precedence over him. But today the guards moved aside instantly and let him go in.

Lord Confalume was at his desk, a broad polished platform of glossy crimson simbajinder-wood rising from a thick podium of black gelimaund. The only illumination was the bright orange glow emanating from a trio of thick spiral-shafted candles of black wax set in heavy iron sconces, and the air was sweet and steamy with the rank piercing fragrance of burning incense, rising in two gray-blue coils of smoke from golden thuribles on either side of the Coronal's seat.

He was involved in a conjuration of some sort. Charts and works of reference covered his desk, and interspersed among them were all manner of instruments and devices having to do with the geomantic arts. Korsibar, who kept people like Sanibak-Thastimoon on hand to deal with such matters for him, had no idea what the purpose of most of those objects might be, though even he recognized the whiskbroom-like ammatepala that was used to sprinkle the water of perception across one's forehead, and the shining coils and posts of an armillary sphere, and the triangular stone vessel known as a veralistia in which one burned the aromatic powders that enhanced one's insight into the future.

Korsibar waited patiently while his father, not looking up,

carried out what seemed to be the conclusion of some lengthy and elaborate tabulation of numbers. And said quietly, when Lord Confalume appeared to be finished, "You wanted to see me, father?"

"A moment more. Just a moment."

Three times in a clockwise way the Coronal rubbed the rohilla that was pinned to his collar. Then he dipped both his thumbs in an ivory vessel containing some bluish fluid and touched them to his eyelids. With bowed head and closed eyes the Coronal murmured something that sounded like the words *"Adabambo, adabamboli, adambo,"* which meant nothing at all to Korsibar, and pressed the tips of his little fingers and thumbs together. Lastly Lord Confalume let his breath come forth from his nostrils in a long series of quick sighing exhalations, so that after a time his lungs were emptied and his head rested on his sunken chest, shoulders slumped, eyes rolled up toward the top of his head.

Korsibar's own belief in the powers of magic was as strong as anyone's. And yet he was surprised and a bit dismayed to see his royal father so deeply enmeshed in these arcane practices, at the cost of who knew what quantity of his waning energies. The expenditure was all too obvious. Lord Confalume's face was drawn and gray, and he seemed tired, though it was still only mid-morning. There were lines of stress along his brow and cheeks that appeared unfamiliar to Korsibar.

The prince and his sister Thismet were the children of the Coronal's late middle age, and there was a gap of many decades between his age and theirs; but that difference in age was only now making itself apparent. Indeed, the Coronal had seemed a good deal younger to Korsibar earlier that day in the ante-chamber to the Hall of Judgment than he looked at this moment; but perhaps that look of youthful middle age had been a mere pretense, a facade he was capable of donning while in the presence of the other princes and dukes, and

41

which he no longer had the strength to maintain in the privacy of this meeting with his son.

Seeing his father this wearied, Korsibar's heart went out to him. The Coronal, he knew, had every reason to be weary, and not just from the exertions of these sorceries. For the past forty-three years, a span of time unimaginable to Korsibar, the Coronal Lord Confalume had had the task of reigning over this giant planet. To be sure, he reigned in the name of the Pontifex, and it was the Pontifex in whom all ultimate responsibility for decision was vested. But the Pontifex lived hidden away in the secrecy and security of the Labyrinth. It was the Coronal who must remain endlessly on public display, holding open court at the Castle atop the Mount, and going forth into the world as well, every six or eight years, to fulfill the custom of the grand processional by which the Coronal presented himself in person in every major city of all three continents.

In making the grand processional it was the junior monarch's task to convey himself beyond the Fifty Cities of the Mount, and onward across the sea to distant Zimroel and its great metropolis of Ni-moya, and grim Piliplok of the terrifyingly straight streets, and Khyntor and Dulorn and flowery Til-omon and Pidruid and all those other faraway places whose existence was barely more than legendary to Korsibar: displaying himself to the multitudes as the living symbol of the system that had governed this gigantic world since the dawn of its historic period so many thousands of years before. Small wonder Lord Confalume looked tired. He had lived long enough to have made the grand processional not once but five times. He had carried all of Majipoor on his shoulders for some years longer than four full decades.

Korsibar stood a long time waiting, and said nothing. And waited some more. And still the Coronal busied himself with his sorcery-things, as though he had forgotten Korsibar was there. And Korsibar waited.

And went on waiting. When the Coronal required one to wait, one waited, and did not question the waiting. Even if he were one's own father.

After a long while Lord Confalume looked up at last, and blinked a couple of times at Korsibar as though he were surprised to see him in the room. Then the Coronal said, with no preamble, "You amazed me more than a little this morning, Korsibar. I never imagined you'd have the slightest objection to starting the games early."

"I confess some amazement at your amazement, father. Do you perceive me as such a shallow thing? Do you look on me as having no sense whatever of proper conduct?"

"Have I ever given you reason to think so?"

"You give me no reason to think otherwise. All my adult life I've simply been left free to amuse myself, like some oversized child. Am I invited to sit in on councils? Am I given high responsibilities and duties? No. No. What I'm given is a happy life of leisure and sport. '—Here, Korsibar: how do you like this fine sword? This saddle, this bow of Khyntor workmanship?—These fiery-tempered racing-mounts have just been sent to us from the breeders at Marraitis, Korsibar: take your pick, boy, the best is none too good for you.— Where will you hunt this season, Korsibar? In the northern marches, perhaps, or will it be in the jungles of Pulidandra?' And so it has been, father, all my life."

The Coronal's tired face seemed to sag into an even deeper weariness as Korsibar's verbal barrage went on and on.

"That was the life you wanted for yourself," he said, when the prince had subsided. "Or so I believed."

"And indeed I did. But what other kind of life could I have chosen to have?"

"You could have been whatever you pleased. You had the finest of princely educations, boy."

"A fine education, yes! And for what purpose, father? I can name a hundred Pontifexes from Dvorn to Vildivar, all in the proper order, and then name fifty more. I've studied the codes of the law, the Decretals and the Synods and the Balances and all and the rest of that. I can draw you maps of Zimroel and Alhanroel and put all the cities in their proper locations. I know the pathways of the stars and I can quote you inspiring passages from all the best epic poets from Furvain to Auliasi. What of it? What good does any of it do me? Should I have written poetry myself? Should I have been a clerk? A philosopher, perhaps?"

The Coronal's eyelids fluttered and closed for a moment, and he pressed the tips of his fingers to his temples. Then he opened his eyes and stared balefully at his son, a hooded, rigorously patient look.

"The Balances, you say. You've studied the Balances. If that's so, then you understand the inner rhythms of our governmental structure and you know why you've been given swords and saddles and fine mounts instead of high public responsibilities. We have no hereditary monarchy here. You picked the wrong father, boy: for you alone, of all the princes of Castle Mount, there can never be any place in the government."

"Not even a seat on the Council?"

"Not even that. One thing leads to another, they would say: put you on the Council and soon you'd want to act as Regent when I'm away from the Castle, or you would propose yourself as High Counsellor, or you'd even aspire to be made Coronal yourself when my turn arrives to move on to the Labyrinth. I would constantly be forced to defend myself against accusations of—"

"Father?"

"—no end of whispering and innuendo, or outright insurrection, even, if—"

"Father, please."

Confalume halted in mid-flow, blinking. "Yes?"

"I do understand all these things. I resigned myself long ago to the realities of my situation. Prestimion will be Coronal, not me: so be it. I never expected to be Coronal, never. Nor wanted it, nor hoped for it. But let me bring you back to the point where this wrangling discussion started, if I may. I asked you whether you really believed I was so stupid that the only thing on my mind was the desire to escape the boredom of this miserable hole by getting on a mount and waving my sword around in some tournament, without a scrap of thought given to custom or tradition or propriety."

The Coronal made no immediate response. His eyes now grew dull with inattention; his face, which had become very grim, seemed to go entirely blank.

At length he said, keeping his voice very low, "Do you resent it that Prestimion is going to become Coronal, Korsibar?"

"Do I envy him, do you mean? Yes. He'll be a king, and who would not envy the man who is to be king? But as for resenting it that he will be Coronal in my place—No. No. That place was never mine to occupy. I know that. There are nine billion men on this planet and I am the only one of whom it was known, from the moment of his birth, that he could never become Coronal."

"And does that make you bitter?"

"Why do you keep asking me these things, father? I understand the law. I yield my non-existent claim on the throne gladly, unhesitatingly, unconditionally, to Prestimion. All I meant to assert before is that I believe that there's more substance to me than I'm generally given credit for having, and

I wish I could be allowed more responsibilities in the government. Or to be more accurate, be allowed some responsibilities at all."

Lord Confalume said, "What's your opinion of Prestimion, actually?"

Now it was Korsibar's turn to pause awhile before speaking.

"A clever man indeed," he said cautiously. "Intelligent. Ambitious."

"Ambitious, yes. But capable?"

"He must be. You've chosen him to succeed you."

"I know what my opinion of Prestimion is. I want to know yours."

"I admire him. His mind is quick and for a small man he's remarkably strong, and exceedingly agile besides. Good with a sword, better even with a bow."

"But do you like him?"

"No."

"Honestly put, at any rate. Do you think he'll make a good Coronal?"

"I hope so."

"We all hope so, Korsibar. Do you *think* so?"

Another pause. After that moment of deep fatigue Lord Confalume's eyes had regained their usual brightness; they searched Korsibar's mercilessly.

"Yes. Yes, I think he probably will."

"Probably, you say."

"I'm no soothsayer, father. I can only guess at what is to come."

"Indeed. The Procurator, you know, thinks that you're Prestimion's sworn enemy."

A muscle throbbed in Korsibar's cheek. "Is that what he's told you?"

"Not in so many words. I refer to his comment of a little

while ago, upstairs, about your opposing the games because holding them was Prestimion's idea."

"Dantirya Sambail is a dangerous troublemaker, father."

"Agreed. But also a very shrewd man. Are you Prestimion's sworn enemy?"

"If I were, father, would I tell you? But no. No. I've been frank with you about Prestimion. I think he's a calculating and manipulative man, a cunning opportunist who can argue on either side of an issue with equal skill, and who has maneuvered himself up out of no position at all and now is about to attain the second highest rank on Majipoor. I find it hard to like men of that sort. But that isn't to say that he doesn't *deserve* the second highest rank on Majipoor. He understands the art of governing better than most. Certainly better than I. Prestimion will become Coronal, and so be it, and I will bow my knee to him like everyone else.—This is an ugly conversation, father. Are these the things you called me here to talk about."

"Yes."

"And the conjuring you were doing when I came in? What was that?"

The Coronal's hands moved flutteringly among the devices on his desk. "An attempt, merely, to determine how much longer the Pontifex is likely to live."

Korsibar smiled. "Are you really so adept a sorcerer now, father?"

"Adept? No, that's not a claim I'd make. But, like many others, I've made a study of the art. I keep measuring my skills against events as they unfold, to see whether I've actually mastered any knack of foretelling the future."

"And have you? You have the true oracular skill, do you think?" Korsibar thought of the reports of him that the sorcerers were said to have brought to his father: that strange prediction, *He will shake the world*. Perhaps it was the Coronal

47

himself who had cast that rune, and now was staring at some singular destiny for his son that Korsibar himself had no way of seeing. "Can we put it to the test?" he asked, happy to see the subject of discussion changing. "Tell me your results, and we'll see what comes to pass. What is the date that you arrived at for the end of Prankipin's lingering?"

"Not any precise one. I'm not that good: perhaps no one is. But it will come, I calculate, within the next nineteen days. Let us keep count, you and I, Korsibar."

"Nineteen days, or even less. And then finally all the waiting will be over, and we can have the ceremonies and Prestimion will be Coronal and you will be Pontifex, and we can all get out of this vile cistern of a place and back to the sweet air of Castle Mount.—All but you, father," Korsibar added, in a softer voice.

"All but me, yes. The Labyrinth will be my home, now."

"And how do you feel about that, may I ask?"

"I've had forty years to get myself used to the idea" Lord Confalume said. "I am indifferent to it."

"Never to emerge into the light of day—never to see the Castle again—"

The Coronal chuckled. "Oh, I can come forth now and then, if I feel like it. Prankipin did, you know. You were only a boy the last time he did: perhaps you've forgotten it. But the Pontifex isn't compelled to stay below ground one hundred percent of the time."

"Still, I wouldn't care for it even so much as one percent of the time. My stay here these weeks past has been quite enough for me."

Lord Confalume smiled. "Luckily for you, Korsibar, living here won't ever be asked of you. The best part of not becoming Coronal is that you know you'll never become Pontifex."

"I should be grateful, then."

"You should."

"And you feel you are ready to take up your new life down here, father?"

"Yes. Completely ready."

"You will be a great Pontifex," said Korsibar. "As you were a great Coronal."

"I thank you for those words," said Lord Confalume. He smiled; he stood. It was a tight, unreal smile, and the Coronal's left hand, clenched at his side, was trembling perceptibly. Something was being left unsaid: something painful to the Coronal, something explosive.

What did the Coronal know, what was it that the Coronal had refrained from telling him?

*You will shake the world.*

It had to have to do with that. But whatever Sanibak-Thastimoon had imagined that Lord Confalume might be going to say to him concerning that mysterious oracular uttering had not been mentioned.

Nor would it be, now. Korsibar was aware that he had been dismissed. He made the formal starburst gesture before his father as Coronal; and then they embraced as father and son, and he turned to leave. He heard the Coronal once again puttering among the geomantic devices on his desk even before he stepped through the doorway.

# 4

Septach Melayn entered the room known as the Melikand Chamber, a narrow curving hall in the imperial sector of the Labyrinth, adjacent to Prestimion's suite of rooms, that had been set aside for the use of the companions of the Coronal-designate. Duke Svor and Gialaurys of Piliplok were already there. "Well," said Septach Melayn as he came in, "I have a little news, at least. Three names have now emerged as candidates for Master of the Games: the Grand Admiral, the Procurator, and our little friend Svor. Or so I have it from one of the Pontifical lackeys."

"Who is a person whom you trust implicitly, I suppose?" Svor asked.

"As much as I would trust my mother," replied Septach Melayn. "Or yours, if I had ever had the pleasure of knowing her." He drew his ornately embroidered cloak, dark blue silk lined with lashings of silver thread, tight about him, and paced with the cat-like lazy grace that was his manner up and down the brightly burnished floor of smooth gray stone in quick, almost mincing steps. As he moved about, Svor and Gialaurys looked at him in their varying ways—Svor with wry amusement, Gialaurys with his usual melancholy suspicion of Septach Melayn's elegance and flamboyance.

They were oddly assorted men, these three dearest friends of the Coronal-designate. In no way did they resemble one another, neither in physique nor manner nor temperament.

Septach Melayn was slim and lanky, with arms and legs so exorbitantly long that they seemed almost attenuated. His humor was volatile, his style delicate and witty. His skin was very fair and his eyes were a pale glittering blue; his golden hair tumbled in carefully constructed ringlets to his shoulders, in what was almost a girlish way; and he affected a small pointed beard and a dandyish little mustache, a mere chiseled line of gold on his upper lip, that were the cause of much knightly amusement behind his back—though never to his face, for Septach Melayn was ever quick to challenge slights and a relentless foe in any sword-fight.

Gialaurys, on the other hand, was a man of ponderous mass, not unusually tall, but extraordinarily thick through the chest and shoulders, with a flat, wide face that confronted the world with a look of the utmost steadiness, like a side of beef. His upper arms were the width of another man's thighs; his fingers had the thickness of fat sausages; his dark hair was close-cropped and his face was clean-shaven except for bristly brown sideburns that descended in thick ominous stripes past his cheekbones.

He too had a reputation as one to be treated with caution— not that he was a swordsman of Septach Melayn's wicked skill, but so great was his physical strength that no opponent could withstand his anger. Gialaurys was dark and brooding in temperament, as befitted one whose foster kin in the unlovely city of Piliplok in Zimroel, the land of his birth, had been a family of bleak-spirited Skandars. Prestimion had met him in Piliplok on his one visit to the western continent, ten years earlier, and by some unpredictable affinity of opposites they had become fast friends at once.

As for Svor, who held the title of Duke of Tolaghai but had no land or wealth to go with it, he was no more than a speck beside the other two: a flimsy, frail little man of inconsequential size, swarthy almost to the point of blackness, as men born under the terrible sun of the southernmost continent often are, with an unruly tangle of dark hair and dark, mischievous eyes and a dark, tangled soul. His nose was thin and sharp and sly, with a hook to it, and his mouth was too narrow for all his teeth, and a short tight beard rimmed his face, though he kept his upper lip shorn. No warrior was Svor, but a politician and schemer and avid lover of women, who dabbled somewhat in sorcery on the side.

In years gone by he had been a companion of the young Korsibar—a kind of pet, in a way, or court jester, whom the big athletic prince liked to keep about him for amusement's sake—but once Prestimion had begun to emerge as the probable next Coronal, Svor had drifted ever so subtly in his direction until by now he was a constant figure in Prestimion's entourage. The shift of allegiance was a fact much remarked upon at the Castle—again, only in private—as an example of Svor's well-known passion for self-aggrandizement and of his expedient looseness of loyalty.

Utterly different though the three men might be from one another, a curious bond of mutual affection linked them all, and each in his way was devoted to the welfare and service of Prestimion. No one doubted that they would emerge as the high lords of the kingdom once Prestimion wore the starburst crown.

Septach Melayn said, "If we speak up now in this business of who is to preside over the games, we might well be able to influence the choice. But does it matter to us?"

"It matters to me," said Gialaurys unhesitatingly, "and it should to you." He spoke in the flat broad accent of eastern Zimroel that seemed so comical elsewhere, but not when it came from Gialaurys's lips, and his voice was a deep gritty rumble that seemed to rise up out of the core of the world. "The Master of the Games determines the pairings. Are you willing to be sent into the field against a series of fools because the Master wishes to embarrass you with mismatches? I don't want the Master using the games to play games of his own. And whenever there's a close call in some contest, we want our own man to be the one who decides the fine points. Lives can depend on it."

"Then you would advise us to put our support behind Duke Svor, I take it," Septach Melayn said.

"Declined," said Duke Svor instantly from the far corner of the room, where he was engaged in a study of esoteric charts inscribed on long rolls of tawny parchment. "I have no idea what the proper pairings ought to be, and—"

"We could tell you," Gialaurys said.

"—and in any event," Svor continued, "I want no part of your silly brawls. The contending sides will forever be shouting in the Master's face; let it be someone else's face."

Septach Melayn smiled. "Very well, Svor. Let it be so." Playfully he said to Gialaurys, "And what do you mean, pray tell, by 'our own man?' Do we have factions here, so that someone can be considered plainly to be Prestimion's man, and someone might be considered altogether unfriendly to him? Are we not all united in the celebration of the new reign."

"You talk like a fool," Gialaurys grunted.

Septach Melayn was unbothered by that. "Surely you'd consider Svor to be our own man, if anyone is; I understand that. But is the Procurator our enemy? Or Admiral Gonivaul?"

"They might be. Either one."

"I fail to understand you."

"There's never a smooth transition from reign to reign. There are always those who have objection, secret or otherwise, to the chosen new Coronal. And may show their objections in unexpected ways."

"Listen to him!" Septach Melayn cried. "The scholar! The

learned historian! Give me examples of such treachery, friend Gialaurys!"

"Well—" Gialaurys pondered for a while, sucking his lower lip deep into his mouth. "When Havilbove became Pontifex," he said after a long while, "and he said that Thraym would be his Coronal, I understand it that some disgruntled lord who bore no love for Thraym launched a conspiracy to put Dizimaule on the throne instead of him, and very nearly—"

"In fact Lord Kanaba was Havilbove's Coronal," said Svor quietly. "Thraym was Coronal three reigns later. Dizimaule lived a thousand years earlier than any of them."

"So I forget the true names or the order of the kings," Gialaurys said, with some heat in his tone now. "But it happened all the same, if not with them then with others. You could look it up. And then there was another case, involving Spurifon, I think, or was it Siminave—"

"All this thinking ill becomes you," Septach Melayn said, and grinned into the back of his beautifully manicured hand. "I assure you, dear friend, that regardless of the private ambitions of the rejected candidates, the new Coronal is always swept up into office by wholehearted acclamation. It has never been any other way. We are a civilized people on this world."

"Are we?" said Prestimion, coming into the room just then. "How good to hear you say so, sweet Septach Melayn. What are you discussing, may I ask?"

"Whom to choose to be Master of the Games. I'm told that it's between Gonivaul and Svor and your dear cousin the Procurator. Gialaurys has been arguing that we can't trust anybody but ourselves even in something like the games, and wants Svor to be Master, so that we can be sure that we'll be put up against the proper people to fight, and that the verdicts will all come down in our favor."

Prestimion glanced at Gialaurys. "Is this so? Are you so apprehensive, Gialaurys?"

"Septach Melayn twists my words, as usual, my lord. But if it's put to me all over again, yes: I would prefer someone I trust as Master to someone that I don't."

"And you trust Svor?" Prestimion said, laughing.

"Svor has already said he will not be it. In that case I would like to see the Procurator Dantirya Sambail given the post."

"The Procurator!" Prestimion cried, bursting into laughter all over again. "The Procurator! You would trust the Procurator, Gialaurys!"

"He's a cousin of yours, my lord, is he not?" said Gialaurys stolidly. "And therefore would make no decision harmful to you or to your friends, or so I would assume."

"He is a cousin much removed," Prestimion answered, as he often did when his relationship to the Procurator was mentioned to him. "And you've called me 'my lord' twice now in half a minute's time. That term belongs to Lord Confalume, at least until a new Coronal has been chosen.— As for my cousin the Procurator, he is truly my kinsman, yes. But if you think you might have anything to fear from the one who is chosen Master of the Games, I would suggest that you throw your support to someone other than he."

"Well, then, Admiral Gonivaul," said Gialaurys without much grace.

"Agreed," Septach Melayn said quickly. "Gonivaul will at least be neutral, if there's any bickering. He cares for nothing and nobody, except, I suppose, for Gonivaul. May we get on now to a discussion of the various events."

"Will there be wrestling?" Gialaurys asked.

"There's always wrestling. Farholt would insist on it."

"Good. I'll wrestle Farholt."

Septach Melayn said, "I had thought we'd put Svor up to that job. You could oppose Farquanor in the fencing-matches."

"Sometimes you fail to be amusing, Septach Melayn," said Gialaurys.

"But no! No!" Svor put in. "Let's confuse everyone. Let us bewilder and bedazzle! Seriously. I will indeed face great hulking Farholt in the wrestling, if only to see the look on his face when I come out against him, and we'll let Gialaurys try his luck with swift-wristed Farquanor in the fencing, and you, Septach Melayn, you can be our lead man next to Prestimion in the two-man chariot races against Korsibar's team."

"I intend to be, as a matter of fact," said Septach Melayn.

"Not the fencing?" Prestimion asked.

"Both," Septach Melayn said. "If there are no objections. And in the chariot races we can—"

There was a tap at the door. Prestimion opened it and peered into the corridor. A woman wearing the narrow mask that marked the servants of the Pontificate stood there, one of those who had been placed in charge of assisting the guests from Castle Mount.

"Are you the Prince Prestimion?" she asked.

"I am."

"There is a Vroon here, sir, one Thalnap Zelifor, who asks present audience of you. He says he has information that will be of great use."

Prestimion's brows furrowed. Looking back over his shoulder, he said to the others, "Were any of you aware that Thalnap Zelifor was at the Labyrinth?"

"Not I," said Septach Melayn.

"He's so small, how could anyone notice him?" Gialaurys said.

"He came in with Gonivaul's people," said Svor. "I've seen him around once or twice."

"By the Divine, I have no use of any kind for that one," Septach Melayn declared. "If you're wise, Prestimion, you'll continue to keep him away from you. We have enough sorcerers buzzing about us as it is, haven't we?"

"He is said to be a seer of exceptional powers," Gialaurys observed.

"Be that as it may," said Septach Melayn. "I dislike even the sight of Vroons. And their smell, for that matter. Beyond which, we all know, this little Thalnap Zelifor is a troublesome treacherous man who tacks in every breeze and who may well be a source of peril to us. He has the soul of a spy."

"But a spy for whom? We have no enemies!" Gialaurys said, with a hearty guffaw. "You explained that to me no more than five minutes ago, is that not so? We are a civilized people on this world, and all of us united in loyalty to those set in authority over us."

Prestimion held up his hand. "Enough, gentlemen, enough! It's a sad affair when we must worry about danger from the likes of Thalnap Zelifor. I think we can spare the creature a moment of our time." To the woman from the Pontificate he said, "Tell the Vroon he can come in."

Thalnap Zelifor was diminutive even for one of his race: a tiny being hardly more than shin-high to a human. The Vroon, fragile and insubstantial of body, had a multitude of flexible rubbery limbs and a narrow, tapering head out of which sprang two blazing golden eyes and a sharp hooked beak of a mouth. From him came the faint, sweet, wistful odor of flowers pressed long ago in a book.

There had been Vroons on Majipoor almost as long as human beings. They were among the first of the various non-human races invited to settle there by the Coronal Lord Melikand, to whom it had become apparent that the human population of the immense world could not grow quickly enough to meet all the needs of a developing civilization. That had been many thousands of years ago, almost in the dawn of Majipoor's history. Vroons had significant and unusual skills: they could link their minds to the minds of others and penetrate deep thoughts, they could move objects about by the power of their inner force alone, and they had given evidence, even in ages less credulous than the present one, of an ability to discern the shape of coming events.

Like most of his people, Thalnap Zelifor claimed to have the gift of second sight, and so far as anyone knew he earned his living primarily by peddling oracles; but no one could ever be quite sure of anything concerning Thalnap Zelifor. At the Castle he was considered to be in the service of Prince Gonivaul the Grand Admiral, but he was just as often found among Korsibar's hangers-on, and more than once before this he had presented himself with some offer of service to Prestimion. Which had always routinely been declined: Prestimion had never been a man to surround himself with wizards in any significant way. It was surprising to see Thalnap Zelifor popping up yet again.

"Well?" said the prince.

Thalnap Zelifor extended one ropy tentacle. On its tip lay a small, highly polished oval plaque, fashioned of the precious green stone known as velathysite. It glowed brightly as if lit by an inner fire. Runes so minute that they were almost invisible to the eye were engraved upon the face of it.

"A gift, excellence. A corymbor, it is, that bears inscriptions of power; it has the capacity to bring you aid in a time of trouble. Wear it on a chain at your throat; touch it when need is upon you, and it will give you the solace that you require."

Septach Melayn snorted. "Gods! Will there never be an end to these fantasies among us? We'll all drown in this tide of superstitious madness!"

"Gently," Prestimion said to him. And to the Vroon: "You know I put little faith in such objects as this."

"I know that, excellence. That is, perhaps, an error on your part."

"Perhaps so."

Prestimion bent forward to take the little green amulet

from Thalnap Zelifor. He rubbed it gingerly this way and that with his fingertip, staring at it warily all the while, as if he suspected that by handling it in such fashion he might conjure up some unsettling thing before his eyes. But he was smiling, also, to say that his show of caution was all pretense; and in any event nothing happened.

Prestimion turned the amulet on edge, commenting admiringly on the fine workmanship of it, and peered briefly at its reverse side, which was blank. Then he tossed it into the air as one might toss a coin, catching it with a quick snap of his wrist and dropping it casually into a pocket of his tunic. "I thank you," he told the Vroon, with deep formality if not with any particular effort at seeming sincere. "And will the need for this be upon me soon, do you think?"

"Forgive me, excellence, but I do."

Septach Melayn snorted again, and turned his back.

The Vroon said softly, so softly that it was necessary to strain to hear him, "What I have come to tell you this day, excellence, is for all Majipoor's sake as much as it is for yours. I know that you yourself have only scorn for me and for the whole of my profession besides; but I think you have the welfare of the world at your heart none the less, and will hear me out if only for that reason."

"And just how much must I pay you to hear your revelations, Thalnap Zelifor?"

"I assure you, Prince Prestimion, that I have no hope of personal gain in this matter."

Septach Melnayn threw back his head and roared his laughter to the vaulted roof of the chamber. "No cost! The advice is free! And dear even at that price, I would say."

Prestimion said, "You should ask me for money, Thalnap Zelifor. I'm suspicious of soothsayers who offer their wares for nothing."

"My lord—"

"That is not my title yet," said Prestimion.

"Excellence, then. I tell you, I did not come here in the hope of earning a fee. Pay me ten weights, if you feel you must pay something."

"Barely enough for a platter of sausages and a glass of beer," Prestimion said. "You value your wisdom very lightly, my friend." He snapped his fingers at Duke Svor. "Pay him."

Svor produced a small square copper-hued coin and handed it over.

"Now, then," said Prestimion.

Thalnap Zelifor said, "What I have to say is this: I looked upon the Great Moon last night, and it was of a scarlet color, as though its face streamed with human blood."

"He saw the Great Moon," came scornfully from Septach Melayn, who was still standing with his back to the others, "although it's on the far side of the world now, where nothing whatsoever that might be in the sky can be seen from this hemisphere, and he saw it from the bottom of the Labyrinth, no less, from down here a mile below the surface. Well done, Vroon! Your sight is sharper even than mine!"

"It was by second sight I saw, my good master. That is a different kind of sight from yours."

Patiently Prestimion said, "And what does it mean, do you think, this show of blood streaming across the face of the Great Moon?"

"A coming war, excellence."

"War. We have no wars, on Majipoor."

"We will," said Thalnap Zelifor.

"Pay heed to him, I beg you!" Gialaurys called out, for Prestimion suddenly was displaying signs of annoyance with this game. "He sees things, prince!"

Septach Melayn came forward abruptly, looming over the Vroon as though about to squash him with the heel of his boot, and said, "Who sent you here, little pest?"

"I came of my own accord," Thalnap Zelifor replied, staring up directly into Septach Melayn's eyes far above him. "For the benefit and welfare of all. Yours included, my good master."

Septach Melayn spat, missing the Vroon by very little, and once more turned away.

In a distant voice Prestimion said, "A war between whom and whom?"

"I can give you no answer to that, excellence. I can tell you only that you do not have a clear path to the throne. There are strong omens of opposition to your candidacy: I read them on every side. The air down here is thick with them. A struggle is brewing. You have a mighty enemy, who waits his time now in secrecy; he will emerge and contend with you for the Castle; all the world will suffer from the strife."

"Ha!" cried Gialaurys. "You hear him, Septach Melayn?"

Prestimion said, "Do you often have such terrible dreams, Thalnap Zelifor?"

"Not so terrible as this one."

"Tell me who this mighty enemy of mine might be, so that I may go to him and embrace him as a friend. For whenever I lose someone's love, I want always to strive to regain it."

"I am unable to give you any names, excellence."

"Unable or unwilling?" Duke Svor asked, from his place across the room.

"Unable. I saw no one's face clearly."

"Who can it be, this rival, this enemy?" Gialaurys asked musingly. His ever-somber visage was dark with concern. Belief ran deep in Gialaurys's nature: the predictions of sorcerers were serious matters to him. "Serithorn, maybe? He has such great estates already that he is practically a king: he may fancy himself as a Coronal as well, descended as he is from so many. Or your cousin the Procurator. He's your kinsman, yes, but we all know what a tricky sort he is. And then, on the other hand, possibly the Vroon's meaning is that—"

"Stop this, Gialaurys," Prestimion said. "You're being too free with these speculations. And as ever much too willing to expend your credulity in unworthy places." Coldly he asked the Vroon, "Is there any other aspect of this revelation you want to share with me?"

"There is nothing else, excellence."

"Good. Then go. Go."

Thalnap Zelifor made a gesture among his many tentacles that might have been some bizarre version of the starburst sign, or might simply have been a stirring of his upper limbs. "As you wish, excellence."

"I thank you for your information, such as it is. And for the amulet."

"I beg you, excellence, take the warning seriously."

"I'll take it as seriously as it deserves," replied Prestimion, and made a curt gesture of dismissal. The Vroon went out.

As the door closed Gialaurys slapped his hand down hard against his meaty thigh. "Korsibar," he exclaimed with sudden explosiveness. "Of course!"

"What?" said Prestimion.

"The enemy. The rival. Korsibar: he's the one! If not Serithorn, if not Dantirya Sambail, it must be Korsibar. Don't you see? It's not so strange to want to be king, if your father before you was one. And so we have a Coronal's son, unwilling to allow someone whom he regards as an upstart to take the throne that he sees as rightly belonging to him."

With a sharpness in his tone that was unusual for him Prestimion said, "Enough and more than enough, Gialaurys! This is all contemptible nonsense."

"I would not be so quick to say so."

"All of it! Nonsense, nonsense, absolute nonsense! The scarlet moon, the secret enemy, the prophecy of war. Who *are* the demons who provide such dependable word of things to come? Where do they live, what's the color of their eyes?" He shook his head sadly. "War, on Majipoor! This is not a world where wars are fought. Not one, Gialaurys, not one war ever in all the thousands of years since the Shapeshifters were defeated. And these preposterous guessing games of yours! Serithorn, you think, is hungering for the throne? Oh, no, no, not him, my friend. His blood is quite sufficiently royal as it is, and he has no liking for toil of any kind. My cousin the Procurator? He enjoys making trouble, yes. But not, I think, that kind of trouble. And Korsibar? *Korsibar?*"

Gialaurys said, "He is a kingly man indeed, Prestimion."

"On the outside, yes. But there's nothing within. A sweet empty-headed man surrounded by a swarm of flatterers and scoundrels. Who has not an idea of his own, and depends on those around him to tell him what to think."

"An exact assessment," said Septach Melayn. "I would have put it in those very words myself."

"In any case," Prestimion continued, "he'd never dream of making a move toward the throne. The son of a Coronal, doing such a thing? It violates all tradition, and Korsibar is no man for defying tradition. He's a dull decent lordling and nothing more, without the necessary spark of evil for such a thing. What he wants from life is sport and pleasure, not the cares of power. The idea's absurd, Gialaurys. Absurd. Put it from your mind."

"What Gialaurys suggests may be absurd, yes," said Duke Svor, "but there's definitely something strange in the air, Prestimion. I can feel it myself: a thick dark ominous cloud gathering close about us."

"You too, Svor?" Prestimion exclaimed, with a gesture of vexation.

"Indeed!"

"Oh, how I wish all this flood of incantations and

prognostications had never been let loose on Majipoor! These talismans and harbingers, these monstrous conjurings! We were a rational people once, so I understand it. Would that we were again. We have Prankipin to blame for this. He was the one that swayed the world toward witchcraft and magic," Prestimion looked gloomily toward Duke Svor. "You try my patience very sorely with these superstitions, friend. You and Gialaurys both."

"Perhaps we do," said Svor. "For that I beg your pardon, Prestimion. None the less, cutting ourselves off from any source of information, esoteric though it may be, seems a mistake to me. That you see no substance in the arcane practices, prince, may not mean that they're altogether devoid of truth. I propose that we put the Vroon on the payroll, for something more than ten weights this time, and ask him to come to us with any further insights he may have."

"Which is exactly what he came here to achieve," Septach Melayn said. "He's obviously looking for a new employer, and who better than the incoming Coronal? No. No. I vote against having anything to do with him. We don't need him and we don't want him. He'll sell himself six times over the same day, if only he can find enough buyers."

Svor held up one hand, palm outward, in disagreement. "In a time of the changing of kings, those in high places should tread cautiously, I think. If there's substance to these Vroonish whisperings, and we spurn him out of mere mistrust of the man himself or of witchery in general, more fools we. There's no need to make him party to our innermost councils: only to toss him a royal or two to retain access to his visions. To me that seems simply prudent."

"And to me," said Gialaurys.

Septach Melayn scowled. "You are both of you much too willing to give credence to such stuff. It's a perilous wizardy time, when lunatic nonsense like this infests even shrewd men like you, Svor. I could gladly take that Vroon and—"

"Calmly, calmly, Septach Melayn," said Prestimion, speaking commandingly but in his most gentle manner of command, for blood and fire had come into Septach Melayn's pale elegant face. "I'm no more eager to have him flapping about us than you are. Nor can I put any faith in this talk of a challenger rising up against me. Such a thing is not going to happen."

"So we all hope and pray," Septach Melayn said.

"So we profoundly believe." Prestimion shuddered, as if he had stepped in something unclean. "By the Divine, I regret having allowed that Vroon to assault our ears with all that foolishness!" He looked toward Duke Svor. "Keep your distance from him, is what I say to you, my friend." And then, looking to the other side: "But do him no harm, Septach Melayn, do you hear? I will not have it."

"As you wish, prince."

"Good. Thank you. And now, if we may, shall we return to the matter of the pairings for the games?"

# 5

The Lady Thismet, sister to Prince Korsibar, had been given one of the most luxurious suites in the Labyrinth's imperial sector for her private chamber, one that ordinarily was reserved for the use of the Coronal's own consort on those rare occasions of state when she might visit the underground capital. But it was an open secret to all the world that the Lady Roxivail, who was wife to Lord Confalume, had long lived apart from the Coronal in a palace of her own on the southerly island of Shambettirantil in the tropical Gulf of Stoien. Though her husband was soon to ascend to the title of Pontifex, she had sent no response to the invitation to attend his investiture, nor did anyone expect her to be present for the ceremony. And so the suite that would have been Roxivail's had been assigned to her daughter Thismet instead.

Within it lay Princess Thismet now, taking her ease in the great glossy tub of porphyry inlaid with patterns of wine-yellow topaz that stood at the center of her bathchamber. From the smooth tubes of green onyx that were its spigots ran a steady pale-pink stream of heated water, the fragrant and silken water of far-off Lake Embolain, carried across two thousand miles of marble piping for the pleasure of the guests of the Pontifex. A triple pair of iridescent green lamps hung above her. The princess lay prettily disposed, breast-deep in the tub with her arms hanging relaxed over its curving rim, so that the two serving-women who knelt just to either side of it could carry out their nightly task of caring for her hands and fingers, the flawless elongated nails of which were enameled afresh each evening in a gleaming platinum hue. Behind her, gently kneading the slender column of her neck, was the Princess Thismet's chief lady-of-honor, Melithyrrh of Amblemorn, her companion since childhood, a woman as fair as Thismet was dark, with a great swirl of golden hair and pale cheeks lightly dappled with a perpetual fine blush.

Usually she and Thismet chattered endlessly; but tonight thus far very little had been said, and that with long periods of silence between each remark. After one of these Melithyrrh said, "The muscles of your back are very tense tonight, lady."

"When I had my rest this afternoon I dreamed, and the dream stays with me and grips me all along my spine."

"It must not have been a very beguiling dream."

To this the Princess Thismet offered no reply.

"A sending of some sort?" asked Melithyrrh, after a few moments more.

"A dream," said Thismet shortly. "Only a dream. Dig your fingers more deeply into my shoulders, would you, good Melithyrrh?"

Again there was silence, while Melithyrrh steadily worked. Thismet closed her eyes and let her head loll backward. Her body was a slender one, sinewy for a woman's, and the muscles lay close to the surface: often, when she had dreamed a disturbing dream, they were knotted and painful for long hours thereafter.

She was Prince Korsibar's twin, born only a few minutes after him, and the kinship between them showed in her shining ebony hair and dark glittering eyes, her prominent sharp-edged cheekbones, her full lips and strong chin, and in the long-limbed proportions of her frame. But whereas Korsibar was a man of towering height, the Lady Thismet was cut to a smaller scale, having her brother's rangy proportions but nothing like his size, and where his skin was leathery and blackened by long exposure to fierce sunlight, hers was extraordinarily smooth, and had the stark whiteness of one who lived only by night. Her whole appearance was one of great delicacy of form and almost a sort of boyishness, other than in the fullness of her breasts and the womanly breadth of her hips.

A third serving-maid entered the chamber and said, "The magus Sanibak-Thastimoon is outside, saying he has been urgently summoned, and asks to be admitted. Shall I show him in?"

Melithyrrh laughed. "Has he lost his mind? Have you? Milady is in her bath."

The girl reddened and stammered something inaudible.

Icily Thismet said, "I requested his immediate presence, Melithyrrh."

"Surely you didn't intend—"

"Immediate," she said. "Am I required by you to maintain my modesty in front of creatures of every sort, Melithyrrh, even those who could never feel desire for women of the human kind? Let him come in."

"Indeed," said Melithyrrh with ostentatious cheeriness, signalling to the serving-maid. The Su-Suheris appeared almost at once, a thin, tall, sharp-angled figure tightly wrapped in a rigid sheath-like tunic of orange parchment bedecked with shining blue beads, from which his pair of narrow emerald-eyed heads jutted like twin conning-towers. He took up a position just to the left of the massive porphyry tub, and, though he was looking down directly at Thismet's clearly revealed nakedness, he displayed no more interest in it than he did in the tub itself.

"Lady?" he said.

"I need your guidance, Sanibak-Thastimoon, in a certain

delicate matter. I hope I can rely upon you. And on your discretion."

From the leftmost head came a quick, barely perceptible nod.

She went on, "You told me once, not long ago, that I was destined for great things—though whether they were great good things or great bad things, you could not or would not say."

"Could not, my lady," said the Su-Suheris. The voice that spoke was the crisp and precisely inflected one of the necromancer's right head.

"*Could* not. Very well. The omens were ambiguous, as such omens all too often are. You told me also that you could see the same ambiguous kind of greatness in my brother's future."

Again Sanibak-Thastimoon briefly nodded, both heads at once.

"This afternoon," Princess Thismet said, "I had a strange dark dream. Perhaps you can speak it for me, Sanibak-Thastimoon. I dreamed that I was home again, that I had somehow returned to the Castle; but I was in some part of the Castle that was unknown to me, on the northern side where almost nobody ever goes. It seemed to me that I was wandering across a broad platform of badly chipped brick that led to a dismal half-ruined wall, and thence to a kind of parapet that gave me a view out to such towns as Huine and Gossif, and whatever city may be beyond those—Tentag, I suppose. There I was, anyhow, in this old and crumbling corner of the Castle, looking outward to cities I had never visited and then in toward the summit of the Mount rising high above me, and wondering how I was ever going to find my way toward those parts of the building where I knew my way around."

She fell silent, and stared at the ceiling of the bathchamber, where an ornate frieze of interwoven flowers and leaves and stalks, eldiron blossoms and tanigales and big fleshy shepitholes, had been carved from sleek curving slabs of sapphire targolite and pale chalcedony.

"Yes, lady?" said Sanibak-Thastimoon, waiting.

Through the Lady Thismet's mind a thousand turbulent images flowed. She saw herself running to and fro on that somber balcony at the edge of the immense sprawling Castle atop the mightiest mountain of Majipoor—the Castle that had been the residence of the Coronals of Majipoor these seven thousand years past, the ever-growing Castle of twenty thousand rooms, or perhaps it was thirty thousand, for who could number them? The Castle that was a great city unto itself, where each Coronal in turn added new rooms of his own to what was already so intricate a building that even residents of many years' standing easily found themselves lost in its seemingly infinite byways. As she herself had become lost, this very day, while she wandered the Castle's unfathomable vastnesses in her dream.

By and by she began to speak again, describing for the Su-Suheris how she had made her way, with the aid of this passerby and that one, through that enormous maze of stony galleries and musty tunnels and corridors and staircases and long echoing courtyards toward the more familiar inner bastions. Again and again the perplexing paths doubled back on themselves and she discovered herself entering some place she had left only a little while before. But always there was someone to help her on her way, and always one of non-human origin. It seemed that persons of every race but her own were there to offer guidance to her: first a pair of scaly forked-tongued Ghayrogs, and then a bright-eyed little Vroon who danced ahead of her on its multitude of ever-recoiling tentacles, and some Liimen, and a Su-Suheris or two, and Hjorts, and a massive Skandar, and someone of a species she could not identify at all. "And even, I think, a Metamorph:

for it was very thin, and had that greenish skin of theirs, and hardly any lips or nose at all. But what would a Metamorph be doing inside the Castle?"

The two manicurists were finished with her now. They rose and left the room. Briefly the princess inspected her gleaming fingernails and found them acceptable; then, indicating to Melithyrrh that she had bathed long enough, she clambered to her feet and stepped from the tub, smiling faintly at the frantic haste with which Melithyrrh rushed to wrap a towel about her. But the towel was gossamer stuff that scarcely hid the contours of her breasts and thighs, nor did the Su-Suheris display so much as a flicker of excitement at the sight of the Lady Thismet's body so skimpily wrapped.

Casually Thismet blotted herself dry and tossed the towel aside. Immediately Melithyrrh came forward to clothe her in a light robe of ivory-colored cambric oversewn with pink strands of tiny, fragile ganibin-shells.

"Imagine me now passing under the Dizimaule Arch and into the Inner Castle," she said to Sanibak-Thastimoon. "And suddenly I was all alone, no one in sight, not any Hjorts nor Ghayrogs nor human people, no one. *No one.* The Inner Castle was utterly deserted. There was a frightening silence, a ghastly silence. A cold wind was blowing across the plaza and strange stars were in the sky, of a kind that I had never seen before, huge bearded stars, stars that trailed bright streams of red flame.

"I was within the heart of the Inner Castle, now, coming up the Ninety-Nine Steps and entering into the centralmost precincts. What I found there was not disposed exactly as the real Inner Castle is, you understand: Lord Siminave's reflecting pool was on the wrong side of the Pinitor Court, and I couldn't see the Vildivar Balconies at all, and somehow Lord Arioc's Watchtower was even more bizarre-looking than it is in fact, with eight or nine tall peaks instead of five, and long looping arms sticking out from every side of it. But I was in the Inner Castle, all right, however much my dreaming mind had changed things around. I could see Stiamot Keep rising up over everything, and Lord Prankipin's big black treasury building in all its spectacular ugliness, and there was my father's garden-house, where all the peculiar plants grow; and then the great door to the royal chambers was before me. All this while, as I walked on and on, I saw no one else. It was as if I was the only person in the entire Castle."

Sanibak-Thastimoon stood statue-still before her, saying nothing, focusing the full concentration of both his heads upon her words.

Steadily, though with an increasing huskiness of voice, the Lady Thismet continued to tell him her tale, describing how in that awesome dreadful solitude she had advanced from room to room within the most sacrosanct precincts of the Castle until at last she stood at the threshold of the throne-room itself.

That was a room she knew very well, for it had been built by the command of her father Lord Confalume at the mid-point of his long, distinguished reign, and all through her girlhood she had watched it under construction, month by month, year by year. The old throne-room, which was said to go back to the very foundation of the Castle in Lord Stiamot's time, had long since been deemed too small and plain for its function; and Lord Confalume had resolved, once the greatness of his achievements was apparent to all, to replace it with a site of true magnificence in which the grandest and most solemn ceremonies of the realm might be held, and for which his name would be remembered through all of time to come. And so he had, amalgamating half a dozen inner rooms of no particular significance into the breathtaking high-vaulted throne-room that was to be his distinctive contribution to the fabric of the Castle.

The floor of it was fashioned not of the usual slabs of

polished stone but rather from the remarkable yellow wood of the gurna, a rare tree of the Khyntor peaks of northern Zimroel, that had the radiant glow of a slow-burning fire and the sheen and grace of fine amber. The beams of the room, gigantic square-timbered ones that jutted out with tremendous force from its ceiling, were gilded with delicately hammered sheets of the fine pink gold that came from the mines of eastern Alhanroel, and inset with huge clustering masses of amethysts and sapphires and moonstones and tourmalines. And on the walls were hung vivid tapestries woven by the most skillful craftsmen of Makroposopos, in which were depicted scenes of the history of Majipoor: its earliest settlement by the voyagers who came across the sea of stars from Old Earth, and then panels that showed the time of the building of the cities and the final conquest of the native Shapeshifters by Lord Stiamot, and finally a group of scenes illustrative of the wondrous expansion of the kingdom under its most recent rulers, who had brought it to its present state of overflowing abundance.

But the heart of the throne-room, the core of the Castle itself, was the grand and lordly Confalume Throne. Atop a grand mahogany pedestal cut with many steps it rested, a high curving seat carved from a single mighty block of black opal in which fiery natural veins of blood-scarlet ruby stood forth in an astonishing tracery. Its sides were flanked by massive silver pillars that supported an overarching canopy of gold lined with blue mother-of-pearl, and looming above all else was the starburst that was the symbol of the Coronal's power, blazing in a splendor of shining white platinum that was tipped at every extremity by spheres of milky-streaked purple onyx.

"The strangest thing of my dream," said the Lady Thismet to the utterly still Sanibak-Thastimoon, "was that there wasn't just the one throne in the throne-room, but two, both of them of identical aspect, facing each other across the entire expanse of the room. One throne was empty; and the other was occupied by a man who wore the robes and starburst crown of a Coronal. His face was in shadows, but even from some distance away I could tell that he was neither my father nor Prestimion; for plainly he was a much bigger man than either one of them, a man of great size and strength indeed.

"He beckoned me forward; and I came to the center of the room and halted there, unsure of what I should do, a little frightened, even, and when I began to make the starburst sign before him he raised one hand as though to make me stop. And said to me, in a deep voice that I knew very well, 'Why do you not take your proper seat, Lady Thismet?' By which he plainly meant the throne at the opposite side of the room. I went to it and climbed the stairs and placed myself upon that opal seat; and in that moment a brilliant light burst down on the room from the highest point of the roof, and I was able then to see that the man wearing the Coronal's crown, the man who was seated on the throne facing mine, was my brother Korsibar."

Once again the Lady Thismet fell silent.

There it was, out in the open at last. Had she been too obvious, too blatant? The silence lingered on and on, and she waited for Sanibak-Thastimoon to offer her his interpretation of her dream; but no interpretation was forthcoming.

Her eyes were bright with yearning. Come, she thought: comprehend my hidden message, you who comprehend everything. Seize the hint I've provided, give me the encouragement to go forward to what I most desire, tell me the thing I want so passionately to hear from you!

But the Su-Suheris remained silent.

"That was the dream, Sanibak-Thastimoon. It ended there. I awoke in the moment of that great light, and my soul was deeply troubled by what I had seen."

"Yes, lady. I understand that."

She waited hopefully once more; and again the Su-Suheris did not speak.

"You have nothing to tell me?" she asked. "Speak me my dream, Sanibak-Thastimoon! Let me know its meaning!"

"You know its meaning already, my lady." And he smiled the Su-Suheris version of a smile with both his faces.

So he perceived, then, the pattern of the tapestry she was weaving! But still, she knew, she had to goad him on to the final revelation. It had to come from him first, that statement of the thing that seethed within her.

Well, she could coax, she could beguile, she could hint. In feigned innocence and puzzlement she said, "Ah, but the most obvious meaning is one that defies all law and logic. Dreams often show visions of what is to come, is that not so? Especially dreams as vivid as this. But this dream goes too far. It seems to say that Korsibar is destined to be Coronal, and not Prestimion. Which is a monstrous impossibility. Everyone knows that such a thing may not be."

"Some dreams are born from our deepest hopes, lady. They show the future we yearn to see, not necessarily the one that is to be. I think this one may have been of that kind."

"And this deep hope, what is that?"

"You wandered long in the Castle, down many a strange path; and ultimately you came to a familiar place, and there you saw your brother crowned and seated on your father's throne. Can it be that you feel within yourself that Prince Korsibar *should* become Coronal?" the Su-Suheris asked, giving her a sharp close look out of the left pair of eyes.

Thismet felt joy rising within her. But she held to her game. "What are you saying? Do you dare put such wildly seditious words in my mouth?"

"I put nothing in your mouth, my lady, except that which I see is already in your soul. Can it be, lady, that in the secrecy of your heart you regret that the choice will not fall upon your brother?" His inflection was flat and even; both of his two faces were entirely without expression. But a terrible pressure was coming from him all the same. "Tell me, lady: is that not the case?"

Yes. Yes.

It was out at last.

Like everyone else, Thismet had taken it for granted that Prestimion would be Coronal; for how could it be otherwise, with the throne forbidden to Korsibar by ancient custom? And yet, and yet, gradually she had come to question the necessity of Prestimion's ascent. Why Prestimion? Why should her mighty brother of the shining brow not be king in succession to their father? Surely he merited the crown, all issues of tradition aside.

These were dangerous thoughts. Thismet had kept them hidden in the sealed fastnesses of her spirit. But as Prankipin's days dwindled, and the imminence of Prestimion's crowning rose on the horizon like Castle Mount itself, she found herself no longer able to suppress the fierce intensity of her feelings. Korsibar should be Coronal, yes! Korsibar, and no other prince. Korsibar! Korsibar!

Where to begin the campaign, though? For that she needed the advice of someone whose range of vision was far broader than her own. Who better than this cold-blooded magus, who served her brother and at times herself? He was the one. He could tell her the path to follow.

He was waiting for her to respond. He knew the nature of the game she had invited him to play with her: that was obvious.

He said, once more, "Is that not true, lady? You think he should be king."

Thismet smiled and drew a deep breath, and the strength to speak out came flooding into her, and boldly she said, "Yes! I will be honest with you, Sanibak-Thastimoon: that is precisely what I believe! It makes no sense to me that Prestimion should be my father's choice instead of Korsibar. Prestimion in place of his own son—his magnificent kingly son—"

She paused. What joy, what relief, finally to have let it all pour forth!

Sanibak-Thastimoon said nothing.

"Custom. Law. I know these things," said Princess Thismet, "But even so—" She shook her head. "There's such a thing as a higher justice in the world, justice that goes beyond mere custom. And by the law of that justice it's right that Korsibar be Coronal. That seems utterly clear to me."

Again she looked questioningly to the Su-Suheris. The four green alien eyes that faced her remained implacably enigmatic.

"Yes," he said, after an eternity. "I do agree, lady."

Her first convert, her first ally. It was a moment for exhilaration and exultation. She could almost have embraced him. Almost.

But there was another matter, too, even more delicate than the other, to thrash out with him.

Thismet breathed deeply once more and said, "The two thrones of my dream. What of that, Sanibak-Thastimoon? My brother beckoned me to take the other throne for myself. But even if Korsibar should somehow become Coronal—I have no idea how, but there must be a way—there'd be no place in the government for me. The sister of the Coronal is without rank in her own right. It was you that told me, remember, that I was destined for greatness, long before I ever dreamed this dream. But in the waking world what throne would there be for me to have?"

"There is greatness in helping one's brother to attain a throne. There is power to be had by standing beside one's brother as he sits upon the throne. You take your dream of two thrones too literally, perhaps, lady."

"Perhaps I do," Thismet said.

She looked toward the richly tiled wall of the chamber as if she were able to see clear through it, and upward also through each of the rings of the Labyrinth, beyond all those ancient subterranean structures—the Court of Pyramids and the Place of Masks and the Hall of Winds and all the rest of them—outward into the open, and off toward the colossal bulk of Castle Mount bestriding the world far to the north. And abruptly all the exhilaration that had possessed her just a moment before departed from her, and she came crashing down out of her joy, and the world went dark for her as though there had been a sudden eclipse.

These fantasies of her dream, she realized, were mere foolish phantoms. None of the things her wanton sleeping mind had imagined would ever come to pass. It was absurd to think that they could. There would be no great position in the realm for her, no, and none for her brother either. The Prince of Muldemar would be king. That was as good as signed and sealed; the inevitability of Prestimion's rule fell like a sword across her soul.

The pattern that her life would surely take once the new reign had begun rose bleakly before her: a soft empty comfort-swaddled life, a meaningless existence of baths and manicures and massages and jeweled idleness, far from the levers of power in the land. Had she been born for nothing more than that? What a sad waste, then!

She knew she must fight it. But how? How?

After a time she said, in a steely tone, "In any event there is no justice in the world, is there, Sanibak-Thastimoon? I know as well as you that it'll be Prestimion who becomes Coronal, and not Korsibar."

"That is something that might reasonably be expected, lady," said Sanibak-Thastimoon placidly.

"And when the throne goes to Prestimion, Korsibar and I

leave the Castle, he to his estate and I to mine; or I might become wife to some powerful prince, I suppose. But there'll be no power in that for me, will there? I will be a great lady, yes, but I am that now; after Prestimion is king I will be a wife, at best. A *wife*, Sanibak-Thastimoon." She spoke the word as though it were an imprecation. "I'll have no voice in anything of any importance outside my own house, and perhaps not even there. It'll be little better for my brother. Our family's influence in this castle ends in the moment when Prestimion puts the crown upon his head."

"The great prince you might marry," the Su-Suheris said, "might well be that same Lord Prestimion, princess, if it is indeed Prestimion who is to be Coronal. And then your power and influence would by no means be at an end."

That suggestion brought a sudden half-smothered gasp of astonishment from the Lady Melithyrrh, who had been standing to one side throughout this entire interchange. She looked toward Thismet, who silenced whatever Melithyrrh might have been about to say with a furious glare and replied, "Are you seriously proposing, Sanibak-Thastimoon, that I give myself in marriage to the very man who is going to take the throne from my brother? The one who's destined to push him into obscurity?"

"I merely raised the possibility, lady."

"Well, see that you raise it never again, if you'd like to keep both those pretty heads attached to that neck of yours." Thismet's eyes flashed him a look of fiery ferocity. Strength and determination were gathering in her again. —"There is another possibility," she said, less severely, in a new and deeper voice.

"Yes, lady?" said Sanibak-Thastimoon, with the most extreme patience. "And what is that?"

Her heart was beating in an astounding thunderous way. Thismet felt herself swaying with an odd vertigo, for she knew she stood now at a precipitous brink. But she compelled herself to maintain an outward appearance of calmness. Moistening her lips thoughtfully, she said, "You agree with me, you say, that Korsibar is better fitted for the throne. Very well. My intention is to see that he attains it."

"And how will you achieve that?" asked the Su-Suheris.

"Consider this, if you will. What the dream was telling me, let me propose, is that what I must do is go to Korsibar and strongly urge him to put himself forth before our father as a candidate for the throne. *Now*, while everything is still in flux: before the old Pontifex dies, before Prestimion is formally named. And our father will yield to him, I think, if Korsibar only makes his case strong enough; and then Korsibar will be Coronal; and in gratitude my brother will name me as one of his high counsellors, so that I may have some role after all in governing the world. Would you not say that that's a plausible interpretation of my dream?" And again, when the Su-Suheris offered no reply: "Would you not say so?"

He nodded, one head after another. And blandly he said, "I will not deny that it is, lady."

Thismet smiled. "It must be, beyond all question," she said, all in a rush. She was ablaze now, flushed and panting. "There can be no other road to greatness for me—is there? How can there be?—but through Korsibar. And it's a known fact that I'm destined for great things. You've told me so yourself. Or do you retract that prophecy now?"

"I retract none of it, lady," said the Su-Suheris quietly. "Your future is displayed in your stars, and obscurity and retirement play no part in the pattern of what is beyond any doubt to come. That is quite certain.—The same is true of your brother's horoscope. '*You will shake the world, Prince Korsibar.*' Those were my words to him, some months ago. Did he never share them with you?"

"No," said Thismet, with some surprise. "I heard nothing about that from him."

"Nevertheless, I did make it known to him. And in recent days your father's own oracles have independently told him the same thing."

"Well, then," she said, "it all becomes clear. The omens converge and confirm one another: all lines lead us to the throne. Tradition will give way to reason; the better man will be chosen. I'll speak with Korsibar this very day."

But then a curious expression passed across both Sanibak-Thastimoon's faces, as if his heads had exchanged glances with one another, though she had not seen his eyes move at all.

Thismet said, "Do you see anything unwise in that?"

"I think it might be wiser, lady, to speak with his friends first, before you bring the matter directly to him."

"Mandrykarn, you mean? Venta? Navigorn?"

"No, not those. They would be worse than useless. I mean the other ones, those two ill-matched brothers, the giant and the little snake. They'll serve the purpose better, I suspect."

Thismet contemplated that for a moment.

"Farholt and Farquanor," she said. "Yes. Yes, perhaps so!" To Melithyrrh she said, "I'll go to my sitting-room now, I think. Send for the brothers; tell them to wait upon me there."

# 6

Korsibar said, "We are agreed, then." He looked to the list in his hand, then to the assembled lords. They had gathered that day in the room of the Labyrinth's imperial sector known as the Old Banquet Hall, which was cut at angles that diminished and swelled curiously from one end to the other, and had many a strangely painted drapery on the wall to enhance the effect of discomforting illusions of distance. "The foot-races and the dueling with batons, first. Following which, the hurdles and hoops and the hammer-throw, both for the men and the women. The archery contest, next, and then the mounted jousting; and after that, the mock battle, and then the boxing and the wrestling matches, with the chariot-racing to come at the very end. Which will be followed by the ceremonial parade upward through the various levels from the Arena to the Court of Globes, where the Master of the Games will award the prizes in the presence of Lord Confalume. And then—"

"It was my understanding that we would have the wrestling earlier in the program," said Gialaurys testily. He had only just arrived in the hall, minutes before. "So it says here on the slip of paper that you see in my hand. The wrestling after the batons, and before the hurdles."

Korsibar looked with an uncertain frown toward Farholt, who had played a closer role in the planning than he had. "That was before," said Farholt, stepping forward and taking

Korsibar's list from him. "It was changed just two hours past, while you were still lingering over your midday ale." Farholt tapped the list and offered Gialaurys a defiant glowering stare. "The lighter sports first, and then the things for sturdier folk."

"I was not consulted," Gialaurys said. "I would rather have it the earlier way." There was a rumble of something close to menace in his voice. He moved a couple of paces closer to the heavy-sinewed Farholt, who bristled visibly and drew himself up to his fullest height. They were the two most sizable figures in the group, both of them mountainous in bulk, Farholt the taller man but Gialaurys of a greater thickness of body, even, than the other. "I prefer to win my wreath sooner rather than later."

"And are you so sure of winning, then?" Farholt asked. "What if it goes against you, and then you must sit sorrowfully through all the rest of the games with the mark of defeat on you, while wreaths are won by others all around?"

Fury gleamed in Gialaurys's eyes. "So that's why you'd prefer to hold back the wrestling closer to the end, Farholt?"

"That was no decision of mine," Farholt retorted. His face, always somewhat florid, had turned a bright red. "But if you mean to suggest—"

"One moment, friends," said Prestimion, moving between the two big men just as it was beginning to seem that the gathering heat of their words would lead to actual strife right here and now. Dwarfed though he was by their hugenesses looming above him, he pressed them each lightly on the chest with his fingertips and pushed them gently apart. "Please, let there be peace in this place, where a Pontifex lies dying close at hand. This is too small a matter for such quarreling. What do you say here, Prince Korsibar?"

"I say that if there's a disagreement, let the Master of the Games decide."

"A good point." Prestimion glanced in the direction of the

Grand Admiral Prince Gonivaul, who had been chosen to be Master that morning by a slender margin over the only other candidate, the Procurator Dantirya Sambail.

The Admiral, one of the senior peers of the land, was linked by ties of blood to the family of Amyntilir, the Pontifex who had held sway three reigns prior to Prankipin. Prince Gonivaul was a tight-faced man of stubborn and parsimonious nature, whose sumptuous private domain lay not far outside the burnt-orange sandstone walls of many-spired Bombifale, which was by general agreement deemed the most beautiful of the cities of Castle Mount. He was long and narrow through the jaw, very much like his famous ancestor, and showed scarcely anything but hair above the shoulders, for a dense and coarse black beard thick as fur covered him cheek and jowl, upward almost to the lower lids of his eyes and the other way deep and heavy down his throat to vanish into his collar; and the hair of his head, of the same thick, rank kind and worn very long, descended across his forehead nearly to his eyebrows. His title of Grand Admiral was a purely ceremonial one; the commerce of the ports lay in his official jurisdiction, but, so far as anyone knew, he had never gone to sea, not even for the journey to Zimroel that most of the princes of the Mount undertook at least once in their lives.

Prestimion said, "Good Admiral and Master, you've heard Prince Korsibar. Will you give us a ruling in this?"

Gonivaul grunted in his beard. His brows lowered and his cheeks screwed upward into a squint until his eyes had all but disappeared within the dark fur that covered so much of his face; and for an inordinate time he seemed lost in what was plainly meant to pass for thought. At long last he said, "Which is the later of the two lists?"

"Mine," Farholt said instantly. "There is no disputing that."

Gonivaul took the slip from him, and the other from Gia-laurys, and studied them both another endless while. Then at length the Admiral said, "We have room for compromise here. The wrestling is moved to the middle of the games, between the hammer-throw and the archery."

Farholt quickly signalled his acceptance; but from Gialaurys there came a grumbling sound, and there might have been something more from him had Prestimion not silenced him with a hiss.

Once the wrangling was over and the preliminary planning for the games completed, servitors entered the room with refreshments for the assembled lords. Others of the Labyrinth's high-born guests who had played no part in the planning session came in now also, for there was to be a general festivity here today in celebration of the impending commencement of the games.

The various princes and dukes and counts moved apart about the hall by twos and threes, gathering by the quaint and curious bits of ancient statuary that were scattered throughout it. They were, supposedly, portraits of Pontifexes and Coronals of ages gone by. While waiting for the wine to be served the guests studied one statue and another, touching them, tracing the outline of a sharp nose or an outthrust chin, speculating on the identities of those whom they were meant to represent. "Arioc," said Gialaurys, pointing at a particularly preposterous-looking one. No, said Duke Oljebbin, that was Stiamot, the conqueror of the Shapeshifters, which led to an extensive dispute between him and Prince Serithorn, who was pleased to count Stiamot among his numerous royal ancestors. Then the scrawny little Farquanor, huge Farholt's brother, identified a statue of a tall man imbued with sublime dignity and nobility as being that of one of *his* ancestors, the Pontifex Guadeloom, bringing a skeptical chuckle from Prince Gonivaul, and so it went from one to another.

"That was done well, your passing that disagreement so quickly to the Admiral," Korsibar said to Prestimion. They stood together at one sharp angle of the seven-sided room beneath a broad sky-blue arch touched with borders of red autumn fire. "Those are two devilish short-tempered men, those two. And they have no tolerance for one another at all. Let the one say 'spring' and the other will instantly say 'winter', let one say 'black' and from the other will come 'white,' and so on through the dictionary for sheer love of contrariness. When they come together in the wrestling, it'll be a spectacle indeed."

"My cousin of Ni-moya expressed the belief the other day that it might be just such a way between you and me as it is between Farholt and Gialaurys," said Prestimion, smiling a little, though barely drawing back his lips. "That is to say, he thinks that we are contrary to the essence; that there's an innate tension between us creates automatic conflict; that you might be expected to oppose a certain thing only because I was the one who had advocated it."

"Ah, no, Prestimion," returned Korsibar, smiling also and with rather more warmth to it. "Do you really believe that to be so?"

"It was the Procurator that said it."

"Yes, but you and I know that it isn't like that with us at all. Do you feel a tension as you stand here beside me? I'm not aware of any. And why should there be? There's no rivalry where rivalry isn't possible." Korsibar clapped his hands to a passing servitor. "Hoy, some wine here!" he called. "The good strong Muldemar wine, from the Prince's own vineyard!"

Many others around the room were watching them closely. Among them was Count Iram of Normork, a slender red-haired man famous for his prowess in chariot-racing: a kinsman of Prince Serithorn's, he was, related also to Lord Confalume's family by marriage. Iram plucked at Septach Melayn's sleeve and said, cocking an eyebrow toward Korsibar and Prestimion, "How strained their smiles are, how hard they work at seeming friendly to each other! And look how gingerly they clink their wine-bowls! As though both of them fear that there'd be an explosion if they were to hit them together a trifle too hard."

"I think those are two men who fear very little," said Septach Melayn.

But Iram persisted. "Beyond question they hold themselves in a very stiff fashion. As well they ought to, I suppose; for what a tremendous lot of awkwardness there must be between them! Prestimion pays deference to Korsibar, since after all Korsibar is the Coronal's son and therefore somewhat royal himself. But Korsibar for his part knows that he has to show respect to Prestimion, who very soon will be a king in his own right and therefore a higher man than Korsibar."

Septach Melayn laughed. "Prestimion will be king, yes. But never, I suspect, will he be a higher man than Korsibar."

Count Iram seemed perplexed at that. His mind was not of the quickest. But then he grasped the point of Septach Melayn's words; for it was plain to see that the long-legged Korsibar rose up far above Prestimion, who came not much more than breast-high to him. Which was all that Septach Melayn had intended, a mere idle jest.

"Higher in that sense, yes," the Count said. "I take your meaning." He offered a polite chuckle for Septach Melayn's feeble play on words.

"It was not a very profound observation," said Septach Melayn.

Indeed he felt a little abashed at his own vapidity. How could anyone speak of Prestimion as inconsequential beside the Coronal's son, even in jest? The smaller man's sturdy breadth of shoulder and invariable air of unshakeable aplomb gave him a commanding look all out of keeping with the meagerness of his stature. And this day in particular Prestimion seemed to glow with the radiance of his advancing destiny. He was dressed in a regal robe of glossy crimson silk belted with emerald green, with a massy golden pendant in the form of a bright-eyed crab hanging from a thick chain on his breast, whereas Korsibar wore only a simple knee-length tunic of white linen that any sausage-vendor might have worn, and open sandals of the most common design. For all his noble height and grandeur of form, Korsibar just now seemed eclipsed, cast into shadow by the flood of light that streamed from Prestimion.

"Be that as it may," Iram went on, "but tell me this, Septach Melayn: does Prestimion privately feel himself more worthy than Korsibar, or does he have secret doubts? And, more to the point: does Korsibar truly think that Prestimion's fit to have the throne? There's much talk going around that Prestimion's coming greatness doesn't sit very well with the Coronal's son."

"And who talks this talk?" asked Septach Melayn.

"Procurator Dantirya Sambail, for one."

"Well, yes, Dantirya Sambail. I heard his famous remark. But there's no substance to it. Venom drips as easily from the Procurator's lips as rainfall does from the sky in the forests of Kajith Kabulon. The moist heavy clouds there have no choice but to let their surplus water spill out each day; and so it is with Dantirya Sambail. He's a mass of hatefulness within, and from time to time he has to vent some of it into the air."

"Dantirya Sambail is the only one who has said it aloud. But everyone thinks it."

"Thinks that Korsibar is resentful of Prestimion?"

"Well, and is there any way for him not to be? When he's such a grand figure of a man, and so much held in esteem everywhere, and the son of a great and beloved king besides?"

"No Coronal's son has ever followed his father to the throne," said Septach Melayn. "None ever will, without bringing calamity down upon us all." Idly he twirled the tip of his little golden beard, and after a moment said, "I agree, Korsibar is very impressive-looking, yes. If Coronals were chosen for their looks, he'd have the job without question. But the law very clearly states that we have no hereditary kingship here, and Korsibar's a law-abiding man. Never has he given any indication of harboring dishonorable ambitions of any sort."

"So you think all's well between him and Prestimion?"

"I have no doubt of it."

"All the same, the air these days is heavy with portents, Septach Melayn."

"Is it, now? Well, better portents in the air than a swarm of dhiims, eh? Because the bite of a dhiim is real, and hurts; but no one's ever seen a portent, let alone been injured by one. Let the loathsome mages chatter all they like. I can see the future every bit as clearly as the best of them, Iram, and this is what I have to tell you: in due time Prestimion is going to come serenely to the throne, and Korsibar will gladly pay homage to him along with all the rest of us."

Count Iram nervously fingered a small bright amulet of gold and sea-dragon ivory that he wore dangling by a little silver chain from the breast of his tunic. "You are very light-hearted about these matters, Septach Melayn."

"Yes. I'm light-hearted about most matters, I suppose. It's my character's biggest flaw." Septach Melayn gave Count Iram a good-humored wink and turned away to find some other conversational partner among a group of younger princes that had collected about the table of wines.

At the opposite end of the room a new figure now appeared, toward whom the attention of a great many instantly began to flow: the Lady Thismet, accompanied by her lady-of-honor Melithyrrh and a little group of her handmaidens. Sanibak-Thastimoon was with her also, garbed in the formal red-and-green livery of Korsibar's service, and the sight of the Su-Suheris magus caused no little whispering in the hall. There were few who failed to find the Su-Suheris folk sinister and forbidding, if only for the strangeness of those double heads.

Like her brother, Thismet had chosen to dress in uncomplicated manner this day, a light cream-white gown of a matte texture, belted in red, with a tracery of red pearls woven into it along her left shoulder to her breast, and for other ornament merely a single sharp manculain spine thrust through the glossy tight-curled darkness of her hair. The simplicity of her costume made a striking effect in this congregation of formally robed lordlings. It was as though she stood in a brilliant spotlight, attracting all eyes to her; and yet she had done nothing at all other than to enter the room, and smile at this one and at that, and to beckon for a bowl of wine.

She spoke for a time with her brother's dear friend Navigorn of Hoikmar, who was regarded almost as Korsibar's equal as a stalwart huntsman, and with Mandrykarn and Venta, those other close hunting-companions of Korsibar's. Then she dismissed them smoothly from her and with one quick imperious glance summoned Farholt to her side, and Farholt's smaller and more malevolent younger brother also, the serpentine Farquanor. These two had been standing with the Procurator Dantirya Sambail and the Coronal's white-haired cousin, Duke Oljebbin of Stoienzar, but they came to her at once, lithe little Farquanor taking up a position at her left hand and big blocky Farholt stationing himself immediately in front of her like a one-man mountain, altogether concealing her from the view of those behind him.

It required some effort to believe that this pair had sprung from the same womb. They were opposites in all ways, hot raucous bellowing Farholt given to all forms of excess and impulse, and icy little Farquanor a quiet man of cunning and caution, who advanced inch by inch through life from one carefully constructed scheme to another. Farholt was huge and fleshy and ponderous of movement, Farquanor slim and taut-skinned and quick. But their kinship could be seen in their eyes, which were of the same flat deadly gray hue, and in the ruddiness of their complexions, and in the prominent jut of their noses, which seemed to spring at a straight line from the midpoint of their foreheads. They had royalty in their ancestry: the long-ago Lord Guadeloom, he who had abruptly and surprisingly been made Coronal as a result of certain curious events surrounding the sudden abdication of the Pontifex Arioc.

Like Lord Confalume, Lord Guadeloom had had a son of more than usual splendor and nobility, Theremon by name. A tradition persisted in the family of Farholt and Farquanor that Guadeloom's son Theremon had been far more deserving to be Coronal after him than any other man. But when it was Lord Guadeloom's time to become Pontifex he had named a mediocre bureaucrat named Calintane to succeed him, putting aside his own son just as all Coronals before him had done.

That decision had rankled in Theremon's descendants throughout the succeeding generations. The hereditary resentment of the family had descended through the long centuries to Farholt and Farquanor, who often when in their cups would hold forth on the fire that still coursed in them when they considered the ancient injustice done their ancestor. The Lady Thismet had long been aware of the passion those two felt on the subject; she found it of special interest at the present moment. They had talked about it most earnestly in her sitting-room only the day before, Farquanor and Farholt and she.

"Concerning the matter that you and I discussed a little while ago—" Thismet said now.

The brothers were instantly attentive, though the flatness and deadness of their eyes seemed to bely the alertness of their features.

She said, with the serenity of a smooth-flowing stream,

"Sanibak-Thastimoon has cast the auguries. The moment is auspicious for making a beginning of great endeavors: the time has arrived to commence our project."

"Here? Now?" Farquanor asked. "In this room?"

"This very room, this very instant."

Farquanor looked warily toward his brother, then to the Su-Suheris, whose faces were as inscrutable as ever, and lastly at Thismet.

"Is this wise?" he asked.

"It is. I am determined." Thismet gestured toward the far side, where Prestimion and Korsibar were still engrossed in their talk, looking like nothing so much as a pair of old friends who had not seen one another in many months and were warmly renewing their acquaintance. "Go to him. Draw him aside. Say to him the things we agreed yesterday you would say."

"And if I'm overheard?" Farquanor asked, his lean hard-angled face clouding, his eyes coming to life with the glint of uncertainty. "What then for me, publicly uttering subversive and indeed seditious notions under Prestimion's very nose?"

"I would assume that you'd utter your utterances in a low guarded voice," Thismet said. "No one's going to overhear you amidst all this noise. And I'll see to it that Prestimion himself is busy elsewhere while you speak with Korsibar."

Farquanor nodded. His moment of unsureness was gone; already, Thismet could see, he was eager for the task. With a flick of her fingertips she sent him on his way, and she watched intently as Farquanor set out across the room, approached Korsibar and Prestimion, spoke briefly with them, doing some pointing and nodding in her direction. Then Prestimion, smiling, broke away and began to head through the crowd toward her. "Leave me," Thismet murmured to Farholt. But she asked Sanibak-Thastimoon to remain with her.

Farquanor and Korsibar, she saw, had now withdrawn a

little way deeper into the room, to a quiet alcove at the next angle of the wall, where the immense hideous flat-faced bust of some primordial Coronal partly concealed them from view. The way they stood, face to face, presenting themselves in profile to the rest of the room, it was impossible for anyone to read their lips. She could see Farquanor saying something to Korsibar, and Korsibar's brow lowering in a heavy frown, and Farquanor speaking on, with many a quick gesture of his hands, while Korsibar leaned forward from the waist as though to hear more clearly what the smaller man was telling him.

Watching them, Thismet felt the rate of her heartbeat accelerating and her throat going dry. The pattern of the years to come—for Korsibar, for her, for the entire world—would very likely be shaped by the words Farquanor was speaking now. For better, for ill, the thing was being set in motion. She stole a quick glance at Sanibak-Thastimoon beside her. He was smiling an eerie double smile at her, as though to say, *All will be well, have no fear.*

Then Prestimion was at her side and saying, with the courteous little gesture of formal obeisance due to her as daughter of the Coronal, "The Count Farquanor tells me you have something you wish me to hear, lady."

"Indeed," she said.

She studied him with carefully hidden care. They had, of course, known each other ever since they were children, but to Thismet Prestimion was just one of the many young lords who thronged the Castle, and not nearly the most interesting of those: she had paid little attention to him over the years. He had always seemed to her nothing more than a self-absorbed lordling on the make, earnest and studious and ambitious, and perhaps a trifle too short to be really attractive, though certainly he was good-looking enough. It was only after Prestimion had begun to emerge a few years ago as the probable candidate for her father's throne that she had given him any serious scrutiny. Mainly Thismet found him irritating, these days; but how much that was because of anything he did or said, and how much simply because she disliked him for the likelihood that he was going to occupy the throne that she wished her brother would have, she could not say.

What surprised her this day, as he stood beside her now perhaps a trifle too closely, was something that she had never in any way felt before: a faint troublesome stirring of response to Prestimion as a man.

He was no taller than he ever was, and he wore his fair hair, as always, in an unflattering way. But he was different today in other ways. Already he had begun to hold himself in a truly regal fashion, but without seeming to be working hard at it, and there was a kingly glint in his eyes, and it seemed almost as though a sort of electricity were playing about his brow. Perhaps the rich splendid garb he wore today had something to do with it: but Thismet knew it was something else that was drawing her, something more elemental, which was nothing but the gathering force of Prestimion's imminent rise to power. There was a magnetism in that. She could feel its pull. A strange pulsation came sweeping upward through her from her loins to her breast, and onward to her head.

Thismet wondered whether Prestimion might feel any corresponding pull himself that came from her. It seemed to her that she detected the signs of that—the movements of his eyes, the shifts of color in his face. It gave her a moment's giddy pleasure.

Which gave way to anger, turned against herself. What absurdity this was! Every atom of her being must be devoted from this time onward to preventing this man from attaining the very power whose mere prospect was so deplorably unsettling her. For him to be drawn to her might be useful to her purpose; for her to be drawn at all to him, nothing but wild folly.

"You know Sanibak-Thastimoon, I think?" Thismet asked, inclining her head slightly in the direction of the Su-Suheris standing just behind her. "Magus to my brother, and occasionally to me as well?"

"I know of him, yes. We have not actually spoken."

Sanibak-Thastimoon bowed to Prestimion, lowering his right head rather more than his left.

Thismet said, "In recent days he has been peering long and hard at the stars, prince, seeking omens for the new reign. He tells me now that he's found auguries that will be of considerable interest to you."

"Has he, now?" said Prestimion, with what seemed like no more than well-mannered formality. Too late, Thismet remembered that Prestimion was said to be skeptical toward all forms of wizardry and omen-seeking. But no matter: her only intention at the moment was to distract him from the conversation between Farquanor and Korsibar that was taking place across the room.

She gestured to the Su-Suheris to speak. Sanibak-Thastimoon made no show of dismay or surprise, although Thismet had not given him any warning of what would be required of him. "What I have determined," said Sanibak-Thastimoon unhesitatingly, "is this: Many great surprises are in store for you, prince—and for us all—in the times that lie ahead."

Prestimion managed a slight elevation of his eyebrows, by way of showing mild curiosity.

"Pleasant surprises, I hope," he said.

"Oh, yes, some of those as well," said Sanibak-Thastimoon.

The prince laughed. "I'm not entirely sure I'm pleased with the sound of that."

He invited the magus to be more specific; and Sanibak-Thastimoon replied sonorously that he would, so far as it was in his power to do so.

Thismet, meanwhile, was looking past Prestimion's shoulder and outward toward her brother and Farquanor. She noted an expression of intense animation on Korsibar's face: he was speaking quickly and with many firm chopping gestures of his hand, while Farquanor, rising almost on tiptoe to reduce the gulf of height between them, appeared to be trying to mollify Korsibar, to soothe him, to reassure him. Suddenly Korsibar turned and stared across the room, directly at Thismet. She fancied that she saw astonishment and bewilderment—and, perhaps, anger—in her brother's eyes; and she felt a great yearning to know without delay what had occurred between him and Farquanor.

Closer at hand, Sanibak-Thastimoon was sharing portents of things to come with Prestimion as fast as he could invent them; but his utterances were couched in the cloudy generalities of his trade, with much murky talk of the stars traveling retrograde in their courses and brazen serpents devouring their own tails, such-and-such happenings and configurations implying the possibility of such-and-such an event and such-and-such a corollary consequence, unless of course they were countermanded by the contrary omen implied by thus and so, and so on, none of this being phrased with any great clarity or specificity.

Prestimion was showing increasing signs of distinct inattention. At an appropriate pause in the narration he thanked the Su-Suheris most graciously for his guidance and excused himself. Then, looking toward Thismet, he gave her a quick dazzling smile and a startling intimate stare that made her feel both flattered and furious at the same time. And then he was gone.

Farquanor now was on his way back to her side of the room.

Her forehead throbbed with apprehension; her brain was spinning in her skull. "Well?" she demanded fiercely.

He seemed drained and wilted, like a plant left too long in the sun. Thismet had never seen him look so shaken. He held up a hand to forestall further pressure from her. Grabbing a bowl of wine from the tray of a passing servitor, he gulped it down before making any answer. She compelled herself to be patient, watching him regain strength and poise until he was again the Farquanor she knew, fearless, resourceful.

"It was very difficult," he said at last. "But I think we have made a start."

Eagerly she gripped him by one forearm. "Quickly! Tell me everything!"

Farquanor paused a long maddening moment. Then at last he said, "I began by observing to him that everyone here was talking about the Procurator's remark, that your brother might feel hostility toward Prestimion and any idea that might come from him. To which your brother responded this, lady: that if the meaning of the Procurator's words was that he felt your brother was inflamed with the desire to be Coronal in Prestimion's stead, then the Procurator was implying treason to him, which is a dastardly charge that your brother utterly rejects."

"Indeed," said Thismet, feeling her spirit sinking within her. "Treason. He used that word. And you said—?"

"I said to him that he himself might not feel that he deserved the throne more than Prestimion, but that there were many others here that did, and that I was proud to say that I was among them. That is treason too, said he, and grew very angry."

"And gave no sign that he might be flattered, as well as angered, by hearing that important people thought that he was worthy of the throne?"

"Not then," Farquanor said.

"Ah. Not *then*."

"I said next that I begged his pardon if I had offended him," Farquanor went on, "and assured him I had no wish whatever to espouse treason, nor the Procurator neither, and most surely not to attribute treasonous thoughts to him. But I asked the good prince your brother to consider that treason is in fact a concept that alters and varies with the circumstances. None would dare call a thing treason, I said, if it were to bring about a worthwhile end. Which made him even more angry, lady. I thought he might strike me.

"I begged him to be calm; I told him again how many there are who believe in his right to have the throne, and that those people felt the succession law is unjust. I spoke of all those famous princes of the past who had been passed over for the Coronal's seat on account of that law, and named a few. They were great names; I was very eloquent on their behalf, and in comparing his virtues with theirs. And gradually I could see him warming to the concept. Toying with it, you might say. Revolving it again and again in his mind as though it were something completely new to him. And finally he said, 'Yes, Farquanor, many a great prince has had to step aside on account of this custom of ours.' "

"Ah. So he has taken the bait, then. The hook is in him."

"Perhaps it is, lady."

"And how was it left between you when you parted from him?"

"You didn't see? There, at the very end of our talk?"

"I was busy at just that moment speaking with Prince Prestimion."

A muscle quivered in Farquanor's fleshless cheek and his eyes betrayed a surge of remembered pain. "I may have moved things along a trifle too swiftly just then, perhaps. I said to him that I was glad to see we were in accord, and that we might profitably hold further discussions on the subject. And also I said that there were those who would be glad to meet with him this afternoon to discuss a course of action leading toward constructive goals."

Thismet leaned eagerly forward, so close that Farquanor's nostrils quivered at the fragrance of her breath.

He said, "The prince reacted badly. It was too much too soon, I think, that final remark. A terrible look came into your brother's eyes, and he reached down and laid his fingertips along both sides of my neck, like *this,* lady, very lightly, so that from a distance one might think it was but a friendly touch. But I knew from the strength of him and the pressure of his hands against me that all he needed to do was flick his wrists and he'd snap my spine as you would a fishbone, and might well do it. And he said to me that he would have no part in any treason against Prestimion and that I must never speak to him of such things again; and then he sent me from him."

"And this, you say, is a good start?"

"I think it is, lady."

"It seems a very bad one to me."

"He was angered at the end, yes, and angry also in the beginning. But betweentimes he was giving the idea serious consideration. I saw that in him. He goes this way and that, lady: it is his nature."

"Yes. I know my brother's nature."

"The thing is planted in him. He'll strive to resist its pull, for as we all know the prince your brother is not one for rising up against the established order. But also it pleases him inwardly that others see him as a king. That was something he may not have allowed himself to dare to believe, but when it comes to him from others, that alters the case for him. He can be turned, lady. I'm certain of it. It would be easy enough for you to see that for yourself. You only need go to him; praise him for the kingliness that you see in him; and watch him closely. His face began to shine with a rosy glow when I spoke to him in that fashion. Oh, yes, lady, yes, yes. He can be turned."

# 7

On the first day of the Pontifical Games the leaders of the kingdom presented themselves formally at the bedside of the Pontifex, who still hovered between life and death, obstinate in his refusal to pass onward and return to the Source of All Things. It was as though they felt a need to ask his permission to commence the games that were by ancient custom supposed to commemorate his departure from the world.

The dying Pontifex lay with eyes closed, face upward, an almost insignificant figure in the great expanse of the canopied imperial bed. His skin had gone gray. The long lobes of his ears had acquired a pendulous droop. His features were expressionless, as though sealed behind bands of bone. Only by his slow, virtually imperceptible breathing did he indicate in any way that he was still alive, and even that appeared to cease for long moments at a time.

It was time for him to go. Everyone was agreed on that. He was unthinkably ancient, with well over a century of life behind him. Forty-odd years as Pontifex, twenty or so as Coronal before that: it was enough.

Prankipin had been a man of tremendous vigor and physical resilience, romantic and visionary of nature, buoyant and joyous of spirit, famous for the warmth and infectious power of his smile. Even his coins portrayed him smiling that wondrous smile; and he appeared to be smiling now as he lay on his deathbed, as though the muscles of his face had long since forgotten any other expression. The Pontifex seemed oddly youthful, too, here in extreme old age. His cheeks and forehead were smooth, almost child-like, all the furrows and corrugations of his long life having vanished in these final weeks.

In the darkened chamber where the old Pontifex lay dying, a luminous hush prevailed. Blue smoke flecked with red sparks coiled upward from tripods in which alien incenses burned, and tables in the shadowy corner of the room were piled high with books of spells and potions and the movements of the stars that the monarch had studied, or had pretended to study. More such volumes lay about him on the floor. A Vroon and a Su-Suheris and a steely-eyed Ghayrog stood sternly beside the bed, unendingly chanting in low soft tones the mysterious incantations that were intended to protect the Pontifex's departing soul as it made itself ready for its voyage.

Everyone in the inner circles of the government, both at the Castle and in the Labyrinth, knew the names of those three aliens. The Vroon was Sifil Thiando; the Ghayrog, Varimaad Klain; the Su-Suheris, Yamin-Dalarad. The three sepulchral-looking beings were the commanders of that immense troop of seers, haruspicators, necromancers, conjurers, and sortilegers that Prankipin had gathered about himself in the final two decades of his reign.

Bedecked with the insignia of their kind, clutching the wands of their art, they held themselves lofty and aloof, clothed in the dark forbidding aura of their own magics, as the members of the Coronal's party prepared to enter the imperial bedchamber. For many years now these three had guided the aging Pontifex in all his most significant decisions; and in recent times it had become apparent to all that they—and not any of the officials of the Pontifical bureaucracy, nor, perhaps, even the Pontifex himself—were the real figures of authority at the court of the Labyrinth. By their imperious stance and commanding mien they left no doubt of that today.

But the three highest ministers of the Pontifical court were also on hand for the ceremony, clustered grimly to the left of the dying man's pillow as if standing guard against the trio to the other side: Orwic Sarped, the Minister of External Affairs, and Segamor, the Pontifex's private secretary, and Kai Kanamat, the High Spokesman of the Pontificate. They were a somber-faced and dismal group. Those three had held their posts for immemorial years and were all three aged and withered, with Kai Kanamat the most shriveled of all, a man who gave the appearance of having been mummified while still alive, mere wizened skin stretched across a flimsy armature of fragile bone.

Once they, and not Prankipin's team of wizards, had been the true wielders of power here. But that time was long gone. Beyond doubt they would all be glad to lay down whatever was left of their responsibilities and disappear into retirement as soon as Prankipin had given up the ghost.

In the room also were the two chief physicians to the Pontifex, Baergax Vor of Aias and Ghelena Gimail. Their time of glory, too, was over. No longer could they claim the gratitude of the entire Labyrinth bureacracy for their skill at sustaining and extending the Pontifex's life. The Pontifex was beyond any kind of repair, now; the administration of the Labyrinth was on the verge of undergoing inevitable change, and all the cozy official niches would be swept clean. Now, standing quite literally in the shadow of the three mages, Baergax Vor and Ghelena Gimail looked like nothing more than hollowed husks, their skills exhausted and their occupation nearly gone from them.

As for the Pontifex himself, he lay like a waxen image of himself, motionless, unseeing, while the great ones of Majipoor made ready to offer him what they all passionately hoped would be their final act of homage.

In the hallway outside the Pontifex's chamber they formed their procession. Lord Confalume, arrayed in the starburst crown and his robe of office, would go in first, of course, with the High Counsellor Duke Oljebbin just behind him, and then the other two senior lords, Serithorn and Gonivaul, side by side. Behind them would walk the hierarch Marcatain, representing the Lady of the Isle of Sleep, who was the third of the three Powers of the Realm; and after her the Procurator Dantirya Sambail, followed by Prince Korsibar and Duke Kanteverel of Bailemoona. Only when all of these had passed into the room would Prince Prestimion at last come in.

That was a thing that would set many tongues to wagging that day, that Korsibar and the rest should have gone in first, and Prestimion after them. But protocol permitted nothing else. All of those who had gone before Prestimion were high officials of the kingdom except for Korsibar, and Korsibar's prominent place in the procession was assured by the fact of his royal birth. Prestimion held no significant place in the government at this point and had not yet been formally named as Coronal-designate. Until the moment that he was, Prestimion was merely a prince of Castle Mount, one of many; his power and prestige lay all in the future.

The signal to enter the Pontifex's chamber was given. Confalume stepped forward, and then Duke Oljebbin, and the rest one by one. And as the grandees of the realm filed past the royal bedside, each in turn kneeling and making the sign of submission and blessing, a strange thing happened. The Pontifex's eyes fluttered open as Korsibar came before him. Agitation was visible on the old man's face. The fingers of his left hand trembled against the bedcovers; he seemed to be trying to move, even to sit up; a thick, bubbling, incoherent sound came from his lips.

Then, most astounding of all, his arm lifted, ever so slowly, and his gaunt quivering hand reached shakily out toward Korsibar, fingers spread wide. Korsibar stood stock-still, staring down in confusion. From old Prankipin came another sound, a deeper one, almost a groan, amazingly prolonged. He appeared to be trying to clutch at Korsibar's wrist. But he could not reach that far. For a long moment that claw-like hand jutted upward into the air, jabbing fiercely toward Korsibar, jerking convulsively, and then it fell back. The Pontifex's eyes filmed over and closed again, and once more the old man in the bed lay still, breathing so lightly that it was almost impossible to tell whether he was still alive.

There was an immediate hubbub in the room.

Prestimion, waiting at the door to the bedchamber for his moment to enter, watched astonished as the three mages moved frantically toward the bed from one side and the two physicians from the other, bending low over the old emperor, their heads close together, each group conferring in urgent whispers in the jargon of its profession. "They'll smother him with all that attention," Prestimion murmured to Count Iram of Normork, as the bedside conference grew more intense. He could hear a frantic clicking of amulets and the almost panicky-sounding recitation of spells, while the doctors appeared to be trying to push the mages away, and one of them finally succeeded in putting a flask of some bluish medicine to the Pontifex's lips.

Then the crisis seemed to pass, perhaps from the medicine, perhaps the spells: who could say? Slowly the wizards and the physicians backed away from the bed. The Pontifex had subsided once again into the depths of his coma.

The Ghayrog magus, Varimaad Klain, beckoned brusquely to Prestimion to enter the room.

He knelt as he had seen the others do before him. And made the sign of the Pontifex, and waited, half afraid that the old man would rise up again in that terrifying way and reach out for him also.

But Prankipin did not move. Prestimion put his head close to him, listening to the faint hoarse sound of his ragged breathing. He muttered the words of the blessing; Prankipin did not respond. Behind the closed lids his eyes were without movement. His waxen-looking face was smooth again, tranquil, smiling that eerie smile.

This is death-in-life, thought Prestimion, appalled. A horror. A horror. A storm of pity and revulsion swept through him. He rose abruptly from the Pontifex's bedside and strode with swift brusque steps toward the room's rear door.


Prestimion's face was bleak as he emerged from the imperial bedchamber. Septach Melayn and Gialaurys met him on the ramp leading upward to the Arena, where the games would commence in little more than an hour; and, seeing the expression on the prince's features, they glanced quickly at each other in alarm.

"What is it, Prestimion, has his majesty died?" Septach Melayn asked. "You look to be half a dead man yourself!"

"Poor Prankipin still lives, more or less," Prestimion replied, grimacing. "More's the sorrow for that. And as for me, no, not dead even by half, only a trifle sick to my stomach. The Pontifex lies there like a marble statue of himself, completely still, eyes closed, hardly breathing, kept alive by the Divine only knows what sorts of tricks. But you can see that he's ready to move along, ready and eager. When Korsibar went past him he came alive for a moment, and actually reached out and tried to grab his wrist—it was an awful moment, that hand of his sticking up from the bed, and the sound he made— like a cry of pain, it was—"

"He'll be at peace soon enough," said Septach Melayn.

"And those wizards," Prestimion said. "By the Divine, friends, my gullet is full of wizardry today, and more than full! If only you had seen them standing there—those three weird ghostly sorcerers, hovering over him as though they owned him, swaying from side to side like serpents about to strike as they muttered their unending gibberish—"

"Only three?"

"Three," said Prestimion. "A Vroon, a Ghayrog, and one of the double-headed ones. They are the three who are said to rule him. And the room all in shadows, and choking with the reeking smoke of incense—books of magic stacked like firewood on every table, and more of them overflowing onto the floor—and the old man altogether lost in dreams in the middle of it all, except for that moment when Korsibar went by him, when it seemed that he briefly awakened, and that rusty horrible screeking noise came from him and he tried to wrap his fingers around Korsibar's wrist—" Prestimion clapped his hand to his throat. "I tell you, I came away nauseated with disgust. The stink of that incense is in my nostrils to this very minute. I feel befouled by it and all else that I saw in that chamber just now. It seems to me as though I've been crawling through a dark tunnel, a place where spiders make their lair."

Septach Melayn touched Prestimion's shoulder comfortingly, and held him there for a moment. "You take it much too hard, friend. There'll be time enough for you to scrape all these sorcerous cobwebs from the world once you're Coronal. But until then you must simply look upon them as the mere vaporous nonsense they are, and not allow them—"

Gialaurys broke in there, red-faced: "Just halt you there, and wait you a moment! You know nothing of these matters, Septach Melayn. Cobwebs, you say? And nonsense? Ah, how simple it is to scoff, when you've had no experience of the higher wisdoms."

"The higher wisdoms indeed," said Septach Melayn lightly.

Gialaurys ignored him. Turning toward Prestimion, the big man said, "And you, prince, who speaks so harshly of these things: be truthful with me, has it been privately agreed between you and Septach Melayn that sorcery will be prohibited when you have the crown? Because if it has been, I ask you to think again. By the Lady, I tell you, Prestimion, these are no mere cobwebs, nor will you sweep them away as readily as you may believe."

"Easily, easily, good Gialaurys," Prestimion said. "Banning wizardry from the land is Septach Melayn's idea, not mine, and I've never said I'd attempt such a thing, however I may feel about it in the inwardness of my heart."

"And in the inwardness of your heart, what?" asked Gialaurys.

"You know that already, good friend. To me these magics are foolish and empty, a mere fraud."

A stormy aspect darkened Gialaurys's face. "A fraud? A mere fraud, prince? You can see nothing real in any of it? Oh, Prestimion, how wrong you are in that! On every side its truths are validated every day. You can deny that if you wish. But that doesn't make it any the less so."

"Perhaps. I am in no position to say," replied Prestimion uncomfortably.

Indeed, even he had from all sides heard reports of inexplicable things, seeming miracles that might well be considered the work of mages. But he clung to the opinion that rational explanations could somehow be had, that these supposed miracles were achieved by the methods of science. Much scientific knowledge had been lost and forgotten in the course of Majipoor's many thousands of years of history, and perhaps some of that had lately been recovered and put to use: the results might well look like magic to people ignorant of the technical means used to produce them.

Then, too, he was willing to concede that the Vroons and

Su-Suheris might have certain special powers of mind, no more magical than eyesight or hearing were among other races, that allowed them to work some of their supposed wonders. But no more than that. And in general Prestimion preferred to reserve his judgment on all these questions.

And so he held up one hand when Gialaurys seemed eager to press the debate further.

"Let there be no more of this," Prestimion said, with the most amiable smile he could muster. "There's no need for us to debate the matter here and now, is there? Let me only say—begging your pardon for any offense to your beliefs, my friend—that I assure you it verged very close on sickening me to behold those parasites clustered around old Prankipin, and very happy I am to be out of that place." He shook his head with vigor, as though to clear it of that stifling haze of incense. "Come: the games will be starting. We should be in the Arena now."

Upward they went through the spiraling levels; and came in time to that huge open space which the Pontifex Dizimaule of ancient times had bestowed upon the Labyrinth, where the Pontifical Games were to be held.

No one knew why Dizimaule had caused this incomprehensible emptiness to be constructed in one of the middle levels of the Labyrinth. He had offered no reason, said the historians of the underground city: had coolly given orders for the clearing of whole acres of existing buildings, and in their place had built—nothing. One could stand in it and look across to the far side and not be able to see the opposite wall, so broad was its span. No interior columns supported its distant ceiling, a fact that had baffled generations of Majipoori architects. When you cupped your hand and shouted, it took half an eternity for the echoes to begin to return, though when they did they went on tumbling and crashing about you for a marvelously long time.

Ordinarily the Arena remained unoccupied and unused. By statute of Dizimaule Pontifex it was forbidden to build anything in it, and no succeeding Pontifex had cared to repeal that law; so there it sat, century after century, purposeless, mystifying. Only upon the death of a Pontifex did anything occur there, for there was no other site in the Labyrinth but the Arena where the traditional Pontifical funeral games could be held.

An enormous many-layered grandstand for the common citizens had sprung up in it virtually overnight, like some fungal growth in a moist forest, all along the Arena's western wall. In the space before it were the structures of the games themselves, the chariot-racing track at the center, with the sandy track for foot-races alongside it, and smaller arenas for boxing and wrestling and the games of special skill up toward the northern end, and an archery course to the south. On the eastern side was the special seating for the visitors from Castle Mount, with an ornate box for the Coronal and his family in the place of honor at the center. Overhead, somewhere midway between the floor and the dimly visible ceiling, clusters of high-powered glowlamps drifted freely, casting brilliant beams of red and golden illumination in this usually dim-lit place.

An usher in a purple robe trimmed with a collar of orange fur, with the little half-mask across his eyes and the bridge of his nose that was the quaint symbol of the Pontifical officials, showed Prestimion and his companions to their place, a booth just to the left of the Coronal's box. Duke Svor was there already, and Prince Serithorn with some members of his staff. Just beyond them the Coronal was smiling and waving to the citizenry from his seat at the center, with Prince Korsibar on one side of him and the Lady Thismet on the other. The

Lady Melithyrrh accompanied Thismet; the Su-Suheris mage Sanibak-Thastimoon sat just behind Korsibar.

On the other side of the royal box Duke Oljebbin of Stoienzar shared a booth with the Counts Farholt and Farquanor, Mandrykarn of Stee, Iram of Normork, and several others. The Procurator Dantirya Sambail arrived moments after Prestimion, very grandly arrayed in bejeweled orange robes more splendid even than Lord Confalume's; he stood for a time studying the arrangements of the seating, and then found a place for himself in Duke Oljebbin's box, along the side closest to Prince Korsibar's seat in the box adjacent.

Prince Gonivaul, as Master of the Games, had a place all to himself, high above everything and set at an angle to the grandstand. He stood looking calmly this way and that, awaiting the proper moment for the start of the games. Then he lifted a silken scarf of dazzling crimson and green and waved it briskly three times over his head.

There was an answering flourish of trumpets and drums and horns and pipes, and from some entranceway in a far-off corner of the Arena came the competitors for the first day's events, riding toward the center of the stadium in a little fleet of floaters. The foot-races would be the opening contest, and then the dueling with batons, both of these being pastimes mainly for the youngest princelings of the Castle.

But as the contestants emerged from their floaters and arranged themselves in parallel lines along the field, kneeling and rising and stretching and dancing in place to ready themselves for their races, other figures appeared and came forward on the field before the Coronal's box.

"Look," Prestimion said, giving Septach Melayn a sharp nudge in the ribs. "Even here, the sorcerers."

Indeed. They were ubiquitous. There was no escaping the reach of the mages any more, not anywhere in the world.

Prestimion watched in deep disgust as brazen tripods were

set up, as colored powders were poured and ignited, as seven long-legged figures clad in the impressive costume of the geomancers who flourished in the High City of Tidias on Castle Mount—the shining robe of golden brocade that was the kalautikoi, the richly woven cloak called the lagustri-more, the towering brass helmet known as the miirthella—struck their stately poses and loudly and resonantly uttered their mystic spells.

"Bythois . . . Sigei . . . Remmer . . . Proiarchis . . ."

"What are they saying?" Prestimion whispered.

Septach Melayn laughed. "How would I know?"

"These are wizards of Tidias, I think, and you are a man of that very city, as I recall."

"I spent no time carousing with wizards when I lived there, nor learning their dark arts," said Septach Melayn. "Gialaurys is your man, if you want a translation."

Prestimion nodded. But he could see big Gialaurys down on his knees, muttering devoutly along with the geomancers as they intoned their incantation. Out of love of Gialaurys Prestimion forced himself to curb his irritation with the lengthy rite that was going on before them.

In any case it was a waste of breath for him to rail against wizardry with anyone other than Septach Melayn. It had begun to seem to Prestimion that he and Septach Melayn were the last two men of Majipoor who had not yielded to the spells of the enchanters. And even the two of them, Prestimion was coming to see, might find it politic to start being more tactful about their distaste for such things. It was wise, he realized, for a Coronal not to place himself too openly in opposition to the temper of the times.

He looked toward the field. The sorcerers and their equip-ment were gone, now, and the foot-races were under way: the sprints first, over almost as soon as they had begun, and then the longer races, up and and around the track and back, one lap, two laps, six laps, ten.

Prestimion recognized very few of the contestants. A great many young knights and guardsmen had come down from Castle Mount as escorts to the royal family and the dukes and lords, and it was from their ranks that most of the foot-racers had come; but he knew only a handful of them by name. His attention quickly wandered. Off to the left he could see them getting ready for the baton-dueling. That sport was more to his taste than the running; he had been a capable hand with the batons himself when he was a boy.

Duke Svor, at Prestimion's side, touched the hem of his sleeve. In a low and oddly throaty voice he said, "Did you sleep well last night, prince?"

"About as usual, I suppose."

"Not I. I dreamed a very troublesome dream."

"Ah," said Prestimion, without much interest. "It's known to happen, I suppose. I'm sorry to hear it." He pointed toward the gathering group of baton-wielders. "Do you see that one on the far side, Svor, in the green? And you, Septach Melayn? Notice how he stands, as though there are coiled springs in his feet. And watch the movements of his wrists. In his mind he's already at work with his baton, and the signal not even given.—I'll put my wager on him, I think. Who'll say five crowns on the first match, and I take the one in the green?"

Gialaurys said doubtfully, "Is it respectful to wager on these games, prince?"

"Why not? Respectful to whom, Gialaurys? The Pontifex? I hardly think he'd care, just now. Five crowns on the green!"

"His name is Mandralisca," said Septach Melayn. "He's one of your cousin's men. A nasty piece of work, like most of those that your cousin likes to have about him."

"The Procurator, you mean? A very remote cousin, that one."

112

"But your cousin all the same, as I understand it. This Mandralisca is his poison-taster, I'm told."

"His what?"

"Stands beside him, sips his drink to make sure that it's safe. I saw him doing it, only the other day."

"Indeed. Well, then, I put five crowns on Dantirya Sambail's poison-taster! Mandralisca, you said his name was?"

"I'll readily put five against him, out of sheer loathing for the man," said Septach Melayn, holding forth a bright coin. "This Mandralisca, I hear, would just as soon stab a man as move aside for him in the road. My money's on the boy in scarlet."

"Concerning this dream of mine, Prestimion," Svor continued, in the low tense voice he had used before. "If I may—"

Prestimion glanced toward him impatiently. "Was it such a dreadful one, then, that you need to spill it forth this instant? Well, then, Svor, go ahead. Go ahead! Tell it to me, and let there be an end on it."

The little man knotted his fingers into the tight curls of his short black beard and screwed his face into the most sour of expressions, so that his thick heavy brows met at the middle in a single dark line. "I dreamed," he said, after a bit, "that the old Pontifex had finally died, and Lord Confalume had come forth in the Court of Thrones and named you to be Coronal before us all, and had removed the starburst crown from his head and was holding it out to you in his hand."

"This is not very dreadful so far," said Prestimion.

On the field four pairs of batonsmen were facing one another in perfect stillness, tautly awaiting the signal, gripping the thin pliant wands of nightflower wood that were their weapons.

"Challenge!" called the referee. "Post! Entry!" Prestimion sat forward as the contests began, his upper body weaving about in his seat as he became attuned to the lively rhythms of the swiftly flashing batons. This was a sport that required quickness of movement and sight and deftness of wrist rather than any special degree of strength. The wooden batons were so light that they could be moved back and forth faster than the lightest rapier. It was necessary to anticipate one's opponent's moves almost as though reading his mind, if one were to have any hope of parrying his thrusts.

Svor, speaking very softly with his head close beside Prestimion's, said, "Prince Korsibar was standing opposite you in the hall, and his hands were raised in readiness to make the starburst sign at you, the moment that Lord Confalume had placed the crown upon your brow. But before that could be done, the dead Pontifex Prankipin entered the hall."

"How very unusual," said Prestimion, listening now with only half an ear. "But of course it was a dream." Turning away from Svor, he tapped Septach Melayn with his elbow and grinned. "Do you see how the poison-taster whips that baton around, now? Your boy in scarlet's a lost cause. And so are your five crowns, I'm afraid."

In a harsh insistent voice that was all rough edges Svor said, "What I saw, prince, was that the old Pontifex came to Lord Confalume and took the Coronal's crown lightly out of his hand. And went not to you but to Prince Korsibar, and gave the crown to him, putting it right in his upraised hands, so that all Korsibar need do was bring the crown toward his forehead and place it there. Which Korsibar proceeded without hesitation to do, and we all stood stunned at the sight of it, but he was wearing the crown, and he who wears the crown is king, and so there was nothing else for us then but to bow down to him and hail him with the old cry, 'Korsibar! Lord Korsibar! Long life to Lord Korsibar!' And suddenly the hall was alight with a glow the color of flame—no, the color of blood, it was, bright fresh blood—and I awoke, sweating from head to foot. But after a time I slept again, and dreamed, and it was the same dream again. The very same."

Scowling, Prestimion said, "Lord Korsibar indeed. In dreams anything is possible, Svor."

On his other side Septach Melayn was shouting, "Scarlet! Yes, Scarlet! Go it, Scarlet!" And then a groan and a curse as the poison-taster suddenly executed a deft double-feint that left his scarlet-clad opponent caught out of position and pivoting on the wrong leg, and sent him down beneath a dizzying barrage of lightning-fast strokes of his baton. "By the Divine, you have it, Prestimion!" said Septach Melayn. With a rueful smile he flipped the five-crown piece into Prestimion's hand.

"I could see his skill at once, from the way he moved even before the contest started. He would be three steps ahead of the other boy at every moment, that I knew." And, leaning again to Svor, Prestimion said, "Forget this miserable dream of yours, and watch the batons, Svor! Who'll give me ten crowns on the poison-taster's next match?"

"One moment more, if you would, Prestimion—" Svor said in that same low conspiratorial tone.

Prestimion was beginning to find Svor's nagging persistence exasperating. "If I would *what?*"

"Matters are more precarious than you understand, I think. Attend me: your future and mine are darkened by the shadow of this dream. Go to the Coronal, I beg you. You must force his hand, or we're surely all lost. Tell him that you fear treachery; ask him to declare you to be Coronal-designate before another day goes by. And if he refuses, stay by his side until he yields to you. Give him no peace so long as he continues to delay. If need be, tell him that you'll openly proclaim yourself his heir without waiting for him, if he won't do it."

"This is unthinkable. Svor. I'll do no such thing."

"You must, Prestimion." Svor's voice was shredded to a hoarse whisper.

"I find your advice unacceptable and unworthy. Force the Coronal's hand? Harass him on my own behalf? Threaten to declare myself the heir, which would be an infamous thing, against all law and precedent? Why? Simply because you ate too many eels last night and had a bad dream? What are you saying, man?"

"And if Korsibar were to seize his father's crown in the moment of Prankipin's death, what then?"

"What's this? Seize the crown?" Prestimion's eyes were wide with amazement. "That's a thing he'd never do.—You make him out most perfidious, Svor. There's nothing of that in him at all. Besides, his father's crown doesn't interest him. Never has. Never will."

"I know Prince Korsibar very well," Svor said. "I was of his company for years, have you forgotten? Perfidious he is not, I agree; but he flutters easily in any breeze. Flattery quickly sways his mind. There are those with grand ambitions of their own who think he should be Coronal, and perhaps already have been at work telling him so. And if he has such things poured in his ear often enough—!"

"No!" Prestimion cried. "That will never happen!" Angrily he swept the air before his face with both his outspread hands. "First that Vroon brought me these omens, and now you. No. I'll not be driven by omens, like some credulous peasant. Let me be, Svor. I love you with all the warmth of my soul, but I tell you that you bother me very greatly just now."

"There was virtue in that dream, prince, I promise you that."

"And if you refuse to put this insufferable dream of yours away this instant," said Prestimion, fuming, now, as his wrath began to spill over in him, "I'll take you by that beard of yours and swing you through the air and pitch you clear over the side of this box. I promise *you* that most sincerely, Svor. An end on it, now. Do you hear me? An end on it!" He glared furiously at Svor and turned his back on him, and looked toward the field.

But Svor's words still rattled in his head. That was, he thought, no fitting advice for the little duke to have given him: inciting him to treasonous insurrection on no evidence other than the urgings of a dream. It was a coward's advice—a traitor's advice, ignoble and bizarre. And foolish besides; for no one forced a Coronal's hand, and the formidable Confalume would surely destroy him if he were to attempt it. No, it was a sorry thing, for Svor to have advocated such rashness—such wild impudence—merely on account of a dream—

Prestimion struggled to cleanse his mind of it.

# 8

The hurdle-racing and the hoop-jumping and the hammer-throw and other such minor sports were the features of the second day, and the third, and the fourth, of the Pontifical Games. Each day the visiting lords and some thousands of the citizens of the Labyrinth assembled in the Arena for that day's diversions. And each day, too, the bulletins from the imperial bedchamber were the same, his majesty the Pontifex's condition remaining unchanged. It was as though his majesty's condition, like the weather in the Labyrinth, was inherently incapable of change, and would vary not in the slightest from here to the end of time.

The fifth and sixth and seventh days were set aside for the wrestling bouts. Two dozen contestants had enrolled. But all attention focused on the final match, the great struggle between the famed wrestlers Gialaurys and Farholt. The stands were full for that contest, and complete silence reigned in the Arena as the two hulking men entered the wrestling ring.

Each had brought a magus with him. Farholt's man was a dark puffy-faced Hjort, one of the many sorcerers of Lord Confalume's retinue, and Gialaurys had chosen one of the brass-helmeted geomancers from Tidias. These two took up positions before the ring with their backs to each other and set about an elaborate and greatly prolonged procedure of casting of spells, with much chanting and drawing of invisible lines on the ground and invocations of unseen forces overhead.

Septach Melayn pointed toward Gialaurys, who knelt with eyes closed and head bowed, making mystic gestures as his geomancer spun his long skein of rituals. With some annoyance in his tone he said, "Our friend truly takes these matters to heart, eh?"

"Rather more so than his opponent, it seems," answered Prestimion: for in fact Farholt appeared to be waiting as impatiently as Prestimion himself for the magical rigmarole to end.

At last the mages withdrew and Farholt and Gialaurys slipped off their robes, revealing their powerful bodies clad in nothing more than loincloths. Each had oiled his skin with sea-dragon oil to keep his opponent from getting a secure purchase on him; and under the brilliant lights of the Arena the contours and ridges of their arms and backs stood out in startling relief, drawing gasps and exclamations of wonder from the onlookers.

"You will wrestle three falls," announced the referee, a Pontifical official named Hayla Tekmanot, no small man himself but diminished into insigificance by the great bulk of the contestants. He slapped each man once on the shoulder with the flat of his hand. "This is the signal that you have won and are to release your hold. And this—" he slapped again, twice in succession "—is the signal that your opponent is unable to continue because of injury, and you are to step back from him at once. Understood?"

Farholt went to the north side of the ring, Gialaurys to the other. The shrill brassy din of gabek-horns sounded in the Arena. Each man performed his obeisance to the Coronal in the center box and bowed to the boxes on either side of Lord Confalume where the other high lords were seated, and, lastly, to the Master of the Games, Prince Gonivaul, high up in his solitary station.

"Let the match begin," declared Hayla Tekmanot, and they

came rushing at each other as if they intended not to wrestle but to kill.

Their giant forms collided in the center of the ring with an impact that could be heard from one end of the Arena to the other. Both men appeared staggered by that bone-cracking crash of flesh against flesh; but they quickly recovered, and took up positions nose to nose, legs firmly planted, each locking his arms about the other's shoulders, each struggling in vain to send the other down to a quick fall. There they stood, stiff, immobile, for many a moment. In this time Farholt could be seen to whisper something in a harsh, rough voice to Gialaurys, who stared at him as though astonished at his words; and then a fierce look of anger came over Gialaurys's features and he replied, something just as coldly and harshly spoken but likewise too low in tone to be heard by any of the onlookers.

The long stasis held. Neither could get the advantage. They were too evenly matched.

Farholt was the taller by a head and his arms were longer, but Gialaurys was somewhat heavier of body and even broader than Farholt across the shoulders, deeper through the chest. Minutes passed; but, try as they could, neither was able to make his rival give ground. Mighty grunts came from them. The muscles of their arms and backs stood out in terrible bulges as though they would leap out through the skin. Sweat ran in torrents down their oiled bodies. Gialaurys seemed to find leverage over Farholt, but Farholt resisted and held his footing, and then it was Gialaurys who swayed ever so slightly against the pressure Farholt exerted.

The deadlock went on and on. A steady rising clamor came from the crowd. Nearly everyone in the royal boxes was standing, now, calling out the name of one or the other. Prestimion looked across to the Coronal's box and saw Prince Korsibar on his feet, wide-eyed, transfixed, shouting, "Farholt!

Farholt!" with frenzied zeal, and then he realized that he was shouting too, perhaps just as frenziedly, crying the name of Gialaurys.

"Look you there," Septach Melayn said. "I think Farholt budges him."

It was so. Farholt's eyes were wild and veins were standing out like thick ropes on his ruddy-hued forehead; but he had indeed managed to pry one of Gialaurys's feet upward from the ground and was straining to lift the other one free. Prestimion saw sudden pallor on Gialaurys's face. He had become as white as Farholt was florid, so that his bristly sideburns stood out as heavy brown bars against his newly bloodless cheeks.

For an instant it seemed that Farholt would succeed in lifting Gialaurys entirely, like a tree pulled up by its roots, and hurl him to the floor of the ring.

But just as Gialaurys's left foot was a moment away from rising, he quickly brought around the other one that was already raised from the ground, and kicked Farholt with it in the hollow of his leg so savagely that Farholt's balance was broken and he was forced to bend that leg forward at the knee. Now it was Farholt who was in danger of toppling. Desperately seeking some sort of grip, he wedged his right hand inside Gialaurys's gaping mouth and tugged at Gialaurys's lower jaw as though he had it in mind to rip it from Gialaurys's face. A dark rivulet of blood ran down Farholt's arm; but whether it was the blood of Gialaurys or Farholt's own, none of the watchers could say.

Svor said, almost to himself, "This should be halted. It is not sport but a disgrace: they will murder each other."

Gialaurys maintained his hold. Grasping Farholt by both shoulders and twisting, he gave him a shove that was meant to send him over on his back.

Farholt spun sideways as he fell. Seizing Gialaurys around

the neck with his free left hand, he pulled him down with him. Each locked in the other's grip, they toppled together, falling headlong and landing side by side, both of them hitting the ground with horrendous force.

"Pin him, Gialaurys!" Prestimion cried. And from the adjoining box came a bellowing from Korsibar: "Farholt! Now! Now! Get him, Farholt!" Farholt's brother Farquanor, who was seated in the royal box today, just behind Prince Korsibar, was on his feet and calling out encouragement to Farholt too, and his narrow face was agleam with a glow of imminent victory.

But, as before, neither wrestler was able to seize advantage over the other. Both men were stunned by the heavy landing they had made; they lay like two felled logs for a long while, then began to stir and slowly came to sitting positions, staring befuddledly at each other. Gialaurys rubbed his jaw and the side of his head; Farholt kneaded his knee and thigh. They were watchful, each poised as if to leap up if the other one did, but neither seemed capable of arising just yet. Hayla Tekmanot knelt between them, briefly conferring with them both. Then the referee rose and walked to the edge of the ring and looked up at Prince Gonivaul.

"I declare the first fall to be a draw," he called. "The contestants will rest for five minutes before proceeding."


"A word with you, prince?" said the Procurator Dantirya Sambail during the interlude between the bouts, inclining his upper body halfway across the low barrier between his box and the one in which Prince Korsibar sat.

Korsibar, his mind still whirling from the heat and intensity of that desperate struggle just concluded, peered up into the Procurator's massive bellicose face and waited for the other to speak.

In an overly amiable tone of man-to-man camaraderie Dantirya Sambail said, "I have a hundred royals riding on your man. Will he prevail, do you think?"

That unwarranted note of easy intimacy caused some anger in Korsibar. He replied steadily, though, "I have fifty on him myself. But I have no more idea than you do who will prevail."

The Procurator pointed across toward the box on the far side, where Prestimion was deep in conversation with Septach Melayn and Prince Serithorn. In the same manner of unearned congeniality as before he said, "Prestimion, so I've been told, has five hundred royals on Gialaurys."

"A princely sum, if that's true. But are you sure? Prestimion's not much of a gambler. Fifty crowns would be more his kind of wager."

"Not crowns but royals, and not fifty but five hundred" said Dantirya Sambail. "I am not mistaken in this." He held a cold roast leg of bilantoon in his hand; he paused now to bite off a chunk of the delicate white meat, and to spit out some bits of skin and gristle. After wiping his lips with the sleeve of his jewel-bedecked robe he said casually, giving Korsibar a slow, icy, malicious stare, "It's not really gambling if you know the outcome in advance, is it?"

"Are you saying that Farholt's been bribed to lose? By the Lady, Dantirya Sambail, you don't know Farholt at all, if you think that he—"

"Not bribed. Drugged, so I hear. A potion designed to work in a gradual way, and to weaken him as the bout proceeds. Of course, it's only a rumor. My cup-bearer Mandralisca heard it, during the batons." The Procurator smiled silkily. "You're right, Korsibar: there's probably no truth to it. And even if there is, well, what's the loss of fifty or a hundred royals to men like ourselves?" He winked and said, once more using the quiet, insinuating voice he had employed at the outset, "In any case, how much like Prestimion it would be to have arranged the outcome in favor of his friend. He looks after his friends, that one, by any means available."

Korsibar made a gesture of indifference, as though to say that these theories were no affair of his, and that he disliked such slanderous talk as the Procurator was offering.

He had never cared for the company of Dantirya Sambail. There were few who did. The Procurator had a certain ferocious air of majesty about him, yes, but to Korsibar he merely seemed base, swinish, a venomous monster of self-regard. Yet of course Dantirya Sambail ruled an immense hereditary domain on the other continent with absolute force, and had to be accepted into the ranks of the great princes on that account: he was the Coronal's subject, at least in name, but he controlled vast wealth and huge resources, and one did not lightly reject his company. Nevertheless Korsibar wished that the Procurator would return to his seat.

"Well," said Dantirya Sambail cheerfully, "we'll see soon enough whether the tale is true. And look, now: our gladiators seem to be getting ready to try a second fall."

Korsibar only nodded.

"I'd pay more attention to Prestimion's antics, if I were you," Dantirya Sambail said, making no move to withdraw. "I hear many strange tales about him, and not just concerning the drugging of wrestlers." His heavy eyelids fluttered with a curious daintiness. "For example, has anyone told you yet that he plans to have you removed, once he's become Coronal?"

The calm words fell upon Korsibar like javelins.

*"What?"*

"Oh, yes. The story's been going around. As soon as he's got the crown on his head, a convenient accident is arranged for you, something during a hunt, perhaps. He can't afford to let you live, you know."

Korsibar felt deep shock that verged on disgust. "These are very offensive lunacies that you're spouting, Dantirya Sambail."

Color came to the Procurator's fleshy face. His lips grew thin; he drew his head downward so that his neck swelled and thickened; and those oddly tender and thoughtful violet-gray eyes of his turned suddenly hard. But his smile remained unwavering. "Ah, no need to be angered at me, dear prince! I'm only repeating what I hear, because perhaps it may be of use to you. And what I hear is that you're a dead man once Majipoor's in his hand."

"This is absurd," Korsibar said curtly.

"Look: if you live, and Prestimion's reign not go so well, you'll always be a threat to him. Does he want all the world muttering about Lord Confalume's glorious son, who might have been Coronal himself, but was passed over? Oh, no, no, no. If times grow hard, and that may very well happen sooner or later, someone will surely cry, 'Put Prestimion aside, make Korsibar Coronal,' and soon they all will be screaming it. You said yourself that Prestimion's no gambler. Your continued existence carries risks for him, for you are perilous to him. He's no man to tolerate risks, or threats, or rivals, or any sort of obstacles. And so—the unfortunate hunting accident, the balcony railing that suddenly isn't there, the collision on the highway, some such thing. Believe me: I know him. He and I are of the same blood."

"I know him too, Dantirya Sambail."

"Perhaps. But I tell you this: if I were Prestimion, I would have you removed from the world."

"If Prestimion were you, very likely he would," said Korsibar. "I praise the Divine that he isn't." The sound of the gabek-horns could be heard across the field, none too soon for Korsibar. He had heard far too much already; he was sickened and revolted by these ugly hypotheses of the Procurator's, and his fingers were trembling with rage, as if they longed by independent will to wrap themselves around Dantirya Sambail's meaty neck. "It's time for the second fall,"

Korsibar said, swinging brusquely away from the other man. "Speak no more to me of these things, Dantirya Sambail."


Farholt came out from his corner this time plainly bent on Gialaurys's immediate destruction. He sprang at once at the heavier man, pushing him back toward the far corner of the ring with sudden unstoppable fury. Gialaurys, who appeared to be puzzled at the wild rage of Farholt's onslaught, planted one foot fore and one aft in a resolute attempt at bracing himself. Farholt backed away a little at that and swung his left elbow around, ramming it savagely into the middle of Gialaurys's face. That brought a howl of pain from him and sent a bright stream of blood running down his face. Gialaurys pressed both his hands to the bridge of his nose.

"Foul!" cried Prestimion, enraged by the blatant stroke. "For shame! Foul!"

But Hayla Tekmanot made no move to halt the contest. He appeared not to have noticed at all. As for Gialaurys, he stood growling and shaking his head to clear it, while at the same time reaching forth one upraised hand to keep Farholt at bay.

Farholt grabbed it just at the wrist, and twisted hard. Gialaurys was forced to pivot so far around that he turned his back on Farholt, who instantly slipped both his arms beneath Gialaurys's armpits and clasped them at Gialaurys's breastbone; and then Farholt pressed his forehead against the back of Gialaurys's skull as though intending to force the head of the shorter man downward until his neck snapped.

A keening scream came from the public grandstands. Svor rose from his seat and called out, "Stop him! Stop him! This is murder!" And Prestimion, gripping the front of the box with both his hands, stood frozen in horror as the relentless downward pressure of Farholt's head against Gialaurys's grew and grew.

Lord Confalume looked toward his son and said, "Your friend the Count fights like a wild beast, Korsibar."

"They are two wild beasts, I would say. But ours is the stronger one, I think."

"I care very little for this match," said the Coronal. "There's too much brutality in it. Who planned this? And why doesn't Hayla Tekmanot do something? Or Prince Gonivaul?" Rising halfway to his feet, Confalume lifted one arm as though to signal the Master of the Games for a halt; but Korsibar caught his father's arm and pulled it back.

And indeed Gialaurys was too thick through the chest for Farholt to contain in this way, and was flexing and reflexing his arms and shoulders now, writhing mightly in an effort to release himself from Farholt's grip. Farholt, despite the great length of his arms, was unable to maintain his hold on Gialaurys's body. In another moment Gialaurys succeeded in breaking free.

The two men lurched back from one another, each circling about the other and making ready for a new assault. Gialaurys appeared to be about to spring when Farholt's open hand flicked out, serpent-quick, to ram itself hard against Gialaurys's already bloodied nose. Farholt thrust all his weight forward. Gialaurys, shocked and numbed by the pain, stood bewildered just long enough for Farholt to take him by the shoulders and spin him with enormous force to the ground. He lay helpless there while Farholt pounced on him and pinned him in place.

"Foul!" Prestimion yelled, outraged, pounding madly on the railing of his box. And Korsibar looked across to Dantirya Sambail in his box beyond, and smiled with one eyebrow lifted, as though to remind the Procurator that certain malignant medicines of Prestimion's had been supposed to be hampering Farholt's performance by this stage in the match.

"This fall goes to Farholt," Hayla Tekmanot announced.

"Yes!" Korsibar called. "Yes!" And from Farquanor, near him in the royal box, came a sharp triumphant whoop of pleasure and approbation.

"No," Prestimion said in a soft voice. "How can it be? Anyone could see that Farholt fouled Gialaurys twice at least."

"It was a bad call," said Septach Melayn. "But look at Gialaurys's eyes. He'll kill Farholt in the third bout."

"Kill him in literal truth," said Svor dourly, "or the other way around. One of them will surely destroy the other. What sort of sport is this? What sort indeed? These men go at it with true blood-hatred for each other, not just the rivalry of sport. Something unusual is happening here today, Prestimion."

Nor would Gialaurys and Farholt wait for the referee to announce the third bout. They were at it already, Gialaurys brushing the surprised Hayla Tekmanot aside with one sweep of his arm and leaping toward Farholt with a terrifying roar. But what they were doing now was no longer even a pretense at wrestling. They struck at each other with their fists, one immense hammer-blow following another. Farholt's mouth was bloodied. He spat out teeth. Roaring still, Gialaurys rushed in close to him, only to be met by a knee rising sharply upward into his groin. He grunted and lurched backward; instantly Farholt fell upon him, clawing at his face and chest with his fingernails; Gialaurys, growling like some truculent steetmoy of the northern mountains, fought back with elbows and chin, and then, coiling himself tightly, reared upward and smashed the top of his head against Farholt's with bone-jarring force, sending Farholt reeling half stupefied off to the edge of the ring.

Duke Svor, urgently grasping Prestimion's arm, said once again, "This needs to be stopped, prince!"

"Yes. I agree." He looked across to the royal box, and called out to the Coronal to bring an end to the contest. Lord Confalume nodded. He signalled to Gonivaul.

From the box on the far side, though, came the jeering voice of Dantirya Sambail: "Ah, I pray you, let it continue, Cousin Prestimion! There's such pleasure in seeing two brave strong men having at it this way!"

As for Prince Gonivaul, he was looking down at the wrestling ring in a detached, almost absent way, as if he were contemplating creatures swimming in some pond in a valley far below him. He stroked his thick beard reflectively, he ran his fingers through the furry hair that tumbled across his forehead; but he offered no response to the Coronal's order. It seemed only now to have come to Prince Gonivaul's attention that anything was going on in the ring at all.

As Gonivaul stood there hesitating, Farholt and Gialaurys came rumbling slowly back toward each other from opposite corners of the ring. They arrived simultaneously at its center and each man, breathing heavily, reached one hand tentatively out toward the other in an uncertain probing way.

They looked like two drunkards far gone in their cups. There was no vitality in their movements. Plainly both of them were at the verge of collapse. Gialaurys touched his fingertips lightly to Farholt's chest and pushed; Farholt swayed and seemed almost to totter, and took two faltering steps backward.

Then he shambled forward again and reached out to give Gialaurys a similar shove. It was Gialaurys's turn to sway and totter. The two men seemed dazed, at the last extremity of exhaustion. Now Gialaurys shoved again, not at all vigorously, and this time Farholt crumpled immediately to the ground. Gialaurys dropped down on top of him, looking barely conscious as he lay across Farholt's chest in a groggy travesty of a grip.

Hayla Tekmanot, kneeling beside them, gave Gialaurys the

slap of victory in this fall. Then the referee looked up at Prince Gonivaul's box.

"One fall to Gialaurys and one to Farholt," he said, "and the first one a draw. So it is an even split, and they are in no condition to continue."

"Is that your opinion?" Gonivaul asked sternly.

Hayla Tekmanot gestured to the two motionless sprawled figures in the ring. "You see them there before you, prince."

Prince Gonivaul appeared for some while to be debating within himself the likelihood of somehow continuing the match. Then he said at last, "Very well. We divide the prize. They are each equal champions in this contest."

Gialaurys rose uncertainly, Farholt a moment later. They stood wobbling in the ring, blinking slowly, as Hayla Tekmanot explained to them the decision of the Master of the Games. With visible reluctance they touched hands; and then they swung about and made their separate ways out of the ring, walking very carefully, as though they were in some danger of falling again.

Gialaurys was undergoing repair by one of the surgeons of the games when Prestimion and his companions arrived in the dressing-room. He looked battered and woebegone, and his nose seemed somewhat out of proper line, but he was conscious and even managed a feeble smile as Prestimion entered.

"How badly are you hurt?" Prestimion asked anxiously.

"Everything bruised and somewhat bent, nothing broken, no permanent harm done" Gialaurys spoke thickly through swollen lips. "But I will tell you straight out that I've had gentler ticklings than this one. What do you hear of Farholt? Did he survive?"

"It would seem so," answered Septach Melayn.

"A pity," said Gialaurys. "He wrestles in a most unchivalrous way. This was not how I was taught to play the sport."

Prestimion put his head close and said in a low tone, "Tell

me this, Gialaurys: what was the thing Farholt whispered to you, as you stood face to face with him at the beginning of the first bout? It seemed to amaze you greatly, and then to make you angry."

"Oh," said Gialaurys. "That." His broad face darkened with a deep frown, which plainly cost him some pain. Slowly he shook his head. "It was a very odd thing, Prestimion. What Farholt said to me was that I was your man—which is true enough—and that he hated all that had to do with you, and therefore would destroy me this day. As he then proceeded nearly to do, when I thought we were only there to wrestle. But he got from me as good as he gave, I think, and perhaps a little more than that."

"He said that? That he hates all that has to do with me?"

"Those were his words, yes. And would destroy me because I am your man."

"We have become two camps already, the camp of Korsibar and the camp of Prestimion," said Duke Svor in a black, dismal voice. "If the wrestling is like this, what will the boxing be, and the jousting? We'll swim in blood before this all is over."

"How strange," Prestimion said, addressing Gialaurys, just as though Svor had not spoken. "How extremely strange, that Farholt would say such a thing." He glanced about at the others. Septach Melayn's face was more somber than usual, and his left hand was uneasily caressing the hilt of the little dress-sword that he had chosen to wear today. As for Duke Svor, his dark eyes had become hard and bleak, and he was looking at Prestimion in a way that communicated the deepest foreboding. "How strange," said Prestimion once more.

# 9

The games were now approaching their midway point; and still the old Pontifex lived on.

Korsibar, calling upon the Coronal in his suite, said, "This is the eighteenth day since that time when I visited you here, father, and you told me then that Prankipin would be dead within nineteen."

"He lingers and lingers, I know," said Lord Confalume.

"Not that I doubt your skill at prognostication. But even the greatest sages have occasionally made errors of calculation. What if he lives another ten days, or twenty?"

"Why, then, the waiting will go on."

"And the games? We're nearly half done with them. Tomorrow will be the archery; the day after tomorrow, the fencing; after that the mounted jousting; then the boxing, then the chariot-racing, and we're done and there must be a grand celebration, with feasting and the bestowing of prizes. This is the problem I saw from the first, father. How can we have a grand celebration, with feasting and parades and all, with Prankipin still on his deathbed? We said when the decision to begin was agreed upon that we'd draw the games out so that they wouldn't finish until after the Pontifex had died. But it may not happen that way."

"I made my calculation again last night," said the Coronal. "It was not perfectly correct before, though close. Now I have more confidence. The Pontifex will die within five days."

132

"How certain are you?"

"The calculation of my experts is the same as mine."

"Ah."

"And, I suspect, that of the Pontifex's own mages also, though they've said nothing on the subject these four days past. But their very silence and withdrawal is suspicious."

"Within five days," said Korsibar. "And then you'll be Pontifex at last. After all these years on the other throne."

"After all these years, yes."

"And Prestimion will be our Coronal."

"Yes," Lord Confalume said. "Prestimion."

The next day was the day of the archery contests. This was Prestimion's particular sport, in which he had always excelled beyond all measure, and no one expected to best him at it. But a contest needs contestants; and so a dozen of the finest archers of the realm gallantly stepped up to the mark alongside the Prince of Muldemar to try their skill.

Count Iram of Normork went first, and acquitted himself creditably enough, after which Mandrykarn of Stee managed a comparable score, and Navigorn of Hoikmar bettered that by some. The next to shoot was the bluff, hearty Earl Kamba of Mazadone, Prestimion's own teacher at the art. Kamba, discharging one arrow after another while scarcely seeming to look at his target, swiftly filled the eye at the center with his shafts, and doffed his cap to the royal box, and merrily left the field.

Now Prestimion stepped forward. The targets were cleared, and he nocked the first of his arrows. His style was very little like Kamba's: he studied the target with care, rocked back and forth a few times on his heels, finally lifted the bow and drew and sighted along it and let fly.

The Lady Thismet, who had come to the games this day

and was seated beside her brother in the Coronal's otherwise empty box, felt a shiver of reluctant admiration as Prestimion's arrow completed its flawless journey. She had no liking for the man but she could not deny his skill. It was a pretty sport, archery, a proper mix of art and bodily coordination and keenness of sight, very much more to her liking than such foolish measures of brute strength as the hammer-toss and certainly more pleasing than wrestling. Her lady-of-honor Melithyrrh had been to see the vile contest between Gialaurys and Farholt, and had tried to tell her of it, with much emphasis on the ferocity and the gore, but Thismet had cut her off after no more than five sentences.

There Prestimion stood at the base-line, trim and lean and so unexpectedly short—she was always surprised to discover how short he was, only a few inches taller than she was herself—but the breadth of his shoulders spoke of the strength of him, and his every movement was the embodiment of grace. She studied him now, taking unanticipated pleasure in the way he selected his arrow and methodically positioned it, and sent it coursing on its unerring way to the target.

Maddeningly, astonishingly, the sudden unwanted image of herself coupling with Prestimion blazed up in her mind like a fire rising to great conflagration out of the merest spark. His fair-skinned body encompassed her darker one; his mouth was pressed tight against hers; her platinum fingernails fiercely raked his back in the wildest throes of ecstasy. Furiously she banished that image and replaced it with one of Prestimion's body hanging from a hook on the wall of the Castle, dangling over an abyss.

"Extraordinary," Korsibar said.

"What is?" said Thismet, taken by surprise.

"His archery, of course!"

"Yes. Yes. The others were good, but Prestimion's in a class by himself, isn't he? You get the feeling that he could hit a bird on the wing, and then put a second arrow through his first one while the bird is still falling."

"I think he could do that," said Korsibar. "I think perhaps I've seen him do it."

"Has he always been as good as this?"

"From the first. That bow he uses: it's Kamba's own. Kamba gave it to Prestimion when he was twelve, saying that it was Prestimion's by right, for he was already the better archer. You could never draw that bow in a million years. I'd be sorely pressed to pull it myself. And the way he makes the arrows go precisely where he wants—"

"Yes," said Thismet. Prestimion had shot the last of his allotted shafts now, and all of them stood clustered at the center of the target, packed so close together that it was a marvel how he had found room to get the last one in.

"I think there's sorcery in it," said Korsibar. "He must have had a spell put on him when he was a boy, that lets him do such magic with the arrows."

"As I've heard it reliably told, Prestimion is no believer in magic."

"Indeed, I've heard it so as well. But what other explanation could there be for skill like his? It *must* be wizardry at work. It must."

Prestimion, looking pleased with himself, went from the field. His place at the line was taken by Hent Mekkiturn, a Skandar of the Procurator's retinue, who wielded a bow at least two yards long from tip to tip as though it were a child's toy. He held it already drawn with his upper arms while fitting the arrow into its place with his lower ones, and when he released his shaft it sped into the target with a loud thudding impact that nearly knocked the bull's-eye from its stand. But the huge Skandar was all strength and little finesse: in no way was he able to match the precision of Prestimion's shooting.

Korsibar said, "I must tell you, Thismet, of a peculiar thing that Dantirya Sambail said to me, while we were watching the wrestling the other day.—Hoy, there, sister, look at this clownish fellow!"

A knight in the costume of Duke Oljebbin's people had come forward to shoot. Evidently he saw himself as something of a comedian: he sent his first arrow high into the air to descend on a curving trajectory into the target, and shot the second one while standing with his back to the mark. For his third, he stood straddle-legged, and discharged the arrow from between his thighs. All three reached the target, though not in any greatly accurate fashion; but it was wonder enough that they reached it at all.

"This is a shameful business," Thismet said, looking away. "He disgraces one of the finest of arts.—What was that remark of the Procurator's that you began to mention a moment ago?"

"Ah. That. A strange and ugly thing."

"Yes, so he is. But what did he *say?*"

Korsibar smiled grimly. "Your tongue is too wicked, sister."

"Forgive me. I have little enough to do, you know, except practice my wit."

The clown was aiming now while lying on his belly. Korsibar shook his head in displeasure. To Thismet he said, leaning close and keeping his voice low, "He told me that he's heard whisperings to the effect that Prestimion will try to have me put to death, after he's Coronal. To make it seem like an accident, of course. But to remove me one way or another, because I'd be a threat to his reign if I lived."

Thismet sharply caught her breath. "Whisperings, you say? Whose whisperings?"

"He didn't say. Very likely the idea exists nowhere but in his own feverish imagination, for Dantirya Sambail's just the sort that would imagine such bestial atrocities. I told him it was a lunatic notion, preposterous and despicable. And asked him not to speak of such stuff to me again."

She stared at him gravely. Then after a moment she said, "If I were in your place, I'd take this thing a little less lightly, Korsibar. Whether he's really heard it whispered about or merely hit upon it all by himself, what the Procurator has told you is sound."

Korsibar said, startled, "What, you also?"

"Indeed. There's logic and substance aplenty in it, brother."

"I find that hard to believe."

"But surely you know that there are a great many people who'd prefer to see you as Coronal and not Prestimion."

"Yes. I know that. Count Farquanor was speaking of that very thing to me not so long ago, the day we all took wine together in the Banquet Hall just before the games began. Offered to start a conspiracy on my behalf, in fact."

"My new young handmaid Aliseeva would join that conspiracy, if ever it were launched," said Thismet, with a little laugh. "And many another. She told me just yesterday that it was a pity you would not be Coronal, for you were ever so much more kingly and handsome than Prestimion. And wished there were some way Prestimion could be set aside in your favor."

"She said that, did she?"

"She and others besides."

"Do they all of them think I'm without the least shred of honor and decency?" demanded Korsibar heatedly. And then, in an altogether different tone: "Aliseeva? The red-haired one with the very pale skin?"

"I see that you've already noticed her. I shouldn't be surprised, I suppose.—What did you tell Count Farquanor that day in the Banquet Hall?"

"What do you think I told him? He was advocating treason!"

"Is it treason to stand by like a fool and be murdered so that Prestimion can be Coronal?"

Korsibar gave her a close, searching look. "You actually do seem to believe that there's something to take seriously, then, in this insane notion of Dantirya Sambail's."

"He's Prestimion's kinsman, remember. He could perhaps be privy to Prestimion's inner mind. And yes, I think it might well be very much in Prestimion's interest to get you out of the way once he has the throne. Or even before."

"Prestimion is a man of decency and honor!"

"Prestimion can counterfeit decency and honor the way he can imitate anything else, I suppose," said Thismet.

"This is very harsh of you, sister."

"Perhaps it is, yes."

Korsibar threw up his hands and looked away.

The clownish archer had gone from the field, now, and his place had been taken by one of Prince Serithorn's sons, a long-limbed young man who set about his shooting with efficiency and skill that came close to matching Prestimion's own. But he too failed to equal the supreme accuracy of Prestimion's work, and his final arrow went astonishingly far astray, grazing the edge of the target and skittering off to the ground, which disqualified him entirely for a prize. The young man left with tears glimmering on his cheeks. The ninth contestant appeared, and the tenth and the eleventh, and then one more. Korsibar and Thismet watched them all come and go without speaking, without even looking toward each other.

As the final archer began his work Korsibar turned once again to Thismet and said abruptly, "Let's say, purely for the sake of the hypothesis, that it is Prestimion's plan to have me put out of the way. What would your advice to me be, in that case?"

Instantly Thismet replied, "Put him out of the way first, of course."

Korsibar gave her a startled look. "I can hardly believe that those words came from your lips, sister. Kill Prestimion, you say?"

"What I said is to put him out of the way. I said nothing about killing."

"Put him out of the way how?"

"By making yourself Coronal before he can get the crown. He'll have no means of striking at you then. The army and the people will be yours."

"Making myself Coronal," Korsibar said, wonderingly.

"Yes! Yes! Listen to your friends, Korsibar! They all feel as I do." The words, so long pent up, came pouring from Thismet in a wild rush, now. "You were made to be a Coronal; you were destined for it; and we'll see to it that you are. You are a prince of a quality very rarely seen before in this world. Everyone knows it; everyone is saying it, wherever I turn. And everyone will rise up for you as soon as the signal is given. We'll strike in a single day. Farquanor will gather support for you among the princes. Farholt and Navigorn will rally the troops behind you. Sanibak-Thastimoon stands ready to weave powerful enchantments to quell all opposition. The moment Prankipin dies, you make your move. You proclaim yourself; you stand before the people as their king and let them hail you; and then you go to father with the whole thing already done and show him that you had no alternative but to stand aside and be slain."

"Hush, Thismet. These are evil words."

"No! No! Listen to me! The omens all point to you! Hasn't Sanibak-Thastimoon told you what he—"

"Yes. Hush. Say no more. I beg you."

"Lord Korsibar, is what you will be!"

"*Enough,* Thismet!" Korsibar held both his clenched fists pressed together at his middle. The muscles of his jaws were knotted as though he were in pain. "No more of this! No more!" Once again he turned from her. His back and shoulders rose like a wall beside her.

But he was beginning to weaken, Thismet knew. She had seen, as Count Farquanor had seen before her, the momentary glint of temptation in his eyes as she had cried out that acclamation of him as Lord Korsibar. How close was he to yielding? Would one final push suffice?

Perhaps. But not just now. She understood the volatility of her brother's character; she knew when he could be nudged toward action, and when he would pull himself back into utter immobility. For the moment she had gone as far as she dared.

"Look," she said. "Prestimion's coming back. Why is that? To claim his prize, I suppose."

"All the prizes will be given at the final celebration," said Korsibar.

"Then why is he out here again now? And he looks as though he's ready to shoot all over again."

That was true enough. Prestimion had his bow in his hand and a full quiver over his shoulder. And now one of the judges was rising with an announcement: The winner of the archery competition, he declared, was Prince Prestimion of Muldemar, who at this time, by universal request, would offer a special additional demonstration of his skills.

"This is very unusual," Korsibar remarked quietly.

"It has to be purely political," said Thismet. "They're making a point of putting him on display, do you see? Letting the people get another little look at their wonderful next Coronal. It's all for show, Korsibar!"

Korsibar's only answer was a wordless sound of acknowledgment.

The same enthusiastic cry was coming at once from many parts of the stands: "Prestimion! Prestimion!" He smiled, saluted the boxes of the nobility, waved toward the crowd with one upraised outspread hand. That radiant, regal glow was on him again. Lifting his bow, he began now a demonstration of the most extraordinary archery, issuing volley after volley with none of his former deliberation, but a series now of rapid shots, coming at the target from a variety of distances and angles and unfailingly achieving his mark.

"*Prestimion! Prestimion!*" came the cry, over and over.

"They love him," Thismet said bitterly.

Korsibar uttered another little grunting affirmation, as though he could not bring himself to speak in actual words. He was staring down rigidly at Prestimion's performance.

Indeed it was a splendid show that Prestimion was putting on, a spectacular demonstration of skill; and the onlookers were responding to it accordingly. Despite herself, Thismet still could not help but react with a certain measure of admiration as well.

But hatred coursed through her also as she watched the compact little prince performing his wonders on the field. His boundless confidence—his sublime smugness—most of all the fact that he was down there at all, making a public show of himself in this way, at what was supposed to be a competitive event, not some theatrical exhibition of one man's prowess— how she detested him for all that! How profoundly she wished that one of those arrows would circle around back on him and skewer him through the throat!

She stole a cautious look at her brother and saw what seemed to be cold rage on his face as well; or annoyance, at least, at Prestimion's arrogance in having allowed himself to be brought forth for this display.

"This offends you, doesn't it?" Thismet said.

"He behaves as if he's Coronal already!"

"As well he might. He will be, soon enough."

"Yes," said Korsibar gloomily. "Four more days and the crown is his."

"You say that as though it's a certainty."

"Father's sure of it. He's cast the runes for Prankipin: four days and the old man'll be dead. Father's completely confident of that. His own mages have confirmed the calculation."

"Four days, then," said Thismet. "And how much time will you have to live, yourself, after that?"

She shot him a wary glance, fearful that it might have been far too soon for her to have returned to the theme of Dantirya Sambail's prediction. But no: no. Korsibar only shrugged.

"He's too proud," Korsibar muttered. "He ought not to be Coronal."

"Who'll stop him, if not you?"

"It would shake the world if I did." Korsibar looked toward her and smiled strangely. "Those were Sanibak-Thastimoon's own words," he said, in an odd way, as though he had forgotten all about them until just now. " *'You will shake the world.'* "

"Shake it, then," said Thismet.

Korsibar stared down at Prestimion, who had just sent two arrows at once speeding toward the target. He said nothing.

"Shake it, then!" Thismet cried. "Shake it or die, Korsibar! Come. Come with me to Sanibak-Thastimoon. There's planning for us to do, and spells to be cast."

"Thismet—"

"Come," she said. "Now. *Now!*"


There were no surprises in the fencing matches the following day. Septach Melayn quelled all rivals with his unsurpassable handling of the rapier, besting Count Farquanor in the final contest by a series of blindingly swift strokes that brought the entire host of onlookers to their feet in homage. The quick-wristed Farquanor was no trifling fencer himself and yet Septach Melayn was everywhere around him at once, mincing and prancing in his most disdainful way as he slipped past

Farquanor's guard again and again. He made it look almost too easy.

Korsibar, too, had an expected triumph in the saber contests, battering his opponents' heavy weapons aside with ease. In the special contests for Skandars—who were too big and had too many arms to compete fairly against humans—it was Habinot Tuvone, the famed fencing-master of Piliplok, who carried off the trophy in the two-sword competition, as had been virtually preordained. And so it went.

The jousting was to be the next day's event, and the atmosphere among the visiting lords was tense and controlled as the time for it approached. No one wanted a repetition of the bloody spectacle that the wrestling match between Gialaurys and Farholt had been; and it would be only too easy, when the armed men were atop their swift battle-mounts, for more carnage to take place under the guise of zeal in the chivalrous arts.

A list of the competitors had been carefully drawn up by the senior lords in such a manner that each team of jousters would consist of an equal mix of men known to be loyal to Prestimion and those who were plainly in Korsibar's entourage. But there would be no way to keep individual princes from attacking opponents of the other camp with the same murderous ferocity with which Farholt had attacked Gialaurys and with which Gialaurys had responded.

The plan was for the ninety contestants to assemble in the Court of Thrones fully armored for the bout, and to be transported in a group to the Arena. Septach Melayn was the first to arrive in that great dungeon-like room of black stone walls that rose to pointed arches, with Count Iram close behind him, and then Farholt and Farquanor together, Navigorn, Mandrykarn, Kanteverel of Bailemoona. There was much joking among them, but of a stiff, clanking, stilted sort. To Septach Melayn it seemed that an overheavy array of Korsibar's people was in the hall thus far, though Korsibar himself had not yet arrived, nor the Coronal his father.

Gradually others of the competitors filtered in, Venta of Haplior and Sibellor of Banglecode, and then the Procurator Dantirya Sambail with three or four of his men, and Earl Kamba of Mazadone. Still mainly Korsibar's men. Septach Melayn looked about for Prestimion and Gialaurys, but they were not yet here, nor Svor, who was unlikely to come: Svor was no jouster.

Dantirya Sambail, who wore conspicuous showy armor of gleaming gold inlaid in red and blue gems with horrific designs of dragons and monsters and a heavy brazen helmet bedecked with tall green plumes, looked to Septach Melayn and said, "Has your prince overslept himself today, friend?"

"That is not his habit. Perhaps he's misplaced his helmet plumes and is searching hard for them: for such plumes are all the fashion this year, I see," said Septach Melayn, with a pointed glance at the Procurator's high-soaring ornaments. "But he'll be in time for the jousting, I think. Being on time is ever his way. For that matter, I see no sign of our great prince Korsibar, or his royal father."

"And yet Korsibar's Su-Suheris wizard is here," Dantirya Sambail said, indicating with a jab of his helmet-plumes the presence of Sanibak-Thastimoon, whose two heads rose up into view in the midst of Farholt, Farquanor, and Navigorn. "Will he be jousting with us, I wonder? He doesn't seem to be in armor. But perhaps sorcerers don't need any."

Septach Melayn frowned. "He has no business in this room today. Why, I wonder, is—"

"Now his lordship comes," said Dantirya Sambail. And the old ceremonial cry went up: "Confalume! Confalume! Lord Confalume!"

The Coronal, in his formal robe of office, green and gold with ermine trim, acknowledged the cheers with brusque little gestures of greeting as he entered the hall. A little group of his court ministers accompanied him, a Vroon and a Hjort and some others. The Hjort, Hjathnis by name, who was unusually officious-looking even for a Hjort, trotted along close beside him carrying the starburst crown on a pillow of maroon velvet.

Iram said, "How weary he looks. This waiting for the change of rule to come has greatly tired him."

"He'll have time to rest soon enough, once Prankipin's gone," said Septach Melayn. "It's a much quieter life being Pontifex than Coronal."

"But when will that be?" asked Kamba. "It begins to look as if the Pontifex Prankipin intends to live forever."

"Cures are available for such intentions, my lord Kamba," Dantirya Sambail said, with a laugh and an ugly grin.

A retort for the Procurator's crassness was on Septach Melayn's lips; but instead he found himself putting his hand to his head and shutting his eyes a moment, for a mysterious fogginess had come suddenly over him. His eyelids felt heavy, his mind was a blur. After a moment it passed.

How very odd, he thought, shaking his head to clear it.

"Make way for Prince Korsibar," a loud voice called. "Make way! Make way!"

In that instant Korsibar appeared in the entryway to the hall, looking flushed and excited.

"News!" he cried, in the first moment of his entry. "I bring you news! The Pontifex Prankipin is dead!"

"You see?" said Dantirya Sambail, grinning his most evil grin. "A solution can always be found, even for immortality!"

"Look you," said Iram to Septach Melayn, with a nod toward Lord Confalume. "The Coronal himself doesn't seem to know anything about this. And where's Prestimion? He should be here for the passing of the crown."

In truth Lord Confalume seemed to have been caught off

guard by the news Korsibar had brought. Every aspect of his expression reflected astonishment and consternation. His hand went to the rohilla he wore at his collar, that ever-present little amulet of strands of gold twined about a bit of jade, and he rubbed the gem at its center again and again with fitful anxious energy.

Septach Melayn said, "Yes, this is Prestimion's moment to be here. A pity that he chose to be late. But I suppose that he—" He halted, perplexed, and swayed a little as a powerful new wave of dizziness swept him. "What? My head, Iram— some kind of damned fuzzy-mindedness coming over me—"

"And me," said Iram.

All around the room it was the same. The entire hall seemed engulfed in a dark cloud. The assembled lords were stumbling about as though asleep on their feet, befogged, hazy-brained, lost in that strange mist of uncomprehension. They spoke, if at all, in murky mumbles.

Then, as abruptly as it had come, the mist cleared. Septach Melayn blinked incredulously at the scene he now beheld.

Korsibar had moved to the rear of the hall and had taken up a position on the steps of the grand seat next to the Pontifex's own throne—the one that the Coronal used when he was present at functions of state in this room. He had seized the starburst crown from Hjathnis the Hjort and was holding the slender, shining royal diadem lightly in his hands, resting on his fingertips. Flanking him like a guard of honor and looking defiantly outward at the rest of the group were Farholt, Farquanor, Navigorn of Hoikmar, and Mandrykarn. The two heads of Sanibak-Thastimoon could be seen jutting up just behind Count Farquanor, very close beside the prince.

Lord Confalume appeared stunned at what had taken place. His face was very pale; his eyes seemed almost glassy. He had come a few uncertain steps toward his son, and his jaws were agape and his hands were turned helplessly outward in a gesture of shock and astonishment. He stared at Korsibar, and at the empty cushion on which the crown had lately rested, and at his son once more. But for a moment no sound could escape his lips except a rasping croak.

Then he pointed a wavering hand in Korsibar's direction and said to him in a hoarse rusty voice, "What are you doing?"

"The Pontifex is dead, father. You are Pontifex now, and I am your Coronal."

"You are—what?" Confalume said, with a gasp that was echoed by a host of others around the room.

He looked like a man who had been shattered by a single blow. He stood dumbstruck in front of his son, his head and shoulders slumped forward, his arms dangling limply at his sides. Where were the force and power of the mighty Lord Confalume now? Gone, all gone in one numbing instant; or so it would seem.

Korsibar held his arms out toward his father in a grand sweeping gesture.

"All hail his majesty Confalume Pontifex!" he cried. It was a cry loud enough to be heard at Castle Mount. "All hail! Confalume Pontifex!"

"All hail his majesty Confalume Pontifex!" the others shouted, or most of them, a very ragged chorus indeed, for the impact of the news was sinking in upon them at a varying rate.

Then Farholt bellowed in a voice that could bend stone walls, "And all hail the Coronal Lord Korsibar! Korsibar! Korsibar! Lord Korsibar!"

There was a moment of astounded silence.

And then: "Korsibar! Korsibar!" went up the cry, from all except a few for whom it was very plainly a difficult matter to give voice to the thing that Farholt wished them to proclaim. "Korsibar! Lord Korsibar!"

In a smooth solemn gesture Korsibar raised the starburst

crown high, held it forth to show it to all who stood before him, and serenely placed it on his own forehead. Whereupon he sat himself on the seat of the Coronal and coolly beckoned to his father to take the Pontifex's throne adjoining him.

"Do you believe this?" Septach Melayn asked.

"We must, I think," replied Count Iram. "Look over there."

Others were pushing their way into the room, now, a swarm of troops of the Coronal's guard, who evidently had taken up positions outside during that time when the minds of everyone within had been embraced by that dark cloud. They were all of them armed. Some deployed themselves along both sides of Korsibar with the plain intention of defending him against any who might raise objection to the sudden coup-d'état; the rest formed two enfilades down the borders of the room. Two, at a gesture from Korsibar, gently took the astounded Confalume by the elbows and prodded him toward the Pontifical throne.

"Come, father," Korsibar said, speaking very tenderly. "Sit beside me for a while, and we will talk; and then we will perform the proper rituals and see old Prankipin into his grave. And then you will take up your new home in this place and I will go back to Castle Mount to assume the responsibilities that now are to be mine."

The guards who were guiding Confalume toward the throne eased him up the three steps that led to it and sat him carefully down. He offered no resistance. He appeared to be without volition of his own, as though he were under some spell; and he had the look of a man who had aged twenty years in ten minutes.

Then came the sounds of a scuffle in the corridor outside. "Get out of my way!" a loud angry voice cried. "Let me in! Let me in!"

"Prestimion, at last," Septach Melayn murmured.

A louder and even angrier voice could be heard next,

stormily threatening mayhem and general destruction if the guards blocking the entrance to the hall did not step aside. It was that of Gialaurys.

Quickly Septach Melayn cut a path for himself to the door, deftly slipping between guardsmen who seemed unwilling to block his movements, or incapable of managing it. Prestimion, looking sweaty and disheveled, said as Septach Melayn approached him, "What's been happening here? I was on my way toward this hall, and I fell into a sort of swoon—and Gialaurys also, both our minds clouded over—and when we returned to ourselves the corridor was full of the Coronal's men, who blocked me from going forward, so that I had to threaten them with all manner of vengeance—"

"Look you there, and see wonders," broke in Septach Melayn, taking him by the arm and swinging him quickly about to face the crowned Korsibar on the Coronal's seat and the bewildered and thunderstruck Confalume on the Pontifical throne beside him.

"What is this?" Prestimion asked in wonder.

Calmly Korsibar said, rising from his royal seat, "The Divine has spoken, Prestimion. Prankipin is dead and my father Confalume now is Pontifex, and I—" He touched his hand lightly to the crown resting on his brow. "I—"

"No!" Gialaurys bellowed. "This is thievery! Thievery! This thing will not be!" Holding his arms upraised and his fingers stiffly outthrust as though he meant to throttle Korsibar with his own hands, he began to move forward with his head lowered like a rumbling bull, only to find himself confronted by the halberds of the front row of Korsibar's guards.

"Step back, Gialaurys," Prestimion said, in a low stern voice. And then, more sharply: "Back! Away from the throne!" And, reluctantly, Gialaurys gave ground.

Then, looking toward Korsibar, Prestimion said, with taut self-control, "You claim to be Coronal, is that it?"

"I *am* Coronal."

To Confalume Prestimion said in an equally quiet tone, "And this is acceptable to you, your majesty?"

Confalume's lips moved, but no words came out. He turned his hands outward and upward in a pathetic gesture of defeat and bewilderment.

Now Prestimion's rage flared high. "What is this, Korsibar, have you put some spell on him?" he demanded fiercely. "He's nothing more than a puppet!"

Farholt, stepping forward, said now with a shameless grin, "You will address him now as *Lord* Korsibar, prince."

Prestimion looked stunned for a moment. Then he smiled, but the smile was a very thin one. *"Lord* Korsibar, then," he said, quietly again, with a barely concealed tinge of mockery imparting an edge to his tone. "Was that properly spoken, Lord Korsibar?"

"I'll kill him!" Gialaurys howled. "I'll tear him apart!"

"You'll do no such thing," said Prestimion, as the line of halberds bristled. He clamped his hand tight about Gialaurys's thick wrist and held him firmly in his place. Smoothly Septach Melayn moved in to press himself up against Gialaurys and restrain him on the other side.

Gialaurys trembled like a shackled titan, but remained where he was.

"Svor saw something very much like this in a dream," Prestimion said in a low voice to Septach Melayn. "I laughed at him. But now we see it also."

"This is not any dream, I fear," Septach Melayn replied. "Or if it is, there'll be no quick awakening from it for us."

"No. And we appear to be friendless in this room today. This is not any place for us to be just now." Prestimion looked across to Korsibar. The world was whirling wildly on its axis, but he forced himself to plant his feet firmly and stand staunchly upright. To Korsibar he said, keeping all that he felt at this dark moment under the tightest of reins and speaking through barely parted lips, "In this time of great loss and mourning I would prefer to reflect in solitude on these great events. I ask your gracious permission to withdraw from the hall, your—lordship."

"Granted."

"Come, then," Prestimion said sharply to Gialaurys, who still looked stunned and numb with fury. "Out of here, now, quickly. And you also, Septach Melayn. Come. Come." And added, under his breath: "While we still can." Prestimion's fingers flicked out toward Korsibar in the starburst sign, which he performed so swiftly that it was little more than a parody of the gesture. Then he swung about and went quickly with his two companions from the room.

# TWO

# THE BOOK OF
# LORD KORSIBAR

# 1

"Did you see his face?" Thismet cried. It was the dazzling hour of triumph. "Like a stone slab, it was. No expression at all, and absolutely gray. A dead man's face." And she squared her shoulders and thrust out her chin and did a scathing imitation of Prestimion's stolid exit from the Court of Thrones, muttering gruffly in a decent counterfeit of Prestimion's strong tenor, "Come, then, Septach Melayn, Gialaurys. Out of here, while we can."

The room shook with laughter. Then Farholt jumped up. Moving stiffly, for he was still badly battered and bruised from that horrendous wrestling match with Gialaurys, he shambled ponderously back and forth before them in the clumsy dangle-armed posture of a great ape of the Gonghar Mountains, pummeling his chest and grunting in a fair semblance of Gialaurys's dark rumbling voice, "I'll kill him! I'll tear him apart!"

A couple of others began now to mimic Septach Melayn's dainty walk, comically exaggerating his feline litheness and overfastidious precision of movement. "Enough of this," said Korsibar, though he was laughing just as heartily as any of the others. "It's bad grace to mock one's fallen rivals."

"A good point, my lord," said Count Farquanor unctuously. "Wisely put, my lord." And the others echoed him: "Wisely put, my lord. A good point, my lord. A very good point, my lord."

The temporary quarters of the new Coronal had been established in the generous suite on the imperial level of the Labyrinth where the former Prince Korsibar had resided since his arrival; and here the new Lord Korsibar was holding court for the first time on the afternoon of his assumption of the crown, seated on an improvised throne while the members of his immediate entourage clustered about him to pay him homage.

One by one they had come forward and knelt and made the starburst sign to him: the Lady Thismet first, and then the brothers Farquanor and Farholt together, and Navigorn and Mandrykarn and Venta and the rest. And Sanibak-Thastimoon as well; for Korsibar was Coronal Lord of the Su-Suheris people of Majipoor now too, and of all the Ghayrogs and Liimen and Hjorts and Vroons and Skandars as well, and even the shapeshifting Metamorphs of the distant Piurifayne forests.

"My lord," they said over and over, greatly relishing the sound of it, interspersing it between every third word they addressed to him: "My lord, my lord, my lord, my lord." And the new Coronal heard and graciously smiled and nodded his acknowledgment of their deference, just as he had seen his father doing since he was a small child. Korsibar had had a better education in being Coronal, perhaps, than anyone who had ever come to the throne before him, at least in the matter of understanding the formalities of the post; for he had had an entire lifetime to study a Coronal's deportment, beginning at his father's knee.

Count Farquanor, eyes bright with the pleasure of victory, approached him and said, "The word has gone out everywhere, my lord, of what has occurred here today. They will all learn of it soon, in every city, on every continent."

He waited, half crouching beside Korsibar as if expecting to be tossed a coin. Korsibar knew what was in Farquanor's mind: he yearned to be named High Counsellor to the

Coronal, which was the highest rank at the Castle below that of Coronal itself. Very likely Korsibar would so name him, when the time for making appointments had come; but it was not yet that time, not this soon. One did not discard the former Coronal's close advisers so hastily: especially when one had come to the throne as irregularly as he had. And his reign was still only in its first moments, after all.

Even now, the news of the change of government was only just beginning to spread—erupting outward upon the world from the claustrophobic confines of the Labyrinth like a column of fiery lava spouting from the black ashy cone of a volcano. Of course it had come by this time to the Castle, where the myriad officials of the Coronal's administrative staff were doubtless looking at one another with astonishment and asking each other in helpless dumbstruck repetition, "Korsibar? How could it have been Korsibar?" And to the fifty glorious cities of the Mount that lay spread out below the Castle, High Morpin of the mirror-slides and juggernauts, and Normork of the great stone wall, and Tolingar where Lord Havilbove's miraculous garden was, and Kazkaz, Sipermit, Frangior, Halanx, Prestimion's own city of Muldemar, and all the rest of them.

And the astonishing news would be continuing onward and onward across the whole continent of Alhanroel, through the teeming valley of the Glayge and the innumerable stilt-legged villages scattered along the silver immensity of Lake Roghoiz, and out to Bailemoona and Alaisor and Stoien and Sintalmond and the airy towns that clung to the grotesque spires of the Ketheron district, and those of the golden hills of Arvyanda, and across the sea to the tremendous cities of Zimroel, the far western continent, cities that were more the stuff of myth and legend than real places to those who dwelled at the Castle—Ni-moya and Til-omon, Pidruid and Piliplok,

Narabal, Khyntor, Sagamalinor, Dulorn. And to parched fiery Suvrael also, and the Isle of the Lady. Everywhere. Everywhere.

Mandrykarn, approaching Korsibar now, said, "If I may ask your majesty—"

"No, not 'your majesty,'" Farquanor interrupted. "'Your lordship.' 'Your majesty' is what one would say to the Pontifex."

"A hundred thousand pardons!" said Mandrykarn with exaggerated punctiliousness, drawing himself up stiffly and looking displeased. Mandrykarn was deep-shouldered and substantial, a man nearly as robustly built as Korsibar himself, and he scowled down at the wiry little Farquanor in unconcealed annoyance. Then, to Korsibar again: "If I may ask *your lordship* a question—?"

"Of course, Mandrykarn."

"What is to be done about the games?"

"Why, we'll continue them where we left off, of course. But first we'll have the funeral for old Prankipin, with all the pomp and grandeur this gloomy place can muster, and then some sort of formal installation ceremony, I suppose, for my father and myself. And then—"

"If I may, my lord—" Mandrykarn said.

Both he and Korsibar looked surprised at that, for Mandrykarn had interrupted the Coronal in mid-sentence, and one was not supposed to do that. But Korsibar quickly smiled to show that he had taken no offense. They were all very new at this business: it was too early to be finicky over protocol.

Korsibar signaled Mandrykarn to continue.

"It occurs to me, lordship, that it might be the part of wisdom to abandon the remainder of the games and begin our journey to Castle Mount as quickly as possible. We can hold more games once we're there. We have no way of knowing what Prestimion's next move may be, my lord. If he should return to the Castle before we do, and raises a dispute against your assumption of power—"

"Do you think Prestimion would do such a thing?" Korsibar asked. "Not I. He respects the law. Under the law I am Coronal now."

"Nevertheless, my lord," Mandrykarn said. "With all respect for your judgment, my lord. If he chooses to challenge the assumption on the grounds that a Coronal's son may not become Coronal after him—"

"That's not law," said Farquanor sharply. "That's merely precedent."

"Precedent that has hardened into law over the past seven thousand years," replied Mandrykarn.

"I stand with Farquanor and his lordship in this," said Navigorn of Hoikmar. "If there's precedent here, it's that the outgoing Coronal chooses and ratifies the ascendance of his successor. Prestimion may argue that the element of choice on the part of Lord Confalume may have been defective, but certainly ratification was there: for did not Confalume sit willingly down on the Pontifical throne beside the crowned Lord Korsibar—"

"Willingly?" Farquanor asked.

"Well, more or less willingly, let us say. And thereby giving implicit recognition to Lord Korsibar by the very fact of making no protest over the assumption."

There was something of a stir in the room at Navigorn's words, not so much over their content as for the fact that he had said them at all. The dark-haired brawny Navigorn was a man of tireless strength and formidable skill in the hunt; but he had never demonstrated much gift for abstract thought before. Nor, for that matter, had Mandrykarn. Korsibar hid his amusement over this sudden dispute behind his hand. Was the coming of the new regime going to transform all his rough-and-ready hunting-comrades into lawyers?

"Still," said Farholt, glowering out from under his massive brows, "what we think the law says and what Prestimion thinks may not be the same. I'm with Mandrykarn here: I vote for calling off the rest of the games and getting ourselves back to the Castle as fast as we can."

Korsibar looked toward the Lady Thismet. "Sister?"

"Yes. Cancel the games. We have more important things to do now. As for Prestimion, he's no danger to us. We control the army. We control the machinery of government. What action can he take against us? Point a finger at you, my lord, and say that you have stolen his crown? It never *was* his crown. And now it's yours. It'll remain that way, my lord, no matter how Prestimion feels about today's events."

"I would go so far as to offer Prestimion a post in the new government," said Farquanor thoughtfully. "To neutralize him—to minimize his resentment—and also to ensure his loyalty."

"Why not High Counsellor?" Mandrykarn suggested, and everyone laughed, all but Farquanor.

Korsibar said, "Yes. A shrewd idea. I'll send for Prestimion in a day or two and ask him to take some Council post. Certainly he's worthy of one, and if he's not too proud to accept, it'll give us a way of keeping a close eye on him. As for the games, Thismet's right: we won't resume them, not here. There'll be time for chariot-racing and jousting later on, at the castle. We bury Prankipin; we consecrate the new Pontifex; we do whatever urgent business must be done and we leave for the Mount. So be it."

"What about your mother, lordship?" Farquanor said.

Korsibar gave him a baffled look. "My mother? What about my mother?"

"She now becomes the Lady of the Isle, my lord."

"By the Divine!" Korsibar cried. "That slipped my mind entirely! The mother of the Coronal—"

"The mother of the Coronal, yes," said Farquanor. "When the Coronal happens to have a living mother, that is, and now that's the case again. So at last old Aunt Kunigarda gets her pension, and the Lady Roxivail will be the Lady of us all."

"The Lady Roxivail," said Mandrykarn, in amazement. "What will she say when she finds out, I'd like to know!"

"And who'll be brave enough to be the one to tell her?" Thismet asked, fighting back a giggle.

The Lady Roxivail was no one's idea of a fitting Lady of the Isle of Sleep. Lord Confalume's beautiful, vain, and imperious wife had separated from the Coronal not long after the birth of her two children and withdrawn to the luxury of her shimmering palace far to the south on the tropic isle of Shambettirantil. Surely never even in her most grandiose dreams had she imagined that the responsibility of becoming a Power of the realm would ever descend upon her. And yet— law and precedent—the Ladyship would indeed have to be offered to her—

"Well," Korsibar said, "we can reserve that problem for a later discussion. Someone who knows more history than I do can tell us tomorrow how long a period of transition is usually allowed between one Lady and the next, and Kunigarda can continue to send dreams to the world until we figure out what to do about replacing her."

"My lord," Farquanor went on, "you will also need to deal quickly with the problem of the senior peers."

"And what problem is that? It seems to me you're finding a great many problems very quickly, Farquanor."

"I mean ensuring their loyalty, lordship. Which involves assuring them of your love and confirming them in their continued posts."

"For the time being, at least," said Mandrykarn.

"For the time being, yes," Farquanor said, eyes glinting with sudden covetousness. "But it would be rash to make them insecure in any way at the outset. I would summon your kinsman Duke Oljebbin within the hour, my lord, and the princes Gonivaul and Serithorn immediately after, and tell them that their role in the government is unchanged."

"Good. See that they're invited here."

"And finally—"

There was a knock, and a servitor appeared. "My lord, the Procurator Dantirya Sambail is here and seeks admission."

Korsibar gave Thismet an uneasy glance, and looked to Farquanor next and saw that he was frowning also. But he could hardly turn the powerful Procurator away from his door.

"Let him come in," Korsibar said.

Dantirya Sambail was still clad in the splendiferous golden armor in which he had attended the gathering in the Court of Thrones, but he held his green-plumed brazen helmet now under his arm in what was perhaps a sort of gesture of deference to the new king. His great freckled ruddy-faced head, topped with its fluffy corona of orange hair, jutted bluntly before him into the room like a battering ram as he made his striding entrance.

He took for himself the place directly in front of Korsibar, which required Farquanor and Mandrykarn to give ground slightly, and stood for a long moment, face to face with the new Coronal, staring at him as though openly taking the measure of him, not as subject before king, but as one equal prince to another.

"So," he said finally. "It does seem that you actually are Coronal now."

"So it seems, and so I am," said Korsibar, pointedly looking toward the floor in front of Dantirya Sambail.

But the Procurator ignored the unambiguous instruction to kneel and render up the sign of homage. "What has your father had to say about this, I wonder?" he asked.

162

"You saw my father sit down beside me in the Court of Thrones. There's implicit recognition in that."

"Ah. Implicit."

"Recognition," said Korsibar irritably. A certain amount of insolence was to be expected from Dantirya Sambail; but he was beginning to exceed expectations.

"You haven't spoken with him since leaving the hall?"

"The Pontifex has withdrawn to his suite," said Korsibar. "I'll visit him in due course. In these early moments of my reign I have much to do, Procurator, decisions to make, responsibilities to discharge—"

"I quite understand that, Prince Korsibar."

"I am Coronal now, procurator."

"Ah. Of course. *Lord* Korsibar, I should have said."

There were exhalations of relief in the room at that. Did that concession from Dantirya Sambail mean that he had chosen not to make trouble over Korsibar's accession? It was a good sign, at any rate.

Again Korsibar glanced down, once more inviting the Procurator to kneel and give homage. A slanting smile spread slowly across Dantirya Sambail's broad heavy-featured face, and he said, "I beg you, my lord, to be forgiven the genuflection. This armor of mine will not easily allow it." And he offered instead, in the most perfunctory way, a quick flashing of fingers in a semblance of the starburst sign.

With a mordant inflection in his tone Korsibar said, "Is there some special purpose to this visit, procurator, other than to offer your formal greeting to the new Coronal Lord?"

"There is."

"Then I await hearing it, Dantirya Sambail."

"My lord," the Procurator said, managing to impart the merest minimum of submissiveness to his dry uncongenial voice, "I assume that there will be festivities of some sort in

163

your honor shortly at the Castle, as is usual at the commencement of a reign."

"I expect so, yes."

"Very good, my lord. I ask to be forgiven if I am not in attendance. It is my hope to withdraw to my own lands of Zimroel for a while." Which caused an immediate sensation, gasps and murmurs and exchanges of meaningful glances. But Dantirya Sambail went on to explain, after a moment, that he intended no disrespect: he was suffering greatly from homesickness, he said, the journey was long, he wanted to get on his way as quickly as possible. "I have been at the Castle these past several years, you know, and it seems appropriate, in a time of the transfer of power, for me to return to the region over which I have responsibility, and look after my duties there. Therefore I humbly request permission to take my leave of you as soon as I have put my affairs at the Castle in order."

"You may do as you wish about that," said Korsibar.

"And furthermore: I ask that when you undertake your first grand processional, you reserve at least a month's time for me, to be my guest at my estate in Ni-moya, so that I can show you some of the extraordinary pleasures that the greatest city of the younger continent has to offer." And added, plainly as an afterthought: "My lord."

"It will be some while before I'll have the opportunity of making the grand processional," Korsibar said.

"I may well be planning a stay of considerable length in Ni-moya, my lord."

"Well, then," said Korsibar. "When I'm ready for the journey, I'll inquire at that time concerning the availability of your hospitality."

"I will await you—my lord."

Again Dantirya Sambail smiled his disagreeable smile, and bowed without attempting to kneel, grandly flourishing his plumed helmet before him, and went from the room, metalled boots clanking heavily against the floor.

"Let him stay in Ni-moya for a hundred years!" Thismet exclaimed, when the Procurator was gone. "Who wants him at the Castle, anyway? How did he get to become father's perpetual house-guest?"

"I think it would be best to have him close at hand, where I can watch him," Korsibar replied. "Perhaps father had something similar in mind. But he'll go where he chooses, I suppose." He shook his head. Something began to pulse behind his eyes and forehead, and a mysterious weariness seemed abruptly to afflict him. The Procurator was an exhausting man. Enduring his insolence without showing rage had been tiring. "Prestimion—Dantirya Sambail—and no doubt others like them, too—I must watch them all, it seems. Eternal vigilance will be necessary. There's more to this thing than I think I realized."

With an edgy impatient gesture he beckoned toward the tall flask of wine on the table beside Navigorn. "Quick, quick, give it to me!"

Between sips he said softly, to Thismet alone, "It seems I have climbed aboard the back of a wild beast, sister, and now I must ride it the rest of my days or it will devour me."

"Do you regret having done it, then?"

"No! Not in the slightest!"

But there must have been some lack of conviction in Korsibar's voice, for she bent her head close to his and said in his ear, "Remember, all this has been foretold." Then, with a glance toward the inscrutable Sanibak-Thastimoon, who was standing alone at the far side of the room: "This is your destiny, brother."

"My destiny, yes."

Korsibar waited for the hot flood of enthusiasm that that word had come to kindle in him in recent days; but this time it was very slow in coming, and he held the bowl out again for wine. The second drink of the young foaming wine warmed him and drove this sudden weariness from his spirit somewhat. He felt that surge of excitement for which he had searched in vain a moment or two before. My destiny. Yes. To which everything else must be subordinate: everything. *Everything.*

# 2

Under the new scheme of things they had, at least, allowed the former Lord Confalume to remain for the time being in the suite of rooms that he had occupied as Coronal. But signs of the sudden metamorphosis that the government of Majipoor had undergone were evident to Prestimion even in the hallway outside. The gigantic Skandars who guarded the Coronal's suite were still on duty, but now, absurdly, they wore the tiny eye-masks that marked them as members of the Pontifical staff. And half a dozen members of the Pontifical bureaucracy were milling about as well in the throng outside Confalume's door.

One of them, a masked Ghayrog with pearl-hued scales, gave him a supercilious look and said, "You claim to have an appointment with his majesty?"

"I am Prince Prestimion of Muldemar. There's an emergency in the land; the Pontifex has agreed to see me, and this is the hour at which I'm to meet with him."

"The Pontifex has sent word that he is very tired, and wishes his appointment schedule to be curtailed."

"Curtail it after I've seen him, then," said Prestimion. "Do you know who I am? Do you know what has happened here today? Go on. Go! Tell his majesty that Prince Prestimion is waiting outside to see him!"

A lengthy conference ensued among the Pontifical officials; then the Ghayrog and another masked figure disappeared into

Confalume's suite, where, very likely, still another lengthy conference took place. Then at last the two officials emerged and the Ghayrog said, "The Pontifex will see you. You may have ten minutes with him."

The great door, glistening with its bright golden LCC monograms that now had become obsolete, swung back and Prestimion stepped within. Confalume sat in deep dejection with his elbows against his simbajinder-wood desk and his head propped morosely against his fists. All about him were his strange implements of sorcery, scattered higgledy-piggledy, some of the elaborate devices overturned and others pushed negligently into untidy heaps.

Very gradually the new Pontifex looked up. His eyes, reddened and raw, met Prestimion's gaze only with the greatest difficulty, held themselves there no longer than a moment, and became downcast again.

"Your majesty," Prestimion said in a frigid voice, making the sign of submission.

"My . . . majesty, yes," said Confalume.

He was no more than the shadow of his former self. His face was bleak and sagging, his whole mien was one of confusion and despair. Poor pitiful man, emperor of the whole world, that could not command his own son.

"Well?" said Prestimion sharply. He struggled to contain the anger that he felt, and the pain. The sudden unimaginable loss of all that he had been working toward was like a blade within him. And even now the reality of it was just beginning to sink in: he knew it would be worse, much worse, for him later on. "Are you actually going to allow this ridiculous business to stand?"

"Please, Prestimion."

"Please? *Please?* The crown is unlawfully stolen from me, from us all, by your own son and you say *'Please, Prestimion'* to me, and nothing more than that?"

"The high spokesman should be here. Kai Kanamat, that's his name, until I've appointed my own." Confalume's voice was thin and faint and hoarse, veering occasionally into an inaudible whisper. "The Pontifex is not supposed to speak directly to citizens, you know. Questions must be addressed to the high spokesman, who will inform the Pontifex—"

"I know these things," Prestimion said. "Save them for later. If you are truly Pontifex, Confalume, what do you plan to do about this usurpation of the crown?"

"This—usurpation—"

"Do you know a better term for it?"

"Prestimion—please—"

Prestimion stared. "Are those tears, your majesty?"

"Please. Please."

"Has Korsibar been to see you yet, since making himself Coronal?"

"He'll come later," said Confalume huskily. "He has appointments to make—meetings—decrees—"

"So you do intend to let it stand, then!"

Confalume made no reply. Randomly he picked some conjuring device from his desk, a thing of silver wires and golden coils, and fondled it in an absent-minded way, the way a child might fondle a toy.

Relentlessly Prestimion said, "Did you have any advance knowledge of what Korsibar had in mind to do?"

"None. None whatever."

"It came like a bolt of lightning, is that it? There you were, and there he was, and you just stood there and let him take the crown from your own head and put it on his, without a word of protest. Is that what happened?"

"Not from my head. It was resting on a cushion. I felt dizzy for a moment and found myself unable to see, and when I was all right again I saw that he had the crown in his hands. I knew nothing before the fact, nothing, Prestimion. I was as surprised as anyone else. More so, even. And then it was done. He had the crown. He had the Coronal's seat. And the hall was full of his soldiers."

"Septach Melayn said that a dizziness came over him too. And I the same, out in the corridor. That was done by sorcery, wouldn't you say?" Prestimion paced furiously back and forth before the desk. He said, wonderstruck, "By the Divine, I don't even believe that true sorcery exists, and here I am crediting this coup to it! But what else could it have been, if not some witching of us all by that two-headed magus of his, casting us into a fog while Korsibar's troops moved into the room and he put his thieving hands on the crown? Such things are impossible: that I know. But what could be more impossible than the stealing of the throne, and look! It has happened!" He came to a halt in front of the former Coronal, leaning downward with his knuckles resting on the surface of the desk, and said vehemently, staring with implacable force into Confalume's eyes, "You are Pontifex of Majipoor now. You have the power to put an end to this monstrous affair with a single command."

"Do I, Prestimion?"

"Who would dare disobey you? You are the Pontifex! Condemn this seizure of the throne by Korsibar; order the imperial guard to reclaim the crown from him; proclaim me the rightful Coronal. I'll do the rest."

"What will you do, Prestimion?"

"Re-establish order. Remove the conspirators from authority and reverse whatever decisions they may already have made. Restore the tranquility of the kingdom."

"He has the army with him," Confalume said.

"The Coronal's guard, perhaps. Not necessarily the general army, and possibly not even the guard. It goes against all reason that your own guardsmen, who were loyal to you unto death only this morning, would now refuse to obey your orders."

"They love Korsibar."

"We all love Korsibar," said Prestimion acidly. "But we have a government of reason and law on this world! No one names himself Coronal and is allowed to have it!—Have you forgotten, Confalume, that the Pontifex is the superior monarch, and that the Pontifex has troops as well as the Coronal, and those troops are entirely under your command?"

"Yes. I know that," Confalume said.

"Order them out, then! Send them against the usurper!"

Confalume looked up at him and stared in silence for a long while. Then he said in the dullest and deadest of tones, "In that case there would be the most bloody of wars, Prestimion."

"Do you think so?"

"I've taken counsel with my own mages," Confalume said. "They say there would be resistance, that if force is used to make Korsibar relinquish what he's taken, he'll use force in return. The omens they cast are all evil ones. Have mercy on me, Prestimion!"

"Mercy?" Prestimion asked, astounded.

But then he understood.

It was folly to think that this Confalume who sat slumped before him now had anything more in common than a name with the great Lord Confalume who had ruled Majipoor with such forcefulness and panache these forty years past. That other Confalume had perished, shattered in a moment by his son's unthinkable treason; this pitiful broken old man here, this remnant, this empty shell, did indeed hold the title of Pontifex of Majipoor, but there was no strength left in him at all. He had collapsed within like some mighty building whose timbers had all slowly gone weak with the dry rot, while still looking grand and splendid on the outside. All his famed vigor and resilience had fled from him.

Confalume, Prestimion realized now, had come to see that

civil war might well be the only way to repair the yawning gulf that Korsibar's audacity—his madness—had opened in the commonwealth. But the price of the restoration of order would almost certainly be the death of his only son. And that was something Confalume could not face.

And so—and so—

"You ask me to accept this criminal act of insurrection in good faith, then, and bow down to Korsibar and accept him as king?"

"I have no other path, Prestimion."

"I was to have been Coronal, not Korsibar."

"The appointment was never formally made."

"Do you deny that you intended it?"

"No—no." Confalume could not meet Prestimion's hot gaze. "You would have been Coronal."

"But instead Korsibar is."

"Yes. Yes. Korsibar. You were the better choice, Prestimion. But what can I do? My blessings go with you, boy. And nothing more. The thing is done. Korsibar holds the power now."

Gialaurys said in a throbbing access of fury, when they were gathered soon afterward in Prestimion's suite, "And are you going to let them put such shame and mockery on you, Prestimion? Is this actually to be borne? If you hadn't stopped me, I'd have struck him down right where he sat on the Coronal's seat in the Court of Thrones. And torn the crown from his head and placed it on your own."

"Three of us, unarmed, and how many of them?" Prestimion asked wearily.

"Tell me again what the new Pontifex plans to do about all this," Svor said.

"He plans to do nothing. He's going to hole himself up here in the Labyrinth and let Korsibar have his way."

"Was he privy to the conspiracy, do you think?" asked Septach Melayn.

"No," said Prestimion, with a vigorous shake of his head. "Beyond all doubt, Confalume knew nothing at all. It was as much of a surprise to him as it was to you or me. And it has been the complete destruction of him. Look upon his face, if you will: he's a broken man. I saw only the ruins of Confalume in there."

"Nevertheless, he holds the highest authority in the land. We must maneuver him toward our side," Septach Melayn said, laying his hand lightly on Prestimion's arm. "This is an unsupportable outrage! We dare not allow it to stand!" His cool blue eyes suddenly became hard and fierce with anger, and two fiery patches of color, standing out like beacons against his fair skin, emerged along the sharp ridges of his cheekbones, and that look of amused contemptuous disdain that was Septach Melayn's usual expression gave way to one of barely contained rage. "We will go to him, you and I, Prestimion, and thrust our faces into his, and make it utterly clear to him that he must immediately—"

"No, my friend," said Prestimion. "No. Don't talk to me of thrusting my face into that of a Pontifex and telling him what he must or must not do. That's blasphemous talk. And in any case it would be useless."

"So Korsibar will be Coronal?" Septach Melayn said, throwing up his hands.

"And we go politely down on our knees before him?" Gialaurys asked. "With a 'Yes, Lord Korsibar,' and a 'No, Lord Korsibar,' and a 'May I lick your boots, Lord Korsibar?' " He clapped his hands together with a sound that could have summoned the dead. "No! I will not abide it, Prestimion!"

"And what will you do, then?"

"Why—why—"

Gialaurys sputtered into puzzled silence. Then he looked up, eyes brightening. "I'll challenge him to a wrestling match! Yes! That's it! Man to man, with the throne of Majipoor as the stake! Three falls, and Oljebbin and Serithorn and Gonivaul as the referees, and—"

"Yes," said Svor wryly. "That certainly is the solution."

"Do you have a better one?" demanded Gialaurys of the little man.

"To leave the Labyrinth as fast as we can, as a first step."

"You were ever a coward, Svor."

Svor smiled a bleak smile. "Careful, friend. There's a considerable difference between cowardice and prudence. But how would you know, having neither of those qualities? It will occur to Korsibar, sooner or later, that he would do well to be rid of us, for Prestimion here is a great impediment to his clear title to the throne. And what better place for achieving our disappearance than this dark and mysterious Labyrinth, where all is levels upon levels that no one understands, and if we were to be taken during the night and led away somewhere into the warrens behind the Hall of Winds to have our throats slit, let's say, or quietly pushed face down into the black lake of the Court of Columns, it would be a very long time before our bodies were found."

"And you think Korsibar would countenance any such damnable thing?" Prestimion asked. "By the Divine, Svor, you have a black view of the human soul, don't you?"

"I have traveled some, and seen a few things."

"And so you believe that Korsibar has the capacity for murder in him."

"Despite his shameless taking of the crown, Korsibar may indeed in other matters be as honorable as you would like to think he is," Svor said coolly. "But there are those in his party who are not. I speak particularly of Count Farquanor. And I remind you also of the Su-Suheris wizard who casts the prince's spells for him. His handsome sister, I think, has a sinister influence over him as well. Korsibar seems wondrous strong and majestic to look upon, but we know that there's a certain lightness within him, and it takes but a gentle breeze to move him easily from one place to another. The same folk who pushed him into seizing the throne can push him into taking our lives."

Prestimion nodded. "Perhaps so," he said, looking darkly downward. His hands opened and closed on air. "You warned me of all this, Svor, and I told you to hold your tongue, that time when you came to me with that dream of dead Prankipin's taking the crown from Confalume and putting it on Korsibar's head. I spurned and ignored you, then, to my great cost. You have greater credit with me now. So be it: we are in danger here, I agree." To the other two he said, "I stand with Duke Svor on this. We'll leave here as soon as is seemly, the moment the old Pontifex is buried."

"Where would you suggest we go?" asked Septach Melayn, addressing Svor.

"We have homes at Castle Mount. I would go there," said Svor, "and test the strength and depth of Korsibar's support within the Castle, and subtly forge such alliances as we can, with this high lord and that one. All the while making great pretense of accepting what has happened, and, yes, freely bending the knee to Korsibar whenever it's required of us."

"And the risk of our being murdered in the night?" Septach Melayn asked.

"There'd be little chance of that at the Castle. That's something that might more easily happen in the Labyrinth than there, where the sun shines brightly on all deeds, and we'd have so many more of our friends about us. And as time goes along, perhaps we will find the opportunity—"

"As time goes along!" Gialaurys cried. "Time! Time! Time!

How long do you think we could contain ourselves, under those conditions? What life would there be for us, with Korsibar lording it over us day after day and month after month? You may bend your knees to him if you wish, Svor, but mine are of stiffer stuff! No, let me go to him now, and smash him down where he stands, even if they kill me on the spot. Majipoor will get its proper Coronal then."

"Gently," Prestimion told him. "Pay attention to Svor's advice."

"Perhaps in due time once we are in residence again at the Castle we will find the opportunity," Svor went on, just as smoothly as though he had not been interrupted at all, "to put together a sufficiency of backers, and then to overthrow Korsibar of a sudden by some quick unexpected stroke. Taking him by surprise at a time when he has come to think of us as loyal subjects, even as he surprised us all this day."

"Aha!" cried Septach Melayn, with a grin. "How dependable you are, Svor! We can always count on you to fall back eventually on the treachery that's so dear to your heart."

"Well, then," said Svor, still unperturbed, "if what I suggest seems despicable to you, let us then be decent law-abiding men, and grovel eagerly before Lord Korsibar every day of our lives and trust to his mercy that he'll allow us to live yet one day more, and one after that. Or, contrariwise, let's have the bold and mighty Gialaurys go to him this very day, whether on the suicidal mission he has just proposed or else, as he offered before, to challenge him to wrestle for the throne."

Septach Melayn said, "Ah, you misunderstand me greatly, Svor. You have my full agreement here: my vote is for treachery also, the blacker the better. We leave the Labyrinth with all despatch; we take up our comfortable lives once more at Castle Mount; we wait for our moment, and then we strike. What do you say to all this, Prestimion?"

"We will leave here, yes," said Prestimion, who in the past

few moments had wandered into some private realm of thought, where all this making and unmaking of kings meant nothing to him, and he had attained a happy, quiet, fruitful life as prince and husband, perhaps, and father some day amidst the serenity of his estate in Muldemar. "We'll go quickly, before our lives can be placed in jeopardy, if it's not already too late for that. And as we journey toward the Castle we'll endeavor to read the will of the people who live along our route, and see whether there's any way we can regain the high place that was meant for us to occupy."

He thrust his hands into the pockets of his tunic and looked from one to the other to the other of them to see whether they were in agreement. And murmured, "Hoy, what's this?" as the fingers of his right hand closed on something small and smooth and unfamiliar in his pocket. He drew it out. It was the little amulet of polished green stone that the Vroon sorcerer Thalnap Zelifor had given him that day which now seemed so long ago, just before the commencement of the games, when he had paid a call on Prestimion to warn him of impending calamity. "I forget how this thing is called. A magic-thing, it is. A gift from Thalnap Zelifor."

"A corymbor," Svor said. "They're said to be useful in time of trouble."

"Yes. Yes, I remember now. Put it on a chain, the Vroon said. Wear it about my throat; stroke it with my finger when I was in need, and it would give me aid." Somberly Prestimion shook his head. "Thalnap Zelifor! There was another one that saw trouble coming, and I paid him no heed. All these visions! All this wizardry! And I paid no heed."

"Blood on the moon, that was what he saw," said Gialaurys. "Do you remember? Omens of war. A secret enemy who would reveal himself and strive against you for the Castle. I said it was Korsibar who was that secret enemy: do you remember, Prestimion? I said it the moment that the Vroon left us."

"And I paid no heed to you either," Prestimion said. "How blind I was! And how clear it all seems to me now, in hindsight. But hindsight is ever clearer than the other kind, is it not so?" He rested the sleek amulet in the palm of his hand a moment, and lightly touched the tip of his finger to the row of minuscule runes inscribed on its face. Then he flipped it through the air to Septach Melayn, who deftly caught it. "You have a good many fine golden chains in your collection of baubles, eh, my lord Septach Melayn? Let me have one for this corymbor, I pray. I'll wear this thing next to my breast, even as Thalnap Zelifor advised, from now on. Who knows? There may be virtue in those tiny lines of sorcery it bears. And surely I need all the help I can get, now. We can have no doubt of that." Prestimion laughed. "Come: let's make ourselves ready to depart from the Labyrinth. And none too soon will it be."

# 3

The way out of the Labyrinth began with the lengthy and circuitous journey upward through the underground city's many levels.

There was indeed a special direct route to the surface that took just a short while to traverse, but that route was reserved entirely for Powers of the Realm; and Prestimion, though he had had high expectations once of leaving the Labyrinth as one of those Powers, was nevertheless still nothing more than one of the many princes of the Castle peerage as he set out now for home.

So for Prestimion and his three companions, and all their comrades and aides and baggage-handlers that had come down with them from the Castle, it was up and up and up the long way—level upon level, ring upon ring, a plodding interminable trek requiring many hours even by floater as they ascended the narrow spiraling roads out of the imperial sector where they had all been lodging these many weeks, and onward through all the strange and musty and darkly lit zones of the famous Labyrinth landmarks. The Court of Globes and the House of Records where the names of all the Coronals and Pontifexes of Majipoor's thirteen thousand years of recorded history were displayed on a great glowing screen, the Place of Masks, the Court of Pyramids, the Hall of Winds, the Pool of Dreams. And upward still, into the densely populated sectors of the city where the common people lived, that multitude of pale and drably clad folk who dwelled forever jammed shoulder to shoulder into the upper circles of the subterranean metropolis. And out, finally, into the world of sunshine and air, of rain and wind, of trees and birds and rivers and hills.

"And may it be a while," said Gialaurys fervently, "before we see that dreary place again!"

"Ah, we'll be back in it gladly when Prestimion is Pontifex," Septach Melayn said, gaily prodding him in the shoulder. "But we'll all be old men with long gray beards by then!"

"Pontifex!" Prestimion snorted. "Let me be Coronal a little while first, if I may, once the present little obstacle is cleared away, before you send me hastening on to the next throne!"

"Oh, yes. By all means, Prestimion: first things first," said Septach Melayn. "Coronal, and then Pontifex!" And they all laughed loudly. But it was more out of relief of being out of the Labyrinth than anything else, for there was little mirth in them just then, but only a great emptiness, and dark uncertainty over what might lie ahead. Just before their departure from the Labyrinth Korsibar had made some surprising noises, yes, about appointing Prestimion to the new government when they had all reached the Castle. But who could say how sincere those promises would turn out to be, once the fluidities of the new situation had hardened into harsh reality?

They had emerged at the northernmost of the seven gateways of the Labyrinth, the one known as the Mouth of Waters, where the River Glayge that descended out of the distant foothills of Castle Mount ran past the city. The usual route north from the Labyrinth to the Mount was by riverboat along the Lower Glayge to the place where it emerged from Lake Roghoiz, and from the far side of Roghoiz onward via the Upper Glayge to the point where the land began to rise significantly and the river was no longer navigable. From there one proceeded by floater-car up through the steepening foothills to the high cities of the great mountain.

The Glayge was a swift and powerful river, but the stretch of it that flowed from Roghoiz southward to the Labyrinth was a mere tame thing, more of a canal than a river. Its banks had been paved long ago, in the remote era of Lord Balas and the Pontifex Kryphon, to control its flow and keep the waters of occasional winter floods from escaping over the barriers that protected the Labyrinth. So the early part of their voyage was a placid one, a sleepy uneventful trip by hired boat through the broad and virtually flat agricultural plain that was the valley of the Lower Glayge.

It was high summer here, a warm bright time, when the golden-green sun of Majipoor hung directly overhead and its brilliance filled all the land. They had almost forgotten about the seasons during their sojourn underground. It had been late spring when they had gone down into the Labyrinth, already a balmy time of the year, for the climate in this entire section of central Alhanroel was never anything but mild. But now the full heat of mid-year was on the valley. Off to the west, where the ruins of Velalisier, the ancient stone capital of the Metamorphs, lay in the midst of a dry barren wasteland, the sun must now be a monstrous frightful eye of flame; and in the far south, along the moist and torrid Aruachosian coast where the Glayge finally emptied into the sea, the air surely was thick with almost tangible humidity.

Here, though, the days were bright and warm but not in any way uncomfortable. To the men so long imprisoned in the joyless artificial depths of the Labyrinth it was a splendid thing to feel the touch of sunlight against their cheeks. To fill their lungs with the sweet gusts of air that came riding on the southerly breezes, carrying the perfume of the myriad flowers of the far-off coastal jungles, yes! Or to stare upward wonder-struck at the immense transparent dome of the sky and watch in admiration as great gliding pink-bellied hieraxes, those huge free-souled birds of the highest zones of the atmosphere, went coasting serenely by overhead, displaying their enormous wings that were more than twice the length of a tall man's body in their spread from tip to tip.

They looked constantly to the north, too, searching for the first sign of Castle Mount rising on the horizon. But that was only hopeful fantasy on their part. Castle Mount stood thirty miles high in the sky, piercing through the atmosphere and jutting up into the other empire that was space; but even so there was no seeing it from this far away.

"Do you espy it yet?" Gialaurys would ask, for he was less well educated than the rest and knew little of scientific things, and Septach Melayn, ever playful, would say, "I wonder, could it be that grayish bit of darkness on our right-hand side?" To which Svor would then reply, "A cloud, Septach Melayn, only a cloud! As you know full well."

And Gialaurys: "If the Mount is so high, why can't it be seen from everywhere on Majipoor?"

To which Prestimion, making a sphere in the air with the out-stretched fingers of both hands: "This is the shape of the world, Gialaurys. And this"—now extending his rigid arms outward from his sides as far as they could go—"is the size of the world, if you are able to imagine it. They say there's no world larger, of any on which mankind can live. They say that Majipoor has ten times the size around the middle of Old Earth, from which we all came so many hundreds of centuries ago."

"What I hear is that it's even bigger still. I'm told that it's twelve or fourteen times greater about the middle than Earth," said Svor.

"Ten times or twelve or fourteen, that makes no important distinction," Prestimion said. "Whichever one it be, this is a huge world, Gialaurys, and as we move across it it curves like *this?"*—making the sphere with his fingers again—"and we are unable to see things that are a great distance from us, because the curve is so vast, and they are hidden on the far side of it. Even the Mount."

"I see no curve," said Gialaurys sulkily. "Look, we sail along the Glayge, and everything lies flat as a board before us, nor are we traveling up a curve as we go, not any that I am able to detect."

"But the top of Castle Mount is higher in the air than we are now, is it not?" Septach Melayn asked.

"The top of Castle Mount is higher than anything."

"Well, then," said Septach Melayn, "the world must curve downward to us from Castle Mount to here, for the Mount is high and we are not. Which is why this river flows only in one direction, down from the Mount toward the Labyrinth and on to Aruachosia, and never up from Aruachosia across the land to the Mount, for how can water flow uphill? But the curve is very gentle because the world is so great, and in making the rim of the circle it must go so and so and so, a gradual extension, so that much of the land looks flat to us, though in fact it is always slightly curving. And slight as it is, over many miles the curve becomes great. Therefore the Mount can't be seen from this far away, concealed from us as it is by so many thousands of miles of the bulging world's curving belly that lie between there and here.—Do I tell it properly, Prestimion?"

"With great elegance and accuracy," Prestimion said. "As you conduct yourself in all things."

"And when will we begin to see Castle Mount, then?" asked Gialaurys, who had been following all this in an ill-tempered, frowning way.

"When we're farther along the curve, closer to home: beyond Pendiwane, certainly, beyond even Makroposopos, possibly not until Mitripond."

"Those cities all are far from here," Gialaurys said.

"Indeed."

"Then if there's no hope of the Mount until Makroposopos, which is so far up the river, tell me this, Prestimion: why did I observe you looking in a northerly direction yourself this morning, just where that darkness is that Svor tells us is nothing but a cloud?"

There was laughter at that; and Prestimion said, grinning also, "Because I'm as eager as you are to look upon the Mount again, Gialaurys, or even more so, and I look toward it even when I know it's too soon to see."

"Then the Divine grant we see it soon," Gialaurys said.


Though towns in great number and even a few cities of some magnitude were clustered along both banks of the Lower Glayge, Prestimion ordered the pilot of his riverboat to pass them by. It was tempting to go ashore and find out how the people of these places had responded to Korsibar's seizure of the crown, yes; but Prestimion preferred to carry out that research farther upstream. He had no idea how much longer Korsibar would linger at the Labyrinth, now that Prankipin was in the ground and Confalume had taken possession of the Pontifical duties, and he wanted no risk of coming into contact with the usurper and his retinue on the way north.

The faster they traveled through the valley of the Lower Glayge, the better: the new Coronal very likely would be pausing at some of these towns and cities to receive homage, and that would provide Prestimion, if he hurried, with an opportunity to return to the Mount well before him. Where, perhaps, if he were the first to arrive, he might find a warm welcome from those who opposed the usurpation.

There was no choice, though, but to halt awhile when they reached the shores of Lake Roghoiz. They would have to change vessels there, for the barge-like flat-hulled riverboats that plied the placid waters of the lower river between Roghoiz and the Labyrinth were unfit to negotiate the swifter and more turbulent stream that was the Upper Glayge. And in all likelihood several days would be needed to arrange to charter a boat to take them the rest of their way upriver.

They came to Lake Roghoiz at dawn, the best time, when the whole broad surface of the immense lake gleamed like a dazzling mirror in the early morning light. Just after sunrise their boat passed through the final lock of the canal and made one last turn where the river took a sharp bend to the east, and then the lake was there before them. It was almost blindingly brilliant in its stunning whiteness as the potent bright glow of daybreak came sweeping out of a gap in the low hills in the distance and went skipping and bounding across the wide expanse of the water, transforming it into a single sheet of silvery splendor.

Roghoiz was gigantic. Whole nations of some smaller world could have been submerged in it, with margin to spare. Every stream of the southwestern slope of Castle Mount drained into the Glayge, which carried all that immeasurable volume of water tumbling down the long steep gradient of the foothill country for thousands of miles, descending through ledge after ledge, terrace after terrace, until at last it came to a place where the land widened into a wide plain. In the center of that plain lay a shallow basin great enough for the river to deliver its burden into it; and that enormous basin was the bed of Lake Roghoiz.

Along the margins of this region of the lake were broad banks of bright orange mud. Here the famous stilt-houses of Lake Roghoiz abounded, forming a string of small fishing villages, hundreds of them—thousands, perhaps—that were home to a lakeside population reaching up into the millions.

In part these stilt-houses of the Roghoiz shore were natural structures, something like the even more renowned tree-houses of Treymone on Alhanroel's western coast. The Treymone people actually lived *within* their trees, though, forming the rooms they occupied out of pliant branches joined together, but those of Roghoiz merely used theirs as platforms upon which to build.

For in the fertile orange silt of the lake's southern shore—and only in that place, in all of Majipoor—there thrived the dyumbataro-tree, whose branches and boughs sprouted not from a single central trunk but at the crown of an immense mass of close-packed pink aerial roots that rose like stilts out of the shoreline ooze. Up came these bare woody roots, scores of them for each tree, to heights of fifteen, twenty, sometimes even thirty feet above the ground; and there, whenever the tree chose to begin its crown, the root-mass widened out into a great wild profusion of ropy vine-like shoots covered with glossy saucer-sized leaves, and flowering stalks that sent scarlet spears thrusting outward at acute angles.

The people of the lake shore had discovered long ago that if a young dyumbataro-tree's upward growth were interrupted by topping at the crown-point—if it were cut there, just as the first growth of leaf-bearing shoots was beginning to appear—it would continue to grow laterally at that point, ultimately creating a flat woody platform eighteen or twenty feet across, the ideal foundation for a house. These they would build from translucent sheets of a thin glossy mineral that was peeled from the sides of cliffs a few miles to the east: they bent this stuff into domes, which they fastened down with wooden hoops and pegs atop the platforms. Inside these they made their dwellings. They were, most of them, crude simple hovels of no more than three or four rooms; but at sunset, when streams of golden-bronze rays struck these domed buildings along their western faces, an effect of extraordinary beauty was created by the blood-red glint of reflected light that rebounded from them.

Prestimion and his companions took lodgings in a modest lakeside hostelry for traveling merchants in the first of these stilt-villages to which they came, a place called Daumry Thike, where they were told they could make their arrangements for a change of transport. It seemed wisest not to advertise his identity, but simply to remain in and about the hostelry in the anonymous guise of a group of young Castle aristocrats heading homeward to the Mount after a visit to the Labyrinth.

The village was situated no more than a hundred yards from the edge of the lake. Here, the silty ground beneath the buildings was perpetually moist. When the storms of the rainy season arrived—they came in autumn, in this region—the lake sometimes expanded well beyond its normal bounds, if the year happened to be an unusually wet one, so that its waters came right up into the village, lapping at the pink stilts and making it necessary to get from one place to another in Daumry Thike by canoe. And in a very wet year, of the sort that might come only once in many centuries, the water might reach almost to the lower stories of the houses: so said the chambermaid who brought them their simple meals of grilled lake-fish and tart young wine.

There had been a flood of that sort in the days of Setiphon and Lord Stanidar, she told them, and another during the time of Dushtar and Lord Vaisha. And in the reign of the Coronal Lord Mavestoi there had been such a deluge that the village had been submerged clear to its rooftops for three days, just when the Coronal himself was here while making his grand processional.

Nilgir Sumanand, who was Prestimion's aide-de-camp, was about to go into the village to set about the task of chartering a riverboat. Since even the chambermaids of this place seemed so well versed in ancient history, Prestimion asked him to try to learn whether these people were equally familiar with current events. When he returned at nightfall, Nilgir Sumanand brought word that the citizens of Daumry Thike did indeed seem to be aware of the recent change of regime. Portraits of the late Pontifex Prankipin were on display outside a goodly number of houses, with the yellow streamers of mourning affixed to them.

"And the new Coronal? What about him?"

"They know that Korsibar has taken the throne. I saw no portraits of him out, though."

"No, of course not," said Prestimion. "Where would they have come from, so soon? But you heard his name mentioned often, did you?"

"Yes." Nilgir Sumanand looked away, abashed. He was a full-bearded gray-haired man of medium height, who had been in the service of Prestimion's father before him in Muldemar. "They were speaking of him, some of them. Not all, but some. A good many, I would say."

"And were they calling him Lord Korsibar, when they spoke of him?"

"Yes," Nilgir Sumanand said, in a husky whisper, wincing as though Prestimion had just uttered some terrible gross obscenity. "Yes, that is what they called him."

"And did they express surprise, would you say, that Korsibar had become Coronal and not someone else? Or distress, or any sort of dismay at all?"

Nilgir Sumanand was slow to reply.

"No," he said, after an awkward span of time had passed. He moistened his lips. "In truth I heard no surprise expressed, sir. There is a new Coronal, and he is Prince Korsibar: and they had no comments to make concerning what has happened, beyond that simple fact."

"Even though Korsibar's the son of the former Coronal?"

"I heard no surprise over that fact, sir," said Nilgir Sumanand again, almost too softly to be heard, and still not looking directly at Prestimion as he spoke.

Septach Melayn said, "There is little to wonder at in this. These are fishermen here, not constitutional lawyers. What do they know of the customs of transition? Or care, so long as the fish continue to take their bait?"

"They know that it isn't a usual thing for a Coronal's son to become Coronal after him," said Gialaurys, biting angrily at his own words.

"They also know," said Svor, "if they know anything much at all about the lordlings of the Castle, that Prince Korsibar cuts a grand and illustrious figure, and looks very much the way they imagine a king ought to look, holding himself well and speaking in a clear kingly voice that has great power and richness, and what better reason can there be for making him Coronal, in the eyes of humble people like these? And they know also that if Lord Confalume chose his own son to be his successor, why, it must have been with the welfare of the populace in mind, for Lord Confalume is beloved everywhere for his wisdom and benevolence."

"No more of this talk, if you will," said Prestimion, for he felt a dark cloud of gloom coming over him, and he loathed that. "Perhaps things will be different as we get nearer to the Mount."

It would be another two days yet before a vessel of the proper sort to take them onward would pass this way. Prestimion and Svor and Gialaurys and Septach Melayn waited out their time in Daumry Thike, spending the long hours peering down from the veranda of their stilt-house at the fat-legged blue-eyed crabs that went crawling across the orange mud, and wagering on which one would be the first to reach a line that they had drawn across their path. In due course the riverboat that Nilgir Sumanand had chartered for them arrived, anchoring a few hundred yards off shore where the water was deep enough. A small creaking ferry carried Prestimion and his companions out to it.

The riverboat was a far sleeker craft than the barge that had brought them up the Glayge from the Labyrinth: narrow-beamed and low-sided and sharply tapered fore and aft, with a triple mast whose brightly painted spars were festooned with garish witch-signs. It was smaller and rather less imposingly appointed than the vessels in which princes of Castle Mount normally made journeys between the Mount and the Labyrinth, but it would do. *Termagant* was the riverboat's name, emblazoned in flaming red letters of jagged baroque style against the lemon-hued wall of its hull, and its captain was Dimithair Vort, a lean, hard-bodied plain-faced woman of Amblemorn, with muscles like a stevedore's and a thick uncouth mop of kinky black hair, to the tips of which she had attached a jingling multitude of small amulets and charms.

"Prestimion," she said, glancing at the names on the passenger manifest. "Which one of you's Prestimion?"

"I am."

"Prestimion of *Muldemar?*"

"The same."

"Brother of mine once took you hunting gharvoles, out in the Thazgarth country back of Mount Baskolo. You and some other great important lords. He's a guide there, my brother, name of Vervis Aktin." She gave Prestimion a coolly appraising look. "I thought you'd be a much taller man."

"I thought I would be too. The Divine had other plans for me."

"My brother said you were the best man with a bow he'd ever seen. Himself excepted, of course. He's the finest archer in the world. Vervis Aktin: do you remember him?"

"Very clearly," said Prestimion. It had been seven years before; Korsibar, with whom he had been more friendly then, had invited Prestimion to join him on a jaunt into the Thazgarth hunting preserve, a dense forest of northeastern Alhanroel, fifteen hundred miles across, where the deadliest of predators were left to roam freely. Septach Melayn had been with them also, and the young and overly wild Earl Belzyn of Bibiroon, who would be killed the following year in a climbing accident.

Vervis Aktin, Prestimion recalled now, had hair of much the same frizzled sort as his sister's, and the same wiry but powerful build, and the same blunt indifference to aristocratic prestige. By the campfire at night he had boasted freely to them of his amatory exploits, his casual seduction of any number of highborn huntresses during the course of expeditions in the preserve; Korsibar had had to silence him before he named actual names. Prestimion remembered him as a tireless guide and, yes, a superb bowman, though not perhaps as supremely gifted as Dimithair Vort claimed.

She led them to their quarters, small simple cabins just below the bridge, where they would make their homes for many days to come. Prestimion would share his with Gialaurys, Duke Svor with Septach Melayn.

"What is your brother doing now?" Prestimion asked her, as she lingered in the doorway, idly watching them.

"Still a guide in Thazgarth. Lost a leg when he got between a mother gharvole and her cub, but that hasn't slowed him down. He was very impressed by you, you know. Not just on account of what you did with a bow. Said that you'd be Coronal some day."

"Perhaps I will," said Prestimion.

"Of course, we're not ready for another one so soon, are we? This new Lord Korsibar's only just settling in. You know him, I suppose?"

"Quite well. He was with your brother and me that time in Thazgarth."

"Was he, now? Old Confalume's son, he is, so I hear. That right? Well, why not, keep it in the family! Divine knows, I'd do the same. You great lords understand how to look out for yourselves." She grinned, showing fierce, sharp-pointed teeth. "My brother always used to tell me—"

But Septach Melayn intervened then, for he disliked such a degree of familiarity as this woman was assuming with Prestimion and the conversation had long since ceased to amuse him. He sent Dimithair Vort on her way and the travelers set about installing themselves in their cabins.

After a time there came the sound of chanting outside. Prestimion peered out and saw half a dozen members of the crew huddled on deck, the captain and some others, passing small stones from hand to hand according to some complex predetermined pattern as they sang. He had seen this done before. It was, some sort of ceremony intended to insure the safety of the voyage, a routine bit of conjuring. The stones were sacred ones, blessed by some shaman whose power the captain trusted.

Prestimion watched the sailors almost tenderly. His rational self was repelled as ever by this further show of superstition, this naive trust in dead stones, but even so he was awed by the purity and intensity of the faith implied in it, a faith in benevolent watchful spirits who could be persuaded to look after one. They were capable of belief in things unseen; he was not; the difference in outlook between him and them was like a wall. Prestimion found himself yearning to share that faith of theirs, which he had never been able even for a moment to feel: and was conscious all the more of the lack, now that the great prize had been snatched from him, and no way visible in the world of reason and natural phenomena by which he could reclaim it. Spirits offered consolation at a time when worldly goals eluded one's grasp. But only if you thought that the spirits existed.

Svor appeared beside him. Prestimion pointed toward the ceremony in progress and touched a finger to his lips. Svor nodded.

The chanting came to an end and the crewmen silently dispersed.

"How real it is to them!" said Prestimion. "How seriously they take the power of those stones!"

"And with good reason," said Svor. "Believe or disbelieve as you choose, I tell you, Prestimion, there are mighty forces to be commanded, if only one knows how. *'I can displace the sky,'*" he intoned, "*'elevate the lands, melt mountains, freeze fountains. I can raise ghosts and bring the gods down to walk among us. I can extinguish the stars and illuminate the bottomless pit.'*"

"Can you, now?" Prestimion said, looking at him strangely. "I had no idea you were such a powerful sorcerer, my lord Svor."

"Ah," said Svor, "I'm merely quoting poetry. Very famous poetry, actually."

"Of course." It came immediately to his mind, now that Svor had given him the hint. "Furvain, isn't it? Yes, of course, Furvain. I should have realized."

"*The Book of Changes*, fifth canto, when the Metamorph priestess appears before Lord Stiamot."

"Yes," Prestimion said, abashed. "Of course." What child had not read that grand epic tale, thousands of years old, that related in such stirring verse the heroic battles of Majipoor's dawn? But extinguishing the stars and illuminating the bottomless pit was the stuff of fable. He had never mistaken Furvain's great poem for historical fact. "I thought you were claiming those powers for yourself," he said, laughing. "Ah,

Svor, Svor, if only someone would witch things back the way they should have been for me, with Korsibar spending his days out hunting in the wilderness and the government safely in my hand! But who can do that for me?"

"Not I," said Svor. "I would if I could."

# 4

On the ninth day of Lord Korsibar's journey northward up the Glayge from the Labyrinth a blue-white star appeared high overhead, one that no one had ever seen before, burning diamond-bright in the forehead of the sky, a great blazing gem that dazzled the eye like a second sun.

Mandrykarn was the first to spy it, half an hour after the evening meal. He was standing by himself on the foredeck of the lead vessel of the nine-ship flotilla, the *Lord Vildivar*. That was the Coronal's own Lower Glayge riverboat, the most splendid of flat-bottomed barges, which had carried the former Lord Confalume to the Labyrinth in the spring and now was carrying the new Lord Korsibar toward the Castle in midsummer. Suddenly in the mildness of the night, as he stood drinking cool gray wine while the darkness gathered and deepened, and gazing idly outward in tranquil mood over the flat monotonous valley, Mandrykarn felt a chill about his head and shoulders. He looked up, and there was the star brilliantly ablaze in a place where no star had been a moment earlier.

Letting out a whoop of surprise and dismay, he brought his hand up so hastily toward the rohilla pinned to the breast of his tunic that he spilled his wine over himself.

A new star? What could that mean, if not impending doom and calamity? For surely that star must be the sign of powerful and dangerous forces that were on the verge of breaking now through the walls of the cosmos, and shortly to descend upon the world.

Stroking the amulet briskly, Mandrykarn murmured a spell against evil that he had learned only the day before from Sanibak-Thastimoon, all the while staring at the strange new star, and experiencing such an access of uncontrollable fear and trembling that after a time he felt acrid shame at his own cowardice.

Count Farquanor materialized from somewhere to stand at his elbow. "Are you taken ill, Mandrykarn?" the serpentine little man asked, with a wicked touch of slyness in his tone. "I heard you cry out. And here you are all pale and shaken."

Mandrykarn said, fighting back that shameful tremor of his body and mastering with furious effort a quaver that had stolen into his voice, "Look above you, Farquanor. What do you see?"

"The sky. Stars. A flock of thimarnas flying homeward very late to their nests."

"You are no astronomer, Farquanor. What is that blue-white star just to the west of the polar meridian?"

"Why, Trinatha, I suppose," said Farquanor. "Or perhaps Phaseil. One or the other, at any rate."

"Trinatha is on the northern horizon, where she belongs. That's Phaseil, there in the east. You are no astronomer, Farquanor."

"And you no drinker. Look, you've spilled your wine all over your front. Boy! Boy! A towel for Count Mandrykarn!— Are you drunk, Mandrykarn?"

"That star in the west was born three minutes ago. I saw it arrive in the sky. Have you ever known such a thing to happen, a star to be born before your eyes?"

Farquanor snickered, a short derisive laugh. "You *are* drunk."

Then came excited shouts from the far side of the deck, and a wild-eyed crewman ran past, pointing skyward and hoarsely calling on everyone to look upward and behold, and other sailors came by just afterward, doing much the same. Sanibak-Thastimoon now emerged on deck also, with the Coronal's sister just a pace or two behind him. They stood together near the rail, peering into the sky, scanning this way and that.

"No, a little more to the west," Mandrykarn called to them. "There. There. Do you see?" He seized the Su-Suheris's arm and aimed it upward, and the mage's two heads followed along the line that Mandrykarn indicated.

Sanibak-Thastimoon was silent for a time, taking in the sight of that sudden star.

"What evil sign do we have here?" Mandrykarn asked him.

"Evil? Why, this is no evil," said Sanibak-Thastimoon. He made a soft sighing sound of satisfaction. "It is the coronation star," he said. "Summon Lord Korsibar."

But Korsibar had already arrived on deck. "What's all this fuss? A new star, someone said. What does that mean? How can there be a new star?"

"*You* are the new star, my lord," declared the Su-Suheris resonantly, both his heads speaking at once in unsettling half-harmony. "You come into the heavens to bring glory to the world. That is *your* starburst in the sky, which honors your advent." And with ferocious vigor he made the starburst sign himself, first at the blue-white star and then at Korsibar himself, doing it three, four, five times in succession, each time calling out, "Korsibar! Korsibar! All hail Lord Korsibar!" Which brought a like response from everyone on deck, so that the air reverberated with the sound of it, "Korsibar! Lord Korsibar!"

In the midst of this clamor Korsibar remained motionless, scarcely even breathing, his eyes riveted on the star. After a moment he took from his forehead the crown, which he had worn almost constantly from the moment of his accession, and pressed it lightly and reverently against his breast. Turning to Thismet, he said, speaking very softly, "Who could have expected this? It means I am truly king!"

"Had you doubted it, brother?"

"No. No . . . Never."

She dropped to her knees beside him, and took the hem of his tunic in her hand and kissed it. The others followed in turn: Mandrykarn first, still so shaken by what he had seen that he nearly lost his balance and toppled forward as he lowered his big body to the deck, and then Farquanor, and Venta, and Earl Kamba, and a moment afterward Farholt and Navigorn and the ship's master, Lynkamor, and five or six more who had come up on deck one by one to see what was happening and discovered a solemn ceremony taking place. Only Sanibak-Thastimoon held himself off to one side, watching the scene with a look of evident approbation, but making no move to take part in it.

When all the rest were done with their homage Korsibar said to the master, "Where are we now, Lynkamor?"

"Just north of Terabessa, my lord, and five hours' journey south of Palaghat."

"Excellent. Palaghat's a good place to make our first public appearance. The coming of that star is a sign that the time has arrived for us to present ourself to the people and be acclaimed by them. Have word sent ahead to Palaghat, then, that in the morning we will go ashore there to offer our blessing and receive the good wishes of the citizenry."

Earl Kamba of Mazadone, who was standing beside Kanteverel of Bailemoona, said quietly, "He speaks of himself now in the plural, I see."

"He is a king," Kanteverel replied. "Kings may speak that way, if they wish."

"Confalume was content to say 'I' and 'me' and 'my,' not 'we' and 'us' and 'our,' when he was Coronal."

Kanteverel cast his eyes heavenward. "Confalume was given no new stars to mark the start of his reign. And Korsibar's still tasting the first pride of kingship. Who can blame him for being full of his own importance, seeing a thing like that come into the sky?"

"So be it," Kamba said, with a chuckle. "Let him speak any way he likes, I suppose, these early days. He's in his finest moments now. The real work of the job hasn't descended on him yet: all he can see so far is the glamor and the glory, the starbursts and the genuflections. He'll find out later about things like the endless long dull reports from pompous provincial governors that he must read, and regulating the supply of grain in far-off places altogether unknown to him, and drawing up a budget for next year's highway and bridge repair, and appointing chamberlains and masters of ceremonies and tax-collectors and ministers and sub-ministers of the royal correspondence and of prisons and frontier forts and weather statistics and weights and measures and on and on through all the rest of it."

Mandrykarn, coming up alongside them but hearing nothing of Kamba's words, laughed and said, "The coronation star, it is! How bright it is, how beautiful! And to think that I took it for an evil omen. Look at me: I spilled my drink all over myself, I was so frightened at the sight of it! But what do I know of such things?" And he laughed again. "See the Coronal, now! His eyes are shining as brightly as that star."

Korsibar stood for a long while staring stiffly upward, his gaze trained on the star as though he could never have enough of the sight of it. Then he offered his arm to the Lady Thismet, and together they went below.

★

Gialaurys, too, saw the new star appear that night, some thousands of miles to the north, where the riverboat *Termagant* was making its way up the Glayge on the far side of Lake Roghoiz. He and Septach Melayn lay sprawled out at their ease on the deck, amusing themselves with a game of tavern dice. It was a calm and pleasant evening, with a soft moist wind blowing down the broad valley toward them from Castle Mount. The engines of the riverboat hummed steadily: the river ran swiftly southward here, descending steeply in its channel as the narrow vessel beat northward against it.

It was Septach Melayn's roll. He swung the cup in his usual showy manner, bringing his arm around in a wide circle and releasing the dice with a dramatic twist of his wrist. They came clattering out, one two three, arranging themselves in a line so precise that it might well have been drawn with a ruler. "The eyes, the hand, the fork," Septach Melayn announced, slapping his hand against the deck in satisfaction. "Ten once again, my mark exactly. You lose two royals, Gialaurys.— Gialaurys? What are you staring at up there?"

"Do you know that star, Septach Melayn?"

"Which? That one, the very bright one out there toward the west. What star is that, Gialaurys?"

"No star at all that I have ever seen. Do new stars suddenly pop into the sky from out of nowhere? For it is a certainty that that one did!"

Septach Melayn, frowning, scrambled to his feet. Pulling his little decorative dagger from his waistband, he held it out at arm's length against the western sky, as though measuring something.

"What are you doing?" Gialaurys asked.

"Spanning the stars, taking their calculation. Look, here's Thorius, and here's big red Xavial, and the distance is one dagger's length from one to the other, exactly as should be. But here's the new one midway between them, where no star

200

ever was of which I know. It is just as you say, Gialaurys. A star out of nowhere."

"A witch-star, is it?"

"A star that has caught on fire, I would sooner say."

"But the stars *are* fire, or so I've heard," said Gialaurys, giving Septach Melayn an uncomprehending look.

"Some fires burn dimly, though, and some very bright. The same with stars: sometimes a dim star flares up greatly of its own accord, and burns ten times as hot as it did before, or perhaps ten thousand times. As with this one, I think. It was there all along, but too faint to reach our notice, and now it has exploded into white-hot flame and probably charred every world that was close about it into ash, and we see it here like a beacon-light suddenly bursting out above us in the night. I'll talk with Svor about this: he knows of such things." And he began to call out to Svor, who was belowdecks. "Come forth, you philosopher! Look you at this mystery in the skies!"

"A witch-star, it is," said Gialaurys again, darkly. "A demon's omen."

"Portending what, do you think?" asked Septach Melayn. "Tell me what this star says to you, for I have no skill at comprehending such things myself. Oh, riddle me this riddle, sweet Gialaurys! What message is for us in that star, if a bringer of omens is what it is?"

"Are you mocking me again, Septach Melayn, as so often you do?"

"No—no," said Septach Melayn. "I mean no mockery."

"Of course you do," said Svor, stepping through the hatch. "You play with poor Gialaurys as though he's a simpleton. Which in truth he's not, though I suppose he lacks some degree of your guile—as do most people, I should say. But play with me instead, my lord Septach Melayn. I'm not so easy."

"Well, then. A new star is in the sky."

"So there is, yes. I see it plain overhead, a little to the west of Thorius. It burns bright and strong."

"And what does such a thing mean to you, Svor, you who give so much credence to wizardry? Tell me, since I have no eyes to see such things myself. Gialaurys calls it a demon's omen. What is the demon trying to tell us, do you think? Do we have harder losses ahead for us, we who have already lost so much?"

"Ah, quite the opposite," said Svor, smiling archly and tugging his fingers hard through the close-clinging curls of his beard. "I am no diviner, O splendid Septach Melayn, but even so I think I can read the skies well enough for an amateur. That star that comes upon us tonight shines out to show the anger of the spirits at the evil thing that Korsibar has done. That star is our salvation. It means the death of Korsibar and the rising of Prestimion."

"And what about it tells you that?" asked Septach Melayn.

"If you have to ask, sweet friend, you will never understand the answer."

To which Septach Melayn responded with nothing more than a grin and a shrug. But from Gialaurys came a quiet wordless sound of agreement with Svor's interpretation. He lowered his head until it touched the planks, and reached forth his hands and made signs to the star, signs of propitiation, signs of welcome.


The city of Palaghat, on the eastern bank of the Glayge, was the largest along the river between the Labyrinth and Lake Roghoiz: an agricultural center where the farmers of the three adjacent provinces brought their produce for shipment to other depots upstream and downstream. Though all this land hereabouts was flat, Palaghat itself stood on a low promontory above the river, which on account of the flatness of everything surrounding it and the dramatic green backdrop of tall leafy mengak-trees behind the city made Palaghat seem to dominate the landscape for many miles about as though it rose atop a veritable Castle Mount.

Coronals and other high officials passing this way often broke their river-journeys at Palaghat, which had better facilities for such exalted guests than any of the other cities of the Lower Glayge. The four-laned brick-paved road that ran from Palaghat's capacious and busy harbor to the center of the city was grandly planted with showy red-boled Havilbove palms along both sides, and bore the ambitious name of the Royal Highway. Today, in honor of the visit of the new Coronal, the trees were bedecked along the entire length of the road with green-and-gold banners bearing the starburst crest. Posters bearing the features of Lord Korsibar might also have been an appropriate part of the roadside display, if only there had been any available in Palaghat; but the choice of Korsibar to be Coronal had not, of course, been in any way expected or expectable, and no portraits of him were yet to be had for copying and general distribution.

Still, it was an impressive enough reception, for all the hasty improvisation of its planning: much clashing of cymbals and blowing of trumpets, and flowers and garlands strewn everywhere along the way, and an escort from port to town comprising hundreds of municipal officials, from the mayor in his velvet robes of state down to bureau chiefs and their clerks, and troupes of solemnly chanting mages in richly brocaded gowns, and thousands of common citizens along the route craning their necks for a look at their new king and lustily crying out, "Korsibar! Korsibar! Lord Korsibar!"

He had almost grown accustomed to it by now.

It had seemed unreal enough in those early days, dreamlike, the constant making of the starburst sign at him, and that yoking of the unfamiliar title "Lord" with his name instead of the "Prince" he had worn all his life, and the secret awe and reverence in the eyes of all those who glanced at him from the corners of their faces, thinking he was looking elsewhere. Each morning when he awoke he expected to find his father standing by his bedside, saying gravely, "Very well, now, Korsibar, it's time to end this little masquerade."

But each day was very much like the one before, a day of starbursts and grovelings, "my lord" this and "yes, lordship" that, and when he had encountered his father, those final days in the Labyrinth, scarcely any words passed between them whatever, those that did being of the most trivial and conventional sort: Confalume, downcast and beaten, showed no sign of desiring to overthrow the strange new state of affairs that his son had brought about in that bold swift stroke in the Court of Thrones.

Even when they said their farewells, just before Korsibar made his departure from the underground city to begin his triumphant journey northward to claim his throne, there had been only one moment when the new Pontifex betrayed any anguish over all these events—when he stared into the eyes of his son and allowed a single blazing flash of fury and mad despair to show, that he who had been the mightiest man in the world just a few weeks earlier should be so overmastered in an instant by his own child. Yet he said nothing overt to indicate repugnance for what Korsibar had done, nor made any kind of remonstration or challenge. It was done; it could not be changed; the power in the world had passed, as it never had before, from father to son.

Palaghat was far from grand, not a patch on the least splendid of the Fifty Cities of Castle Mount. But in its provincial way it was a decent pretty place, high white terraces along its riverfront side, luxuriant greenery, a sturdy city wall fashioned of pink granite blocks, with a great abundance of ornamental parapets and embrasures and crenelations and machicolations, and heraldic dragons and great-horned gabalungs delineated along its face in gold and lapis lazuli.

The mayor of the city was Ildikar Weng, a plump, perspiring, red-faced, thick-lipped man with an absurd continuous fringe of curling golden hair all about his head and cheeks and chin. He sat beside Korsibar during the floater ride uphill from the harbor to the hostelry that had been set aside for the royal party, his gaze trained unwaveringly on the Coronal in a look of utter admiration and servile regard, while at the same time he waved and nodded constantly to the people flanking the road as though their cheers were directed not to Lord Korsibar but to him.

In an unending flow of babbling chatter the mayor labored to demonstrate to Korsibar that he was a man comfortable in the company of Coronals as well as lesser lords—sprinkling his conversation with reminiscences of the visits that other grandees had made to Palaghat during his administration, with much talk along the lines of how "the magnificent Lord Confalume your father always preferred a certain wine, that I will gladly provide also for you," and that "we have always found it a time of special pleasure when the High Counsellor Duke Oljebbin is in Palaghat," and "as I said to the Grand Admiral, when he questioned me about a certain rare fish of these waters that was very much to his taste—" Ildikar Weng boasted even of a visit from the late Pontifex, for Prankipin had been given to leaving the Labyrinth occasionally, at least to travel as far as here, though not in many years.

Korsibar found his patience quickly ebbing. Was this what it meant to be Coronal, to listen to the prattle of fools such as this, wherever he might go from this day forward?

He forced himself to listen politely enough, for a time. But then the mayor went too far. "And then," he said, "two years past we enjoyed a visit from the splendid and charming Prince Prestimion, in which the prince said, as I remember it—"

"Spare us what the splendid and charming prince said, if you will," said Korsibar untenderly, with an imprecation under his breath.

Ildikar Weng turned pale at the Coronal's rough tone, and then a moment later flushed bright red. He blinked and goggled at Korsibar.

"Lordship? Have I given offense in some way?"

"If it is offensive that we are required to hear anecdotes about every petty idiot of a Castle lordling who's ever belched or puked at one of your dreary feasts, yes, you have given offense. Do you think our ear never grows weary of this kind of noise being poured into it?"

"Lordship, lordship, lordship!" the mayor cried, flinging his hands about in the air. He was so agitated that he seemed on the verge of tumbling out of the open-topped floater. "I meant no harm, lordship! A thousand pardons! A hundred thousand! I understood Prince Prestimion to be your dear friend, and so I thought you would want to hear—" Korsibar stared at him even more stonily. Ildikar Weng's eyes bulged with horror. He let his voice trickle off into silence. He seemed about to weep.

Korsibar saw that he had been too hard. But what now? Apologize? Offer soothing reassurances that no offense had been given or taken? A Coronal could hardly apologize; and, if he did, it would only guarantee a fresh torrent of this stuff in the mile or so that remained before they reached their destination.

Thismet, who was seated on the mayor's far side, rescued the moment by saying, "His lordship is very weary now, good sir mayor, and perhaps would prefer to be left in silence for a time. He was awake far into the night signing decrees and papers of appointment, and you know what heavy toil that can be, especially at the beginning of a term of office."

"I am covered in shame for my thoughtlessness."

"No need. But speak with me instead, for now. Tell me: these handsome palm trees by the side of the road, with the red trunks? Something similar, I think, grows in Lord Havilbove's garden, by Tolingar Barrier on Castle Mount."

"It is the very same tree, lady, whose seeds we were given in Lord Tharamond's time," said Ildikar Weng, and he launched into a lengthy disquisition on how and why the seeds had been obtained, and what difficulties of culture had been met with in the process of establishing them here in Paraghat. Korsibar, in great relief, sat back against his soft cushion of crimson leather and let himself slip into a dozing trance, thinking of nothing very much at all, as the shouts of "Korsibar! Lord Korsibar!" blew past him on the breeze that rose from the river.

And then they were at the guest-palace, and he was alone in his room at last. The royal suite was altogether worthy of a king: five grand rooms with glistening walls of green jasper lightly dotted with blood-red spots, and draperies of Gemmel-thrave weave, so fine that spiders might have done it, framing the great windows through which a spectacular view of the city, the port, and the river could be had.

This was his chance to slip out of his clothes for a time, and bathe and rest before the inevitable banqueting and speechifying was begun. He was wearing a white stole of steetmoy fur over a green doublet, the Coronal's usual colors; but there had been no time for proper tailoring, and the costume was ill-fitting, and too heavy for this summer day, besides. Lifting the stole from his shoulders, he set it aside on a wooden rack, thinking that he would have few enough chances to dress and undress himself once he was at the Castle with all the myriads of royal servitors attending him constantly.

As Korsibar began to undo the lacings of his doublet his eye fell upon a mirror beside the bed, and he paused to study his features in it, searching to see whether he had taken on the full commanding lineaments of royalty yet. To be a successful king, he knew, it was important as a bare minimum at least to *look* like a king. His father, though not a man of grand stature, had that look. It had often been said of Lord Confalume that a visitor from another planet could appear in a crowded reception at the court, and he would know at once which man in the throng was the Coronal, whether or not Lord Confalume had bothered to wear his crown that day.

Of course, the crown helped. Korsibar moved it slightly, straightening it, for it had become somewhat atilt during the ride from the harbor.

Thismet's voice came from behind him, suddenly: "You like the look of it, do you, brother? But you should take it off and let it rest from time to time, don't you think?"

"And you should knock before entering the Coronal's chambers, even if he is your own twin brother."

"Ah, but I did knock, twice. You were so busy admiring yourself that you didn't hear, I suppose. And when I got no answer I thought I would come in. Or shall we have shame between us now that you are king, that never existed between us before?"

Korsibar took off the crown and laid it on the bed.

"Perhaps I wear it too much," he said, with a grin. "But I'm not yet so much at home in it that I like to be without it."

"Father wore it only now and then."

"Father was Coronal for twice as many years as either of us has been alive, Thismet. Let me be king six months, at least, before I begin taking this crown for granted."

"As you wish, my lord," Thismet said, with a gesture of exaggerated submissiveness. She came to his side, looking up at him far above her with excited glowing eyes and taking hold of him by both his wrists, and said, "Oh, Korsibar, Korsibar, do you believe it, yet?"

"Only some of the time."

"The same for me. Lord Korsibar! Coronal Lord of Majipoor! How easy it all was! Oh, we will put our mark on this world, won't we, you and I! We will do such marvelous things, Korsibar, now that all this has been given into our hands!"

"So we will, sister."

"But you must take care not to be so haughty, brother."

"Haughty, am I?"

"You were very cruel to that fat red-faced mayor."

"He chewed too long on my ear, with his tales of playing host to father, and Prankipin, and Oljebbin, and this one and that one, and finally Prestimion—ah, that was too much, mentioning Prestimion!"

"He thought you loved Prestimion."

"Certainly I hold no hatred for him, and never have. But to throw his name at me just then—what slyness was meant there, what hidden implication?"

"None, I think."

"When it was known everywhere that Prestimion was to have been the next Coronal?"

"No," Thismet said. She lifted her hand and ticked off points on her fingers. "One, what is known everywhere at the Castle is not necessarily general knowledge in the valley of the Lower Glayge. Two, there's no reason in the universe for the mayor to be sly and mocking with you about Prestimion. He has everything to lose and nothing to gain from such mockery. Three, the mayor's much too stupid to have any hidden motives at all. And four—pay attention to me, brother!—four, kings must be tolerant of having their ears chewed by fools, because every fool in the kingdom will try to do it, and some will of necessity succeed. Your father didn't win the love of the world's people by snarling and snapping at them. No great Coronal ever has. I want you to be a great Coronal, Korsibar."

"And so I will be."

"Well, then," she said. "Suffer fools more gladly. The Divine made millions and millions of them, and gave you to them to be their king."

She made the starburst at him again, more sincerely than before, and kissed the tips of her fingers to him and went from the room. He enjoyed two hours' respite before his duties came seeking him again. Hardly had he bathed and dressed but Oljebbin came to see him, with some papers that must be signed and dispatched to the Castle, which he did without reading them, for Oljebbin said they were only matters of routine. And then it was Farholt, who had brought plans with him for the seating arrangements at that evening's municipal banquet in Korsibar's honor; and after him Farquanor, who lingered for a time once more irritatingly angling for the High Counsellorship by indirection and innuendo, so that Korsibar wanted to cry out to him in fury to be gone. Then came Dantirya Sambail, who had heard a crude foul joke about Prestimion and Septach Melayn and felt the need of sharing it with the Coronal that very minute.

In the afternoon Korsibar held court in the garden of the guest-palace—doing without his crown, this time, just to see what it was like to leave it off, whether he would still feel fully royal without it—and received homage from a delegation of landowners and great farmers from the surrounding countryside. Then he had a little while to enjoy a quiet drink in his rooms with Mandrykarn and Venta and a few other intimate friends, and after that it was time for the banquet, and too much heavy wine and too much rich food, piles of stewed vegetables and great slabs of some pale meat marinated in spicy wine and sweetened thereafter by jujuga-fruit, and then an elaborately diplomatic speech by the very much chastened Mayor Ildikar Weng that mentioned Prankipin and Confalume and other previous distinguished visitors to Paraghat not at all, and dwelled with inordinate optimism on the grand achievements that the Coronal Lord Korsibar would accomplish.

To which Korsibar responded courteously enough, though briefly. He left the main task of speaking to Gonivaul and Oljebbin and Farquanor, all of whom spoke in artfully empty words of the great things that the new regime proposed to bring about and the wonderful benefits that would surely accrue for the citizens of the district of the Lower Glayge Valley.

No speaker failed to mention the new star that had come into the sky the night before. "Lord Korsibar's star," they called it. All hailed it as a sign of the greatness of the hour, the bright promise of the wondrous new era now commencing. Afterward, when they gathered for a time under the night sky before retiring to their rooms, Korsibar looked toward it again and again, fixing his eyes on its brightness and thinking, *Lord Korsibar's star. Lord Korsibar's star.* And was flooded once more with a sense of the grandness of the destiny that had swept him to this high place, and would carry him onward through all his life as Coronal, past whatever obstacle he might be called upon to face.


During the night Korsibar had a sending of the Lady, the first such that he had had in many years.

It was rare for the Lady to direct her attention to princes of the Mount. Her chief responsibility was to the ordinary citizens, who looked to her sendings for comfort and guidance. But she came to him now. The moment he closed his eyes Korsibar felt himself drawn downward into a vortex of swirling blue with an eye of gold at its farther end; he knew that resistance was futile, and he let himself drift freely, passing through that golden eye into a place of mist and shadow.

The Lady Kunigarda was in that place, which was the octagonal chamber with walls of white stone that lay at the center of her dwelling at Inner Temple, atop the highest terrace of the Isle of Sleep. She was strolling by the eight-sided pool in the middle of that chamber: a woman of advanced years, strikingly like her brother Confalume in appearance, strong-featured, with gray eyes set far apart and broad cheekbones and a wide, commanding mouth.

He knew her at once. His father's elder sister, she was, who had been elevated to the rank of Lady of the Isle when Korsibar and Thismet were still small children, and whose reign as a Power of Majipoor must now end with the coming of the new regime. He had met her only three times in his life. She was a person of formidable strength and determination, every bit as regal as her royal brother Confalume.

She stared at him now through veils of dream with some severity in her gaze and said, "You sleep in the bed of a king, Korsibar. Tell me, how is that?"

"I *am* a king, Lady," he replied, using the voice of dreams that he had been taught to use in childhood. "Did you see my star? It's a king's star. Lord Korsibar's star."

"Yes," she said. "Lord Korsibar's star. I have seen it too, Korsibar." And began to speak of its coming, and of him, and his sister also, and of his father the newly made Pontifex, and of the comings and goings of Coronals and Pontifexes across thousands of years, and of many other things. But there were such twists and turns in the pattern of her long discourse that Korsibar could barely grasp the logic of her words with his sleeping mind, and then was unable to follow it at all. She seemed to be speaking always of two or three contradictory things at once, so that every sentence had its own antithesis and cancellation buried somewhere within it and would not

212

let him discern any thread running consistently from front to back.

Then she stopped, and gave him a long cool steady look and was gone, leaving him staring into an empty room; and moments later he awoke, confused and troubled. It seemed to Korsibar that the stern old woman's presence was still resonating in his soul, like the afterclamor of a great bell once the bell itself has ceased tolling. He struggled to wring some sense from the dream, attempting to retrace in his mind the tortuous path that her words had taken.

She had acknowledged him as legitimate Coronal, he was sure of that; for she had referred to him several times as *Lord* Korsibar, had she not, and to Confalume as Pontifex? On the other hand she had made reference once to his father as a "prisoner." The prisoner of the Labyrinth, as the Pontifex was sometimes said to be, or the prisoner of recent events? The meaning was ambiguous. There were other ambiguities, too, blurry and indeterminate fragments of augury, possibly implying coming hardships and reverses. But hardships and reverses for whom? Was she talking about Prestimion, who had already experienced them, or about him, or about someone else entirely?

The dream left Korsibar frightened and uneasy. Though he could not say why, because he had understood so little of it, it seemed to open mysterious abysses of dark possibility for him, harbingers of a transformation of his fortunes for the worse; here at the summit of Majipoor the only direction he could go now was downward, and as he reflected on the dream it seemed to him that it was warning him of troublesome shoals ahead. But was that so, or was he merely giving way to a sudden spate of doubt to balance his supreme success? He did not know. It was so long since he had paid attention to a dream of any sort, or had consulted a dream-speaker to help him understand one, that he had forgotten whatever he might once have known of the technique of interpreting them.

He toyed with the idea of calling in Sanibak-Thastimoon and asking for a speaking of the dream. But he realized that the details of it were fleeing so rapidly from his mind that there would soon be nothing for the Su-Suheris to work with. And gradually the discomfort went from him.

The dream is a good omen, he told himself firmly, upon some further reflection when morning came.

It means that the Lady Kunigarda recognizes my ascendancy, and will lend me her hand in these the early days of my reign.

Yes. Yes. A good omen, definitely a good omen.

Yes. Yes!

"Did you sleep well, brother?" Thismet asked him, at breakfast.

"I had a sending of the Lady," he said. She looked at him in sudden alarm; and, farther down the long table, the heavy domed head of the Procurator Dantirya Sambail turned his way also, with an expression of deep interest. Korsibar smiled. "All is well," he said calmly. "The Lady gave me assurances of her love and full support. We will flourish and prevail: there is no doubt of that, none whatever."

# 5

Midsummer eve, a magical night, the sun high in the sky far into the evening watch, the Great Moon and two of the smaller ones shining brightly as well, and in the loftiest vault of the heavens the three immense red stars that formed the buckle of the constellation known as Cantimpreil plainly visible despite the competing radiance of sun and moons. The new star was there, too, the fierce white one burning blue through all the competing illumination, the star that Svor had prophesied was the star of good omen for Prestimion's cause.

Prestimion, though, alone on the *Termagant*'s deck at this late hour, pacing back and forth, his eyes brilliantly alert, all his senses tuned and receptive, felt little joy at the beauty of the night, its mingled lights and its host of conflicting shadows. Joy was a quality that seemed to have gone from him. His great anger over the events in the Court of Thrones had subsided into a calm steady sense of ongoing disappointment, a sort of perpetual inner chill replacing the earlier hot rage; but the price of that stark self-control was, it seemed, a general loss of emotion, an absence of the ability to respond to pleasure as well as to pain.

He watched the sun go down at last. The Great Moon moved across the sky until it disappeared beyond the eastern hills, and the stars took possession of the sky, the lesser ones now as well as the mighty red trio of Cantimpreil. That strange new blue-white one drilled unyieldingly down out of the center of the heavens like a blazing spike. For a time he dozed in a deck chair; and then, seemingly only moments after sundown, it was morning again and the coppery-pink light of dawn was moving toward him across the valley of the Upper Glayge.

The river was very wide here. Off to Prestimion's left, where darkness still held sway, a nest of deeply eroded canyons rose one upon another beyond the water's edge in muddled mists, with bright streams of vapor beginning to boil off their rims like unfurling banners as the sunrise reached them. In the other direction lay the great riverfront city of Pendiwane, its multitude of conical red-tiled roofs ablaze in the glory of the onrushing morning. Not far beyond, a little way on to the north, lay something dark along the river's western side that he knew must be the shoreline of Makroposopos, the center of the textile arts. Tapestries and draperies and weavings of many other sorts emanated from there that were eagerly sought after throughout the world.

Captain Dimithair Vort was managing a good pace for them up the river. Castle Mount itself would be in view before much longer; and, soon enough, they would be commencing the ascent of its incomprehensible bulk, making their way to the royal dwelling at its summit, where—where—Svor appeared suddenly beside him, rising up as if out of nowhere. "You are up and about very early this morning, Prestimion," Svor said.

"I seem to have spent the night on deck."

"Did kindly spirits visit you here?"

Without even trying to feign amusement Prestimion said, "I saw only stars and moons, Svor, and also sunlight to an extraordinary hour. No spirits whatever, none."

"Ah, but they saw you."

"Perhaps they did," said Prestimion, in a flat cool tone meant to indicate an utter lack of interest.

"And afterward they came to me as I slept. May I tell you my dream, Prestimion?"

Prestimion sighed. "If it pleases you to do so, Svor."

Svor said, "It was as a manculain that the spirit came to me, the fat little red-spined sort of manculain that we have in Suvrael, with a thousand sharp daggers jutting from its back and two big yellow eyes looking out almost sadly amidst that mass of dangerous needles. I was crossing a great sparse lonely plain, and it came scurrying up beside me, all bristling and threatening. But I could see that it meant no real harm, that that was simply the way it looked; and it said to me in the most friendly way, *'You seek something, Svor. What is it that you seek?'* I told the manculain what I sought was a crown, not for myself but the crown that you had lost in the Labyrinth, which I would find for you again. To which it replied—are you listening to me, Prestimion?"

"Certainly. You have my most complete attention."

Svor let that pass. "It said to me, *'If you would find it, inquire after it in the city of Triggoin.'*"

"Triggoin."

"You know of Triggoin, Prestimion?"

He nodded somberly. "The wizards' own city, so I've heard, where the mages flock and swarm together in perpetual coven, and all manner of witchcrafts hold sway, and spirit-fires burn blue in the air by day and by night. Somewhere deep in the far north, beyond the desert, it is: by Sintalmond or Michimang, as I understand it. It's not a place I've ever thought of visiting."

"It is a place of many fascinations and wonders."

"Ah, you've been there, Svor?"

"In dreams, only. Three times now my sleeping mind has been to Triggoin."

"Perhaps tonight once you've closed those beady eyes of yours you'll be kind enough to undertake a fourth journey to it, then. And ask questions there on my behalf in regard to my lost crown, as the kindly manculain told you to do. Eh, Svor?" Prestimion laughed, but his eyes were empty of all jollity. "And what you'll learn from the good sorcerers of Triggoin, I very much suspect, is that the crown we seek is just a few thousand miles behind us on the Glayge, and we need only send word nicely and courteously to Lord Korsibar and he'll ship it ahead to us."

Gialaurys emerged then on deck and said, with a look of keen attention, "What's this about Triggoin?"

"The good Duke Svor has discovered in his slumbers that we must make inquiries there concerning ways of recovering the crown, and they will inform us as to how we may find it," Prestimion explained. "But of course, Svor, we haven't actually *lost* the crown, because we never *had* the crown, and what was never ours can hardly be said to be capable of recovery. This carelessness in the use of words can be dangerous to a sorcerer, I'm told. Misplace a single trifling word in one of your spells, or even a syllable, and you may find one of your own demons rending you limb from limb, in the erroneous belief that you instructed him to do so."

Gialaurys said, unceremoniously brushing aside Prestimion's heavy attempt at drollery with a brusque swipe of his hand, "I would listen to Svor. If he's had a dream telling us that we can get help in Triggoin, we should go to Triggoin."

"And if the dream had told us to make inquiries of the Metamorphs in Ilirivoyne, or to seek the aid of the wild men in the snowy mountains of the Khyntor Marches, would you be just as eager to go to one of those places?" Prestimion asked, once more with a mocking edge to his voice.

"The dream said Triggoin," Gialaurys said doggedly. "I

would surely go to Triggoin, if we don't find the support we hope for at the Castle."

He clung to that idea, endlessly expounding and elaborating on it, as the *Termagant* made its swift way past Pendiwane and began its approach to Makroposopos, where Dimithair Vort proposed to stop briefly for provisions. Svor's dream of Triggoin had inflamed Gialaurys with enthusiasm and hope. His eyes took on a brightness and fervor that they had not shown in weeks, at the mere thought of that place in the far north.

The wizards of Triggoin would put the troubled world to rights, Gialaurys insisted. His faith in them, he said, was boundless. The mastery of all secrets of power was to be had at Triggoin. He had long intended, in fact, some day to make a pilgrimage to that place, purely for the good of his spirit, and to give himself over there to one high magus or another as a humble body-servant, so that he might learn something of the arts himself as fee for his employ. Surely Prestimion would not reject the help of Triggoin out of hand, if all else failed: surely not! Surely! The force of all those potent sorcerers joined in a single endeavor would provide Prestimion with the strength he needed to restore the commonwealth to its proper condition. He believed that with all his soul, did Gialaurys. And so on and on in that vein until the riverboat was almost into Makroposopos harbor.

But then came an ugly surprise. For the weavers of Makroposopos had been busy of late, it seemed; and all along the waterfront hung billowing flags bearing portraits that were recognizably portraits of Korsibar, with banners beside them in the royal colors, green and gold. Plainly the arrival of the new Coronal was imminent in Makroposopos, and they were hurriedly making ready to greet him in fitting style.

Prestimion said to Dimithair Vort, "Can we call at some other city farther upstream for the things you need?"

"At Apocrune, yes, or Stangard Falls. We can wait even until Nimivan, maybe. Though the others would be better."

"Let it be Apocrune or Stangard Falls, then," Prestimion instructed the captain. "Or Nimivan, or one of those places, whatever you say." And they sailed onward without stopping at Makroposopos.

The sight of those innumerable portraits of Korsibar fluttering along the piers of Makroposopos aroused Gialaurys' temper even more. All fantasies of Triggoin's wizardly aid went from his mind; what he advocated now was that they go on to the Castle as swiftly as they could, and simply and straightforwardly lay claim to it as the rightful seat of the Coronal Lord Prestimion, striking with the same preemptive boldness as Korsibar had shown that day in the Labyrinth.

"We will fashion a crown for you somehow," he told Prestimion, "and you'll walk right through the Dizimaule Arch wearing it on your head, with us beside you, armed to the teeth and making starbursts at every step of the way."

"A crown," said Prestimion. "Starbursts."

"Yes. A crown! And when they come out from within to see who is arriving, you'll proclaim yourself before them all as Lord Prestimion the authentic Coronal, as was intended all the while by Lord Confalume, and make them kneel down before you, which they will do when they see the true kingliness of you. In that moment it will become clear to them that Korsibar's actions have no force of law and he is a false king. And you will seat yourself on the throne and accept the homage of the Castle and there will be an end to all this foolishness."

"So easily achieved," said Svor softly. "Bravo, Gialaurys!"

"Yes, bravo!" cried Septach Melayn in an altogether different tone. His eyes flashed as though with lightning. It was plain that he too was for the moment swept up in the rude audacity of the scheme. His rage at the usurpation had from the first moment of it been nearly as strong as that of Gialaurys.

The plan could not fail, said Septach Melayn. The Castle officials were mere spineless cowards and idlers, he said, who had no more courage among them than a herd of blaves and less stiffness to their bones than a swamp-dwelling gromwark. It made no difference to them who was Coronal, Lord Korsibar or Lord Prestimion; they required only someone to tell them what to do, and whichever man got there first would fill that need for them. While Korsibar dallied along the Glayge, enjoying the pleasures of royal feasts as the guest of the people of Pendiwane or Makroposopos or Apocrune, Prestimion could snatch the Castle and the throne as easily as plucking thokka-berries from a vine.

This hearty show of support kindled fresh excitement in Gialaurys. For some minutes the two of them spoke back and forth between themselves in rising fervor, until they had made it seem for each other that it would be the easiest thing in the world to turn Prestimion into an anointed Coronal merely by an appeal to justice and reason.

Then finally, when after long minutes of harangue they had begun to lose some of their heat and momentum, Svor turned to them and said, his eyes glittering with devastating scorn, "This is the maddest nonsense and folly, my lords. Have you both taken leave of your senses? If the throne could be had by any prince who walked in and demanded it, we'd have a new Coronal every time the old one departed from the Castle for as much as a day."

They stared at him, startled at the force of his mocking tone, making no response.

"Consider also," Prestimion added, "that the Pontifex Confalume has not openly condemned his son's seizure of the throne, and never will. 'The thing is done,' is what the Pontifex told me when we were in the Labyrinth. 'Korsibar holds the power now.' And so he does."

"Illegally," Septach Melayn said.

"And what legal claim do I have, pray tell? Was I ever publicly named as Coronal-designate? Korsibar, at least, has the Pontifex's blessing. In the eyes of the people I would be the one who'd be regarded as the usurper, not Korsibar, if I somehow managed to take possession of the Castle. *If.*"

Septach Melayn and Gialaurys looked blankly at each other, and once more said nothing; and after a time Septach Melayn reluctantly acknowledged with a little shrug the wisdom of what Prestimion had said.

To them both Svor said sharply, "Attend me here. We have a strategy in place already, which is to go to the Castle as loyal subjects of the Coronal Lord Korsibar, and pretend to bow the knee to him, and all the while slowly and quietly attempt to build support for his overthrow and replacement by Prince Prestimion. That will take time: years, perhaps, until Korsibar's inadequacies are fully demonstrated. But I pray you, let us follow our plan, for it's the best that we have; and let there be no more hotheaded talk of simply announcing Prestimion to be the king and expecting the Castle folk to lie down and yield."

More Korsibar banners were on show at Apocrune, and at Prestimion's orders they sailed on past; but Dimithair Vort pointed out that it was necessary now for her to reprovision the riverboat somewhere, and the best thing was to make landfall at the town of Stangard Falls. Prestimion gave his assent. But he was pleased to note that no Korsibar-faces greeted them there as the *Termagant* dropped its anchor at the pier.

There were two wondrous things to be seen at Stangard

Falls. One of them was the Falls itself: for here there was a tremendous rift in the surface of the world, with the land falling away sharply toward the west. Whatever colossal geological event had shattered the terrain at Stangard had also thrust a giant mile-long boulder upward in the midst of the river's course: a single smooth slab of pink granite that had the shape of a fat loaf of bread resting on its side, which divided the Glayge here into two flows. One, east of that titanic monolith, was the river proper, sweeping smoothly and grandly on southward beyond the town in its majestic progress toward the distant sea. The other, the western branch, was a much lesser but still powerful stream that went plunging off swiftly at a sharp angle to the river's main bed. The course followed by that secondary stream carried it over the edge of the rift, thus creating a cascade that had an unbroken milky drop of seven thousand feet, uncountable millions of tons of water per second hurtling down that great declivity into a basin far below.

The roaring of the waters at Stangard Falls, the sound of that great plunge and the terrible crashing impact it made when it struck the stony bed below, could be heard far up and down the river, hundreds of miles away; and at close range, anywhere within a mile or so of the point where that western fork of the Glayge went over the edge, that sound was intolerable. Observation platforms were mounted to either side of that place where that river began its mad descent, so that visitors could stand there and look downward as the foaming waters fell on and on and onward still to be lost in the spuming rainbow-flecked turbulence at the bottom. But they had to cover their ears with thick padding as they watched, or they would be irreparably deafened by the noise of it all.

Prestimion and his companions had no special interest in experiencing the majesty of Stangard Falls just then. It was the other noteworthy sight of Stangard Falls that drew them now: for here, on the side of the river away from the Falls themselves, travelers were granted the first awesome view of Castle Mount rising in the north-east.

You needed only to take an eastward turn on the river just opposite the shining pink monolith that created the Falls, and there it was, standing unanswerably before you, dominating beyond all measure the great sloping plateau from which it rose. Up and up and up went the land as you looked to the north, and then came that sudden heartstopping leap to supreme height, imparting a mysterious visionary grandeur to the scene. At Stangard Falls the glittering gray-white mass of stone that was Castle Mount seemed to float in the air as though it belonged to some other world, a world that was lowering itself by gradual stages into the sky of Majipoor.

It was by far the greatest mountain of Majipoor, and, perhaps, the largest of any world in all the universe. Farther upriver, the Mount had the look of a vast wall hanging over-head and blotting out the heavens like a vertical continent. But in this part of the Glayge Valley the traveler was still separated from it by a thousand miles, or more. From here one might to some degree comprehend it as an actual moun-tain that tapered upward from a broad base to the narrow summit, with a band of cloud about its middle. And even, almost, to persuade oneself that one could make out glinting hints of some of the fifty mighty cities that clung to its flanks, and the sprawling Castle atop its highest peak, thirty miles up.

"At last!" Gialaurys cried. "Can there be anything else so splendid anywhere? I feel such a chill of wonder whenever I look upon it that I could weep." And he struck Svor, who was standing beside him, a great wallop between the shoulder-blades that nearly flung him flying through the air. "Eh, my brave Svor? What do you say? Is that not the grandest sight in the universe! Lift up your eyes to it, Svor! Lift up your eyes!"

"It is a very fine sight indeed, extremely splendid," said Svor, coughing, and hitching up first one shoulder and then the other as if putting them back into their proper alignment. "It is truly a magnificent sight, my friend, and I admire it most considerably, even though you have perhaps loosened my teeth somewhat in your enthusiasm."

Prestimion's eyes were glistening as he looked toward that monarch of mountains. He said nothing, only stared, as minutes passed. Septach Melayn, coming up behind him, lowered his head to the shorter man's ear and said quietly, "Behold your Castle, my lord."

Prestimion nodded. Still he said nothing.


Their stay in the town of Stangard Falls was brief, as brief as they were able to make it. Nilgir Sumanand, who went ashore with the captain, reported that portraits of Lord Korsibar were on display here too. They were not as common as at Makroposopos, but they were indication enough that the people had been apprised of the change of reign and had accepted it with good enough grace.

They went onward. City after city thronged this fertile valley: Nimivan and Threiz, Hydasp and Davanampiya and Mitripond and Storp. The shores of the Glayge were home to millions of people. But now the valley began to shade into the foothills of the Mount. The land was rising perceptibly here as the broad plateau that bore Castle Mount commenced its steep upward tilt toward the colossal upthrust limb that was the mountain itself. When they looked northward at the river it appeared now to be descending toward them out of the sky, and at times the *Termagant* seemed to be sailing straight upward, valiantly climbing a wall of water.

Tributaries could be seen coming into the Glayge now on both sides, subsidiary rivers and riverlets running down from the higher reaches of the Mount. As they proceeded past each of these confluences the Glayge itself dwindled, becoming a much narrower stream, for the river on which they now traveled was in essence only one of the many that flowed together to constitute the main body of the Glayge behind them. The river towns—Jerrik, Ganbole, Sattinor, Vrove—were different here too, mere fishing villages, mostly, instead of great thriving cities, all but hidden in the dense blackish-green foliage of foothill forests that came right down to the river's edge.

At Amblemorn the part of the journey that they could make by riverboat ended. The Glayge no longer existed as a coherent river beyond this point: this was its source, where it was born out of a tangled swarm of small shallow rivulets coming down from many regions of the Mount. They bade farewell to Dimithair Vort and her crew, and set about hiring floater-cars to take them the rest of the way to the Castle.

Arranging that took several days. There was no choice for them but to cool their heels in Amblemorn, a huge ancient city where the narrow winding streets wove one upon another in dense intricate snarls and the cobbled walls were thickly overgrown with woody-trunked vines.

Of the Fifty Cities that bespeckled the breast of the Mount, Amblemorn was the oldest. Pioneering settlers had begun the conquest of the Mount here some twelve thousand years before, clambering up the naked rocks and putting into place the machines that brought warmth and light and a breathable atmosphere to these formerly bleak heights. Bit by bit they had extended their upward sway until eventually the whole gigantic Mount lay wrapped in an eternal balmy springtime, even the uppermost realm that jutted into the darkness of space. There was in the center of Amblemorn a monument of jet-black Velathyntu marble, set in a garden of smooth-trunked halatinga trees perpetually crowned with a glory of crimson-and-gold flowers, that bore lettering on it announcing that this was the place where the old timber-line had been:

### ABOVE HERE ALL WAS BARREN ONCE

Green-and-gold banners of the new Coronal were flying everywhere in Amblemorn. Someone had attached one, even, to the pedestal of the monument.

Prestimion attempted to ignore it. He focused his attention on that tall and glossy marble shaft and let his mind wander back across the thirteen thousand years of Majipoor, back to the founding of the world, the coming of the first settlers, the planting of the early cities; and then this conquest of the Mount, the extension of the human sphere into the once-uninhabitable high reaches, raw and stony and airless, of this unthinkably huge mountain. What an achievement that had been! And then to live in peace and harmony all these thousands of years on this giant planet, this warm and beautiful world, building city after city of such size and splendor and magnificence, finding room for fifteen billion souls without despoiling the marvelous richness of the land—

There were others at the monument too, citizens of Amblemorn. He saw someone looking at him and imagined that person thinking, *That was Prestimion who was to have been Coronal, but now is no one.* And his blood ran hot in him for a moment, and his head was all aswirl with the fury of intolerable loss.

But then his iron control reasserted itself. No, Prestimion told himself: no, they have no idea here who I am, and if they do, what of it? It is no shame not to be Coronal. And a time will come when the world is right-side up again, perhaps, and all will be well: or else I will die attempting it, and none of this will matter any longer to me.

The travelers lost no time getting on the road once the floaters were assembled and ready.

From Amblemorn there were various routes upward. The Fifty Cities were arrayed around the sides of the Mount in levels, forming four big rings, with great expanses of open space separating one ring from the next. Amblemorn was one of the twelve Slope Cities, as those of the bottommost ring were known. From it rose two main highways of approximately equal directness, one passing through its neighboring city to the west, Dundilmir, and the other going eastward past Normork and Morvole. They chose the Dundilmir road, which was less heavily traveled and took them around the gloriously strange zone of red lava flows and smoking fumaroles and spuming geysers known as the Fiery Valley to a place where they could gain access to a good road leading further upward.

The angle of ascent beyond the Fiery Valley was a relatively gentle one, and it was a journey of a hundred miles along the flank of the Mount to the level of the nine Free Cities, the next urban ring. This road led them a quarter-turn around the haunch of the mountain even farther toward the west, where the chief cities were Castlethorn, Gimkandale, and Vugel.

Septach Melayn argued for the Castlethorn road, but Svor pointed out that that one was a slow one because it wound back and forth upon itself so many times; and so Prestimion and his companions went up and around it, traveling by way of the next city to the west. That was Gimkandale, famous for its floating terraces that looked out toward the gray desert lands of middle Alhanroel. The travelers were some ninety degrees around Castle Mount from their starting point at the source of the Glayge, there. Again a choice of routes confronted them; and after some debate they took the steep path along the starkly serrated palisade of Stiamot Battlements, where the wild saber-fanged hryssa-wolves bayed night and day from the porches of their inaccessible caves, and thence through the forest of glassy-leaved trees that grew beside Siminave Highway, leading to Strave, Greel, and Minimool, which were the closest of the eleven Guardian Cities.

There were further indications all along the way that the rise to power of Lord Korsibar was not unknown in these higher levels, and apparently had met with no opposition. Prestimion paid little notice. But Gialaurys, seeing the banners of Korsibar fluttering here and there, would mutter now and again and clench his fists and look upslope, eyes red with rage.

He raised no new discussion, however, of his optimistic if implausible plan to take the throne for Prestimion by the mere declaration of his kingship as an accomplished fact. Prestimion had made it clear that he wanted such talk to cease. Plainly the scheme continued to simmer within Gialaurys, though, and even in Septach Melayn.

They were nearly halfway up the Mount now. A dozen miles of vertical ascent and many hundreds of miles of lateral travel remained before they would come into the true high country, which was hidden from them down here by the mantle of white clouds that perpetually screened the midriff of the mountain. But already they were far above the lowlands of the continent. The air at this height was crisp and electric, with a quality of light that could not be duplicated at lower altitudes. In every direction the towers and battlements of the great Mount cities could be seen, clinging boldly to enormous ledges and scarps and outcroppings on the face of the mountain; and everything was outlined in a brilliant tracery of radiant color.

Their road took them between Strave, where architects

were looked upon as demigods and no building was in any manner like any other, and Greel, its very opposite of a place, limited by strict construction codes to five shapes for houses and no more. A straight ribbon of a highway, bright as glass in the midday sun, led onward from there, ever higher, into the level of the nine Inner Cities.

The choice of route now was beginning to become limited for them: the mountain was narrowing rapidly, here in the cloud-covered upper fringes of the midzone country. Any of the nine High Cities could be reached from any point below, but above the High Cities the landscape became so jagged that traversing it could be managed only in the most favorable places, and just a handful of roads continued beyond their level to that of the Castle itself. Of those, by far the best was the one that went via Bombifale to High Morpin, where the Castle road began. So they made their way on a long diagonal across the face of the Mount to the great tableland known as Bombifale Plain, below lovely Bombifale itself, the city of the Grand Admiral Gonivaul. A multitude of Korsibar banners oppressed them at every town along the road, all the way from Greel.

The evening was already too far gone into moonless night when they came to Bombifale for them to feel the full beauty of the place, which was the work of Lord Pinitor of distant antiquity, the only Coronal in all of Majipoor's history who had come from Bombifale. Pinitor had never ceased to expand and glorify his native city. Long plodding trains of pack animals had hauled untold tons of orange sandstone up the Mount from the desert back of Velalisier to build the scalloped city walls that thrust far out over the plain; and an even greater effort had gone into the mining and transportation of the imposing diamond-shaped slabs of blue seaspar that were inlaid in those walls, for seaspar was found only along the shores of the Great Sea on Alhanroel's remote and inhospitable eastern coast. It was by the order of the Coronal Lord Pinitor, too, that scores of enormously tall slender towers sharp as needles had been erected atop the city battlements for many miles, giving Bombifale a profile unlike that of any other city in the world.

But little of that was apparent to the tired travelers now. It was late and dark. The one conspicuous thing was the new star, shining high above them, burning fiercely against the blackness. "See, it follows us everywhere!" cried Svor jovially. That was the star which to Svor was a star of good omen. But Prestimion, looking up wearily at that hard insistent glare now, was much less certain of that. It had been too strange in the manner of its coming, and was too potent in its savage brightness.

They found rooms for themselves and all their party at a small drab inn near the city's outer edge. Once they were settled they ordered up a meal from the surly, reluctant landlord, who agreed to serve them at this hour only when he realized that among this group of late-coming guests was no less a grandee than the Prince of Muldemar.

A couple of sullen Hjort girls waited on them, along with a limping, one-eyed, black-bearded man whose scars and scowls gave indication that he had come out very much on the short side of some bloody brawl years ago. As he set Prestimion's flask of wine and bowl of stewed meat down before him, he bent low and peered full in Prestimion's face, staring intently at him with that lone bloodshot eye as though Prestimion were a being of a kind that never had been seen on Majipoor before.

For an intolerably long moment he held that stare, and Prestimion looked levelly back. Then the man's fingers shot out quickly in a hasty and rudimentary version of the starburst sign, and he grinned a broad ugly grin, showing yellow snaggled teeth, and went shuffling away toward the kitchen.

Gialaurys, who had seen it, rose halfway from his seat. "I'll kill him, my lord! I'll rip his head from his shoulders!"

Prestimion restrained him by the wrist. "Peace, Gialaurys. No pulling off of heads, and no calling me 'my lord.'"

"But he mocked you!"

"Perhaps not. Perhaps he is my secret adherent."

Gialaurys laughed a harsh bitter laugh. "Your secret adherent, yes. No doubt he is, and a fine figure of a man, too. Take down his name, then, and make him your High Counsellor when you are king."

"Peace," Prestimion said. "Peace, Gialaurys."

But he was wounded and angry too; for there could have been no intention in the one-eyed man's mind other than to mock. Had he fallen so far, that servants in a shabby inn felt free to make sport of him? Prestimion kept his feelings to himself; but he was glad to leave that place in the morning, and glad also that he had no cause to see that one-eyed man again before he left, for he knew that he might not be so forbearing at a second offense.

It was only a long day's journey up from Bombifale to the lowest reaches of the Castle. Gialaurys, sizzling still over the insult in the tavern, held forth much of the way once more on his notion that Prestimion must assert his right to the throne immediately and forcefully. Prestimion would not hear of it. "You can leave the floater and walk the rest of the way to the summit," he said, "if you can find no other topic for discussion than this." Gialaurys ungracefully subsided, though he began again an hour later, and had to be silenced once more.

This was familiar territory now: they had traversed it dozens, even hundreds, of times, often coming down from the Castle on this steep mountain road made of bright red flagstones to enjoy the many delights of the rich and luxury-loving cities in the heavily populated belt just below it. High

Morpin was the chief pleasure-city of the Mount, where lords young and old amused themselves on the mirror-slides and the juggernauts and in the fantastic caverns of the power-tunnels, and sat afterward under canopies of spun gold to sip sweet wines and nibble cold sherbets.

But there would be no rides on the juggernauts today, and no wines and sherbets. They bypassed High Morpin entirely and hastened onward along the ten-mile stretch of road called the Grand Calintane Highway, which ran through fields of ever-blooming flowers to the borders of the Castle domain.

The summit of the Mount was in sight, now.

This was the furthermost realm of Majipoor, which once had stood far out into the eternal frigid night of space, before the construction of the weather-machines. But the weaving of a soft mild atmosphere around this ultimate peak of the Mount had done nothing to gentle its fierce sharp topography: the craggy summit was made up of an intricate array of slender, dagger-tipped sub-peaks of hardest basalt, stabbing upward at the sky like a myriad of black stalagmites. In the center of all these stony spikes, rising up high above them, was one final great upwelling of granite, a huge rounded hump at the very tip of the mountain that formed the foundation for the Coronal's royal residence.

The Castle! The immense unchartable bewildering Castle of uncountable thousands of rooms, virtually a city in itself, that covered so many hundreds of acres! It clung to the mountaintop like a great sprawling chaotic monster of brick and masonry, sending random tentacles roaming in every direction down the slope.

The Grand Calintane Highway came to the Castle at its southern wing, terminating in the great open space known as the Dizimaule Plaza. The pavement here was of smooth green porcelain cobblestones, and a huge starburst in golden tilework lay at its center. On its far side was the mighty Dizimaule

Arch, through which all visitors to the Castle must pass when entering.

There was a guardpost here, just to the left of the arch, and a tall gate with elaborate iron grillwork mounted with giant hinges set in the sides of the arch itself. That gate was always open; it was purely ornamental, for no invading armies were expected ever to present themselves at the entrance to the Castle, on this world that had known only peace for so long.

The gate was closed, now. It stood shut in front of them like a palisade of spears embedded in the ground to block their forward path.

"Do you see that?" Prestimion asked, in a voice choking with wonderment. "Closed? Have you ever known that gate to be closed before?"

"Never," Gialaurys said.

"Never," said Svor. "It comes as news to me that it can be closed at all."

"Yet there it is," rumbled Gialaurys. "It stands in our faces with its great padlock on it. What is this, my lord? How can they close the gate on us? The Castle is our home!"

"Ah, is it?" said Prestimion softly.

Septach Melayn, meanwhile, had stepped to the inner side of the plaza, just by the guardhouse door, and was rapping on it with the flat of his sword. There was no immediate response. Septach Melayn rapped again, more vigorously this time, and shouted to get the attention of those within.

After a little while the guardhouse door slowly opened, and two men dressed in the garb of officials of the Castle chancellery moved out into view. One was a Hjort, cold-eyed and somber, with an extraordinarily broad mouth and thick pebble-textured olive-hued skin; the other, a human, was scarcely prettier, for his face was almost as flat and wide as the Hjort's and he wore the sparse tufts of his reddish hair arrayed in stiff tall spikes all over his skull. Both wore swords, of the decorative kind that had come lately into great popularity at the Castle.

"What game is this?" Septach Melayn asked at once. "Open the gate for us!"

"The gate is closed," replied the Hjort complacently.

"I've already observed that it is, else I'd not waste my breath asking. Open it, and it would be wise not to make me ask a third time."

The spike-haired one said, "The Dizimaule gate is closed by order of the Coronal Lord Korsibar. We are told that it is to remain closed until he has reached the Castle himself and taken up residence in it."

"Is it, now?" said Septach Melayn. His hand went to the pommel of the sword that dangled at his side. "Do you have any idea who we are? I see plainly that you don't."

"The gate is closed to all comers, no matter who they be," said the Hjort, now with some tension in his tone. "Those are the orders we have received from the High Counsellor Duke Oljebbin, who is en route from the Labyrinth, traveling in the party of the Coronal. No one may enter until they are here. No one."

Gialaurys caught his breath sharply at that, and took a step or two forward to put himself at Septach Melayn's side; and Prestimion, though he remained in his place farther back, made a noise low in his throat like the growl of an angered dog. The two chancellery men looked increasingly uneasy. Some uniformed guardsmen now began to appear from within and take up positions alongside them before the gate.

Speaking mildly, though restraining himself was an effort, Prestimion said, "I am the Prince Prestimion of Muldemar, as I think you know. I have apartments within the Castle and I wish to have access to them. As do my companions here, whose names I think you also know."

The Hjort made a Hjortish nod. "I know you, Prince

Prestimion. But nevertheless I am not permitted to open this gate, not for you nor anyone, until the Coronal is here."

"You hideous toad, *this* is the Coronal who stands here before you!" Gialaurys shouted, and rushed toward him with the fury of a maddened bull. "Down and give worship! Down and give worship!"

Two guardsmen moved quickly in to protect the Hjort. Gialaurys seized one of them without an instant's hesitation and hurled him head first through the air so that he fetched up against the guardhouse door. He struck it with a terrible cracking sound and lay still.

The other, who was armed with a vibration-sword, went for his weapon but was slow in activating it: Gialaurys caught him by the left arm, spun him around, and yanked the arm sharply upward, snapping it like a twig. As the man began to crumple in shock Gialaurys struck him hard across the throat, a sharp powerful blow with the edge of his hand, and he fell down motionless also on the plaza pavement.

"Come on, the rest of you!" Gialaurys cried to the other guards, who stared in awe and astonishment at their two dead comrades. Gialaurys beckoned them challengingly to come toward him, but none of them moved.

Septach Melayn, meanwhile, had his sword out and was dancing in a cold but sportive rage about the Hjort and the other chancellery man, moving with a theatrical flamboyance: artfully nipping out again and again at them with the tip of his blade, menacing them with taunting grimaces and lightly pinking them here and there without actually inflicting a serious wound. His long thin spidery arms flashed like pistons, lashing out tirelessly. There was no defense against him. There never was. The two chancellery men had their own swords drawn too, but they were flimsy ornamental ones with scarcely any substance, and they held them like the utter novices that they were. Septach Melayn, laughing, flicked the Hjort's sword from his hand with a quick sidewise swipe of his own, and disarmed the spike-haired man just as easily an instant afterward.

"Now," he said, "I will draw one nice stripe after another down your flesh, until someone quickly chooses to open that gate for us." And he began by cutting open the Hjort's blue official jerkin from shoulder to waistband.

An alarm was sounding somewhere. Shouts could be heard from behind the gate.

The second chancellery man had turned and was trying to get past Gialaurys and the clutter of motionless guards standing between him and the guardhouse door. Septach Melayn raised his sword and began to bring it slicing down between the man's shoulderblades; but the blow was interrupted by Prestimion, who drew his own sword from its sheath and tapped it against Septach Melayn's. Septach Melayn halted his stroke and whirled about, slipping automatically into a posture of defense. But upon seeing that it was Prestimion who had interfered with him he lowered his weapon.

"This is idiocy," Prestimion told him. "Back to the floater, Septach Melayn! We can't fight the whole Castle. There'll be a hundred guards here in another five minutes."

"So there will indeed," said Septach Melayn, with a smile. He gave the red-haired chancellery man a thrust in the rear with his boot to send him lurching toward the guardhouse, whirled the astounded Hjort around and shoved him in the same direction, and caught Gialaurys by the arm in time to keep him from charging the guardsmen once more. Svor, who had watched the entire incident from his usual safe position on the sidelines, now trotted forth and took Gialaurys by the other arm; and he and Septach Melayn led him away, while Gialaurys continued loudly swearing that he would wreak havoc on all and sundry foes.

They re-entered their floater, and Prestimion signalled to

those in the other vehicles farther across the plaza to turn quickly and head back down the highway.

"Where shall we go?" asked Septach Melayn.

"Muldemar," Prestimion said. "At least there the gate will be open for us."

# 6

The High City of Muldemar lay nestled in a soft and greatly favored zone of the upper reaches of Castle Mount on the southeastern face of the mountain. Here a secondary peak, which in any other region of the planet would have been a considerable mountain in its own right, jutted up from the flank of the Mount to create on its inner slope a broad sheltered pocket, a great hollow fold, where the soil was rich and deep and the waters that flowed from within the giant mountain came forth generously in a plenitude of springs and streams.

The ancestors of Prince Prestimion's ancestors had settled in this part of Castle Mount nine thousand years before, when the Mount was still a place where newcomers could stake out domains for themselves, and the Castle itself had not yet been begun. There were no princes in Muldemar then, only a family of ambitious farmers who had come up from the lowlands around Gebelmoal bearing grapevines of good quality that they hoped could be transplanted to the Mount.

At Gebelmoal those vines had yielded a decent red wine of fair body and character; but on the Mount the alternation of sunlight and periods of cool mist was perfect for their cultivation, and it became quickly apparent, even from the earliest vintages, that the wine of Muldemar was going to be extraordinary in nature, thick and strong and complex, a wine for kings and emperors to cherish. The harvests were abundant, the yield of the grapes was lavish, their flavor uniquely pungent and bright. And yet, so popular did the wine of Muldemar prove to be, it was centuries before the vineyards there could be expanded sufficiently to meet the demand, despite every effort of the proprietors to expand production. Until that day came when supply and demand were at last in balance, one had to place one's order for Muldemar wine a decade or more in advance, and wait in turn, hoping that that year's vintage would be up to the quality of its predecessors. It always was.

Plain hardworking farmers will eventually turn into knights, and knights into counts and earls and dukes, and dukes into princes and sometimes kings, if only they stay prosperous and hold their land long enough. When that great hero of antiquity Lord Stiamot had in his later years transferred the royal capital from the High City of Stee on the slopes to the very summit of the mountain and built the first Castle there atop the Mount to celebrate his conquest of the Metamorph Shapeshifters, the ancestors of the ancestors of Prestimion had already come to hold noble rank as a reward for the quality of their wine and, perhaps, for the quantities of it that they had supplied to some earlier Coronal's festivities. Lord Stiamot it was who transformed the Count of Muldemar into the Duke of Muldemar, supposedly out of delight over some special cask of wine that was served at the Castle's dedication ceremony.

Some later Coronal—the historical record was uncharacteristically unclear on the point, and no one was quite sure whether it had been Lord Struin or Lord Spurifon or even Lord Thraym—had further ennobled the Muldemar duke of his time by making him a prince. But there were no greater titles to be seen on the family escutcheon. Never had there been a Coronal from the Muldemar line. Prestimion would have been the first, but for the intervention of Korsibar.

"So I am not to be Lady of the Isle after all, it seems," said Prestimion's mother the Princess Therissa, with a smile that betrayed relief as well as regret, when Prestimion and his party had arrived at his family's great hillside estate looking down over the broad sprawling acres of the huge Muldemar vineyard. "And I had already resigned myself to leaving this place, too, and was beginning even to pack a few things for the journey. Well, it will be no hardship for me to remain here. Is it a great disappointment to you, Prestimion?"

"I have had worse ones," he said. "I was promised a racing-mount once, and then father changed his mind and I received some set of fat history-books instead. I was ten years old then; the wound still festers in me."

They both laughed heartily. It had always been a close and loving family here. Prestimion embraced his mother, who was twelve years a widow now but still seemed beautiful and young, with a serene oval face and glossy black hair that she wore tightly drawn back and braided behind. A simply designed jewel of the highest beauty and value rested on the bosom of her white gown: a huge and flawless pigeon's-blood ruby, deep red tinged with purple, that was set in a hoop of gold with two sparkling little haigus-eye stones mounted as companions beside it. It was the Muldemar Ruby, the gift of the Coronal Lord Arioc, that had been in the family four thousand years.

But Prestimion noticed also that his mother wore an unfamiliar talisman encircling her left sleeve just by her wrist, a golden band inlaid with shards of emerald. It was something that might have seemed merely to be another ornament, but for the fact that the emerald shards spelled out mystic runes. They were much like the runes carved on the little corymbor amulet that the Vroon Thalnap Zelifor had given him in the Labyrinth, and which, mainly to humor Gialaurys and Duke Svor, he wore now around his neck on Septach Melayn's golden chain. She had not had any such thing when he last saw her in the early part of the year.

These witchery-things are everywhere now, Prestimion thought: even here, even on his own mother's arm. And not worn in jest, he suspected, as was the corymbor dangling by his throat.

"What will you do now, Prestimion?" she asked him, as she walked with him to his rooms.

"Now? Now I'll rest here, and eat well and drink well and swim and sleep, and watch how the Coronal Lord Korsibar conducts himself on his throne. And consider my options, carefully and with much thought."

"You'll abide by his stealing of the crown, then? For that is what he did, I hear: stole it, took it right out of his father's own hand without the slightest show of shame. And Confalume allowing it just as shamelessly."

"He took it from the Hjort crown-bearer Hjathnis, in fact, while his father stood to one side all dumbfounded and amazed. And the others too, for they were every one under some spell then that clouded their minds as it happened. Septach Melayn was there and saw it. But no matter: Korsibar has the crown. Confalume is unwilling to raise objection, or incapable of it, or both. The deed is done. The world accepts it. The people have raised banners in honor of Korsibar all along the Glayge. The Castle guards themselves turned me away at Dizimaule Arch: why do you think I am here, mother, instead of there? They turned me away!"

"That goes beyond all belief."

"So it does. But believe it anyway, mother. I do. Korsibar is Coronal."

"I know that boy well. He's brave and handsome and tall; but he lacks the capacity for the task. To look like a king is insufficient; he needs to be a king within. And he is not that."

"This is true," said Prestimion. "But he has the crown. The Castle and the throne await him."

"A Coronal's son may not follow his father that way. That is the ancient law."

"A Coronal's son is doing that very thing, mother, even as we stand here talking. And it is not law, only custom."

The Princess Therissa stared at Prestimion in flat amazement. "You amaze me, Prestimion. Are you going to allow it to happen, without even a protest? You'll do nothing at all?"

"I said I would consider my options, mother."

"Which means what?"

"What I intend to do," he said, "is summon certain high men of the kingdom here to Muldemar and sound them out, and learn from them how strong their support of Korsibar really is. I mean such as Duke Oljebbin, and Serithorn, and Gonivaul. And also, I think, Dantirya Sambail."

"That monster," said the Princess Therissa.

"A monster, yes, but a bold and powerful monster, and also, I remind you, a kinsman of ours. I'll speak with these men. I'll fill them full of our finest vintages and see if they are in Korsibar's pocket, or can be pried free of him, yes or no, if they will give me an answer. And then I'll form some plan for my future, if I'm to have one. But for now I am only Prince of Muldemar, and that in itself is no little thing." He smiled and touched the talisman at his mother's wrist.—"Is this new?" he asked.

"I've had it these two months past."

"Elegant work. Who is the goldsmith?"

"I have no idea. It was given me by the magus Galbifond. Did you know we have a magus here now?"

"No."

"To help us foresee patterns of rainfall and mist, and to judge the proper day for picking the grapes. He's an expert winemaker: knows all the true spells."

"The true spells," Prestimion said, wincing. "Ah."

"He told me also that you would not become Coronal

when the old Pontifex died. I learned that from him no more than five days after you set out toward the Labyrinth."

"Ah," said Prestimion again. "It seems that everyone knew that except me."

There was no part of the vale of Muldemar that was anything less than lovely, but the vineyards and estate of the princes of Muldemar occupied the choicest position of all. The princely lands were situated in the best protected shelter, nestling up against the flank of the Mount itself so close that it was impossible to see the Castle from the manor house, because one would have to look up almost straight overhead. Here only sweet winds blew and gentle mists came. And here, in the perpetually green domain between Kudarmar Ridge and the well-behaved little Zemulikkaz River, the lands of the princely family ran for mile after mile, culminating in the splendor and magnificence of Muldemar House itself, a great white-walled structure of two hundred rooms whose three main wings were topped with lofty black towers.

Prestimion had been born at Muldemar House, but, like most of the princes of the high families, had lived much of his life at the Castle, taking his education there and returning here only a few months out of the year. Since his father's death he was technically the head of the family, and took care to be here on all major family occasions, but his rapid rise to the status of heir-presumptive to Lord Confalume had required his presence at the Castle much of the time in recent years.

Now all that was over; and it was far from displeasing to be back in his own suite of rooms again. He had a generous private apartment within the house, on the second level, facing the sweeping vista of Sambattinola Hill. Long curving windows of faceted quartz carved by the subtlest craftsmen of Stee flooded the rooms with brilliant light; the walls of the rooms were lavishly covered with mural paintings in delicate pale tones, azure and amethyst and topaz pink, endless interwoven floral traceries in the intricate and curiously eye-tickling mode of the artisans of Haplior.

Here Prestimion bathed and rested and dressed, and received visits from his three younger brothers. They had become virtual strangers to him after his long absence, and had grown almost beyond recognition in just this one year.

Each of the three professed his fury at Korsibar's villainous theft of the throne. Teotas, who at fifteen was the youngest, was the one most heated in his insistence that Prestimion make immediate war against Confalume's lawless son, and most eager to die if need be in defense of his brother's crown. Eighteen-year-old Abrigant, who stood head and shoulders above all his brothers, was nearly as vehement. Even the artful and paradox-loving Taradath, at twenty-three the closest to Prestimion's age and thus far in life much more given to the writing of ironic verse than the mastering of the skills of warfare, seemed aflame with a passion for vengeance.

Prestimion embraced them all, and assured each in turn that he would play a prominent role in any action that might be undertaken. But he sent them away from him without having offered any clear indication of what kind of action that might be.

In truth he had no idea. It was far too soon for the making of plans, if indeed there were any that needed making.

He spent the first weeks of his return in pleasant idleness, and at times felt the pain of his bitter disappointment giving way to a lighter mood, the first he had known since the events at the Labyrinth.

It seemed unwise to leave the estate at all and enter the great city of Muldemar adjacent to it, since he wanted neither to hear the people of Muldemar swearing allegiance to Lord Korsibar nor passionately urging him—for he would be easily recognized there—to make civil war on the usurper. So he passed his days swimming in the cool Zemulikkaz, and strolling in the park surrounding Muldemar House, and hunting bilantoons and khamgars in the family preserve. Septach Melayn and Gialaurys were in constant attendance on him; Svor also, a little later, for first he made a brief sojourn to the nearby city of Frangior, where there was a woman he liked to visit. When Svor came back from there he seemed dejected, and said to Prestimion, "It is all Korsibar out there. He has arrived at the Castle now and is kinging it in great glory there. His face is posted up everywhere in Frangior."

"And in Muldemar city too?" asked Prestimion.

"Fewer posters there, but there are some. And some portraits of you also, though they keep getting taken down. There's much sentiment in the city in your favor."

"I would expect so," Prestimion said. "But I intend to give it no encouragement."

Sometimes in hours of solitude Prestimion browsed in Muldemar House's capacious library, leafing through the books of history he had found so unwelcome as a boyhood gift. Their pages were full of vivid accounts of the deeds of heroes of ages past, the establishment of the Pontificate under Dvorn and the bold exploration of Castle Mount in the days when it was still uninhabitable and the war of Stiamot against the Shapeshifters, and the expeditions into the torrid south and the frigid north and across the uncrossable Great Sea. Prestimion's eyes took on a blurry glaze as he turned past sheet upon sheet of the annals of Coronals and Pontifexes whose names meant little or nothing to him: Hemias, Scaul, Methirasp, Hunzimar, Meyk, and many a dozen more. But of previous usurpations of the throne he could find no mention at all.

"Can it be," he said to Svor one day, "that we are such a

virtuous people that never once in thirteen thousand years before this has someone wrongfully seized the throne?"

"Surely we are a kingdom of holy saints," said Svor piously, rolling his eyes upward.

"Surely not," said Prestimion.

"Well, then," Svor said, tapping his knuckles against the dusty leatherbound book in Prestimion's hand, "perhaps it's the case that certain dark episodes of our history have somehow been lost along the way, and are missing from these heavy tomes?"

"Lost by accident, you think, Svor?"

"By accident or purpose. How can I say?" But it was clear from the roguish look in Svor's dark eyes that he was hinting at some deliberate suppression of truth. Prestimion let the point pass. Svor was ever willing to postulate rascalry and conspiracies without foundation, simply because his own feverishly intense mind wheeled eternally in such devious circles. Nevertheless, even Prestimion found it difficult to believe that this was the first time in those thousands of years that there been an illicit taking of the Coronal's crown.

There were, of course, the capsules of the Register of Souls, stored in the House of Records of the Labyrinth, where ever since Lord Stiamot's time people had deposited imprints of their innermost memories. The unedited data of those capsules might yield truer accounts of ancient events than these massive but untrustworthy volumes of historical scholarship. But the Register of Souls was sealed against casual access, and in any event its capsules were so multitudinous, numbering up into the many billions, that unless one already knew where one wanted to look one would probably be unable to find anything useful in them: there was no general index, no way of scanning through them for such a topic as "royal throne, usurpation of." And a random search across an archive that was seven thousand years deep might well require seven thousand years to produce anything useful.

Prestimion put the issue from his mind. It was not really that important, after all. As the Pontifex Confalume had said most regretfully but emphatically, the thing was done. Korsibar held the power now. Seeing nothing else for it, Prestimion gave himself over to the pleasures of his home and the company of his family and the fellowship of his friends, biding his time.


The High Counsellor Duke Oljebbin, when the summons came to him from Prestimion inviting him to pay a call on him at Muldemar, happened to be in the presence of that other senior peer, Serithorn of Samivole. They were strolling together on the terrace of Oljebbin's office just off the Pinitor Court, close to the core of the Castle, hard by Stiamot Keep that was the oldest wing of all. Oljebbin and Serithorn and the Grand Admiral Gonivaul, along with some other high officials of the Confalume regime, would be lunching later this day with a few of the new men of Lord Korsibar's government, Farquanor and Farholt, and Mandrykarn of Stee, and one or two others.

A knight-initiate in Oljebbin's service approached him on the terrace bearing an envelope of gray vellum, sealed with a splash of bright purple wax. Duke Oljebbin took it without comment and slipped it into a fold of his robe.

"A love-letter from Prestimion?" Serithorn asked.

Oljebbin gave him a sour look. "If I could see through closed envelopes, I'd tell you. But I don't have the knack. Do you?"

"It looks very much like a letter I had from Prestimion myself, no more than an hour past. Go on, Oljebbin. Open it. I'll look the other way, if you prefer."

It was always like this between them: a chilly sort of banter, a long friendship in which sharp teeth were showing in every smile. The Duke Oljebbin and the Prince Serithorn were both some years past the age of fifty, and had known each other, so it seemed, since before their births. They had both from an early age been important members of the Royal Council.

Oljebbin, whose great estate near Stoienzar in Alhanroel's southern districts was a demesne of such extravagant luxury that even he felt almost abashed to visit it, was Confalume's cousin on his mother's side. Very likely he would have been Coronal himself had the Pontifex Prankipin not lived to such a great old age. But Prankipin had conducted himself as though he was all but immortal, and Confalume had put in forty-three years as Coronal instead of the customary fifteen or twenty; and Oljebbin, after two decades as Lord Confalume's High Counsellor and heir-presumptive, had had to confess that he no longer had any yearning for the throne. That had been the beginning of Prestimion's spectacular if abortive rise to prominence.

Oljebbin himself had suggested Prestimion to Confalume as a successor. To be a power behind the throne was one of the great pleasures of his life. He was a wide-shouldered, deep-voiced man much given to wearing elaborately brocaded robes of rich colors suitable as complements to his remarkable shock of thick white hair: his eyes were warm and shrewd, his features somewhat small and pinched in relation to the grandeur of that hair, and his manner was one of lordliness bordering on the extremes of self-admiration.

Serithorn, to the contrary, had never for an instant wanted to be Coronal, and therefore had spent all his life in the innermost circles of power, where everyone sought him out with confidences because he was no threat to anyone. He was a prince of one of Majipoor's oldest families, tracing an impressive if somewhat tenuous line of ancestry back to Lord

Stiamot, but also counting such ancient kings as Kanaba, Struin, and Geppin as ornaments of his family tree.

He had, so rumor maintained, courted Prestimion's mother before Prestimion's father married her; he remained a close friend of the family. Serithorn was the wealthiest private citizen of the realm, with estates in every part of Alhanroel and much land in Zimroel as well. His bearing was elegant, his style light and easy. He was fair-haired, smooth-skinned, and trim and compact of form, somewhat like Prestimion in that way, though his stance was more relaxed, lacking in that sense of energy compressed and contained that was so marked a characteristic of Prestimion. Never had Serithorn been seen to take any matter with any great seriousness; but those who knew him well knew that that was only a pose. He had great properties to defend, and, like most men of that sort, he was profoundly conservative at heart, a stubborn defender of the ways he knew and cherished.

Duke Oljebbin scanned the letter once quickly, and then read it again rather more carefully, before sharing its contents with Serithorn.

"From Prestimion, as you correctly supposed," he said finally.

"Yes. And he invites you to dine with him at Muldemar?"

"Indeed. A tasting of the new vintage. And to hunt in his preserve."

"It was the same with me," Serithorn said. "Well, we know the quality of his wine."

Oljebbin regarded the prince with care.

"You intend to go, then?"

"Why, yes. Is Prestimion not our friend, and is his hospitality something that can be nonchalantly refused?"

Tapping the letter lightly against the fingertips of his left hand, Oljebbin said, "These are the early days of a new reign. Would you not say that we owe it to Lord Korsibar to remain in constant attendance at the Castle at this time, so that we can offer him the benefits of our wisdom?"

Serithorn smiled naughtily. "You fear his displeasure, do you, if you go to Muldemar?"

"I fear nothing in this world, Serithorn, as you very well know. But I would not casually offend the Coronal."

"In a word, then, the answer to my question seems to be 'Yes.' "

Oljebbin's lips quirked in a quick cool smile that showed little in the way of amusement.

"Until we know what Lord Korsibar's true attitude toward Prestimion is," he said, "it could be construed as an act of provocation for us to be paying calls upon him."

"Korsibar has offered Prestimion a post in the government. The offer was made while we all were still in the Labyrinth."

"And declined, I hear. In any case the offer was an obligatory one, mere politeness. You know that, I know that, and obviously Prestimion knows that. I said we needed to know Korsibar's *true* attitude toward Prestimion."

"We can very readily guess what that is. But he'll never dare act on it. He'll try to neutralize Prestimion, but he wouldn't dare harm him.—I hadn't heard, by the way, that Korsibar's invitation was rejected by Prestimion."

"Not accepted, at any rate."

"Not yet. Prestimion has some calculations of his own to make, don't you think? Why else are we asked to Muldemar?"

With his voice kept low Oljebbin said, taking Serithorn by the arm and leading him to the edge of the terrace, "Tell me this. What will you say, if Prestimion should have some insurrection against Lord Korsibar in mind, and wants to learn from us whether he has our backing?"

"I doubt that he'll be so forthcoming so soon."

"There's already been that skirmish at the gates, when Prestimion found himself turned away by the guards. There'll be other little skirmishes, wouldn't you say? And then perhaps something bigger. Don't you think he intends eventually to rise against Korsibar?"

"I think he detests what Korsibar has done. As do I, Oljebbin: as do I. And, I think, you as well."

"Yes, I do understand the difference between right and wrong, Serithorn. I agree that Korsibar's assumption of the crown was a rash and most improper thing."

"Not just improper. Unlawful."

Oljebbin shook his head. "I won't go that far. There's no formal law of succession. Which is a great omission in our constitution, we all now realize. But what he did was improper. Unwarrantable and unjustifiable. An astonishing contravention of tradition."

"Well, at least you still have some shred of honesty left intact somewhere within you, Oljebbin."

"How kind of you to say so. But you're avoiding my question. Will Prestimion placidly accept the situation as it now exists, and, if he doesn't, whose side will be you on?"

"I feel as you do that the seizure of the throne was a monstrous despicable thing, and I abhor it," said Serithorn, speaking with a heat that was unusual for him. But he damped that fervor instantly with a simultaneous wry smile. "Of course, he's a very popular monster. The people were fond of Prestimion too, but they've taken to Korsibar very quickly. And they lack our nice sense of precedent and custom when it comes to matters at Castle Mount: all they want is a sturdy, good-looking Coronal who can flash a bright smile at them when he rides in the processional through the streets of their city. Korsibar is that."

In some annoyance Oljebbin said, "Give me a direct answer, Serithorn. Suppose Prestimion says he wants your help in a rebellion. What will you tell him?"

"This is very tactless of you to ask."

"I ask it anyway. We are beyond tact here, you and I."

"Take this as your answer, then. I have no idea what Prestimion has in mind to do. I've twice already said that I regard Korsibar's usurpation as an abomination. But he is the anointed Coronal now, and an uprising against him is treasonous. One wrong can lead to another, and then to others, until all the world is turned on end, and I have more to lose than anyone."

"So you'd try to remain neutral in any struggle between Prestimion and Korsibar for the throne?"

"At least until I see which faction's likely to win. I think," he went on carefully, "that that is your position too, Oljebbin."

"Ah. Finally you speak in a straightforward way. But if you intend to remain neutral, why accept Prestimion's invitation?"

"He hasn't yet been proscribed, has he? I admire his wine; his hospitality is generous; he is my dear friend. As is his mother. If by some chance he determines one day to make war against Korsibar, and the Divine should smile upon him and bring him to victory, I wouldn't want to have it on his mind that I snubbed him at a time that I knew must be difficult and painful for him. So I'll go. A social call, with no political undertones."

"I see."

"You, on the other hand, are Lord Korsibar's actual High Counsellor, and I realize that that makes your position more ticklish than mine."

"Does it? In what way?"

"Nothing that the High Counsellor does is without its political implications, especially at a time like this. By going, you'd seem to be conferring more importance on Prestimion than Korsibar may want him to have just now. Korsibar wouldn't appreciate that. If you want to continue to hold on to your post, you might not care to offend him."

"What do you mean, if I want to continue to hold on to my post?" said Oljebbin, bristling.

Serithorn smiled benignly. "He's carried you over from the Confalume government, yes. But for how long? Farquanor's hungry for your position: you know that. Give him some excuse to undermine you with Korsibar and he will."

"I'm assured of my counsellorship as long as I want it. And—I remind you once more, Serithorn—I fear no one. Particularly not Count Farquanor."

"Come with me to Muldemar, then."

Oljebbin was silent for a time, glowering down with displeasure at Serithorn. Then he arrived abruptly at his decision.

"Done," he said. "We'll go there together."


Prestimion said, "In this cask at my right hand is the famous wine of the tenth year of Prankipin and Lord Confalume, which by common agreement is the best this century. In this one is the wine of the year Thirty Prankipin Lord Confalume, which also is highly regarded by the connoisseurs, in particular for its unusual color and fragrance, although still relatively young and with much greatness yet to develop. And this cask—" He tapped an especially dusty barrel of archaic make, which tapered toward its ends at unusually sharp angles—"In this," he said, "is our last remaining stock of the oldest wine we have, which dates from, if I read this faded tag properly, Eleven Amyntilir Lord Kelimiphon, that is to say, two hundred and some years ago. Its body is perhaps a little thin by now, but I had it brought up, Admiral Gonivaul, so that you might sample a wine that was in its prime when your great ancestor was Pontifex."

He looked about the room, singling out each of his guests in turn for a warm smile and a close intense look: Gonivaul first, who had been the first to arrive that afternoon, and then Oljebbin and Serithorn, who had come in the same floater an hour later.

"Finally," said Prestimion, "we have here the first cask of this year's vintage. It represents, of course, mere potential, rather than actual accomplishment, at this point. But I know that men of your perceptiveness and experience of wine will understand how to judge this wine for what it promises, not for what it is at the moment. And I can tell you that my good cellarmaster here believes that when the wine of Forty-three Prankipin Lord Confalume has reached the summit of its destiny, it will be a match for the best that has ever been produced here. My lords, let us begin with this new wine first, and proceed backward in time until we come to the ancient one."

They were gathered in the tasting-room of Muldemar House, a dark and cavernous subterranean vault of green basalt, where rack upon rack of bottles stretched on and on into the dimness. The room extended no little distance into the side of Castle Mount itself, and both sides of it were lined with the greatest wines of Muldemar, a treasure valued in the many millions of royals. Prestimion had with him Septach Melayn, Gialaurys, and Svor, and also his brother Taradath. His three guests had come unaccompanied. A fourth had been invited, the Procurator Dantirya Sambail, but he had sent word that he had been unavoidably delayed by responsibilities at the Castle, and would arrive in a day or two.

"If you please, cellarmaster," Prestimion said.

Abeleth Glayn was the cellarmaster at Muldemar House, and had been for over fifty years: a gaunt, skeletal man with the palest of blue eyes and straggly white locks, who liked to say that he had consumed more of the best wine in the world than any man who had ever lived. As he leaned forward to open the spigot on the first cask he paused an instant to touch the rohilla mounted on his surplice over his breastbone, and to make a quick little witchery-sign with his left forefinger and thumb, and to whisper something incantatory under his breath. Prestimion allowed none of his annoyance over this display of superstition to show. He loved old Abeleth Glayn dearly, and tolerated him in everything.

The wine was drawn, and passed around. They all imitated the cellarmaster in tasting the wine and spitting it out unswallowed, for that was, they knew, the wine-taster's proper way; and in any event this wine was too green for drinking yet. But they nodded sagely, and uttered their praise. "It will be a marvel," said Oljebbin sonorously, and Serithorn said, "I'll have ten casks for my cellar, if I may," and dark shaggy-haired Gonivaul, whose palate was no more cultivated than a Ghayrog's and who was widely believed not to be able to tell wine from ale nor either one from fermented dragon-milk, solemnly offered the opinion that this would be a vintage of inestimable virtue indeed.

Prestimion clapped his hands. Slabs of bread were brought with which they could clear their mouths, and a light repast of smoked sea-dragon meat sliced very thin and sauced in a marinade of delicate meirva-blossom petals. When they had eaten a little, he ordered the pouring of the impressive second wine, which he said ought not to be spat out; and after that had been duly consumed and commented on, a course of spiced fish was served, along with Stoienzar oysters that still were slowly moving in their shells. With this they sampled the great wine of Ten Prankipin Lord Confalume, which drew the appropriate expressions of awe, and much talk of Dantirya Sambail's misfortune at not being here to drink it.

Svor said privately to Septach Melayn, "If the same wine were to come out of each cask, would any of them, I wonder, know the difference?"

"Be quiet, O irreverent one," Septach Melayn replied, affecting a look of extreme horror. "These are very great connoisseurs, and the wisest men of the realm besides."

They went at last on to the antique wine of Amyntilir's

day, which somewhere in its two centuries of life had evidently parted with whatever merit it might once have had. This did not keep the Grand Admiral Gonivaul from praising it beyond all measure, and in fact coming close to tears of joy over Prestimion's kindness in making available to him this tangible memorial to the greatest member of his family.

"Let us now go upstairs," said Prestimion, "and join my mother and some other friends for dinner; and then afterward some brandy awaits us that I think you'll find rewarding."

The name of Korsibar had not yet been mentioned that evening. At dinner, with the great table in the banquet hall set for eighteen and one rich course after another steadily arriving, the talk was all of hunting and the coming grape-harvest and the new season's exhibition of soul-paintings, and not a syllable spoken concerning the change in government. Nor was it to be until very much later, many hours after dinner, when the original smaller group from the wine-tasting was gathered once more in the glass-paneled study where a century's worth of Muldemar brandy was racked in lovely hand-blown globelets, and Prestimion had served a generous portion of his hundred-year-old stock to all.

"What news is there from the Castle?" he asked, very mildly, with no edge to his voice whatever, and addressing his question to no one in particular.

There was a long silence in the room. The three guests variously studied the contents of their brandy glasses or sipped at their drinks in extreme concentration. Prestimion smiled pleasantly, waiting for a reply as though he had asked something utterly innocent, a question about the weather, perhaps.

"It is a very busy time there," said Oljebbin finally, when the lack of response was beginning to become significant.

"Is it, now?"

"The housecleaning that always takes place when the regime changes," said the duke. He seemed uncharacteristically

257

uncomfortable at being the center of attention. "You can imagine it: the bureaucrats scuttling around, securing their places if they feel in danger of losing them, or striving for upward movement while all is still in flux."

"And in which category do you place yourself, my lord Oljebbin?" asked Svor, taking a maidenly sip of his brandy.

Oljebbin stiffened. "The High Counsellor is something more than a bureaucrat, would you not say, my lord Svor? But as a matter of fact I have been reconfirmed in my office by the new Coronal."

"Well! We should drink to that!" cried Septach Melayn, and lifted his drink with a reckless flourish. "To the High Counsellor Oljebbin, once and again!"

"Oljebbin!" they all called, brandishing their brandy-bowls. "Oljebbin! The High Counsellor!" And drank deep to cover the inanity of that hollow toast.

Prestimion said afterward, "And the Coronal? He settles easily and well into his new duties, I hope?"

Again an uneasy silence. Again, great attention paid to the brandy-bowls.

Serithorn, upon receiving an urgent glare from Oljebbin, said somewhat restively, "He's getting accustomed to the job bit by bit. It is, of course, a heavy burden."

"The heaviest he's ever lifted, and then some," grunted Gialaurys. "Man should be careful what he picks up, if he know not how strong he really be."

Prestimion poured another round of brandy all around: newer stuff, dealt out with a free hand.

"Of course the people welcome Korsibar's ascent," he said, as they tipped back their bowls once more. "I saw, all the way up the Glayge, how quick they were to put his portrait out and celebrate his coming. He is very well received, I think." And flashed his eyes from one to another of the visitors, quickly, as if to let them know that there were deeper currents to the bland stream of his conversation. But they already understood that.

Gonivaul, who looked flushed with excess of food and drink wherever his reddening face could be seen through his dense thatches of hair and beard, said in a thickened voice, "It is a honeymoon time for him now. Every new Coronal is accorded that. But when his decrees begin to fall upon the land, the common folk may be singing different songs."

"Not only the common folk," said Serithorn, reaching out to have his bowl filled yet again. He was growing flushed also, and inflamed about the eyes.

"Oh?" asked Septach Melayn. "Is there reason for such men as yourselves to be apprehensive?"

Serithorn shrugged. "Any great change such as this must be weighed and analyzed carefully, my lord Septach Melayn. Lord Korsibar is, after all, one of us. We have no reason to doubt that we'll enjoy the same privileges under him that we've known before. But one never knows what reforms and rearrangements a new Coronal has in mind. None of us has ever experienced a change of Coronal before, let me remind you."

"How true," said Prestimion. "What a strange time this is for us all.—Let me introduce you to our special aromatic brandy, now, shall I? We store it six years in keppinong-wood casks after it's distilled, with a couple of ganni-berries dropped into it to add a little spice." He gestured to Septach Melayn, who brought out fresh drinking-bowls, and a new round went to each of them. Prestimion watched carefully as they drank, as if concerned that they appreciate it to the fullest. Then he said bluntly, "And you, my lords? How do you find the changes, personally? Tell me, are you fully contented with them?"

Oljebbin looked warily to Serithorn, and Serithorn to Gonivaul, and the Grand Admiral to Oljebbin. Whose turn was it to make the awkward answer to the embarrassing question?

There were no clear replies, only temporizing mumbles.

Prestimion pressed onward. "And the mode of Korsibar's accession: how did that strike you? Is it a good idea, do you think, for Coronals to elect themselves?"

Oljebbin let air escape slowly from his lips. This was coming down to the heart of the matter at last, and he was not in any way pleased by it. But he said nothing. Nor did Gonivaul.

Serithorn it was who spoke at last, after another endless while: "Does my lord Prestimion intend to have us speak treason here?"

Prestimion's eyebrows rose. "Treason? What treason? I asked a straightforward question of political philosophy. I solicited your opinions on an issue of governmental theory. Should members of the government not hold beliefs concerning constitutional matters, and feel free to speak of them among friends? And certainly you're among friends here, Prince Serithorn!"

"Yes. So loving a friend that he's filled me full of great wine and fine food and splendid brandy until I'm near to bursting," Serithorn said. He arose and yawned elaborately. "And more than ready for sleep, also, I think. Perhaps it would be better to discuss these constitutional matters and issues of philosophy in the morning. If you'll excuse me, prince—"

"Wait, Serithorn!" cried Gonivaul, in a ferocious voice.

The usually cool and aloof Grand Admiral was on his feet, wobbling more than a bit from too much drink, holding himself erect with evident effort. His eyes were blazing, his face as hot and blustery as the irascible Count Farholt's might have been in full wrath. Swinging about on Serithorn and half spilling his liquor as he did so, he said hoarsely, slurring his words a little, "We've been sitting here all night drinking Prestimion's wines and playing these little games with him.

Now the time of truth's at hand, and you'll stay for it." And, looking toward Prestimion: "Well, prince? Where are we heading here? Are you telling us that it's your intention not to abide by the crowning of Korsibar, and asking us where we will stand if you rise against him?"

Oljebbin instantly went as tense as a metal rod. He sat bolt upright and blurted, "You're drunk, Gonivaul. For the love of the Divine, sit down, or—or—"

"Be quiet," Gonivaul said. "We are entitled to know. Well, Prestimion? Give me an answer!"

Oljebbin, aghast, rose unsteadily to his feet and took a few weaving steps in Gonivaul's direction as though meaning to silence him by direct force. Serithorn caught him by the hand and pulled him back to his seat. Then, to Prestimion, Serithorn said, "Very well, prince. I wish we had not reached this point, but I suppose it was where we were meant to go. I too would like to hear your answer to the Admiral's question."

"Good," said Prestimion. "You will have it." And, calmly: "My position on Korsibar is precisely what you would suppose it to be. I regard him as an illegitimate Coronal, wrongfully come to power."

"And mean to overthrow him?" Gonivaul asked.

"I would like to see him overthrown, yes. Yes. His rule will bring disaster upon us all, so I do believe. But putting him aside isn't something that can be done with the waving of a wand."

"Are you asking for our help, then?" said Serithorn. "Be straightforward with us."

"I have never been anything other than straightforward with you, Prince Serithorn. And I remind you that I haven't ever said I intend to make any move against Korsibar. But if there should be an uprising—if there *should* be one, I say—I would put all my energies and resources to it. I would like to think that you three would do the same."

Prestimion's eyes traveled from Gonivaul to Serithorn, from Serithorn to Oljebbin.

Slowly and uncomfortably Serithorn said, "You know that we share your distaste for the methods by which Korsibar reached the throne. We are men who love the old traditional ways, we three. We find it hard to approve of his unconscionable and, as you say, illegitimate acts."

"Indeed," said Oljebbin.

"Hear, hear!" Gonivaul cried, slumping back heavily into his chair.

"So I may think of you as being with me?" Prestimion asked.

"With you in what?" said Serithorn at once. "In disapproval of Korsibar's usurpation? Absolutely! We deplore it." Oljebbin nodded vociferously at that, and Gonivaul also. "Of course," Serithorn went on, "we must move cautiously at present. Power resides with Korsibar, and he's understandably on his guard in this transitional time. We'll do nothing hasty or rash."

"I understand," said Prestimion. "But when the moment arrives, if it does—"

"Everything in my power to return this world to the proper path. I promise you that with all my heart."

"I also," said Oljebbin.

"And I," Gonivaul said. "You know that, Prestimion. I will do my duty. At whatever risk to my personal position. What—ever—risk. What—ever." His tongue was thick; he stumbled over his words. He sank back in his seat and closed his eyes. A moment later he seemed to be snoring.

"Perhaps this is enough for now," Prestimion said quietly, to Svor and Septach Melayn.

He got to his feet. "My lords—the time has come, I think, to conclude our brandy-tasting. My lords—?"

Gonivaul was deep in sleep. Oljebbin appeared to be nearly as far gone, and Serithorn, though still awake and in command of himself, was visibly struggling as he made his way toward the door. At Prestimion's suggestion Gialaurys raised the Grand Admiral to his feet and guided him from the room. Septach Melayn offered his assistance to the wobbly Oljebbin, and Prestimion instructed Taradath with a quick gesture to give Prince Serithorn such aid as he might need.

He and Svor remained after the others had gone, for one last drop of brandy before making an end to the evening.

"What do you think, my wily friend?" Prestimion said. "Are they with me or aren't they?"

"Oh, with you, with you, by all means!"

"You think? Truly?"

Svor smiled and held up one hand. "Oh, yes, Prestimion, they are definitely with you, these three great and long-established lords. They said so themselves, and so it must be true. You heard them. That is, they are with you so long as they sit here in your house and drink your brandy. Once they're back in the Castle, it might be a different story, I suspect."

"I think so also. But will they betray me, do you think?"

"I doubt that. They'll wait and see what you do, and keep all their options open. If you move against Korsibar, and seem to have a chance of winning, they'll join you: but not until you're plainly on your way to victory. And if you don't appear to stand a chance, why, they'll deny under oath that they ever said a word to you about lifting a finger on your behalf. Or so it seems to me."

"And to me," said Prestimion.


Dawn promised a flawless early-morning day, and indeed the promise was fulfilled, but it was many hours after the dawn before any of Prestimion's guests presented themselves. They breakfasted at a time best fitted for lunch, and in the afternoon, under warm emerald sunlight, they hunted happily in the Muldemar preserve, bringing down a host of bilantoons and sigimoins and other such small animals, which were carried off by Prestimion's people to be prepared for that evening's dinner. That night there was no mention of the subjects that had arisen the evening before, but only of light and easy things, as befitted wealthy lords enjoying a brief holiday in the countryside.

A day more and they were gone, back to the Castle. An hour after the last of them had left came an outrider to Muldemar House to announce that the Procurator of Ni-moya was approaching, and then shortly the Procurator himself, with an entourage of some fifty or sixty folk, or perhaps even a few more than that.

Prestimion felt only amusement at such cool audacity. "At least it wasn't five hundred," he remarked, upon going to the gate to greet Dantirya Sambail and discovering him in the midst of this unexpected horde. "But I think we can find room for them all. Are you making a grand processional, cousin?"

"That would be premature of me, cousin. No one has yet offered me a crown." The Procurator was richly dressed, as usual, bare-headed but with a gleaming and costly jerkin of black leather, covered all over with bright diamond-shaped sequins, that rose almost to his chin, and a breastplate of gold chased with silver, on which were inscribed loose curvilinear symbols of some sort unknown to Prestimion. "But I won't be taxing your resources unduly," he said, as they went within. "This will be only a brief visit. I expect to be on my way in the morning."

"So soon?" Prestimion said. "Why, feel free to stay as long as you wish!"

"That *is* as long as I wish. I have a considerable journey

ahead of me, which is why I come upon you with all this great number. I'm on my way back to Ni-moya."

"Before the coronation ceremony?"

"The Coronal has graciously excused me from attending, on account of the length of the voyage. I haven't been home for three years or thereabouts, you know, and I miss the place. Lord Korsibar believes it would be a good idea for me to make myself visible in Zimroel right now, by way of carrying the word of what's been happening here. Korsibar isn't well known on the other continent, you understand. I'm to vouch for his merits among my people."

"Which you'll do most loyally, with all your heart and soul, I know," said Prestimion. "Well, come join me below, and let me try you with the new vintage, and one or two older ones. We had quite a grand feast here, the other evening, Oljebbin and Gonivaul and Serithorn and I. A pity you missed it."

"I think it was Gonivaul that passed me on the road, a little way back."

"It was an interesting evening that we had."

"Interesting? Those three?" Dantirya Sambail let out a gust of scornful laughter. "But in your position you need all the friends you can find, I suppose." He turned to one of his servants and whispered something: the man ran off, and returned an instant later with a member of the Procurator's following, a lean, swarthy, hawk-nosed tight-jacketed man. Prestimion was sure he had seen him somewhere before. "Where's this wine of yours, Prestimion?" Dantirya Sambail asked.

"The best is in the cellar."

"Let's be for it, then. Come along with us, Mandralisca."

*Mandralisca.* Prestimion remembered now. The poison-taster, the quick-eyed green-jacketed batonsman of the Labyrinth games on whom Prestimion had wagered five crowns with Septach Melayn. He was an evil-faced man, grim and bleak, with thin, austere lips and hard-angled cheekbones. The taster was staring coldly and levelly at Prestimion as though assessing the probability that the prince had prepared a deadly draught for his master.

Prestimion felt a hot surge of fury run through him. For all his tight control his voice was like a whiplash as he said, "We have no need of this man, Procurator."

"He goes everywhere with me. He is my—"

"Poison-taster, yes. So I have already been told. Do you mistrust me that much, cousin?"

Dantirya Sambail's pale fleshy cheeks went crimson. "This is my ancient custom, ever to have him taste for me first."

"My ancient custom," said Prestimion, "is to open my house only to those I love. And very rarely do I poison any of those."

His eyes met Dantirya Sambail's squarely, and remained locked against them a long moment, radiating anger and injured pride and searing contempt. Neither man spoke. Then the Procurator, as though having made some inward calculation, looked away, and smiled, and said in a soft conciliatory voice, "Well, then, Prestimion. I would not give offense to my dear kinsman. For you I will dispense with my ancient custom, and so be it." He made a flicking gesture with his left hand, and the poison-taster, after throwing a chilly inquiring glance at Dantirya Sambail and one of utter malevolence at Prestimion, went slinking away.

"Come, now," Prestimion said. "To the cellar, and I'll let you have a bowl or two of our finest."

Together they descended into the dark catacomb.

"You made reference upstairs to the position I am in," Prestimion said, opening a flask and pouring. He was more tranquil now, and at his ease with the Procurator. "And what position would that be?"

"An indecently uncomfortable one, I would think. Crown

snatched right out from under your nose: makes a man look a fool before fifteen billion people." Dantirya Sambail drank heartily and smacked his lips. "At least you've got your vineyards to support you, though! Fill this again, will you?"

"So you are more trusting now, after the first taste? What if it's a slow-acting poison?"

"Then you and I will go from the world in one and the same hour," said Dantirya Sambail, "for I saw you drink of the identical stuff you gave me. But I never doubted you, cousin."

"Then why Mandralisca?"

"I told you. It is my habit, my ancient custom. Forgive me, cousin," said Dantirya Sambail, looking soulfully blave-eyed at him, all meek and repentant. "If this is poison, it is the finest for flavor the world has ever seen. I pray you give me another draught; for if it doesn't kill me, it will give me keen pleasure." The Procurator laughed again, thrusting his strong-featured face upward into Prestimion's, and grinning a broad savage grin as Prestimion refilled his bowl to the brim. "And where are those three comrades of yours, the spider-legged dandified swordsman whom no one can touch, and the great ape of a wrestler, and the other one, the sneaky little Tolaghai duke? I thought you were never apart from them."

"They've gone off hunting. We had no notice of your coming, you know. But they'll be with us presently. Meanwhile we can talk, kinsman to kinsman, with none of your flunkeys around to listen to us." Prestimion contemplated his bowl a moment. "I look a fool, you said. Is that so? Do I really seem such a fool to all the world, Dantirya Sambail? I was never named Coronal-designate, you know. Korsibar stole the crown, sure enough: but can it be said that he stole it from me?"

"If it please you, cousin, he stole it from the air, then," said Dantirya Sambail. He reached out and helped himself to yet another bowl of wine. Standing close by Prestimion, he seemed to loom, not so much on account of his height as from the massiveness of his torso and the confidence of his spread-legged stance. The pale skin of his heavy-featured face was already turning ruddy and glistening from the drink, making his dusting of orange freckles seem less apparent, and creating an even deeper contrast with his extraordinary violet-hued eyes. But the steadiness of those eyes told Prestimion that the Procurator was still altogether sober, however he might seem affected outwardly by the wine. In a cheerful, almost friendly tone he said, "What are your plans, eh, Prestimion? Will you try to knock Korsibar from his perch, do you think?"

"I had hoped you might advise me on that," said Prestimion smoothly.

"You do have plans, then!"

"Not plans. Intentions. Not intentions, either: *possible intentions.*"

"Which will require a possible army, and powerful possible allies. Here, drink with me, cousin, keep pace, don't leave me to do it all!—Tell me what's in your heart, dear Prestimion!"

"Would that be wise of me?"

"I trusted you with my life when I drank your wine. Speak, and fear nothing, cousin."

"I will be very blunt and plain with you, then."

"Do be. By all means, do."

It was no secret to anyone that Dantirya Sambail was the blackest of scoundrels; but Prestimion had long since learned that one good way to disarm a villain was to open your heart utterly to him. He was therefore resolved to be totally frank with the Procurator.

"Item one," Prestimion said, "I should have been Coronal. There's no one from one end of the planet to the other who would deny that. I am the best qualified candidate. Korsibar is far from that."

"And item two?"

"Item two, Korsibar's done something foul and dark and blasphemous by crowning himself like that. Such deeds inevitably are repaid on high. Perhaps, if luck is with us, he'll undo himself swiftly through his own stupidity and arrogance: a very bad combination, that. But otherwise he will in time bring the anger of the Divine crashing down upon us all, if we allow him to reign unchecked."

Dantirya Sambail said, with a comical blink, "The anger of the Divine, you say? The anger of the Divine? Ah, cousin, and all this time I mistook you for a rational, skeptical man!"

"It's well known I have no use for sorcerers and such-like flummery. To that extent I'm a skeptic; but that doesn't mean I'm godless, Dantirya Sambail. There are forces in the universe that punish evil: this I do believe. The world will suffer if Korsibar's left to go unopposed. My own private ambitions aside, I feel he must be taken down, for the good of all."

"Ah," said the Procurator, lifting his shaggy red brows high. And an instant later said again, as he often did: "Ah.—Is there an item three?"

"Those two are enough. There you have it, within the span of two minutes." Prestimion helped himself to wine, and gave Dantirya Sambail more, when the bowl was held out to him for it. "My plans. My intentions. A profession of my faith, even. What will you do, run back to Korsibar and give him warning, now?"

"Hardly," the Procurator said. "Am I such a treacherous pig, that I'd give testimony against my own kinsman? But you face a perilous hard task here."

"How hard, would you say?" Prestimion asked, staring once more into his wine-bowl and swirling it about. "Give me your most realistic assessment. Shield me from nothing."

"I am ever a realistic man, cousin. Disagreeable, perhaps, but realistic." The Procurator held up his thick-fingered hand

and ticked his points off one by one. "Item, as you would say: Korsibar holds the Castle, which is close on unassailable and has great value in people's hearts all across the land. Item: with control of the Castle goes control of the Castle guard. Item: the army too is with him, for the army is a great headless beast, loyal to whichever man it is that wears the crown, and Korsibar is the one who wears it now. Item: Korsibar is a fine dashing fellow and the general populace seems to admire him. Item: he's been well schooled in Castle protocols and routines all his life. All in all he'll probably make a decent enough Coronal."

"On that last we are not in agreement."

"So I understand. But I'm less given to trusting to the mercy and wisdom of the Divine than you are. I think Korsibar can probably do the job, more or less. He's got such as Oljebbin and Serithorn around him to remind him of the proper way, and crafty little Farquanor's a shrewd asset too, whether you like him or not. That Su-Suheris magus of Korsibar's is another clever architect of strategy, very dangerous indeed. And there's also the sister to reckon with, don't forget."

"Thismet?" Prestimion said, in surprise. "What about her?"

"You don't know? That one's the true force in that family," Dantirya Sambail said, with a flash of his square stubby teeth. "Who was it, do you think, pushed poor blockhead Korsibar into grabbing for the crown in the first place? The sister! The lovely Lady Thismet herself! Whispering in his ear, all the while we were in the Labyrinth, poking him and prodding him and nudging him and chivvying him, filling what passes for his mind with much inflammatory talk of his surpassing virtues and lofty destiny, shoving him onward and onward until he had no choice but to make his move. Ah, she's a fierce one, that sister."

"You have this for a fact?"

The Procurator turned his hands outward in a gesture of

pious sincerity. "I have it on the finest of authority, that is, my own. I overheard them conniving together myself, during the Games. He's as helpless as a grazing blave before her. She drives him like a herdsman, and he goes where she says."

"He's a secret weakling, that I know. But I never knew her to be so strong-willed."

"You never knew her, cousin. She loves Korsibar above all else. Her twin, after all: entwined together in their mother's womb. Would surprise me not, if there were not something incestuous between them, even. But also there's her hatred for you to add to the equation."

Prestimion was unexpectedly stung by that. That Thismet would have loyalty to her brother, and ambitions on his behalf, was no surprise. But loyalty and ambition for the one should not necessarily translate themselves into loathing for the other.

"Hatred—for me—?"

"Did you ever refuse her, Prestimion?"

"I've known her many years. But never in any close way. I admire her beauty and grace and wit, of course, as does everyone else. Perhaps more than most. Nothing's passed between us, though, not ever, of an intimate kind."

"That may be the problem. She may have been saying something to you all along that you've been unwilling to hear. They will hold terrible grudges against a man who does that to them, you know. But be that as it may: those are your obstacles. The world is with Korsibar. You have nothing to your own advantage but your conviction that you are the true and proper Coronal, and your superior intelligence and determination, and, I suppose, your faith that the Divine wants to see you sitting on the throne. Though I must say that in that case the Divine has taken a very strange way of putting you there. If the Divine were more direct in attaining the fulfillment of its will, Prestimion, it would be a duller world, I suppose, but I'd have less difficulty believing in the existence of such great supernatural forces that govern our destinies. Eh?"

"You think I'll fail at gaining the throne?"

"I said only that it would be far from easy. But go, plunge into it, make the attempt. I am with you, if you do."

"You? You're on your way to Zimroel even now to make the way easier for Korsibar!"

"So he's asked me to do. What I will really do there is a different matter."

"Let me understand this. Are you actually offering me a pledge of support?" Prestimion asked, incredulous.

"There's a bond of blood between us, boy. And also love."

"Love?"

"Dantirya Sambail leaned toward Prestimion and smiled the warmest of smiles. "Surely you know I love you, cousin! I see my own beloved mother when I look at yours: they could have been sisters. We are nearly of one flesh, you and I." Those strange violet eyes stared into Prestimion's with incandescent intensity. There was terrible sinister force there: but also that mysterious tenderness. "You are all I would have wanted to be, if I could not have been myself. What joy it would give me to behold you atop the Castle in the place of that ninny Korsibar! And I will do all in my power to put you there."

"What a fearsome monster you are, Dantirya Sambail!"

"Ah, yes, that too. But I am *your* monster, dearest Prestimion." Yet again he refilled his bowl without being asked. "Come sail for Zimroel with me this very hour. Ni-moya will be the base from which you launch your war against Korsibar. Together we'll raise an army of a million men; we'll build a thousand ships; we'll stand side by side as we cross the sea, and we'll march together toward the Castle like the brothers we truly are, and not the distant and sometimes unfriendly cousins the world imagines us to be. Eh, Prestimion? Is that not a wonderful vision?"

"Wonderful, yes." Prestimion chuckled. Coolly he said, "You want to goad me into strife with Korsibar so that he and I will destroy each other, which will leave a clear path to the throne for you. Is that not it?"

"If I had wanted the throne, ever, I would simply have asked Lord Confalume to give it to me when he was tired of sitting on it. I'd have done that long before you were old enough to get your hands all the way around a woman's breasts." The Procurator's face was scarlet now, but his voice was steady; he seemed calm, and merely amused. "Who else was in line for it? That fool of an Oljebbin? Confalume would have put the crown on a Skandar before he gave it to him. But no, no, I had no use for Castle Mount. The Coronal can have that, and I have Zimroel, and we are both content."

"Especially if you can say that the Coronal owes his crown to you, eh?"

"Ah, you impugn me and impugn me, dear Prestimion. You waste too much precious breath attacking my motives, which sometimes in fact are pure ones. Perhaps this good wine of yours muddles your mind. Let us come to basics: you want to be king, and I offer you my help, both as your loving kinsman who would support you in all things, and also out of a powerful conviction that the throne is rightfully yours. The forces at my disposal are not inconsiderable. Tell me here and now: do you accept my offer or refuse it?"

"What do you think? I accept it."

"What a sensible boy. Now, then: will you come with me to Zimroel and create a military base for yourself there?"

"No, that I will not. Once I leave Alhanroel it may not be so easy for me to return. And this is my home; I'm most at ease here. I'll stay here, at least for the time being."

"Whatever way you would have it, then." Dantirya Sambail

smiled broadly and brought one great hand down with a loud clap against the table. "There! Done! It's wearisome hard work, offering you help. Will you feed me, now, at least?"

"Of course. Come."

As they left the cellar the Procurator said, "Oh, and one thing more. The Coronal Lord Korsibar intends to summon you shortly to the Castle to attend his coronation ceremonies."

"Does he, now?"

"I have it from Farquanor himself. Iram of Normork will be carrying the invitation. Perhaps he's already on his way to Muldemar. What will you tell him, cousin, when it comes?"

"Why, that I'll go." Prestimion threw him a quizzical look. "What would you have me do, cousin?"

"To go, of course. Anything else would be a coward's course. Unless, that is, you plan to reveal your breach with Lord Korsibar so soon."

"It's far too early for that."

"Then you have no choice but to go to the Castle, eh?"

"Exactly."

"It pleases me greatly that we're of a mind.—And now, Prestimion: food. No small quantity of it, if you please."

"You have my promise on that, cousin. I know your appetites, I think."


They feasted well at Muldemar House that night, though Prestimion had had more than enough to eat and drink already, these few days, with the guests who had been to him before Dantirya Sambail. But he held his own, and saw the Procurator and his retinue off in good grace the next day, after which he retired to his study with his three companions to assess the meaning of the meetings that had just been held. For hours they spoke, and might have gone on far into the evening without even troubling to have dinner; but then came an interruption, a servant knocking at the door with word for Prince Prestimion.

"Count Iram of Normork is here," he said. "He bears a message for you from the Coronal Lord."

THREE

# THE BOOK OF CHANGES

# 1

Korsibar had been in residence at the Castle for five days before he first brought himself to climb the steps that led to the Confalume Throne.

The throne was his by legitimate right: he had no doubt of that, or hardly any. Now and again, in the night, he awakened in a chilly sweat, having had some new sending of the Lady to unsettle his sleep, or even just a troubled recurrent dream that did not seem to be a sending, in which someone had arisen before him and pointed a jabbing finger and said to him, "Why is your father's crown sitting there above your ears, Prince Korsibar?" But in his waking hours he had no difficulty looking upon himself as king. He had the crown, which he wore some part of every day, so that others would get accustomed to seeing him with it. He garbed himself in a Coronal's robes, green and gold, with ermine trim. When he went to and fro in the halls they all made starbursts to him, and averted their eyes, and said, "Yes, my lord," and "Of course, my lord," to everything he might choose to say.

Yes, he was the Coronal Lord. There could no doubt of it. A little residual surprise over it still lurked in his soul, perhaps: for he had been from the day of his birth simply *Prince* Korsibar with no hope of rising to anything beyond that, and now all of a sudden he was *Lord* Korsibar, and the swiftness and newness of it clung to him. But there was no denying those starbursts, or those averted eyes. He was truly Coronal.

All the same, he somehow refrained from ascending the throne itself, those first four days.

There was a great deal for him to do away from the throne-room. Supervising the transfer of his private quarters, for one thing, from his old suite on the far side of the Pinitor Court to the Coronal's much grander apartments, a virtual palace within the Castle, in the wing known as Lord Thraym's Tower.

Korsibar had often wandered those splendid rooms, of course. But then they had been filled with his father's uncountable hoard of strange and rare things, the little dragon-ivory sculptures that he loved so much and the shimmering statuettes of spun glass and the collections of prehistoric artifacts and the mounted insects, bright as jewels, in their frames, and the massive volumes of esoteric lore and all the rest, the fine porcelains and the incomparable Makroposopos weavings and the cabinet containing silver coins of all the rulers, Pontifex on one side and Coronal on the other, going back to the dawn of time.

None of that was here now, though, for Lord Confalume had known when he went down to the Labyrinth to await Prankipin's death that he was never going to return to Lord Thraym's Tower as Coronal: he had taken many of his collections with him on the journey, and the rest had gone into storage, or into the Castle museum. So Korsibar found the Coronal's rooms bare and strangely forbidding when he entered them for the first time after coming to the throne. He had never noticed, before, how offputting those harsh groins of gray-green stone could seem, how bleak the bare black flagstone floors.

Therefore in these first days he had set about filling the place with things of his own. He had never been much of an acquirer, though. Lord Confalume, in his forty-three years at the Castle, had insatiably collected whatever had struck his fancy, and there had been all the gifts flooding in from every quarter of the world besides.

But by choice and temperament Korsibar owned very little other than his wardrobe of fine clothing and his array of hunting and sporting equipment, his bows and swords and the like. His furniture was commonplace—Thismet had often chided him about that—and of paintings, bowls, carvings, draperies, and the like he had hardly anything at all, and what little there was of it quite ordinary. That needed to be remedied. Living in bare stone rooms of such magnitude as these would be a depressing business. He called for Count Farquanor, who was glad to be of service in almost any capacity, and said, "Find me something to fill this place. Get pieces out of the museum, if you have to. But nothing famous, nothing that will attract envious comment. Let them be decent-looking things, that's all I ask, no eyesores, nothing radical, just pleasant things that will make these rooms look like a place where somebody actually lives."

Farquanor's idea of what constituted an eyesore and what was a decent-looking thing, it seemed, was somewhat different from Korsibar's. So there was a considerable coming and going of furnishings in those first few days, and that took up time.

Then, too, there was the job of becoming familiar with the Coronal's official suite, not as his father's occasional visitor but as the man who actually sat behind the splendid palisander desk with the starburst-like grain in it, and did whatever work was supposed to be done at that desk.

There had not yet been time, of course, for any legislation to be reaching him. The Council had been in suspension all during the period of Prankipin's slow decline, and would remain in abeyance until Korsibar had had time to reconfirm the members that he was holding over and to appoint the new ones that he meant to select. All he had done thus far was to tell Oljebbin that he could go on being High Counsellor.

Sooner or later he would need to ask Oljebbin to step down, and replace him, he supposed, with Farquanor; but there was time for that later.

Still, even if there were no new laws yet for him to read and approve, there were other matters requiring his attention, trivial things, appointments of provincial administrators to confirm, routine proclamations of various local holidays—there were a hundred different holidays a day all over the world, it seemed, this festival in Narabal and this one in Bailemoona and that one in Gorbidit and something else in Ganiboon, and the Coronal had to scribble his name on a piece of paper to make each one official. He did some of that. He received delegations from the mayors of half a dozen of the Inner Cities, too—it was too soon for the delegations from more distant cities to get to the Castle—and listened solemnly as they expressed their confidence in the benefits and wonders that his reign would bring forth.

And also there were the coronation festivities to plan, the games and feasts and such. All that had been given over to Mandrykarn and Venta and Count Iram, but they kept running in constantly to consult him about this matter or that, unwilling so early in the new regime to risk employing their own judgment.

And so on, and so on. Would it be like this all the time, or was this simply the combined effect of the old Coronal's having been away from the Castle for so many months, and the new one needing to perform all manner of new-Coronal tasks?

But at last on the fifth day there came a few open hours; and it occurred to him that this might be a good opportunity to investigate the throne. To try it out for size, so to speak.

He went alone. He knew the way well; he had been present at the building of this place when a boy, had looked on day by day as it took form. A clutter of little rooms that went back to early times at the Castle led up to it, a robing-room of Lord Vildivar's time, a judgment-hall that was said to go back to Lord Haspar. Lord Confalume had planned eventually to replace them with chambers that were more fitting accompaniment for the throne-room beyond. Perhaps I will do that, Korsibar thought. The Coronal always does some reconstruction hereabouts.

Down a shadowy stone-arched passageway, turn left, across a chapel of some sort, turn right, and there it was: the great gold-sheathed ceiling beams, the glowing floor of yellow gurna-wood, the inlaid gems, the tapestries. Everything was shining with an inner light, even in the near-darkness of the vast empty room. And there, against the far wall, rose the Confalume Throne in solitary grandeur, that giant block of ruby-streaked black opal atop the stepped pedestal of dark mahogany. Korsibar stood a time in wonder before it, letting his hand rest lightly on one of the silver pillars that upheld the golden canopy above it. Then he took a step, and another, and another. His legs were quivering a little from his knees to his ankles.

Up.

Turn. Face the hall.

*Sit.*

That was all it took. Climb up, sit down. He placed his arms on the two satin-smooth rests and looked across the way, through the dimness, toward the tapestry of Lord Stiamot accepting the submission of the Metamorphs that hung on the opposite wall.

"Stiamot!" he said. His voice carried easily, echoing in the empty hall. "Dizimaule! Kryphon!" Coronals, ancient ones, great ones.

Then, saying it slowly, enjoying the majestic sound the rolling syllables of his father's name made as they came from

283

his tongue, "Confalume. Con-fa-lume." And then, loudly, resonantly: "Korsibar! *Lord* Korsibar, Coronal of Majipoor."

"Long live Lord Korsibar!" came an answering voice out of the shadows somewhere to his left, astonishing him so much he nearly bolted from the throne.

Korsibar's face flamed scarlet in embarrassment at being overheard in his puerile self-congratulation. He squinted and stared.

"Who—Thismet? Is that you?"

"I saw you go in, and I followed after you." She stepped out into plainer view. "Taking the measure of it, are you? How does it feel, sitting there?"

"Strange. Very strange. But quite acceptable."

"Yes. I would imagine so. Get up and let me try it."

"You know I can't do that. The throne—this is a conse-crated seat, Thismet!"

"Yes. Of course it is. Sit up straighter, Korsibar. You've got your right shoulder lower than your left. That's better. You're the king, now. You have to sit straight. A decent show of majesty, that's what's necessary. —Do you know, I dreamed one night while we were still at the Labyrinth, that I came sleepwalking into the throne-room and found you sitting just like this, all by yourself in the darkness?"

"Did you, now?" Korsibar said, making no great show of interest. She was always dreaming things, Thismet was.

"Yes. Only it was so dark that I didn't recognize you at first. I stood right here, where I am now. And there was a second throne identical to this one, a twin throne, Korsibar, behind me against the far wall where the Stiamot tapestry is now. I made the starburst sign to you; and you pointed across the room to the other throne, and said that that was my seat over there and asked me why I didn't go to it. So I sat down on it and a great light began to shine down from the ceiling, and then finally I could see that it was you on this throne,

wearing the Coronal's crown. And that was when I first understood that you were going to be Coronal."

"A very prophetic dream."

"Yes. And a second throne, Korsibar, one for me! Wasn't
*that* an interesting feature?"

"Dreams, yes, they show us all sorts of unusual things," he
said, in an offhanded way. He stroked the arm-rests again.
"This was something that *I* never dreamed of, sister. I wouldn't
have dared to! But how good it feels to be sitting here.
Coronal! The Coronal Lord Korsibar! Imagine it!"

"Let me try it, Korsibar."

"It isn't possible. It would be blasphemous."

"There was a second throne in my dream, and you told
me to sit on that."

"In your dream, yes," Korsibar said.

# 2

S vor said, fingering the elaborately embellished invitation
that Count Iram had brought, "Then you really mean
to go, Prestimion? You'll actually do this thing?"

"There's no other path I can take," said Prestimion. They
were gathered, the four of them, in Prestimion's shooting-
range on the stable-side of Muldemar House, where he had
been at targets since the departure of Korsibar's envoy two
hours before.

Septach Melayn said to Svor, "The Coronal of Majipoor
invites the Prince of Muldemar to attend the festivities at the
Castle. Forget which Coronal, forget which prince. To refuse
such an invitation would be unpardonable at any time. But to
refuse it now would be virtually an act of war."

"And are we not already at war?" asked Gialaurys. "Were
we not driven away from the Castle by armed men when we
sought peacefully to enter it?"

Prestimion said, "That was before Korsibar had possession.
He was unsure of himself then, and of our intentions. Now
he's firmly in control. He invites the princes of the Mount to
attend him. I have to go."

"And bend the knee before him?" Gialaurys cried. "What
a humiliation, prince!"

"It's humiliating, yes. But no more so than having to slink
away from the Labyrinth by ourselves, when all the rest
accompanied the new Coronal on his glorious journey up the

Glayge." Prestimion, smiling bleakly, ran one finger two or three times along the string of his bow. "The throne has gone to Korsibar. *That* is the true humiliation. All else dangles down from that as amulets dangle from a chain."

Svor said, "As you surely know, I have some little skill at geomancy, Prestimion. I've drawn the runes for this adventure you propose. Would you hear my findings?"

"Hear, yes. Give credence to, probably not."

Svor smiled patiently. "As you choose. The chart," he said, "shows that we would be putting ourselves into peril by going to the Castle at this time."

"Putting ourselves into peril!" cried Septach Melayn, with a great burst of high-pitched laughter. "Four men riding into a castle held by a whole army of our enemies, and you need to draw charts to tell us that the trip's dangerous? Ah, Svor, Svor, what a keen-eyed seer you are! But it's a peril I think can be faced."

"And if he takes hold of us straightaway, and strikes off our heads?" Svor asked.

"Such things are not done," said Prestimion. "But even if they were, Korsibar is not of that sort. Is that what your chart foretells for us, that we lose our heads?"

"Not explicitly. Only great peril."

"We know already that that's so," Prestimion said. "Be that as it may: I must go, Svor. Septach Melayn has said he'll accompany me; and I hope you and Gialaurys will also, despite the gloomy forecasts of your charts. This trip to the Castle may yet prove a death-trap for us, but I think not. And to ignore the invitation is open defiance. The time's not yet come for such a breach with Korsibar."

Gialaurys said, "Oh, defy him, Prestimion, defy him out-right, and let there be an end to this pussyfooting! The Procurator promises you troops. Let us get ourselves out of here, and form a battle line somewhere out in a safe part of Alhanroel, in the plains beyond the Trikkala Mountains or even farther, along the Alaisor coast if that's the best place, and have Dantirya Sambail send us his army there, and we'll march on the Castle and take it, and that will be that."

Prestimion said, laughing, "As simply as that? No, Gialaurys. I don't want to bring war into the world unless there's no other way. This new government has no legitimacy: it'll fall of its own failings. Give Korsibar enough rope, I say, and let him tie the noose around his throat himself. I've waited this long for the throne; I can wait a little while longer, rather than plunging us all into a war that will surely harm winners nearly as much as losers."

"If you are bound on this course," Svor said, his eyes suddenly brightening, "then I have a suggestion."

"Let me hear it, then."

"Korsibar took the crown in the Court of Thrones by having his wizard Sanibak-Thastimoon cast a spell that clouded minds, and when all was clear again, the crown had passed to him and there was no gainsaying it. Septach Melayn was there: his mind was one of those clouded. Very well. What is gained by sorcery can be lost by sorcery. I have a spell taught me by one who knows such things, will reduce Korsibar to a babbling idiot. We go to him at the Castle; stand before him as he sits upon the throne; I say the words and make the movements, and all his capacity is lost, such as it is. When they perceive what has happened—"

"No," said Prestimion.

"There'll be no option but to make you king in his stead."

"No, Svor. No. Even if I believed that such a spell would do the task, do I want it to be said, a thousand years after, that one thief stole the crown from another? If the throne's to be mine, it'll come to me the way it came to Confalume and Prankipin and all those who went before them. Not by witchery, not by fraud."

"Prince, I beg you—"

"A third time, no. And no again." Prestimion lifted his bow and put an arrow in place, and sent it straight to the heart of the target. And another, and a third after that to split the shaft. Then he said, "I pray you, friends, make yourselves ready now for the trip to the Castle, if you plan to come with me. And if you will not go, well, that should not be cause for woe between us. But one way or the other, I must leave you now: I have word that my mother would speak with me before I go."

The Princess Therissa was in her reading-gallery on the third floor of the great house, a little library apart from the formal one downstairs. This was a quiet nook lined on all walls with shelves of dark wood crowded with her favorite books, and furnished with banquettes covered in soft red leather where she was fond of spending long hours during the season of mists, reading by herself or to any of her children who happened to be with her. It was a place much beloved by Prestimion himself.

But when he entered it now his eye took in two immediate strangenesses.

For one, there were some big leather-bound books with iron clasps stacked on the old table in the middle of the room, books that he had not seen in here before but which looked very much like those texts of sorcery and incantation that he had seen so copiously strewn about beside the death-bed of the Pontifex Prankipin. That was a dark sign, that his mother should have given herself over so thoroughly to these writings. For another, the Princess Therissa was not alone. The lank and stoop-shouldered figure of a haggard old white-haired man stood beside her. It was this man who had been pointed out to Prestimion soon after his arrival: Galbifond, his mother's newly hired diviner, he who had been taken on to give advice on the likelihood of rainfall in the vineyard and the proper time for gathering the harvest.

Prestimion remembered him from time past, now. He was a one-time field hand, who had left their employ a few years back and gone off to Stee or Vilimong or some such place. Where he had learned the craft of magery, Prestimion supposed; all very fine, if that was what he desired for himself—but what was he doing here, in his mother's little reading-gallery, for this private meeting between mother and son?

The Princess Therissa said, as he came in, "Prestimion, this is Galbifond. I told you of him: our magus, who is so helpful to us these days."

"I recall him from olden times. He was a picker of grapes then, I think."

Galbifond bowed gravely. "The prince's recollection is extremely acute. That is indeed what I was."

"And now moved up somewhat higher in the world. Well, good for you: a man should strive to improve his place." Prestimion glanced toward his mother. "I see you're even more deeply given to sorcerous matters than I supposed. These great books here are full of spells, are they? The late Pontifex collected such texts also. They lay all around him in his final bedroom."

The princess said, "You would find them instructive reading, Prestimion, if only you took the trouble to look into them. But we can discuss that another time. Tell me: you are determined to go to the Castle, is that correct?"

"Yes, mother, I am determined."

"Do you see no risk in it?"

"There's risk in sauntering down a pretty garden path beneath a sambon-tree that's laden with ripe cones ready to drop. But that doesn't make us go helmeted through the garden. Svor opposes going to the Castle on the grounds that

290

we'll be walking into a trap, and Svor's often right about such things, but nevertheless I mean to overrule him here. I do mean to go, mother. It seems the politic thing to do, to be cordial to Korsibar and not snap my fingers in his face. Do you disagree? Does this wizard of yours have further discouragement for me?"

"See for yourself, and interpret it as you will," said the Princess Therissa.

She nodded to the magus, who produced a broad plain white bowl and poured into it a pale fluid, a watery sort of stuff with a faint pink sheen. He put his hands to the rim of the bowl and said five short words in a language unknown to Prestimion, and then Prestimion's own name, inflected in an archaic grammatical mode that made it sound unfamiliar even to Prestimion; and then he sprinkled a handful of some grayish powder into the pink fluid. It clouded over instantly, so that its surface became like slate.

"If you would look into it, excellence," said the magus Galbifond.

Prestimion stared down into the smooth impenetrable surface. There was a stirring in it, and then a clearing; and suddenly he had a view, as though in a painting hanging on a wall, of a narrow valley, a sizable lake at its center, and armies running to and fro along its shores in great confusion, with the figures of dead and dying men lying scattered all about like so much litter. Everything was in wild disorder; it was impossible for him to make out details, to tell who was fighting against whom, or where the scene was taking place. But it was plainly a scene of terrible slaughter and murderous chaos.

Then the battlefield image faded, and there appeared on the smooth surface of the fluid in the bowl a view of a bleak and forbidding gray landscape, empty, gritty, and drab, with distant hills standing far apart from one another, like isolated jagged teeth rising against the pale sky. That was all, gray against gray. There were no figures in view, no structures, only that awful desolate tract, delineated with marvelous sharpness of detail.

"Quite an impressive trick," Prestimion said. "How do you do it?"

"Look closer, excellence. If you would."

The focus had refined itself to dwell on a narrower segment of the same scene. The hills on the horizon were smaller now, farther away. He saw a sharper depiction of that barren land: reddish soil, a scattering of eroded wedge-shaped boulders like the skeletal remnants of a ruined city, a single lone tree with bare twisted limbs jutting away from the trunk in lunatic angles, as though they had been stuck on at random. A szambra-tree, it was. Trees of that sort, Prestimion knew, grew mainly in the Valmambra Desert of the north, a place where rain scarcely ever fell.

He looked closer yet, and saw a tiny figure trudging across that wasteland toward that single tree: a man nearly spent with fatigue, from the looks of him, one who was forcing himself onward in utter exhaustion, with a supreme effort. His face was not visible; but from the rear he seemed square-shouldered and sturdy, built somewhat low to the ground. His hair was golden, and cut short. He wore a ragged jerkin and bedraggled leather leggings, and carried a pack on his back, and a bow slung beside it.

"I think I know that man," Prestimion said, with a smile.

"As well you should, excellence," Galbifond replied.

"And what am I doing in the Valmambra, then, wandering by myself? It's an unkind place to go strolling in alone."

"You have the look of a fugitive, I think," said the Princess Therissa. "That desert is far to the north of here, on the other side of Castle Mount, and no one enters it willingly. You are fleeing, Prestimion."

As he watched, the sky at the upper end of the bowl turned

blood-red, and darkness began to fall, and great soaring birds of evil aspect came into view, coasting above him. The little man at the center of the image who was himself knelt down against some scraggly bush, as though settling in for the night. Then a second figure appeared, just a dot against the horizon, too small to make out clearly: but it seemed to Prestimion, from the lanky shape and attenuated limbs of him, that this might be Septach Melayn. He came closer; but just then the image went black, and Prestimion found himself staring at nothing at all, a bowl of blue-gray fluid rimmed round by a dull red glow, like that of a dying fire. And then even that was gone and he saw only gray.

"It's a clever trick," Prestimion said again. "I ask you once more, how are these pictures generated?"

Galbifond said, tapping the rim of the bowl, "I believe, excellence, that we behold you here traveling in the direction of Triggoin, which lies beyond the Valmambra. That city is where I learned the art of this bowl: you may learn it also, when you are in Triggoin."

"I am supposed to inquire about how to go about gaining my lost crown, too, when I am in Triggoin," said Prestimion with a wry smile. "My friend Svor had that advice in a dream, that we should inquire into such matters in the city of Triggoin. So it seems from this vision and that one that I am surely bound for Triggoin, eh?"

"As a desperate fugitive," said the Princess Therissa. "After some dreadful battle. This is the future that awaits you if you go to the Castle now. A wanderer in that miserable desert."

"And if I don't go? What future then for me, Galbifond?"

"Good prince, I can show you only what I can show you."

"Indeed. This is the only future I have, is that it? Then I must follow along my path, I suppose."

"Prestimion—"

"It's all set down here for me, mother, by the prophecies

of your very own magus. There's trouble coming, it seems: but even so, it would appear that I'll survive my visit to Korsibar's court, at any rate, because here I am well beyond the Mount, making my way out through the Valmambra. Heigh-ho! It's settled, then. Off I go to the Castle, because I can be certain now that no harm will come to me there. One less thing to worry about. And afterward—afterward—" He looked toward his mother and smiled. "Well, afterward is afterward, eh? One thing at a time."

# 3

The Lady Thismet's private apartments at the Castle were close by the ones where her brother had resided in his days as a prince: just across the Pinitor Court from the innermost sector, looking down from the Vildivar Balconies on the long, narrow reflecting pool that had been built in Lord Siminave's time. Here, amidst all the little luxuries that she had gathered in her busy life of self-indulgences, her velvet hangings and her cushions and divans covered in rare furs, her cases of rings and necklaces set with all manner of precious gems and her wardrobes of the most costly gowns and cloaks and bonnets, Thismet waited for the Lady Melithyrrh to return. She had sent her lady-of-honor an hour before to bring Sanibak-Thastimoon to her; and Melithyrrh had not yet come back.

Then Melithyrrh appeared, alone, with high color blazing in her pale fair cheeks and her cool blue eyes aflame with anger.

"He will be with you presently, my lady," she said.

"Presently? An hour's wait, and he says only *'presently?'* "

"I sat a long while in his antechamber. They said he was holding a meeting, could not be troubled now. I sent word in that it was the Coronal's sister who wished to trouble him, and they made me wait another endless span. And brought back a message to me finally that the magus was deeply pained to cause any distress for the Lady Thismet, but that he was engaged in a conference of the high sorcerers of the realm, and certain conjurations were under way that could not for any reason be interrupted, and he would be at your service in the first moment of his availability thereafter." The Lady Melithyrrh's eyes flared again with fury, and her bosom heaved. "Whereupon," she continued, "I sent one message more, and was so bold as to say that the Lady Thismet was unaccustomed to being left in delay, and would speak sharply with the Coronal Lord her brother if the delay were to become any greater."

"You did well," Thismet said.

"This time I think I put some fear into him. At any rate, the person who was bearing these messages to and fro came back and said that I was to go inside, so that I could see with my own eyes how serious a conjuration was under way. Which I did."

"And was it a mighty working of spells, then?" Thismet asked.

"Of that, I have no knowledge to judge. But certainly it was a grand convocation. This was in Sanibak-Thastimoon's own rooms, where he has all the peculiar devices and machineries of his craft arrayed on level upon level two stories high; and the air in there, my lady, was so thick with blue smoke and the reek of incense that I thought I would choke on it, and I carry it still in every fold of my gown. And what a crowd was in there! Fifty sorcerers, or I miss my count. There were two more of the Su-Suheris kind, and a whole pack of Vroons, and human ones also, those ones of Tidias that wear the tall brass hats, and some great hairy beast of a man bigger even than the Count Farholt, and uglier, and others besides, not only conjurers and diviners who had been in Lord Confalume's court, but new ones, ones I had never seen before and never want to see again, all of them gathered around Sanibak-Thastimoon and chanting some recitation with their hands clasped together about the circle, and loudly crying out sudden strange words. 'Bythois!', they cried, and 'Remmer!', and such as that. And Sanibak-Thastimoon gestured to me as though to say, 'Do you see, Lady Melithyrrh? This is serious business we are involved in here.' So I left. But I have his promise that he will be with you presently, and that as quickly as he is able."

"Well," said Thismet, made a little uneasy by all that she had heard. "He's never been slow to come to me before. I think of him as my special ally, Melithyrrh, the sharer of my inmost secrets. Has something changed, I wonder, now that Korsibar is king?"

"Perhaps not. Perhaps the Su-Suheris loves you as much as before, but was genuinely enmeshed in his wizardries just then, and it would truly have been perilous to break off. I hope so, for his sake and especially yours. Certainly it was a great outpouring of smoke and chanting in there, enough to let loose fifty score frightful demons upon the land, or to bring plague and drought to a dozen continents the size of Alhanroel.—But I must tell you, lady, I have never liked your Su-Suheris, nor any of these chanting mages, in fact. They frighten me. And he in particular seems cold and dangerous."

"Cold, yes. His kind are all like that. But dangerous? He's a friend to me, Melithyrrh. He serves me faithfully and guides me well, so far as I know. I have great trust in him." There came a knocking just then at the door. "Here he is, I think. You see? He came as quickly as he could."

Indeed, it was Sanibak-Thastimoon, who overflowed with apologies for his tardiness and begged the Lady Thismet's forgiveness in a manner altogether unlike him in its abjectness. That made Thismet uncomfortable all in itself. He had been engaged, he said, in casting the great prognosis for the new reign's first year, the grand oracle by which the Coronal's policies would be framed. The Coronal's entire staff of geomancers and seers had been employed in the task; it could not have been interrupted even for the Coronal himself, or great harm would have come to the realm.

"Very well," Thismet said. "So be it: I'm not to take priority over such matters, I suppose. But are you free to talk awhile with me now, Sanibak-Thastimoon?"

"I am completely at your service, lady."

"Tell me, then: do you remember the dream I had at the Labyrinth, of the two thrones in the throne-room?"

"Of course."

"The other day I saw Lord Korsibar go into that room— it was the first time he had been there, I think, since coming back to the Castle—and seat himself on the throne, as though to accustom himself to it. I went in after him. We spoke, for a bit, of his attaining the kingship, and what joy that was. Then I told him of my dream: the second throne, the one he had bade me ascend. He heard me out, but from his manner I saw he was hardly even pretending that my words had any importance. He made no comment at all, except to say that the dreaming mind dreams all sorts of things. I asked him, next, to let me sit on the throne myself; and he told me that was impossible, and we went out of the room. What do you make of this, Sanibak-Thastimoon?"

"Only the Coronal may sit on the Coronal's throne, lady. That is a long-standing custom."

"No one would have known but he and me. Korsibar and I are of one flesh, Sanibak-Thastimoon. We lived in our mother's belly together, wrapped for nine months in each other's arms. Surely he could have allowed—"

"It would have been a blasphemy. No doubt he would have liked to let you mount it; but he feared doing it, and for sufficient reason."

"Yes. He did say it was blasphemous. Let that part of it

pass, then. But what about his ignoring my dream of the second throne?"

"What about it, my lady?"

"Am I to have no power in the realm? Nothing's been said to me about that, not a syllable, since our return from the Labyrinth. I am still the Lady Thismet, with no other rank or title; the difference simply is that I who was the Coronal's daughter am now the next Coronal's sister. But I am nothing and no one in my own right. Nor does the Coronal even seek my advice on matters of state these days, though he did so many times in the first few days after his ascent."

"Perhaps he will again."

"No. He turns only to his men, now. You told me long ago that I was marked for greatness, Sanibak-Thastimoon. You told me that again when you spoke my dream for me in the Labyrinth. What did that second throne in my dream mean, if not that some high post would be set aside for me?"

The Su-Suheris regarded her gravely, in that unreadable, emotionless way of all his race. "When I spoke your dream in the Labyrinth, lady, I cautioned you not to interpret it too literally. I said there is greatness involved in the making of a king, as well as in the being of one. Your brother would not be Coronal today but for your role in urging him onward. You and I both know that."

"And that's all I'm going to have? The knowledge that I've helped to put Korsibar on the throne, and nothing more? No power in my own hands? No post in the government? A life of continued idleness, only?"

"We discussed this in the Labyrinth, my lady. And you acted; and Korsibar is king." The Su-Suheris looked at her blandly, almost indifferently. "I hardly know what to say, lady, more than that."

"You, at a loss for words!"

Sanibak-Thastimoon offered her a double smile that seemed freighted with irony, but nothing else.

"Help me, Sanibak-Thastimoon. I have a good mind; I have a powerful will; I am something other than a mere ornament. I feel that I deserve a place in this government. Help me make that come about."

From him, now, the Su-Suheris shrug: the drawing of the slim forked neck downward upon the chest, the hooking of the six-fingered hands inward on the wrists. His eyes were four gleaming emeralds, as impenetrable as ever. "It is Korsibar that is king, not I, lady. He makes the appointments. What you ask is a radical departure from all custom and tradition."

"Of course it is. But so is Korsibar's coming to the throne. Speak to him. Tell him what I want. Advise him to grant it. You can do that; and he'll listen. You and I are the people he listens to more than anyone in the world; but this is something that I can't ask for myself, not directly. Do it for me. Will you do that, Sanibak-Thastimoon?"

"He is the Coronal Lord, my lady. I can ask; but I can't promise that he will agree."

"Ask, at least," she said. "Ask."

He went out.

To Melithyrrh, Thismet said, "You heard it all. What do you think? Will he help me?"

"This is your special ally, you said? The sharer of your inmost secrets? He shares your secrets, yes: he knows everyone's secrets. But an ally? I think not, lady."

"He said he would speak with Korsibar for me."

"He said he would tell Lord Korsibar what you wanted, that I concede. But I heard no pledge that he would advise Lord Korsibar to grant your request, or that he would do anything at all to bring it about."

"He promised exactly that!"

"No, lady," Melithyrrh said. "You wanted to hear him

promise that, but I was listening also, and I heard nothing of that kind. He said he would ask. That was all: that he would ask. He also declared that what you desire goes against all custom and tradition. He'll do nothing to help you, this ally of yours. Trust me on that."

Thismet was silent a long while, replaying in her mind her conversation with the Su-Suheris, searching and failing to find the assurances that in fact she understood now were not there.

Then at last she said, beginning to pace now around the room, "What should I do, Melithyrrh?"

"There are other sorcerers. I think this one is lost to you: I think he is entirely Korsibar's creature now that Korsibar is Coronal."

"This is painful, if it's so. I've thought of Sanibak-Thastimoon as being as loyal to me as he is to my brother."

"That may have been the case once. But no longer, I think. His loyalty is with the Coronal. He'll serve you also, yes, but not against Korsibar's interests." Melithyrrh was deep in thought a moment. "Do you know the Vroon, Thalnap Zelifor?"

"Prince Gonivaul's wizard, you mean?"

"He's been in Gonivaul's service, yes. But the Grand Admiral is famed for his niggardly way with money. Thalnap Zelifor's been sniffing about the Castle for a new patron for a long while, now. Came to one of Korsibar's people, Count Venta, I think; but was turned away, out of Venta's dislike of Vroons. Came to me afterward, to ask if you'd hire him. But I sent him away also."

"You never told me that."

"Was of no importance, my lady. At that time you were deep in love with the wizardry of Sanibak-Thastimoon: why hire another? But now the case is altered. The Su-Suheris is merely a conduit, passing your secrets on to your brother: do you see that, lady?"

"Perhaps. Perhaps." She picked up a handful of her rings, put them down, picked them up again. Her fingers closed tight about them.

Melithyrrh said, "In any conflict between the Coronal and the Coronal's sister, Sanibak-Thastimoon will inevitably take the Coronal's side. There is no other way for him. No appeal will sway him; no bribery will buy him. You need a wizard of your own, one who owes no loyalty elsewhere."

"And you think this Vroon is the right one?"

"His abilities in the art are second to none, so it's said. It isn't only spells: who can say what value the casting of spells really has? But there's more to sorcery than spells. The Vroons have powers of mind that exceed all others. They say he's even built a sort of machine that allows him to see right into people's souls. And apart from that, he knows everyone, has his nose everywhere."

"Vroons have no noses," said Thismet, laughing. "Only those horrible beaks."

"You understand my meaning. I'll go to him, if I may. Set forth your cause to him. Enlist him in your service, and offer him good enough pay so that he won't be tempted to sell what he learns from you to Lord Korsibar. May I do that, lady?"

Thismet nodded. "Do it, yes. Hire him for me. Bring him to me straightaway. Oh, Melithyrrh, Melithyrrh, I want so much to be a queen!"

# 4

And now atop Castle Mount it was the third day of the joyous coronation festival. Feasting and celebration and the pleasures of the gaming-fields were the tasks of the moment for the knights and lords of the Castle.

The spirit of these games was entirely different from that of the ones that had lately been held in the Labyrinth while the old Pontifex was dying. Those other games had taken place in the strange and dark and mysterious subterranean enclosure that was Pontifex Dizimaule's Arena, at a time of worldwide tension and uneasiness; but these games of Lord Korsibar's coronation were being staged on the broad sunny greensward of Vildivar Close, just below the Ninety-Nine Steps, where there was a splendid view of the topmost reaches of the Castle and the great arching brilliant blue-green vault of the open sky beyond. And they were meant as a happy festival, a brave celebration of new beginnings instead of the marking of an end, with drums and trumpets and jugglers and tumblers and fireworks by night, and laughter and delight and good hot sunshine by day, and plenty of strong wine flowing all the while, both day and night.

A towering grandstand had been erected along three sides of the Close, with a splendid high seat for the Coronal Lord Korsibar in the front row at the center of everything, an imitation in lustrous gamandrus-wood of the Confalume Throne within. On the opposite side of the courtyard, facing it directly, was a second throne-like structure of equal height and grandeur for the use of the Pontifex Confalume, who had come to the Castle the day before from the Labyrinth to attend the coronation of his own son, as no Pontifex had ever done before him. And on the third side, the one to the left of the Coronal's throne, was yet a third great seat, this one belonging to the newly installed Lady of the Isle of Dreams, the Coronal's mother Roxivail, who had this very morning arrived from her tropical retreat on the isle of Shambettirantil in the Gulf of Stoien.

The Lady Roxivail had not been present at the Castle for more years than anyone could recall, nor had anyone ever expected to see her there again. But here she was now, a small, dark woman whose great beauty was still altogether untouched by the years, a magnificent figure in her extraordinary gown of dazzling white silk with flaring sleeves and trim of deepest purple, to whom all eyes were magnetically attracted. She sat with royal grace looking serenely toward her royal husband and her royal son. The three Powers of the Realm gathered here this day, and all of the same family: who could have imagined such a thing?

Behind the seats of the Powers were those of their counsellors and aides: for Korsibar, his High Counsellor Duke Oljebbin, carried over from the old regime, and the senior peers Gonivaul and Serithorn as well, but also the new great men of the kingdom, Farquanor, Farholt, Mandrykarn, Navigorn, Count Venta of Haplior. The sorcerer Sanibak-Thastimoon was close by Korsibar too, whispering occasionally in his ear out of one mouth or the other, and several of the other sorcerers of the Castle staff.

A much smaller group of aides flanked the Pontifex Confalume, for he had been accompanied from the Labyrinth only by the venerable Orwic Sarped, who had been the late Pontifex Prankipin's Minister of External Affairs and for the moment was still in that office, and by the iron-faced Heszmon Gorse of Triggoin, who for many years had been Confalume's chief magus. No replacement yet had been named for Kai Kanamat, the High Spokesman of the Pontificate under Prankipin, who had resigned his post the day after Prankipin's death, or for most of the other high Pontifical officials of the previous regime. Rumor at the Castle had it that Confalume was trying to persuade Duke Oljebbin to transfer himself to the Labyrinth and become his High Spokesman, but that Oljebbin had thus far resisted the invitation.

As for the Lady Roxivail, no one had accompanied her who had any connection with the administration of the Isle of Sleep. Only her own ladies-of-honor and mages sat beside her. There had not been time for her to make the journey to the Isle and accept the reins of power from the outgoing Lady Kunigarda, nor to designate hierarchs from the Lady's staff to take part with her in the coronation ceremonies.

Indeed, much was being whispered about whether the Lady Kunigarda would gracefully surrender those reins at all, which she had held so long. The hierarch Marcatain, who had been her representative at the Labyrinth for the funeral ceremonies of Prankipin, had returned to the Isle immediately upon Prankipin's death, instead of going up to the Castle for the coronation of Korsibar. That was taken by some as a sign that the Lady Kunigarda did not plan to recognize Korsibar's accession to the throne, nor would she give up her own Ladyship to a successor whose appointment she regarded as illegitimate. But there had been no public statements concerning any of this.

Various other great nobles of the realm and intimates of the new Coronal had choice seats not far from the three Powers and their immediate staffs: Duke Kanteverel of Bailemoona, Earl Kamba of Mazadone, Count Iram of Normork,

Dembitave of Tidias, Fisiolo of Stee, Prince Thaszthasz who governed in rainy Kajith Kabulon, and many another.

Among this group, too, was the Lady Thismet, who had sat through the first two days of the festival with a notably glum expression on her lovely face, one that had not gone unremarked by the more keenly perceptive onlookers. Her lady-of-honor Melithyrrh sat to one side of her and Thalnap Zelifor, the little Vroon wizard newly hired into her service, on the other, and she said almost nothing to anyone else, nor smiled nor seemed in any way gracious, even when Lord Korsibar himself came by, radiant with his new regal glory, to offer her a bowl of shimmering golden wine. "You would think," said Kanteverel of Bailemoona to Kamba of Mazadone, "that Prestimion had become Coronal and not Korsibar, the way Thismet's sulking!"

"Perhaps she wanted a grander seat," Earl Kamba said. "There's her brother high up on a nice throne, and her father has one too, and her mother, even: but here she is sitting with the ordinary ruck of dukes and princes like all the rest of us."

"The other three are Powers of the Realm," Duke Dembitave of Tidias pointed out. "What's she compared to that? A princess, only, and that only by courtesy of her father's rank."

"What I think," said the blunt and always irreverent Count Fisiolo of Stee, "is that what's bothering her is the way her mother looks. Roxivail was last seen around here—what?—twenty years ago. Thismet probably figured she must be a withered old hag by now, no competition at all. And then she shows up, and she looks more like Thismet's sister than her mother, and she's wearing a fancier dress than Thismet besides."

And they all laughed, for the Lady Thismet's vanity was well known to every one of them.

At one remove farther from the central area were the seats reserved for high municipal officials. The mayors of most of the Fifty Cities of the Mount were there, and those of some of the more distant cities, ones in the Glayge Valley and the Stoienzar Peninsula. But the outermost cities of Alhanroel— such places as Sefarad and Alaisor, Michimang, Bizfern, and all those on the far side of Mount Zygnor—were only sparsely represented, and of the immense population of the great metropolises of far-off Zimroel there were no representatives at all; the coronation had been announced so swiftly that there was no way for anyone from the western continent to reach the Castle in time.

Missing also from the coronation festivities were Dantirya Sambail, who was said to be on his way to Ni-moya bearing official word that a new government had taken power, and Prince Prestimion of Muldemar, who had been invited but had not yet appeared. On this the third day of the celebration, just as the games of hammer-toss and hoop-hurdling had ended and the field was being made ready for the first jousting, Farquanor went clambering up to the Coronal's high seat and said to Korsibar, "He's here at last, with his three friends. Arrived an hour ago; went straight to his old apartments."

"Does he know the games are in progress?"

"He does, my lord. Is planning to be in attendance soon."

"Send a formal escort for him. Guard of honor, banners, princely regalia, everything. And clear a seat for him, for the four of them, close by us." Korsibar glanced around to his left. "There. Those seats are open, just beyond Venta and Mandrykarn. Put them there."

"That is Kanteverel's seat, lordship, and Thaszthasz's, I think."

"Sit them somewhere else today, if they show up. Prestimion's to be treated with soft gloves, do you understand? An honored guest. Every courtesy."

Farquanor saluted and left. Not long after, a stir in the crowd signalled the appearance at the gateway to the games field of Prince Prestimion, flanked by Gialaurys and Septach Melayn, with Duke Svor a short distance to the rear. All four were distinctively clad for this special occasion, Prestimion in golden leggings tight as scabbards, and an ivory jacket worked with silver threads, over which he wore an open cloak of purple velvet. The other three were nearly as splendid. An escort of a dozen strapping men of the Coronal's guard, five of them Skandars and the rest human, formed a living wall about them as they marched onto the field and were shown to the seats that Farquanor had set aside for them.

Korsibar leaned forward and across the frame of his throne-like chair, smiling jovially, waving to Prestimion, calling out to him as to his dearest friend, telling him how pleased he was to see Prestimion here this day, how much he had regretted the absence of his company on the first two days of the games.

Prestimion replied with a cool formal smile and a few words of gratitude for the welcome he had received. He offered Korsibar no starbursts.

Korsibar made note of that. He made note also that his sister, in her place across the way, was staring at Prestimion with terrible strange intensity, as though he were some demon incarnate who had materialized just now for the sole purpose of blighting the coronation festivities. She sat forward in her seat, her gaze fixed, jaw set, shoulders hunched rigidly. It was as if she had eyes for Prestimion alone, no one but Prestimion.


Three jousting contests had been scheduled for that afternoon: Kovac Derocha of Normork and Belditan of Gimkandale against Yegan of Low Morpin and Duke Oljebbin's middle son, Alexiar of Stoien, and then two young brothers, counts of the Mavestoi line, contending with the grizzled old Duke of Sisivondal and his son, and after them a bout pitting Lethmon Yearlock of Sterinmor and his formidable one-eyed brother

Grayven against unruly Viscount Edgan of Guand and his kinsman Warghan Blais, the Laureate Master of the Twelve Lakes. Kovac Derocha and Belditan had already come out onto the field on their mounts and were going up and down to accustom themselves to the animals, and Yegan and Alexiar could be seen at the paddock, getting ready to emerge.

But then the ponderous figure of Count Farholt came between Korsibar and the sunlight, and the huge man said, "My lord, I have a request to make."

"Make it, then."

"Gialaurys is here. I challenge him to single combat."

There was a wild look of fierce bloodthirsty murderousness on Farholt's face. Korsibar, his mind hearkening back to that grim wrestling-match in the Labyrinth, said, glowering, "These are happy celebrations, Farholt, not occasions for blood-vengeance. We'll have no unseemly gore spilled on this field today."

"My lord, I want only to—"

"No. We forbid it."

Farholt, his eyes burning with rage, turned to Sanibak-Thastimoon, who sat nearby, and cried, "I beg you, reason with him, my lord magus! He denies me out of hand, and why? Gialaurys is my enemy. I ask for him."

"The Coronal Lord has spoken," said the Su-Suheris dispassionately. "You may not do it, then."

"Why? Why?" Farholt's face had reddened. He sputtered and spat. "Here's a chance for us to be rid of that ape for good! Let me have him! Let me, my lord!"

"There will be no carnage here today," replied Korsibar, letting his annoyance now become more apparent. "Sit down, Farholt."

Sanibak-Thastimoon said, when Farholt had gone off still grumbling to his place, "You did well, lordship. No one wants to see those two face each other again so soon. But he's right that Gialaurys is an enemy, and not only Farholt's enemy. There's danger in that one for our entire cause."

"Danger? How so? All goes well for us here."

"At the moment. But Gialaurys is far more warlike than his master. He seethes with resentment over the taking of the crown; and has the capacity to stir Prestimion's anger, and perhaps to drive him one day into rebellion, even. Let me deal with him, my lord."

"What have you in mind?"

"Single combat's the way, as Farholt says. We can rid us of him most innocently. There can be accidents in a joust, that look not at all like murder."

"You heard me say, no carnage here today!"

"Not at Farholt's hand, no. Would look like open war, Farholt to strike down Prestimion's man before Prestimion's eyes, after what passed between Farholt and Gialaurys at the Labyrinth. But I have a man will do the work, and make it look all accidental, and no one the wiser." Sanibak-Thastimoon indicated a magus sitting with the group of sorcerers near the front railing of the stands, a man of Zimroel, Gebel Thibek by name, big and long-limbed and sturdy, but not known to Korsibar as a sporting man in any way.

Frowning, Korsibar said, "Him? That's no jouster there, that's one of your mages! Gialaurys will throw him halfway to Suvrael with one swipe of his lance."

"He has his skills, my lord."

Korsibar contemplated the tips of his fingers. "Is this wise, Sanibak-Thastimoon?"

"Your situation is more precarious than you realize, my lord. And this Gialaurys is one great reason for that. Allow me to remove him."

On the field, the first match had begun. Korsibar hesitated a long while, giving his attention outwardly to the contestants before him, observing Kovac Derocha and Yegan of Low

Morpin circling one another on their frisking mounts, and Belditan of Gimkandale touching lances testingly with Alexiar of Stoien. Then he looked up at the Su-Suheris. "Whatever you think is best," he said.

The unscheduled bout of single combat was inserted into the day's program in the third position, following the contest between the two Mavestoi counts and the father-and-son pair from Sisivondal. Gialaurys, taken by surprise by the challenge from a man he did not know, and not in any way garbed for jousting just now, needed time to return to his quarters for the proper costume. But he accepted the invitation readily enough, practically in the same breath as it was offered. To Prestimion, who expressed some uneasiness over the suddeness and unexpectedness of all this, Gialaurys said, "I've been idle long enough, my friend. Here's a chance to show all these Korsibar-loving folk here that I know which end of the lance to hold."

He went off to change, and to select a mount from the ones in the royal stables and to test a few weapons for strength and balance.

The first contest still was under way. Kovac Derocha of Normork had unseated his man, and stood to one side, waiting for the outcome of the bout between Belditan and Alexiar. If Belditan should fall, Kovac Derocha would take on Alexiar. But it looked as though neither man was capable of throwing the other. Five times they came down the field toward one another, and five times they clashed lances and went lurching onward, still atop their mounts. It was not a pretty display. Prestimion, growing restless, left his place and went across to speak with a few of the lords he had not seen since the Labyrinth, Kamba and Fisiolo and some others.

Duke Svor, remaining in his seat next to Septach Melayn, turned to him and said, "This challenge troubles me."

"And me also. Who is this Gebel Thibek? He was sitting among the mages before he came up here to challenge Gialaurys."

"A magus is what he is, my friend. I know of him: one of Sanibak-Thastimoon's following."

"I thought we jousted only with men of breeding here."

"A high-born magus, then, perhaps," said Svor. "If there be such a thing. But it's not this man's ancestry that troubles me. It's his skill."

"There's none better at jousting than Gialaurys."

"I'm not speaking of skill at jousting."

"Ah," said Septach Melayn. "You think there's treachery here?"

Svor's eyes took on a sly brightness. "We are among honorable folk, are we not? But it's always good to be ready for the unexpected." And Septach Melayn nodded his agreement to that, and smiled, and sat forward on his seat.

Prestimion returned a moment later. He seemed easier of mood than he had been a little while before. "All the talk is of Roxivail and Thismet over there," he said, settling into his seat. "How lovely the Lady Roxivail looks, and what a sour face the Lady Thismet is wearing today."

"She has a good magus, the Lady Roxivail does," Septach Melayn said, with a wink. "Beauty such as that at an age such as hers comes out of the conjurer's bag of tricks, wouldn't you say? Why, she's forty, at least. Forty-five, even."

"Somewhat more than that, I hear," said Svor. "But she's had nothing to do, all those years down in sultry Shambettirantil, other than to take the beauty-waters and bathe in the shining beauty-mud and, yes, I suppose, have spells of juvenescence said over her day and night." Svor laughed somberly. "I can imagine the dreams she'll bring, when she takes over as Lady of the Isle! A face like that, stealing into your sleeping soul. Those eyes—that wanton smile—"

"And then behold the daughter," Prestimion said. "That angry glare of Thismet's! How it twists and distorts her face! The way she stares and stares, as if she can't forgive her mother for looking that way. Or for being here at all, I suppose. But what did they think, when they stole the crown for Korsibar? Roxivail would be Lady of the Isle, then, and would have to come forth from her own little distant island: did that not occur to them?"

"It seems to me," said Septach Melayn, "that the Lady Thismet has mainly been looking toward you, Prestimion, and not to her mother at all. See, she's staring this way now! And not with a loving face, no, not loving at all, eh, Prestimion? A troublesome woman, with troublesome thoughts behind that pretty brow."

A little roughly Prestimion said, "Does she fear I'll reach across and snatch the crown from her beloved brother's head as we all sit here? Not that the thought hasn't crossed my mind, but—ah, look, here's Gialaurys, now!"

The big man, clad in a jousting costume, came riding out on the field just then astride a racing-mount so spirited and fierce that it seemed more like a fire-breathing demon than any sort of beast of burden. Its legs were long and slender, its narrow back was razorsharp; its sleek hide was a bright purple verging on red, and its yellow red-rimmed eyes were devilish ferocious ones. Behind him rode the magus Gebel Thibek on a sturdy-looking but far less fiery steed, one better suited, perhaps, for a long journey over difficult country than for the rapid charges and reversals of a joust.

Gialaurys seemed to have the measure of his animal, though any lesser mountsman would very likely have been thrown in his first moments. He sat with confidence toward the front of the natural saddle that interrupted the mount's narrow spinal ridge and his legs were dug deep into its barrel of ribs, and he held himself upright, balanced well, with his long lance resting lightly in the crook of his arm. The mount, though plainly indignant at being ridden at all, seemed to recognize Gialaurys's mastery and to give him some respect for it.

Whoever had raised this animal had bred a fiendish one of volcanic energy and hair-trigger temperament. Racing-mounts, like the slower, stockier breeds of their species used for ordinary transportation and hauling, were artificial creatures designed for human convenience long ago, through usage of ancient science not very different from witchcraft and now wholly forgotten. Though the art of making them was lost, such synthetic things as mounts were able to perpetuate themselves through normal reproduction, as natural animals do, and various types had arisen by selective breeding. Of these the racing-mount was the finest kind, reserved entirely for the use of the lordlings of Castle Mount. But there could not have been many capable of handling this one.

Gialaurys and Gebel Thibek faced each other from opposite sides of the field, saluted, and swept forward on their first charge. The speed of Gialaurys's mount was so much greater than that of the other man's that they came together nearly two thirds of the way down toward Gebel Thibek's end of the field. As was customary, they offered no attack on this first pass, merely touching lance-tips and continuing on. But then both men spun about; as they made their return passes Gialaurys raised his lance in his familiar pattern of thrust; his mount was moving so swiftly that all its hooves seemed to travel off the ground at once. Gebel Thibek, waiting for the attack, appeared slow and uncertain, and held his lance clumsily, its sharp tip drooping.

"Here it comes," Prestimion said. "Thrust and overthrow."

But no. Gialaurys brought his powerful lance forward and downward, aiming it at the dark circle at the center of Gebel

Thibek's padded leather jerkin. And then something miscarried: at the last instant Gebel Thibek brought his own lance up in a surprising parry, sliding it smoothly along the shaft of Gialaurys's and deflecting it so that it went harmlessly past him.

"How was that possible?" Septach Melayn asked, astonished. "Is there some sorcery at work here?"

"Unexpected skill, I'd say," replied Prestimion. "The man's no petty jouster. I wonder why we've never heard of him."

Another pass was already under way. Once more Gialaurys guided his mount with supreme effectiveness; once more Gebel Thibek's defensive movements appeared awkward and inept. And yet when the two men came together, this time in mid-field, Gialaurys's lance wavered strangely in its thrust and his opponent brushed it easily aside with a loud contemptuous thwack that brought cheers from the men about Korsibar and gasps of amazement from Prestimion and Septach Melayn.

"Something is very much amiss here," Prestimion murmured.

Indeed there was. Gialaurys was sitting oddly now, canted off to one side, dangling nearly halfway out of his saddle. He held his lance much too far down its handle, as though he had never held one before. And he had surrendered some of his control over his high-spirited mount, which was cantering about in finicky strides as if thinking of attempting to throw its rider.

"He carries himself like a drunken man, suddenly," Septach Melayn said.

"Not Gialaurys," said Prestimion. "He would never have gone out there with wine in him."

"It's not wine that does this to him," said Svor. "Do you see, below the helmet, the magus's lips are moving? He's speaking to Gialaurys. Weaving some spell, perhaps? Why did

315

they send a magus to challenge him, and not someone like Farholt, unless they planned to use spells?"

Gialaurys now was riding away, back to his end of the field—badly, drunkenly. He looked like a buffoon, as he had never been seen to look before. From the grandstand on the other side the sound of raucous jeering could be heard. Gibel Thibek, taking his place in mid-field, called out Gialaurys's name three times, and three times jabbed his lance toward him in the air, the signal for his opponent to turn and charge. It was apparent that Gialaurys was struggling with his mount, trying to swing it about and finally succeeding.

Once more they rode toward each other. Gialaurys shook his head as if to free it from a shrouding of mist. He barely managed to parry Gebel Thibek's thrust, which was heading for his heart: he offered none of his own.

Those lances came to sharp points. A blow in the wrong place, or one not properly parried, could be fatal. And Gialaurys seemed suddenly incapable of defending himself. His condition was worsening steadily: he had no grip on himself. Another moment and he would topple to the ground without even being struck, from the way things looked.

Prestimion began to rise. "This has to be stopped," he said, looking across to Navigorn, who was Master of the Games today, and signalling for his attention. "Gialaurys is in no shape for this match." But Navigorn was looking the other way.

Duke Svor's hand caught Prestimion's wrist.

"Look there," he said.

Septach Melayn, in three quick leaps, had descended from the grandstand and was down on the field, roaring and staggering about like a man who has drunk six flasks of wine in five minutes and hopes to find a seventh. His sword was out; he was waving it wildly about. The crowd began to yell.

At the sight of that bare steel shaft Gialaurys's mount balked and reared, all but throwing him. His lance fell from his grasp but he hung on somehow to the mount's heavy mane as the high-strung animal ran frantically to and fro. Gebel Thibek's more stolid steed held its ground. The magus called out angrily to Septach Melayn to quit the field, to which Septach Melayn replied with coarse drunken insults and a lunging thrust of his sword through the empty air. Gebel Thibek responded with a powerful jab of his lance, one plainly meant not to warn but to kill. If Septach Melayn had not leaped aside with the utmost agility, he would have been skewered through the breast.

"What?" Septach Melayn cried, thick-voiced, still capering like one who has lost his senses. "Is this a demon here atop this mount? Yes! Yes, a demon!" He snatched up Gialaurys's fallen lance and swung it in a wide lateral circle, catching Gibel Thibek under one arm and knocking him to the ground. "A demon!" Septach Melayn cried again. "It must be exorcised!" The sorcerer, rising uncertainly to his feet, backed away from him, making signs and incantations against him. But Septach Melayn, grinning like a madman, came running forward in quick hopping skips and without breaking stride put his sword through Gebel Thibek's middle so that it jutted forth six inches out of his back.

A great shout of amazement and horror went up. Guardsmen began to run out on the field. Septach Melayn, reeling back and still moving spraddle-legged like a drunkard, looked down wide-eyed at his sword and his sword-arm as though they had struck Gebel Thibek down of their own accord. He made his way through the confusion on the field and, reaching the side of the grandstand, cried out, looking up at Korsibar, "My lord! My lord, it was an accident—forgive me, my lord, I thought this man was some demon putting an enchantment on my friend—"

Then Prestimion was on the field beside him, with his arm thrown over Septach Melayn's shoulders, leading him off. "The filthy wizard!" Septach Melayn muttered, speaking into

Prestimion's ear alone, and no drunkenness in his tone now. "Another moment and he'd have put that weapon of his right through Gialaurys, as I did with him!"

"Come. Hurry," Prestimion said.

And he too looked up at Korsibar, whose face was stern and grim and black with anger. Prestimion managed to don an expression of shock and anguish. "My lord—how terrible this is—he's had far too much wine, his mind is altogether in a fog. He had no idea what he was doing. All he saw was his friend in great peril, or so it seemed to him."

"Forgive me!" Septach Melayn moaned again, in the most piteous quavering voice that anyone had ever heard from him. "I beg you, lord, forgive me! Forgive!"

# 5

fterward, in Prestimion's apartments, Gialaurys said
furiously, "By the Lady, I should have killed him
straightaway at that first pass, instead of politely
touching lances with him. But I was not trained to do such
slaughter in the name of sport, and how was I to know what
scheme he had in mind? Though I learned soon enough, by
the Lady! This was the wrestling-match of the Labyrinth all
over again, only with a deadlier weapon than Farholt's arms
and hands, this time. When I approached him at the second
pass he was already whispering his spells at me. And then I
thought, it is all over with me, my mind is clouding over and
my strength is gone, I will perish here in front of everyone
and they all will think I had forgotten all my skills since last I
jousted. I would have killed him, if I could. But I was too
much befogged by him."

He was trembling and white-faced with anger. Prestimion
handed him a flask of wine, and he drained it without bothering to pour any into a drinking-bowl, and tossed it aside.

Svor said, "To go up against a magus in a contest like that
was madness. I should have warned you to refuse."

"No one ever listens to your warnings, Svor," said Septach
Melayn lightly. "It is your fate. But at least that one will cast
no spells on us tomorrow."

"This was all of it madness," Prestimion said darkly. "The
accepting of the challenge and the killing of the magus both.

You're lucky not to be in the Castle dungeon tonight, Septach Melayn."

"He gave me provocation, after all. Everyone saw that. He aimed the lance at me to kill, when I was only a silly drunkard disrupting the match. Who could deny it was self-defense when I struck him down?"

"You went out there intending to kill him," Prestimion said.

"Yes. So I did. But he was there to kill Gialaurys. Would you have preferred that he had?"

Prestimion opened his mouth to reply, but no words came, and he closed it again.

Gialaurys said, "It would surely have been my death. He was chanting words at me, binding me in the grip of demons— I could barely see, it was all I could do to stay atop my mount—" He reached out for another flask of wine. "I knew I would die. But I couldn't make myself run away. I felt no fear, only anger at having been gulled this way. It was their plan to kill me. If Septach Melayn hadn't gone out to interfere, I'd be with the Source tonight."

"Whose plan?" asked Prestimion sharply. "Korsibar's, you think?"

Gialaurys shook his head. "You keep telling us he's an honorable man. Steals the throne, yes, but a man of honor all the same. Well, then, he loves us all: let us say that. It was Sanibak-Thastimoon who sent the magus against me. And next, I vow, he'll be trying his witchcraft against you."

"Ah, just let him try!" Prestimion said, laughing.

"He will! Do you see how the Castle is full of sorcerers for these games? The smell of incense-smoke is everywhere, and wherever you turn someone's chanting in a corridor. Did you not see that, as we were coming in? He's got half of Confalume's mages still on his payroll, and all of his own, and new ones we've never seen before. This is to be a reign of wizardry, Prestimion! This vast host of sorcerers is here at the Castle to frighten and intimidate anyone who might say Korsibar's not the legal king: and this was the first blow against the four of us, who are Korsibar's known enemies. The next will be aimed at you, my friend. Let us get ourselves from here at once."

"Go, then," Prestimion said. "I won't keep you, not any of you. You need not stay. But I must."

"While spells are woven against your life?"

"Spells! What do I care about spells?" Prestimion cried. "Oh, Gialaurys, Gialaurys, must I coddle your foolishness forever? It's all mere silly noise, these incantations. There are no demons! There is no witchcraft!"

"And what happened to me on the jousting field, then? What was that, a sudden sunstroke?"

"There's such a thing as hypnotic illusion," said Prestimion, "and that was what the magus worked against you. You were half ready to believe any words of his, anyway: more than half ready. So he used your own credulity against you, and hypnotized you to make you feel feeble and confused."

Gialaurys butted his clenched fists together and let his breath run from him in a sigh of frustration. "Call it hypnosis, call it magic—ah, what difference do the words make? He took control of my mind. As was their plan. Oh, Prestimion, you are so clever, and I am so dim of wit, or so Septach Melayn likes to tell me, and yet everything seems clear to me that you and he refuse to see. There is magic in this world, and it works, and you must believe that or die!"

"Must I, now?" said Prestimion calmly. "We have fought this battle before, you and I."

Gialaurys closed his eyes and drew a deep breath or two. Then he said, more evenly, "Let it pass. Believe or not, as the spirit impels you. But grant me at least that we are in danger here. Why was Septach Melayn not arrested for killing a man on the jousting field? Not because it was in self-defense, but because Korsibar knew that he had sent the magus out there to murder me, and feared that in any investigation it would come out! I say again, we should quit this place tonight."

"We are in no danger so long as we keep our wits about us," said Prestimion stubbornly. "How can I leave here on the very first day of my arrival? The thing is not possible. I owe Korsibar the courtesy of attending these events: he is Coronal, however he came by it, and this is his coronation time, and I am a prince of his nobility. But I tell you once more: you need not stay, none of you." He looked at each of them close and hard. "Go, if you like. Go."

"Say it once more and there'll be a brawl," said Septach Melayn. "We came here with you. We'll stay with you. At least I will, for one.—Gialaurys?"

"It would be wisest to go, I think. But I will stay, if you and Prestimion do."

"And you, Svor?" Septach Melayn demanded.

The small man ran his hand carefully through the close-knit curls of his beard. "This place is unsafe for us, as I told you before we ever came, and as today's events confirm. But we were none of us born to live forever. I'll stay also, Prestimion, though not with much joy in the thought."


The Lady Thismet and Thalnap Zelifor walked together on the terrace outside her rooms, where a golden view of the slopes below the Castle opened out magnificently to the east. The sky was mottled and cloud-strewn this day as the long afternoon gradually descended toward night, and dull thunder boomed faintly somewhere downslope, where a storm must be going on above one of the Guardian Cities, or even farther below. Here, though, the air was mild and untroubled. Thismet strolled slowly, adjusting her pace to that of the diminutive

Vroon, and now and again glanced down at the small creature as though he were some amusing pet trailing along at her ankles. But she knew he was something quite other than that.

She had told him everything. Now she depended on him to show her the proper path to follow. This hideous little alien *thing* no heavier than a mass of feathers, so tiny it could almost stand on the palm of her hand, with its horde of writhing little limbs and its ugly head and fierce little curving beak and those two huge yellow eyes whose pupils were eerie horizontal black stripes: her mentor now, her only savior.

"You've looked at the horoscope I had from Sanibak-Thastimoon?" she asked.

"Not only looked at it, but studied it top and bottom and sideways. Not only did that, but cast the runes for you myself, from the numbers you gave me."

"And?"

"Total confirmation. He is a superb craftsman, is Sanibak-Thastimoon. There's no one finer exists anywhere, dealing in such arts as these."

"Would that I still trusted him. I trusted him once, more than anyone in the world. But that was folly. He was my brother's minion always, and gave me only such scraps from Korsibar's table as would not be missed, out of courtesy to me, perhaps, but never out of any sort of loyalty. *You* are the only one I trust, Thalnap Zelifor. You and the Lady Meli-thyrrh." Her eyes grew very bright. "Total confirmation, is it? He said a great destiny awaited me. And you found the same?"

"Look you," he said. He flung half a dozen of his myriad tentacles upward to encircle his head, and swept them swiftly about in a pattern too intricate for her eye to follow; and suddenly, somehow, there sprang into being in the air before them a brilliant show of colored light, intense pulsing greens and deep throbbing violets and sharp spearing reds, with dazzling lines of black and yellow cutting across this background tapestry like comets lancing through the firmament. It could have been a map of some undiscovered continent. "Here is your chart, lady, and your line is the yellow. And this is Lord Korsibar's destiny-line, the black one. See, see, how they rise from the same point, your line and his: for you and he were womb-mates, and that links you forever in these findings. Here, you see, in this region where the lines twist and turn around each other and go both of them only in a straight path, this is your happy childhood and his, the long sweet idle times at the Castle, the pampered days of the indolent young prince and princess—pardon me for the ugly word, milady, but it is so, there is no getting about that, and I must be utterly honest with you or what value is there to my service? Indolent is what you were. Begging your forgiveness for saying so."

"Spare me politeness," said Thismet. "I prefer truth." Her eyes were already racing ahead, seeking to know the trajectory of those yellow and black lines, but the pattern was confusing to her: it needed a magus to speak it, she realized.

"Now follow here," he said. "And here, and here, and here. Your lines, which have been flat, now begin to rise. The Pontifex sickens. Your father must ascend to the senior throne. Prestimion will be Coronal. But no, no, your destiny-line and Korsibar's will not permit that. It is his time at last, and yours. See, here, you and he rise steadily day by day, and your line lies just beneath his, supporting his, thrusting him higher—"

"As indeed I did, when I put the idea of taking the crown into his mind."

"Yes. Yes. And here he is, trending ever upward, Coronal Lord of Majipoor." The black line, thicker now, rose like a skyrocket toward the heavens in a sudden spike, stark against the shimmer of red and green behind it in the air.

"And my line? Where has that gone?" She searched desperately; but all was confusion and swirls of color. "I saw it just a moment ago, the yellow, but now—now—"

"Ah, milady. At this edge of the chart we stand at what we call in our profession a nexus, a juncture of possible futures where nothing is certain, for opposing pulls are strong and outcomes are subject to the taking of great decisions that still are held in abeyance."

"I paid you well," said Thismet coldly, "to give me certainties, not junctures of possibility."

She peered down at him. There was a savage pounding behind her temples; her fingers and toes were cold, and the muscles of her lips and cheeks ached from all the scowling she had done of late. This had not been an easy time for her, these first weeks back at the Castle, when she had hoped only for triumph and joy.

Had it been a mistake, investing so much faith in this new wizard? He had not given much satisfaction to his previous employers, had he? And now she had fastened on him as though he and he alone held the key to all the mysteries of the universe.

"Lady, lady, lady," the Vroon said, with a flurry of his ropy limbs. "All depends on you! Here is your moment! Seize it!" He pointed to the muddled left-hand side of the chart, where Thismet could make out nothing comprehensible. "Everything is made plain here. The issue must be joined, and no more time can be wasted. From the moment of your conceptions, your destiny has been irretrievably entwined with his, and so it is shown here to continue for you and for him to the end of your days—unless you fail to take proper action now. Inaction will separate the lines. —You have told me that what you most truly want is a place of power in the realm."

"Yes. That is my hope and desire. Now tell me this, if you can: If my line is entwined with his, as you say—and Sanibak-Thastimoon said the same—then why is it that Korsibar is Coronal, and I—I am nothing at all?"

"You have no position just now, perhaps. But are meant for great things, lady, if only you reach out to seize them."

"Yes, and what things are those? High Counsellor, perhaps? That'll be Farquanor, I suppose. Member of the Council? Korsibar hasn't said a word about that to me. He looks pained whenever I come near him, these days. He knows I want something from him, and he seems resolved not to give it to me. But why? Why? I made him king. Don't I deserve a reward?"

Thalnap Zelifor said, "Have you made any specific request of him, milady?"

"How can I? What am I supposed to ask for? I told him of the dream I had, the one of the two thrones, he and I sitting facing each other in the throne-room. He laughed and said it was just a dream, that all sorts of wild fantasies come to us in dreams. Then I sent word to him again, by way of Sanibak-Thastimoon, that I hoped for a place in the government. No answer came."

"And what place was it that you asked for?"

"Why, no particular one. One that carried with it some power, that was all."

"There is your error, lady. And that is why the chart has entered this zone of uncertainty."

"Tell me, then, what demand I should have made."

"You dreamed, you said, of a throne-room with two identical thrones in it. There you have your answer." The Vroon was looking triumphantly upward at her, his bulging golden eyes bright with vehement assertion. "A joint reign! You and your brother, who shared space within your mother's belly, must share the power of the government as Coronals together! What other meaning could your dream have had?"

Thismet's mouth drooped open in astonishment. "Are you serious?"

"Are you, my lady?"

"When I told that dream to Sanibak-Thastimoon, he cautioned me against interpreting any dream literally. Now you tell me to take it precisely at its face value."

"Yes. That I do."

"There's never been a joint Coronalship. There's never been a woman on the throne."

"There's never been a son succeeding his father, either, as I do understand."

She gaped at him. In all her fantasies of power it had never occurred to her to seek to make that dream of hers come true to the letter. It had been enough merely to dare to imagine her brother as king; for herself, the most she had ever hoped for was some key post in his government, not—despite what she had seen in that dream—a throne of her own. It was lunacy to want that. Thus far Korsibar had ignored even her mildest hints for some place of authority. And this—this—

"Look at the chart, lady!" cried Thalnap Zelifor. She looked. Nothing made sense. It was only meaningless zigzagging lines. "There it all is, lying before you like a path paved with the stars of heaven! This is no moment for timidity. Go to him. Tell him of your true ambitions. Insist on their fulfillment, my lady. He is not a strong man, your brother. He can resist only up to a point; and then, when a stronger force presses against him, he capitulates. You know that, my lady."

"Yes. I do. And I am a stronger force."

"That you are, indeed. So go to him."

Why not? Why not?

Her head was reeling. Lights and color swirled before her. The chart that the Vroon had conjured up in the air opened out and widened until it filled all the sky. She had said to Melithyrrh not long before that she wanted to be queen; but what had she meant by that? The word had simply leaped to her lips. Queen? There were no queens on Majipoor. But Coronal Lords were kings, and a Coronal who was a woman would be a queen, was that not so? Coronal in her own right, yes! Royal daughter of her royal father, royal sister of her royal brother, occupant of that second throne that would be built for her in her father's wondrous throne-room.

Why not?

*Why not?*

Korsibar said, "You may come in, sister."

He spread his hands against the great desk of red palisander that had been his father's, and Lord Prankipin's before that, and one king's and another's ever since this splendid official suite had been constructed for the Coronal's use in the reign of that great builder Lord Dizimaule, and watched as Thismet entered, making her way in swift businesslike fashion toward him across the huge room, over the inlays of semotan-wood and bannikop and ghazyn with which the floor was decorated.

Then she stood before him, tiny and dangerous. She was always potentially explosive. His other half, his female self, his companion in the womb, beautiful, forceful, full of unfocused energies. She frightened him. She was a constant threat to him, now and ever. He was so very tired, after these hectic weeks and this nightmarish blundered thing of Septach Melayn and the magus, this terrible miscalculation, just the other day on the jousting field. And by the hard glitter of her dark eyes, the way she held her shoulders now, the jutting angle of her chin, he knew she had not come here simply to pass the time of day.

She had pushed him into becoming Coronal. What would she push him into now?

"You look awful, brother," was how she began.

"Do I? Are you surprised? That ghastly mess? The killing right under our noses?"

"Why haven't you had Septach Melayn arrested, then?"

"He was drunk. It was all an accident."

"So he claimed, yes."

"I believe him," said Korsibar steadfastly. "What do you want, Thismet? In ten minutes Farquanor will be here with more papers for me to sign."

"Ten minutes for your sister, is that all? Well, perhaps I can tell you what I have to tell you in that." She gave him a look that he knew all too well, and said, after a pause that was only too eloquent, "The horoscope that Sanibak-Thastimoon cast for you, the one that said you would shake the world: were you aware that he cast a similar one for me, Korsibar?"

"Well, and why should it not be similar? We were born in the same hour. Nearly the same moment. The stars were in identical configuration when we were conceived. And you *have* shaken the world, sister. Your destiny is fulfilled in me."

"In you." Said very flatly.

He glanced at the crown, which lay next to him on the desk. He wore it less and less often these days. "I sit upon the Coronal's throne, and it was your doing that put me there. But for your urging, your shrewd counsel, your confidence in the chances of my success, I would never have attempted it."

"This fulfills *your* destiny, not mine. The runes of my future show me following your path."

"And so you have. I am Coronal; you stand alongside me now as I take the governance of the world upon my shoulders."

"Alongside you? A little distance behind you, I would say, Korsibar."

He had feared something like this. But the exact direction of her drift was still uncertain.

"I pray you, Thismet, come to your point. I've already told you that Farquanor will be here any moment, and bringing a host of documents that must be—"

"I could deal with those documents," she said.

"The Coronal's sister has no authority to do such a thing."

"My point exactly. You are king; I am nothing that I was not before." Thismet leaned forward, resting her closed fists on the desk, thrusting her face aggressively toward his. "Thalnap Zelifor has cast my horoscope anew. It confirms the findings of Sanibak-Thastimoon. We follow identical trajectories, you and I. I was born for greatness in my own right, and this is my hour." She paused a moment; and then astounding words burst from her: "Make me Coronal in joint reign with you, Korsibar."

The blunt incredible request hit him with the force of a mace striking against his mid-section.

This was worse than he had expected: worse even than he could have imagined. He felt her words with actual physical pain. "Can you be serious, Thismet?" he said, when he had regained his breath.

"You know that I am."

"Yes," he said leadenly. "Yes, I think I do."

He stared at her, unable to find words.

A knock came at the door. The voice of his major-domo sounded from without. "My lord, it is my lord Farquanor for you!"

"Tell him to wait a moment!" Korsibar returned, in a voice hoarse and strangled with perplexity and rage. Thismet waited motionless for his reply. Her eyes, implacable, gleamed like polished stone.

Slowly, holding himself tightly in check, he said after a time, "What you ask is no small request, sister. There's no historical precedent for any such sharing of the throne."

"I understand that. Many things have happened lately that have no historical precedent."

"Yes. Yes. But for a prince to succeed his father as king is not wholly unnatural. For a woman to occupy the Coronal's throne, though—"

"To *share* the Coronal's throne."

"Put it however you wish. It has never happened before."

"I ask you to consider it. Would you do that?"

He was utterly amazed. Diplomatically he said, "I would need a chance to explore the constitutional issues that may be involved, do you see? And to consult with grayer heads than mine or yours, and have their opinion concerning what sort of consequences in the world in general we could anticipate if we undertook such a move. The people have peacefully accepted my irregular coming to the throne, I think. But if I ask them now to go another step, and accept you also—"

"A very daring step, yes," she said, and he was unable to tell whether there was irony in her tone.

"Let me have a little time, is all I ask. Time to study your request. To obtain wise advice."

She gave him a long, cool, skeptical look.

He knew her well enough to realize that she was prepared to make a great nuisance of herself over this, or something worse than a nuisance, until she had her way. She knew him well enough, he suspected, to understand that his request for a reflective delay was very likely his way of refusing her. But for the moment it would be a standoff: he was sure of that.

"How much time, do you think, will you require for your constitutional researches?"

A shrug. "I don't have any precise idea. This comes with great suddenness, Thismet, at a moment when I have Prestimion on my hands here with his situation unresolved, and also, I remind you, our mother and father both, and am still new to my crown besides, with all the challenges that that poses. But you have my word: I understand your need and I'll give it the most careful consideration."

There was a knocking again from the hallway—impatient, now.

"A moment!" Korsibar bellowed, glaring at the door. "I am with the Lady Thismet!"

He looked toward her again. He still could hardly believe she had made this request of him. It seemed to him now that behind the beautiful mask of her face there lurked a demon's intensity.

"We'll talk further of this before long," he promised her soothingly, summoning a warm smile from some deep reservoir of his soul. And added, at her frown: "We'll do it soon. Very soon, Thismet. You have my word."

"Yes," she said. "So I do."

She skewered him with one last penetrating look. Then she whirled about and quickly crossed the long room and was gone, nearly colliding with Farquanor as he entered. The little man carried a chin-high stack of papers, so unwieldy that it was all he could do to manage a one-handed starburst over the top of them. "My lord—" he began.

"Put them down there," said Korsibar. He closed his eyes for a moment and drew three deep breaths. Then he said, "The Vroon wizard, Thalnap Zelifor—you know which one I mean, Farquanor?"

"Gonivaul's man, I think."

"Gonivaul's no longer. He's in my sister's employ, and filling her ears with grotesque nonsense, of a sort which does neither her nor me any kind of good service. Have him arrested and detained. And take care of it quickly and quietly."

"On what grounds, my lord?"

"A complaint has been filed against him, let us say, of practicing dark arts against innocent victims. No need to name the accuser. Just get him and lock him up in in the lower vaults and leave him there until I've had time to speak with him, and to explain to him how he can best correct his attitudes. Do it now, Farquanor. We can look at these papers afterward. Go. *Now!*"

# 6

Anger and fear and a rush of wild excitement coursed through Thismet as she made her way swiftly from her brother's office.

For better, for worse, she had made her throw of the dice. And now she must live with the consequences of her act.

No peace would be possible between Korsibar and her, she knew, until the issue was settled. That much was certain. The request, once made, could neither be withdrawn nor forgotten, only accepted or refused. He was aware that she was serious; the look of dismay and dread that had come over him as she voiced her demand had told her that much. He already understood what sort of adversary she could be.

But, she wondered, had she taken his new kingship too lightly into account? All her life and his, she had known how to have her way with Korsibar, for he could never refuse her anything: indeed, could rarely refuse anything to anyone who asked him sweetly enough, or firmly enough. Now, though, he was not simply her handsome but pliant brother Korsibar, but Coronal Lord of Majipoor.

The crown, Thismet had read, sometimes ennobled and exalted its wearer. There were old tales of what a lazy wastrel Prince Kanaba had been, until the Pontifex Havilbove picked him to be his Coronal and he instantly put aside his roistering ways and adopted the gravity of a king. And then there was Lord Siminave: also, supposedly, a drunkard and a gambler until the crown came to him, and then he was as stern and righteous as a monk forever after. Or Lord Kryphon, who was said to have been a weakling totally under the sway of his sinister friend Ferithrain until the day after his coronation, when without warning he exiled Ferithrain forever to Suvrael. Would Korsibar, too, find sudden unexpected strength of character now that he was king?

Pondering all these things, asking herself over and again whether she had damaged herself irreparably by launching this bold and maybe overbold assault on Korsibar's sole possession of the royal authority, she rushed in an agitated way through the Inner Castle, from Pinitor Court to silly Lord Arioc's silly tower to her father's garden-house, and from there downward along the Guadeloom Parapet to Vildivar Close, and up the Ninety-Nine Steps again and into the inner structure once more, past chapels and armories and courtyards and parade-grounds, until she found herself in front of one of the entrances to the enormous brick-walled library founded by Lord Stiamot that ran like a long coiling serpent back and forth through the core of the Castle from one side to the other and around and around again.

Any book that had ever been published on any civilized world was kept here, so they said. Shriveled old librarians who were little more than huge brains with dry sticks of withered limbs attached shuffled around all day long in there, dusting and arranging and pausing now and then to peer appreciatively at some choice obscure item of their own near-infinite collections.

The sign over the entrance proclaimed that this was the history section. Thismet had not set foot in any part of the library for years. Impulsively she rushed inside now, not knowing why, thinking perhaps to find an ancient chronicler's neglected book of annals in which she would discover an account of a Coronal's sister, thousands of years before, who had in some strange way come to be given a crown of her own. So hastily did she sweep through the doorway that she went crashing with a force that took her breath away into a short, sturdily built man who was leaving the building just as rapidly.

The impact, which she received against her shoulder and left breast, was severe enough to send her spinning around. A strong hand caught hold of her just as she was about to strike the vestibule wall, and steadied her.

She reached one hand toward the wall to help herself regain her balance. "Forgive me," she said, still a little dazed. "I'm terribly sorry. I should have been paying attention to where I—"

Prestimion, it was. Trim and tidy in a well-cut close jacket of some soft white leather and pale green leggings trimmed with swirling strips of orange velour.

"Are you all right?" he asked.

"Just—a bit shaken—" she said.

He stood before her smiling pleasantly. The collision did not seem to have harmed him. Three books were clasped under his left arm and several more lay at his feet. Thismet offered him a brief uneasy smile of courtesy. Her breast ached where it had struck against him, and she wanted to rub it, but not in front of him. She began to go around him, but he held up one hand to stay her.

"Please. As long as we've run into each other like this. Can I have a word with you, Thismet?"

"Here? Now?"

"Please," he said again. Smoothly he scooped up his fallen books and in the same easy gesture stowed them with the others under his arm and offered his free arm to her. It was impossible for her to resist. She had for the moment exhausted all her ferocity in her confrontation with Korsibar. He led her within, and to one of the little cubicles where scholars sat poring over the tomes that they had requisitioned from the endless stacks that went tunneling down from here into the heart of the Castle Mount.

They sat opposite each other, with his little heap of books stacked up between them like a barricade. Thismet was intensely aware of Prestimion's keen close-set greenish-blue eyes, his narrow face and thin determined lips, the great breadth of his shoulders. He would be more handsome, she thought, if his hair were glossier. But even so he was a handsome man. The thought surprised her, that she should think such a thing at all.

He said, "Are you angry with me over something, Thismet?"

"Angry? What makes you think that?"

"I saw you across the way, at the tournament, the other day. You were glaring. Your face was all drawn up in what I took to be fury. I thought it was your mother you were glaring at, but Septach Melayn maintained that that was not so, that you were looking at me."

"He was wrong. I have no quarrel with you, Prestimion."

"With your mother, is it, then?"

He said it with a light and merry smile. She tried to match it as she said, "My mother is a difficult woman, and it's not easy for me, seeing her again after all these years. But no, no, I have no particular quarrel with her, either. Or with anyone. I am at peace with the world. If I looked tense at Vildivar Close, Prestimion, it was on account of the jousting itself, my fear that someone would be hurt. I've never been able to find pleasure in watching these savage amusements you lords love so much." It was an outright lie, every bit of it, and Prestimion's brow flickered a bit, perhaps, at the sound of it; but she went smoothly onward. "If anything," she said, "I would expect that *you* would be the one holding some anger toward me. Or toward my brother, at least. But you seem the soul of amiability."

"You and I have always been good friends, haven't we, Thismet?"

That was another lie, at least as far from the truth as hers. She met it with a demure smile, and even a blush.

He went on, speaking in the same good-natured way, "As for the ascent of Korsibar to the throne, well, I was as startled by that as everyone else, or perhaps a little more so. That I freely admit. But angry? Just as well be angry at the rain, for getting you wet. It is done; it is the reality of things. Korsibar is our Coronal and I wish him long life and a happy reign. Who could want anything else for him?"

She allowed her smile to grow more sly.

"You feel no resentment at all, you say?"

"Disappointment would be a better term. You know I had hoped to be king."

"Yes. Everyone knew that."

"But things fell out otherwise for me, and so be it. There are other pleasures in life beyond sitting on a throne and issuing decrees, and I hope now to indulge in them."

His gaze rested on her face in a disconcerting way. Once again, as had happened in the Labyrinth, she found herself stirred unexpectedly by desire for him.

That had infuriated and appalled her then; but then Prestimion had been the enemy, the rival. That was all behind them now. Even if she discounted two thirds of what he had been telling her here, it still seemed to her that he had come gracefully to terms with his displacement. And she saw distinct signs that he was attracted to her as well. She found herself wondering what use she might be able to make out of that in her own struggle with Korsibar.

But even as she was thinking these things he rose and gathered his books under his arm again. "Well," he said. "You've put my mind at ease. I would never want there to be unfriendliness between us, Thismet."

"No," she said, looking toward him as he left the cubicle. "By all means, let there be no unfriendliness between us."


The major-domo said, "The Lady Roxivail your mother is here, Lord Korsibar."

She was a startling sight. Delicate of build, small and dark and preternaturally beautiful, Roxivail was so much like Thismet that it might almost have been thought that she, and not her son Korsibar, was Thismet's true twin. Her black curling hair had that same rich glossy sheen, her eyes the same diabolical sparkle. She entered Korsibar's office clad in a short clinging robe of shining black satin subtly worked with purple figures, all ruffles and lace and beaded filigree-work, and a bodice cut down so deep that her breasts stood forth from it all but bare, high and round and firm like a girl's. The sweet thick aroma of attar-of-funisar came from the hollow of her throat. She was tanned a deep rich color wherever her skin could be seen, as if she went naked half the day on her sunny isle of Shambettirantil.

Korsibar looked at her in astonishment.

"You should cover yourself before me, mother."

"Why? Am I so ugly?"

"You are my mother."

"And must I dress in some particular fashion, on that account? I'm not accustomed to dressing like an old woman, nor do I see any reason for matronly modesty before you. We are strangers to each other, Korsibar. You were a baby when I left this place. I feel very little like anyone's mother."

"Nevertheless, my mother is what you are. Cover yourself."

"The sight of my body disturbs you? Forgive me, then," she said, with a coquettish smile. She knew she had unsettled him, and she was enjoying it.

Korsibar could see now why Lord Confalume had not greatly regretted her leaving of him.

He continued to stare coldly. The smile turned to an impish grin; and she drew a fold of satin down over her bosom. "I've come to say goodbye," she said. "In two days' time I leave to begin my journey to the Isle of the Lady. Where an ugly struggle awaits me, I think, with your aunt the Lady Kunigarda."

"A struggle? For the Ladyship?"

"No messages of welcome have come from her. No emissaries from her staff offering to accompany me to the Isle. No mention of the instruction that must be given me if I am to perform the Lady's functions. No indication of any sort that she recognizes you as Coronal, or that she intends to stand down from her post."

"Ah," said Korsibar. He had learned that already, the value to a king of that noncommittal *ah*.

"Of course, she'll have to stand down, like it or not, once I'm there. You're king and I'm your mother and the rules are the rules: the mother of the Coronal becomes Lady of the Isle, and that's that. Still, I think there'll be trouble first. She's tough and stringy and hard, is Kunigarda, and gives nothing up easily. I remember her well from the old days."

"If she refuses to yield to you," said Korsibar, "I'll send orders for her to give over."

Roxivail laughed. It was a sharp-edged brittle laugh that grated on him like a file. "It is precisely because she doesn't regard you as a legitimate Coronal that she's not likely to turn the Ladyship over to me. Why, then, would an order from you make one twig's bit of difference to her? But leave her to me, Korsibar. I'll bring matters around to where they ought to be."

"You actually want to be Lady of the Isle, then, mother?"

She seemed taken by surprise by that. A moment went by

before she said, "Yes! Of course I do! Why would you ask such a thing?"

He said, nonplussed, "You much preferred the comforts of your island in the Gulf, is what I had heard. Your lavish palace, your soft warm breezes and bright sunlight, your good life of luxury and idleness."

"A palace and breezes and sunlight I can also have on the Isle of Dreams, and luxury too, if I want it. As for idleness, I've had enough of that for one lifetime."

"Ah," he said again.

"I never expected to be Lady of the Isle, you understand, or anything else, ever, but myself. Lord Confalume's estranged wife, is who I was. But what kind of identity is that? Known to the world only by the name of the man I once was married to? When I lived at the Castle I had nothing to do from dawn to dark, and little enough after that. And so it's been for me in Shambettirantil, too. Well, then, Korsibar, somehow you made yourself Coronal, and that makes me Lady of the Isle, for which I'm eternally grateful to you. At last I have a role to play in the world. Oh, I'm looking forward to the Ladyship, all right. Make no mistake on that, my son."

"I see," he said.

She was just like Thismet in spirit as well as body, then. A beautiful idle woman, too intelligent for her own good, hungry for power. Not that he had ever had any doubt of it, but plainly Roxivail was her daughter's mother.

She said offhandedly, "How has Confalume taken all of this, by the way?"

"All of what?"

"This. You snatching the crown out of his hands and putting it on your own head when Prankipin died. That's what you did, isn't it? That's what they're saying, at any rate. We spoke, Confalume and I, just for a few minutes the other day: the first words that have passed between us in twenty years, I think. He seemed altogether changed. He's like a shadow of the man I knew. All the stuffing's gone from him. Is he sick, do you think?"

"His health is fine, as far as I know."

"But he let you make yourself Coronal? He didn't object at all? Prestimion was supposed to get it, from what I heard. Why didn't Confalume speak out right then and there to prevent you from doing what you did?"

"It was already done," said Korsibar. "There was a feeling among us—Thismet, Farquanor, some others, and I—that Prestimion wasn't right for the throne, that he was too proud a man, too full of himself. And in some way not truly regal: he doesn't hold himself apart from others, as I think a king must do. He mingles too readily with too many. And so I acted. And it happened so swiftly that father could not or would not stop it. He let it be; and here we are."

" 'Proud and full of himself.' That's how I'd describe your father, too. I never liked Confalume, you know? I'm not talking about love, boy. I never even *liked* him. Stiff and pompous, so terribly conscious of what a great Coronal he was. Sleeping with him was like sleeping with the Stiamot Monument. So I woke up one morning not long after you and your sister were born, and I said to myself that there was no longer any reason to stay here, that I had little interest in rearing babies and even less in being the Coronal's consort, and so I left.—But it astonishes me, all the same, that Confalume would have let you pull that trick of crowning yourself Coronal. He must be getting old."

"He is not young," said Korsibar solemnly. He glanced in a hopeful way toward the door, wishing someone would knock and interrupt this. But he had no appointments scheduled for the rest of the day. "Well, mother—" he said.

"Don't be afraid, I'll be gone soon enough. I have just a few little words of motherly advice for you, first."

Korsibar smiled for the first time since she had entered the room. "Better late than never, is that it?"

"Perhaps motherly advice is the wrong term. Counsel of state might be more accurate. We are both Powers of the Realm, now. This is political advice."

"Very well."

"First. Marry Thismet off as fast as you can. Give her to one of your good-looking young lords—that Navigorn, for example. Or your friend Mandrykarn, the one from Stee. Someone robust enough to satisfy her, and loyal enough to you that he won't start intriguing against you the moment he's married to the Coronal's sister. You can't let her stay single. Beautiful single women are restless creatures, and restless women make trouble. I should know, Korsibar."

"Thismet's restlessness has already begun to show," Korsibar said. "I'll take your advice under consideration, and I thank you for it."

"Two," she said. "Get rid of Prestimion."

His head jerked about in surprise. "Get rid—"

"Absolutely. Don't just banish him. See to it that he disappears *permanently*. There's someone on your staff who'll know how to do that, I assume."

"Farquanor, I would think. Or Sanibak-Thastimoon. But Prestimion's no danger! He seems to have accepted the loss of the crown very well indeed."

"Has he?"

"Oh, he's hurt, no question about that. But he's a practical man, a realist. I'm king and I have the army behind me, and what can he do about it? He's a decent clean-souled man. I've always thought of him as a friend."

"A friend," Roxivail repeated scornfully.

"Yes, a friend! What do you know, mother? All these people are just names to you, but I've lived with them all my life. Surely Prestimion thinks he would have made the better

342

Coronal: how could he not? But it's over and done with. The throne has passed from father to me, and Prestimion knows that that can't be undone. I wouldn't harm him, not for anything. I intend to offer him a high place in the government, in fact, to pacify him, to ease whatever resentments he's still carrying around."

"Get rid of him," Roxivail said once more. "You can't buy a man like that with a Council seat. He's another proud one, another who's swollen with himself. I knew his father: a proud man too, as bad as Confalume that way. Prestimion's the same. If he's been friendly to you lately, it's only because he's biding his time, waiting to make his move. I tell you, Korsibar, he won't rest until he's standing on top of your dead body trying your crown on for size. Have him killed."

Korsibar shook his head. "I took the bad advice of the magus Sanibak-Thastimoon and we made an attempt at killing Prestimion's friend Gialaurys on the jousting field. It couldn't have worked out worse for us. I'm done with killing, mother. Prestimion means me no harm; and I'll do no harm to him."

"Do as you please, then," she said, with a gesture of indifference. "But test him in some way, I would suggest, to see if he's as benevolently inclined toward you as you imagine. And do it soon."

"I'll give that some thought." He kneaded his knuckles together and wished her ten thousand miles away. "Do you have any further advice for me?"

"This is enough, I think. Come: get up from that desk, boy. Give your mother a farewell kiss." Her eyes sparkled maliciously. She pressed herself tight against him as they embraced, wriggling a little, flattening her breasts against his chest. Her kiss was not a motherly one. He released her quickly; and quickly she was gone.

★

Prestimion said, "Another summons from Korsibar. This time to a private audience in the Confalume throne-room."

"Concerning what?" asked Svor. He stood against the great outcurving window of Prestimion's suite in the Castle, a comfortable apartment in the building of white brick known as Munnerak Tower on the Castle's eastern face, that was set aside for the residences of princes of Prestimion's rank. It was mid-morning. Shafts of golden-green light streamed through the faceted glass behind him.

"Concerning the place he means to offer me in the government," Prestimion replied. "This following on the discussion I had with him our last day in the Labyrinth, when he said I'd eventually be invited to hold a high place in his reign."

"Be careful," said Septach Melayn. "Favors from your enemy often have poison at their centers."

"By which you mean what?" Prestimion asked.

"His goal is to compromise you, I suspect, by making you complicit in his capture of the crown. When you've been sitting there at his right hand in the Council-chamber for a time, giving your assent to his laws and decrees and appointments, and then one morning you rise up against him and call for his overthrow, you'll look merely ungrateful and treasonous, an overly ambitious underling spitefully attacking his master."

"Whereas if I continue to hold myself aloof from him, neither openly rebelling nor accepting any post from him, I maintain my distance from a regime that I intend in time to brand as unlawful. Yes. I see that. And what if he doesn't permit me to maintain that distance?"

"How would he do that?" asked Septach Melayn.

"By taking the position," said Svor before Prestimion could reply, "that anyone who isn't with him is against him. Surely Farquanor will have put that idea in Korsibar's head already: try to buy Prestimion's loyalty by pulling him close with some important role in the government, and if Prestimion should refuse, interpreting that as a sign that Prestimion means sooner or later to make trouble. That's the advice *I* would give Prestimion, if the situations were reversed."

"Yes," said Septach Melayn, drawing the word out slowly. He held his dress-sword across his knee, and was polishing its bright steel lightly with a strip of chamois. "Two peas of a pod, you and Count Farquanor. Put your beard on his face and I don't see how we could tell the two of you apart."

Gialaurys, who had been silent a long while, said to Prestimion now, "When is this audience with Korsibar to happen?"

"Today. An hour from now."

"Just the two of you, you and he?"

"So far as I know."

"Take a dagger, then," said Gialaurys. "Stand there next to him, and listen close to all he tells you, and smile and nod and give him no cause for distress, and then when everything is warm and friendly between you, pull out the dagger and put it in his heart, and put the crown on your head and announce yourself to be Coronal."

"Bravo, Gialaurys!" cried Septach Melayn. "You must have been taking lessons in treacherousness and perfidy from our beloved Duke Svor! And you are an apt pupil, it seems."

"The treacherousness," said Gialaurys coldly, "is all Korsibar's, for stealing the crown. This would only put matters to rights again. Where's the shame in that?"

"Do you think Korsibar will have no guards nearby?" Prestimion said. His voice was very mild; he was more amused than angered by Gialaurys's suggestion, outrageous though it was. "I cut him down, and the next moment my body lies next to his on the throne-room floor. It will have been a very short reign for me. But I know you mean this as loving counsel, Gialaurys. You want me to be Coronal, I think, even more than I want it myself."

"What will you do, then, when you come before Korsibar?" asked Svor.

Prestimion said, frowning, "I have no clear plan, yet. What would you suggest for me, any of you, short of hiding daggers in my bosom?"

"Best not to go at all," said Septach Melayn. "Failing that, to do much listening and little speaking, and when he makes you the offer, to say that you need time to consider it, that you must speak with your mother the Lady Therissa first, and see if you are needed more urgently at your Muldemar estate than here."

"Good. That buys me a little time, but only a little."

"I wish I had some shrewder thing devised for you," Septach Melayn said.

"As do I."

"This audience, you say, is in the throne-room?" Svor asked. "Not the Coronal's office?"

"The throne-room, yes," Prestimion said.

Svor's expression darkened. He turned a little, so that he was staring out the window instead of looking at Prestimion. "I see trouble in this. He fears you; the royal office, grand as it is, evidently isn't grand enough for him for this meeting; he wants all the majesty of the throne-room surrounding him when he addresses you. Which is a sign of weakness in his soul. An enemy whose soul is weak but who nevertheless has great power at his command is more deadly than a strong one. He'll strike out of fear, like a cornered snake. Take care, Prestimion."

"Yes. That I surely will." He threw open the door of his great wardrobe closet and studied the array of garments within. "The next great problem, gentlemen: shall I dress in something rich and grand, as befits a high prince summoned before a Coronal? Or will it trouble him if I do, and shall I dress more modestly, like the humble vassal he no doubt would like me to be, which will put him at his ease?" Prestimion laughed. "And yet I don't want him to take me too lightly. Perhaps the middle range is best, in this as in all other things."

He chose, in the end, simple but costly clothing, a white silken tunic that looked more like cotton, and gray hose of the same deceptive material, and an ordinary red cape cunningly worked around its borders—but only there—with figures in cloth of gold, and plain leather buskins. At the last moment he drew forth the green stone amulet of Thalnap Zelifor, the corymbor on the golden chain, and slipped it around his neck.

Gialaurys and Septach Melayn accompanied him as far as the Inner Castle, leaving him at the entrance to the throne-room precinct itself. Duke Svor, having a prior meeting with a lady of Duke Kanteverel's following—for that was a great thing with Svor, the attention he paid to ladies, and they to him—did not go with them.

Korsibar was esconced most magnificently atop the Confalume Throne when Prestimion entered. He wore a grand robe of rich scarlet velvet over his Coronal's colors of green and white, and the starburst crown gleamed on his brow with the brilliance of the new star in the heavens that had signalled his advent, and he held himself sternly upright in his seat to accentuate the grandeur of his powerful form. About his throat was the Vildivar Necklace, its golden links ablaze with sapphire and ruby and topaz, and his belt of black serpent-skin was studded with tourmalines and blue quartz, and on his finger was the massive fiery ring that had been Lord Moazlimon's, a great diamond set round with jasper and onyx. It was exactly as Svor had said it would be, Prestimion thought: Korsibar, uncertain of himself within that kingly exterior of his, had opted for the full theatricality of his position in some fevered hope of maintaining an advantage over him thereby.

Well, he was impressive, that much had to be granted. And of course the throne itself was the most majestic possible

setting for a king. Prestimion, looking at it now, felt a fresh
pang of anguish and loss, knowing that this was to have
been his. The massive slab of black opal, that great mahogany
pedestal, the silver pillars, the golden canopy, the glister of the
gems encrusting the ceiling-beams, the tapestries, the shining
floor, everything: Confalume must have poured the wealth of
five provinces into this room.

Building it, all unknowingly, for his own son. His own son.

Korsibar said, "Come closer, Prestimion. The echoes in
here are very bad, if you stand so far away."

Prestimion advanced another couple of steps. There was
no one in the room other than he and Korsibar, though an
ample body of guards stood just outside. The enthroned Korsibar loomed far above him. Prestimion had to look up, up,
up, to meet his eyes.

"Well, Prestimion—" Korsibar began.

And stopped again. For Prestimion had not knelt; Prestimion had not made the starburst; Prestimion had not shown
in any way that he was in the presence of his king.

*Take care, Prestimion,* Svor had advised.

Yes. Yes. But in this moment of confrontation Prestimion
felt a terrible paralysis coming over him, and at the same time
fury rising like a red column within his frozen body.

He could not kneel to this man.

He could not make the starburst.

This was the first time he had been alone with Korsibar
since before that awful day when Korsibar had stolen the
crown. Then they had been friends, more or less, two carefree
young princes of the Castle; but now one was a king and one
was not, one sat high up on a throne of black opal with a
crown on his head and a robe of scarlet velvet on his shoulders
and the other stood humbly below him in a simple tunic and
buskins. The immense *wrongness* of all that now took possession
of Prestimion here in the overwhelming grandeur of Lord

Confalume's throne-room. He struggled fiercely to maintain his self-control. But he felt himself losing the struggle.

Korsibar said, "I know how difficult this must be for you, Prestimion."

"Yes." Very tightly.

"You should say, 'Yes, my lord.'"

Prestimion moistened his lips. "I know that I should."

"Say it, then."

"Korsibar—"

"*Lord* Korsibar."

"Can you really know how hard this is for me? As you sit there on the throne, with the jewelry of past kings all over you and the crown resting on your brow—"

"I am the Coronal Lord, Prestimion."

"You have the throne, yes. You wear the crown."

Color came into Korsibar's swarthy face. This is going all wrong, Prestimion thought. He was heading for the brink of an abyss, and there was no calling himself back. Unconsciously his hand stole to the Vroonish amulet at his breast, and he rubbed up and down along its cool green surface until he realized what he was doing, and then he took his hand away.

"Please, Prestimion. A Coronal shouldn't say 'please,' but there it is. I want us to be friends. I want you to hold high power in the land, to sit in the Council with me and offer all that you have to offer, which is considerable. But there are certain formalities that have to be observed."

"Your father said 'please' to me too, when I went to him in the Labyrinth to ask him if he meant to allow your taking of the crown to stand. 'Please, Prestimion,' he said, and began to weep. So now I've heard that word from a Coronal and a Pontifex too. If indeed you are a Coronal, Korsibar."

Korsibar sucked his breath in sharply.

"Prestimion—this is very dangerous, Prestimion—"

"Yes."

He was over the brink, now. There was no returning from it: he must plunge all the way.

"I was warned against doing this," said Korsibar. "Nevertheless, I felt I owed you a place on the Council. It's yours if you want it, still. But you must tell me that you recognize me as Coronal, and show me that you do."

"No," Prestimion said, staring steadily and coldly upward at the man on the throne.

"No?"

"This is too much to ask of me."

"It is essential, Prestimion. Or there will be a terrible breach between us."

"Creating a breach was not what I meant to do, I think, when I decided to come here today. I had no wish to thwart you. But actually seeing you on the throne changes everything for me: it allows me no other choice but to say what I have said. I'll take that Council seat, Korsibar, if you are still willing to give it to me, for I think it would be best that you and I work together to avoid chaos in the world, and it is not my desire to be the one who brings that chaos down upon us."

"Which gives me great pleasure to hear."

"I am not done," said Prestimion inexorably. "You should know that I will take that Council seat with the understanding that it's an interim Council, the Council of an unlawful regime, which is operating only until the present constitutional situation is made regular. I tell you, Korsibar, that I regard the world as having no legitimate Coronal at this time."

There. The words had been said. It was like throwing a gauntlet. Going back was impossible, now.

Korsibar stared. A vein stood out in high relief on his forehead, as though his skull were about to explode. His face was bright with heat. It had taken on a deeper scarlet hue than that of his robe.

For a moment he appeared unable to speak.

Then, in a dark, congested voice: "Will you not retreat from that statement, Prestimion?"

Prestimion, looking up unwaveringly at him, made no response.

Korsibar nodded grimly. Into the dread silence came a grunt from him as of a great pent-up force being released, and then the sharp sound of Korsibar clapping his hands a single time; and as the echoing vibrations of that clap went forth, a squadron of guardsmen rushed into the room. They had been waiting and ready, Prestimion realized, in some hidden chamber. Korsibar, livid, rose to his full height and pointed to him, and cried in a voice like thunder, "Here is a traitor! Arrest him! Take him to the Castle vaults!"


Septach Melayn was in his chambers, feinting at shadows with his rapier to keep his eye sharp and his balance pure, as he was wont to do for at least an hour every day, when Gialaurys came bursting in without announcement, crying, "Prestimion's taken! He's chained up in one of Lord Sangamor's tunnels!"

"What's this? What?" Septach Melayn sheathed his weapon and bounded across the room, catching up the loose front of Gialaurys's doublet in his fist and thrusting his face into that of the other man. "Taken? How? Why?"

"He had the audience with Korsibar, and it went badly. Angry words were spoken. And then Korsibar called for his guardsmen, and had Prestimion carried off to be arraigned for high treason. I have this from Serithorn's nephew Akbalik, who was waiting in the antechamber to speak with Korsibar, and heard the whole thing."

"Taken," said Septach Melayn again, in wonder. "Who would think that that hollow fool Korsibar could ever find the courage? No, I withdraw that, he has foolishness aplenty, but no dearth of bravery in him, either. A bad thing it is, too, to have great courage without overmuch wisdom to temper it." As he spoke he moved busily around the room, collecting some weapons, a few garments, other stray possessions, and thrusting them into a sack. "What madness this thing is! It's the two-headed wizard that put him up to it, or perhaps Farquanor, who has enough evil guile in his soul to fill *three* heads," he said. And a moment afterward: "Well, then, we must flee this place, you and I."

"And leave Prestimion hanging in chains?" said Gialaurys in an tone of disbelief. "Surely not."

"Do you imagine that you and I by ourselves can fight our way to his side and bring about his release?" Septach Melayn asked, laughing. "The two of us against all the Castle? It would be the wildest sort of folly."

"But if we raised an outcry and a protest, and won the support of such as Oljebbin and Serithorn—"

"We'd never get the chance. There's room in those dungeons for plenty more beyond Prestimion, my friend, and at this moment places are probably cleared for both of us. We'll be able to do him little service if we're hanging there beside him."

"Would they dare?"

"Even Korsibar's shrewd enough to know that doing a thing by halves is a certain way to fail at it. He's tried already to have you killed right in front of everyone, or have you forgotten that? And now he's made his move against Prestimion: how can he let us remain free? He'll want to put us all away in one swoop." Septach Melayn gave the heavyset man an impatient shove. "Come, Gialaurys, come! We need to be outside. From there we can work to win support for him, and freedom. Move that great bulk of yours, and let's be on our way, while we still have the chance."

"Yes. Perhaps we should. Where to, though?"

"Ah," Septach Melayn said, for that was a question he had not yet asked of himself. But after only an instant's thought he said, "Muldemar, and Prestimion's mother and brothers. They have to be told what's happened; and after that there'll be time to decide what to do next." He shook his head angrily. "What a reversal and change of fortune this is, that he who should be sitting on the high throne is hurled into the deep vaults instead!"

"And Svor?" asked Gialaurys. "What of him?"

Septach Melayn made a wry face. "He's off with one of his whores, some Bailemoona woman Kanteverel gave him. Who knows where he's gone with her? We can't spare the time to search from bedroom to bedroom all over the Castle. I'll leave word for him of what's taken place: it's the best that we can do for him. What do you say to that?"

"You have my agreement on it. Svor will have to look after himself."

"Go to your rooms, then, gather whatever things you'll be taking with you. We should leave the Castle by the Gossif side, down the Spurifon parapet—you know the one I mean?—and out the old road that leads toward Huine. Going out Dizimaule way's too risky: that's where they'll set up the roadblock first. But if the Divine's with us they won't even think of the Gossif side until after we're gone."

"A good plan. I'll meet you in fifteen minutes by Kanaba Stairs, that go down behind the old parade-grounds."

"Ten."

"Ten, then."

"And if I'm not there when you arrive, make your way out of the Castle on your own and head for Muldemar without me. I'll do the same if you're late. We dare not wait for each other." A warm flash of comradely love came into Septach Melayn's eyes, and he grasped Gialaurys's treetrunk of an arm with his, gripping it from the great swelling muscle, and the other hand clasping Gialaurys for a moment about the back and shoulders. Then they hastened into the hallway.

All was clear out there. Gialaurys ran off toward the right, where his chambers lay, and Septach Melayn went the other way, out into the open space that was the Kryphon Cloister, which led to the tumbledown remains of Balas Bastion, with a maze of pathways beyond it that would take him around to the northern side of the Castle.

His expectation was that the very hugeness and intricacy of the Castle would work in his favor. He had no doubt now that guards were already out looking for him, and for Svor and Gialaurys also; but first they had to find him, and he was in motion through the almost infinite passageways and underpasses and crosswalks of the great building, so that their only hope was to stumble upon him by chance somewhere between his chambers and whichever exit from the Castle he chose to take. There were many of those, though most were rarely used. Septach Melayn knew the Castle well, and was quick-minded as well as quick on his feet. He moved steadily forward. Now and again he saw groups of guardsmen in the distance, but they did not seem to see him and perhaps did not even yet know that he was being sought; and in any case it was always possible to find some alternative route that took him toward his goal.

All went well, though his path was somewhat more circuitous than the one he had originally planned to take, on account of the deviations made necessary by these glimpses he had of guardsmen ahead. He sprinted easily and swiftly through a courtyard whose name he had forgotten, where a host of headless eroded marble statues bearing the stains of five thousand years had been piled in a sad heap, and over a bridge that he thought was called Lady Thiin's Overpass, and down a spiraling brick-edged rampart to the Tower of Trumpets, which led to the staircase that would put him on the Castle's outer face.

There, to his great annoyance, he encountered four men in the colors of the Coronal's guard, who arrayed themselves at the head of the stairs as though they meant to block his way. That did indeed seem to be their intention. Their stance was a distinctly unfriendly one.

"Put up your weapons and let me pass," he told them without a moment's pause. "I have no time to waste in talk."

"And where are you going, in such a hurry?" asked one, who had on a captain's helmet.

"No time, either, to answer questions. Step aside: you will regret it if you hinder me. I am Septach Melayn."

"We know your name. You are the very one we seek," said the captain, though he looked glum enough about it, and the man who stood beside the captain seemed downright dejected at the thought of doing battle with so famous a swordsman as Septach Melayn. "Come with us peacefully. By order of the Coronal Lord Korsibar you are herewith—"

"You have had your warning," said Septach Melayn, and drew.

His arm was still warm from the rapier practice of a little while before, and more than ready. He parried a wide wobbly thrust from the captain as though it were a child's, and put the point of his sword into the man's cheek, then pivoted and sliced down into another guardsman's shoulder on his backsweep, and took three fingers from a third with one quick flick of his hand, all of it accomplished in his lazy-looking way, that seemed so effortless and easy. The fourth guardsman was armed with a small gray metal device, an energy-thrower, which he tried desperately to aim and fire. But he must never have been faced with the need to use the thing before. His attempts to operate the activator catch were hampered by the violent shaking of his entire arm. Septach Melayn severed it at the wrist and stepped around him as the man began to set up the uncomprehending wailing that usually followed upon such events.

The whole thing had taken no more than a few moments. But the noise coming from his maimed victims was attracting other guardsmen now; Septach Melayn could see them overhead, heading down the spiral rampart toward him. He circled quickly to his left, past the ruined eastern face of the Tower of Trumpets, and was gratified to find a huge dry underground cistern there, running deep and long, with a glimmer of daylight showing at its far end. Crawling quickly into it, he ran some fifty paces and scrambled up into the light, emerging on a lower level in a place he could not at first recognize, but which he saw to be the back end of Spurifon Parapet. That was the very place he sought. There was no sign of Gialaurys. Very likely he had been here already, and gone onward upon seeing that his companion was going to be late; but on the off chance that Gialaurys might be even tardier yet, Septach Melayn lingered at the parapet a few minutes, until he caught sight of a fresh group of guardsmen moving about two levels higher up.

It was foolish to stay longer. The residential quarters of the guardsmen were close by this district. A party of them might come upon him without even looking for him, simply while going off duty, and then he would have to spill more blood. Better to move along, and swiftly.

Septach Melayn darted down the slope of the parapet and through the small, ancient arched gateway that gave exit from the Castle on its little-used northern side. The road to Huine stretched before him. If he took it downslope a little way and then went circling about eastward, it would bring him to the juncture with the Gossif road, and Gossif was adjacent among the Inner Cities to Tidias, which was Septach Melayn's own birthplace; and not far beyond Tidias was Muldemar. It was his deeply felt hope to see Gialaurys again when he reached there. The task of springing Prestimion free of Korsibar's grasp was not one that he would care to tackle by himself.

He looked back. Still no Gialaurys. Let him be safe out of the Castle already, thought Septach Melayn. May the Divine speed him on his way. And turned his own lanky legs toward the road that led down the Mount's long shoulder.

FOUR

# THE BOOK OF RECKONINGS

# 1

No one had any idea what use Lord Sangamor had had in mind for the tunnels that came to bear his name, when he ordered the construction of them three and a half thousand years earlier. They were situated on the western face of the Mount in a middle level of the Castle, where a tall spire of rock that was virtually a mountain in its own right jutted from the main formation. That high spire— it too was named for Sangamor—was so angular and sharp that it was unusable, and in fact next to unclimbable; but at its base Lord Sangamor had installed a series of low-roofed underground chambers, each connected to the next, that ran from the Castle proper to Sangamor Peak and completely encircled that spire where it sprang from the Mount.

The material out of which these chambers had been constructed was as mysterious as their purpose. Their walls and roofs were lined with paving-blocks of some radiant synthetic stone that gave off, of its own accord, vivid emanations of color. One chamber was constantly lit by a pulsating maroon glow, another by a brilliant emerald, another saffron, another a powerful rufous hue, another sulphur-toned, another a bright bursting orange, and so on and on.

The secret of the inherent luminosity of these blocks, which had not dimmed in the slightest in all the millennia since Lord Sangamor's distant time, was one of the many that had been lost by the craftsmen of Majipoor over the centuries. The effect of the lights and colors of Lord Sangamor's tunnels was an extremely beautiful one, but also, since they never dimmed even for a moment, by day or by night, it very quickly became exhausting and even distressing to experience it: there was always that great inescapable throbbing sweep of *color* coming from those walls, hour after hour, day after day, so powerful that it was visible even when one closed one's eyes to it. That perpetual radiance was, in fact, a torment if one had to endure it for any great length of time.

And so—since the tunnels were set apart from all the rest of the Castle by the peculiar topography of this region of the Mount and since no other use had ever been found for them, and comfort was not an important factor to consider where prisoners were concerned—they came after some centuries to be employed from time to time as dungeons for the storage of individuals whom the Coronal regarded as excessively obstreperous, or too inconvenient in some other way to be left at large.

Prestimion had seen the Sangamor tunnels once, long ago, while touring odd corners of the Castle in his boyhood under the auspices of his late father. No one was imprisoned in them then; no one had been, apparently, for some two or three hundred years, not since the time of the Coronal Lord Amyntilir. But the endless waves of color were impressively beautiful if somewhat overwhelming, and the rows of empty shackles mounted against the walls were impressive also in a different way, and so too were the tales that Prestimion's father told him of this rebellious prince and that hot-headed young duke who had been chained up here in the time of some ancient Coronal desirous of restoring decorum at his court.

It had never occurred to Prestimion that he might find himself chained up here himself one day. This place was a medieval relic, not something that was in everyday use. But here he was, dangling from a wall that radiated a spectacularly vibrant ruby tone, with his arms spread wide and manacles clamped tight about his wrists and ankles. It struck him almost as funny, now and again. Korsibar, blustering with rage, ordering him off to the dungeons! What was next? The heads-man's block?

But of course there was nothing funny about it. He was at Korsibar's mercy. Nobody knew what went on down here. At any moment some henchman of the Coronal's might come in here and slit his throat, and there would be nothing he could do to defend himself. He had been here, he supposed, six or eight hours by now, in unbroken solitude. Perhaps they simply meant to leave him here until he starved to death. Or, perhaps, until those unyielding pulsating waves of red, red, red, endlessly bounding and rebounding from every surface about him, drove him into screaming insanity.

So it would seem. The hours passed, and no one came.

Then, astonishingly, a small quiet furry voice said out of the maddening sea of color opposite him, "Do you happen to have your corymbor with you, Prince Prestimion?"

"What?" His voice was husky from disuse. "Who said that? Where are you?"

"Just across the way. Thalnap Zelifor. Do you remember me, excellence?"

"The Vroonish wizard, yes. I remember you all too well." Prestimion, peering into that obstinate light, blinked, and blinked again, and struggled to focus his eyes. But all he could see was that surging ocean of redness. "If you're there, you've made yourself invisible, somehow."

"Oh, no. You could see me, if you tried. Close your eyes for a time, and open them very quickly, excellence, and you'll make me out. I'm a prisoner here too, you see.—It amazed me no end when they brought *you* in here," the voice out of the red glow continued. "I knew the pattern of your stars was an unfavorable one, but I didn't think it was *that* unfavorable. Do you see me yet?"

"No," Prestimion said. He shut his eyes and counted to ten, and opened them, and saw nothing but the waves of redness. He closed his eyes again, and counted this time to twenty, and decided to count twenty more. When he opened them then, he was able just barely to make out the indistinct shape of the little many-tentacled creature straight across the room from him, manacled to the wall even as he was, with the gyves fastened about two of his biggest tentacles. Thalnap Zelifor was hanging, though, three or four feet off the floor, because he was so small and the manacles had been installed for the purpose of restraining individuals of normal human size.

The redness closed in again.

"I saw you for a moment, at least," Prestimion said. He stared somberly into the pulsating radiance. "It was definitely you," he said. "You who came to me to tell me in the Labyrinth that I had no clear path to the throne, that you saw omens of opposition on all sides, that I had a mighty enemy who was waiting in secrecy to overthrow me. You knew—by what means, I dare not guess—what was going to happen. It's fitting, I suppose, that we'd meet next in the same dungeon. You could predict my downfall, but not your own, eh?" He narrowed his eyes, trying without success to make out the Vroon across the way. "How long have you been in here?"

"Three days, I think. Perhaps four."

"Have they fed you?"

"Occasionally," said the Vroon. "Not terribly often. I asked you before, prince: do you happen to have your corymbor with you? The little green amulet I gave you, is what I mean."

"Yes. As a matter of fact, I do. On a chain about my throat."

"When they come to give you your food, they'll have to

free your hands so you can eat. Rub the corymbor, then, and implore the force it controls to smile upon you. That should dispose the guards more favorably to you, and perhaps they'll feed you more often, or even bring you something better than the usual swill. I should tell you that the food here is abominable; and the guards are utter ruffians."

"Your corymbor wasn't much help to me a little while ago when I was in the throne-room with Korsibar. I touched it once, as he and I were just beginning our dispute. But things only got worse and worse."

"You touched it with the intention of using its power, did you? You commended yourself to its strength, and told it your specific need?"

"I did none of that. It never occurred to me. I merely touched it, as one might scratch at an itch while one is talking."

"Well, then," said Thalnap Zelifor, as though to say that Prestimion's error was manifestly obvious.

They were silent for a time.

"Why have they locked you up in here?" asked Prestimion, eventually.

"That isn't clear to me. It's through some grievous act of injustice, of that I'm sure. But who's responsible has not been shown me. I only know that I'm innocent of the charge, whatever it may be."

"Undoubtedly," said Prestimion.

"I was, for a while," said the Vroon, "employed as an adviser to the Lady Thismet, and perhaps some of the things I suggested she say to her brother may have been offensive or troubling to him, and he had me put away to keep me from giving her further advice. That could well be. On the other hand, there was the matter of a debt I had incurred, money owing to Prince Gonivaul, who had been financing some of my research. You know how Gonivaul is about money. He may have asked the Coronal to put me here in punishment for my failure to repay him his loan, though how doing that will get him his money back is far from clear to me."

"It would seem," said Prestimion, "that there's a great deal is unclear to you. For one of your profession, that's not much of a recommendation. I thought all knowledge was an open book to you sorcerers. And yet you're not even sure why you've been chained to this wall."

"It is an imperfect science, excellence," said Thalnap Zelifor dolorously.

"Oh, a science, is it?"

"Oh, yes, most assuredly a science. To you it may seem to be all demon-worship and conjuring, but to us it is a matter of understanding and obeying the basic laws of the universe, which are rooted in utterly rational foundations."

"Indeed. Rational foundations, you say. You must teach me about this, if we are in here very long.—You would prefer to call yourself an engineer, I take it, rather than a wizard?"

"To me they are nearly the same thing, O prince. Three hundred years ago an engineer is what I would have been, and no doubt of that. The very research I was doing for the Grand Admiral Gonivaul was purely technical in nature: the invention and construction of a mechanical device."

"A mechanical device that would perform acts of sorcery?"

"A device that would allow one mind to make direct contact with another. Through scientific means, not through any kind of incantation or invocation of demons, I would be able to look into your mind, prince, and see what thoughts were there, and to place thoughts of my own devising in you."

Prestimion felt a little shiver of fear. Perhaps it was for the best, he told himself, that Thalnap Zelifor was chained up here hanging on this wall.

"You've actually perfected such a thing?"

"The research, I fear, is not quite complete, excellence. It wanted still a little more work—but the shortage of funds, you see—Prince Gonivaul's unwillingness to advance me the few additional royals I needed—"

"Yes. A great blow that must have been to you. And would you care to tell me what use the Grand Admiral Gonivaul was going to make of this device, once you had finished inventing it?"

"For that, I think, you would have to ask Prince Gonivaul."

"Or use your mind-reading machine, more likely," Prestimion said. "Gonivaul's not one to bare his secrets freely to anyone." For a time he was silent. And then: "Do you happen to have among your repertoire of spells one that will make this damnable red light a little less offensive to the eye?"

"The corymbor, I believe, could have that effect."

"But of course my hands aren't free to touch the corymbor, are they?"

"What a pity," said Thalnap Zelifor. "But here—the guards are coming." Indeed Prestimion heard footsteps, and the opening of gates. "You'll be fed now, and your hands will be freed, at least for a little while. That will be your chance."

Three guards, bristling with weapons, entered the chamber. One stood by the entrance with folded arms, watching grimly; one unlocked the manacles about Prestimion's wrists, and held out a bowl of cold nasty gruel to him to take and drink down; the third brought a plate of food to the Vroon, who scrabbled eagerly in it with one of his free tentacles. While Prestimion ate, and it was no easy thing to get that thin bitter stuff down, he surreptitiously slipped one hand within the bosom of his tunic and—feeling not only foolish but contemptible, a betrayer of all he believed—gave the corymbor a couple of perfunctory strokes with his finger, and then a couple of strokes more.

"Is this stuff the best you can find for me?" he asked his guard. "Do you think you could get me anything that doesn't curdle in the stomach?"

The guard's only reply was a cold, bleak stare.

When the bowl of gruel was empty the guard took it from Prestimion and returned his hands to their manacles, and all three left the chamber. They had not spoken a word all the while.

"The lights are just as strong," Prestimion said. "And the guards seemed not at all friendly."

"You touched the corymbor, prince?"

"Several times, yes."

"And asked the power that is resident in it to look favorably upon your needs, did you?"

"I simply stroked it," Prestimion admitted. "To do more than that was something I could not bring myself to do. I confess that the invoking of imaginary powers is something that doesn't come easily to me."

"Well, then," said Thalnap Zelifor again.


Svor, returning late that afternoon from his pleasant assignation with the voluptuous Heisse Vaneille of Bailemoona, found all his satisfaction turning immediately to dust when he learned, as he quickly did, that Prestimion was a prisoner in the Sangamor vaults and that Gialaurys and Septach Melayn were nowhere to be found anywhere in the Castle.

Prince Serithorn's useful gray-eyed nephew Akbalik, who was his source for all this, suggested that Duke Svor might do well to flee the Castle himself without much further delay.

"Is there a proscription declared against the faction of Prestimion?" Svor asked him.

Akbalik, who was calm and judicious of nature, said only, "Not that I've heard. There was some dispute between the Coronal and Prince Prestimion in the throne-room and Lord Korsibar ordered the prince to be imprisoned: that I can tell you absolutely. What became of the other two, I can only guess. Some guardsmen, I understand, were badly damaged in a sword-scuffle near one of the back gates. It's not unreasonable to think they got in Septach Melayn's way as they were leaving."

"No doubt. So they are gone, and I am left here alone."

"It might not be wise for you to stay, either," he said again.

Svor nodded. He sat quietly for a time, considering the range of possibilities that stretched before him, none of them cheerful and most of them perilous. That the interview between Korsibar and Prestimion had ended in calamity did not surprise him. It was disheartening to Svor to see how Prestimion insisted again and again on thrusting his head into demons' lairs, despite the warnings Svor repeatedly offered him. But Prestimion was not a man to put much credence, or any, in omens and forecasts; and thrusting himself knowingly into the lairs of demons seemed to be an integral aspect of his personality. Svor was of a different cast of mind entirely: comprehending Prestimion was not always an easy thing for him.

Now it was his own future that had to be spied out and understood, Svor knew, or he was lost. The auguries were ambiguous.

At length he reached his decision. "I'll seek immediate audience with Korsibar myself," he told Akbalik.

"Do you think that's wise?"

"Wiser than any other course. I'm not one for slashing my way out of the Castle like Septach Melayn, or throwing guardsmen around like twelvepins in the fashion of Gialaurys. If Korsibar wants to imprison me, so be it. But I think I can talk my way around that: and I see no other path for myself."

And so Svor requested—and, somewhat to his surprise, was immediately granted—entry to the Coronal's office. Two armed Skandar guardsmen stood protectively beside the Coronal's palisander desk, as though Gialaurys's brave talk of leaping upon Korsibar with a dagger had drifted through the corridors to Korsibar's ears. He felt dwarfed before those giant aliens and the commanding figure of Korsibar between them. But that was no new thing for him, to be among bigger and stronger men. Slender and wiry and frail though he was, he had held his ground among them well enough thus far.

Korsibar himself looked drained and enervated, sallow-faced, with a stark, haunted look in his eyes. He had a string of amber beads in his left hand and was toying with them in a nervous, compulsive way, passing them one by one between his long powerful fingers. The crown lay in a corner of the desk like a discarded toy.

He said in a strange subdued way as Svor took up a position before the desk, "Have you come here to defy me too, old friend?"

"Is that what happened? Prestimion defied you?"

"I offered him a Council seat. He spurned me and told me to my face that I was an unlawful illegitimate Coronal. How could I tolerate that?—Give me a starburst, Svor, I pray you. I am king here, remember."

This costs me nothing, Svor reflected. He brought his hands upward in the gesture of respect.

Korsibar's face, which had been stern and tense and drawn, softened with relief. "Thank you. I wouldn't want to have to imprison you also."

"The rumor's true, then? Prestimion is chained in the vaults?"

"For a little while. I'll bring him up in a day or two and speak with him again. I want him to see reason, Svor. The world hails me as king. My father himself recognizes my accession. There's nothing he can gain but grief by interposing himself between me and the throne now. Do you agree?"

"There will be grief, yes. I have no doubt of that.—

Where are Gialaurys and Septach Melayn? In the vaults with Prestimion?"

"They are fled, I think," replied Korsibar. "Certainly Septach Melayn is gone—he fought with four guardsmen as he left, and chopped them into sausage-meat—and no one's seen Gialaurys since midday. I had no quarrel with either of them. I would only have asked a starburst or two from them, and that they call me 'my lord' when they spoke to me. You should say it too, Svor: 'My lord.' "

"If it pleases you, my lord."

"Not because it pleases me, but because it is my proper title of respect. One says those words when one addresses the Coronal."

"Yes, my lord."

Korsibar managed a pale smile. "Oh, Svor, Svor, you are the least trustworthy man who ever walked this planet, and I love you even so! Do you know how much I miss you? We were such warm friends; we drank of the same cup, we embraced the same women, we stayed up all through the night many a time telling wild stories, and ran to the river to swim at dawn. And then you went to Prestimion. Why did you leave me for him, Svor?"

"I never left you, my lord. You stand great in my heart, as much as ever. But I find much pleasure in Prestimion's company. And that of Gialaurys, and Septach Melayn, for whom I feel a great fondness and a deep interest in the ways of their minds, though I have little in common with either of them. Nor does either of them have much commonality with the other of them, for that matter. They are of two very different kinds."

"What they have in common is their feeling that Prestimion ought to be Coronal. And you also, I suppose."

"I've made the starburst to you, my lord."

"You would make it to these Skandars, if you felt need of

it.—What will you do now, Svor, with Prestimion in the vaults?"

"You said you would let him out in a day or two, my lord."

"Or three or four. First I'll want a starburst out of him too, Svor, and a little sincerity behind it."

"He may be in the vaults a long while, then," Svor said.

"So be it, then," said Korsibar. "We can have only one Coronal at a time in this world."

Svor said, after standing a moment in thought, "If it's not your intent to release Prestimion shortly, my lord, and I suspect that it is not, then I ask your lordship's permission to leave the Castle."

"And go where? You have no estate anywhere, do you, Svor? Only the apartments I provided for you here, in the days of our friendship, is that right?"

"A small suite has also been set aside for me in Muldemar House. I would go there, I suppose."

"To join Septach Melayn and Gialaurys, and conspire with them against me on Prestimion's behalf?"

"I have no idea where Septach Melayn and Gialaurys have gone, my lord. I feel uncomfortable at the Castle now, is all, knowing that Prestimion is in chains somewhere beneath my feet, and that I myself am free only at your pleasure, which at any moment may be withdrawn. You say you love me, my lord: very well, let me go. Muldemar is a quiet pretty place, and the wine is good, and the Princess Therissa makes me feel welcome there. By your leave, my lord, I would go to Muldemar. I say nothing of conspiring against you."

"But you will. I know that."

"I say nothing of that, my lord."

Korsibar tossed his beads aside, and stretched both his arms across the table toward Svor in a gesture of surprising warmth and vulnerability. A flashing energy came briefly into his weary eyes. "Listen to me," he said. "Go to Muldemar, if you like,

Svor. You have my permission, and Farquanor will give you a scrip of safe-conduct, if you ask him. I would never do you harm. Do you understand that, Svor? We were friends once, and in the name of that friendship I tell you now, I would never do you harm. But do me no harm either. I am Coronal, not Prestimion. That has already been decided. Do me no treasons, Svor. Conspire me no conspiracies. And if one should spring up anyway, I pray you, Svor, bring it to my ear. If not out of some vestige of affection for the friendship that once existed between us, then for the loyalty that you owe me as your king, and for your love for this world of ours of Majipoor. For Prestimion to make war against me for the throne would do irreparable damage to all the world, whichever one of us were to emerge wearing the crown."

"I have no doubt of that, my lord," said Svor. He made the starburst again, unasked. "And I thank you for your many kindnesses to me, past and present. May I go?"

Korsibar dismissed him with a weary wave of his hand. Svor lost no time removing himself from the Coronal's presence.

# 2

After a long and arduous journey by foot down from the summit of the Mount, Septach Melayn arrived grimy and ragged and footsore at Muldemar House, where news of Prestimion's incarceration had already come, and was conveyed at once to one of the guest apartments. There he bathed and lightly supped and took some wine, and changed into a fresh doublet and hose that belonged to Abrigant, Prestimion's second brother, who was nearly as tall as he was himself. Afterward in the great hall of the house, where heavy red draperies closed them in on all sides, he gave Prestimion's mother and all his brothers such news as he had, which was very little: only that the prince and Korsibar had had hot words at a private meeting, and Korsibar had clapped him straightaway into the Sangamor tunnels. That did not come as news to them.

"It was little use our staying," he told them. "Korsibar would only have put us away in chains also."

"You did well to flee while you could," agreed the Princess Therissa. "But this is very rash of Korsibar, so shamefully to detain a great prince of the realm this way. Can't he see how this high-handedness threatens all the other lords of the Castle?"

"He gave no thought to what he was doing, I think. Svor saw the picture clearly, as so often he does: is a weakness in Korsibar's soul, said Svor, will make him strike of a sudden where no strike is called for, sheerly out of the fear that's in him. So he was ready to lash out overseverely, at any provocation Prestimion might give. And I think Prestimion may well have given him one."

"Of what sort?" the Princess Therissa asked.

"Korsibar did offer Prestimion a Council seat, or some such high post as that, at that meeting between them in the throneroom: this much we know. And Prestimion, I would wager, did angrily throw the appointment back at him like a rotting fish."

"Prestimion would have done that, yes," said the warlike brother Abrigant, with glee in his eyes.

"Ah, was not wise to do, when Korsibar sits so high, and fears Prestimion so much," said Septach Melayn. "But Prestimion's more impulsive these days than he was before, and sometimes too fiery, to his great cost."

"There's always been hot fire in him," said the Princess Therissa, "that with great effort he keeps always banked and within its bounds; but it must have been too much for him to hold his control, seeing Korsibar on Lord Confalume's throne, and deigning to give a mere Council seat to him whose seat should have been that same throne."

Septach Melayn nodded. "You have it precisely, milady. We warned Prestimion not to go to the meeting at all, for it would only compromise and endanger him; or if he did, to withhold any immediate answer to whatever offer might come, but say he wanted to take counsel at Muldemar House over whether to accept it or no. That would have bought him a little time. Yet I think he could not hold his temper, Prestimion. It must have galled him even to make the starburst to Korsibar, or to bend the knee and call him 'my lord.' Yes. That's where it all broke down, right there, I think: right at the very beginning, when the homage was due."

"I agree. He would never kneel gladly to Korsibar," said Prestimion's brother Taradath.

"No," said Septach Melayn. "That he would not. His anger is too great, and his pain."

"Pain?" the Princess Therissa.

"Oh, yes, milady. Prestimion is in terrible pain over the loss of the crown. You'd never know it, were you talking with him: is calm and easy, takes a philosophical approach. But within him all is wrath and fire." Septach Melayn held forth his wine-bowl, and Taradath filled it brimming. "Korsibar will do no real harm to Prestimion, I think. Is full of confusion and uncertainty, Korsibar is, finding himself suddenly king who never should have been there. Follows this one's advice and then that one's, having no clear path of his own in mind. But I think his heart is warm toward Prestimion despite all, and would not ever bring himself to injure him. A few days more and he'll see there's no sense in keeping him in the vaults, and will let him come forth."

"The Divine grant you be right in that," the Princess Therissa said.

"Korsibar's done him plenty of injury already, by stealing the throne from him," said Abrigant. "I'd have lost my temper too, standing there before Korsibar and expected to make starbursts to him."

"Prestimion should have had a knife with him," said the fierce youngest brother, Teotas, "and gone up the steps of the throne and cut the thieving Korsibar's throat with it!"

"You are not the first to suggest something of that sort," Septach Melayn said, smiling. "Which reminds me: has any word come here from Gialaurys? We were separated as we left the Castle. This place was where we agreed to meet."

"Nothing," said the Princess Therissa.

"And Svor? From him, anything?"

She shook her head again. But Prince Taradath said, "Not

so, mother. Word has arrived within the hour from Duke Svor, who says that he is safe and has permission from Lord Korsibar to leave the Castle, and will be coming shortly to Muldemar House. He says there's no news of Prestimion but he has strong reason to believe Korsibar has no thought of taking his life."

Septach Melayn tapped the dark obsidian tabletop with pleasure. "Svor safe! So Korsibar's not forgotten his old love for his slippery little friend of former days. This is good news: means, perhaps, that Korsibar's softening after his burst of wrath, and Prestimion's release will not be far behind. But I fear for Gialaurys even so. Is too quick to seek a battle, that one, and may have taken on more than even he could handle on the way to the Castle gate."

But just then came a servant at the door, with word of another guest at Muldemar House; and it was Gialaurys, looking even more threadbare than Septach Melayn had been at his own arrival a little while earlier, and a great swollen purplish welt down the left side of his face. He seemed cheerful enough, though, such as cheerful was, to a man of Gialaurys's brooding nature. He embraced Septach Melayn with bone-cracking joy and downed three bowls of ruby wine running within the first ten minutes of his presence there.

Septach Melayn told him of Svor's message, and asked Gialaurys of his escape from the Castle. That had been easily enough accomplished, said Gialaurys, except that he had found the approach to the Gossif gate too thick with guardsmen, and had gone instead around to the Halanx side, where guards had had time to assemble also and were waiting for him. So there had been a brawl, and he feared that he had returned a few of the guardsmen to the Source, which he regretted, but they would not give him a free path and so had left him no choice. "You know the long-nosed lieutenant of the guards, Himbergaze?" Gialaurys asked. "I knocked him over the side of Canaberu Keep, and he made a very loud landing below. Will not, I think, be doing much guarding again. That's how I got this." He tapped the great welt on his cheek.

"He struck you in the face?" Septach Melayn asked.

Gialaurys chuckled. "The other way round. I butted him with my head, as he came at me to grapple me. Went flying up all amazed, and over the parapet's edge. I wish I'd done that to Farholt when we wrestled at the Pontifex's games." He rose and surveyed the tatters of his clothing unhappily. "On my way down the Mount I came through the thorn forest of Quisquis: not a pleasant route. Look at me now!"

"This is Prince Abrigant's doublet I'm wearing," said Septach Melayn, with a glance about at Prestimion's three willowy brothers. "My journey here left me on the ragged side also. But I think there's no clothing here vast enough for you, my friend. Perhaps one of the hostlers can fetch you a spare tent that milady's seamstresses can stitch into trousers for you."

"You are ever the jolly one," Gialaurys said, with no jot of amusement in his voice.

But the Princess Therissa told them then that new garments could be fashioned for him swiftly enough; and they were, by morning. By morning, also, Duke Svor was at the gates of Muldemar House, having come at the head of a caravan of five pack-mounts, bringing a load of goods, among them a welcome array of clothing that he had fetched from the rooms of Gialaurys and Septach Melayn.

He told them of his conversation with Korsibar, and of his hopes of Prestimion's imminent release.

"What are they saying at the Castle," asked Septach Melayn, "about Korsibar's arresting him? What does Serithorn say, or Oljebbin?"

"Not very much," Svor replied. "You understand, I lost little time in getting myself away from there, and didn't go about the place discussing the matter with a great many folk. But from what I did hear, it seems everyone is too astonished to speak out, and is pretending that all is proceeding in ordinary fashion, while waiting to see what Korsibar does next."

"As it has been since this thing began," said Gialaurys darkly. "Korsibar snatches the crown, and no one speaks out against him, not even Confalume himself, everybody waiting timidly to see what happens next. So Korsibar comes to the Castle and takes possession of the government unchallenged. Now Korsibar throws Prestimion in the dungeon, and it's the same. Are they all such cowards? Why doesn't Oljebbin rise up, or Gonivaul, or anyone, and cry out against these unlawful follies?"

Septach Melayn said, "You sat here in this very house and listened to the stirring words of the brave Oljebbin, and the fearless Gonivaul, and the courageous Serithorn too, with your own ears. One after another they told us they would wait and see, and observe the doings of Korsibar very carefully before taking any position, and make no moves against him until it was appropriate to do so. 'We will do nothing hasty or rash,' said Serithorn, or was it Gonivaul? I forget which one. But it was the same words out of all their mouths."

"They promised to support Prestimion if he rose against Korsibar," Gialaurys said.

"In a lukewarm pigeonhearted way," said Svor. "Hedged all around with ifs and buts and maybes, and nothing said about supporting Prestimion if Korsibar rose against *him*. Ah, what do you think, Gialaurys? That those feeble-spirited comfort-loving old men will stand up and bluster and rage against the detention of Prestimion, when Korsibar need do nothing more than snap his fingers and they'll be down in the Sangamor tunnels themselves a moment later? Korsibar holds all the advantage. The high lords fear him and mistrust each other. In all the land, there's only one aside from Prestimion who dares to stand up to Korsibar and who might help us wrest Prestimion free of Korsibar's grasp. Of course, he's no angel himself."

"The Procurator, you mean?" said Septach Melayn.

"Who else? If we're to make any sort of opposition to Korsibar, it can only be done with the help of Dantirya Sambail. He's Prestimion's kinsman, after all: who better to demand Prestimion's release? There's a powerful man, with powerful armies at his back,and wealth and determination besides, and five times as clever as Korsibar as well."

"And also much personal charm and sweetness of soul," said Septach Melayn. "Not to mention his great beauty and love of small animals. What a fine ally he would be, Svor!"

"In any case, Dantirya Sambail is far out at sea at this moment, heading toward Zimroel," Gialaurys said. "Even if he turned around the moment he landed at Piliplok, it would be months before he could get all the way back here. Assuming he would even want to do it."

"Ah, no," Svor said. "He's not at sea at all. Is my understanding he went no more than halfway to Alaisor port, and word reached him of Prestimion's being taken captive. Canceled his voyage at once, and began to march immediately back toward the Mount."

"You know this for fact?" Septach Melayn asked.

"I know nothing for fact except the number of my fingers and toes," responded Svor, "and there are days when even that is in doubt. But I heard it from reliable people in Muldemar city, as I was coming through there this morning, that Dantirya Sambail with all his horde of followers is heading this way. Is it so? I could cast some runes on it, but you'd not believe those findings either, eh, Septach Melayn? So all we can do is wait. Here sit we, and Dantirya Sambail will come, or else he will not. I've told you what we know."

"What price will he ask, do you think, for getting Prestimion out of that dungeon?" Gialaurys said. "He does nothing without exacting a good price."

Septach Melayn said, "A good point. Prestimion will be greatly beholden to him, and the reckoning will be an expensive one. If Prestimion ever comes to power in the world, Dantirya Sambail will sit at his right hand. Well, and nothing can be done about it, unless we can magic Prestimion out of that cellar without the Procurator's help, and we can't. Here sit we, as Svor says, and wait to watch what unfolds."

"It is a pleasant place to sit, at least," said Svor. "And the wine is very good."

The days passed, and news of varying sorts came daily to Muldemar House, not all of it totally trustworthy. Prince Prestimion, they were told, would be released on Seaday next; no, it would be Moonday; no, Threeday. But Prestimion was not released, not on Threeday nor on Fourday, nor on any day at all. From Akbalik came word that Prince Serithorn had visited Prestimion in the vaults, and that Prestimion seemed healthy enough, though much amazed at Korsibar's temerity at holding him prisoner like that, and unhappy about the quality and quantity of the fare, which had given him a pale and somewhat haggard look. As for Lord Korsibar, he had been glimpsed very little of late: he kept to his private chambers, and Navigorn and Farquanor and Mandrykarn were often seen going to him, but life at court seemed to be at a standstill during this strange time of crisis. The Lady Thismet, too, was rarely seen in public. A tale had come forth, from one lady-of-honor to another and then through a circuitous chain of gossipers, that Thismet and her brother Lord Korsibar were estranged over some matter and that the breach was a deep and serious one.

"I have here a letter from my friend the Lady Heisse Vaneille of Bailemoona saying that the quarrel is over Prestimion," reported Svor. "It seems the Lady Thismet has begged most tearfully for Prestimion to be set free, declaring that Prestimion is very close to her heart and she would not have him locked away like this. Which so infuriated the Coronal that he threatened to have *her* locked away too in some other part of the tunnels."

"They will all be chained up in the Sangamor if this continues," said Septach Melayn, with a grin. He gave Svor a questioning look. "Do you know anything about this, you man of the ladies? I mean this sudden affection that has sprung up between Thismet and Prestimion. It was my belief she detested him."

"Anything's possible, where men and women are concerned," said Svor. "I tell you only what Heisse Vaneille told me."

"A very reliable informant is she, this slut of yours?" Septach Melayn asked.

Svor peered sourly at the swordsman and said, "You do her a great injustice. She is a fine woman of the best family of Bailemoona. But let me continue my news, for there is more. The Pontifex Confalume has left the Castle to return to his duties in the Labyrinth."

"Turning a blind eye once again to his son's crimes," said Septach Melayn.

Gialaurys said darkly, "He's under some spell of sorcery, the Pontifex is. There's no other explanation for the way he carries himself these days. This is not anything like the Confalume of old, to be such a supine thing; but Sanibak-Thastimoon, or some other wizard even more sinister in Korsibar's employ, has put a magic on him. I know that for a surety."

"You may well be right," said Svor. "Further: the Lady

Roxivail also is gone, on her way to Alaisor to take a ship to the Isle of Sleep and assume her role as Lady of the Isle."

"May the Lady Kunigarda greet her with spears," Septach Melayn said.

"There is also," said Svor, "news of the Procurator Dantirya Sambail. Those earlier reports that I had that he had turned back from Alaisor are correct. He is marching toward the Mount with all his followers. He and his party have been seen in Coragem, and Tedesca, and Klatre, and Bland. Word is that he'll be at Pivrarch or Lontano in another week and will make his ascent of the Mount from that side, coming here to Muldemar to confer with us—he knows that we are safe, and here—before going to the Castle to confront Lord Korsibar. He's already sent a message ahead to Korsibar, says the Lady Heisse Vaneille, who has it from Akbalik, notifying him of his displeasure at Prestimion's internment."

"If this is true," said Septach Melayn, "he might send a message to us also, letting us in on some knowledge of his plans."

But no message came. What came instead was Dantirya Sambail himself, presenting himself as he had before at Muldemar House without warning, a dark presence in the middle of a warm sunny afternoon, accompanied by his horde of followers and requesting food and wine and lodging for them all.

The Procurator, resplendent as always in his peacock clothes, high-waisted yellow doublet this time with winged sleeves and cuffs of lace above blue velvet breeches, and long-tipped turquoise shoes with trimming of yellow satin ribbon, gathered with Septach Melayn and Svor and Gialaurys and the brothers of Prestimion in the long room that was known as the cabinet of arms, where a hundred ornate antique bows that Prestimion had collected, and a great assortment of fanciful arrows, were mounted along the white granite walls. The

Procurator's hatchet-faced poison-taster Mandralisca hovered as ever at his left elbow.

As chamberlains of the house poured cool wine of a fine vintage for them all, Dantirya Sambail said, after drinking deep and greedily once it had been pronounced safe for him, "What do you hear lately of my cousin Prestimion? Is he being treated well? Are there any plans for his release?"

"We have no direct news," replied Septach Melayn. "Only the tales at second-hand, or third. We're told that he's reasonably well, but that news is several weeks old. No visitors have been permitted him lately."

The Procurator sat heavily forward and dug his thumbs deep into his pink fleshy jowls, and ran his hand slowly up the great shining dome of his forehead. Then he beckoned for still more wine. His bowl was filled yet again; Mandralisca took his little sip; Dantirya Sambail drained the rest at a long voracious gulp. Displeasure and even disgust was evident on the faces of several of the brothers of Prestimion.

He said, at length, "You three are his beloved minions, and you three"—with a sour glare sweeping over Taradath and Abrigant and Teotas—"are his brothers. Yet all six of you sit lazily here at Muldemar House doing nothing. Why is that? Why are you not at the Castle filling the air with protests over the disgraceful treatment being given the Prince Prestimion? I never heard it said of you that you were lacking in courage, Septach Melayn. Or you in guile, Duke Svor."

"We were waiting for you," said Septach Melayn. "You are the missing piece in the puzzle. We go ourselves, and we'd be popped into the manacles faster than you can drink a bowl of Prestimion's wine, for what are we but mere appurtenances to Prestimion? But you are no one's appurtenance. This is not a matter of courage nor of guile, Dantirya Sambail, but of power. You alone have the power to make Korsibar relent. I speak of the army at your command in Zimroel."

"Ah," the Procurator said. "So this is my task. I suspected as much. You'll come with me, at least?"

"If you think it's best that we do, yes. Certainly," Septach Melayn said.

"You three, then, come," said Dantirya Sambail, indicating Septach Melayn, Svor, and Gialaurys.

"And what of us?" asked Abrigant, with some heat in his voice.

"I think not. Your work is to make Muldemar House safe and ready for your brother's return. Begin gathering the men of your city and preparing them for the possibility of battle."

"Battle?" said Septach Melayn and Gialaurys in the same breath, both of them instantly excited. Svor said nothing, but his gaze turned distant under his heavy brows.

"Battle, yes. If Korsibar won't give us Prestimion willingly, we'll take him by force. And then the fat will truly be in the fire, eh?" The Procurator grinned a wolfish grin. "I want thirty strong men-at-arms from among your people," he said to Taradath and Abrigant, "and I want them dressed in the same livery as my own company."

"Muldemar people in Ni-moya colors?" said the scholarly Taradath immediately, bristling. "How could we allow a thing like that?" And the tall fiery young Abrigant came halfway out of his seat in rage.

Dantirya Sambail waved one broad meaty hand. "Peace, cousins, peace. I mean no offense. I want only to achieve your brother's freedom. Attend me, here: I have seventy-six men of my own. You give me thirty more, begins to seem an impressive force, enough to make Korsibar take notice. But if they wear my colors they are merely my traveling retinue, the ones I had with me at the Labyrinth to accompany me to the Pontifex's funeral. Is innocent enough, that. I show up at the Castle now accompanied by a second troop of men in Muldemar colors, it seems more like we are mustering an army against the Coronal in his own home, which is a threat no Coronal could ever abide. You follow me, do you? The extra men will be useful, but we disguise them a little to avoid a premature onset of hostilities."

The brothers still were restless and unsure.

"Do it," Svor urged them. "It is a good plan." And to Dantirya Sambail he said, "Take fifty instead of thirty, perhaps?"

"Thirty should be enough," the Procurator replied. "For now."

Svor had not expected to be back at the Castle so soon. But Dantirya Sambail was an irresistible force; and so here he stood with Dantirya Sambail before Korsibar in the old Stiamot throne-room, which the new Coronal apparently had begun using lately for most audiences instead of the far more imposing one that his father had built. It was an austere little room, stark and simple—a low throne of plain white marble, benches beside it for the Coronal's ministers, a triangular floor of smooth gray paving-blocks covered by a purple-and-gray Makroposopos carpet that copied some ancient design.

Count Farquanor was seated to one side of Korsibar, and Sanibak-Thastimoon at the other. In the facing group, Svor and Septach Melayn stood at the Procurator's right hand, and the poison-taster Mandralisca at his left. Gialaurys was not with them; he had announced defiantly beforehand that he would not bow and make starbursts to Korsibar, and so he was below, with the hundred men in Dantirya Sambail's colors who had accompanied them to the Castle.

Korsibar seemed oddly diminished, after these additional weeks of his kingship. Much of his old swashbuckling vitality had vanished, and he looked wan and gray-faced now. His shoulders were slumped, his skin showed an indoor pallor and not its customary sun-darkened hue, his cheekbones stood out sharply. Though there still was an outward look of force and strength about him, his jaws were clenched and his eyes were ringed by dark shadows and rigidly set as though he had been applying that strength lately to a burden far too great even for him. He seemed a haunted man.

It was Duke Svor's task to guard against Sanibak-Thastimoon putting a mind-clouding spell on them as he had done at the taking of the crown in the Labyrinth. For, as Dantirya Sambail had pointed out, Svor had the knack of sniffing out sorcery, even if he was unable to perform much of it himself, and so he would defend them against treachery. Svor stared at the Su-Suheris now, offering him now and again a dark warning glance, as though to say, *I am on to your tricks, try none of them this day! And Septach Melayn is here with his sword for those two necks of yours, if you do.*

Dantirya Sambail, standing splay-legged directly in front of Korsibar with his massive head thrust aggressively forward, began: "You received my message, I think, my lord, concerning the detention of my cousin Prestimion?"

"The message reached us, yes." Korsibar delivered those words very coolly.

"It was some weeks ago I sent it. I am informed, my lord, that Prince Prestimion continues to be detained."

"The prince is in a condition of rebellion against our authority. When he cures that condition, he'll be released, Dantirya Sambail. Not before."

"Ah," said the Procurator. "And how may he accomplish that, my lord?"

"When you entered our presence, you made the starburst to us, and knelt, and greeted us as 'my lord.' The Duke Svor very kindly did the same, and even the Count Septach Melayn. We must have the same courtesy from the Prince Prestimion; and then he will be a free man again."

Dantirya Sambail said, "He has refused you the ceremony due a Coronal? Is that it?"

"He has refused, yes. I sat upon the Confalume throne itself and asked him—more like a suppliant than like a king—to give me my due." Anger glinted in Korsibar's eyes. But, Svor noticed, for the moment he had stopped referring to himself in the royal plural. "As one old friend to another, I asked him, and said it was simply that which is due me, for I am king. And he said to me that I was not king."

"He said that, did he?"

"To my face. My regime is unlawful, he said. The world has no legitimate Coronal at this time, he said."

"Ah. He said those things."

"He did, and I said to him to take back the words, and he left them untaken; and so he is in the vaults, and I will leave him there until such time as he tells me that he recognizes me as true Coronal."

"Ah. *Ah*." And then Dantirya Sambail asked: "May I have leave to speak with him, my lord?"

"No, you may not."

"It might be," said Dantirya Sambail, "that I could persuade him to yield in this matter."

"I allowed him some visitors at first. But he has had no company of any kind for the past nineteen days, other than a certain highly annoying Vroon who is chained in the same vault as his. I prefer to keep him in this semi-solitude until his resolve to defy me has melted entirely."

"I might hasten its melting, my lord," the Procurator said. "Show him where the path of reason lies, and—"

"No, Dantirya Sambail. No. No. No. Must I say the word yet again? Then I shall: *No*." And Korsibar's lips clamped tight shut on that final emphatic syllable.

It seemed to Svor, watching this exchange from his place at the side, that Korsibar had been on the verge of threatening the Procurator with imprisonment himself, if he persisted in this course of argument, but had bit back the words at the last moment before uttering them. It seemed to Svor, also, that Dantirya Sambail had understood that the threat was imminent, and was ready for it. But the words went unspoken, and so did the hot response that Dantirya Sambail held in waiting for them.

In the little silence that followed, the Procurator, who had been standing motionless like a great block of stone before Korsibar, turned now and spoke a word to Mandralisca. He nodded and made a hasty starburst to the Coronal, and went from the room. Then Dantirya Sambail said, in a pleasant easy tone just as if he and the Coronal had not a moment before been at loggerheads, "Tell me, then, my lord, is my beloved cousin reported to be in good state, after these weeks in the vaults? For he is very dear to me, and his well-being is of high importance to me."

"We're not starving him, Dantirya Sambail. Nor torturing him, nor harming him in any other way except to interfere with his freedom to come and go as he pleases. Which freedom he can have again readily enough in a moment, for the price of a starburst and a bended knee."

"I would like assurances, my lord, that he's been faring well under the stress of his confinement."

Count Farquanor leaned across, at this, and whispered something to Sanibak-Thastimoon. The Su-Suheris responded with a double nod and turned to speak with Korsibar. But Korsibar shook him off and said icily to Dantirya Sambail, "You have just had such assurances, Procurator."

Then Dantirya Sambail: "You told me only what you were not doing to him, my lord, not how he actually was faring."

Farquanor now it was who said, in a cold, harsh voice, "Is it your purpose to give offense to the Coronal, Dantirya Sambail? Your precious cousin Prestimion—a very distant cousin, is that not so?—is intact and well. Be comfortable on that point, and give over this questioning. Not even the Procurator of Ni-moya may subject the Coronal to vexation of this sort."

And from Korsibar: "Why are you here at all, Dantirya Sambail? You told me that you were returning to Zimroel out of a terrible homesickness, and to carry the word of Lord Korsibar's accession to your people there. Instead we find you back at the Castle only a few months after taking your leave. Why is that?"

"You know why I'm here," Dantirya Sambail replied evenly. "But it would vex the Coronal if I stated it once more, and I am forbidden by Count Farquanor's own decree to vex the Coronal."

"May I have leave to speak, lordship?" Septach Melayn asked, who had been silent all this while. "We are at an impasse here. But I have a compromise to propose."

"Speak, then," Korsibar said.

"Prestimion, so I understand it, has given offense by refusing you proper obeisance. Very well. But you hope to extract that obeisance from him under compulsion, my lord, and surely you know Prestimion well enough to realize that he'll never give it that way."

"He is an unyielding man, yes," Korsibar acknowledged.

"Well, then: you have in return charged him with rebellion and sentenced him to imprisonment until he repents, and since he won't repent he'll languish in the vaults until he dies, which may be sooner rather than later if that place is as wearisome as I've heard. Then the word will go out that the Coronal Lord Korsibar has done his former rival Prince Prestimion of Muldemar to death for sedition, and how will that look in the world, considering how well loved Prestimion is in all the provinces of Majipoor? Forgive me, my lord, but I tell you it will be interpreted as a vile act, that can only injure the love that the people bear for you in these the earliest days of your reign."

"Enough. I seek an end on this. What is the compromise you suggest, Septach Melayn?" asked Korsibar, in a voice ragged with strain.

"That we will make no open protest against the treatment that Prestimion has received at your hands, but also that you give him to us this day, my lord, and let us go back to Muldemar with him. In that place it may well happen that his mother and his brothers and we can convince him of the grave error of his ways. You can never accomplish that in the dungeons, my lord, never, but we, perhaps, reasoning with him calmly and persuasively—"

And Korsibar: "This is your idea of compromise? You must think I'm a fool. There is no possibility whatever that—"

"Lordship!" cried a hoarse voice outside. The door burst open and two guardsmen came running in, panting and disheveled. "The prisoner—they've broken into the vaults—"

Korsibar, gaping, sat as if stunned. Farquanor was on his feet, red-faced, shouting. Even the impassive Sanibak-Thastimoon seemed swept by surprise and dismay. An instant later Mandralisca rushed into the room and to Dantirya Sambail's side, and whispered into his ear. Dantirya Sambail listened, frowning at first, and then smiling.

Serenely the Procurator said, looking up now at Korsibar, "It seems there has been some sort of skirmish, my lord, between my men and a group of your guardsmen. It appears to have taken place at the entrance to Lord Sangamor's tunnels, and during the unfortunate brawling the sealed gateway to the tunnels was damaged to a certain degree, so that entry became possible. I am saddened to say that I believe there have been casualties. Also a Skandar archer in my service evidently chose this opportunity to determine whether his fellow archer Prince Prestimion had been treated properly during his imprisonment, and, finding the prince not in completely satis-factory condition, has removed him from the vaults so that he can receive the medical care he apparently needs."

The placid way he announced all this left Svor rapt with astonishment and admiration. Dantirya Sambail's complacent calmness seemed to have wrapped Korsibar in some spell of remarkable acquiescence to the thing that had happened in the vaults. Korsibar's mouth opened and closed again, but no words came forth. Inner conflicts made themselves apparent in the roiling of his features and the knotting of his forehead; and yet he offered, for the moment, no response to this amazing news, even though it connoted virtual insurrection against his authority. As Korsibar remained silent Farquanor seemed to come to the verge of speaking out, but Korsibar waved him to silence with a brusque imperious gesture.

Dantirya Sambail spoke on, smoothly, easily into the vacuum of authority that Korsibar was leaving for him:

"It is a delicate situation, lordship. What I propose, there-fore, is that we agree at once on the compromise just put forth by Count Septach Melayn. There will be peace between the faction of the Coronal and the faction of Prince Prestimion henceforward, and no recriminations on either side for what has occurred; and I will take Prince Prestimion into my own custody immediately, and will make myself personally respons-ible for his good behavior."

Sanibak-Thastimoon stirred uneasily now as though con-sidering some action. Svor, looking toward him, made a small threatening witchcraft-sign in the air with his forefinger and thumb. The Su-Suheris, subsiding, became once more as still as a statue. Farquanor, though still glowering at the edge of eruption, held himself also in check. All eyes went to Korsibar.

And Korsibar, taking this in all frozen-faced, stared the wide-eyed glassy stare of one who is face to face with a deadly serpent that has already begun to weave in readiness to strike.

He was adrift like a dreamer, unable to move or respond; and the dream was not a good one.

For here he was being mocked and defied most outrageously in his own throne-room by Dantirya Sambail. And yet it seemed he dared not show that he was offended. That struck Svor as incredible. Perhaps because Korsibar was still insecure in his own stolen crown and incapable this day of going up against the wishes of the crass and violent and dangerous Procurator of Ni-moya, whose power was so great and who was capable, when provoked, of any action at all. Whatever the reason, Korsibar seemed paralyzed in the face of this monstrous show of contempt for his power.

Svor held his breath in amazement. He could scarce believe that this was taking place, for all that Dantirya Sambail had told them concerning his intentions just an hour before they had entered here.

The Procurator continued in the same tranquil way:

"It is my intention, my lord, to withdraw from this place at once and once more undertake my journey on your behalf to Zimroel; and it is my plan to permit Count Septach Melayn and his companion Duke Svor to remove Prince Prestimion at once from the Castle and take him to Muldemar House, where he can recuperate from his recent hardships at leisure. After which, I'm altogether sure that every attempt will be made to persuade the prince to undertake the acts of homage that are incumbent upon him as your lordship's obedient subject, and that these attempts will prove successful."

With a splendid flourish Dantirya Sambail presented the numbed-looking Korsibar with a flurry of starbursts and a deep bow. "I bid you good day and a long life, my lord, and I offer all regards for the success of your reign." And he turned to go from the room.

Korsibar, who still seemed unable to speak, made a small gesture of acceptance and assent with his left hand, and sank back in a defeated way against his royal seat. Svor, feeling a sweeping admiration for Dantirya Sambail's consummate audacity of a sort he had rarely felt before, looked at the Procurator in wonder and awe.

So it came to pass, then, that they walked out of Korsibar's presence unscathed, Svor and Septach Melayn and Dantirya Sambail, and also that Prestimion had his freedom, by gift of his fierce-hearted kinsman the Procurator. But for this gift, they all knew, there would be a good price exacted.

And when they were safely through the Castle gates, and riding down to Muldemar once more, the Procurator said to the pale and haggard Prestimion, "We are now at war with Korsibar, cousin, would you not think? For surely he will not long tolerate what I've just done. Collect you an army, and I will do the same."

# 3

After a week at Muldemar House, during which time he and his henchmen ate and drank like a herd of snuffling insatiable habbagogs rooting through a field of succulent crops just come to ripeness, Dantirya Sambail took himself off toward Alhanroel's western coast to await armies that he had called up by swift messengers out of his native continent. "I pledge you an enormous force of fighting men at your disposal, such as has never been seen on this world," the Procurator told Prestimion grandiloquently. "My own stout brothers Gaviad and Gaviundar will be your generals, and you'll have lieutenants of the most fearsome valor."

Prestimion was glad to see him go. He bore a grudging fascinated fondness for his strange and ruthless kinsman, and was grateful, of course, for his rescue, but had no great love for extended doses of his company: especially not now, when he felt so weak and weary, and had such a heavy making of plans to do. The Procurator would only be a drain on his already impaired vigor at a time like this.

The prince's face was lean and gaunt from the weeks of his captivity, his eyeballs sunken in on their sockets, his skin a drab grayish tone, his golden hair dull and lifeless. He had acquired a tremor of the hands, and dared not approach his archery-course at all, out of fear that his great skill had rusted away in Lord Sangamor's vaults. Most of the day, those first few days, he rested in his bedchamber like a sick old man, with the draperies of heavy blue velour pulled back so that he could enjoy the beauty of the green hill beyond the curving window of faceted quartz, and that the beneficent rays of the sun flooding in might speed the replenishing of his greatly lessened resources.

His friends had been aghast at the sight of him when he first came forth from the vaults. Gialaurys was incoherent with fury. Svor's fingers coiled about one another like anguished serpents. But now they were in Muldemar, and as ever, Septach Melayn bubbled over with optimism. "A little decent food in you, a few sips of wine each day, Prestimion—fresh air, the river, the sun—look, you begin to heal already, and you're only newly free!—Were they starving you in there, is that it?"

Prestimion smiled wryly. "Starving would have been no worse, I think, than eating the stuff they gave me. Such slops I wouldn't feed to mintuns scavenging in the streets! A thin sour soup of old cabbage it was, most of the time, with fragments of the Divine only knows what sort of tired meat swimming in it—pfaugh! And the light: that terrible throbbing light, Septach Melayn, hammering at me out of the walls every hour and every minute of every day and every night! That was the worst of it, far beyond the awful food. If I never see anything red again, it'll be a hundred years too soon."

"They say the unending light of the tunnels was put in those stones by some ancient magic now forgotten," Svor observed. "And the magic that turns it off has been forgotten also."

Prestimion shrugged. "Magic, science—who knows where the distinction lies? It is a dreadful thing, that light. It hits you hard as a fist. There is no hiding from it. You close your eyes and still you see it behind your lids, and you feel it day and night. I'd have gone mad altogether but for the little green amulet of Thalnap Zelifor, which gave me some defense." A bemused look came over him. "He told me how it was used.

I would stroke the thing with my fingertip, in this fashion, every mealtime when they unshackled my hands. And as I did so I said secretly, inside my head, as though I were praying to the Divine: *Let my eyes be eased, let me have some rest.* And after a fashion it worked, do you know? Bad as things were for me, I think they would have been even worse without my having done that. Though who or what I was praying to, I could not guess: not the Divine, surely.—What became of that little Vroon, anyway?"

"He's here at Muldemar House," said Septach Melayn.

"Here? How did that happen?"

"He was freed when you were, and in the confusion attached himself to us, and came along with us from the Castle."

"Well," said Prestimion, smiling, "there's no harm in that, I suppose. I came to like him more than a little, in all that time while we were penned up facing each other on the walls of our tunnel."

"You are a very tolerant and kindly man," said Svor. "You find things to like in the most surprising people."

"Even the vile Korsibar," said Gialaurys, with a furious grimace. "You continued to have good words for him even after he did you out of your throne. But not, I think, any longer."

"No." And red wrath flared up in Prestimion's eyes. He had reached some turning point in that prison, that much was evident. "For a long while I thought of him as a decent simple man who was pushed onward in an evil course by villains and monsters; but I see now that a man who pays heed to monsters ultimately makes himself one also. Korsibar had no mercy on me, merely because I'd not grovel before him as he sat on his stolen throne. And I'll have none on him when things are reversed. There will be a reckoning now, and a heavy one, for all that has happened."

"Well, now! Well! So the sweet Prestimion we love is now the savage vengeful Prestimion who will do battle to take his rightful seat at the Castle," said Septach Melayn. "I take this for the best of news. Plainly it was Korsibar's most foolish day, out of a great many such, when he thrust you into that dungeon. For now it will be war."

"It will be war now, yes," Prestimion said.

He drew from his bedside table a coiled chart and spread it out on his knees facing them to show them the plan. It was the map of Alhanroel, done in a multitude of bright colors, with many a fancy scrolling ornament and curlicue. He tapped it at the place where Castle Mount was drawn in deep stark purple rising high above all else.

"We must isolate the Castle before we attack its false Coronal. This we will do both by words and by deeds. There will be a proclamation, first, in my name and in that of the present Lady of the Isle of Dreams, to the effect that Korsibar holds the Castle against all law and precedent, by dint of having worked a sorcery against his father Lord Confalume in the hour of Prankipin's death, and that he is a false usurper and traitor against the will of the Divine, who must be cast down from the great height that he has illicitly made his own."

"The present Lady of the Isle?" Svor said. "You mean Kunigarda, I suppose, and not Roxivail. But do you actually have her support, Prestimion?"

"I will. She's come to me three times in dreams, these past four weeks, to tell me so. I'll have a message on its way to her quickly, confirming that I'm free and intend to challenge Korsibar's claim to be Coronal. And I will request a public statement from her, declaring that she recognizes me as Coronal Lord and has vowed never to give up her own place at the Isle to the illegally designated Roxivail, but only to my own mother once I am installed at the Castle. To which I think she will agree."

And Septach Melayn: "This business of claiming that Korsibar worked magic against Confalume when he grabbed the crown—do you believe that, Prestimion? Or are you only saying it for the sake of impressing the credulous?"

"It makes no difference what I believe in the privacy of my heart. You know that the mass of the people give credence to sorcery. If I charge that Confalume was ensorceled, that'll help turn them against Korsibar, which is my goal. No one wants a Coronal who improperly got his crown by dint of witchcraft."

"But it was by magic, anyway," said Gialaurys. "Oh, Prestimion, when will you believe the evidence that rises in mountains on all sides of you?"

Prestimion merely smiled. But it was a very wan smile.

Turning stubbornly to Septach Melayn, Gialaurys said, "You were there when it happened. Your own mind was clouded by the spell. Do you deny there was magic at work?"

"Something put a mist over my mind, that I freely admit. Whether it was magic or something else, I'm in no position to tell you." A wicked twinkle entered Septach Melayn's eyes. "My mind was clouded, Gialaurys. Since that was so, how could I know what was clouding it?"

Impatiently Prestimion said, tapping his chart again, "To continue. We proclaim the illegitimacy of Korsibar's reign, and descend the Mount to begin its encirclement. I'll announce myself as Coronal first in the city of Amblemorn, by the black marble monument that marks the old timber-line, where the ancient conquest of the Mount first began: for we will be commencing a new conquest of the Mount in that place. In Amblemorn I'll call for volunteers for my army. We'll have a host of Muldemar men with us, well armed, in case there's any trouble with local troops; but I think that Amblemorn will come over to us easily enough. From Amblemorn we proceed down the rest of the way to the foot of the Mount, at the place where the Glayge has its source. Then we move this way, to the west, going steadily rightward around the base of the Mount through each of the great foothill cities in its turn, Vilimong, Estotilaup, Simbilfant, Ghrav, and onward clear around the entire circuit." He jabbed his finger again and again to the chart, calling off the names. "Arkilon. Pruiz. Pivrarch. Lontano. Da. And here we come to Hazen, Megenthorp, Bevel, Salimorgen, Demigon Glade, and finally Matrician, where good Duke Fengiraz will open his arms to us, and Gordal, and then we are back at the Glayge, below Amblemorn, with the road to the Castle opening before us. How many people live in all those foothill cities? Fifty million? More, I would think. They'll flock to our banner: I know they will. And at the same time Dantirya Sambail will have come from Zimroel with his armies, and his warlike brothers Gaviad and Gaviundar, to join forces with us at the western base of the Mount. Meanwhile atop the Mount itself they will hear what is happening, and will they rally behind Korsibar against me? I think not. They'll tell each other that Lord Prestimion has the mandate of the Divine, and that Lord Korsibar is a false Coronal; and they will leave his side in droves. Then we begin to ascend the Mount."

He burst out suddenly then in a fit of coughing, and groped for the bowl at his bedside. Gialaurys handed it to him. Prestimion drank deeply, and took breath deep into his lungs, and closed his eyes a moment to regain his poise.

"There. What do you think, my friends?"

"I think you should have more rest," said Svor.

"Yes, and then? The plan?"

"Is no way it can fail," said Septach Melayn.

"Agreed," Gialaurys said. "The Divine is on our side."

"Indeed," said Svor, when the others looked toward him. But there was just the smallest hitch of hesitation in his response. And he said then, "First you should rest, Prestimion, and restore yourself. Then we'll march forth and see how it fares for us in this war."

How it fared was cheering enough at first. At Amblemorn, where Prestimion and his family had always been much beloved, there was a delegation to greet him with warm enthusiasm when he came down the road from Dundilmir. "Prestimion!" they cried, with hands upthrust in starbursts. "Lord Prestimion! Long live Lord Prestimion!" That was the first time any of the citizenry had called him that and made the starburst, and, smiling, he accepted the homage with modesty and confidence.

The banners of Korsibar that had been all over Amblemorn at Prestimion's last visit were gone, now, and they had Prestimion banners up instead in the same royal colors of green and gold. No doubt these were the ones they had planned to hoist when Prankipin died, and had hurriedly stored away when the throne so surprisingly went to Korsibar. Prestimion stood by the black stone shaft of the timber-line monument and solemnly pledged himself to restore the world to its proper state, and they cried out his name again and vowed to support his claim. And when he moved on down the Mount and made his westward turn to the foothill city of Vilimong with a great horde of men of Muldemar and some from Amblemorn at his back, everything was much the same, Vilimong hailing him gladly as the true Coronal and swelling his army by another regiment of fighters.

It was at Estotilaup, the next city beyond Vilimong at the foot of the Mount, that trouble first occurred.

Estotilaup was Confalume's ancestral city, and they felt a fierce pride in him there, which had carried over to his son Korsibar. It was a city of tall narrow white towers with pointed tops of red tile, ringed around by a formidable high gate of black iron palisades; and when Prestimion arrived before it, the gate stood ajar, but not by much, and was blocked to him by fifty men in the uniform of the municipal proctors who stood with folded arms outside it. A larger party of somber-faced armed troops was visible behind them, just within the palisade.

Duke Svor went forward and said, "This is the Coronal Lord Prestimion, who seeks entrance to your city and a meeting with your mayor."

"The Coronal Lord is Lord Korsibar," the chief of proctors replied, peering unhappily at the multitudes of armed men who stood behind Svor on the plain, "and we know Prestimion only as a prince of one of the cities of the Mount. If he has come here to subvert the throne, he will not be admitted."

Svor carried this news to Prestimion, who responded that they might well not care to recognize him as Coronal here, but even so they had no right to refuse entry to their city to the Prince of Muldemar. "Tell them that," said Prestimion.

"And let them see that we'll force entry if entry is denied us," said Septach Melayn, with more than a little vigor.

He raised his arm as though to signal to the frontmost detachment of Prestimion's troops that they should move closer to the gate. But Prestimion caught him midway between wrist and elbow and drew the arm downward. "No," he said sharply. "We'll force nothing here, not this soon. There's time to draw blood later, if we must; but I have no yearning to make war on innocent uncomprehending folk at Estotilaup gates."

"This is foolishness, my lord," said Septach Melayn.

"You call me 'my lord,' and you call me a fool also, all in the same breath?"

"Indeed. For you are my Coronal, and I am pledged to you to the death," the long-legged swordsman answered him. "But for all that you are a fool, if you think you can back away from conflict here, and force it at your convenience another day. Show these people of Estotilaup here and now that you are their king, who will not be turned away at their gate."

"I am with Septach Melayn on this," said Gialaurys.

"You both will quarrel with me?"

"When you are wrong, yes," said Gialaurys. "And here you are most gravely wrong."

"Well," said Prestimion, and laughed. "If this is my beginning at kingship, when I am bearded and defied by my own dearest companions, it will be a rocky reign." And to Svor he said, "Tell them that we will have entry, and no two ways about it." And instructed Septach Melayn to stand behind Svor with a squadron of some two hundred men, but to refrain from launching any hostile action unless attacked.

He himself withdrew to one side, and waited.

What happened then was unclear even to those who were in the thickest of it. Prestimion, standing apart, saw Svor in hot negotiation with the chief of proctors, the two men face to face and gesturing; and then suddenly there was an angry flurry of some sort, though hard to say where it began. The Estotilaup troops came rushing forward among the proctors, and Septach Melayn's men charged toward the gate also in one and the same instant. Swords flashed and there was the thrusting of spears and here and there the bright flaring red beams of those unreliable but deadly weapons, energy-throwers. Prestimion saw Septach Melayn towering over all the rest, wielding his rapier in a blaze of furious activity, the blade flashing with such rapidity the eye could scarce follow it, and drawing blood with every thrust, while with the other hand he plucked little Duke Svor up high, out of the midst of the melee. Several soldiers of each force were down with flowing wounds on the field. A man of Estotilaup staggered out of the brawl, staring uncomprehendingly at the red stump of his arm.

Prestimion began to lunge forward, heading for the gate. But he had taken no more than three steps before Gialaurys caught him about the chest and held him back.

"My lord? Where are you going?"

"This has to be stopped, Gialaurys."

"Then tell me so, and I will stop it. You are not to be put at risk here, my lord." He released Prestimion and ran in thunderous steps to the gate, where he forced his way into the muddled throng and came to Septach Melayn's side. Prestimion saw them conferring in the midst of the battle. The confusion continued another few moments more, until the order to withdraw had reached all of Prestimion's men. Then, suddenly, the clangor and shouting ceased; the Estotilaup men went rushing back within their gate and slammed it shut, and Gialaurys and Septach Melayn returned at the head of Prestimion's troops. Svor was huddled between them, looking pale and wan, for he was not built to a warrior's scale and lacked all appetite for bloodshed.

"They will not admit us except we make them do it," Svor reported. "On this they are resolved. Men have died already today to keep us out of this place, and many more will perish on both sides, I think, if we make a further attempt."

"Then we will give it over for now," said Prestimion, with a sharp glare of warning meant for Septach Melayn. "The next time we come here, they will roll out a precious carpet of Makroposopos for me to tread upon as I enter. But for now, I want no warfare made against my own people, is that clear? We will win their acceptance by the force of our righteousness, or else not at all." And he gave orders to draw back and march on to Simbilfant, which was the next city in their circuit of the Mount. Two men of their company had been killed, one of Muldemar and one of Amblemorn, and four wounded, in the skirmish; of the men of Estotilaup there were at least five seen dead or dying on the field.

"This troubles me," said Gialaurys quietly to Septach Melayn, as they returned to their floaters. "Can it be that he has no stomach for battle?" And Septach Melayn frowned and nodded, and replied that he had the same concern.

But Svor had overheard, and he laughed and said, "Him? Is a fighter, no doubting it! And will slash and slaughter with the best of you, when the time comes. Is not yet the time, is what he thinks. Is not fully reconciled within his soul, either, to the knowledge that he will reach the throne only by sailing on a river of blood."

"Just as I say," replied Gialaurys. "No love for battle."

"No love for it, but a good willingness, when battle's the only way," Svor said. "Wait and see. I know the man at least as well as you. When battle's the only way, even I will have a sword in my hand."

"You?" cried Septach Melayn, with a great guffaw.

"You will instruct me," said Svor solemnly.


Matters went better for them at Simbilfant of the famous vanishing lake, which was a busy mercantile city through which much wine of Muldemar traditionally was shipped, and held Prestimion in high favor. Word had already reached there of Prestimion's claim to the crown, and the hegemon of the town, which was what their mayor was called, had a great banquet waiting for him, and green-and-gold banners everywhere, and two thousand men in arms ready to join his forces, with the promise of many more afterward. And, just as though he were a visiting Coronal, they staged a disappearance of the vanishing lake for him, rolling aside the great boulders that blocked the volcanic sluices beneath it so that the whole lake seemed to go gurgling down into the depths of the planet, leaving a bare gaping crater of sulphrous yellow rock ringed round with white granite ridges, only to come roaring back with tremendous force an hour later.

"This is like making a grand processional," said Prestimion, "and here I am not even crowned yet."

The reception was friendly also at nearby Ghrav, though not quite so warm or eager—it was plain that the mayor felt himself caught between Prestimion and Korsibar as between the two grinding-stones of a mill, and did not care for it. But he was hospitable enough, and, in a cautious way, sympathetic to Prestimion's claim. Then they moved along toward Arkilon, where four million people clustered in a wide green valley flanked by low, wooded hills. There was a notable university there; it was a city of unworldly scholars and archivists and book-publishers, and there was no reason to expect much in the way of opposition there. But as they approached it under the brightness of a hot autumn sun the sharp-eyed Septach Melayn pointed to the hilltop on the side closest to the Mount, and all up and down that hillside were troops of the Coronal's force, like a horde of ants spilling everywhere over the sloping contours.

"They are ten men for every one of ours, I would hazard," said Septach Melayn. "The whole western garrison is here, and some men from other districts too, it would seem. And they hold the high ground, too. Are we prepared for this?"

"Is Korsibar?" Gialaurys asked. "He's brandishing a fist at us with this army. But will he do anything more than brandish?"

"Send forth a messenger," said Prestimion, looking soberly up at that huge hilltop force. "Call him forth. We'll have a parley."

A herald duly went forth; and, by twilight time, riders came down from the hill to meet with Prestimion at an agreed point midway between the two armies. But Korsibar was not among them. The two chief lords who appeared were Navigorn of Hoikmar, in a grand and formidable warlike costume of stiff and glossy black leather tipped with scarlet plumes, and Kanteverel of Bailemoona, looking rather less belligerent in a loose flowing tunic of orange and yellow stripes, fastened about the waist with an ornate golden chain. Prestimion was surprised and in no way pleased to see the easygoing good-natured Kanteverel here at the head of Korsibar's garrison-force. The round smooth face of the Duke of Bailemoona seemed strangely bleak, now, with none of its customary good humor.

"Where is Korsibar?" Prestimion said at once.

Stonily Navigorn replied, looking down at Prestimion from his considerable height, *"Lord* Korsibar is at the Castle, where he belongs. He charges us bring you back with us so that you can defend your recent actions before him."

"And what actions are those, pray tell?"

It was Kanteverel who replied, speaking calmly as always, but not showing now the warm easy smile that was his hallmark, "You know what they are, Prestimion. You can't run all over the foothill towns proclaiming yourself Coronal and levying troops without getting Korsibar's attention, you know. What do you think you're up to, anyway?"

"Korsibar knows that already. I don't recognize him as Coronal and I offer myself before all the world as the legitimate holder of the throne."

"For the love of the Lady, be reasonable, Prestimion!" Kanteverel said, letting a flicker of his old cajoling smile show. "Your position's absurd. No one ever named you king. However Korsibar may have come to the crown, there's no question he's Coronal now, which everyone concedes." And Navigorn said, speaking over Kanteverel with a haughty crackle in his voice, "You are Prince of Muldemar, Prestimion, and nothing more, and never will be more. Lord Korsibar has the blessing of the Pontifex Confalume, who confirmed him in his kingship at the Labyrinth according to all the ancient laws."

"Confalume's his father. How does *that* fit with the ancient laws? And in any case Confalume doesn't know what he's doing. Korsibar's had his conjurers wrap a mass of spells around Confalume's mind that make him into a doddering senile idiot."

That drew laughter from Kanteverel. "You, Prestimion, telling us that this has all been achieved by sorcery? Next we'll hear you've hired a staff of mages yourself!"

"Enough. I have business in Arkilon," Prestimion said coolly. He glanced toward the great army on the hill. "Do you mean to prevent me?"

"You have business at the Castle," said Navigorn. He spoke firmly enough, though his look was an uneasy one, as though he disliked this situation and regretted the collision that both factions knew was coming. "When you were set free at Dantirya Sambail's request, it was under his pledge of your good behavior, for which he made himself personally responsible. Now the Procurator is gone to Ni-moya, we hear; and your good behavior, it seems, consists of raising armies to bring civil war in the world. Your freedom is revoked, Prestimion. I order you in Lord Korsibar's name to come with us at once."

There was a moment of uncertain silence. Prestimion had been accompanied to the meeting only by Septach Melayn, Svor, Gialaurys, and five men-at-arms. With Navigorn and Kanteverel were the lords Sibellor of Banglecode and Malarich Merobaudes, and five men-at-arms also. The men of the two groups shifted about warily. Was there to be a scuffle right here on the field of parley? There had never been anything but friendship among them; but where was that friendship now? Prestimion stared levelly at Navigorn, whose dark face was a stony mask, and then threw a quick glance at Septach

Melayn, who smiled and rested his hand on the hilt of his sword.

Prestimion wondered whether Navigorn might indeed have some wild idea of trying to seize him here. It would be a fool's act, if so. The advantage, if it came to that, lay with him. His companions at the parley were the stronger; his troops, if he needed them, were not far away.

"I have no intention of going with you," said Prestimion after a little. "You knew that when you came out here. Let's waste no more breath on these formalities, Navigorn. We'll need it for what is to follow."

"And what is that?" Navigorn asked.

"How can I say? I tell you only that Lord Korsibar is not Lord Korsibar to me, but only *Prince* Korsibar, and I reject his authority over me. I would like now to end this meeting."

"As you wish," said Navigorn bleakly, and made no move to apprehend him as Prestimion turned to return to his own lines.

As they walked away, Prestimion said to Septach Melayn, "This is not going to be quite like a grand processional after all, is it? We will have the war, it seems, sooner than we bargained for."

"Sooner than Korsibar bargains for, either," Gialaurys said. "If Navigorn and Kanteverel are the best generals he can find at short notice, we'll beat them into surrender this very day."

"Kanteverel's here only to wheedle," said Svor. "Navigorn's the general, and he's the one will call the tune, if there's to be a battle today."

"What is the plan?" Septach Melayn asked.

"We continue on to Arkilon," said Prestimion. "They'll have to come down the hill to stop us. If they do, we make them regret that they tried."

# 4

L ord Korsibar was in his great bath of alabaster and chalcedony, disporting himself in the warm bubbling water with his sister's handmaiden, the red-haired Aliseeva of the milky skin, when word was brought to him that Count Farquanor was waiting outside with important news. There had been a military engagement at Arkilon, it seemed, and Farquanor had had word from the field.

"I will be back quickly," Korsibar told the girl. He robed himself and went out into the antechamber, where mosaic sea-dragons were inscribed on the white-tiled walls in many fine bits of blue and green and red glass, and saw at once from the look of smugness on little Farquanor's lean and wolfish face that the news must be good.

"Well?" he said at once. "Is Prestimion taken?"

"Escaped into the open country, my lord. Navigorn was too merciful, I think. But the rebel force has suffered great losses, and is in severe retreat."

"Septach Melayn dead, at least? Gialaurys?"

Farquanor said, with apology in his voice, "None of those, lordship, nor Svor, either. But a multitude of casualties for them—I have some names, but the only one I know is that of Gardomir of Amblemorn—and the back of the resistance broken. The war is over in its very first encounter, it would seem."

"Tell me," said Korsibar.

Farquanor ran his hand down the long sharp blade of his nose, that sprang so startlingly from his brow. "Here is the valley of Arkilon," he said, drawing pictures in the air. "The city, here. The Vormisdas hill, where our troops are situated, here. Prestimion over here on the plain, with a raggle-taggle army that he has put together out of Amblemorn and Vilimong and some other places, and a bunch of wine-makers from Muldemar at the center of it. There is a parley; Navigorn delivers the message; Prestimion defies it, as we all expected. And then—"

Prestimion, he said, having turned his back on Navigorn after the parley, had attempted to continue his march through the flatlands toward Arkilon. Navigorn had brought his army quickly down from its hilltop position, a battalion of small floaters at the center that were equipped with low-caliber energy-throwers, flanked by two squadrons of mounted spearsmen, and the mass of the infantry held back to the rear. Prestimion had no cavalry at all, and his troops were more of a casual aggregation than a trained army; the best he could do was give an order to scatter and surround, so that there would be no center for Navigorn's floaters to attack, and try to throw Navigorn's men into confusion by coming upon them from every side at once.

But that was of no avail. The early ferocity of Prestimion's onslaught took Navigorn by surprise, but Navigorn's men were better armed and better skilled, and very much more numerous; and after a few difficult moments they fought the rebel forces off with great success. The floaters held their formation, the spearsmen prevented any serious incursion into their ranks by the rebels, and even before the royal infantrymen had had a chance to reach the field, the tide of the battle had become clear and Prestimion's men were in unruly retreat, fleeing helter-skelter, some toward Arkilon and others back in the direction of Ghrav and some off in a third direction entirely.

"But Prestimion and his three minions got safely away?" Korsibar asked, when Farquanor paused.

"Alas, yes. Navigorn had given orders that none of them be harmed, only captured. It was too kind of him, lordship. Had someone like my brother Farholt had charge of the day, I think we'd have seen a different result. Surely Farholt would—"

"Spare me the advertisement of your brother's virtues," said Korsibar unsmilingly. "Capturing them would have been sufficient. But they failed even at that?"

"They had Septach Melayn held in close quarters in the middle of the field for a time, with Hosmar Varang, the captain of the spearsmen, giving him great menace, and Earl Alexid of Strave, on foot, penning him up from the other side with two other men."

"But he got away even so?"

"He cut Hosmar Varang down from his mount and gave him a deep slice near the armpit that will take a year to repair, and killed Alexid outright and slashed the other two so that they were left counting their fingers and hard pressed to find ten between them. And—entirely untouched, himself—leaped upon Hosmar Varang's mount, snatching up the loathsome little mongrel Duke Svor whom he loves like a baby, and off they went at high speed into the woods, seeing that the battle was lost and there was no sense in remaining."

"Four of them against his one, and he prevails? The man is in league with demons. No, he is a demon himself! And Alexid dead?" Korsibar grew more somber at that. He had hunted with Alexid of Strave beside him many times, in the jungles of the south and on the bare purple slopes of the northern mountains: a lean restless man, quick and capable with a javelin. This was suddenly very real, to hear Alexid had perished. "What other losses did we suffer, of men I would know?" Korsibar asked; but then, seeing Farquanor unfolding what seemed to be a considerable list, hastily waved him into silence. "Prestimion, you say, is fled into Arkilon?"

"Into the forest to the west of it. They are all four of them in there, I think, with the other survivors, and thought to be moving further westward yet."

"Later today," said Korsibar, "I will issue a proclamation naming Prestimion as traitor to the realm, with a price of three thousand royals to anyone who brings him in alive."

"Dead or alive," amended Farquanor immediately, with a ferocious gleam coming into his cool gray eyes.

"Has it come to that, already?" Korsibar asked, pensive a moment. "Yes. Yes, I suppose it has. Well, then. Five thousand silver royals, dead or alive, for Prestimion, and three thousand for any of the other three. Send word to Navigorn that he's to undertake close pursuit. And Farholt will have a second army, to chase Prestimion up the other side of the world, if need be, and we'll catch him between. This will all be over in another ten days, I think."

"The Divine favors our cause, lordship," said Farquanor in his oiliest tone. He made the starburst and withdrew, leaving Korsibar free to return to the bathchamber.

"Pleasing news?" asked red-haired Aliseeva, peering winsomely over the side of the tub.

"It might have been better," Korsibar said. "But yes: yes. Pleasing news."


From the royal chamber Count Farquanor made his way at once to the apartments of the Lady Thismet. She had asked him not long before to keep her apprised of news of the rebellion; and this first report of victory would serve as good pretext for other matters he hoped to put before her.

The Lady Melithyrrh admitted him. Thismet was in her nine-sided drawing room of the ice-green jade walls, with an array of golden rings set with various precious stones laid out before her on a low table as though she were choosing between them for the evening's wear; and she was richly dressed in a dark hooded gown of green velvet hanging in heavy folds, with a high-waisted close bodice and close-fitting sleeves with great puffed wings at her wrists. But her lovely face was taut and drawn, as it so often was these days, with a bitter clenched set to her delicate jaw, and Farquanor saw the glitter of a perpetual anger shining in her eyes. What was it that angered her so?

He said, after a bow, "Navigorn and Kanteverel have clashed with Prestimion before Arkilon, lady. Prestimion's forces are utterly ruined and your brother's high cause has triumphed."

Briefly Thismet's nostrils flared with excitement and color rose in her face.

"And Prestimion? What of him?" she asked, quickly, tensely.

"It was the first thing your royal brother wanted to hear from me, too. And the answer is that he is escaped, he is. Off into the forest with Septach Melayn and the rest of that crew, more's the pity. But his army is dispersed and the rebellion, I think, at its end even in its beginning."

She grew quickly calm again, lips curling under, color fading to her usual pallor. "Is it," she said, without any questioning inflection to her tone. And looked at him blankly for a moment, and turned her attention back to her rings, as though she had no further interest in speaking with him.

But, since she had not actually dismissed him, he continued to stand before her, and after a little while said, "I thought the news of our victory would please you, lady."

"And so it does." Tonelessly, once again, as though she was speaking in her sleep. "Many men are dead, I suppose, and blood satisfactorily distributed all over the field? Yes, this is very pleasing to me, Farquanor. I do so love to hear of the shedding of blood."

That was very strange of her. But she had been nothing but strange since this bleak mood had come upon her these many weeks back. Well, then, he thought, enough of battle news. There was the other subject to deal with.

He counted off a few numbers in his mind and drew a deep breath, and said, "Thismet, may I speak to you as a friend? For I think we have been friends, you and I."

She looked up, amazed. "You call me Thismet? I am the Coronal's sister!"

"You were another Coronal's daughter, once, and I called you Thismet then, sometimes."

"When we were children, perhaps. What is this, Farquanor? You presume a great deal of a sudden."

"I mean no offense, lady. I mean only to help you, if I can."

"To help me?"

The musculature along the width of Farquanor's shoulders tightened into a rigid iron constriction. Now he must make the leap, or forever despise himself. "It seems to me," he said, weighing every word and judging its probable impact with all the craft at his command, "that you may have fallen somewhat out of favor in recent months with the Lord Korsibar your brother. Forgive me if I am in error here: but I am not the least observant man in this Castle, and to my way of thinking I see an estrangement lately between you and him."

Thismet's eyes flicked upward in a wary glance.

"And if there is?" she asked. "I don't say that there is, but if it should be so, what then?"

Piously Farquanor said, "It would be a matter for great regret, royal brother and royal sister at odds with each other. And—forgive me, lady, if I speak too close to your soul—I think that something like that must be the case, for I no longer see you at the Coronal's side at formal functions, nor does he smile when he speaks with you in public, nor do you *ever* smile these days, but hold yourself always tense and grim. It has been that way with you for more than one season now."

She looked away, toying with her rings again. In a dull-toned voice she said, "And if the Coronal and I have had some small disagreement, what is that to you, Farquanor?"

"You know how I labored at your side to make Lord Korsibar what he is today. It made me feel a great closeness to the two of you, as I schemed and connived at your behest to nudge him toward the throne. If the result of all my scheming has been only to drive a wedge between brother and sister, the sorrow is on me for it. But I have a solution to propose, lady."

"Do you?" she said, distantly.

It was the moment to make the great attempt. How many times had he rehearsed this in his mind, he could not count. But now at last the words came streaming forth from him.

"If you were to marry me, lady, that could serve to bind up the breach that has opened between you and Lord Korsibar."

She had put five rings into the palm of her hand, a ruby one and an emerald and a sapphire and one of many-faceted diamond and one of golden-green chrysoprase; and at Farquanor's words she jerked so convulsively that the rings went clattering forth in a spill of brilliance to the floor.

*"Marry* you?"

There was no swerving from this now. He was resolved to hold firmly to his course.

"You are without a consort. It is widely said in the Castle that this is much to be regretted, considering your grace and beauty and high birth. And also it is said that of late you seem adrift, all moorings severed, no destination in view and no way of reaching any, now that so much power has devolved upon your brother and you yourself are left in no fixed position. But how can a woman without a husband, even the Coronal's sister, find a proper place in the court? A significant marriage is the answer. I offer myself to you."

She seemed stunned. But he had expected that. This was coming upon her without the slightest preparation. He waited, neither smiling nor scowling, watching the unreadable play of turbulent emotions come and go on her face, seeing the color rise there, the changing glintings of her eyes.

After a time she said, "Do you really have such an elevated opinion of yourself, Farquanor? You think that by marrying you I would *raise* my status at the court?"

"I leave my ancient royal ancestry out of consideration here. But since you speak so rarely with your brother these days, perhaps you are unaware that I am soon to be made High Counsellor, once old Oljebbin has reconciled himself to the retirement that is being thrust upon him."

"You have my warmest congratulation."

"The High Counsellor—and his wife—are second only to the Coronal in the social order of the Castle. Furthermore, as your brother's most intimate adviser, I'd be in an excellent position to mediate whatever dispute it is that has damaged the affection that should prevail between you. But there's more to it than that: the High Counsellor is in the plain line of succession to the throne. If Confalume were to die, I might well be named Coronal when Korsibar went to the Labyrinth; which would greatly enhance your own position, not merely the Coronal's sister now, but the Coronal's own wife—"

Thismet gave him a disbelieving stare. "This has gone on long enough," she said, bending now to scoop up her fallen rings with one angry sweep of her hand. Then, looking up fiercely at him, she said, "Successor to my brother? I would not have you even if you were proclaimed successor to the Divine."

Farquanor gasped as though he had been struck.

"Lady—" he said. "Lady—" And his voice trailed off into inaudibility.

In a tone of savage mockery she said, "Nothing has so amazed me as this present conversation since I was a child, and was told of the method by which children are conceived. Marry you? You? How could you have imagined such a thing! And why would I accept? Are we in any way a fitting couple? Do you in truth see yourself as a match for me? How could you possibly be? You're such a *small* man, Farquanor!"

He drew himself up as tall as he could. "Not of a size with your brother, say, or Navigorn, or Mandrykarn. But I am no dwarf, either, lady. We would look well together, you and I. I remind you that you are not greatly large yourself. You come barely shoulder-high to me, I would say."

"Do you think I'm speaking of height?" she said. "Well, then, an idiot as well." She shook her hand in the air at him. "Go. I beg you, go. Quickly, now. I tell you: go. Before you make me say something truly cruel."


Korsibar was in his private study, an hour later, when the Lady Thismet came to him. It was the first meeting she had had alone with him in a very long while, not since she had shared with him the horoscope that Thalnap Zelifor had prepared for her. They had not spoken of that matter since. Plainly he was not going to yield to her request without a battle, and with Prestimion loose in the land and speaking of rebellion she hesitated to tax him again with the matter just now. But it had not left her mind.

As she entered, he seemed uncertain and ill at ease, as though he feared she had come here to begin some new discussion of her having a throne of her own. Thismet suspected he would have preferred to forbid her his presence entirely, but did not care to impose so substantial a prohibition on his own sister. And in any case it was trouble of a different sort that she planned to make for him today.

He had some maps beside him, and a stack of official reports.

"News from the battlefield?" she asked. "Details of the great victory?"

"You've heard, then?"

"Count Farquanor was kind enough to bring me some word of it just now."

"We'll have Prestimion back here in chains by Seaday next, is my guess. And then a course of instruction in proper behavior will begin for him that he'll hew to for the rest of his life."

He returned to his scrutiny of his charts. She said, after watching him for a moment with displeasure, "Attend to me, Korsibar."

"What is it, sister?" Without looking up. "I hope you haven't chosen this moment to renew your demand for—"

"No, nothing to do with that. I want you to dismiss Farquanor and banish him from the Castle."

Now he did look up indeed, and stared at her in complete astonishment.

"You are ever full of surprises, sister. You want me to dismiss—"

"Farquanor. Yes. That's what I said, to dismiss him. He's not deserving of any place in this court."

Korsibar seemed to grope for words a moment.

"Not deserving of a place?" he said, finally. "On the contrary, Thismet. Farquanor's not a lovable man, but very useful, and I mean to use him. Oljebbin's finally agreed to step down at the turn of the year, and Farquanor will be High Counsellor. I owe him that much; and 'twill shut him up, to have the thing he's dreamed of so long."

"Not shut him up enough," said Thismet. "He's just been to see me, Korsibar. Has asked me to marry him."

"What?" Korsibar blinked and smiled as though in nothing more than mild surprise; and then, as he weighed her words again and the impact of them sank in, the smile turned to laughter, and the laughter to great heavy racking guffaws, and a slapping of his thigh until he could get himself under control once again. "Marry you?" he said at last. "Well, well, well: bold little Farquanor! Who'd have thought him capable of it?"

"The man's a snake. I never want to see his narrow little face again. You refuse me many things, Korsibar, but don't refuse me this one: send him from the Castle."

"Ah, no, sister, no, no! It would not do."

"No?" she said.

"Farquanor is very valuable to me. He's overreached himself here, perhaps: should certainly have discussed this thing with me, at least, before he went sniffing off to you. It is a bold request, I agree. A match beyond his level, perhaps. But he's a shrewd and crafty counsellor. I couldn't do without him, especially now, with Prestimion still at large out there, perhaps planning some new rampage now that he's slipped away from Navigorn. I need a man like Farquanor, full of spite and mischief, to lay my plans for me: can't only have great noble-souled clods around when you're king, don't you see?—You could do worse, in any case, than to marry him."

"I would sooner marry some Liiman peddling sausages on the streets."

"Oh. Oh. The flashing Thismet eye! The bared teeth! Well, then, reject him, sister, if that's how you feel about him. By no means would I force him on you."

"Do you think I haven't rejected him already? But I want you to get him forever out of my sight."

Korsibar pressed his fingertips against his temples. "I've explained to you how valuable he is to me. If you like, I'll rebuke him, yes, tell him to put the idea entirely out of his mind forever, send him to you to crawl and snivel a little by way of apologizing for his impudence. But I won't get rid of him. And you *should* marry, anyway. It's time for it, and even a little past the time, perhaps. Marry Navigorn, for example. Fine and noble and decent, that one."

"I'm not interested in marrying anyone." Thismet altered the tone of her voice, deepening it, putting somewhat of an edge on it. "You know what I want, Korsibar."

She saw him quail. But she pushed onward all the same. If he would not satisfy her in the one matter, she would harry him on the other.

"Give me a crown," she said. "Make me Coronal in joint reign with you."

"That thing again?" He clamped his lips and his face grew dark with anger. "You know that that can never be."

"A simple decree—as easily as you took the crown the day Prankipin died, you could—"

"No. Never, Thismet. Never. Never!" Korsibar gave her a long deadly furious look; and then he sprang from his seat and paced in agitation before her. He was bubbling with rage. "By the Divine, sister, don't plague me with this business of a crown again, or I tell you I'll marry you to little Farquanor myself! I'll put your hand in his and proclaim you man and wife before all the world, and if he has to strap you down to have his consummation of you, it'll be no grief to me. This is a solemn pledge, Thismet. One more word about this lunacy of your being Coronal, and you are Farquanor's bride!"

She stared at him, horror-stricken.

He was silent a time. She saw the anger gradually subsiding in him, but his face now was stony. "Listen closely to me," Korsibar said, more calmly now. "There is a rebellion in the land against my reign. I must destroy Prestimion, which I will do, which in fact I am well on my way to doing. When that's done, I'll stand unchallenged here as Coronal of Majipoor, and when I come fully into my kingship it will be mine, and mine alone. Do you understand that, Thismet? I will not go before the world and say that I am building another throne at this Castle and that a woman will occupy it as my equal. For you to ask to be joint Coronal is as bizarre as for Farquanor to ask for you in marriage. He will not be your husband unless by your obstinacy you make me give you to him; and you will not be Coronal, not under any circumstances whatever. That is my final word on the subject. *Final*. And if you will excuse me now, sister, the good Sanibak-Thastimoon waits outside to see me on a matter of high importance, and I would not delay him any longer—"

# 5

In the hour of his defeat by Arkilon plain the skies opened on Prestimion, and pelted him with one of the heavy rains of autumn that were so common in these parts. So he rode long and hard under a driving deluge far into the night, accompanied by only a few dozen of his men; and he was soaked to the bone and in a sorry frame of mind indeed when he reached, finally, the forest of Moorwath by Arkilon's western flank. This was the place that he and Septach Melayn had chosen as their gathering-place, should the battle at Arkilon go badly for them. In his pre-battle mood of optimism he had never truly foreseen an outcome that might cause him to be spending this night beneath the tall and fat-trunked vakumba-trees of Moorwath; but here he was, lame and wet and weary in the darkness.

"There is somewhat more to making war, it seems," he said sorrowfully to his aide-de-camp Nilgir Sumanand, "than merely proclaiming the righteousness of one's cause."

"It was only the first skirmish, my lord," replied Nilgir Sumanand in a quiet tactful way. "There will be many more encounters on the field for us, and happier ones, before the task is done."

Prestimion said dourly, "But look how badly we're damaged already! Where's Gialaurys? And Septach Melayn—I had a glimpse of him far across the field, in the midst of a pack of enemies. By the Divine, if Septach Melayn has fallen—"

"He is safe somewhere nearby in the forest, of that I'm certain, and will find us before long. The man's not yet born who can lay a weapon to him, my lord."

It was welcome reassurance. But Prestimion brushed it aside and snapped, with more anger in his voice than he would have preferred to display, "Enough of calling me 'my lord'! It galls me to hear the phrase. Some Coronal am I, sitting here in the rain under these dripping vakumbas!" And then, quickly and in a softer tone, for he was abashed at having chafed this good loyal man with such harshness: "I've had to swallow down many an unpalatable thing, haven't I, Nilgir Sumanand, since my fortunes changed? This was surely not the plan I charted for myself when I first set out to win greatness in the world."

The rain seemed to be ending now. Through the huge heavy gray leaves overhead, leathery-skinned on their upper sides and furry below, he saw faint white shafts of moonlight peeping through. But the night was cold and the ground was sodden, and his thigh throbbed mercilessly; for he had taken a sudden blow across the fleshiest part of it in one wild melee, one of Navigorn's men galloping past and slashing him with a riding-crop as he went. Better that than the blade of a sword, Prestimion told himself, yet he was limping all the same.

"Do we have glowfloats with us?" he asked Nilgir Sumanand. "Tie them to these trees, if we do. They'll guide others of our people toward us in the night who might be wandering hereabouts."

"And if they guide Navigorn to us instead, excellence?"

"It would be a very rash general who led his troops into a dark forest like this by night, not knowing what sort of ambush is waiting for him. No, Navigorn and his men are getting grandly drunk in Arkilon just now. Put up some glowfloats, Nilgir Sumanand." And soon there were globes of reddish light hanging from the lowest branches of the nearby trees;

and in a little while, just as Prestimion had hoped, the lights began to draw the straggling fragments of his army, by twos and threes at first, or sometimes as many as a dozen.

It was midnight when Gialaurys appeared. He came alone. His sleeve was in tatters and a raw bloody cut showed through. His mood was so grim that even Prestimion hesitated to speak with him; shrugging off an offer to bind his wound, Gialaurys sat down by himself and took from his torn jacket the green fruit of a vakumba, one that he must have pulled from a low-lying branch or even picked off the ground, and began to gnaw and rip at it in a snarling frightful way, cramming the flesh of it into his mouth as though he were no more than a beast of the fields.

A little while after, Kaymuin Rettra of Amblemorn arrived, with a detachment of Skandars and some human men of his city, and then Nemeron Dalk from Vilimong, with fifty more, and almost on their heels was Count Ofmar of Ghrav, followed by many of his people, and some Simbilfant folk, and the three sons of the vineyard overseer Rufiel Kisimir, leading a whole host of men of Muldemar, who surrounded Prestimion with loud cries of joy. And the noise of all these as they gathered in the one encampment under the fat vakumba-trees brought others, on through the night. So the army was not as utterly destroyed as Prestimion had feared, and he took some heart from that. There was scarcely anyone who had not taken some injury in the battle, and some of those serious. But all of them came before Prestimion, even the wounded ones, and earnestly vowed to go on fighting in his cause until the end.

Of Septach Melayn and Svor, though, there was no sign.

Toward morning Prestimion slept a little. Dawn was slow coming in this latitude, for Castle Mount lay straight eastward of here, and the rising sun had to climb above that thirty-mile-high wall before its light could penetrate the forest. At last Prestimion felt warmth on his face; and when he opened his eyes the first he saw was Duke Svor's hooked nose and devilish toothy grin, and then Septach Melayn, as cool and elegant as if he were on his way to a banquet at the Castle, with not a single golden hair out of place and his clothes unmussed. The Vroonish wizard Thalnap Zelifor was perched pleasantly on Septach Melayn's left shoulder.

The swordsman smiled down at Prestimion and said, "Have you rested well, O peerless prince?"

"Not so well as you," Prestimion said, coming creakily to a sitting position and brushing the mud from himself. "This hotel is less gracious, I think, than the luxurious inn where you must have spent the night."

"Luxurious indeed. It was all of pink marble and black onyx," replied Septach Melayn, "with sweet handmaidens galore, and a feast of bilantoons' tongues steeped in dragon-milk that I'll not soon forget." He knelt beside Prestimion, allowing the Vroon to jump down to the ground, and said in a less airy way, "Did you take any injury in the battle, Prestimion?"

"Only to my pride, and a bruise to my thigh that will have me aching a day or two. And you?"

Septach Melayn said, with a wink, "My thumb is sore, from pressing too tight against the hilt of my blade in the thick of the fray, as I cut down Alexid of Strave. Otherwise nothing."

"Alexid is dead?"

"And many others, on both sides. There'll be more."

Svor said, "You don't ask me about my wounds, Prestimion."

"Ah, and were you fighting valiantly too, my friend?"

"I thought I would test myself as a warrior. So I went into the midst. In the veriest heat and turmoil of it, I came up against Duke Kanteverel, my face right up against his."

"And you bit his nose?" Prestimion asked.

"You are unkind. I drew on him—I had never drawn in anger before—and he looked at me and said, 'Svor, do you mean to kill me, who gave you the lovely Lady Heisse Vaneille? For I have lost my weapon and am at your mercy.' And nowhere in my heart could I find hatred for him, so I took him by the shoulder and spun him around, and shoved him with all my strength, and sent him staggering toward his own side of the field. Did I fail you greatly, Prestimion? I could have killed him there and then. But I am no killer, I think."

Prestimion answered, with a shake of his head, "What would it have mattered, killing Kanteverel? He's no more a fighter than you. But stay behind the lines, Svor, in our next battle. You'll be happier there. So, I think, will we." Prestimion looked toward Thalnap Zelifor and said, "And you, companion of my prison-chamber? Did you do mighty work with *your* sword?"

"I could wield five at once," said the Vroon, waving his many tentacles about, "but they would be no greater than needles, and all I could achieve with them would be the pricking of shins. No, I shed no blood yesterday, Prestimion. What I did on your behalf was cast spells for your success. But for me the outcome would have been even worse."

"Even worse?" Prestimion said, with a little chuckle. "Well, then, you have my gratitude."

"Be grateful for this, too: I've thrown the divining-sticks to see the outcome of your next battle. It was a favorable pattern. You will win a great victory against overwhelming odds."

"Hear, hear!" cried Septach Melayn.

And Prestimion said, "I would embrace sorcery with all my heart, my friend, if I could hear prophecies of that kind from my mages all the time."

★

The coming of a warm bright morning and the return of his dear friends gave a great lift to Prestimion's spirit, and he began to put the grief of the battle at Arkilon behind him. All day stragglers continued to arrive, until he had something of the semblance of an army again, weary and battered and muddied though it was.

They would have to leave the forest quickly, Prestimion knew. It was rash to assume that Navigorn would let them camp here unchallenged for long. But where to go? They had no maps with them; and none of them had much acquaintance with the great open stretches of territory that lay west of Arkilon, but for the great and celebrated Gulikap Fountain just beyond the forest, which was well known to all.

Some information came from Nemeron Dalk of Vilimong, a man of some years, who had traveled from time to time in those lands. He knew the names of rivers and hills, and roughly where they lay in relation to one another. Elimotis Gan, who hailed from Simbilfant, had some knowledge of the region also. And one of the skills that Thalnap Zelifor claimed was the casting of inquiry-spells that permitted the divining of correct roadways and routes. In mid-morning these three, with Septach Melayn and Prestimion and Svor, came together to draw up a route of march.

The Vroon lit some little cubes of a brown stuff that looked like sugar, but which he said was the incense of sorcery, and wriggled his tentacles and stared into the distance, murmuring softly to himself. And after a time he began to describe the lay of the land beyond them as he claimed to perceive it in his incense-visions, and Elimotis Gan and Nemeron Dalk provided amplification and correction, and Septach Melayn sketched out a rough chart of it from their words with the tip of his sword on a bare damp patch of soil, smoothing out his errors with the toe of his boot.

"These hills here—hills, are they, or mountains?—what are they called?" Prestimion asked, pointing to a line on Septach Melayn's map that ran boldly for a great distance from north to south.

"The Trikkalas," said Elimotis Gan. "More mountains than hills, I would say. Yes, very definitely mountains."

"Can they be easily crossed if we were to march due west from here?"

Elimotis Gan, who was a short wiry man with a look of great vigor about him, exchanged a glance with the robust, sturdy Nemeron Dalk. It seemed to Prestimion that it was a very pessimistic look that passed between them.

Nemeron Dalk said, "The Sisivondal highway runs through here," he said, pointing to the lower end of the line, which marked the southern end of the mountains, "and this is the Sintalmond road, here, in the north. In the middle, which is where you say you want to go, the range is at its highest and most jagged, and there's only the pass known as Ekesta, which is to say, in the dialect of the region, 'Accursed.' "

"A pretty name," said Septach Melayn.

"Not a pretty road," Elimotis Gan said. "A rough trail, very steep, I hear, little to eat along the way, and packs of hungry vorzaks to harass travelers at night."

"But direct," Prestimion said. "This is what I ultimately want to reach, this broad river here, on the far side of the mountains. It's the Jhelum, isn't it?"

"The Jhelum, yes," said Nemeron Dalk.

"Good," said Prestimion. "We head westward and take your accursed pass through the Trikkalas, and throw stones at the damned vorzaks if they bother us, and when we come out on the other side of the mountains we cross the river after what ought to be a much easier march below the pass. And then we can sit ourselves down here, beyond the Jhelum's western bank, in what I think is the Marraitis meadowland, where the best fighting-mounts are bred and schooled. Do you see my drift?"

"We will need a cavalry, if we intend to fight again," said Septach Melayn.

"Exactly. We requisition a host of mounts from the Marraitis folk, and we send off messengers to any city that may be favorable to our cause, asking for volunteers, and we build and train a real army, not just the sort of randomly assembled horde that Navigorn cut to pieces yesterday. Eventually Korsibar will find out where we are, and he'll send an army after us. But he won't send it over the mountain pass, if it's as nasty a place as these two gentlemen say it is. They'll go south or north of the mountains, instead, which will take them many months; and so by crossing by way of the Ekesta ourselves, we'll get ourselves a head start, bringing us into the western country far ahead of them and giving ourselves time to prepare, at the cost of just the little extra effort of traveling the hardest route."

"How do you see this pass?" Svor asked Thalnap Zelifor. "Can it be taken, do you think?"

The Vroon lifted his tentacles again, and went through some sort of conjuring motions. "It will be difficult, but not impossible," he replied, after a bit.

"Difficult but not impossible: good enough," said Prestimion, with a smile. "I choose to believe that you have the true gift and I accept your findings as accurate and trustworthy." He looked around at the others. "Are we agreed, then? Ekesta pass to the Jhelum, and across the river by some means that we'll worry about later, and make our headquarters in the Marraitis meadows? And by the time we go into battle again, the Divine willing, we'll have a proper army to throw against the usurper."

"Not to mention the reinforcements that Dantirya Sambail will surely have sent us from Zimroel by then," said Svor.

"There's a wicked look in your eye as you say that," said Septach Melayn. "Do you doubt that the Procurator's armies will come?"

"There's always a wicked look in my eye," Svor answered. "It's not my fault: I was born that way."

"Spare us this byplay, if you please, both of you," said Prestimion crisply. "The Divine willing, the Procurator will keep his word. Our task now is to get to Marraitis and make ourselves more ready for war than we were yesterday. What may come afterward is something to fret about in its appropriate hour."

At midday their baggage-train came into the forest, such of it as remained intact, bearing the belongings and weaponry that had been following them through the foothill cities. It was good to have fresh clothing, and such other things that they had lacked in their night in the woods. Another few hundred stragglers found them, also; and then, when it appeared certain that there was no one else who would be rejoining them here, Prestimion gave the order to begin the westward march toward the Trikkala Mountains and the Jhelum River beyond.

Beyond the forest all was ordinary farming land for a while, but soon the landscape grew strange, for they were approaching the famous Gulikap Fountain. First came the bubbling up of warm springs, that scalded the ground into moist brown bareness, and then spouting geysers, and chalky terraces, like clustered bathtubs, holding sheets of water pervaded by algae of many colors, red and green and blue and all mixtures thereof.

Prestimion paused in wonder to watch black steam spouting hundreds of feet from a purse-shaped fumarole. Then they crossed a dead plateau of glassy sediments, zigzagging to avoid gaping vents that were giving off foul rotting gases.

"Beyond doubt I could acquire a belief in demons in a place like this," said Prestimion, and he was near halfway to being serious. "This countryside is like a piece out of some other world, brought here by some dread enchanter's whim."

Svor, who had been here before, only smiled, and told him to wait and see what lay ahead.

They were passing now around an intricate array of thermal pools that gurgled and heaved and moaned and seemed about to deluge them with boiling fluids. The sky here was gray-blue with smoke even at midday, and the air had a bitter chemical reek. The sun could not be seen. Their skins were covered quickly with dark grimy exhalations; Prestimion watched Septach Melayn draw his fingernails lightly across his cheek, and leave pale tracks in the murk. Yet this place, horrid as it was, was inhabited. Many-legged slithering things with shining rosy hides moved about everywhere, close to the ground, looking up and studying them warily through rows of beady black eyes that bulged above their foreheads.

A shelf of blunt rock closed in this place of geysers and hot pools at its farther end, stretching off to north and south. They scrambled quickly up it, despite the myriad loose stones that made footing tricky, and descended on the cliff's western face into a zone so extraordinary that Prestimion knew they must be at the domain of the Fountain itself.

By the deep light of the smoke-filtered sun he saw a completely naked flatland: not a bush, not a tree, not a rock, only a level span of land running from the extreme left to the extreme right, and curving away from them over the belly of the world. The soil was brick-red. And straight ahead of them on the plain rose a tremendous column of light bursting from the ground and rising with perfect straightness, like a great marble pillar, losing its upper end in the lofty atmosphere. The column was half a mile in width, Prestimion guessed, and had the sheen of polished stone.

"Look you," Svor said. "It is the Gulikap."

Not stone, no, Prestimion realized: an upwelling of sheer energy, rather. Motion was evident within its depths: huge sectors of it swirled, clashed, tangled, blended. Colors shifted randomly, now red predominating, now blue, now green, now brown. Some areas of the column appeared more dense in texture than others. Sparks often detached themselves and fluttered off to perish. The column at its uncertain summit blended imperceptibly with the clouds, darkening and staining them. There was a constant hissing, crackling sound in the air, as of an electric discharge.

Prestimion found that single mighty rod of brilliance in the midst of this forlorn plain an overwhelming sight. It was a scepter of power; it was a focus of change and creation; it was an axis of might on which the entire giant planet could spin.

"What would happen to me, do you think, if I were to touch it?" he asked Svor.

"You would be dissolved in an instant. The particles of your body would dance forever in that column of light."

They went as close as they dared. It was possible to see now that a broad calcified rim, bone-white, porcelain-smooth, surrounded the Fountain. The incredible surge of many-colored light came roaring up through that rim from some immense dark abyss. What forces were at play down there, Prestimion could scarcely begin to guess. But, staring wonder-ingly at this mighty thing that lay before them, he was struck as though for the first time with a sense of the majestic splendor of his native world, of the overwhelming beauty and grandeur of it, of Majipoor's infinite variety of marvels. And felt great sadness that some of that beauty and grandeur must now be marred by warfare. Yet there was no choice. There was a disharmony in the world that had to be cured, and war was the only way.

He contemplated the Fountain a long while. Then he gave the order to move on around it and continue the westward march.

# 6

They were thirteen days crossing the Ekesta Pass, which Nemeron Dalk said was faster than any crossing of it that he had ever heard of; they marched day and night with scarcely any pause, as if Navigorn's troops were treading on their heels. It was a considerable ordeal, but, as Thalnap Zelifor had predicted, not an impossible one, only very difficult.

The Trikkalas were rugged mountains that rose to jagged points like those of a lizard's crest, and the road across the pass was nothing more than a rough trail, in some places much less than that. There was little up here to eat, and most of that provided not much in the way of nourishment and even less in the way of pleasure, and the air was dry and cool and thin, so that at times even breathing was painful. But they marched swiftly and without complaint, and carried out the crossing without incident. Even the much-dreaded vorzaks kept their distance, confining themselves to a furious yipping and baying from the safety of their hilltop caves. At last the travelers came down on the far side of the hills in a mood of gratitude and relief.

Now they were in open country, lightly wooded, with towns here and there sparsely scattered. The air was softer here, for they were entering into the valley of the Jhelum, and tributary streams flowed past them on every side.

The Jhelum itself was broad and swift, too wide for bridging in this region. But there were no rapids or other evident hazards, and they set about building boats and rafts from the abundant trees that lined the shore. It took three days to get all the men and equipment across.

The only troublesome moment came when the great blunt shining head and long thick neck of a gappapaspe rose from the water no more than twenty yards in front of Gialaurys's boat; the gigantic thing loomed up high above them like an ogre, filling the sky and bringing some of the men close to panic. But all it did was stare. Gappapaspes were harmless browsers on river-weeds and bottom-muck; the only danger they posed the travelers was that if one of them should come to the surface directly beneath a raft or boat, it would shatter it like matchsticks and hurl them into the water, where less harmless creatures might be waiting. But they saw only the one lone behemoth, which after a time slid down out of view again and vanished in the gray-brown depths.

West of the river they found themselves in settled country again, bustling cities of medium size surrounded by agricultural zones; and here, as soon as Prestimion announced himself to the people, they greeted him as a deliverer and as their Coronal. In these parts people knew little of Korsibar, and found it hard to understand how he had been able to take possession of the throne, when a Coronal's son was never supposed to follow his father to the kingship. Among these good conservative countryfolk Prestimion was gladly hailed as the rightful king and they flocked eagerly to his standard.

He set up his camp as he had planned, in the great Marraitis meadowlands, where for thousands of years the finest mounts of Majipoor had been reared. The best breeders came to him with their herds of strong fighting animals, and freely made the most spirited of them available for his cavalry.

Word went forth far and wide, too, that Prestimion was collecting an army to march on Castle Mount and overthrow the false Coronal; and the response was enthusiastic. Hardly a day went by without a detachment of troops from some city of the region arriving at his camp. "I would rather die here with you than abide that unlawful man in the Castle," is what they told him, over and over again. And so Prestimion welcomed gladly into their midst such men as the white-bearded Duke Miaule of Hither Miaule, with some five hundred green-jacketed warriors skilled at handling mounts, and Thurm of Sirynx with a thousand more all clad in that city's turquoise stripes, and the radiant young golden-haired Spalirises, son of Spalirises of Tumbrax, at the head of a great force, and Gynim of Tapilpil with a corps of sling-casters in purple jerkins, and bold Abantes of Pytho and Talauus of Naibilis, and many more of that caliber; and also troops from Thannard and Zarang and Abisoane and two dozen other places that Prestimion had never heard of, but whose assistance he welcomed all the same. The outpouring of support amazed and gratified him greatly. His brothers Abigant and Taradath came too, with what seemed like half the able-bodied men of Muldemar city. They said that Teotas, the youngest brother, would have joined them also, but that their mother the Princess Therissa refused to let him go.

And finally came the news he had anticipated most keenly, without ever quite daring to believe that he would ever hear it: word that a huge army under the command of Gaviad and Gaviundar, the brothers to Dantirya Sambail, had landed some weeks ago at Alaisor and was making its way quickly overland to Marraitis to join the growing rebel force. Dantirya Sambail himself, the message added, had been delayed in Ni-moya by the responsibilities he held as Procurator there, but would be leaving Zimroel shortly and would affiliate himself with Prestimion's armies as quickly as he could.

Was it so? Yes. Yes. Hot on the heels of this message, the

outriders of the Zimroel force appeared, and then the bulk of
the army, with the Procurator's two brothers riding at its head.

"This is quite a pair, these brothers of Dantirya Sambail,"
said Gialaurys softly to Septach Melayn, watching them arrive.
"They are of the same pretty breed as their elder brother, are
they not?"

"Even prettier, far prettier," said Septach Melayn. "They
are true paragons of beauty."

Gaviad and Gaviundar shared Dantirya Sambail's ruddy
orange hair and freckled complexion, and they were as gloriously ugly as he was, though in differing ways. Gaviad, the
older of the two, was short and thick, watery-eyed and
blubbery-faced, with a great red blob of a nose and a coarse
fiery mustache jutting out like tufts of copper wire beneath it
above marvelously fleshy sagging lips; he was a heavy man, of
monstrous appetites, with a chest like a drum and a belly like
a swollen sack. His brother Gaviundar was much taller, of a
height nearly approaching Septach Melayn's, and his face was
broad and perpetually flushed, with small cruel blue-green
eyes flanked by the largest and thickest ears any human had
ever been given, ears that were like wagon-wheels. He
had gone bald very young: all that remained of his hair was
two astonishing bristly tufts springing far out from the sides
of his head. But as if to compensate he had grown himself a
dense and tangled reddish-yellow beard, so huge that birds
could hide in it, that tumbled like a cataract down to the
middle of his chest. He was, like Gaviad, an inordinate eater
and a man with a colossal capacity for drink; but Gaviundar
held his wine well, whereas stumpy little Gaviad, it quickly
became evident, took great pleasure in drinking himself into
a stupor as frequently as possible.

That could be tolerated, Prestimion decided, as long as the
man could fight. And in any event the brothers had come
with a great horde of troops that they had raised along along

the eastern coast of Zimroel, mainly from Piliplok and Nimoya but from twenty other cities as well.

All through the autumn and winter and on into spring Prestimion labored to meld these variously assorted soldiers into a single effective fighting force. The one question now was when and how to move against Korsibar.

Prestimion inclined to his original strategy of marching through the foothills of Castle Mount, making the circuit once again from Simbilfant to Ghrav to Arkilon to Pruiz and all the way around past Lontano and Da back to Vilimong, this time at the head of a large and ever-increasing army that eventually would go swarming up the side of Castle Mount and demand Korsibar's abdication. But Gialaurys had a different course in mind. "Let us wait here in the middle of Alhanroel for Korsibar to come out and chastise us," he said. "We smash his army beyond all repair, out here far from the Mount; and then we proceed at will to the Castle, accepting the surrender of any troops we might encounter along the way."

There was merit in both plans. Prestimion arrived at no quick decision.

Then one day Duke Svor came to him and said, "We have reliable despatches from the other side of the Jhelum. Two large armies, far greater even than our own, are approaching us: one under Farholt, taking the southern route around the Trikkalas, and the other led by Navigorn, traveling the northern way. Farholt brings with him an enormous force of war-mollitors. Once they've crossed the river, they plan to come up behind us, one army from above and one from below, and catch us between them and grind us to pieces."

"Then our strategy is settled," Gialaurys said. "We'll meet them here at Marraitis, as I proposed."

"No," said Prestimion. "If we wait for them here until they've joined forces, we're lost. Big as our army is, we're outnumbered by far, if we can believe reports. Either they'll shatter us here in the meadowlands, if that's so, or they'll drive us eastward until they can shove us into the river."

"What do you suggest, then?" asked Septach Melayn.

Prestimion said to Svor, "Which army is likely to reach the Jhelum first?"

"Farholt's, I would say. The southern route is quicker."

"Good. Let him come. We'll feed him to his own mollitors. What I propose is this: we cross the Jhelum first, while he's still camped on the eastern shore building his boats, and come around behind him. The one thing Farholt isn't going to be expecting from us is an attack on his *eastern* flank."

"Can we get there quickly enough?" Septach Melayn asked.

"We got here quickly enough, didn't we?" Prestimion said.


That night Prestimion wandered the camp by himself, pausing now to speak with Valirad Visto, who had charge of the mounts, and with Duke Miaule of Miaule, and Thurm of Sirynx and Destinn Javad of Glaunt, and even going over into the Zimroel force to pass some time with Gaviad and Gaviundar. Gaviad was long gone in drink by the time Prestimion got there, but big shaggy-bearded Gaviundar greeted Prestimion as though they were not simply distant kinsmen but actual brothers, giving him an enveloping embrace out of which emanated a great stink of garlic and dried sea-dragon meat. "We have waited much too long in life to get to know each other," Gaviundar bellowed. "But we will be good close friends once you are installed at the Castle, eh, Prestimion?" He had been drinking too, it seemed. And he said also, "My brother the Procurator thinks you are the finest man in the world, bar none. He looks forward to the day you ascend the throne as keenly as though it were he who were being made Coronal rather than you."

"I'm grateful for all his assistance," said Prestimion. "And yours, and that of your brother too," he added, with a glance at Gaviad, who sat in full armor slumped forward with his face in his plate, snoring loudly enough to summon lovesick gappapaspes from the distant river.

And when he had returned to his own side of the camp Prestimion went from this tent to that one, restless, far from any desire for sleep, though it was very late, now. He spoke with his brother Taradath, for a while, and then with Septach Melayn, and with young Spalirises, who could scarcely contain himself in his eagerness to see action.

A light was still shining in the tent of Thalnap Zelifor; and when Prestimion looked in there he found the Vroon wizard at his work-table, bent intently over something that looked somewhat like a kind of rohilla—an intricate circular weavery of bright gold wires and bits of crystal, it was, but far too big to be any sort of an amulet, ten times a rohilla's size, more like a crown than anything else. "What is this?" Prestimion asked. "Some new kind of witchery-device? Are you conjuring up success for us with this in our attack on Farholt?"

"No witchery here, O Prestimion. Do you remember that I told you, when we were prisoners together in the tunnels, that I was building a mechanism by which I could amplify the waves coming from people's minds, and read their thoughts, and put thoughts of my own into their heads?"

"The thing that Gonivaul had hired you to devise, yes. Is this it?"

"That is an attempt to reconstruct it," said the Vroon. "I left my half-finished trial model and all my notes behind in the Castle when we so suddenly took our leave of the place. But I have started again on it, and have been working at it all the while we've been here."

"With what purpose in mind?"

"Why, the purpose of reaching out across the Jhelum and

441

making contact with the minds of our enemies as they approach us, and perceiving their strategies and intentions."

"Ah," said Prestimion. "What a useful thing! And are you able to do it?"

"Not yet," the Vroon said sadly. "Certain essential parts remain in my room at the Castle with all my other machines both perfected and incomplete, and I have not yet found a way of replicating them here. But I continue to work. It is my great hope, O Prestimion, to present you with this wondrous device before long, as recompense for your saving my life at the Castle."

"Was Dantirya Sambail who saved your life, not I," said Prestimion, grinning. "And that only by accident, I think. He was the one forced Korsibar's hand, and you were freed by the same stroke that sprang me from that dungeon. But no matter: finish your device, and you'll be well rewarded for it. We are not so numerous and mighty here that we wouldn't benefit from being able to read our enemies' minds."

He bade Thalnap Zelifor goodnight, and left him still bent over his coils of golden wire. In his own tent Prestimion sat for a while, thinking about what was to come, and then in time he felt sleep steal over him at last, and dreams as well.

What he dreamed was that he held the planet that was Majipoor in the palm of his hand like an orb, and he looked down at the world in his hand and perceived it to be a vast and intricately embroidered tapestry that was hanging in some dim and shadowy stone hall where a fire flickered. Despite the gloomy darkness of that hall the details of the tapestry stood out with marvelous clarity. By the flickering of the firelight he saw in it all manner of elaborately woven elves and demons and strange beasts and birds moving to and fro in dark forests and thickets of thorny scrub and, here and there, a brilliantly blossoming glade. In its weave he made out glints of sunlight and starlight, and bright patches of gold, and the gleam of wondrous jewels, and the differing sheens of human hair and the scales of serpents. And everything was wondrous beyond all understanding, haloed around with an aura of supreme beauty.

The dream remained with him when he woke, holding him in an eerie magical grasp. But then he went to the door of his tent and looked out, and it was gray and raining out there, not at all magical. Not merely raining: *pouring*. A deluge.

Rains accompanied them all the way back to the Jhelum, day after day. The world seemed to have turned to an ocean of slippery mud. "I would rather cross that accursed Ekesta pass ten times running, than travel through this," Gialaurys said, cursing; but they traveled onward anyway, through a dreadful realm of soggy dank marshland that had been easy fields on their journey westward the year before. Between one night and the next, winter had arrived in the Jhelum Valley, and winter was a season of never-halting rain in this region, it seemed.

Then they came to the Jhelum itself; and found it in wild spate, high above its old level and far outside its former boundaries, and running with a terrible turbulence where beforetimes it had merely been very swift.

The boats and rafts that they had left for themselves by the shore in the autumn had all been swept away by the flooding. But they were in need of new ones anyway, for they were vastly greater in number now than the army that had come across the river in the other direction; and so they set about once more building boats, and chopping saplings and lashing them into rafts. But would it be possible to cross at all, until after the rains? Already that looked doubtful; and the river grew ever higher every day.

Prestimion called for volunteers to make the crossing and

spy out the situation on the far side. A thousand men stepped forward; Prestimion picked six, and sent them off on a sturdy little raft, and watched anxiously as they bobbed and tossed on the stormy swollen river. It was so wide now that it was nearly impossible to see all the way to the other shore through the unending rain; but Septach Melayn, posted in a watch-tower, stared into the distant dimness and said finally, "Yes, they are across!"

They were gone six days. Then they returned with news that Farholt's army had reached the Jhelum also, and was camped by its edge, thirty miles downriver from them, waiting for the weather to improve.

"How many are there?" Prestimion asked.

"It would have taken all week again to count them."

"And the mollitors?"

"They have hundreds with them," said one of the spies. "A thousand, maybe."

That was ominous news. Mollitors were the deadliest of all beasts-of-war: colossal armor-plated creatures of synthetic origin, first created, like mounts and energy-throwers and airborne vehicles and many other such things, in the ancient times when scientific skills had been greater on Majipoor, and sustained ever since by natural breeding of the old stock. Wide-bodied short-legged things with purple leathery hides hard as iron, they had savage curved claws that could rip a tree apart the way a child might pull leaves from a plant, and massive heads with huge heavy irresistible jaws designed for rending and crushing. Though they had little intelligence, their strength was so formidable that it was all but impossible to withstand it. And Farholt had brought hundreds of them to the shore of the Jhelum. Thousands, it might be.

Prestimion said to Septach Melayn, "Take four battalions—no, take five, cavalry and footsoldiers both—and get you down south to the riverbank opposite Farholt's camp, with plenty of our best mounts. Set up fortifications there, and drill your troops, and make sure you're seen and heard as you shout your commands. Let there be much clatter every day, and all night long too. Build boats, with all the hammering you can manage. Blow your trumpets; beat your drums, march up and down along the shore. Have your men sing battle-songs, if you can invent some, with all their might. Send spies out by night on the water to stare into Farholt's encampment. Do everything, in short, that would announce to Farholt that you are on the verge of crossing the river and attacking him. Everything, that is, except actually to attack."

"Great noise will come from us," Septach Melayn vowed.

"On the third day, launch your boats toward Farholt by night, preferably in the rain, if it's still raining, and take no pains to be silent about that, either. But turn back after a hundred strokes of the oars. The next night, go out a hundred fifty strokes into the river, and turn back again. Do the same the following night as well. But that night the attack will be no feint."

"I understand," said Septach Melayn.

Prestimion, meanwhile, assembled his own assault group, seven battalions of his finest infantrymen and archers, with the remainder of the cavalry force to ride behind them. It took two days to make everything ready; the morning after that he led them seventeen miles upstream, to a place where his reconnaissance men had discovered a large and heavily wooded island in the midst of the river. That would make the crossing easier, having such a place midway to halt. Nor would they be seen there while they regrouped behind the trees, even if Farholt's scouts were ranging that far up the river. By night, using boats and rafts, he crossed with all his troops over to the island, pausing there to survey and rearrange his force, then proceeding onward about two hours before midnight to the Jhelum's eastern shore.

The night was moonless; there was no illumination except from the terrifying bolts of lightning that flashed again and again. Rain came in torrents, driven sidewise into their faces by the relentless wind. But that wind blew from the west and carried their little boats swiftly across. Prestimion made his crossing in one of the smallest boats, accompanied only by Gialaurys and his brother Taradath: they talked of nothing but the coming battle.

Forty-seven miles of muddy riverbank separated them now from Farholt's encampment.

"Now," Prestimion said, "we begin our march."

There was no dry moment, all the way south; slipping and sliding through the mud was the only mode of progress, and yet they marched. When they made camp it was in miserable sodden mud; when they marched again, it was through driving rain. Yet they were all of good cheer.

Septach Melayn was in place by now; he had made his first feint across the river; Farholt, if he had any sense, would have his strongest forces lined up along the riverbank, looking outward toward Septach Melayn's camp and ready to beat off the lunatic onslaught from the west whenever Septach Melayn actually deigned to launch it.

But first—first—

Under cover of darkness and storm Prestimion advanced steadily down the eastern shore until he was within striking distance of Farholt's encampment. It was a heavy gamble: would Septach Melayn be a sufficient distraction? And would he, once he began his crossing of the river, be able to make it safely to the other side? And would the rest of the army be in the right place at the right time for the culminating stroke? Prestimion could only time his own attack with care, and hope for the best.

He led the troop of archers himself, with Taradath at his side. Gialaurys, on his right flank, had charge of the javelin-men, and to his left were the long spears, under Thurm and golden Spalirises. Duke Miaule of Miaule would lead the cavalry, holding back in the rear until the question of the mollitors was resolved, for even the finest war-mounts were in dire fear of mollitors and would be useless if the great monsters were to charge.

"Come, now," said Prestimion, and led the way forward against Farholt.

It was almost a perfect surprise attack.

Farholt indeed had deployed the heart of his force along the riverbank, waiting for Septach Melayn. For two nights the false crossings had put Farholt's men on full alert, and then the supposed attack had come to nothing, so that it began to seem to the royalist forces that Septach Melayn intended merely to feint night after night. There was, inevitably, a decline of vigilance on Farholt's side; but still he kept his line intact along the river, with the bulk of the mollitors in readiness to hurl the rebels back into the river if ever they attempted to come ashore.

This night, though, Septach Melayn's attack was no feint. And while he led his boats past the midpoint of the river and toward the waiting royalists, Prestimion's band of archers came down into Farholt's camp from the other side. If it had been a complete surprise, the battle might have ended with a rout in its first minutes; but some men of Farholt, happening by chance to be following some strayed mounts into the woods that lay just to the north of the camp, saw by the light of a lightning-bolt Prestimion's men descending a low hill toward them, and ran screaming back to camp to sound the alarm. And so Farholt was granted just enough time to redeploy one segment of his force to meet the unexpected incursion from his rear.

"Look, brother," said Prestimion to Taradath between two great thunderclaps. "They come running to their deaths." And he drew and put an arrow into one of Farholt's captains; and Taradath, aiming right after him, felled another.

The slaughter was fearful. A hail of arrows fell upon Farholt's bewildered men as they charged uphill through the mud in the darkness. Of the mollitors, there was no sign: it seemed they were still down at the water's edge, waiting for Septach Melayn. So it was safe for Prestimion to bring the cavalry into play, and he sent word to Miaule to move his division forward.

Farholt, aware now of the magnitude of the unexpected attack behind him, was desperately dividing his forces, sending battalion after battalion to meet the thrust of Prestimion's men. Plainly he had underestimated the size of the rebel army, nor had he expected them to come upon him from two sides at once; and most of his own men were still camped for the night, struggling slowly to make ready for battle. Prestimion now signalled Thurm and Spalirises to swing into action with the spearmen, and Gialaurys from the other side to enfold the royalists with his javelins. "We have them!" he called out to Prestimion in a great booming shout that could be heard from one side of the battlefield to the other. "Prestimion! Prestimion! All hail Lord Prestimion!"

Now Farholt's men were falling back under the diabolical onslaught of Prestimion's archers, while the infantrymen on both flanks herded the royalists toward the center of the camp. Septach Melayn was on shore now: that much was evident from the wild trumpeting of the mollitors in the distance. Prestimion, standing in the thick of things, found himself wondering in an astounded bemused way whether they might be able to put the royalist army entirely to flight all at once, here at the very beginning of the struggle, as his force and Septach Melayn's came together like the halves of a nutcracker with the royalists between them.

But that would be too simple to hope for, he knew. He pushed such thoughts from his mind and gave all his concentration to his bow. The arrows flew forth, and nearly every one found its mark.

Who these men were that he was bringing down, Prestimion attempted not to consider, though he could not help recognizing some. He saw the stunned look on the face of Hyle of Espledawn, and another who might have been Travin of Ginoissa, as he pierced them through. But there was no time to regret such things now. He aimed again, at a man holding an energy-thrower. There were a few such weapons in Farholt's army, and very dangerous weapons they were; but they were wildly erratic also, for the art of making them, having been lost a thousand years before, was but newly revived and not yet with much skill. The man had the muzzle of his weapon pointed at Prestimion from fifty yards' distance. But Prestimion put a shaft through his throat while he was still fumbling with the buttons and studs that controlled its beam.

Shouts came from Prestimion's left. He glanced down that way and saw that the momentum of the battle, which had been all with the his forces at first, had begun to change. Farholt's people were rallying; or, at least, were holding their own.

No longer, now, was Prestimion's band of archers gleefully advancing with utter freedom on Farholt's camp. The sheer mass of Farholt's army was too great. Caught between Septach Melayn's landing-party and Prestimion's rear-guard attack, they had no place to go; and now they were standing firm between the forest and the river. The suddenness of the double attack had turned them into little more than a mob, but they were an armed and sturdy mob, and they feared for their lives. So they held their ground, butting up against their attackers and refusing to yield an inch. They were locked face to face with them the way Farholt and Gialaurys once had been in that wrestling match long ago in the Labyrinth.

Archers were no longer of much use in this sort of struggle. Preeminence had passed to the battalions led by Gialaurys, Spalirises, and Thurm, who needed less space for the use of their weapons. They prodded and jabbed with their spears and javelins, while Miaule's cavalrymen rode about the outside of the melee, hacking with swords and axes at Farholt's men from above.

Prestimion made his way to Gialaurys's side. "Clear a path for me to the waterfront," he said. "My archers will be of more value down there."

Gialaurys—grinning broadly, soaked through and through with rain and sweat—nodded and drew a platoon of his javelin-men from the main fray. Prestimion saw his brother Taradath just to his side, and pulled at his sleeve. "There's work for us down by the water's edge," he said. And off they went, with their corps of archers behind them, around the left side of the camp under cover of the javelin platoon, and down the gentle muddy slope to the river.

It was madness down there. Septach Melayn had come ashore, as instructed, with his footsoldiers only; the presence of cavalry battalions on the other bank had been intended only to mislead Farholt. But the invading force had been met, after its struggle with the roaring flood that was the river, with an implacable line of mollitors. The ponderous war-beasts ranged up and down the shore, clawing, stamping, impaling. Septach Melayn's men were fighting back with spears and javelins, striking upward in the hope of hitting some vulnerable spot beneath their body-armor. But all was mud and blood and driving rain and Prestimion saw fallen soldiers everywhere.

"Aim for the mollitor-drivers," he called to his men. For every mollitor had its driver seated in the saddle formed by natural folds of the shoulder-armor, who by signals delivered with a mallet was able more or less to control his monstrous beast. Prestimion's archers now began to pick them off, sending them tumbling one by one into the mud beneath their own animals' clawed hooves. The mollitors, confused without their drivers and hemmed in an ever-narrowing space, moved in bewildered circles, trampling their own side; and then, unable to tell friend from foe, wheeled about and erupted in a charge away from the waterfront that carried them right into Farholt's own cavalry, which was riding down to the shore in a counterattack.

Prestimion fought his way inward until he stood next to Septach Melayn. The tall swordsmen was fighting with wild exhilaration, slashing gleefully and to terrible effect. "I had not thought it would go so well," he said, laughing. "They are ours, Prestimion! Ours!"

Yes. The battle was won. And now came the final blow. The regiments of Zimroel had been held in reserve; now, under Gaviad and Gaviundar, these troops were crossing the river in a multitude of boats and descending onto a shore no longer guarded by mollitors. Eyes agleam, their hideous faces shining with the joy of battle, the two ghastly brothers seemed transported with ecstasy as they led their men ashore.

What followed was butchery, not fighting.

The royalist army—an army no longer—went into wild retreat as this newest and most utterly unexpected of reinforcements appeared in their midst. The battlefield had become a bedlam of fallen mounts and wounded men and maddened uncontrolled mollitors, and rebel warriors rising up on all sides. Farholt's forces swirled about wildly in an attempt to break into retreat while the rebels mowed them down on all sides. This was war of a ferocity no one had expected, and they were unprepared to hold their places in the face of such a bloodletting. When an opening appeared to the eastward, the royalist army melted away into it, first by the tens and twenties, then hundreds at a time taking to their heels and disappearing into the rainy darkness.

Prestimion caught sight of Farholt himself, a gigantic furious figure wielding an immense sword and bellowing orders. Gialaurys had spied him too, and set out in his direction with murder in his eyes. Prestimion called to him to come back, but it was no use, for he had little voice left and Gialaurys was already beyond the range of it.

But then Farholt vanished in a swirl of confusion. Prestimion saw Gialaurys standing alone, looking about, searching for the man who was his particular enemy, unable to find him.

The first light of dawn was in the sky. It showed the muddy field red with blood, bodies everywhere, Farholt's proud army streaming off in chaos toward the east leaving mounts and mollitors and weapons behind.

"All done," said Prestimion. "And done very well."

# 7

The battle by the riverbank had been a great victory for the rebel cause, but not without high cost. By brightening day, as the rains gradually halted and the warm sun appeared, the victors tallied their dead. Kaymuin Rettra of Amblemorn had fallen, and Count Ofmar of Ghrav; and one of the sons of Rufiel Kisimir was dead, and another gravely wounded. That useful guide Elimotis Gan of Simbilfant had perished also, and the master spearsman Telthyb Forst, and many more. Nor was Prestimion any less grieved when he saw the bodies of those who had died on the other side, for though they had chosen to oppose him for Korsibar's sake, nevertheless they were men he had known for years, some since boyhood, and once had looked upon as good friends. Among them was Count Iram of Normork's younger brother Lamiran, and Thivvid Karsp of Stee, who was close kin to Count Fisiolo, and also such great men as Belditan of Gimkandale and Viscount Edgan of Guand and Sinjian of Steppilor. But Farholt, it seemed, had escaped, he and most of his commanders, fleeing back in disarray toward Castle Mount.

"These are all grave losses, both ours and theirs, and I mourn them all," Prestimion said somberly to Duke Svor, after they had had the rites for them. "And how it galls me that they won't be the last! How many deaths must there be, do you think, before Korsibar steps aside and allows us to prevail?"

"Korsibar's, for one," said Septach Melayn. "Do you

453

seriously think, Prestimion, that he's merely going to resign in your favor, now that he's lost a battle? Did you renounce your hopes, that time he smashed us at Arkilon?"

Prestimion made no reply, but only stared. That this war could only end with Korsibar's death, or his, was something that he had understood from the first; and yet he could not easily abide the reality of it. It was a formidable thing to contemplate, that Korsibar must die for peace to be restored. And when he thought of all else that must be accomplished before that time, it seemed to him as challenging as making the ascent of Castle Mount on foot.

"And also a second army under Navigorn waits for us by the Jhelum to the north," Gialaurys pointed out. "We'll be back in the field before we have time to catch our breaths, and it may not go as nicely for us the next time."

But it appeared that they would have time to catch their breaths after all; for news soon came from messengers out of the east that Korsibar had withdrawn Navigorn's army from its position along the riverbank, and was holding meetings at the Castle to discuss the best manner of prosecuting the campaign against the rebels. The winter rains were a hindrance to battle just now in any case. So there would be a respite. The next battle, whenever it came, would at least find Prestimion's forces rested and ready.

Prestimion set about now replenishing his army, and winning the support of the citizenry here in the hinterlands.

Dantirya Sambail had failed to arrive as promised. That was a problem. The Procurator had sent messages instead: he was, he said, finding affairs at home more complex than he had expected, but he hoped to conclude matters there quickly and join the rebel forces no later than in spring. Meanwhile he offered Prestimion his felicitations over the great victory at the Jhelum, about which he had heard in full detail from his brothers, and expressed the firm belief that Prestimion's road to the Castle and the throne would be marked by steady success all the way. Which was all well and good, but Prestimion found Dantirya Sambail's absence troubling. He was capable of being on too many sides at once, was Dantirya Sambail.

After waiting out the wet season by the Jhelum, gathering provisions and receiving an additional complement of mounts from the Marraitis breeders, Prestimion began to move in a generally northerly direction into the Salinakk district of central Alhanroel, a plateau region of mild breezes, low hills, and a generally dry, sandy terrain. His goal was the populous city of Thasmin Kortu, the capital of the province of Kenna Kortu, which lay just beyond Salinakk. Duke Keftia of Thasmin Kortu, who was related by ties of marriage to the Princess Therissa, had sent letters to Prestimion by the Jhelum declaring sympathy to Prestimion's cause and inviting him to use his city as his home base as he prepared his campaign against the usurper.

Between the Jhelum and Thasmin Kortu, however, lay the many cities and towns of the Salinakk, and much of that region was loyal to Korsibar. The scouts Prestimion had sent ahead had seen the banners of Korsibar widely displayed there.

But there was little overt opposition, at first, to Prestimion's advance into that province. For one thing, he had Farholt's corps of mollitors with him. It had hardly seemed prudent to let the terrifying war-beasts go roaming loose along the banks of the Jhelum when he could make use of them himself. So he had had them all rounded up and had impressed Farholt's surviving mollitor-drivers into his own army.

The villagers of the Salinakk, seeing this formidable army approach, gave Prestimion a cordial enough welcome. At a place called Thelga, they hailed him with seeming sincerity as Coronal, and showed him an easier route through the Salinakk than he had planned to take, via Hurkgoz and Diskhema and past the dreary salt-flats of Lake Guurduur.

There was only one engagement of any note along this way: at the hilltop fort of Magalissa, where a garrison of army troops was stationed. Prestimion sent word to them that as Coronal he claimed their services, to which they replied with a defiant shower of arrows.

"We should not tolerate such behavior," said Septach Melayn pleasantly, and went out with five hundred men to deal with them. It was a tricky task—an uphill charge against an entrenched position, and with no cavalry support, the hill being too rough and steep for mounts to ascend—but the Magalissa garrison turned out to have little real longing for battle and its surrender came quickly.

After that the rebel force moved quickly northward over the sandy plateau, through a region of small streams cutting across bare tawny soil, and tiny villages screened by stands of narrow upright vribin-trees closely planted side by side. In time they came to Lake Guurduur, a grim dead lake covered by a whitish scum of salt. Baleful red-eyed salt-creatures with jointed legs and scorpion tails held high crawled slowly about there, defying them with clicking jaws to intrude on their domain; but Prestimion had no wish to be Coronal of the salt-creatures, and let them be. And in five days more he came to the crossroads town of Kelenissa, which guarded the approach to Kenna Kortu Province and the main road to Duke Keftia's city farther to the north.

Two rivers began here, the Quarintis and the Quariotis, one flowing east and the other west and both of them emerging from the same huge limestone cavern that sat like a gaping white mouth against the sandy soil. Above it on the hillside where Kelenissa town was situated all was green and lush and blooming, a welcome sight after the mud of the Jhelum Valley and the barrenness of the Salinakk plateau.

They found here an ancient stone palace of some Coronal earlier even than Stiamot, all in ruins, and a forest where strange wild animals wandered freely. A man of Kelenissa who was hunting there told Prestimion that the Coronal who had built the palace, whose name he did not know, had had a great park full of such beasts here. The park had been maintained for thousands of years after his time as a zoological preserve, but now the animals lived on their own, for the walls of the park had crumbled away.

The same man pointed to Septach Melayn, who was standing to one side carefully adjusting the hang of his sword in its baldrick in that finicky way of his, and said to Prestimion, "That very tall man there, with the fancy golden ringlets and the little pointed beard: can he be Prince Prestimion, who claims to be Coronal? For there's something I should tell him, if that's the case."

Prestimion laughed. "He looks to be a kingly man, does he not? And in truth he's Prestimion's other self, or one of them, for that is Prestimion too over there, that dark little man with the beard so tightly curled, and that one there also, the great-shouldered one whose hair is cut so short. But in fact I am the one who was born to the name, so tell me whatever it is that you think Prince Prestimion needs to know."

The Kelenissa man, bewildered by Prestimion's airy and fanciful response, looked frowning from Septach Melayn to Svor to Gialaurys and then to Prestimion again; and then he said, "Well, whichever of you is indeed the prince, let it be known to him that two great armies of the other Coronal Lord whose name is Korsibar are marching at this moment toward this city to take him captive and return him to Castle Mount for trial as a rebel, and that we here have received orders from this Lord Korsibar instructing us to give all assistance to them when they arrive, and no help to the rebel Prestimion. Tell that to Prince Prestimion, if you will." And the man turned and trudged away, leaving Prestimion sorry he had been so flippant and playful with him.

So their respite was over. Quickly Prestimion consulted Thalnap Zelifor, who did indeed seem to have some skill at casting his mind out into distant places and spying out knowledge. The Vroon gestured busily with his tentacles, bringing a dim bluish glow into the air before him, and after a few moments of intent concentration reported that two armies in fact were converging on them once more, forces even larger than the one Farholt had led. Mandrykarn and Farholt were the generals of the southern force, marching up through such places as Castinga and Nyaas and Purmande, while Navigorn was coming at them once more from the north.

"And which is closest to us now?" Prestimion asked.

"Navigorn. His is the greater army, as well."

"We'll carry the war to him, without waiting for him to get here," said Prestimion at once, for the victory at the Jhelum still coursed hot in his veins. "He hurt us once at Arkilon, but we'll take him this time. And afterward deal with Mandrykarn and Farholt."

Septach Melayn and Gialaurys were in agreement: strike quickly, before the two advancing armies could unite. The brothers Gaviad and Gaviundar were less eager for it. "It's too soon to fight again," said Gaviad, who even here at this morning hour had already been at his wine, or so it seemed from the thick-tonguedness of him. "Our brother the Procurator will come to us before long with additional men."

"Wait, yes," said Gaviundar. "He is a great wondrous asset to our cause, our brother is."

"And have you any date for his arrival among us?" asked Septach Melayn, a little testily. "He seems somewhat overdue already, would you not agree?"

"Be patient, lad, patient!" said Gaviad, peering up at Septach Melayn out of reddened bleary eyes and pulling at the wiry tufts of his mustache. "Dantirya Sambail won't be much longer now: my oath upon it." And he drew forth a new flask of wine and set to work.

Nor did the argument for immediate attack find favor with Svor. "We feel strong and high-spirited now, after the river-battle and this easy march north. But are we strong enough, Prestimion? Would it not be wiser to draw back into the west, perhaps as far as the coast, even, and build ourselves a bigger army yet, before we take them on?"

"Which would give them opportunity, also, to build their own forces," said Gialaurys. "No. I say hit them now, flatten them with our mollitors, send them slinking back to Korsibar in tatters as we did with Farholt's army. Two such defeats running and the people will begin to tell each other that the hand of the Divine is against the usurper. Wait, and it'll only give him more time to make himself look like a legitimate king."

There was a silence then; and into it, in a low voice edged with melancholy, Svor said, "Legitimate—illegitimate— ah, my good lords, how much blood do we intend to shed over these words? How many wounds, how many deaths? If only Majipoor were not saddled with this devilish thing of a monarchy at all!"

"Saddled, Svor?" said Septach Melayn. "And devilish? A strange choice of words. What are you saying?"

"Let us suppose," Svor replied, "that we had no lifelong kings here at all, but only a Coronal who served by the choice of the high lords and princes, perhaps, for a term of six years, or perhaps eight. And then he would step down from the throne and another be chosen in his place. With such a system, we would tolerate Korsibar's holding of the throne, irregular though it may be, with the agreement that after his six years, or eight, he would go his way, and Prestimion could have the crown. And after Prestimion, someone else, six or eight years farther on. If that were so we would not have this war, and fine men dying on muddy fields, and before long cities burning as well, I think."

"What you say is lunacy," retorted Gialaurys. "A recipe for chaos and nothing else. Kingship should be embodied in one great man, and that man hold the throne so long as he lives, and then go to the Labyrinth and have the higher throne to the end of his life. It is the only way, if we are to have a stable government in the world."

"And also," said Septach Melayn, "consider this: under your scheme the Coronal would lose all power in the last year or two of his reign, as everyone came to see that he was soon no longer to be king; for why fear him, with his time almost up? And another thing: we would always have men jostling for the succession, hardly one Coronal on the throne but five or six others already angling to take his place after his term of office. Gialaurys is right, Svor: a crazy system. Let us hear no more of the idea."

Prestimion called upon them then to return to the theme of their meeting, whether or no to launch an attack on Navigorn's army. It was so resolved, though the brothers Gaviad and Gaviundar remained cool to it; and scouts were sent out in several directions. Soon Prestimion had word from them confirming the essence of Thalnap Zelifor's spell-casting. Navigorn was five days' march north and east of them, at a flat dry place called Stymphinor. He had with him an army of dismaying size, and, said the scouts, an entire large corps of wizards and mages as well.

"Give me one good man with a sword and another with a spear," said Prestimion scornfully, "and they can handle a dozen wizards apiece. These men in brazen hats hold no terror for me."

Let Navigorn use such things if he wished, he declared.

He himself would depend on more conventional tactics: good sturdy weapons of bright sharp steel, and not such things as ammatelapalas and veralistias and rohillas and other such magical devices of the ignorant and credulous. "We'll attack at once," he said. "In surprise lies our best hope." And they straightaway got themselves ready for battle.

They set out then to the east, following the course of the Quarintis as long as they could, then going up a little way into the hills north of the river that led into Stymphinor, where Navigorn lay encamped.

On the eve of the battle Thalnap Zelifor came to Prestimion, who sat going over the plan of attack in his tent with Septach Melayn, and asked him whether he wished him to cast a spell favorable to their cause that night. "No," Prestimion replied. "Have you not heard me say again and again that such things are for Navigorn, perhaps, but not for me?"

"I had come to think that you were beginning in recent weeks to see merit in our art," said the Vroon.

"I tolerate a little conjuring around me, yes," Prestimion said, "but only because others whom I love wished me to permit it. I am far from a convert to your magic, Thalnap Zelifor. Military skill and plain good luck are worth more to me than a whole legion of demons and spirits and other such invisible and nonexistent forces."

But to his surprise Septach Melayn took a different position. "Ah, let the spells be cast, Prestimion," he said. "There's no harm in it, is there? What will it cost us to have this Vroon wriggle his tentacles a bit, and make the air glow blue, and mutter some words that might help us on the field?"

Prestimion gave him a strange look. Never before had he heard Septach Melayn say a word in favor of sorcery. But Septach Melayn was right to the extent that such witchery cost nothing but a little effort on the part of the Vroon; and so Prestimion gave his permission. Thalnap Zelifor went off to his quarters to cast the spell; and Prestimion and Septach Melayn began once more to study their plan of battle.

An hour later the Vroon reappeared. His big yellow eyes seemed more than usually solemn and earnest, as though he had labored long and hard at his task.

"Well?" Prestimion said. "Is it done? Are all the demons properly invoked?"

"The runes are cast, yes," said Thalnap Zelifor. "And now I come to you about another matter entirely."

"Go on," said Prestimion. "Speak, then."

"I told you, my lord, that I had left the incomplete model of my thought-perceiving device at the Castle, and many another mechanism that could be of use to you in the struggle ahead. I ask your permission to return immediately to the Castle—setting out this very night if you will allow it—and fetch those things."

Septach Melayn laughed. "You'll be hanging by chains in the Sangamor tunnels again five minutes after you get there. And that's if you're lucky. Korsibar knows you're with us; he'll charge you with treason the moment he sees you."

"Not if I claim to be defecting to his side," said the Vroon.

"Defecting?" said Prestimion, startled.

"In pretense only, I assure you," the Vroon said hastily. "I announce to him that I can see no merit in your claim to be Coronal, and offer him my services. Perhaps I'll share with him, also, some purported strategic plans of yours—which I have invented myself. He won't harm me then. And then I'll go into my room and gather up all my devices and mechanisms, and when the time is right I'll slip away again and come back to you with them. That will give you—after I've completed the last step or two of my research, of course— the power through me of looking into Korsibar's mind, or Navigorn's, or the mind of anyone you please, and seeing the innermost secrets hidden there."

Prestimion looked uneasily toward Septach Melayn. "This is all too devious for me. Pretending to defect? Will Korsibar be so innocent as to believe that? And then managing to leave the Castle under his very nose, and coming back here with these magicky machines of yours?"

"I have explained," said Thalnap Zelifor with dignity, "that there is no magic to them, but only science."

"Let him go, if he thinks he can do it," Septach Melayn said. "We have other things to deal with tonight, Prestimion."

"Yes. Yes. All right, you can go to the Castle, Thalnap Zelifor." Impatiently Prestimion waved the Vroon away. "Do you want an escort?" he asked, as Thalnap Zelifor backed from the tent. "I can spare you two men of Muldemar who were wounded at the Jhelum, and won't be fighting tomorrow anyway. Speak to Taradath about them. And get you back here with your machines as quickly as you can."

Thalnap Zelifor made a reverent starburst and departed.


The engagement began at sunrise: a bright clear sky, a brilliant hot sun. The whole formidable corps of mollitors was at the ready in the fore of the rebel force, each great beast with its rider perched above, ready to send the animal careering forward at the signal from Prestimion. The two armies were facing one another on a wide, flat, open field, broken only by a few spindly bushes and occasional outcroppings of rock: a perfect place, thought Prestimion, for charging mollitors. He himself stood off to the left with his archers, set back a short distance from the line of battle; his spearsmen and slingers were in the center, led by Gialaurys and Septach Melayn, and they likewise were set back a little way. The cavalry, under Duke Miaule, waited hidden in a defile well over to the right.

It was Prestimion's plan to be quick and economical about the battle, because they were so greatly outnumbered.

Therefore he meant to strike the enemy not at his weakest but at his strongest point, in the very center.

An oblique advance was what he proposed: the center and left held back in the early moments, the mollitors coming on first to put Navigorn's front line into disarray, and then, when a gap had developed there, to bring the cavalry in from the right for the decisive charge, with the other two wings pouncing in their wake. Overwhelming force at the decisive point: that would be their strategy. Once more the army from Zimroel under the command of the brothers of the Procurator would be kept in the rear to provide the final overwhelming assault and to do the mopping-up as Navigorn's routed men retreated.

Prestimion could see Navigorn across the way, standing at the head of his forces: an imposing dark-haired figure very much like Korsibar himself in appearance, bold and swaggering, grinning with confidence, with green-cloaked shoulders thrown back, deep chest swelling proudly beneath armor of gleaming silver scales, eyes even from so far away visibly bright with the joy of battle and an eagerness to be moving forward. A worthy enemy, Prestimion thought. A pity that they must be enemies, though.

He gave the order for the charge. The mollitors moved forward. Their heavy hooves made a sound as of a thousand hammers striking a thousand anvils.

Then a dozen or more of Navigorn's brazen-hatted sorcerers, impressively garbed in golden kalautikois and scarlet-and-green lagustrimores, came suddenly into view. Prestimion saw them standing side by side on one of the rocky ledges above the battlefield. They were holding in their left hands great coiling bronze horns of an unfamiliar kind; and as the mollitors began their charge, the mages put the mouthpieces of those horns to their lips and brought forth such a devilish screech that Prestimion thought the heavens would crack apart from it. It was as though some witchery were at work to amplify the noise of those horns beyond the capacity of human lungs to create. That sound—again, again, again—wailed all about them like the crack of doom.

And the mollitors, some of them, at least, were flung into confusion.

Those at the frontmost of the charge halted abruptly when that terrible blast of sound hit them, turning away from it and running wildly in any direction that would not take them closer to the evil screeching. Some ran to the left, bursting into the midst of Prestimion's archers, who scattered before them. Some ran to the right, vanishing amidst clouds of dust into the gully where Prestimion's cavalry lay concealed, which surely would drive the mounts into a panic of their own. And some, perhaps braver or simply more stupid than the others, went plunging onward toward Navigorn's front line; but the royalist army simply stepped aside, creating aisles through which the oncoming mollitors could pass, and letting them go rampaging harmlessly on and on into the open fields beyond.

For an instant Prestimion stood stupefied by the utter failure of the charge. Then he lifted his bow and with the mightiest shot of his life, stretching the bow almost to its breaking point, struck one of Navigorn's mages off his rock, the arrow making its way easily into the rich brocade of his kalautikoi and the shaft emerging a foot through on the other side. The man tumbled and fell without uttering a word and his horn of burnished bronze went clattering down beside him.

But Prestimion's wondrous shot was the last happy moment of the day for the rebels. The real momentum lay with the royalist side. As the mollitors scattered, Navigorn's cavalrymen came thundering forward, with the infantry just behind, wielding their javelins and spears with awful effect. "Hold your formations!" Prestimion shouted. Septach Melayn, far across the way, called out the same command. But the rebel front line was breaking up. Prestimion watched his men turning and flooding backward into the second line, and to his horror saw that for a time a bizarre struggle was raging among his own men. For the second line, unable in the heat of the fray to distinguish friend from foe, was striking at those who came rushing into them, not realizing that they were their own fleeing companions.

Prestimion looked about for a messenger and caught sight of his fleet-footed brother Abrigant. "Get yourself to Gaviundar," he ordered. "Tell them that all's lost unless they join the battle immediately."

Abrigant nodded and ran off toward the rear.

Navigorn was a masterly general, Prestimion saw now. He had complete control of every instant of the battle. His cavalry had sent the rebel front line into rout; his infantrymen were going at it fiercely, hand to hand, with Prestimion's second line, which by now had reconstituted itself and was offering strong resistance; and now Navigorn's own second line was coming forward, not along the expected wide front but instead as a lethal concentrated wedge, smashing ruthlessly into the heart of the rebel line. There was no stopping them. Prestimion and his men filled the air with arrows, but the best archers in the world could not have halted that advance.

The slaughter went on and on.

Where were Gaviundar and drunken Gaviad? Crouching over a flask of wine somewhere safe behind the lines? Prestimion had a glimpse of Gialaurys skewering men with his spear, and Septach Melayn's tireless flashing sword hard at work elsewhere, but it was hopeless. It seemed to him even that blood was streaming down Septach Melayn's arm, he who had never known a wound in his life. They were beaten.

"Sound the retreat," Prestimion called.

Just as the signal to withdraw went out, Abrigant came

running up alongside him. "The Zimroel army is coming!" the boy said, panting.

"Now? Where have they been all this while?"

"Gaviundar misunderstood. He thought you would not want him until after the cavalry had gone into action. And Gaviad—"

Prestimion scowled and shook his head. "Never mind. I've already called retreat. Get you to safety, boy. We're done for here."

# 8

A sudden nasty disturbance of some sort was going on in the corridor outside the High Counsellor Farquanor's office in the Pinitor Court. The High Counsellor, looking up in annoyance at this interruption of his work, heard the clacking of boots against the stone floor of the hallway, blustering angry shouts, the clatter of running feet coming from several directions. Then an astonishingly familiar voice rose above the melee, an impossible voice, loud and raucous and harsh, crying out, "Easy, there, easy! Get those filthy hands off me or I'll have them chopped from your wrists! I am no sack of calimbots to be thrust about by you this way."

Farquanor rushed to the door, peered out, gaped in amazement.

"Dantirya Sambail? What are *you* doing here?"

"Ah, the High Counsellor. Ah. Please instruct your men in the proper courtesy due a high lord of the realm, if you will."

It was beyond comprehension. The Procurator of Ni-moya, in magnificent traveling robes of lustrous green velvet over flaring yellow breeches, was grinning diabolically at him from out of the midst of a bewildered-looking group of Castle guardsmen, some of whom were holding drawn weapons. For all the splendor of his garb, the Procurator looked dusty-faced and creased as though from a long hard journey. Five or six men in the boldly colored livery worn by Dantirya Sambail's people were nearby, as travel-worn as their master. They were being pressed against the wall by even more guardsmen. Farquanor recognized Mandralisca, the sharp-faced poison-taster, among them.

"What is this?" Farquanor demanded, turning to the highest-ranking guardsman in the group, a Hjort named Kyargitis, who had the perpetually glum face and bulging eyes of his kind. Kyagartis looked more than usually unhappy just now. His thick orange tongue was flicking nervously back and forth over the many rows of rubbery chewing-cartilage that filled his capacious mouth.

"The Procurator and these men of his obtained admission to the Castle through Dizimaule Gate—I will make full investigation, Count Farquanor, I promise you that—and succeeded in getting all the way to the vestibule of the Pinitor Court before they were challenged," said the Hjort, puffing with chagrin. "He insisted on seeing you. There was a scuffle—it was necessary to restrain him physically—"

Farquanor, altogether baffled by this inexplicable materialization outside his door of the last man he might have expected to see in this hallway today—the audacity of Dantirya Sambail's marching into the Castle with this little handful of men and expecting anything other than immediate arrest—gave the Procurator a sharp look. "Have you come here to assassinate me?"

"Why would I do that?" said Dantirya Sambail, all charm and friendliness now. "Do you think I covet your post?" The Procurator's mysterious amethyst eyes fastened on Farquanor's, giving him such a fierce blast of that strange outreaching tenderness of his that Farquanor had to struggle to keep from flinching before it. "No, Farquanor, my business is not with you, except indirectly. I'm here to speak with the Coronal on a matter of the highest importance. And so, since protocol requires that I apply myself to the Coronal's High

469

Counsellor—my congratulations, by the way, on your appointment: he took his time about it, eh?—I came up here to the Pinitor to see if I could find you, and—"

"Protocol?" Farquanor said, still bemused with amazement at the sight of this man here at a time like this. "There's no protocol for granting audience to rebels against the crown! You are proscribed, Dantirya Sambail: are you not aware of that? The only appointment you have is in the Sangamor tunnels! How could you imagine anything else?"

"Tell Lord Korsibar I'm here and would see him," rejoined the Procurator coolly, in a tone one might use in speaking with a footman.

"Lord Korsibar is busy at present with—"

"Tell him that I'm here and that I bring him his means of victory in the present insurrection," Dantirya Sambail said, and he was even less cordial now than he had been a moment before. "Tell him those exact words. And I promise you, Farquanor, if you do me any interference in bringing about my conference with the Coronal, if you delay me by so much as another heartbeat and a half, I will see to it ultimately that you not only are removed from your present high office but are very slowly flayed of every inch of your skin, which will be wrapped in strips about your face until you smother from it. This is my very solemn promise, Count Farquanor, which I am most unlikely to fail to keep."

Farquanor stared a moment, and then another, without replying. It seemed to him that behind the Procurator's usual arrogance and bluster lay some extraordinary intensity of tension and unease. Nor was a threat of that nature from a man of Dantirya Sambail's sort to be taken casually.

This strange visit was a matter, Count Farquanor began to realize, that went beyond his scope of office. It would be wisest not to interpose any pretensions of his own. In a formal frosty tone he said, "I will notify Lord Korsibar that you are in the Castle, and he will see you or not, as he chooses, Dantirya Sambail."

"Why are you here?" Korsibar asked, as surprised as Farquanor had been just a short while before. "I never wanted to see you again, after you forced Prestimion from my grasp. And I hardly thought to have you come calling at a time like this. Should you not be fighting against me now beside your loathsome brothers in Salinakk?"

"I am not your enemy, my lord," said Dantirya Sambail. "Nor are they."

"You call me 'my lord?' "

"I do."

The meeting was taking place not in the throne-room or in the Coronal's private office but in Lord Kryphon's Grand Hall, a long and dark and narrow room much less grand than its name suggested, where wall-charts of the campaign against Prestimion were hung and constantly updated.

Korsibar spent much of his time in this room these days. He sat slouched now in a low chair of some antique kind, with twining lizards of wrought iron for its arms. The only movements he made were those of his eyes, which shifted restlessly from side to side in their deep sockets; other than that he was utterly still. With one hand he gripped the yawning fanged head of the lizard that was the left-hand armrest, and with the other he held his head propped upright with a finger pressed against his cheekbone, hidden deep within his thick beard. Korsibar had let his beard grow in full lately, something he had never done before, though Aliseeva and other women of the court had told him that it made him look much older than his years; indeed, there were even a few bright strands of white glistening in its blackness. That was something new. But

471

this was a taxing time beyond anything for which his comfort-able early life had prepared him.

Sanibak-Thastimoon was with him, and Prince Serithorn and Count Iram and Venta of Haplior, and several of his other close advisers. Two Skandar guardsman hovered close beside Korsibar in case the Procurator had some mischief in mind. Dantirya Sambail stood squarely before the Coronal in that customary cocky spread-legged stance of his, arms pulled back behind him and head thrust forward. Count Farquanor, looking sour-faced and strangely sallow, stood just behind him.

Slowly, for he was very tired this day, Korsibar said, "I am your lord, so you say, and you are not my enemy, so you also say, and yet your armies hold the field against mine. Why is it that they don't seem to know you're not my enemy, Dantirya Sambail?"

The Procurator nodded toward the wall-charts. "Have my brothers' soldiers done your troops much harm?"

"At the Jhelum battle they did. I have this from Farholt."

"And at the battle by Stymphinor, what there?"

"That battle was a short one. Navigorn had Prestimion beaten in the first half hour. We had few casualties there."

"Send to Navigorn, my lord, and ask him whether the troops of Zimroel saw action against him at all at Stymphinor. Tell him that I claim it is the case that the armies under the command of my brothers Gaviad and Gaviundar never entered the fray, that day, but held back, rather, until the issue was settled against Prestimion, and see what he says."

Korsibar knotted his fingers in his beard, and tugged at it somewhat after the fashion of Duke Svor, from whom, so he suspected, he had learned that mannerism. There was a terrible hammering behind his eyes. After a little while he replied, "If there were soldiers of yours at Stymphinor pledged to Prestimion, then why were they not fighting that day?"

"Because I told them not to," said the Procurator. "I will

not deny, my lord, that I allied myself with Prestimion in the first days of his rebellion. He is my kinsman: you know that. The ties of blood drew me to him. But I never had any great love for his cause."

"And yet you gave him troops."

"I gave him troops, yes, because I had pledged him I would do so, and at the Jhelum I let them fight against your army. But it was only a pretense, to swell him up with pride over an easy victory, and make him ready for the crushing. At the next battle my soldiers came too late to fight, and that was at my order too."

"What's this?" cried Korsibar. "Oh, you serpent!"

"But *your* serpent, my lord. Prestimion's cause is hopeless. That was clear to me from the start and it seems beyond dispute now. He is one man against a world; you have the backing of the people, and you will prevail. He may win a battle here and there, but his doom is certain."

"You have that from your soothsayers?" Korsibar asked, with a quick glance at Sanibak-Thastimoon.

"I have it from *here,* my lord," replied Dantirya Sambail, tapping his great gleaming freckled forehead. "Every ounce of wisdom I have in here, and there's more than a little, tells me that Prestimion is attempting the impossible by trying to overturn your regime. And so I withdraw my pledge of aid to him: for I am not one who is given to toiling at impossible tasks. I've come here to you—at great personal inconvenience, my lord, which you can see from my rumpled look; traveling back and forth with such speed across the vastness of Alhanroel as I've been doing all this year and last, not to mention crossing the sea a couple of times, is no easy thing for a man of my years—for the sake of presenting you with the key to victory and putting an end to the strife that embroils the world."

"The key to victory," Korsibar repeated tonelessly. "What can you mean by that?" This conversation was becoming abhorrent to him. Dealing with Dantirya Sambail was like wrestling with manculains: there were deadly spines all over the man. He looked around the room for guidance, to Sanibak-Thastimoon, Iram, Serithorn, Farquanor. But their faces were as rigid as masks and their eyes told him nothing. "What would you have me do, Dantirya Sambail?"

"For one thing, you must take the field yourself."

"Will you bite us both?" Korsibar demanded. "First you work treachery against your cousin, and then you try to lure me out of the Castle into the open, where anyone who cares to aim a javelin at me can—"

Dantirya Sambail grinned a tigerish grin. "Put your suspicions aside, my lord. You'll come to no harm. Let me show you what I have in mind.—Is this the map of the battle zone? Yes: good. Here's Prestimion, somewhere between Stymphinor and Klorn and moving to the northwest, I assume with the goal of reaching Alaisor and recruiting new troops for himself along the coast. Here's the army of Mandrykarn and Farholt, somewhere around Purmande and heading toward him from below; and here's Navigorn, to his east, pursuing him also. Perhaps Mandrykarn and Farholt will trap him in central Alhanroel, perhaps not: more likely not, but they'll force him northward. Do you agree?"

"Go on," said Korsibar.

"As he runs from place to place, trying to elude the two armies coming after him from this side and from this, word now reaches him that you yourself, the Coronal Lord Korsibar, have assembled yet a third army and have gone into the field yourself at the head of it. Look, here is the River Iyann, my lord. Here is the great Mavestoi Dam, and here is the reservoir behind it, Lake Mavestoi. Now, my lord, you take up your position in the hills above the dam; and then you let the word leak out to Prestimion's spies that you are camped there, planning to descend on him from the north and destroy him."

Dantirya Sambail's violet eyes were glowing now with excitement: they seemed almost incandescent. "His position is desperate, but he sees one last hope for himself! If he can attack your camp, and manage to kill or capture you, he has at one stroke ended the war. Ringed all about him are the hostile forces of Mandrykarn and Farholt and Navigorn, but with you removed from the scene they would have no choice but to yield the throne to him."

"So you bait a trap for him with me," said Korsibar. "And he comes marching up the Iyann to take the bait. Yes, but what if he succeeds in snatching it, Dantirya Sambail? What if he *does* overthrow me with his one desperate final stroke? I'm not within his reach so long as I remain at the Castle, but once I'm in the field he has a chance at me. Not that I fear him, or anyone; but it's only prudent for me to stay beyond range of some sudden wild thrust until this affair is done with."

"Ah, no, my lord, no need to fret over that. Prestimion will fall into the trap and be destroyed, and no risk to yourself at any time. Here, my lord—let me show you—"

# 9

For Prestimion it was a time of steady retreat, and of the healing of wounds.

The losses at Stymphinor had not been as great as he first had feared, but they were serious enough. Of his officers he had lost Abantes of Pytho and the fearless Matsenor son of Mattathis, and also Thuya of Gabell, the Ghayrog Vexinud Kreszh, and an old playmate of his Muldemar childhood, Kimnan Tanain. A good many soldiers of the line had perished also; but the core of his army was still intact, though battered and to some degree demoralized.

And also Septach Melayn had taken a deep cut in the upper part of his sword-arm, which was an event that caused much wonder and dismay among Prestimion's men. It was like the humbling of a god. No one had ever touched steel to Septach Melayn's skin before, in all his years of mastery of the sport of swordsmanship. But the battle at Stymphinor had not been any sort of sporting event; and now Septach Melayn sat shirtless and pale and grimacing while one of the surgeons closed the long red slash for him with glossy black thread.

Was that an omen of their ultimate defeat, the peerless Septach Melayn wounded? The men were muttering darkly and making conjure-signs to ward off the demons that they feared were closing in on them.

"I'll go among them," said Septach Melayn good-humoredly, "and show them I'm well, and tell them that I'm

476

relieved to discover that I'm mortal after all. Will make me less cocksure next time I'm in a fray, I'll say: for indeed over the years I'd come to think I could best any opponent in the world without half trying."

"As surely you can," said Prestimion, who had learned that morning that Septach Melayn had taken his wound while fighting four men at once, and, despite the hindrance to his arm, had slain all four of them before leaving the field with the greatest reluctance in order to seek a poultice for the cut.

The behavior of the Zimroel armies, that had been so slow to take the field at Stymphinor, was another concern for Prestimion. He summoned Gaviad and Gaviundar to berate them for their laxness; but the fleshy-faced brothers were so penitent and abject that he withheld most of the anger he had had in readiness for them. Stocky thick-bodied Gaviad of the pendulous lips and jutting mustache was cold sober, for a novelty, and said over and over that his troops had been ready, but he had been waiting for news of the cavalry charge before sending them forward, since that had been the plan; and tall big-eared strutting Gaviundar of the bald head and great tangled orange beard actually wept at dismay for having failed to bring in his men in timely fashion. So Prestimion forgave them. But he kept in mind whose brothers they were, and, fearing always the tricksiness that ran in the Procurator's blood, warned them that he would tolerate no excuses at the next engagement with the royalists.

Which he prayed would not occur soon. His men needed time to rest and repair themselves; and he hoped also for additional troops to join his cause. Encouraging messages had reached him from Alaisor on the western coast, which was the port through which the family of Muldemar shipped its wine to Zimroel, and where he had many close connections both of business and of family: the leading folk of Alaisor, he was told, favored the rebel cause over Korsibar's, and were raising an army to fight for him. Good news came from elsewhere in western Alhanroel, too: all up and down the coast, in Steenorp and Kikil, in Klai, in Kimoise, in other cities too, people were debating the merits of the two claimants to the throne and more and more of them were giving the nod to Prestimion, for they had had time now to consider the means by which Korsibar had come to be Coronal, and that did not sit well with them.

All this was fine indeed; but those cities of the western provinces were very far away, and the armies of Mandrykarn and Farholt and Navigorn were close behind. What Prestimion needed now to do was head swiftly to the north and west, to the land of his supporters along the coast, and make rendezvous with them before the enemies to his rear could fall upon him and bring an end to his whole rebellion. With all possible haste, then, he took himself upward and outward across the continent, moving farther away from Castle Mount and the throne he desired with every passing day.

They were approaching the valley of the River Iyann, which flowed out of the north country and made a westward turn here that took it to the sea at Alaisor, when Duke Svor came to Prestimion and said, "I have found certain persons who can do some useful scouting on our behalf, I think. They claim to have learned certain information already that may be valuable for us to know about."

"Do we have some shortage of scouts, Svor, that we need to hire strangers?"

"We have none like these," Svor said. And beckoned forward a bony-faced man of extraordinary height, at least a head taller than any man in the camp, but so lean and long-limbed that he seemed as frail as a wand, that could be snapped in two by a good heavy shove. His hair was very dark and cropped short, and his aspect was a dark one too, swarthy skin almost like Svor's own, and a coarse thick beard blackening

478

his heavy-jawed face. He gave his name as Gornoth Gehayn and said he was a man of the nearby town of Thaipnir on the tributary river of the same name. Behind him stood three more men almost identical to him in their great height and gauntness and dark aspects, but they seemed no more than half his age; and behind them was a long cart drawn by a pair of mounts. Four large square boxes covered by leather shrouds rested on the cart's bed.

"What is this?" Prestimion asked brusquely, for he was in an uneasy mood and short of patience just then.

"Your lordship," said Gornoth Gehayn in a thin high reedy voice, "we be trainers of hieraxes, my sons and I, who make them fly where we will, and ride clinging to their backs. It is a secret art private to our family, which we have been a long while in mastering. We go far and wide, and see many strange things."

"Hieraxes?" Prestimion said, taken aback. "You fly on hieraxes?"

Gornoth Gehayn made a grand sweeping gesture; and one of his sons leaped up on the cart and pulled back the shroud that covered the hindmost box. Which stood revealed as a steel cage that held a huge bird, one with vast gray wings folded over its body like a cloak, and big glittering blue eyes that gleamed outward between the bars of the cage like angry sapphires.

Prestimion caught his breath in surprise. He had seen hieraxes before, on many occasions, when traveling between Castle Mount and the Labyrinth. They were gigantic predatory creatures of the upper air, that glided lazily on the warm atmospheric currents high above the Glayge Valley, scarcely flapping their wings as they coasted from place to place and now and again snapping some unfortunate smaller bird out of the sky with a swift movement of their long beaks. In their way they were graceful and very beautiful, at least aloft, though they seemed nothing more than bony monsters huddled here in their cages. But he had never known a hierax to be taken captive, and the thought of men riding on their backs as though they were tame well-bred mounts was beyond belief.

"These are somewhat different from the hieraxes of the east," Gornoth Gehayn explained, as his son raised the portcullis of the bird's great cage. "These are the black-bellied ones of the Iyann region, which are bigger and much stronger than the pink ones of the Glayge, and so intelligent that they can be trained to obey. We take their eggs from the nest, and raise them and train them to our will, all for the pleasure of going aloft. Shall I demonstrate, my lord?"

"Go on."

At a cue from Gornoth Gehayn's son the huge bird came waddling awkwardly from its cage. It seemed barely to know how to unfurl the enormous wings that were wrapped tight about its body, and its long thin legs were plainly unaccustomed to movement on the ground. But after a moment it got its wings to open, and Prestimion emitted an astonished hiss as he saw those long and arching pinions unfold and unfold and unfold until they were spread out for an unthinkable distance on either side of the bird's substantial elongated body.

Immediately the son of Gornoth Gehayn, a boy so long and lean and light that he seemed almost to be the bird's own kin himself, sprang lithely forward and seized the hierax delicately but firmly just at the place where the powerful wings sprouted from the bird's muscular shoulders, and lay himself down sprawling along its back with his head just beside its own. Then there was a flapping of wings, a wild thumping beating of them on the ground, and after a moment's seeming struggle the hierax leaped up a short way above the ground, and then two instants later was coursing upward through the air, with Gornoth Gehayn's son still clinging to it.

It swept strongly higher almost at a straight line, and circled once overhead far above them, and shot off northward with phenomenal speed so that bird and rider soon were lost to view.

Gialaurys, who had joined Prestimion and Svor just as the boy had let the bird from its cage, laughed and said to Gornoth Gehayn, "Will you ever see either of them again? For I think the bird will fly off to the Great Moon with him."

"There is no danger," the man replied. "He's been flying these hieraxes of ours since he was six years old." Gornoth Gehayn gestured toward the cart and said to Gialaurys, "We have three other birds, my good lord. Would you care to go aloft yourself?"

"Gladly would I, and I thank you for the invitation," said Gialaurys with a bright gleeful grin that was far from typical of his wintry nature. "But I suspect I might be somewhat too heavy for the creature to bear." And he tapped his bull-like chest and each of his powerful shoulders. "A smaller man, perhaps, would be better. Such as you, my lord Duke Svor."

Prestimion joined in also: "Yes, Svor! Go up there, tell us what you see!"

"Some other day, I think," said Svor. "But look—look—is that the boy returning?" He pointed toward the sky; and indeed it was possible now to see a dark spot high above, which resolved itself against the brightness of the air into the wide-spread curving wings and long black-feathered body of the hierax, and then, as it descended, the son of Gornoth Gehayn could be seen still clinging to the bird's back. They landed a few moments later, bird and boy, and the boy jumped off, flushed, beaming with pleasure, exhilarated by his flight.

"What have you seen?" his father asked him.

"The armies, again. Marching up and down, drilling beside the lake."

"Armies?" Prestimion said quickly.

Svor leaned close to him. "I told you they'd discovered information that would be useful to us."

The fliers had indeed been making reconnaissance flights up the valley of the Iyann all week, once they had noticed the military movements north of their town, and they had learned a great deal already, all of which they were pleased to make available to Prestimion for just a few silver royals. A great force of men, they said, had come riding lately in floaters across the land out of the east, men with weapons and armor; and upon reaching the Iyann they had gone straight up along the part of the river that flowed down from the north, until they had reached Mavestoi Dam, at the foot of the great reservoir that held the water supply for much of this province.

They were camped now all along the dam's rim, and up both sides of the lake behind it. Each day one of the sons of Gornoth Gehayn had flown up there to see what was taking place—Gornoth Gehayn himself no longer went aloft, he said; he was too old for the game—and each day they saw additional troops arriving and digging in.

"The interesting thing," Svor said, "is that three days ago one of the boys swooped low and saw a man in the center of the camp, a tall dark-haired man wearing a Coronal's clothes, the green and gold with trim of white fur; and it seemed to him that he saw something flashing on the dark-haired man's brow that might just have been a crown."

Prestimion gasped. "Korsibar? Korsibar himself is out here?"

"So it would appear."

"Can it be? I thought he'd stay safe and snug in the Castle as long as he had men like Navigorn and Farholt to fight his battles for him."

"It seems," said Svor, "that he has come to fight this one himself. Or so our airborne spies tell us."

"Why is it, I wonder," said Prestimion, frowning, "that Korsibar's men allow these birds to fly low and spy them out, and make no attempt to shoot them down? I suppose they see only the hierax from below, and not the rider clinging to its back, and give it no heed. Well, no matter: if this is true, Svor, opportunity's in our grasp, would you not say? We'll send word to our friend Duke Horpidan of Alaisor to hurry those troops, and gather them in, and make an attempt on Korsibar while he's here. It's our one great chance. Seize him and the war's over, simple as that."

"I'll bring him as a prisoner to you myself," said Septach Melayn, whose wound was healing quickly and who was eager to be wielding his sword once again.

Each day, now, the hieraxes went forth; and each day they returned with further reports of the activities at Lake Mavestoi. The army there, they said, was a considerable one, though all three of Gornoth Gehayn's sons were of the opinion that Prestimion's own army was larger still. They had set up tents and were chopping down the trees around the lake to use for fortifications; and, yes, the man in the vestments of a Coronal could readily be seen whenever they flew over the camp, moving vigorously about in the midst of the soldiers, directing things.

Prestimion longed to hop on the back of one of these hieraxes himself, and verify that with his own eyes: but when he spoke of it to Gialaurys and Septach Melayn, sounding more than half serious, they rose up in wrath against him and told him that they would slaughter Gornoth Gehayn's birds with their own hands should he make any motion to go near them. And Prestimion promised them that he would not; but still he yearned for attempting it, both for what he might learn concerning his enemy and also for the sheer wonder and splendor of flying through the air.

There once had been airborne vessels on Majipoor, a very long time ago: Lord Stiamot, so it was said, had fought his war against the Shapeshifters from the air, setting fire to their villages by dropping burning brands on them and driving them into captivity. The skill of making flying machines had been lost in the distant past, though, and to get from place to place on the enormous planet it was necessary to crawl along by floater or mount-drawn vehicle, and no one but these bony lads from the district of the Iyann knew what it was like to go up above the surface of the world. Prestimion bitterly envied them.

But there would be no hierax-flying for him. He knew it was a skill you had to be born to, and learn as a child; and perhaps he was too sturdily built for the birds to carry. And in any event he had a war to fight, and soon.

They had decided not to wait for the reinforcements from the west. While they waited, Korsibar's other armies would be coming upon them from the east, and if the forces of Mandrykarn and Farholt and Navigorn were given the opportunity to join with those under Korsibar's command, they would have no hope against them. The thing to do was to strike at once, against an army apparently not as numerous as their own.

"Had Thalnap Zelifor not left us," Gialaurys said, "we could be using his witcheries to see into Korsibar's camp and count their number. And also to learn the best route by which to attack."

"We see the camp through the actual eyes of these boys," Prestimion told him, "which is better than glimpsing it by sorcery. As for the route, this is Gornoth Gehayn's home country, and he has drawn good maps for us. Thalnap Zelifor will return one of these days, bringing those thought-reading devices of his. But we'll finish Korsibar off without his help, I think."

They bent low over the maps. There were paths through the forests on both sides of the river leading up to the dam. Come up by night, on a night when no moons were in the sky; station half the cavalry on the east bank, half on the west; at a signal, ride into Korsibar's camp and attack from both sides at once. Prestimion would have his archers atop mounts for this engagement: come riding in, riddle the enemy with arrows as you came. That would be a sure producer of terror, men on mountback with bows. And then the heavy infantry, Gaviad coming in from the east side, Gaviundar from the west—the Divine preserve them if they were slow this time!— a series of massive strokes, one after another, Septach Melayn's bright sword cutting a path into the royalist camp, Gialaurys with his spear—

Yes. Yes. What wild miscalculation of Korsibar's was it that had delivered the usurper by his own free will into their hands?

"There'll be no moons shining three days hence," Svor announced, after consulting his almanacs and almagests.

"Then that's our night," said Prestimion.

The Iyann here was a narrow river, not very deep, easy to ford. Most of its flow out of the north was choked off by the dam that Lord Mavestoi had constructed here eight hundred years before. It was simple enough for Prestimion to divide his forces, sending half to either bank. He took up a position on the eastern shore, with his mounted archers; Gialaurys was behind him with the heavy infantry, and Gaviad's army in back of those. On the river's western side was the regular cavalry detachment under Duke Miaule of Miaule, with Septach Melayn's battalions accompanying them, and the army of Gaviundar poised to the rear for the second thrust.

The night's only illumination was that of the stars, which in this part of the world shone with particular brilliance. There were the great stars that everyone knew, Trinatha up to the north, and Phaseil in the eastern sky and its twin Phasilin in the west, and Thorius and blazing red Xavial marking the midpoint of the heavens. Somewhere out there, too, was the little yellow star of Old Earth, though there was no agreement on which one that really was; and then, too, the new star, the fierce blue-white star that had appeared to the world while Korsibar and Prestimion were making their separate journeys northward up the Glayge to Castle Mount, was in plain view straight overhead, piercing the sky like a furious staring eye.

By the light of those stars, and especially that of the new star, the long, narrow white band that was Mavestoi Dam could be seen at the head of the valley above them, running between the dark cliffs. It was there that Prestimion and his men must climb this night, up into those forested bluffs, then inward and downward upon the unsuspecting royalists in their camp. Looking upward now, Prestimion thought he could make out tiny figures moving along the dam's concrete rim. Sentries, no doubt. Did they have any idea that twin armies were stealing toward them along both sides of the river below? Very likely not. There was no sense of urgency or alarm in their movements: just some men, tiny as matchsticks from here, steadily pacing up and down along the crest of the dam.

Prestimion checked the positions of the stars. Trinatha, Thorius, Xavial, all in alignment. Time to get going, now. He raised his hand, held it high a moment, lowered it. Began to move forward, up the pathway beside the river. On the western shore Duke Miaule's forces were in motion also.

Upward. Upward.

The Divine grant us its favor, Prestimion thought, and we will finish this struggle tonight and bring sanity back into the world.

"What's that?" Svor said. "Thunder?"

Prestimion looked around, puzzled. A dull booming sound, indeed. But the night was clear, cloudless. There had been no lightning; there was no storm.

"Brother? *Brother!*"

Taradath, coming up the path. "Not so loud!" Prestimion said, in a harsh whisper. "What is it?"

"Gaviad—the Zimroel men—"

"Yes?"

Another boom, louder than the first.

"I've just had word—they're heading out. Marching away from the river as fast as they can."

"Heading—out?" said Prestimion. "But—what—?"

Svor said, "Look up there. The dam!"

*Boom. Boom. Boom.*

No figures could be seen along the dam's crest now. Only a quick burst of red, like a flare going off, and then a dark jagged crack, and what looked like a triangular chip taken out of the face of that white concrete wall.

*Boom.* Louder than all the others.

Svor cried, in a ragged voice, "They're blowing up the dam, Prestimion! They'll send the whole lake down on us!"

"But that would flood a hundred villages, and—" Prestimion replied, and said no more after that, but only gaped in disbelief, for by the lurid light of the explosions above them he could see the whole face of the dam crumbling, and a stupefying torrent of water descending through the darkness toward the valley below and all his men.

FIVE

# THE BOOK OF WIZARDS

# 1

This was surely the bleakest place in all the world, Prestimion thought, save only those terrible deserts of the continent of Suvrael where no one in his right mind would ever want to go.

It was a gray land that he was walking through in this black hour. The sky overhead was gray, the dry ground beneath his feet was gray, the very wind was gray with a burden of fine silt as it swept roaring out of the east. The only color in this place came from the plants, which seemed to be striking back against the universal grayness with some furious determination of their own. Big rigid dome-shaped fungi, a deathly yellow in hue, exploded into clouds of brilliant green spores whenever he trampled on one; the tough sparse saw-edged grass was an angry carmine; the trees, tall and narrow as spears, had gleaming blue leaves shaped like spines, and constantly dropped a rain of viscous pink sap that burned him like acid whenever he passed incautiously within reach of it.

Low chalky hills that had the look of stubby teeth formed chains across the far horizon. The open country between them was flat and dry and unpromising, no lakes, no streams, only an occasional brackish spring oozing out of some salt-encrusted crack in the ground.

He had been walking for days, so many that he had lost count of them. His tongue was thick and swollen from thirst and his eyelids were so puffed that he looked out between them as if through slitted windows. Sweat streamed on him constantly; caked dust clung everywhere to his sticky skin; the force of the sun became a metallic clangor sounding in his head. And through his mind ran, over and over without cease, the remembered images of the cataclysm that had destroyed his army and, for all he knew, robbed him of his dearest friends.

That merciless white wall of water riding down the hillside toward them, with the great sundered chunks of Mavestoi Dam coming down with it—

The terrified mounts bucking and rearing—scattering in every direction—the infantrymen desperately running, seeking high ground—screams in the night—the sound of that falling water, the inexorable *sound* of it, like the Great Moon itself rushing down upon them through the air to crush them all—

Prestimion had scarcely any recollection of how he himself had managed to survive the destruction of the dam. He remembered the first tongue of foaming water swirling along the ground toward him clearly enough, and remembered, too, the greater rush of water behind it. His mount struggling to stay upright and failing, pitching over, kicking frantically in the sudden lake that had begun to engulf it. Then his memories were unclear for a time. He knew he had been unable to right the animal or to steady it in any way, and that eventually he had been swept out of the saddle and away from the sinking mount by the force of the water. And then— swimming? Yes, he must have made his way somehow across the breast of the rising flood, through all the turbulence of it, great masses of water constantly falling on him like boulders and smashing him under. Being hurled down deep, his lungs filling, and fighting his way up again, again, again. But he had no memory of that at all. Remembered, only, emerging at last onto dry land, crawling up on some rocky outcropping that must have been, an hour earlier, part of the cliff below the dam, and lying there for an endless time, gasping and puking, fighting for breath, sick and dizzy from all the water he had gulped down.

Then—Korsibar's men coming down into the flood zone, seeking out the dazed survivors, slaughtering them like pigs.

He had no idea how he had escaped that. His weapons all had been lost in the water. Perhaps he had found safety under some overhanging ledge, or behind some bush. All he remembered was that he had come through it alive, somehow. Making his way from the battle scene, from that place along the water's edge where shouting warriors ran about, where the figures of dead or gravely wounded men lay strewn across the land like straws.

That was not the first time Prestimion had beheld that grim landscape of death. He had seen it once before, he knew: long ago in Muldemar House, in the pleasant peace and privacy of his mother's reading-gallery, that time when the magus Galbifond had had him look into a bowl of some pallid fluid. Galbifond had muttered incantations and had shown him that very battlefield, that same scene of frightful chaos. Prestimion had not known, then, whose armies they were that contended there: but now it was clear that one was Korsibar's and the other his, and that Korsibar by working a monstrously evil deed had been the victor.

But he himself had survived the flood and the debacle that had followed it. In the eye of his mind he saw himself limping away from the battlefield where nothing now remained but the evidence of disaster. Coming forth at last into a quieter place where no one was in sight anywhere, neither friend nor foe. Climbing some steep rocky path that took him upward along the course of the river, past the shattered dam, past the palisades of Korsibar's encampment.

Alone, as the dreadful dawn after that dreadful night had arrived, Prestimion had looked down and behind him, thinking, *Taradath? Abrigant?* And thinking then, also: *Svor? Gialaurys? Septach Melayn?*

Why had he ever wanted to be Coronal? Had he not been happy enough as Prince of Muldemar? Two of his brothers almost certainly dead, his three dear friends swept away in that deluge, the lives lost of thousands of men who had supported his cause, and for what? For what? So that he might sit upon a great ruby-streaked block of black opal instead of some other man, and have people kneel and make inane gesticulations before him, and listen solemnly as he issued decrees?

He was numbed, stunned, by the death and destruction that his determination to wrest the crown from Korsibar had caused. How many had perished for his sake? His overweening ambition had made martyrs of thousands of good people. Majipoor had never been a warlike world; since the pacification of the Shapeshifters seven thousand years before, its people had lived placidly, in happy harmony, and those who were of a warring nature could find release on the jousting-fields and other such rough sports. But now, behold! Because of his determination that he and not the other man should rule, war had come to the world, and men were in their graves who should have had long lives ahead.

Now there was nothing left for him but to march onward into this unknown country in the hope of avoiding the fury of Korsibar's men, and reach some safe place where he might rest and recover himself, and then he would consider how he meant to spend whatever time might remain to him in the world.


In the days that followed, and for days after that, roots and leaves and little white acrid fruits were the only food Prestimion had. Then at last on the far side of the chalky hills the country changed a little, the land becoming pale brown streaked with red: a sign, perhaps, of fertility. There was a grayish silty little river running here from east to west that was split into three forks. Along the riverbanks the plants had shining green foliage, and some of them carried fat purplish fruits with wrinkled skins. Prestimion tried one and it did him no harm, so he ate several others before sleeping, and when he found himself still alive and unpoisoned in the morning he had some more, and collected others to carry with him in a fold of his jerkin.

This was a harsh untamed land. He had no idea of what it was called. Danger lurked everywhere. He stumbled across some loose boughs and nearly fell, and when he caught his balance he looked down and saw himself at the verge of a pit, with glittering red eyes and flashing yellow claws waiting below. Later in the day a long swaybacked beast covered in thick brown scales that looked as hard as rock rushed wildly out of nowhere, swinging its small dull-eyed head from side to side like a club; but it went running past him as though in search of juicier prey. And afterward was a comic hopping creature with merry golden eyes and absurd tiny forearms, but from its tail there sprang a spike that squirted poison into the plump gray lizards that it hunted. A day or two later came a swarm of winged insects, as dazzling as colored jewels, that filled the air with a milky spray, and when a bird flew into that deadly mist it let its wings droop and plummeted ground-ward like a stone.

Farther on, the terrain changed again. Now it was broken land, cut by gullies and steep canyons. The bones of the world lay exposed here, great dark stripes cutting through the soft reddish rocks of the hillsides. Sprawling shrubs with white woolly leaves clung to the ground like a dense coating of fur. There were great trees with thick black trunks and wide-spreading crowns of yellow leaves.

And there was a village here, in a sheltered place at the floor of a narrow canyon.

The people were all Ghayrogs, the gray-scaled reptilian-looking folk with forked, flickering scarlet tongues. There were a few hundred of them, living widely scattered up and down the canyon along a stretch a couple of miles long. This dry country seemed to be what they liked: Ghayrogs often settled in inhospitable parts of Majipoor that reminded them of their home districts on their native world.

They were friendly enough here. They gave Prestimion a place to sleep, and food that was edible enough, though strange, and he was able even to acquire a bow and some arrows to hunt with once he continued along his journey, and a pack to store provisions in when he wandered onward.

Of Coronals, and civil wars, these people knew nothing at all. The names "Prestimion" and "Korsibar" and even "Confalume" and "Prankipin" had no significance for them. They lived out here as though on a planet of their own.

He asked them where he was, and they said, in thick hissing accents that he could barely comprehend, "This is the town of Valmambra, where the desert of the same name begins."

It was like the turning of a key in a door, hearing that name, *Valmambra*.

Once again Prestimion's mind went back, far back into what seemed like another life, to that quiet hour spent in his mother's reading-gallery in Muldemar House. His mother there, and the stoop-shouldered white-haired magus Galbifond. The bowl of slate-colored fluid in which Galbifond had shown him—how?—that all-too-accurate vision of the battle by the shores of the Iyann, the slaughter of his army by Korsibar's.

But that vision had had a second part, Prestimion remembered now. The battlefield image had faded; the bowl had shown him some grim and bleak landscape, bleaker even than the one he had recently passed. A scattering of isolated jagged hills. Reddish soil, wedge-shaped boulders. The twisted sparse-leaved form of a single szambra-tree writhing before him against the cloudless sky. A tree of the Valmambra Desert and nowhere else, was the szambra-tree. And look! That tiny figure of a man, plodding wearily through the wasteland, every step an effort for him: that short square-shouldered man, golden hair cut short, ragged jerkin, carrying a pack, a bow, a few arrows: himself. Galbifond had let him see it all, there in Muldemar House. Himself, a lonely weary refugee, setting out on foot across the Valmambra toward the wizard-city of Triggoin. Triggoin, where Svor, in a dream, had once been told that Prestimion might learn how to gain the crown that he had lost.

Galbifond had shown all this to him long ago in the depths of that bowl, the battle, the defeat, the trek northward through the desert; and now those very things were coming to pass.

So he must follow his destiny, willy-nilly.

"I have business in the city of Triggoin," he said to the Ghayrogs of this village that lay at the edge of the desert that he knew now he must cross. "Can you tell me how to find the road that leads there?"

The Valmambra was in every way identical to the place Galbifond had shown him in the vision of the bowl—the hills, the boulders, the few twisted trees growing in the reddish soil. But the bowl had been able only to *show* him the desert; it could not make him feel it. And Prestimion felt it now. It had seemed to him that he had been marching through a desert almost all the time since beginning his northward journey, but he saw now that what he had taken for a desert was a gentle park, a paradise, even, compared with the Valmambra. For the terrain that lay behind him had merely been dry broken country, empty because hardly anybody cared to live there. The Valmambra was true desert indeed and it was empty because it was virtually uninhabitable.

Triggoin, the Ghayrogs told him, lay in a straight track to the north, on the far side of the desert. He need only guide himself by the stars at night, keep Phaseil to his right and Phasilin to his left and head constantly for the white gleam of Trinatha in the northern sky. After a time he would come to a little village called Jaggereen, another Ghayrog town, which was the only settlement within the Valmambra proper. They would tell him at Jaggereen how to proceed onward to Triggoin.

All that sounded uncomplicated enough. But the Ghayrogs had not prepared him, any more than Galbifond had, for the austerities of the Valmambra. Had not prepared him for the merciless dryness of the land, where you could go three days at a time without finding a source of water, and what you found then would be brackish. For the air, as dry as the sand beneath his feet, so that breathing it parched the nostrils and made the tongue raw and tender. For the heat of day, which seemed as fierce to Prestimion as he supposed the fabled heat of Suvrael must be. For the chill of night, when the clear air released to the sky all the warmth that had poured in by day, and left him huddled and shivering in whatever shelter he managed to find. For the scarcity of anything to eat, nothing at all for two or three days at a time, then only miserable little dry berries and the stems of some low crooked plant with spiny leaves and—occasionally, very occasionally—the stringy meat of the small gray hopping creature with great curving ears the size of its own head that was the only kind of animal life that seemed to live here. Their hearing was so sensitive that it was impossible for Prestimion to stalk them. But now and again he saw one motionless on a hillside across some barren ravine, and by releasing his arrow swiftly in the direction which he thought the animal would run once it heard the sound of the singing shaft heading its way, he was able to bring it down.

Triggoin was supposed to be on the far side of the desert, but the desert appeared to have no end. Prestimion grew weaker and weaker as the demands the Valmambra placed on his already overtaxed body far exceeded the quantity of food and water he was able to find. He was assailed by fever and dizziness, so that the landscape rocked and lurched before him like the breast of a wild sea; his vision grew blurred, so there was no way for him to use his bow; his feet and legs swelled, making every step an aching torment. The clangor coming from the sun's inexorable light began again, and would not cease. He imagined the sound of thunder in a place that knew no rainstorms. Great oscillating rings of green light surrounded the sun, filling half the sky, or so it seemed to him. Sun-blisters sprang up along his back and shoulders, and after he lay dozing face downward on the sand for a time when he felt too dizzy to go forward, he arose reddened and swollen from neck to ankles, feeling half cooked, or more than half.

A day or two later he ate something hard and blue, a nut of some kind, that stung his mouth and made his eyelids puff to three times their thickness. He was set upon by a cloud of small golden flies, like a mist of bright metal, that bit him in a hundred places and raised blisters. He came to a tangle of impassable brambles many miles wide that barred his path, so that he had to go a long distance to the east before he found a way to continue on his northward route.

He dreamed of Muldemar House, his bed, his stone bathtub, his wine, his soft clean clothes. He dreamed of his friends. One night in his dreams Thismet came to him and danced and opened her bodice to show him small round breasts tipped with hard dark nipples.

He woke retching, one morning, and spent what seemed

like an hour vomiting thin white fluid. He woke sobbing once, which astonished him. The leather of his boots began to split. His toes stuck out; he stubbed one and it bled for two days.

He tried not to think of where he was or what was happening to him. He did not want to consider the prospect that he would die out here, forgotten and unburied.

For a whole day he thought he was Coronal, and wondered why he was not at the Castle. Then he remembered the truth.

Three lean-shanked animals squatted beside him one night as he waited for sleep at the edge of a dry gully, and made cackling sounds that seemed almost like laughter. They had sharp teeth; he wondered if they would fall upon him and eat him. But they did not. They laughed at him some more, and walked in circles around him, and one by one emitted little piles of bright green turds. Then they moved along. They had no use for him.

He came to a river of sand running through the desert. In the midday sun it blazed like a long line of white fire from the quartz crystals that were in it. He knelt and scooped it up in his hands as though it were water, and let it run through his fingers, and once again wept.

He stumbled over a gnarled shrub and twisted his leg. His knee swelled like a balloon. For two days he could put no weight on it, nor could he walk. He crawled. In a broad open place under the merciless sun he was attacked by a huge carrion-bird, a thing somewhat like a milufta, with terrible bloodshot eyes and a long bare red neck that had loose skin hanging from it in ruffled folds, and a beak like the edge of a scythe. It came flapping down out of the sky, shrieking as though it had nothing to eat in a month, and tried to wrap him in its great ragged-edged wings. "Not dead yet!" Prestimion cried, and rolled over and kicked at it with his good leg. "Not dead, not dead, not dead!"

Evidently it didn't care. The bird seemed crazed. It must have gone without food so long that it was willing to kill to eat, though it was plainly a carrion-bird. It clawed at him with curved yellow talons and drew blood from him in half a dozen places. It snapped at his throat, at his eyes. It tore at him and ripped a strip of flesh from his arm, and came back for more. "Not dead yet!" Prestimion kept saying, as he struggled to beat the bird away from him. "Not dead!" It was the first time he had spoken aloud in days.

The reek of its breath sickened him and the pain where it had ripped him was like a line of white fire. He lay on his back and kicked and pummeled at it as it fluttered and flurried about him. If it would only fly upward a little way he would try to put an arrow through its belly; but no, no, it hovered close against him, frantically biting and clawing, wounding him again and again, until somehow in a burst of desperate fury he caught it by its long scrawny neck, wrapped one arm about it and brought a rock down against its skull over and over with his other hand.

It fell away from him and lay limply, flapping its wings slowly for a time, and then no longer moving. When it was done with the last of its death-spasms Prestimion rose and walked over to it, and saw that it was a monster nearly as big as he was. The thought came to him that its meat might be edible; but the thought of eating that creature was so revolting to him that he began to vomit once again, and vomited up the emptiness that was within him for an endless time.

Afterward he bandaged the deepest wound with cloth torn from his undershirt. And then he arose and went limping onward. Before long he ceased to note the pain, though blood seeped through all day to his outer garments. He had begun to forget how to feel pain.

But then one day he was simply unable to go on at all.

It seemed to him that he must have been heading in the

proper direction all this while, but there was no sign yet of the village of Jaggereen, and he had had nothing at all to eat in several days, no leaves, no roots, no insects or crawling things, even, and no water except what he had been able to lick from a flat rock that had a tiny trickle running along its face from somewhere. And now his strength was exhausted. This was, he knew, the end. All his proud ambitions would reach their termination in this forlorn place, and no one would ever know what had become of him, and in time the world would forget that there had ever been such a person as Prestimion of Muldemar, who might once have had his name inscribed in the list of kings.

He lay down in the shade of a tall rock and placed his pack on one side of him and his bow on the other, and closed his eyes, and waited. How long, he wondered, would it take death to come for him? An hour? A day? Already he felt time slowing to a halt. His mouth had the taste of dust and his breaths came so infrequently that each one was a surprise to him. Once in a while he opened his eyes and saw only a vague reddish swirl before him. Then for a long time he lay quite still, and the mere idea of movement struck him as impossible of fulfillment, and it occurred to him that he might already be dead. But no, no, he heard himself draw another breath.

I should write my name beside my body, he told himself, so that when they find my bones they will know whose bones these were.

He opened his eyes. Impossible to focus them. The red swirl, again. Behind it, the glare of the sun, resounding in his consciousness like a metal gong in the sky. Turned slightly toward the left. Extended a trembling finger, slowly and shakily traced the first letter of his name in the sand. The second letter, the third. Halted there, tried to remember what the fourth letter was. A voice from overhead said, "You write an 's' next."

"Thank you," Prestimion said.

"And after it a 't,' " said another, deeper voice, in the heavy accents of the city of Piliplok.

"I know that voice," Prestimion murmured.

"Yes. You do. And you know mine also.—Pick him up, Gialaurys. Let's waste no time getting him to the village."

"Svor? Is that you?"

"Yes. And Gialaurys."

"So you died also? And are we at the Source together, then?"

"If the village of Jaggereen is the Source, then we are at the Source, yes," said Svor. "Or three hundred yards away, for that is how close you are to Jaggereen." Prestimion felt himself being lifted and cradled in powerful arms. It seemed to him he had no weight at all. "Do you have him securely, Gialaurys?" The voice of Svor, again. "Good. Hold him well. If you drop him, I think he'll break into a hundred pieces."

He was two weeks healing at Jaggereen, which was a town of flimsy wickerwork shacks sprouting from the Valmambra sands at the one place in all that desert land where fresh water rose to the surface from hidden springs. For the first week he lay on a bed of twigs, sleeping most of the time, awakening now and then to take sips of some strange sweet soup that Svor spooned out to him or to nibble at bits of a curious spongy Ghayrog bread. Then his strength began to return, and he left the bed and walked slowly about the room leaning on Gialaurys's arm, and after a week of that he felt ready to move about on his own power, though he still was far from well.

"It was Gialaurys that saved me when the dam broke," Svor told him. "Snatched me up from the water, carried me away on his back as we fled Korsibar's men. And sustained me in the desert. But for him I'd have died ten different times between there and here."

"As usual he lies," said Gialaurys, though there was no rancor in his stolid voice. "Is a much tougher creature than he'd like us to think, is Svor. Needs no food to speak of and precious little water, and scrambles like a zamfigir over rocks and gullies, and half a dozen times caught little animals with his bare hands that made dinner for us both. We had a hard time coming through this way, but it would have been much harder, but for him. And you had the hardest journey of all, looks like. Another hour, and—well, we found you, is the important thing. And we three still live, when so many have perished."

Svor said, "Korsibar will have much to answer for, breaking that dam. I saw men being swept away by the force of the water on every side, or carried under because they had never learned to swim. Many thousands are dead, I fear. And those just in our own army; but the water will have flooded out into the countryside, where unsuspecting farmers must have been drowned in their beds."

"Not only Korsibar will be called to account," said Gialaurys. "Surely it was Dantirya Sambail that put him up to the breaking of the dam: Korsibar would never have hatched such evil of his own."

"Dantirya Sambail?" said Prestimion. "Why would he have—?"

And then he remembered: the eerie moment of the first explosions, when he had thought it was merely thunder he heard, and his brother Taradath had come to him to report that Gaviad's army was on the march. Marching *away* from the river, as though Gaviad had been warned of what was to befall the dam. In the chaos of the moment Prestimion had put that from his mind, and had not thought of it again until it was recalled to him now. "Yes," he said. "Of course! Playing each side against the other for his own advantage. Very likely it was he who counselled Korsibar to take up a position behind that dam; and the Procurator also who kindly sent us those hierax-men, so we would know Korsibar was there, and follow him toward the dam in order that we'd be below it when the lake fell upon us. While telling his two despicable brothers to pull their armies away at the last moment before the breaking of the dam, and save their worthless selves. Who else but Dantirya Sambail could conceive such a plan? By the Lady, I'll cut him apart inch by inch if ever I capture him!"

"You shouldn't shout like that," Svor said. "You're quite weak yet."

Prestimion ignored that. "Who else survives? Do you know?"

"Of those who were west of the river, a good many, I think," said Svor. "Korsibar's troops were slower coming down that side than on ours, and there was time for Miaule and his people to get away, if they were able to stay ahead of the rushing water."

"Then there's hope for Septach Melayn?"

"Ah, much more than hope," Svor said. "The Ghayrogs have told us of him, both at Valmambra and here at Jaggereen. He came dancing through the desert well ahead of us, cool and lively as though it were a quick, pleasant journey such as the one from the Castle to High Morpin, and has long since gone on beyond here. He'll be waiting for us at Triggoin."

"Triggoin?" Prestimion said. "Why would he have gone to Triggoin?"

"The vision you were shown at Muldemar House said that Triggoin was where you would go one day, after some great battle. And I dreamed it also," said Svor. "He must have expected that Triggoin was where we would all go, after the catastrophe by the dam. In any case, it's certainly Triggoin where he has taken himself now: the Ghayrogs said he left here bound on a northward track."

Prestimion laughed. "And is there already, most likely. Septach Melayn among the sorcerers—what a curious idea that is! Will we see him wearing a wizard's robes, do you think, when we get there, and making mystic signs at us by way of greeting? It would be his idea of amusement." And then he said, in a darker tone, "I wonder how my brothers fared."

"Abrigant, surely, escaped with Miaule," Gialaurys said. "Things went much easier for those who were on that side of the river, as Svor has already told you."

There was an uncomfortable silence, then.

"And Taradath?" Prestimion asked, finally. "He was with me when the dam began to break. I never saw him after the water separated us."

Quietly Gialaurys said, "I tried to save him, I swear before the Divine that I did. I had one arm about him and the other about Svor. But then came another surge of the water, and he was ripped from my grasp.—I tell you, Prestimion, I would have held him if I could, but it would have cost me my arm, and then he would have been swept away anyway."

Prestimion felt a leaden weight suddenly where his heart had been. But he hid his feelings and put the best face on things he could, saying, "Even though the water was so very strong, it may yet be that he swam to safety."

"Yes. Maybe so," said Gialaurys carefully, in a voice that left no doubt how unlikely he thought that was.

"You ought to rest now," said Svor, before Prestimion could make any further inquiries. "Your strength is not yet what it should be. And a difficult journey still awaits us, once you are ready to travel again."

# 2

Triggoin of the sorcerers lay well beyond the desert's northern margin, nestled pleasantly in a green valley beside a circular lake bright as glass, with a heavily wooded double-humped mountain rising in back of it. Viewed from the last turn of the hilltop highway that approached it from the south, it seemed no more than an ordinary place, one that could have been any medium-sized city at all, anywhere on Majipoor. A gentle breeze was blowing, cool and fresh and sweet, and the grassy borders of the road were glistening from the fall of a recent light rain. All his life Prestimion had heard dire tales of Triggoin, of the flame-red sky and the blue spirit-fires that burned in its air by day and by night and the strange shrieks and sobs of disembodied entities that resounded constantly there. But he could detect no sign of such things now as he and Svor and Gialaurys made their descent toward the cheerful-looking and even pretty city below them. After the bleakness and horrors of the Valmambra, though, almost any place would have looked cheerful and pretty, he reflected.

"So we are here at last," Gialaurys said. "And here we will find magicians to hire to our service, and perhaps will even learn a trick or two of magic ourselves that will send Korsibar running in fright to his mother, eh?"

"I envy you the certainty of your faith in magic," said

Prestimion. "Even here at the very borders of Triggoin I still resist the idea that there's any merit to it."

"Ah, just accept the evidence of your eyes, Prestimion! Wherever you look about you in the world, you see sorcery at work, and the work it does is real!"

"Wherever I look I see deceit and illusion, Gialaurys, which lead the world ever deeper into darkness."

"Was it deceit when your mother's magus showed you your very self pictured in that bowl, crossing the Valmambra? Was it deceit when Thalnap Zelifor came to us in the Labyrinth to warn you of the secret enemy who would contend with you for the Castle, and of the terrible war that would break out? Was it deceit when—"

"Spare me the rest," Prestimion said, holding up one hand. "It will be a wearisome story, rehearsing all the omens I failed to heed on the road that brought us from there to here, and I'm weary enough these days as it is. Let me be, Gialaurys. My soul relinquishes its doubt very slowly, it seems. But perhaps I'll experience a great conversion out of my skepticism here: who knows?"

"I'll pay some magus a rich fee to give me a spell that will bring you to your senses," said Gialaurys.

"Yes," Prestimion said. "I think you have the solution now: use sorcery to lead me to belief in sorcery's merits. That may be the only way it can be done." And all three of them laughed. But they laughed in different ways, for Svor and Gialaurys had long been believers, and the robust tone of their laughter seemed to be expressing their confidence that Prestimion would go out of Triggoin a different man from the one who was entering it. But Prestimion's laughter was thin and hollow. Any laughter that came from him these days was forced laughter. There was little mirth left in him after the calamity of the Mavestoi Dam.

*

The city looked less cheery and innocent once they were inside its walls. A cobbled plaza just within the gate led to a dark chaos of medieval streets that went winding off in a dozen directions, all of them coiling tightly in upon themselves so that it was impossible to see more than a few dozen yards down any of them.

The style of construction here ran to narrow five-story mustard-colored buildings of an ancient-looking sort, all jammed one against another, most with gabled roofs and blank-looking facades pierced only by the tiniest of windows. Now and then a shadowy passageway separated two buildings, and these passageways seemed occupied. Whispers could be heard coming from them, and occasionally hooded eyes, bright and keen-looking and unfriendly, peered out of them. Sometimes two pairs of green eyes looked out, for there were many Su-Suheris folk in these streets, and also an unusually great number of Vroons. But everyone, human and alien alike, carried himself with an air of being privy to the great mysteries of the universe. These are people, Prestimion thought, who walk and talk daily with invisible spirits, and have no doubts of themselves as they consort with phantoms. He had never felt so profoundly ill at ease in his life.

"You seem to know where you're going," he said to Svor, as they marched single file through the streets, which were too narrow and crowded to let them walk three abreast. "I thought you'd never been here except in dreams."

"But they were vivid dreams," said Svor. "I have some idea of what to expect. Look, here's a hostelry. We should take rooms, first."

"Here?" Prestimion cried. It was a dark, grimy, slouchsided building that looked to be five thousand years old. "This would be no fitting place for pigs!"

"We are not in Muldemar now, O Prestimion," said Svor

very softly. "This place will do, I think, and it's not likely that we'll find a better one hereabouts."

The rooms were small, with low ceilings and small windows that admitted the barest nip of light, and they smelled of rank spices and stale meat, as though previous boarders had been in the habit of cooking their meals in them. But the lodgings Prestimion had had in the Valmambra left him little disposed to quibble over these, which seemed palatial enough in comparison with lying half frozen under the open sky in the desert, or sleeping in some wickerwork Ghayrog hut through which sandy winds blew all night. The place was reasonably clean, at least, with decent lavatory facilities just down the hall, and Prestimion's mattress, though it rested right on the stone floor and seemed both stiff and clammy, had clean sheets on it and a relatively insignificant population of bugs and ticks.

"I'll return shortly," said Svor, after they were settled. He was gone an hour and a half. When he came back, he brought with him a frail white-haired man clad in simple dark robes, who from the look of him might have been two hundred years old, or even two thousand: so thin that any vagrant wind might have carried him away, and with pale skin whiter than the whitest paper, and almost transparent. Svor introduced him as Gominik Halvor, who had been, he said, his instructor in the wizardly arts, long ago; and added that he was the father of Heszmon Gorse, who was chief magus to the former Coronal Lord Confalume.

"His father!" Prestimion blurted, astonished. It had always seemed to him that the somber and aloof Heszmon Gorse must be the fifth or tenth oldest man in the world, and it had never occurred to him that Heszmon Gorse's *father* too might still be alive. But Gominik Halvor seemed incurious about the reason for Prestimion's outburst. He merely smiled, and studied Prestimion a moment with small dark eyes, very bright and shining, that were half-buried within the wrinkles and folds of his ancient face.

Svor said, indicating Prestimion, "This is Polivand of Muldemar. And this—" with a nod toward Gialaurys— "is Gheveldin of Piliplok. There will be a fourth student also, who has not yet joined us, but we believe he is somewhere in Triggoin. We are ready to begin our course of studies at any time."

"The seventh hour of the night will be an auspicious time to start," said Gominik Halvor. His voice was another surprise: not the faint reedy whistling one might expect from someone so ancient, but the strong and deep voice of a man in the prime of life. Looking from Prestimion to Gialaurys he said, "You, Gheveldin: I see that you have had some initiation already into our mysteries. But Polivand here has the aura of an utter novice."

"That is what I am," said Prestimion. "I have no skills at magic whatever, nor any knowledge of its secrets."

"So I see, if you call our arts 'magic.' We prefer to speak of them as our 'philosophy', or else as our 'science.' "

"Philosophy, then. I stand corrected and beg your pardon."

"Are you fully prepared, do you think, to open your mind to our disciplines?" the old man asked.

"Well—" Prestimion hesitated. He was not at all prepared for that, or for any other aspect of this conversation: Svor had led him without warning into some scheme beyond his understanding.

And indeed it was Svor who quickly spoke over Prestimion's uncertain pause: "Count Polivand is deeply interested in every aspect of the great philosophy, master. He has never had opportunity to study it before; but he has come to Triggoin for that express purpose now. As have we all. And dedicate ourselves now to be your most devoted pupils."

Prestimion remained silent as arrangements were concluded

for the beginning of their education in wizardry. But then, when Gominik Halvor was gone, he whirled on Svor and said, "What's all this about our studying magic with this man? I thought we were going to *hire* sorcerers here, not apprentice ourselves to them! And why these names—Polivand, Gheveldin?"

"Peace, Prestimion. A certain amount of pretense is necessary for us now. Orders have been issued for the arrest of all those who rebelled against the government of Lord Korsibar: aren't you aware of that? Even in Triggoin, we aren't completely beyond his grasp. You can't simply come sauntering in here and announce yourself to be Prince Prestimion of Muldemar, and call for sorcerers to flock to your side and give you aid in your rebellion, without bringing down trouble upon yourself."

"And if this Gominik Halvor is such a powerful magus, how, then, will he fail to discern our true identities?"

"Of course he knows who you are," Svor said.

"But—then—"

"We have to take care not to implicate him. Suppose the authorities go to him and say, 'Do you know anything of the whereabouts of the proscribed fugitive rebel Prince Prestimion, who is thought to be in this city?' No, he can say: he has never had contact with anyone of that name. And so forth."

"I see. So I am Polivand and Gialaurys is Gheveldin. Very well. And by what name are we supposed to call you?"

"Svor," said Svor.

"But you just said—"

"My name is not posted on the list of wanted fugitives, Prestimion. Korsibar has promised me immunity from prosecution, out of respect for the old friendship between him and me. Since I'm not sought for and Gominik Halvor knows who I am anyway, I've not bothered to assume any pretended identity with him. Does that trouble you, that Korsibar's willing to overlook my allegiance to you? Does it make you suspect my loyalty in any way?"

"Korsibar's a fool, and you are my friend, and I have no doubts of where your loyalties lie. If he wants to exempt you from the proscription, so be it. But why have you signed me up for a course of studies in magic, Svor? Is this some little prank of yours?"

"We'll need to stay hidden here until we know it's safe to emerge, and the city authorities will require some plausible reason for our presence. Studying sorcery's not only a way of passing the time, it gives us some appearance of legitimacy in our residence here. You might find it illuminating, besides."

"I might, yes. And blaves would fly, too, if only you knew how to grow wings on them. So now I am to be a scholar of the mysterious arts! Ah, Svor, Svor—"

A knock at the door interrupted his words.

A ringing voice outside, a voice they all knew very well, called, "Are these the lodgings of Count Polivand of Muldemar!"

Gialaurys reached the door first and threw it wide. A slender and extremely tall man in the elegant clothes of a courtier of the Mount—a doublet of green velvet in the Bombifale style, with high-standing collar and a small ruff above—stood smiling there.

"Septach Melayn!" Gialaurys cried.

He bowed gracefully and entered. Prestimion rushed to him and embraced him. "Svor and Gialaurys told me you had survived," Prestimion said. "But still—I was afraid for so long that you had drowned in the flood—"

"I move quickly when dying's the alternative. How have you fared, Prestimion?"

"Not entirely well, to speak the truth."

"No. I'm not surprised."

"And you must not call me 'Prestimion,' here. I'm Count Polivand of Muldemar. Gialaurys is now Gheveldin. Svor will explain. He's still Svor, by the way. We are all enrolled as students of wizardry, I'll have you know, and our tutor is—I am speaking nothing but the truth, Septach Melayn, however strange it may sound—the father of Confalume's ancient magus Heszmon Gorse. The *father*."

"Students of wizardry," said Septach Melayn in a musing way, as though Prestimion had just announced that they were all soon to become women, or Skandars, or sea-dragons, perhaps. "A quaint pastime for you, Prestimion. I wish you joy of it."

"You'll be enrolled in our scholarly pursuits also, Septach Melayn," said Svor. "Your name is now Simrok Morlin, and you are a man of Gimkandale, not of Tidias." He explained the reason for these subterfuges; and Septach Melayn, in high good humor, gave his assent to the plan and swore to be the most assiduous student of them all, and to come away from Triggoin a true master in the diabolic sciences.

Then Prestimion asked him how he had known where to find them; to which Septach Melayn replied that a messenger had come to him a little while before in his own lodgings, which by coincidence were just three streets away, and had told him the address where certain great friends of his were to be found. The messenger, said Septach Melayn, had given him the card of his employer, which Septach Melayn produced and showed him. It was the card of the magus Gominik Halvor.

"We never told him your name!" said Prestimion. "How would he have known—?"

"Ah, Prestimion," Gialaurys said. "What did I tell you? The evidence lies all about you, and still you refuse to credit the reality of what these mages do!"

Prestimion shrugged. He had no wish to debate the issue any further with Gialaurys, now or ever again.

The inn where they had lodged had a dining hall, where they went for some meat and wine before their first lesson with Gominik Halvor was to commence. Septach Melayn regaled them with tales of his escape from the flood and his swift journey north and of his light-hearted adventures in Triggoin while waiting for them to arrive, for, he said, he had never once doubted that they would show up here sooner or later. He made everything sound like the easiest and lightest of exploits, which was his style in everything; but Prestimion could see that he was deliberately making light of it all—the awful debacle of the breaking of the dam, the hardships of his journey through the desert, the uneasy hours of his time alone in Triggoin. It was plain that Septach Melayn had already perceived the darkness of Prestimion's mood, and did not want to darken it further with tales of losses and suffering.

Prestimion ate little, and drank less. Though he had struggled constantly since his recovery in Jaggereen against the doleful bleakness that had enfolded his soul, he found himself making little headway with it.

He had no idea what he would do now. For the first time in his life he was utterly without a plan.

For the time being he wanted only to live quietly, far from the Castle, far from all exercise of power, far from everything he had been in the days when he was Prestimion of Muldemar. He saw it as fitting that the shipwreck of his destiny should have cast him up in Triggoin, this place so antithetical to his nature and to all his beliefs. It would be an appropriate penance, having to take refuge here among the magicians.

"Penance?" Septach Melayn cried, when after a time Prestimion began to give voice to some of these somber thoughts. "Penance for what? For serving the cause of righteousness against that of evil?"

"You think that was it? That I rose up against Korsibar purely because I believed I was the rightful Coronal and he a wicked usurper?"

"Tell me it was anything else," said Septach Melayn, "that it was sheerly out of the lust for power that you did it, say, and then I'll give you the sword that I wear here on my hip, and you can put it through my gut, Prestimion. Pardon me: *Polivand*. I know you and I know why you did as you did. Korsibar's theft of the crown was a crime against all civilization. You had no choice but to stand up in opposition to it. No guilt attaches on that account, Prestimion: no blame whatever."

"Listen to him, and take his words into your heart," Gialaurys said. "You belabor yourself for no sensible reason, Prestimion."

"Polivand," Svor corrected. "Come, now, gentlemen. It's time for our first lesson in sorcery."


Gominik Halvor's lodgings were plainly those of a personage of consequence. He occupied seven or eight large rooms, or even more, at the top of a lofty stone tower in central Triggoin that looked down on the entire panorama of the city. There Gominik Halvor had brought together a great collection of equipment of strange and esoteric nature, alembics and crucibles, flasks holding curious fluids and powders, metal boxes containing ointments and creams, iron plates on which cryptic characters were inscribed, retorts and beakers, hour-glasses, weighing-scales, armillary spheres and astrolabes, ammatepilas, hexaphores, phalangaria, ambivials. Besides these things—and there were many more devices also, of all manner of strange sorts—there were whole rooms of shelves lined with the great leather-bound books of the kind that Prestimion had already seen at the late Pontifex's bedside and in his mother's own reading-gallery, and which no doubt were highly valued everywhere in the world by the cognoscenti of these arts. And there were still other rooms in which they were not invited to look.

"I address myself first to your skepticism," is how Gominik Halvor began, glancing in Prestimion's direction and then in Septach Melayn's. "You needn't deny your feelings: I see them revealed plainly enough in your faces. They need not be a hindrance to your studies here. Listen to my words, and test them against the results I achieve. What we of Triggoin practice is a science, which is to say, its methods follow strict discipline and the results we attain are capable of empirical analysis. Reserve your judgment; watch and examine; do not be too quick to challenge that which you do not understand."

He launched now into a tale of his own studies and travels, which seemed to have taken him to every region of the world, though Prestimion knew it would take five lifetimes as long as Gominik Halvor's to accomplish that. But he spoke of voyaging in the Great Sea, to a place where the sky was lit bright as day with the strange ghostly light of the stars Giskhernar and Hautaama that were never seen over land, and watching the giant blue serpents of the depths wrestling with twenty-legged monsters that dwelled in perpetual whirlpools. He spoke of his journey to the Isle of Gapeligo, of which Prestimion had never heard, where the fires of the inner world burst forth unceasingly in a deafening upsurge of white flame. He spoke of his explorations in the dank and steaming rainforests of Kajith Kabulon, gathering certain herbs of immeasurable value that were unknown even to the residents of that district. And he told also of the time he had spent among the Piurivars, the Metamorph aborigines, in their jungled province of Piurifayne on Zimroel, where Lord Stiamot had penned their ancestors up long ago at the conclusion of the Shapeshifter War.

The old mage's improbably deep and sturdy voice had been

rolling on and on, lulling them into complacency; but this mention of living among the Metamorphs brought Prestimion up short with surprise. The Metamorphs had little commerce with the outside world and did not welcome visitors of the human sort into their reservation. Yet Gominik Halvor gave them to believe that he had spent years among them.

"These demons everyone speaks of," he said: "We know now of what nature they are, and I will share that knowledge with you. They are the prehistoric inhabitants of this world, its first masters, in fact—undying creatures of the ancient days before mankind ever came to Majipoor, who roamed free until the Shapeshifters locked them up under terrible spells twenty thousand years ago. Those locks can be opened with the right words, and those spirits can be made to do our bidding; and then we send them back to the dark place from which we pulled them. Watch," said Gominik Halvor, and spoke words in no language Prestimion had ever heard. *"Goiba-liiud yei thenioth kalypritiaar,"* he said, and *"Idryerimos uriliaad faldiz tilimoin gamoosth,"* and there was a stirring in the air, and a dimly visible, half-translucent figure appeared in the middle of the room before them, something with spikes for hair and pools of light for eyes. "This is Theddim," said the magus, "who presides over the coursing of the blood through our hearts." And indeed Prestimion felt his own heart beginning to pound and thump, though whether it was the doing of the demon Theddim or merely his dismay at being present at such a rite, he could not say. Then the magus uttered other words and the apparition was gone.

Gominik Halvor told them of other demons also, Thua Nizirit the demon of delirium, and scaly-faced Ginitiis, and Ruhid of the great dangling snout, who brought ease from fever, and Mimim, who facilitated the recapture of lost knowledge, and Kakilak, the benign demon who soothed those who were troubled by seizures. These beings, the magus said, could be only imperfectly controlled; but even so, they were often of great service to those who understood the techniques of summoning them.

He offered his four students, at their nightly lessons, some hint of those techniques—merely skimming the surface of his science, he told them, for they were still in the preliminary phases of their studies. "These are the three classes of demons," he said: "the valisteroi, who escaped the power of the Metamorph spells and live beyond the sphere of the sun, and will not heed our commands under any circumstances; and the kalisteroi, who are partly free, and are the spirits whose dwelling place is between the air and the Great Moon, and who sometimes favor us with their sympathies; and the irgalisteroi, who are the demons of the subterranean world whom the Metamorphs subjugated, and whom we can sometimes turn to our uses, though they are dangerous angry beings and must be invoked only by the adept, for they will devour any others."

As they returned from that lesson Prestimion said quietly to Septach Melayn, "We should tread carefully, for there are irgalisteroi under our feet. Did you ever realize, Septach Melayn, that we shared our world with so many invisible beings?"

"I would take them all to this tavern here for flasks of wine at my expense, if they would show themselves to me this moment," said Septach Melayn. And Gialaurys, walking a few paces ahead, called back angrily to them not to blaspheme, lest in their brazenness they call trouble down upon themselves, when they had already experienced trouble enough.

Patiently Gominik Halvor unfolded his mysteries before them, night after night. He told them of amulets and knots and ligatures, and of the magical powers of stones, and how to concoct healing potions; he taught them a spell for walking through fire, and a way to banish warts, and recipes for ridding oneself of coughs, of headaches, of pains in the bowels, of the sting of a scorpion. He explained the rules of gathering herbs, how certain plants must be picked before sunrise, and others only under the light of one of the lesser moons, and others only with the thumb and forefinger of the left hand. Prestimion yearned to ask why that was so, what would befall if one used the other hand and other fingers; but he had pledged himself to listen and observe, and not to express doubt or scorn.

The course went on and on. How to interpret the movements of the stars in their courses; how to cast the sticks to tell the shape of things to come; how to detect the lies of perjurers by making them hold certain white reeds in their hands; words of power to use against the attack of beasts in the forest; using senior demons to threaten and control junior ones; neutralizing the spells of rival magicians with devices made of wax and hair; which plants to use in testing the purity of metals, and which to make tinctures from for long life or great sexual vitality, and how to ensure a bountiful harvest, and how to ward off the depradations of thieves. There was even a spell to reverse the flow of rivers. ("Quickly, quickly," Prestimion said, but only silently, to himself: "Let it be done at the Iyann, and let all those dead men walk again as the lake runs back into itself from below the dam.") He instructed them in the use of rohillas and veralistias, and in the merits of corymbors, and made Prestimion bring his own amulet forth from beneath his jerkin, using it to illustrate his lecture with some quick conjurations that caused—or so he hinted—a rainstorm that had begun an hour before to dwindle and reach an end.

There was no end to the wonders that Gominik Halvor paraded before them, although his actual demonstrations of technique were few and far between. And to Prestimion's way of thinking the results he attained could almost always be explained away, if one were willing to work at it, in some mundane fashion not involving incantations and charms.

Prestimion and Septach Melayn had much private sport with all this at first, often making up witchcrafts of their own when the other two were out of earshot. "Cure toothache," said Septach Melayn, "by spitting in a gromwark's mouth and turning three times left to right." And Prestimion: "A slowness of digestion is dealt with by counting falling stars in the sky, and squatting down on the ground just as the eleventh star of the night streaks past." Then Septach Melayn: "To keep one's nose from running, kiss the nose of a steetmoy precisely at the stroke of noon." And there were many more, until they grew tired of the game.

It was good diversion for Prestimion, these early unhappy days in Triggoin, to go night after night to the magus and listen to his recitations. But gradually, as Gominik Halvor not only expounded on the arts of divination and the summoning of spirits but led his pupils to make modest experiments of their own in such things, Prestimion began feeling a strange sense of distress. While much of what Gominik Halvor had to say still struck him as the wildest of lunatic fantasy, he kept encountering odd little examples of the apparent efficacy of certain spells. Those were hard to explain away.

And also, looking back over all that had befallen him, it was hard for him any longer to argue away all the various dire prophecies and forecasts that Svor had made for him, and Thalnap Zelifor, and this one and that one, in the days before Korsibar's taking of the crown. Then too there was the vision given him by his mother's magus Galbifond, which had plainly showed him the battle of the Mavestoi and his flight into the Valmambra. All of which he had scoffed at, and all of which, ignored, had paved the way to his present disaster.

Under Gominik Halvor he was arriving at certain misty forecasts of his own. Once again he looked into a bowl of the kind Galbifond had showed him; and though the things it showed him now were far murkier than that other vision, they hinted at his going forth from Triggoin eventually and resuming his quest for the throne, and of further great battles, and of many more deaths, and of some immense ultimate event whose nature he could not comprehend at all, but which seemed almost to hint at the end of the world, a time of blankness and blackness beyond which nothing could be seen.

"What is this?" he said to Gominik Halvor, of that last apocalyptic revelation. "What am I seeing, here?"

But Gominik Halvor peered into the bowl for no more than half a second, and said in a tone of the greatest indifference, "Sometimes what looks inexplicable is merely meaningless, my good Count Polivand. And not everything that a novice conjures up has meaning. I advise you to put this from your mind."

Which Prestimion attempted to do. But it stayed with him, that swirling vortex of nothingness churning in the bowl. The fact that he was working small sorceries of his own had already begun to unsettle him; the fact that they showed him, and Gominik Halvor, things that were incomprehensible but ominous, unsettled him even more. He felt feverish and strange much of the time, now. He sometimes felt that his mind might be breaking up. To Septach Melayn, who had been his only ally in skepticism, and who remained invincibly closed-minded even now, Prestimion said one rainy night when they had sat up late together and had shared some bowls of wine, "I have built all my life about the certainties of reason, Septach Melayn, and I find that my faith in those certainties is threatened now."

"Is it, Prestimion? Are you succumbing to your own incantations, then?"

"I confess that much of what Gominik Halvor says is beginning to make sense to me. But that statement itself makes no sense to me!"

"A sad plight, to be driven into madness by contradictions of your own devising. Relax, old friend. What these wizards spout is half madness and half fraud, and there's no need to take either half seriously. I never have, and never will, and neither should you. Since I was a boy I've discarded and cast off from myself everything that didn't seem to fit my understanding of how the world really is."

"I can no longer do that," said Prestimion. "Or perhaps my understanding of how the world really is has begun to change, here in this city of sorcerers. I do think I'm coming to believe these folks, at least somewhat."

"Then I pity you."

"Spare me that," Prestimion said. He hunched forward, so that his face was close against Septach Melayn's across the table. In a quiet voice he said, "Day by day I try to find the strength to leave here and resume my struggle with Korsibar. I'm a long way from that now, but the desire has begun to possess me again. Korsibar must not be allowed to hold his stolen crown: of that I'm as convinced as ever. The fate of the world may depend on what I do, once I've gone from here; and I may well need the help of sorcerers, which once I foreswore, in gaining my purposes."

"Well, then, use them, Prestimion! I never said that I discarded anything that might be of use."

"But you have no faith in sorcerers, Septach Melayn. So how can you advise them for me?"

"*You* have the faith. What I believe is unimportant."

"Faith? I said only that I believe a little of what they—"

"If you believe any at all, you are converted to their creed. You've hooked yourself as deeply as Svor or Gialaurys or any of the rest of them. You'll be wearing a tall brass hat next, and robes with mystic symbols on them."

"Are you mocking me?" Prestimion asked, feeling himself grow heated.

"Would I do such a thing?"

"Yes. Yes, I think you would. You're sitting here laughing at me, Septach Melayn."

"Do you take offense? Shall we go outside and fight?"

"With swords, perhaps?"

"Any weapon you prefer, Prestimion. Swords, yes, if you're in a suicidal mood. Or rocks, or pieces of raw meat. Or we could stand in the street and cast spells at each other until one of us falls down with a paralytic ague." And with that he began to laugh, and after a moment Prestimion also, and then with one impulse they reached their hands across the table and clasped them, still laughing.

But behind his laughter Prestimion was still heartsore and full of confusion, and it was a long time that night before sleep found him. Somehow, he thought, he had lost his path, and was wandering in a desert far more bewildering and hostile, even, than the one he had crossed, a month or two before, in coming here to Triggoin.

# 3

The High Counsellor Farquanor said, "The wizard Thalnap Zelifor is outside, and asks an audience with you, lordship. Shall I send him away?"

The High Counsellor's face had a curdled look. He had never made any attempt to disguise his distaste for the little Vroon.

But Korsibar said, "He's here at my request. Let him come in. And take yourself away afterward."

That last did not make Farquanor's expression any sweeter. He stalked without a word to the door—it was the stark and severe little Stiamot throne-room, where Korsibar spent most of his working hours nowadays—and went out, holding the door open just long enough for Thalnap Zelifor to slip inside.

"Lordship?" the Vroon said, his yellow eyes going wide as he made his starburst before the Coronal. "Lordship, are you well?"

That took Korsibar aback, that his distress should be so easily seen. He had been awake all this night past, turning restlessly and unable to find a position of comfort, and more than a few other nights recently before that one.

"Do I look ill, Thalnap Zelifor?"

"You look—weary. Pale. Dark borders beneath your eyes. I have a spell to improve sleep, my lord."

"Does it give a sleep without dreams?"

"There is no spell for that," said the Vroon.

"Then I'll do without it. My dreams are dreadful ones, that bring me awake and sweating with fear again and again; and when I'm awake things are no better." Korsibar's brow was clouded and his jaw was clenched; he sat over at one side of Lord Stiamot's ancient unadorned marble throne, his shoulders hunched high with tension, his fisted hands pressing against each other, clamped knuckle to knuckle. "A thousand times a night I see that dam breaking," he said bleakly, looking off toward the bare stone wall. "The water spilling forth below me, flooding into nearby farms along the river, into villages— so many dead, Thalnap Zelifor, Prestimion's men and all those villagers also—"

"The dam was Dantirya Sambail's doing, my lord."

"The dam was his idea, which he slipped into my mind like a trickle of poison to infect my soul; but I gave the order. The guilt is mine."

"Guilt? My lord, you were fighting a rebellion!"

"Yes," Korsibar said, looking away, closing his eyes a moment. "A rebellion. Well, Prestimion's dead, now, or so it's generally thought. The rebellion's over. But when will I sleep again? And still I have Dantirya Sambail wandering around here, plaguing me with his schemes, and my sister also, who smoulders with wrath against me and won't be pacified, and the secret faction of my enemies, too—I know there's one; I know I'm being conspired against; for all I know Farquanor and Farholt, or maybe Oljebbin, or some others whose names I've never heard, are at this moment scheming to replace me with some brother of Prestimion, or with the Procurator himself—"

"My lord—"

"Tell me," Korsibar said, "do you conspire against me too?"

"I, my lord?"

"You come and go, you move from one side to another, you always have: you sell yourself now to Gonivaul, to Thismet, to

Prestimion. And now you come back to the Castle claiming to have defected from Prestimion's side and sell yourself again to me. What is there about me that causes such swarms of tricky folk to attach themselves to me? First there was sly little Svor, whom I loved and who leaped from me to Prestimion's bosom, and then Farquanor, who'll say anything to anyone so long as it does him some good, and then Dantirya Sambail, who managed to betray his cousin Prestimion and do great harm to me at the same time by talking me into bringing down that dam, a thing which I would gladly undo if I could undo any act of my life."

"My lord—"

But Korsibar could not halt his flow. "Even my own magus, Sanibak-Thastimoon: he seems loyal enough, but there's treachery in him somewhere, that I know. And Oljebbin. Gonivaul. I trust none of them. Navigorn, I suppose: he's a true friend. And Mandrykarn. Venta, perhaps. Iram. But even they seem to have turned from me, since the dam, though they pretend still to love me as before." He paused at last, and stared balefully down at the Vroon. "Shall I trust you, Thalnap Zelifor? Why should I?"

"Because no one else but you in this Castle or outside it will protect me, my lord. You are my bulwark. My own self-interest leads me to be your faithful servant."

Korsibar managed a faint smile at that. "Good. That has some ring of honesty to it." He gave the Vroon a sidelong look and said, "Have you heard the rumors that Prestimion survived the flood, and lives in hiding somewhere in the north at this very moment?"

"Yes, my lord, I have."

"Do you think it's true? Sanibak-Thastimoon does. He's cast the runes and uttered his spells and sent his mind forth roving, and he says it's very likely Prestimion's alive."

"Sanibak-Thastimoon is a master of these arts, my lord."

"Yes. So he is. He's being tactful; but if he says he thinks there's a possibility that Prestimion lives, then what he means is he knows perfectly well that he does. Well, I'm not troubled by that. I never wanted Prestimion dead. I was fond of him: do you know that, Thalnap Zelifor? I admired him. I would have named him to my Council. But no, no, he had to refuse, and tell me that I'm an unlawful Coronal, and start an uprising against me. None of that was necessary. He could have had his Council seat and a happy life at his vineyards." A second time Korsibar closed his eyes, for a longer while, now. They ached. They ached all day and all night, from the pounding of his fevered mind behind them.

He looked out toward the Vroon after a time and said, very quietly, "Do the people hate me, do you think?"

"What, my lord?" said the Vroon, surprised.

"In the cities. Up and down the Mount, and outward across the land: what are they saying about me? Do they think I'm a tyrant? A monster? They know about the dam: do they understand that it was an act of war, that Prestimion's uprising had to be stopped, or do they think I'm a criminal for having done it? My getting the throne: what do they think about that? Are they coming to feel Prestimion should have had it? I fear what they may be whispering out there. I dread it. What can you tell me about that, Thalnap Zelifor?"

"I have not left the Castle, my lord, since I came back to it from Prestimion's camp. And that was before the event at Lake Mavestoi."

"Can you cast your mind out there by means of some sorcery, as Sanibak-Thastimoon does, and tell me what the people say about me?"

"I can do better than that, my lord. I can make it possible for you to go into the world yourself and move secretly among them, so that you can listen with your own ears.

Korsibar sat forward, his heart suddenly racing. "What? Outside the Castle, secretly?"

"Indeed. To Bombifale for half a day, let's say, or Halanx, or Minimool. In perfect safety, no one aware that it's the Coronal who's in their midst."

"How is this possible?"

Thalnap Zelifor said, "You know, my lord, that in my workshop in the Tampkaree Tower are many devices of my own design, not magical devices but scientific ones, all of which have to do with the transmission of thought from one mind to another?"

"Yes. So you've told me."

"They are, unfortunately, incomplete, most of them. But I've finished one lately that would, I think, be of great value to you in precisely the regard you've mentioned. One that casts an illusion—that allows a perfect deception of identity—"


Arranging for his departure from the Castle was no simple thing, Coronal though he was. It was necessary first to let word go forth to all his staff that he would be retiring to his bedchamber at the hour of thus-and-so on the evening of thus-and-so for a period of solemn meditation on the condition of the world, and that he must not be disturbed by anyone under any circumstances whatever until he had emerged, even if a day or more were to elapse.

Korsibar needed also to have one of the court secretaries order a high-speed floater to be made available at the south gate, on demand, for the use of the Vroon Thalnap Zelifor and his driver. Another essential step was the invention of a Su-Suheris on the Coronal's staff who had a certificate providing him with the right of departure and access at the Castle. Thalnap Zelifor had designed his machine to give its user the guise of a member of the two-headed folk, for the sake of better mystification, since they all looked very much alike to people of other races.

Each of these steps had to be carried out in independence of all the others, so that no one would think to connect the retreat of the Coronal to his bedchamber with the comings and goings of the Vroon wizard and his Su-Suheris driver. Several days were required to put everything in place. But that gave Korsibar time to master the trick of Thalnap Zelifor's shapechanging device.

It was a small instrument, shaped much like a decorative dagger, that a man could wear at his hip without attracting attention. In using it one had first to sweep the mind free of all distraction and inner noise, so that the device might attune itself to its user's mental functioning. Then one merely put one's hand over the hilt of the little dagger and slid downward on the switch that activated it; and took care to hold the switch in the downward position all the while the machine was in use.

"Is there no way to lock it in place?" Korsibar asked.

"None. I am still working on that aspect of it. But it's no great thing to keep your hand on that little lever for a few short hours, is it, lordship?"

"I suppose not. Let me try it, now."

"Clear your mind of thought, my lord."

"Not so easily done. But I'll try," said Korsibar. He strapped the device to his side, and closed his eyes, and set his mind adrift in a featureless sea, where all was gray above and below, and there was nothing whatever to behold. When he thought he had properly quieted all the noises of his mind, he moved the switch downward and held it there.

Across the room from him was a mirror, and after a time he thought to glance into it. But he saw only his own reflection. He tried again, dipping again into that gray sea and drifting calmly on the breast of it, and after a time he was so calm that he nearly forgot what he was trying to do; but then it came to him and he moved the switch again, and again the face of Lord Korsibar looked back at him from the mirror across the way.

"It isn't working, Thalnap Zelifor."

"On the contrary, my lord. To my eyes you are the Su-Suheris Kurnak-Munikaad, precisely as it says on this official certificate. And quite a splendid figure you are, as Su-Suheris figures go. You look like the very twin of Sanibak-Thastimoon."

"I see only myself in the mirror." He touched his hand to his head. It felt like his own. Mustache, beard: Su-Suheris folk had no beards. Nor was there any second head that he could detect. "Nothing has changed in me," said Korsibar. "I have only one head. My flesh feels like human flesh."

"Of course, lordship! You are not changed at all. What has changed is the way you appear to others. To any onlooker you are—but come, let me show you—"

They went into the hall. Korsibar kept his hand pressed to the switch at his hip. A chambermaid passed just then; and Thalnap Zelifor said to her, "Lord Korsibar has entered into his retreat, and no one is to approach his door until he comes forth again."

"I'll send the word around, sir," said the chambermaid. She glanced without sign of recognition at Korsibar, and looked away. She gave no indication whatever that she saw the Coronal of Majipoor standing beside the Vroon at that very moment.

"So I am a Su-Suheris now," said Korsibar, feeling the first flicker of amusement he had known in many weeks. "Or seem that way to others, at any rate. Well done, Thalnap Zelifor! Let's be on our way!"

Thalnap Zelifor had already ordered up the floater, and it was waiting at Dizimaule Plaza when he and Korsibar emerged from the Castle. None of the Castle servants whom they had encountered as they moved outward through the building had paid any attention to them: no starbursts, no genuflections. It was only a Vroon and a Su-Suheris, members of the Castle staff like themselves, bound on some errand of their own.

Korsibar did not want to be absent overlong on this first excursion, and so they directed themselves to High Morpin, which was the city of the Mount closest to the Castle itself, a ride of less than an hour away. A sense of great relief and freedom came over him as the floater went soaring down the Grand Calintane Highway and the fantastic many-limbed monster that was the Castle dwindled behind him. He had not been at the controls of a floater since becoming Coronal, and it was pleasant to be guiding one now. He scarcely ever was allowed to do anything for himself any longer: there were people to drive for him, people to cut his meat for him and pour his wine, even people to dress and undress him. For the moment, at least, he was a free man again.

He had reverted to his own appearance once they had left the Castle. But Thalnap Zelifor reminded him that he would have to be in the Su-Suheris form if any floaters came near them on the road. "I understand," Korsibar said, and every few minutes he would reach down to touch the little switch. "Is it still working? Did I turn into a Su-Suheris?"

"You are the very image of one, my lord," declared Thalnap Zelifor.

Soon the golden airy webwork out of which the streets of the pleasure-city of High Morpin were constructed could be seen gleaming on the slope of the Mount to their left. They parked the floater at the edge of the city, near the great fountain that had been built in the reign of Korsibar's father that unendingly sent spears of tinted water shooting hundreds of feet into the air, and walked into the heart of the city. "Am I all right?" Korsibar asked nervously, again and again. "I have no way of telling, you know, whether this thing of yours is functioning correctly."

"When people begin kneeling down before you and making starbursts, my lord, you'll know that something is wrong. But for the moment you seem to be unnoticed here."

It was nearly midnight, but the pleasure-city bustled with eager throngs of amusement-seekers. Korsibar allowed the Vroon to perch on his shoulder, to spare him from being trampled. Although tempted, Korsibar did not try any of the rides and games himself—it seemed inappropriate, somehow, for a stern and dour Su-Suheris to be disporting himself on the mirror-slides or in the power-tunnels—but simply moved about through the crowds, one hand kept constantly on the switch of the Vroon's device, marveling that it was possible for the Coronal of Majipoor to walk here undisturbed.

More than once he caught sight of some holidaying gentleman of the court—Woolock Fals of Gossif, Count Gosbeck, Iram of Normork—and braced himself to be hailed by them, but they went by him with nothing more than the most casual of fleeting glances. This was indeed a wondrous magic, Korsibar thought. Or else the work of science, as Thalnap Zelifor insisted: but he was hard pressed to comprehend the difference.

As he walked, he listened to what was being said.

The Coronal and his policies were not the most common topics of conversation in High Morpin that night. At least an hour had gone by before Korsibar heard his name at all. But then, stopping in the doorway of a tavern, he heard someone call out lustily, "Let's drink to the Coronal!" And from elsewhere in the hall came the cry, "Lord Korsibar! Lord Korsibar!" and cheers, and the clinking of glasses. Had they recognized him amongst them? No. No. They all were looking the other way. They were simply drinking toasts to his name. But if they were offering toasts to the Coronal's health in the pleasure-city of High Morpin, could there be much substance to the rumors he had heard of a general displeasure with his administration?

Several more times in the course of the night Korsibar heard his name mentioned, and even smatterings of political talk. Someone said in a knowing tone that he had heard Dantirya Sambail was hoping to make himself High Counsellor in place of Farquanor, with an eye toward becoming Coronal himself some day when old Confalume died and Korsibar went to be Pontifex. But another replied just as knowingly, "Lord Korsibar'll never put the Procurator so high. Never. Procurator's too dangerous: Korsibar will send him packing home to Ni-moya. He knows how to deal with troublesome characters, Korsibar does. Look what he did to Prestimion!"

When Korsibar and Thalnap Zelifor slipped back untroubled by the guards into the Castle in the hours just before dawn, his mood was one of exhilaration and triumph. What he had heard at High Morpin had allayed his worst fears. "You have rescued me from the depths of despair," Korsibar told the Vroon, and handed him a purse of silver royals. "But for that machine of yours—ah, I'd have been lost indeed." And walked off whistling happily to his chambers, having taken on once more his own form.

But new doubts came creeping in, in the days that followed. The reassurance that Korsibar had found in High Morpin quickly faded; he needed to go forth once more, and make certain that those words of affection and loyalty that he had heard there were not mere exceptions and anomalies in a climate of general disapproval of his government.

And so go forth he did, arranging everything as he had before, setting out this time in mid-afternoon and spending a long evening in Bombifale of the orange sandstone walls, where for hours and hours he listened with care but overheard nothing that mattered in any way to him, and then once more caught scraps of a conversation devoted to a flattering estimation of his reign.

So, then! His fears were all for nothing!

It was clear to him now and unarguably certain that he was a proper Coronal, that he had the support of the populace, that even the dreadful stroke by which he had shattered the armies of Prestimion had not cost him the love of the people.

For Korsibar now it became an addiction, these ventures into the cities of the Mount by stealth to hear himself being praised. He made a third trip, to glowing Halanx, and a fourth to High Morpin again, and then to Sipermit just below the Castle on the side of the Mount opposite to High Morpin. It was in Sipermit that Korsibar slipped up at last, and let his hand stray from the switch of Thalnap Zelifor's device, one moonlit night in the statuary garden of Lord Makhario as he leaned forward straining his ears to pick up some bit of talk of current affairs that was just beyond the range of his hearing.

*"Lordship!"* Thalnap Zelifor whispered urgently.

"Please," said Korsibar. "Can't you see I'm trying to listen to what they're—"

"Lordship! The switch!"

"Ah, the switch!" Korsibar cried, appalled at his own stupidity. "For the love of the Divine!" Both his hands, he realized, were free, and he was standing in plain view in the bright moonlight not far from twelve or fifteen citizens of the city of Sipermit, not as the two-headed saunterer of a moment before, but as the Coronal Lord Korsibar in his green-and-white robe of office. Hastily he thrust his hand down to the device at his side and shoved the switch into place. But not before he saw the incredulous gapes and stares of half a dozen onlookers nearby.

"You are concealed again. But we should leave here quickly, lordship," said Thalnap Zelifor.

"Yes. Yes. Cast a spell on them, will you? Make their minds grow cloudy, so they come to disbelieve what they just saw."

"I will try to do that," the Vroon said. But there was an element of uncertainty in his tone, a certain disturbing lack of confidence, that aroused great disquiet and apprehension in Korsibar as he strode hastily from the park.

# 4

In the third month of his stay in Triggoin Prestimion felt that he had come to the point of desperation, the utter low ebb of the troublesome voyage through the world on which he had been bound since the day that Korsibar had snatched the starburst crown from him in the Labyrinth.

His mind was full of hazy sorceries, now, half-digested, minimally understood. Gominik Halvor's nightly teachings had both illuminated and muddled him; for Prestimion by this time had come both to believe and to disbelieve in that world of invisible spirits that so many people had told him lay just beyond the wall of human perception. Here in Triggoin he had seen, again and again and again, the apparent inexplicable efficacy of certain spells and enchantments, of certain amulets and devices, of ointments and potions and herbal powders and mixtures of powdered minerals. He saw stones that glowed strange colors in the dark and gave off heat. He watched bizarre demons dancing in the white light of black candles. He saw much more besides, much of it maddeningly plausible. And, seeing all this, it was ever harder for him to say, "This is unreal, this is pretense, this is delusion, this is folly," when the evidence of his eyes told him otherwise.

And yet—yet—

Prestimion noted evidence also of everything he had always denounced: frauds of all sorts, things that beyond any doubt were unrealities, pretenses, delusions, follies. He peered into factories in this town where crude statuettes and portraits of imaginary gods and demons were manufactured by bored squatting craftsmen in untold quantities for sale to the credulous, and watched their products being boxed and taken to the loading piers to be shipped everywhere in the world. He leafed through cheap, badly printed books of curses intended to harass one's enemies and incantations to bring prosperity or a child of a desired sex or some other yearned-for thing, that plainly were turned out by unscrupulous hacks to be sold to credulous fools.

He heard Gominik Halvor admit that it was useful for a successful magus to study certain techniques of sleight-of-hand and hypnotism. And he listened also to young boastful student mages in the taverns speaking of the tricks they had lately mastered, the making of waxen image-figures that stood unharmed in fireplaces and sang in unknown tongues, the spell that seemed to open doors into adjacent universes, the conjuring of levitations and disappearances and wondrous appearances, all of them by their own admission managed by deceptive mechanical means. These youths offered to sell their fraudulations to one another for stiff prices: "Fifty royals for the dancing waters!" they cried. "Sixty for the floating ghosts!" All of which confirmed and reconfirmed Prestimion's original innate skeptical views. But against that he had to place the new knowledge that he had acquired himself from Gominik Halvor, incomplete and misunderstood though it was, that did indeed seem to open real doors into real places that lay beyond reality. And that new knowledge, the things he could in no way refute even though they contradicted all that he had always believed, shook him to the core.

By night came turbulent dreams in which malevolent and horrific creatures coursed through his mind. He saw a great black crab biting the corner of the sun, and a giant serpent with a thousand legs slithering up over the edge of the world onto the land, and swarms of insects with the faces of wolves, and many other things of that kind, so that often he awoke sweating and trembling, and a time came when he feared sleeping altogether.

But on other nights, sometimes, there were kindlier dreams, sendings from the Lady of the Isle. These were puzzling to him in their own way, for he had heard that Korsibar's mother the Lady Roxivail was now installed on the Isle of Dreams and had taken command of the machineries by which sendings went forth to the world, and the former Lady Kunigarda had fled instead of taking up residence in the Terrace of Shadows on the Isle where former Ladies were supposed to dwell. But these sendings that came to Prestimion now were unquestionable sendings of the Lady Kunigarda. He recognized her firm but gentle touch, the iron purity of her spirit. Were there now *two* Ladies of the Isle, each of them equipped with the transmitting devices by which the Lady sent her visions into the minds of the world's sleepers?

In the dreams that came from Kunigarda he found himself wandering again in the Valmambra, a ragged weary man staggering at the outer edge of exhaustion from one hideous szambra-tree to the next in that endless desolation. But instead of that blazing clangorous sun in the sky there was the shining smiling face of the Lady Kunigarda, and her voice came to him, saying, "Yes, Prestimion, go onward, go on to the place you are meant to reach, you are not yet at the end of your energy." And she would say to him also, "You must go on. You are the world's redeemer, Prestimion, from whom we will have our salvation." And then also, as he tottered at the brink of collapse in his journey through that dread land of little water and burning sand, crying out that he had no more strength, that he would perish here: "Walk on, Lord Prestimion our true Coronal, until you reach the throne."

Madness, was it? The megalomaniacal follies of his own

troubled mind? He reminded himself that Korsibar was Coronal, and he a bewildered fugitive hiding under a name he often could not remember in this eerie city of wizards.

He was lost in confusions.

And becoming estranged from his friends as well. His partial embrace of sorceries had put him apart from Septach Melayn, whose irreverent wit and dancing-master mannerisms no longer amused him. But even Svor and Gialaurys, for all their love of him and their joy at seeing him come over at least a little way to their beliefs, had grown very distant from his soul. Prestimion held them guilty in a fashion for having brought this torrent of incomprehensible contradiction down upon him. Why had he chosen believers to be his companions? Why had he not limited himself to the company of cheerful materialist men like Septach Melayn? He was doing Svor and Gialaurys a great injustice by this, he knew; but so frayed were the moorings of his heart that he shrank away even from them, which was something they were altogether unable to understand.

No question of it, he had lost his way entirely. He was wandering hopelessly in a terrible desert. His only comfort was in the sendings that came from Kunigarda; and they were few and far between, and gave him no help in fulfilling the high destiny whose compulsions, he was coming to admit, still plagued him.

Then one night there came to him in a dream not the Lady Kunigarda but the magus Gominik Halvor, who stood before him as he lay sleeping in his dismal little room and said to him, "This must not go on any longer. The time has come for you to seek guidance." And when Prestimion awakened he knew that it had been a true dream: that he had wandered long enough without purpose or understanding in this chaos, and guidance now must be sought.

*

On a night when no moons were in the sky, but only the potent cold blaze of the ten million million stars, Prestimion rose in the hour after midnight and quietly left his little low-ceilinged room, carrying under his arm a small bundle of things that he had been collecting over the previous ten days. He went out from the inn and made his way through the tangled winding streets of Triggoin, no longer as much of a mystery to him as they had been when he first came here, and left the city by the gate known as Trinatha gate at the northern side of town, which faced the white star of that name.

There was a pleasant open park here, up against the double-humped mountain that lay just north of the city, a place of meadows and streams and some copses of leafy trees. No one, or hardly anyone, went to that park at this hour. And he wanted to be away from the city and its inhabitants, its crowded narrow old buildings impregnated with five thousand years of magic, its multitude of sorcerers casting spells day and night, its jostling invisible hordes of demons and ghosts and spirits. The park, close though it was by sorcerous Triggoin, was a peaceful place. Prestimion needed to be calm: as calm as was possible for him to be just now.

In a quiet grassy place between two little groves of trees, where a trickling stream so narrow that he could hop across it went flowing by, he set down his bundle and knelt beside it. He did not dare allow himself to think. Thinking, now, would be fatal to his purpose.

The strange new star that had burst into the sky while he was making the journey between the Labyrinth and the Castle was almost directly overhead, bathing him in the great intensity of its light. He could feel its blue-white fire streaming down upon him. It was a welcome sensation, a purifying sensation. "Lord Korsibar's Star" was what they were calling that star, or so he had heard, but to Prestimion it seemed there was nothing at all of Korsibar in its brilliant radiance. It was a star of change, a star of great transformation, yes: but it was not Lord Korsibar's Star and never would be.

"Help me," he whispered.

Prestimion understood that he was praying, a thing he had never done before in his life. He did not ask to know to whom he prayed.

He knelt a long while in that prayer, first looking down at the soft thick dewy grass, which looked almost black in the starlight though in fact its true color was closer to scarlet, and then very slowly lifting his head, looking up, straight up, into the eye of the new star.

"Help me."

He had learned some words, and he spoke them now. *"Voro liuro yad thearchivoliia,"* he said, and said them backwards too, *"Thearchivoliia yad liuro voro."* And heard a rumbling in the distance, as of thunder, though the night was clear and dry. He said then also the Five Words that had never been written down, and the Three Words that *could* never be written down. Then he took from his bundle the balls of colored twine that he had brought with him, and carefully laid out strips of different colors according to certain patterns that he had learned.

When the patterns were complete he looked up at the sky again, but this time with his eyes closed, and he uttered Names that he had heard others utter before, but never had expected to be speaking himself.

"Bythois!" he said, and waited a moment, and said also, "Proiarchis!" There were two loud rumbles of thunder. Prestimion did not ask himself why. "Sigei!" he said, and waited.

And then:

*"Remmer!"*

At that last and most puissant of Names there was a crack of thunder and a flash of lightning that danced across the sky, of such a brightness that he could see it even behind the lids of his closed eyes.

From his pack now he took the herbs he had brought with him, the powdered circaris leaves and the seeds of the cobily and the dried jangars, and sprinkled them into the palm of his hand and licked them into his mouth. Which smarted and stung for a moment, until he found the flask that contained the oil of gallicundi, and drank that down, which eased the stinging somewhat. There was only the pardao-berry to eat after that, which he did; and then he waited. Sweat rose in beads on his forehead and streamed down his face. A powerful dizziness overcame him, so that his head reeled and spun and the world was whirling three ways at once. And still he waited, kneeling in the soft grass, head turned to the sky, eyes shut.

After a time he opened his eyes and saw that a greenish-yellow mist had arisen and that there were four moons in the sky that he had never seen before, three small pale angular ones that were like white slivers and a greater, redder one in the midst of those. That fourth one was diamond-shaped, and from its four sharp corners came a sparkling blue-white radiance much like the light of the new star. Prestimion fixed his eyes on that and after a little while felt himself beginning to rise. He drifted up above the feathery hilltops of the two-humped mountain that overlooked Triggoin, and shortly saw the city spread out far below him, flat, like a mere sketch of itself. And went higher still, so that distant Castle Mount stood out against the night like a lantern, and a bright bronzy glow appeared to him in the east beyond it where the cities on the other side of the Mount were already opening to the new day.

Higher yet. He was above the realm of clouds. The world billowed like a carpet of thick fog beneath him.

The stars here burned with a brilliance beyond all comprehension. The air, which had for a time during his ascent been engulfed in a dazzling whiteness, grew dark again, and then darker than dark, and became very cold. He was in a kingdom of perpetual night. This was, he knew, the border of heaven; and as he soared through it he saw apparitions and portents all about him, great armies of fierce men wielding spears and swords who were battling on every side, and streaks of bloody lightning coursing among them, and swirling lights like comets ripped from the firmament plunging wildly downward toward the world below.

He was freezing, now. His hair, streaming out behind him, was stiff with ice. His blood had ceased to move in his veins. But there was no pain for him, and fear was wholly absent from his spirit. He was in a kind of ecstasy. Upward and upward he continued, until a band of blackness had closed around him and not even the stars were visible. There was nothing in the sky but Majipoor itself, like a child's ball beneath him, turning slowly, a thing all green and blue and brown, and he could make out the great dark wedge that was Alhanroel and the long wide green continent that was Zimroel and the little Isle of Dreams lying between them, with tawny Suvrael hanging below; and then the world turned and he saw only the Great Sea, that no one had ever crossed from one side to the other, a vast emerald scar spanning the world's middle. And then Alhanroel came into view again; for the world was turning ever faster and faster, the continents and the sea that lay between them spinning by again and again and again.

It was his. It was meant to be his, and he was meant for it. All doubts of that dropped forever from his soul. This was the thing he sought; this was what he had come to find, up here at reality's edge. His. The world was his, and he was the world's, and it hovered before him in the air within his reach.

Prestimion reached down and touched it.

It hopped up into his hand, that little ball that was the world, and he held it carefully there, and looked at it closely, and breathed upon it. And said to it, "I am Prestimion who would heal you. But first I must heal myself." And knew that he would. A great door had swung open in his soul that had been closed until now by iron bars.

He was very cold now, almost frozen; yet even so there still were rivers of sweat running down his body. But his way was clear. He saw the path that would carry him to the warmth, if only he had the will and the strength to follow it. And he knew that he did.

He released the little world and let it go spinning away from him in the darkness.

Then he saw a light above him. The new star was shining again, but now it had a face, and its face was that of the Lady Kunigarda, and he could hear her voice, saying softly, "Come, Prestimion. A little farther. I'm not so far away. A little farther yet. Farther. Farther—"

"Farther. Farther."

"This is far enough, I would think," a deep and robust voice above him said. "Come, Prestimion. Open your eyes."

For a moment he was unable to see; and then he perceived Gialaurys standing beside him, with Svor and Septach Melayn a short distance away. It was mid-morning, at least. The sun was high; the dew was gone from the grass. There was a griping anguished grumbling in his stomach, as though he had not eaten for weeks, and his throat was dry and his eyes felt swollen.

"Take my hand," said Gialaurys. "Up. Up."

"We've been searching for you since before dawn," Svor said. "Finally we asked Gominik Halvor, and he said to look in the park. But it's a big park."

Prestimion rose and took a few wobbling steps. Then he stumbled and nearly fell into the stream nearby, but Septach

Melayn came forward quickly and gracefully and caught him and steadied him on his feet.

"You've been playing with dangerous toys, haven't you, Prestimion?" he said, and gestured toward the array of herbs and the patterns of twine on the ground, making no attempt at concealing his scorn. "But you'll be all right, I think. A good meal, and some rest—"

"You should try these things, Septach Melayn," said Prestimion, managing a thin smile. He spoke with some difficulty: his voice was rusty and harsh, not yet fully under his control again. "You'd be in for some surprises. Circaris leaves and cobily and some dried jangars, to start with, and then—"

"Thank you, no. Would take the edge off my swordsmanship, I think, to dabble in such medicines as those. What nonsense have you been amusing yourself with out here, Prestimion?"

"Let him be," said Gialaurys gruffly. "Come. Let's go back to the inn."

"Can you walk?" Svor asked, peering into Prestimion's face in an anxious way.

"I'm fine, Svor." He held his arms outstretched before himself. "Look: a straight line, step step step step. Is that satisfactory to you?" Prestimion laughed. He gathered up the things he had brought with him and stuffed them into his pack. He felt very calm, very peaceful, after the night's adventure. His path was altogether clear. He need only take the first step, and then the second. A straight line, yes, step step step step.

"Would you like to hear the news?" Svor said, as they walked back together toward town.

"What news is that?" Prestimion asked.

"The proclamation of the Lady Kunigarda, concerning the state of the government. Septach Melayn heard it announced in a tavern last night, and we came to your room to tell you, but you were gone; and then began the business of searching for you all over town. How will we get our night's sleep back that you owe us, Prestimion?"

"Tell me the proclamation, Svor!"

"Oh, yes. That. It seems that the Lady has fled from the Isle, taking with her the mechanisms by which sendings are made; and announces that by means of those devices she will continue to guide the souls of the world, naming herself Lady-in-Exile. And also she has spoken out against Korsibar, and against her brother the Pontifex Confalume too. She gives the name of usurper to Korsibar. 'The false Coronal, the usurper Korsibar' is what she calls him. Her own nephew! As for Confalume, she denounces his supine acceptance of Korsibar's taking of the throne. They have brought the displeasure of the Divine upon the world, she says. She's called on all citizens of Majipoor to rise up at once and cast Korsibar aside. She means to make war on him herself, by sendings and other methods also."

"All this from Kunigarda?" Prestimion said, amazed. It seemed to him that this was still part of his dream, that he lay yet asleep on the grass beside the stream, holding the little ball that was Majipoor in his hand. "And what has become of Kunigarda, I wonder? Has she been proscribed too?"

"She's left the Isle," said Septach Melayn. "She's somewhere in southern Alhanroel right now, and making her way north. She has announced that she means to find you and join forces with you: for you are the rightful Coronal of Majipoor, Prestimion—so says the Lady Kunigarda. Which we would have been happy to tell you last night, my friend, except that you felt it needful to spend a night sleeping in the park with a belly full of—what did you say? Circaris leaves and cobily?" A great gust of roaring derisive laughter came from him. "Has all this been achieved by means of witchcraft, I wonder, this making of an alliance with Confalume's own sister? Did you come out here to invoke Proiarchis and Remmer on your behalf, and did those great beings look upon you with favor, Prestimion, and give you the world to hold in your hand like a toy?"

Prestimion made no reply. But a secret smile played quickly across his face.

# 5

"It was in Lord Makhario's statuary garden in Sipermit that I saw it, when I was on holiday there," said Sebbigan Kless of Perimor, who was a manufacturer of doublets and hose in that busy city on the lower slope of Castle Mount. His companion, who was listening as intently as though Sebbigan Kless had just told him that the Mount was about to break loose from the planet and drift off into space, was the jobber and wholesaler Aibeil Gammis of Stee, an important distributor of Sebbigan Kless's products in several of the Free Cities a little way higher on the mountain. "There was this Su-Suheris walking in the garden, with the smallest Vroon you could imagine sitting on his shoulder. Well, you can't help stealing a glance at a Su-Suheris whenever you see one, can you?—such weird bastards, those two pointy heads sticking up out of that neck—and for one to have a Vroon riding on his shoulder was pretty strange too, but, let me tell you, that was nothing at all compared to seeing the Su-Suheris *flicker* all of a sudden, and then—" Two days later, when Aibeil Gammis had returned to Stee and was going over inventories at his warehouse with his accountant, a man named Hazil Scroith who claimed some sort of tenuous kinship with a younger brother of the Duke of Alaisor, he said, "If we were smart, you know, we'd start getting up a line of goods to sell to the Metamorphs. After all, we've got one as our Coronal, now."

"A Metamorph? What are you talking about?"

"Well, I had this from Sebbigan Kless himself, and Sebbigan Kless is no tippler, you know, so I doubt that he was making it up. It seems he was visiting Sipermit, you know, to see that jiggly little Zimroel girl that he doesn't want his wife to find out about, and they were in the park where the sexy statues are when just as you please the Coronal comes strolling through, Korsibar himself, only he's disguised as a Su-Suheris. Well, you ask, how does a human being manage to make himself look like a seven-foot-tall monster with two heads, and how did Sebbigan Kless manage to discover that the seven-foot-tall monster was in fact our beloved Coronal? And the answer, my friend, is that the Coronal isn't a human at all, but has to be a Shapeshifter, because Sebbigan Kless actually saw him change form—it was just for a moment, mind you, but Sebbigan Kless isn't a man whose eyes deceive him—the Su-Suheris turned into the Coronal, who looked very surprised to find himself revealed that way, and turned himself back into a Su-Suheris just as fast as I can tell you the story! But it was done and seen. A Shapeshifter! No wonder Korsibar was able to put the hex on Confalume and all those lords in the Labyrinth! He wasn't Korsibar at all, was he, but some kind of thing out of the Metamorph country! Or can it be that Confalume's a Shapeshifter too? That we've had a whole family of Shapeshifters running the world for the last forty years? And if that's true, let me tell you—"

Which revelations Hazil Scroith duly reported in his next letter to his wife's nephew Jispard Demaive, who was not the younger brother of the Duke of Alaisor at all but who did indeed have a clerical post in the duke's Ministry of Prisons and Warehouses. "We are all buzzing here with the news," wrote Hazil Scroith, "that the Coronal Lord Korsibar is in fact a Metamorph, the real Korsibar evidently having been done away with while his father was still Coronal. Word of this comes from an absolutely reputable source in Stee who was able to observe the supposed Lord Korsibar *changing shape in a public park*—is that not incredible?—and turning himself very quickly from human form to that of a Su-Suheris and immediately back again. Why he would do such a thing in plain view of others is hard to understand, dear nephew, but who has ever understood the way the minds of the Meta-morphs work?

"Anyway, the tale is all over the Mount now, and nobody is discussing anything else. Just yesterday a salesman who was here from Normork told me the latest bit of news, which is that the Su-Suheris sorcerer Sanibak-Thastimoon, who has been standing at our new Coronal's elbow ever since he came to the throne, is a Metamorph also! Both of them are impos-tors, the king and his magus too, and where will it end? Will we find that the whole government is shot through and through with Shapeshifters pretending to be human? It stuns the mind. The whole crowd of them up there at the Castle nothing but masquerading Metamorphs!"

"Horpidan, Duke of Alaisor, to the esteemed Grand Admiral Prince Gonivaul.

"Dear Uncle:
"You will be astonished, I think, by the remarkable story that has been floating around Alaisor for the past few weeks. I had it from one of the chamberlains in my Customs office, who says that he's heard it from at least two dozen people this week alone. The essence of it is that the entire pack of you at the Castle, from Korsibar and his Council on down, are a bunch of Metamorphs:

we are asked to believe that a squadron of aboriginals secretly infiltrated the Castle sometime during Lord Confalume's reign and one by one killed off the leading men of the realm and took their places. That includes Confalume himself, apparently. Which would explain why the former Coronal was so acquiescent when Korsibar, or the creature that we understood to be Korsibar, made his astonishing grab of the throne. It was all arranged between them—a Metamorph conspiracy to gain control of Majipoor! And, if you can believe the stories, it has brilliantly succeeded.

"According to the newest versions of the story, the only one they didn't manage to replace with one of their own was poor Prince Prestimion. He slipped out of their grasp, somehow. But they were able, at least, to push him aside in favor of Korsibar when the Coronalship became vacant, and when Prestimion threatened to expose the whole foul conspiracy they drove him into exile and eventually, so it seems, killed him by blowing up that dam when he was camped below it on the Iyann, getting ready to launch a campaign to set things to rights. Seamier and seamier, uncle!

"Of course it's all crazy nonsense, this Metamorph thing, isn't it? The mere gabble of ignorant provincial rumor-mongers? I would certainly hope so, although everybody who tells the story is willing to swear by all that's holy that Korsibar was definitely seen changing shapes right out in the open in some public park in Stee or Halanx or one of the other big Mount cities. Supposedly there are witnesses, affidavits, et cetera.

"Put my mind at rest, uncle, I beg you. If the story is true, then presumably *you* are a Metamorph in disguise too. Are you? I'd be saddened to hear that, because you have always been one of my favorite relatives, not to mention being the head of our family since the death of my father, and it would upset me terribly to learn that you are in fact some repellent soft-boned noseless *thing* out of the jungles of Ilirivoyne. Please let me know the truth, one way or another.

"Your affectionate nephew—I hope—

"Horpidan, Alaisor."

And in Sisivondal they were saying—
In Bailemoona—
In Sefarad—
In Sippulgar—

Korsibar, pacing endlessly, whirled without warning and advanced toward Farquanor as though he meant to rend him limb from limb. Farquanor, quailing, took a quick couple of steps backward, then felt himself butting against the wall of the throne-chamber.

"These stories, Farquanor! These impossible ridiculous stories about me—"

"Lies, my lord," said Farquanor, trembling. "Every one of them, a lie!"

Korsibar stared, wonderstruck.

"Thank you," he said acidly, after a little while. "I had begun to believe the truth of them myself, but you have greatly reassured me, Count Farquanor. How pleased I am to know I'm not a Shapeshifter after all."

"I only meant, my lord, that—"

"You meant! You meant! You meant!"

"My lord, I beg you, take hold of yourself!"

"I'll take hold of you, and hurl you from here to Zimroel, if you don't stop spouting nonsense. You are my High

Counsellor, Farquanor. I call upon you for advice, and you spout platitudes instead. Tell me: what are we to do about these lunatic tales that are heard suddenly on all sides?"

"Ignore them, my lord."

"Ignore? Not deny?"

"They are too contemptible to deny. Can you imagine it, going before the world and saying, 'I am not a Shapeshifter'? Such a denial only gives life to the thing. Let it die of its own absurdity, my lord."

"You think it will?"

Farquanor took a deep breath. He felt uncomfortably confined, with Korsibar's great bulk looming before him and the wall only inches behind him. And the Coronal seemed to be almost at the edge of madness: face rigid with tension, eyes bulging, altogether looking like a man driven to distraction by the responsibilities of the office he had seized for himself and by the annoyance of this most curious of rumors concerning him. It would not take much to cause him to snap entirely and erupt into wild violence. One wrong word, Farquanor thought, and he will squash me against this wall like a bug.

Carefully he said, forcing a look of urgent concern and deep sympathy to his face, "My lord, I have no doubt of it. It's no more than the momentary madness of the season. Let it dry up and blow away; and the people will hail you gladly as their lord, as they have since the beginning. This I promise you, my lord. Remain true to your own self, and no lies will attach themselves to you."

"Ah," said Korsibar, in relief. And then, almost as though he had caught the habit from Dantirya Sambail, said again, after a moment, "Ah."

Oljebbin said, "Serithorn, may I have a word with you?"

Serithorn, who was examining a tray of ancient carved

kebbel-stones that had been brought to him an hour before by a dealer in antiquities from Gimkandale, glanced up at the former High Counsellor and said pleasantly, "You look very hot and bothered, old man. Is anything wrong?"

"Wrong? Wrong? Oh, no, nothing at all!" Oljebbin came fully into Serithorn's study—both men still maintained their lavish suites at the Castle, though they no longer held significant posts in the government—and slapped his hand down on the desk so fiercely that the kebbel-stones leaped about in the tray. "Do you see this hand, Serithorn? Does that look to you like a Metamorph's hand?"

"For the love of the Divine, Oljebbin!"

"Does it? Can I make it wriggle and shift? Sprout another seven or eight fingers, maybe? Turn it into a Skandar's hand if I feel like it? What about you, Serithorn? Let's see your hand! If I twist it hard enough, will it change?"

"You're overwrought, Oljebbin. Sit down and have some wine with me. This absurd tale about Lord Korsibar—"

"Not just Korsibar. Gonivaul's been to see me. The thing is spreading like a plague. Do you know what they're telling each other in places like Alaisor and Sisivondal? That we're all Metamorphs, every last one of us, you and me and Gonivaul and Farquanor and Farholt and Dantirya Sambail—"

"Well," said Serithorn, "I wouldn't care to speak for Farquanor and Farholt, and Gonivaul may very likely be a Metamorph for all I know, although if he is he's a deucedly hairy one; and as for Dantirya Sambail, I never thought he was a human being in the first place. But I tell you flat out that I am myself and nothing other than myself, as incapable of changing shapes as I am of making love to twenty women the same night, and I'm reasonably confident that you are quite genuine too. Reasonably confident, I say. I don't have serious doubts of you. I'd be willing to accept any oath that you'd care to swear as to your humanity at face value, old friend, and never once thereafter would I let anyone try to make me believe that you were actually—"

"Serithorn, for once in your life be serious!" cried Oljebbin explosively.

"Very well." The little smile that was Serithorn's usual expression gave way to a look of dour glowering intensity worthy of Farholt or Gialaurys. "I am serious, now."

"Thank you. Listen to me: of *course* I don't believe that Korsibar's a Metamorph, or that you are, or that I may be one myself and simply haven't noticed. It's all too ridiculous for words. But the fact is that five or ten billion people out there seem to think he is. Gonivaul's been making inquiries and the story's all over Alhanroel by now, in at least a dozen different permutations, each one more preposterous than the next. What effect do you think this is having on Korsibar's legitimacy in the eyes of those five billion people? Don't you think he's hideously compromised by it? He takes the throne by unconstitutional means, for which he's already being denounced up and down the land by nobody less than the former Lady of the Isle, Kunigarda herself, who's spouting subversive sendings day and night. And then it becomes widely believed that he's not only not human but is in fact a *Shape-shifter* who's disguised himself as Korsibar—" Oljebbin ran both his hands agitatedly through his thick shock of white hair. "Prestimion's alive, did you know that?" he asked. "And is about to make a second try at claiming the throne."

Serithorn's elegant facade of unshakeable poise gave way to a gasp of astonishment.

*"Alive?"*

"Yes. This is confirmed, just today. I don't think the Coronal knows it yet: Farquanor's afraid to tell him, apparently. Prestimion has been in Triggoin, it seems, but now, according to Gonivaul, he's out and marching around again somewhere in western Alhanroel, patching together those pieces of the rebel army that Korsibar didn't drown, and recruiting a new—"

There was a knock at the door.

"Gonivaul," Oljebbin said. "I asked him to join me here."

"Come in, admiral!" Serithorn called, and Prince Gonivaul strode into the room. His shaggy-bearded face was grim and stormy.

"Has Oljebbin told you—" he began.

"Yes," Serithorn said. "We're all supposed to be Metamorphs. Well, we aren't, and that's that. But what's this business about Prestimion being alive? "

"He is. That's definite. He's come out of the north— Triggoin, I hear—and has set up headquarters for himself in the plains between Gloyn and Marakeeba, which are places somewhere on the far side of the Trikkalas. He's collecting a new army there, with the notion of marching to Castle Mount, gathering up a billion or so rebel soldiers along the way, and pushing Korsibar off the throne."

"Is he the one behind this lunatic thing of Korsibar's being a Metamorph?" Serithorn asked.

Gonivaul shrugged. "I can't say. There's probably no connection. But certainly he'll be willing to make damaging use of it as propaganda. 'Accept me as your true Coronal in place of this creature who pretends to be Korsibar,' he'll say. 'The person you take for Korsibar is not only an unlawful Coronal but an evil Metamorph impostor!' And people will gobble it up.—There's a germ of truth, I think, in this Metamorph fable, anyway."

"There is?" said Oljebbin and Serithorn at one and the same instant.

"Oh, not literally," Gonivaul said. "But Korsibar's been very thick these last few months with the Vroon Thalnap Zelifor, who used to work for me once upon a time, and who, as you may recall, got himself into big trouble with

Korsibar last year by putting some kind of wild ideas into the Lady Thismet's head and after that by running off to join Prestimion. When the Vroon came scooting back here after Prestimion's defeat at Stymphinor he managed somehow to talk his way into Korsibar's good graces, don't ask me how, and has been right up there in prestige with Sanibak-Thastimoon on his staff of mages ever since.

"Well, this Thalnap Zelifor is very good with gadgets, and I happen to know that something he was working on when he was in my pay was a device that would allow the wearer to seem to change shape. Not *actual* shapeshifting, mind you, just the illusion of it. Now, there definitely seems to be some escapade of Korsibar's at the bottom of all these stories—he was seen changing shapes in Bombifale or Bibiroon or somewhere by a vacationing businessman who doesn't seem to have had any reason to be inventing the tale, and he says Korsibar had a Vroon with him at the time. My guess is that he and Thalnap Zelifor slipped away from the Castle to experiment with this machine, and got careless with it just as the businessman happened by. After which the story started circulating that—"

"All right," Oljebbin said. "Whether it did or didn't happen that way, the main thing is that the story's traveling like wildfire and doing Korsibar a lot of harm. Metamorphs are feared and detested everywhere. He'll have a hard time scrubbing away the taint. True or false, this business is bound to weaken Korsibar's position with the common folk, which is weak enough already now that Kunigarda's been speaking out against him. With Prestimion suddenly back in the picture, what I want to know from you two is this: is this the moment for *us* to withdraw our support from Korsibar too?"

"In favor of Prestimion?" Serithorn asked, eyebrows lifting in-surprise.

"No," said Oljebbin sharply. "In favor of Prankipin's

embalmed corpse. In favor of the statue of Lord Stiamot, maybe. Who do you think I'm talking about, Serithorn?"

"Prestimion doesn't have a chance of becoming Coronal, not now, not ever," said Serithorn in a quiet emphatic tone.

"You say this?" asked Oljebbin. "You, his good friend for so long, his mother's *very* good friend?"

Serithorn reddened faintly at that. But his voice remained calm as he replied, "There's a curse of some sort on Prestimion. Anybody who couldn't keep an idiot like Korsibar from nudging him aside when the throne became vacant and the whole world was expecting him to become Coronal is plainly marked by the gods for misfortune. Now that he's back in view and heading this way, something will go wrong again. Korsibar will dump another reservoir on him or a stray arrow will get him or he'll be eaten by vorzaks as he comes over the mountains. Mark my words, Prestimion won't have any more success this time than he did before."

"So if we were to back him," Oljebbin said, "we'd be cutting our own throats?"

"Essentially," said Serithorn.

"But that would leave us with a Coronal who half the world believes is a Metamorph! There's no way Korsibar can stand up in front of everybody and prove he *isn't* one, is there? This numbskull rumor will eventually do irreparable harm to his ability to govern, if it hasn't already, and then—"

"You're forgetting someone," Gonivaul said.

Oljebbin stared. "What do you mean?"

"The name of Dantirya Sambail hasn't been mentioned at all since I entered the room. Korsibar's done for, I agree: these wild stories never get properly contradicted, and sooner or later everybody out there will have been made permanently suspicious of him. As for Prestimion, I share Serithorn's view of him: he's simply a poor unlucky devil and I can't believe he'll ever manage to get the throne he so richly deserves to have. That leaves the Procurator. Since the Mavestoi business he's quietly pushed Farquanor and everybody else aside and has made himself Korsibar's chief adviser, at least unofficially. Now Korsibar is having political problems in the provinces because of this bizarre Metamorph thing. All right: either Dantirya Sambail will very shortly overthrow Korsibar himself—'for the good of Majipoor,' as he'll piously tell everybody—or else, in the coming war with Prestimion, Dantirya Sambail will advise Korsibar right into some terrible calamity. One way or the other, Korsibar goes out of the picture before long and Dantirya Sambail emerges on top. If we're smart, and we are, we'll cultivate the friendship of Dantirya Sambail at this particular point in time.—What do you think, Serithorn?"

"I agree completely. Korsibar's position is suddenly very wobbly, not that it was tremendously strong in the first place, because of the legalities, Coronal's son becoming Coronal, and all that. Prestimion's isn't any better. He was never officially named Coronal-designate, after all. So, even if he's the winner in this new war that's shaping up, he's got no very valid claim himself. Dantirya Sambail, on the other hand, can argue that as Procurator of Ni-moya he stands second only to the Pontifex Confalume, and therefore is the logical and legitimate heir to the Coronal's throne."

"Very well thought out," said Oljebbin. "At last I make out a pattern in all this chaos. Our strategy, my lords, is to pledge our undying support in the coming challenge for the throne to our beloved Lord Korsibar and his loyal ally the Procurator of Ni-moya, and roundly condemn the audacity of the criminal upstart Prestimion. If Korsibar somehow survives and remains on the throne, he'll be indebted to us forever. If he doesn't, he'll almost certainly be replaced as Coronal by Dantirya Sambail, who also will be grateful to have had our help. Either way, we're on the winning side. Are we agreed, gentlemen?"

"Absolutely," said Gonivaul at once.

"Let us drink to it," said Serithorn, pulling a dusty bottle of wine from his cabinet. "Good Muldemar wine, as it happens, Prestimion's own. Fifteen years old.—To peace, gentlemen! To everlasting peace and harmony in the world!"

# 6

Thismet said, "Have you heard these stories, Meli-thyrrh, that say that my brother is a Metamorph?"

"What foolishness they are, my lady!"

"Yes. Foolishness indeed. If he is a Metamorph, then what am I, who was hatched in the same womb as he?"

"The stories, as I hear them, have it that he was *replaced* by a Metamorph secretly as a grown man, not that he was born one. But all of it is nonsense. You should pay no attention, my lady."

"True. I shouldn't. But it's so hard, Melithyrrh!"

Thismet rose from her divan and crossed the room to the octagonal window that gave a view of Lord Siminave's dazzling reflecting pool, and then, pivoting restlessly, went to the other side, opening her wardrobe's fragrant doors of shimmak-wood to reveal all her wealth of clothing within, the scores of brocaded robes and jeweled gowns and bodices and chemises and cassocks and all the rest, everything fashioned from her own design by the most skilled clothing-makers of Majipoor. She had worn many of them only once or twice, some not at all; and now they needed to be refitted, so lean and gaunt had she become in these sour days. She barely ate any longer; she scarcely slept. Korsibar's coming to the throne, which had seemed such a glorious thing to her once, had been the ruination of them both.

Melithyrrh said, "My lady, please—this pacing, this constant fretting of yours—"

"I've had to swallow too much, Melithyrrh! Traitors and villains on all sides. The sorcerer Sanibak-Thastimoon, who deludes me into thinking great things are in store for me, and turns his back on me at the first opportunity! The other sorcerer, Thalnap Zelifor, who goads me into giving offense to my brother, and then leaves me altogether, and when he returns is suddenly my brother's devoted servant! Or the vile Farquanor, who comes right into these rooms—he stood over there, in the jade drawing room—I should have had the floor scrubbed with acid afterward—and says to me, cool as ice, 'Marry me, Thismet, it will improve your social standing at the Castle.' Calling me *Thismet,* as though I were a serving-wench! And going unpunished for it when I denounced him to Korsibar."

"My lady—"

"And Korsibar," Thismet went on. "My wonderful heroic brother, who made himself Coronal simply because I told him to do it, and who rewards me by making me an exile within the very walls of the Castle, ignored, excluded, shunted about with impunity, while he surrounds himself with cheats and liars and treacherous traitors who are leading him to destruction, men like Dantirya Sambail lording it around the Castle now as though he were Coronal and Pontifex both at once—too much, Melithyrrh, much too much! I can abide this place and these people no longer." She drifted on into the room adjacent, where her treasures of jewelry were housed, her wondrous rings and pendants and necklaces that were the equal of the best that any Coronal's consort had ever possessed, and stood with her delicate white hands plunged deep amongst them as though it was some hoard of buried treasure that she had just uncovered. After a time she said in a much quieter voice, "Melithyrrh, will you accompany me on a little journey?"

"Of course, my lady. A few days in High Morpin, perhaps—they'll do you a world of good. Or a visit to the gardens at Tolingar—a holiday in Bombifale—"

"No," Thismet said. "Not Bombifale, not Tolingar. Nor High Morpin neither. A longer journey is what I have in mind. Do you know where Gloyn is, Melithyrrh?"

"Gloyn?" Melithyrrh repeated blankly, as though Thismet had spoken the name of some other planet.

"Gloyn. It's a city, or maybe a town, in western Alhanroel, across the Trikkala Mountains, but this side of Alaisor."

"I've never heard of it," said Melithyrrh, mystified.

"No. Nor I, before this day. But I have a mind to go there now. To leave tomorrow, just you and I together. Come, let's pack some things. You can operate a floater, can't you? And I'm fairly sure I can. I can't tell you how eager I am to get away from this place—out into the fresh air, a little adventure of our own, the first one I've ever had: just you and me, Melithyrrh—"

"May I ask, lady, what attraction there is in Gloyn?"

"Prestimion," Thismet said.


In the end she took much less with her than she would have imagined possible to travel with, almost none of her elegant robes and gowns, only simple rough clothes that would be useful in the place where she was going, and just a handful of baubles, a few rings and necklaces to remind her that she was the owner of such things. But also she took a small jewel-handled dagger that she could strap along the inside of her left arm, and, after some thought, an energy-thrower she had borrowed in a moment of foresight from the weapons storehouse, a month before. She had no clear idea of how to use it, and had heard that the things were terribly unreliable in any case, but she supposed it would serve to frighten away anyone who might think that two young women traveling by themselves were easy prey.

Operating the floater was the most challenging part. She had never driven one herself or even paid much attention to what the driver was doing as she was taken about. Nor, as it developed, had Melithyrrh had any experience in driving. But there couldn't be much to it, could there? *Start, stop, up, down, slower, faster*—that was about it, she thought. At an hour when Korsibar and the others were having another of their interminable Council meetings—they were always having long meetings nowadays, what with Prestimion's new rebellion gathering strength in the west and this absurd ongoing crisis of the Metamorph rumors—Thismet requisitioned a pleasure-floater from the captain of the guards, and she and Melithyrrh went down to Dizimaule Plaza together to pick it up.

The guardsman who brought the floater around looked at them a little strangely when he realized they had no driver of their own with them. But it was not his place to ask questions of the Coronal's sister. He helped them load their baggage in the storage compartment, and held the door open for them.

"You drive it first," Thismet whispered.

"Me? But—my lady—"

"They'll think something's really wrong if I sit down in front of the controls. Go on!"

"Yes, my lady."

Melithyrrh studied the panel of controls for a moment. Eight or nine knobs, none of them identified. She took a long deep breath and touched one. Nothing happened. The guardsman was staring open-mouthed at them. Surely he had never seen two ladies of rank get into a floater before on their own.

Melithyrhh pressed another knob. A humming sound came from below them.

"Those are the rotors starting up," said Thismet. "Now touch the knob to the left of it."

It was only a guess, but a good one. The nose of the floater came up six inches from the ground, eight inches, ten. And kept on rising.

"Let go of it!" Thismet cried. The floater descended a bit and leveled off. "Now the next knob to the left!" That one sent the floater jolting violently backward. Thismet snatched Melithyrrh's hand from the knob and put her own on the one just to the right of the rotor control. Just as violently, the floater began moving forward. The guardsman, who had backed away from the vehicle at its first lurch, stood off to one side, mouth gaping even wider. "Here we go!" Thismet exclaimed, as the floater went cruising uncertainly off toward the Grand Calintane Highway.

"I think I have the essence of the thing now," Melithyrrh said. "This one makes it go faster, this one slows it down. And this one turns it to the—right? No, the left, I guess. So this one must be—"

"You're doing very well," Thismet said. And indeed she was. The floater was remaining level in relation to the ground now, and moving smoothly down the center of the highway track. A sign loomed up. High Morpin to the left, Halanx to the right. "Take the Halanx road," Thismet ordered. Melithyrrh touched a knob. The floater veered to the right, not too jerkily. "You see?" said Thismet. "Nothing to it at all. We're on our way."

Getting off the Mount was the first task. They needed to go west once they were in the flatlands: that meant leaving the Mount by the Dundilmir side of things, Thismet knew. But Dundilmir was a Slope City, far down near the bottom of the Mount. To get there they had to make their way first through the three higher levels, the Inner Cities, the Guardian Cities, the Free Cities. She had a vague idea of a route that ran down through Banglecode to Hoikmar or Greel and another that led downward from there to Castlethorn or Gimkandale, which ought to take them to Dundilmir and thence to ground level. But her knowledge of Mount geography was imperfect and did not at all include an awareness of the intricate spires and secondary peaks that complicated travel up and down the sides of the immense mountain. One couldn't simply go from Point A to Point B because they were in a straight line on a map; one had to find a road that actually connected them, and sometimes that involved going halfway around the Mount. And so they spent their first night, unexpectedly, at an inn in the city of Guand, which Thismet and never visited in her life, and which they arrived in under the mistaken impression that they had taken the Banglecode road out of Halanx.

The inn was the best they could find, but it was something less than luxurious. From the innkeeper came impertinent stares, even though they had dressed as unflatteringly as they knew how, with all color washed from their faces and their hair pulled severely back. The room was small and bleak and there were stains on the walls and the bedding did not seem fresh. The dinner they bought for themselves there was unthinkably bad, unknown pale meat fried in grease. All night there were sounds of laughter and bedsprings from adjacent rooms.

"Will it be like this, do you imagine, all the way to Gloyn?" Thismet asked.

"Worse, my lady. This is still Castle Mount."

When the time came to pay the reckoning Thismet discovered she had brought no money with her. Money was not something a Coronal's sister was accustomed to carrying. Fortunately, Melithyrrh had a purse of royals with her; but it seemed a small purse, and Thismet began to think they would be pawning her jewelry to pay for these miserable lodging-houses as the journey went on. Things would get worse, yes, Thismet saw.

Somehow they found their way down the Mount. Somehow they located roads that would take them westward, though they had no maps and no skill at traveling. "We should look for highway signs that say 'Alaisor,'" Thismet said. "Alaisor is in the west." But Melithyrrh pointed out that Alaisor was thousands of miles away—eight thousand miles, ten, perhaps, all the way out by the sea—and was not likely to be shown on highway signs this far inland. So they tried to think of other cities closer to the Mount that lay in the right direction. "Arkilon," Thismet suggested, remembering that there had been a big battle there the year before and that she had seen on the map that it was west of the Mount. So they went to Arkilon.

There they found a traveler staying at their inn who suggested that they go south to Sisivondal next, and drew a little chart for them showing how it would avoid the difficult crossing of the Trikkala Mountains if they did that. "You are very kind," said Thismet, smiling, a phrase and a smile which he mistook, putting his hand boldly on her thigh as they sat together at table, so that she had to let him see the dagger strapped within the sleeve of her blouse. After that he was more polite. But the imprint of that roaming hand burned against her skin for hours thereafter.

They went to Sisivondal. It was the ugliest place Thismet had ever seen. Not even in nightmares had she conceived anything more hideous. This time their hotel room was a barren stuffy box. It seemed all but airless; but when they opened the window a fine rain of sand came sifting in on them.

Roads led from Sisivondal in all directions. A maze of signs confronted them.

"Which way is Gloyn?" Thismet asked, dispirited. "I never imagined that Majipoor was so big!"

"It is the biggest world in all the heavens," said Melithyrrh. "The biggest where people of the human sort can live, at least."

"And we must travel it alone, two pampered women."

"It was our choice, lady."

"Yes. There was no other, was there?"

No. No choice. She knew she had come to the end of her time at the court, that place which once had been so lovely and had somehow been transformed into a place of disappointment and rebuke. Already the Castle and all its horrors seemed far away: the skulking leering Farquanor, the snorting bestial Procurator, the treacherous mages, the noble brother who had treated her so ignobly when she had asked him for a place in his government. She scarcely missed her jade drawing room and her alabaster tub, her robes and bangles, her whole luxurious empty life. She was done with all that. It was dead. Over. A new life was what she sought now, and would find in the west. But still—this endless wearying journey—that impudent hand on her thigh, burning like a flame—the shabby hotels, the dreary roads, the ghastly food—

The territory around Sisivondal was a vast dusty wasteland. A dry hot dusty wind blew across it all the time. They kept the floater sealed tight and yet, when Thismet glanced at Melithyrrh, she could see Melithyrrh's golden hair coated with a sandy film, and knew that hers must be like that also. Grit in her eyes, grit between her teeth, grit along her arms and down between her breasts. Her skin was dry; her throat was dry. Her soul itself was parched. She had never felt so filthy, so bedraggled, so unglamorous, so little like anything that anyone would recognize as the Lady Thismet of Lord Confalume's Castle. They drove on and on, praying that this grim sandy plain would come to an end eventually; and eventually it did, and the air grew sweet and the world became Majipoor-beautiful again.

"We are nearing Gloyn at last, I hope," Thismet said, one magnificent sunlit morning as they passed through a land of glistening green fields.

They stopped for information at a farm where some mysterious-looking plant with purple leaves was being grown in fields that stretched onward, one after another, out of sight. Gloyn? Gloyn? Ah, yes, Gloyn! That was on the road to Marakeeba, was it not? Well, then, they had passed the highway for Gloyn seven hundred miles ago. Go back to Kessilroge, turn right there and go three hundred miles, watch for signs for Gannamunda, and at Gannamunda look for the Hunzimar Highway—

Very well. Back to Kessilroge.


The Vale of Gloyn was the place where Prestimion's army lay encamped, a great broad savanna in west-central Alhanroel, almost equidistant between the Mount and the seacoast at Alaisor. All this flat peaceful land was covered by huge carpets of coppery-hued, shin-high gattaga-grass, the blades of which were so close-knit and thick that when you walked upon it you left a trail that could be seen half an hour afterward; and those hundreds of miles of gattaga-grass were home to immense herds of grazing animals that lived there as they had lived a hundred thousand years before, or a million.

Duke Svor, who had ridden out of camp alone that day, was standing near the sharp peak of one of the dwarf mountains that were scattered across the plain, ship-sized piles of rock eighty or a hundred feet high rising like little stony islands above the grass. From that vantage point he looked out now on these herds in wonder.

The gattaga-grass spread to the limits of his vision. Here,

close at hand, were ten or twenty or fifty thousand of the large, stocky, flat-faced quadrupeds called klimbergeysts, whose hides were dappled with shifting patterns of red and gold. They looked like so many thousands of sunsets wandering freely in the plain. Off to his left was a glade of tall, spiky gray trees where dozens of long-necked browsers that stood close to fifty feet high were feeding on the tender top leaves. He had no idea of the name of these animals. Their long slender legs were rigid and angular, with three sets of equidistant knees; their necks were as flexible as serpents, topped by heads that were little more than gigantic mouths topped with dim, uneasy eyes. Untiringly they ripped the soft growth from the towering trees, and just as untiringly the trees put forth new leaves as soon as the browsers passed by.

On the other side of him Svor observed a squat tank-shaped thing with gleaming armored hide, not very different in appearance from a mollitor but obviously much less warlike, moving placidly along the margin of a swampy area where the pink shoots of some water-plant were sprouting. Beyond it, at the opening of a secondary valley that had two of the little island-mountains serving as its gateway, he saw another huge grazing herd, these being the broad-nosed pig-like animals that were called vongiforin, snuffling about in the gattaga for the small sweet seeds on which they fed. The sun was warm and mild; fleecy clouds drifted overhead; a light soft breeze was blowing out of the south.

An idyllic scene, Svor thought.

Almost idyllic, anyway. He noted the presence, atop one of the nearby island-mountains, of a trio of slim, tawny hunting-animals, kepjitaljis, who were eyeing the grazing vongiforin with interest. The kepjitaljis—a mother and two cubs, he supposed—were long and tapering, with harsh wedge-shaped heads, bright eyes like red stars, fierce-clawed forearms, and great powerful hind legs that could propel them swiftly forward

571

in inexorable hopping motions. He had seen the same trio two days before, lying growling and bloody-mouthed in a heap of gnawed ribs. No doubt they would be feeding again before very long.

Behind him, on the far side of the miniature mountain that he had made his lookout post, was Prestimion's camp.

This new army was bigger than any of its predecessors, and continued to grow daily as volunteers from every part of Alhanroel came flocking to the rebel banner. Survivors of Prestimion's shattered army from the Iyann had been the first to enroll, and there were more of those than Prestimion had dared to suspect: gathered here, once again, were Duke Miaule of Hither Miaule, and golden-haired Spalirises of Tumbrax, and sturdy Gynim of Tapilpil with his band of sling-casters, and many others of that hardy crew, every one of them brimming with tales of their escape from the raging flood-waters and all athrob with desire for vengeance on the cowardly enemy who had brought the reservoir tumbling down upon them.

But there were others, now, a myriad of others: a legion of men from the southern lands, Stoien and Aruachosia and Vrist, and a host from misty Vrambikat that was far to the east on the other side of Castle Mount, and men of towns at the base of the Mount itself, Megenthorp and Bevel and Da, and troops of the city of Matrician where Fengiraz, whose mother had been the dearest childhood friend of Prestimion's mother, had his flourishing dukedom, and Gornoth Gehayn and his fearless sons, with their trained hieraxes, out of the west country to serve as airborne spies. And still more came every day; and every day Prestimion and Gialaurys and Septach Melayn toiled from dusk to dark to weld them into a single force that would shortly begin its march eastward to make war against the false Coronal.

Some of these men had come to Gloyn out of love of Prestimion, and some out of anger over the illicit taking of the throne by Korsibar, and a good many because they had heard the whispered tales now circulating of Korsibar's being a Metamorph in disguise and would not allow such a thing to stand. Some were only looking for adventure; some hoped to better their lot. And more than a few had given allegiance to Prestimion's force of rebels out of simple repugnance for Korsibar's dastardly breaking of the Mavestoi Dam. In that last group was a contingent of farmers of the Iyann Valley, all of whom had lost kinsmen in the flooding, and who, although they were not in any way soldierly by inclination or training, had come to Gloyn bearing hatchets and spades and pitchforks and whatever other implements of husbandry they thought could be put to good use against the usurper and his army.

It was a wondrous fine army that was coming together here, and Svor, looking back upon it from his hilltop place, was greatly gladdened to see it spread out here below him, parading up and down and practicing its maneuvers of attack and defense. The knowledge that Prestimion had regained his sense of purpose after those dark months in Triggoin gave Svor great joy; for it was the hope of his heart that his friend would prosper and triumph and take his rightful place on the Confalume Throne.

But for his own part Svor had had a sufficiency of observing these military matters lately and wanted a little respite from them. Since he was no soldier himself, he had little role in this drilling and marching and drawing up of battle plans, nor did he take much pleasure in the responsibilities assigned to him; and his own idleness was coming to chafe him. He longed for his rooms in the Castle, for his books and his charts of the stars, and for his ladies. Especially for them; for great energy coursed through Duke Svor's wiry little body, energy that he long ago had learned was most readily released in a woman's arms. In his day he had had covert romantic passages with many a great lady of the Castle, and many a tryst in the

surrounding cities of the Mount, and even in the grim Labyrinth he had managed to find companions in pleasure.

But there were no women in Prestimion's camp at Gloyn,
nor were there cities nearby where he might find any. Restlessness was growing in Svor, now, on that account. Which was
why he had gone riding out this day by himself into the
savanna that lay north and west of the camp, not with any
goal in mind, but only to rid himself, if he could, of the
tension that his idleness and his solitary nights in this place
had engendered in him.

So he had borrowed a mount from the cavalry stockade
and had come up here atop this little mountain to look out
into the open country beyond the camp; and now, choosing
his destination randomly, he went riding off into the adjacent
valley where that herd of vongiforin was grazing.

It was low-lying, somewhat moist country in there. The
vongiforin were innumerable, a sea of them stretching off to
the horizon, with occasional sub-herds of klimbergeysts and
other animals grazing among them. They were all peaceful
beasts, and they moved obligingly aside, making unmusical
little snorting sounds, as Svor's mount made its way through
their midst. He rode for perhaps half an hour in a
northwesterly direction. Then, seeing another of the little
island-mountains before him, he tethered his mount at its base
and scrambled up the side of it to survey the terrain that lay
still farther beyond him.

A surprising sight greeted him there.

Another valley lay below, a broad expanse of coppery
gattaga-grass divided here and there by small streams. In the
midst of it, some three hundred yards to the north, Svor was
startled to behold a dusty and somewhat dented floater sitting
at a sorry angle in a boggy patch, as though it had been
allowed to drive too close to the surface of the land and had
fouled its rotors with mud. Two women stood beside it—

young ones, from the looks of them. There did not seem to be anyone else with them. One was fair-haired, one was dark; and even at this distance Svor could see by their stance that they were troubled and perplexed by the plight of their vehicle.

Two women, traveling alone by floater in this unpopulated trackless countryside of vongimorins and klimbergeysts and sharp-clawed kepjitaljis? An unlikely sight; but one that definitely bore investigation.

Svor hurried back to his mount and rode quickly toward the stranded floater.

# 7

There was no vegetation here other than grass and the women saw him coming when he was still some distance away. They stared and pointed at him, and moved cautiously together against the flank of the floater as Svor approached. Yes, definitely young, Svor saw now. Shabbily dressed, but both of them quite shapely, and they carried themselves well. The dark-haired one in particular, he thought, held herself with great elegance and self-possession. But what in the name of the Divine were they doing here? This was no place for women. The only likely explanation was that they had journeyed here unbidden to be with their lovers or husbands in Prestimion's army, which was a rash and unwise thing for them to have done.

And then he was close enough to make out their faces. "By all the gods and demons!" Svor cried hoarsely, astonished beyond all reckoning. "My lady," he said. "How did *you* come to be—"

"Get down from that mount and stand beside it with both your hands in the air," Thismet said. She gripped a small energy-thrower in her hand, aimed at the mid-point of his chest.

"My lady, I am unarmed," Svor said, quickly dismounting. "And I would mean you no harm in any case. Please—that weapon is dangerous—"

"Just stand where you are, my lord duke." Her face seemed cold and hard. "I'm looking for Prestimion's camp."

"Behind us." He gestured with his head. The energy-thrower struck cold dread into him; he wished she would put it aside.

"Far?"

"Less than an hour's ride."

"Take us there, Svor."

"Of course, my lady. If you please, the weapon—there is no need—"

"I suppose." She lowered the energy-thrower and slipped it into a holder at her side. Her voice softened a little. "I was afraid you might slay us out of hand, thinking I was doing some spying for my brother. But spying is hardly my purpose in coming here."

Svor wondered if he dared ask her what that purpose was. Her presence here was altogether mystifying. They had not had an easy journey of it, that much was sure. Both Thismet and Melithyrrh were grimy and drawn and disheveled to a degree that made them almost unrecognizable. The simple peasant clothes that they wore were dirty and torn; their faces were stained, their hair was all asnarl; they both looked badly undernourished and they did not seem to have slept for several days. The intensity of Thismet's great beauty, shining through the blowziness, was undiminished. But she was a frightful sight and the Lady Melithyrrh no better. Why in the world had they come? Could their presence here be part of some deadly trick that the enemy had devised? He could see the little dagger that was fastened along the inside of her arm, showing through where the sleeve of her blouse was torn. But even if she had no sinister ideas in mind, the sudden appearance of Korsibar's sister at Gloyn was incomprehensible.

Lowering his arms, Svor caught hold of the reins of his mount.

"I can carry only one of you at a time, my lady."

"I'll wait here by the floater," Melithyrrh said immediately. "Take my lady, and send someone back here quickly for me."

"Is this agreeable to you?" he asked Thismet.

"It will have to be," she said. "Tell me, Svor: How does Prince Prestimion fare?"

"Well, my lady. Very well."

"He has a goodly army assembled by now, does he?"

"I ask your pardon. You'll have to judge that for yourself. I must regard you as an enemy, lady, and I ought not be telling you details of—"

"I'm not an enemy, Svor."

He stared and said nothing.

"My brother's a fool and his advisers are villains. I want no further part of any of them. Why do you think Melithyrrh and I have come traveling halfway across Alhanroel to be here? A nightmare of a trip it was, too. Sleeping in the most horrid of hovels, eating the most dreadful slop, fending off the advances of any number of coarse, vulgar—" She paused. "And then to wreck the floater just a few miles from the end of our journey! We were at our wits' end, Svor, when you came along.—Is there a place nearby, do you think, where I could wash myself a little before you take me before Prestimion? This coating of filth I have on me disgusts me. I haven't bathed in two days, or perhaps three. Never before in my life have I been as dirty as this."

"A stream lies just over there," Svor said, nodding to his left.

"Show us."

He led them a hundred feet through the thick grass. It was the stream that fed the bog in which they had stranded their floater; its flow was swift and clean.

"Stand over there by your mount," said Thismet. "Turn your back and keep it turned."

"I give you my word," Svor said.

Only once while they were bathing did he steal a look at them, and that when he could no longer force himself not to. A single glance over his shoulder showed him the two of them knee-deep in the stream, incandescently naked, Melithyrrh with her back to him scooping up water in her shirt and pouring it over Thismet, who stood turned to one side. The sight of Melithyrrh's pale full buttocks and the Lady Thismet's round flawless breasts seared itself unforgettably into Svor's mind, and after all these weeks of solitary life it left him weak-kneed and trembling.

"Are you all right, Svor?" asked Thismet, when she and Melithyrrh, looking cleaner and much refreshed, returned from the stream's edge. "You seem sickly, all of a sudden."

"I had an ague last week," he said. "I am not fully recovered from it, I suppose." He assisted Thismet into the saddle of the mount, and hopped up close behind her, his thighs against her haunches, his arm tight around her waist. This too stirred him close to madness. He called out to the Lady Melithyrrh not to wander from the place, but to remain by the floater until someone had come for her, and spurred the mount forward.

As they made their way through the thick herds of vongi-forin and klimbergeysts Svor said, after a time, "You are completely estranged from your brother, my lady?"

"It would not be far wrong to put it that way. I left the Castle without notifying him, but Korsibar must know by now where I've gone. A day came, suddenly, when I could no longer stand being there among them all. A loathing for the place rose in my throat, and I thought, *We were wrong to take the throne from Prestimion. It was a terrible sin against the will of the Divine. I'll go to him and tell him that, and beg his forgiveness.* Which is what I mean to do. Do you think he'll accept it, Svor?"

"Prince Prestimion has only the kindest thoughts for you, my lady," Svor said mildly. "I have no doubt he'll be pleased and delighted beyond all measure to hear of your change of heart."

But he wondered again if this were all some elaborate scheme of Korsibar's against Prestimion—or, what was more likely, a plot of Dantirya Sambail's on Korsibar's behalf. How could it be, though? What possible benefit could accrue to Korsibar from sending his sister and her lady-of-honor across thousands of miles by themselves to Prestimion's camp? Did she have some wild notion of thrusting that dagger of hers into Prestimion's heart the moment she came within reach of him? Somehow Svor did not want to believe that of her. Especially when he sat here like this astride the mount staring at the slender nape of her neck, with his thighs pressed up against her flesh and his arm grasping her middle just below her breasts.

His mind was lost for a moment in a frenzied swirl of desire and impossible yearning. And then he found himself saying softly, into the lovely ear that was only inches from his lips, "My lady, may I tell you something?"

"What is it, Svor?"

"If you are truly of our faction now, lady, then it may be that I can offer you my protection in this unkind place."

"Your protection, Svor?" Her head was turned away from him; but it seemed to him that she was smiling. "Why, what protection would you be, in this camp of rough soldiers?"

He chose not to take offense. "I mean that you would have my company, that you would not be left alone to be troubled by others who might come upon you, my lady. Do I make myself fully clear?" He was trembling like a lovesick boy, he who had made his way through life always with a clear confident sense of how to attain his destination. "Let me tell you, lady, that ever since I first came to the Castle, I have felt the deepest and most honorable love for—"

"Oh, Svor. Not you too!"

That was not encouraging. But he pushed desperately onward, letting the words spill out unchecked. "Of course I could say nothing of it, especially after the coolness began to develop between your brother and the prince. But at all times, lady, have I looked upon you with unequaled delight—with great love in my heart—with a sincere and eager and all-consuming desire to claim you for my own—"

With surprising gentleness in her tone Thismet said, "And to how many women before me, Svor, have you professed the same sincere and eager desire?"

"I speak not only of desire but of marriage, my lady. And the answer to your question is, not one, not a single one."

She was silent for a time that seemed to tick on for ten thousand years. Then she said, "This is a passing odd place to be asking for my hand, my lord duke: crunched together as we are on this mount, riding through the back end of nowhere with wild animals snorting and snuffling all about us, me in rags and you clutching me from behind. Farquanor, at least, made *his* proposal in more appropriate surroundings."

"Farquanor?" In horror.

"Oh, don't worry, Svor. I refused him. Indignantly, as a matter of fact. I refuse you more kindly, for you are a better man than Farquanor by far. But you are not for me. I'm not sure whether there's a man who is; but at any rate I know you are not the one. Take that without bitterness, Svor, and let's speak no more of this ever again."

"So be it," said Svor, as amazed at his own temerity in having let all this pour forth from him as he was by the softness of her response.

"You might apply yourself to the Lady Melithyrrh," Thismet said, a little while afterward. "Now that she and I are no longer at court, she feels greatly adrift; and she might look favorably on your advances. Whether she wants a husband, I can't say; but whether you truly want a wife is equally doubtful. I think you might do well to approach her, at least."

"I thank you for the suggestion, my lady."

"I wish you well with it, Svor." And then, a bit later, as though she had not already asked it just a short time before: "Will Prince Prestimion believe that my repentance is sincere, do you think?"

Prestimion had not felt such astonishment since the day so long ago when he had come striding into the Court of Thrones to see Korsibar seated on the Coronal's seat with the starburst crown on his head. Thismet here in the camp? Asking him to see him now, alone in his tent?

It seemed unreal that she could be here in this remote place. Surely it must be the work of sorcerers, this apparition that stood before him now. But no, she was real, he felt no doubt of that. Dressed in little more than rags, she was. Her hair unkempt. Devoid of all jewelry, all cosmetic adornment. Her face drawn and weary. She looked now more like a scullery-maid than like the daughter of one king and the sister of another; but the regal grace of her, the fiery eyes, those lips, the finely molded features, all told him that this was the undeniable Thismet. Here. Against all probability, here in Gloyn.

"I should tell you, my lord, that I come into your presence armed," she said. She drew back her tattered sleeve, revealing the little scabbard that was attached to her arm. Unclipping it, she tossed it casually across to Svor. "That was only to defend myself while I traveled, my lord. I am not here to do you harm. There are no other weapons on me." She smiled, in a sly inviting way that sent shivers through him. "I am willing to be searched, if you wish it."

But something other than her flirtatiousness had caught his attention. "Twice now you have called me 'my lord.' What do you mean by that phrase, Thismet?"

"Why, what everyone means by it, my lord. The same that is meant by this." And she raised both her hands in the starburst gesture, smiling all the while and staring directly into Prestimion's eyes.

He said slowly, after a bit, "You repudiate your brother's claim, do you, Thismet?"

"That I do most sincerely, my lord."

"Call me Prestimion, as before."

"Prestimion, then. As before." Her eyes flashed. It was like staring into lightning. "But I recognize you as Coronal Lord of Majipoor. Those clownish men at the Castle—those fools and villains—I have no allegiance to them any longer."

"Come closer," Prestimion said.

Svor, who was watching from a discreet distance, said, "Perhaps it would be a good idea to search her first, my lord."

"You think?" Prestimion smiled. "Another dagger hidden on her somewhere, is that it?"

"Come and search me, then, Prestimion!" Thismet said, her eyes bright as beacons. "Who knows? I may have a second dagger hidden here"—and she placed her hand between her breasts— "or *here*." With her hand against the base of her belly, fingers splayed out wide. "Come look, my lord! See whether I'm still armed!"

"You have weapons enough on you, I think," said Prestimion, "and those are indeed the places where you carry them. And I do believe I'm in great peril from them." He grinned and said, "Since I have your leave to do it, Thismet, I think I will conduct a little search for them, yes."

"My lord—" said Svor.

"Peace," Prestimion said to him. And to Thismet: "But first tell me truly why you're here."

"Why, to forge an alliance with you," she said, blunt and outspoken now, not an atom of coquettishness in her tone. "There was a time when I wanted Korsibar to be king in your place, not because I thought you were unworthy of it, but only because I was hungry to see my brother on the throne. That was a great error, and it shames me now to think of the role I played in bringing it about. He is still my brother and I still have a sister's love for him; but he should never have been king. I'll proclaim that gladly before all the world. Standing by your side, Prestimion, I'll hail you as Coronal Lord."

He thought he understood her now.

"And what role do you see for yourself," he asked carefully, "when I am on the Confalume Throne?"

"I have been a Coronal's daughter and a Coronal's sister," she said. "No one in all our history could have said such a thing before me. I would set myself apart even further from all others by becoming a Coronal's consort as well."

From Svor came a gasp. Prestimion himself was taken aback by her straightforwardness. There was no coy diplomacy here, only the directness of ultimate will.

"I see," he said. "An alliance of the most literal sort." And saw in the eye of his mind not the weary travelworn Thismet who stood before him now, but the radiant glorious Thismet of the Castle, dressed in some fine gown of thin white satin with glittering bands of gold about her throat; and then, still in his mind's eye, the light of tall tapers came shining through that gown from behind her and laid bare to him the supple curves of breast and belly and thigh. Such a torrent of passion came crashing through his soul in that instant that for a moment Prestimion thought he was below the Mavestoi Dam once again and the reservoir was pouring down upon him a second time.

Then he glanced toward Svor. Saw the warning look; the troubled frown. Svor, the man of ladies, so knowing in all the ways of desire, telling him, no doubt, to beware the sorceries of this woman's body, which might well be more powerful than the most potent spell known to the high magus Gominik Halvor or any of his colleagues in the realm of magic.

Yes. Very likely. But still—still—

Then Thismet said, into the continuing silence, "My lord, if I might have an hour to myself, and a basin of warm water, and my clean clothes brought to me from the floater that lies wrecked in the valley beyond this one—"

"Of course. To be done at once. Go into my tent, Thismet."

"We already have sent for the baggage from the floater," Svor said. "And also for the Lady Melithyrrh, who waits there with it."

Prestimion nodded. "Good." And to the aide-de-camp Nilgir Sumanand, who was nearby, he said, "See to it that the Lady Thismet is given all that she needs to refresh herself. She's had a long and difficult journey here."

Svor said, when the others had gone inside, "What will you do, Prestimion?"

"What do you think I'll do? What would you do yourself, in my place?"

"I understand," said Svor. "Who would resist?" A thin rueful smile. Softly Svor said, "I won't conceal from you, my friend, that I'm in love with her myself. Long have been. As has everyone else at the Castle, I suppose. But I'll content myself, like the good subordinate I am, with the Lady Melithyrrh."

"One could do worse," said Prestimion.

"Indeed." Svor glanced toward the tent. "You trust yourself alone with her?"

"I think so. Yes. I don't really expect her to try to murder me."

"Very likely not. But she is dangerous, Prestimion."

"Perhaps so. It's a risk I'll take."

"And if all goes well, will you actually make her your consort, do you think?"

Prestimion smiled and clapped Svor on the shoulder. "One thing at a time, Svor, one thing at a time! But it would make good political sense, wouldn't it? The triumphant Lord Prestimion taking the daughter of the Pontifex Confalume as his bride, to close the breach in the commonwealth that foolish Korsibar has opened? I like that idea. Good political sense, yes. But also—the lady, purely for her own sake—"

"As you said just now, Prestimion, one could do worse."

"One could, indeed."

He told Svor then that he wanted some time alone; and Svor withdrew.

Drawing his cloak about him, Prestimion paced by himself undisturbed through the camp, revolving in his mind this strange new turn of events.

Thismet!

How odd, how unexpected. She was using him, of course, for some manner of revenge against Korsibar; no doubt Korsibar had disappointed her in something, or perhaps had tried to force her into a marriage that was not to her liking, or in any event had created enough displeasure in her to send her racing across the world to the arms of his great enemy. Well, so be it. It was surely possible for them to come to terms, for their mutual benefit. They understood each other, Thismet and he. She would use him, and he would use her. There was no better match for him to make, and all the world knew it.

And then, of course, questions of politics aside, there was Thismet herself to weigh into the bargain. That fiery, passionate woman whom he had watched hungrily from a distance for so long: coming to him at last, here, now. Offering herself to him. He had lived like a monk long enough. This was not something lightly to be refused.

"Prestimion? Is that you, all muffled up in that cloak?"

Septach Melayn, it was, coming up behind him. "Yes," he said. "You've spied me out."

"Svor has told me about Thismet."

"Yes."

"She's the most beautiful woman in the world, I suppose. I do congratulate you. But trouble follows her wherever she goes."

"I know that, Septach Melayn."

"Do we want that trouble following us right into the midst of our army, Prestimion? Here on the eve of battle, practically?"

"Let me be the judge of that."

"Gialaurys and I have just been speaking of this, and——"

"Well, speak no more. She's bathing in my tent, and when she's ready to be visited I intend to go to her there, and let such trouble follow me as it will. But speak no more." Prestimion went up beside Septach Melayn and laid his hand on the other man's arm, just by the wrist. Gently he said, smiling all the while, but there was more than a little force in his tone also, "Listen to me, old friend. I don't instruct you in how to use your sword. Pray don't instruct me in the use of mine."

And then at last they stood face to face, alone in his tent. She had bathed, and had changed into a simple sheer white gown, with nothing beneath. He could see the dark points of her nipples rising against its thin fabric, and the deeper darkness at her loins. Yet without her jewelry and cosmetic adornments there was a strange purity about her now: an odd word to use in connection with Thismet, purity, but there it was.

The bravado she had displayed an hour before, inviting him to search her for concealed weapons and all of that, seemed entirely gone from her. To Prestimion she appeared tense, uncertain, almost frightened. He had never seen her like that before, not ever. But he understood. He felt somewhat like that himself. The possibility suddenly took wing in him that there might be something more to their coming together than blunt conspiratorial power-hunger, and something more to it, too, than mere physical gratification. Perhaps. Perhaps.

She said, "I was the one put Korsibar up to taking the crown. Did you know that, Prestimion? I stood behind him and pushed. He would never have done it, but for me."

"Dantirya Sambail said something of the sort to me about that," he said. "It makes no difference. This is not the moment to speak of it."

"It was a great mistake. I know that now. He was not a fitting man to be king."

"This isn't the moment to speak of such matters," Prestimion said again. "Leave them for the historians to discuss, Thismet." He took a step toward her, arms outstretched. Coolly she waved him away, telling him with a quick gesture to remain where he was. And then, with a smile that was like the sun emerging after a storm, she slipped the sheer white gown from her body and stood bare before him.

She seemed so small: scarcely breast-high to him, with slender limbs, and a waist that emphasized the fragility of her body by the sharpness of its inward curve above the flaring hips. And yet even so her body looked taut and trim and strong, an athlete's body, wide shoulders like her brother's, lean sinewy muscles, elegant graceful proportions. But for all that she was utterly feminine. Her breasts were small but full and round and high, with little hard nipples, virginal-looking ones. Her skin was dusky. Her hair below had the same glossy glint as above, a dense, curling black thatch.

She was perfect. He had never imagined such beauty.

"So many years we were strangers to each other," she murmured. " 'Good morning, Lady Thismet,' you would say, and I, 'Hello, Prince Prestimion,' and that was all. All those years at the Castle, nothing more than that. What a waste! What a sad and foolish waste of our youth!"

"We're still young, Thismet. There's plenty of time to make new beginnings now." Once more he stepped close to her, and this time she made no retreat. His hands ran across the satin smoothness of her skin. She pressed her lips tight to his and he felt the fiery dart of her tongue, and her fingers raking his back.

"Prestimion—Prestimion—"

"Yes."

# 8

Two more weeks passed in the camp at Gloyn. Then came word from the scouts Prestimion maintained all across the land that Lord Korsibar had come down out of the Mount with an enormous army and had begun marching westward. The hierax-riding sons of Gornath Gehayn went aloft on the backs of their giant birds and confirmed it: a great troop of warriors, coming this way.

A pair of messages reached Prestimion's camp not long afterward, written on the crisp parchment paper used by Coronals, and bearing the starburst seal.

One was addressed to Prestimion himself, and warned him to end his rebellion once and for all and surrender himself immediately to the nearest agents of the government so that he might be put on trial for treason. The penalty for failure to surrender, Prestimion was told, was death upon capture for him and for all his high captains who claimed allegiance to him; if he alone yielded himself now, the lives of his chief officers would be spared.

The other message was for the Lady Thismet. It informed her that her august and gracious brother the Coronal Lord Korsibar forgave her for her transgression in having gone to consort with the enemy, and was herewith offering her a pledge of safe conduct across the continent if she chose to return to the Castle and resume her former life of ease and content at the court.

"Well, then," Prestimion said lightheartedly, when he had read both these documents aloud to his officers, "our choices are clear, aren't they? I'll leave for the eastern provinces at once, and go before Korsibar wherever I find him and throw myself upon his mercy. And I'll take his sister with me and deliver her up safely to him, notifying him with solemn oaths that I return her in the same condition in which she came to me."

There was laughter from all sides of the campfire, and the loudest of all came from Thismet.

The wine, no fine Muldemar stuff now but only the good rough blue-gray wine of nearby Chistiok Province that came in long flasks made of klimbergeyst-leather, was passed around the circle once again, and they all sat quietly for a while, drinking. Then Gialaurys said, "Do you intend to wait here for Korsibar to come here to us, Prestimion, or do you think it's better to carry the war to him wherever we find him?"

"To him," said Prestimion unhesitatingly. "This flat country is no place to fight a great battle. We'd all go running foolishly hither and yon."

"And it would disturb the animals of these pleasant plains," said Septach Melayn. "They've had enough trouble on our account already. Prestimion's right: we go to him."

Prestimion looked about the group.

"Is there opposition? I hear none. Very well: we break camp at dawn tomorrow."

That was a massive task, for it was a mighty army now that had come together in the peaceful Vale of Gloyn. It took more than a single day to strike the tents and load the floaters and wagons and assemble the pack-animals and get the great eastward journey under way.

But a far mightier army, by all reports of Prestimion's agents in the field, was heading toward them. Not only had Korsibar mobilized the general army of the provinces surrounding the Mount, but also he had at his service the armies brought from Zimroel by Dantirya Sambail under the command of his brothers Gaviad and Gaviundar, and, furthermore, the private forces controlled by the lords Oljebbin, Gonivaul, and Serithorn.

"Even Serithorn!" Prestimion said. "Gonivaul I can understand: he's never been a great friend of mine. Oljebbin, well, he's cousin to Korsibar's father, after all. But Serithorn—Serithorn—"

"This is Dantirya Sambail's doing," said Septach Melayn. "Since the breaking of the dam, he's been at the Castle, stirring up the lords into confusion. Surely they're all frightened of opposing him. If Dantirya Sambail has cast in his lot with Korsibar, how can they dare do otherwise?"

"Which says much for the power of family ties," Duke Svor observed. "For the Procurator, as I recall, is some cousin of yours, is he not, Prestimion?"

"A very distant one," replied Prestimion. "And growing more distant every hour. Well, it makes no difference, a few more private armies here and there standing with Korsibar. The people are with us, eh? The world's had nothing but trouble since Korsibar made himself Coronal, and everyone knows it. The hands of citizens lifted against citizens, the crops falling off because men are marching up and down bearing weapons when they should be tilling the fields, the government in paralysis—an inept Coronal and a bewildered Pontifex—"

"There's the most pitiful thing of all," said Gialaurys. "Old Confalume who was such a splendid Coronal, now reduced to wreck and ruin as he hides in the Labyrinth while his magnificent worthless son brings the world down around himself! What must he think? I feel such sorrow, that Confalume's great reign should have ended in this miserable turmoil."

Svor said, "Perhaps he perceives very little of what's been going on. I like to think that some magus of Korsibar's—Sanibak-Thastimoon, most likely—has cast a perpetual veil over his mind, and the old man goes through his days and nights as though in a dream. But it's sad all the same, for those of us who remember what Confalume once was."

"Sad indeed, Svor. What a strange road we've all traveled since then!—Yes, boy?" Prestimion said.

A messenger had come running up, bearing a rolled scroll in his hand. Prestimion took it from him and read it through.

"A new edict from Lord Korsibar, is it?" Septach Melayn asked.

"No, nothing like that. It's from our venerable maguses Gomrik Halvor and his son. They've cast the runes for our enterprise. The most auspicious place for us to engage Korsibar in battle, they say, is between the Trikkalas and the Mount, at a place called Thegomar Edge, by Stifgad Lake in the province of Ganibairda."

"I know that place," said Gynim of Tapilpil. "We reach it by way of Sisivondal, and southeastward from there in the direction of Ludin Forest. The people there raise stajja and lusavender, and other such basic things. That's where your strongest support lies, my lord, with the farming folk who want nothing more than for the world to return to normal."

"Then we'll take ourselves to Thegomar Edge," Prestimion said, "and invite Korsibar to visit us there."

"Tell me, Prestimion," said Septach Melayn, "do the good mages offer us any reading of the omens foretelling the success of our venture?"

"Oh, yes," Prestimion said, with the quickest of glances at the scroll in his hand, a mere flick of his eyes. "Everything augurs favorably for us. On our way, then! The province of Ganibairda! Stifgad Lake! Thegomar Edge!"

The eastward march had something of the character of a grand processional about it for Prestimion. The people of the cities along his path hailed him almost everywhere as a liberator as he rode in an open floater in their midst with Thismet beside him, and cheered him onward to his rendezvous with Korsibar.

These were the people who had felt such fear when news first went out that the Pontifex Prankipin was dying; and those fears had proved to be justified. Trouble of some sort would follow the old emperor's death, they had believed; and the trouble had come. Their maguses had told them that there would be chaos; and there was. From every province came reports of factional strife, diminished crops, widespread anxiety and even panic.

It was clear to Prestimion that the people of Majipoor were sorely weary by now of the strife between the rival kings, which had brought such harm to the general prosperity in this time of uncertainty and hostility. And also he saw that the enormity of Korsibar's sin in appointing himself Coronal had belatedly had its impact on the common folk of the world. A growing number of them now understood Korsibar to be the author of their troubles, and not just those who subscribed to the tale of his being a secret Shapeshifter, though there were plenty enough of those. There was no one who did not desperately want the world to be restored. They looked to Prestimion as the one to put things in balance.

And also there were the nightly sendings of the Lady Kunigarda, attacking Korsibar and Confalume and praising Prestimion. Kunigarda's words still carried great weight in the world, especially since the new Lady of the Isle, Roxivail, had not yet begun to speak to their minds. Roxivail had taken possession of the Isle, it seemed; but she had not yet managed to establish herself there in the functions of the Lady.

Despite all these things in his favor, Prestimion felt no assurance that the crown of Majipoor was going to topple into his hand like ripe fruit from a tree. The people might be with him, yes. Popular support for his cause might well be increasing every day. But there was no automatic victory in that. It still remained for him to deal with the full power of Korsibar's army. An awesome foe waited for him in the east.

The journey east retraced of necessity much of the route that Thismet and Melithyrrh had taken during their flight from the Castle. The women were not at all pleased at that, seeing all those drab rural places once again that stirred such dark memories of hardship in them, but there was no help for it, and at least they were traveling this time in more comfort and safety than before. One city after another went by: Khatrian, Fristh, Drone, Hunzimar—Gannamunda, Kessilroge, Skeil— they were in the dry dusty plateau of Sisivondal now, and then Sisivondal city—

At Sisivondal, that dreary place of giant warehouses of a single design, where the streets were lined with grim dull camaganda palms and prosaic lumma-lumma bushes by way of decoration, the cultists who went by the name of the Beholders staged a great festival for Prestimion, what they called the Procession of the Mysteries. It would have been a grave insult to refuse, and so he let himself be given the place of honor as the singers and dancers came forth, the girls in white who scattered halatinga blossoms on the ground, the giantess in winged costume who bore the two-headed holy wooden staff, the veiled initiates with waxed and shaven heads.

The mayor of the city explained each step in the ceremony to him, and Prestimion nodded solemnly and watched with the greatest show of deep interest. Impassively he looked on, saying little, as the sacred implements of the Beholders were carried before him, the lamp of flame, the serpent of palm fronds, the disembodied human hand with the middle finger bent backward, and the enormous male organ carved from wood and all the rest. Even after Triggoin, Prestimion found these things unsettling. There was a madness to the frenzy of the dancers, and a strangeness to the objects they revered, that were difficult for him to accept.

"Behold and worship!" the marchers cried.

And, while Prestimion watched in silence, the answering cry came from the onlookers: "We behold! We behold!"

The Ark of the Mysteries was next, carried on a wooden pole by two great Skandars, and then, on his cart of ebony and silver, the masked Messenger of the Mysteries himself, naked, painted black down one side and gold down the other, carrying the serpent-entwined staff of his power in one hand and a whip in the other.

"Behold and worship!" the Messenger cried.

And from the Mayor of Sisivondal at Prestimion's side came the response: "We behold! We behold!"

Thismet cried it also, this time: "We behold! We behold!" And nudged Prestimion sharply with her elbow, and nudged him again, until at last he cried it out too: "We behold!"


And now Thegomar Edge, by Stifgad Lake, in Ganibairda.

In this place a high hill, steep and heavily forested on its eastern face, sloped down more gently to the west into a broad marshy region called Beldak that had the lake lying at its back. The road from the west came running around the border of the lake and traversed the marsh to ascend the Thegomar hill, going across the summit of it near its southern side.

All during the night Prestimion marched eastward through the farming land of Ganibairda Province toward Thegomar, and just at dawn, as he was nearing the western shore of the lake, news was brought to him that Korsibar was already here with his formidable force and in position on the hill.

"How did they know we were heading this way?" Septach Melayn demanded angrily. "Who is the spy in our midst? Smoke him out, and flay him alive!"

"We are not the only ones with scouts in the field," said Prestimion calmly. "Or maguses to search for the omens, for that matter. We have our information and Korsibar has his. It makes no difference."

"But he holds the high ground," Septach Melayn pointed out.

Prestimion was undisturbed even by that. "We've charged high places from below before, haven't we? And this time he has no reservoir to drop on us."

He gave the command, and they continued their advance into Beldak marsh as the morning was born above them.

By first light they could see Korsibar's forces on high. The whole crest of the hill seemed to be bristling with the spears of an infinite sea of men. At the center, two gigantic banners were unfurled: the green-and-gold one that marked the presence of the Coronal of Majipoor, and just to its side a second one in royal blue and vivid scarlet on which was emblazoned the dragon emblem of the ancient family to which Korsibar belonged. Other banners fluttered elsewhere on the hill: one at the northern end that Prestimion recognized as Serithorn's, with Oljebbin's a little way to the south of it, and the banner of Gonivaul beyond that.

And on the far side of Korsibar's dragon-banner, down by the southern end of Thegomar Edge, there rose a rippling banner of pale crimson nearly as great in size as Korsibar's own, with a blood-red moon in its center. It was the banner of the clan of Dantirya Sambail. Prestimion had never thought to see that banner arrayed against him.

He ordered the deployment of the troops to begin at once. In mid-morning, while this was still under way, a man came riding out from Korsibar's side of the field bearing a herald's white flag. The message he carried was from the Grand Admiral Gonivaul, who called upon Prestimion to send a representative to mid-field for an immediate parley. He suggested Duke Svor as an appropriate choice, indeed particularly requested that Svor be sent.

"Gonivaul's forsworn six times over," Gialaurys said at once. "Why waste breath parleying with any such as he?"

"And what will he offer us?" Septach Melayn asked. "Pardons for all, and great estates at the Mount, if we swear to be good children and make no more trouble in the land? Send him your glove, Prestimion."

But Prestimion shook his head. "We should hear what they have to tell us. It does us no harm to listen. Svor, will you go?"

The little duke shrugged. "If you wish me to, of course I will."

So Svor rode out to a point in the middle of the open field, and waited there a time, and eventually he caught sight of Gonivaul descending the hill road and approaching him over the marshy ground. The Grand Admiral was so bulked out in armor that he seemed more burly even than Farholt or Gialaurys, and his helmet came down over his forehead so that nothing showed of his face except his eyes and dense black beard. His long jutting jaw thrust outward at Svor like a javelin.

He dropped down heavily beside his mount and for a time simply stood staring at Svor, who waited in silence. Then the Admiral said, "I come at Korsibar's request, and he specifically asked that I speak with you. He loves you still, Svor: do you know that? He talks often of the friendship that there was between the two of you in days gone by. He greatly fears that harm will come to you in the battle today. That possibility much disturbs him."

"Why, then," said Svor, "if that's how he feels, he can disband his troops and take himself elsewhere in peace, and all will be well."

Gonivaul did not seem amused. "The Coronal Lord Korsibar has sent me out here because he offers his hand to you in peace, Svor. For once, put your mockery aside. It may save your life."

"Is that what this parley is about? Nothing more than a personal invitation to me to surrender?"

"Not to surrender, but to return your allegiance to the great lord who once was your friend. Prestimion's doomed, Svor. We know that and in your heart you must surely know that too. Look at our army, and the position it occupies. Look at his. You know what today's outcome will be. Why die for him? When we die, we are dead forever, Svor. The dead drink no wine and they know no lovers' embraces."

"The last time I saw you," said Svor, "it was in Muldemar House, where we all drank wine aplenty, especially you, and I listened to you pledge yourself most warmly to Prestimion. You would do your duty, you told him, and help return the world to the proper path. You would do so whatever risk to your personal position might be entailed. Those were your own words, Admiral. Of course, you were a little tipsy when you spoke them, but that was what you said. I see that the pursuit of your duty has somehow brought you to the side of the field opposite Prestimion's. And now you want me to do the same? To turn my back on him and come back over to the other side with you this minute?"

"Hardly that, Svor," said Gonivaul in a stony voice. "Nothing so blatant."

"What, then?"

"Remain on your side of the field during the battle. You can hardly do otherwise. But in the thick of the fray, go among Prestimion's captains and let them know one by one that they'll be treated well by Korsibar if they cast off their allegiance to Prestimion as the day goes along. Tell them there's no reason to give up their lives in a lost cause, and that rewards await them if they abandon it. Do it quietly; but do it. Provide us your cooperation and Korsibar will reward you beyond your wildest dreams, Svor. You need only make your request of him, and it will be yours. Nothing will be denied you. *Nothing*. Not even a place in the Coronal's own family, should you want that. Do you understand what I'm telling you, Svor?"

"I think that I do."

"Or else continue on your present course, and you'll surely die today on the battlefield, along with Prestimion and Septach Melayn and all the rest. That much is certain. The stars have shown us our victory. There can be no doubt of the outcome."

"None, eh?"

"None." Gonivaul undid his helmet, so that the thick fur of his head sprang from its confinement, and extended his hand to Svor. "You have our offer. Say to me that you'll give it thought; and then we should return to our places."

Svor touched his hand briefly to Gonivaul's.

"It will have the most careful consideration," he said. "Tell that to the Coronal Lord Korsibar. And tell him also that I remember the old days of our friendship with the greatest warmth."

He turned away and clambered atop his mount and rode back toward Prestimion's lines, thinking with some astonishment of what it would be like to be brother-in-law to the Coronal, and husband to the Lady Thismet; and all he would have to do to achieve it was to commit an act of treason against Prestimion no greater than those already done by Gonivaul and Oljebbin and Serithorn and Dantirya Sambail. A nice transaction, that would be. Treason was epidemic these days.

"Well?" Prestimion asked, when Svor had returned. "What was it that he told you?"

"That I would be well rewarded if I defected, and brought some of your captains over to Korsibar's side with me."

"Ah," said Prestimion. "He told you that. How well rewarded, exactly?"

"Very well indeed," said Svor simply, and no more than that.

"And what did you tell him, then?" asked Septach Melayn.

"Why, that I would give his offer the most careful consideration," said Svor. "No sensible man would have said anything else."

# 9

All that day and far into the night the two armies faced each other across Beldak marsh without moving; and as dawn drew near Prestimion gave the order for the ascent of Thegomar Edge.

"They are well set forth," said Septach Melayn.

"So I see. We'll strike again at their strongest point: break them there, and the rest will yield quickly enough."

The loyalist forces were ranged in one great solid mass from end to end of the hill's crest, packed shoulder to shoulder to form a solid wall of shields. Korsibar's frontmost men, clad in chain mail and wielding spears, javelins, two-edged swords, and heavy long-handled axes, were a fearsome sight. It was still too early to see what lay behind them, but Prestimion had intimations of an enormous horde of men, stretching on and on into the forest on the eastern side of Thegomar, and when the hierax-men went up on their birds they confirmed that guess: troops stretched out to the east as far as could be seen.

"The Divine be with you today," said Thismet, as he made ready to enter the field; and she kissed him tenderly in front of all the men. But he could see conflict and tension on her face, and fear lurking in her eyes, and he knew that her fear was not only for him. There was a bond between this brother and sister that he could only just begin to understand.

Prestimion's own force was drawn up in three divisions. In

the center were the battle-hardened men of the earlier contests, under his own command, with Septach Melayn and Gialaurys beside him. To his left were the troops of Spalirises of Tumbrax and the men of six foothill towns, with Prestimion's brother Abrigant in general charge, and on the other flank was Gynim of Tapilpil and his band of sling-casters at the apex of a mass of more recently recruited warriors. In each division the light-armed foot-soldiers armed with bows and crossbows were in the front, heavy-armed infantry with spears in the second rank, and cavalry in the rear.

"Up the slope, now," Prestimion ordered. "Smash through that wall of shields in our first assault, and we'll drive them panicking into the woods."

At first light the advance began, covered by Prestimion's archers. The arrows flew: uphill only, with little reply from above, for Korsibar evidently had very few archers in his force. The rebel foot-soldiers went running joyously toward the enemy with Prestimion's heavier infantry pounding along behind them, bellowing a raucous chant of victory.

But the shield-wall held. That line was stronger and far more determined than Prestimion had supposed.

His front line crashed against it and it staunchly stood its ground, an impenetrable barrier, and the attackers were met with a fierce tumult of missiles of every kind, javelins, lances, axes, spears, the whole ancient armamentarium of weaponry, more suited to some primitive land than to this great kingdom. And then in one place near its left end the wall of shields suddenly parted, and there came forth a battery of energy-throwers hurling bright red bolts into the rightmost wing of Prestimion's force. That was a frightening sight. Clumsy and difficult to use though the energy-throwers were, as likely to explode in the faces of their own handlers as to do damage to an enemy, nevertheless they raised a great clamor, and where they were effective at all they did terrible damage.

"Hold firm!" Prestimion cried. "They are untrustworthy things, those machines! It's scarcely possible to aim them straight!"

But it was hard to hold firm, and all but impossible to go forward, in the face of those bright destructive blurts of raw power, random and wild though they seemed to be. Few of Prestimion's men had faced energy-throwers before. The confidence that had carried them swiftly and eagerly uphill wavered and slipped from them. There was uncertainty among them; and soon there was disruption and then chaos on the rebel right flank, men giving way, breaking formation, turning and fleeing down the hill into the marshy land at the foot of the slope.

Prestimion could feel the turning of the tide almost as a tangible thing. It seemed to him that his entire force might be transformed in a moment from a confident advancing army into one in frantic retreat, and the battle lost right here. Already Korsibar's cavalry had come out from behind gaps in the shield-wall and was beginning a slow and steady advance down the hill, doing terrible damage as they came.

He rode back and forth, trying to be everywhere at once, even the front line, urging his men to hold steady. Then he heard his mount make a soft sighing sound of a kind he had never heard a mount make before, and it sank down on its forequarters so suddenly that he nearly was pitched forward over its head. A fountain of blood rushed from its breast where some lucky stroke of a spear had caught it. He freed himself from his stirrups just in time, leaping to the ground as the animal fell to its side.

"Prestimion! Behind you!"

He whirled with all his speed. And saw the cold eye and hatchet face of Mandralisca the poison-taster, rushing fiercely upon him with upraised sword. Prestimion managed a quick lunging parry, and parried another thrust instantly afterward. And another, and another, and another, without pause.

Dantirya Sambail has sent his man down into the heart of the battle particularly to kill me, Prestimion realized. I will bear that in mind later, if there is a later for me.

This Mandralisca, plainly, was a demon of a swordsman, every bit as good with steel as he had been that day at the Labyrinth games with the wooden baton. Prestimion had not forgotten the poison-taster's deft movements then, the dizzying feints and pivots, the swiftness of his wrists, the baton-strokes quick as lightning. Those skills of Mandralisca's had won Prestimion five crowns from Septach Melayn that day. But he had never expected to have them turned against him in deadly battle.

Mandralisca launched a new flurry of thrusts. Prestimion parried, and parried again, and managed a quick thrust of his own, which the poison-taster avoided with the greatest agility. Now Prestimion pressed his moment of advantage. Mandralisca was better on the attack than he was on defense, but his speed served him well enough in that quarter too; and after each parry he came back on the attack, as ferocious as before. Septach Melayn himself would have been hard put to deal with him. Prestimion knew of no one else about whom that could be said.

They moved back and forth across the crowded noisy field in a private little arena entirely their own. Quick as he himself was, it was all that Prestimion could do to ward off Mandralisca's diabolically swift thrusts. Again, again, again the sword came at him; each time Prestimion managed to parry, but only barely fast enough, and his own thrusts fell ever short of the mark as Mandralisca darted mockingly away from them. The poison-taster's speed was formidable; his handling of his weapon was unorthodox but masterly. It was impossible for Prestimion to pay heed to the battle while his own life was in jeopardy. He had a distant sense of swirling forces, of chaos everywhere; but for him the struggle had come down to a single opponent.

And for a moment it seemed that all was up for him. The poison-taster came at him with such a dazzling flurry of thrusts, seemingly from five directions at once, that Prestimion for all his whirling and bobbing could not avoid them all. A hot line of pain ran along his left arm as Mandralisca's blade sliced into him. He swung about and dropped into a purely defensive stance as the poison-taster came at him again for a finishing stroke; and succeeded this time in beating the blade away, and even in regaining the offensive.

But Mandralisca seemed suddenly to be tiring now. He was like a spirited racer who was at his best in brief spurts, Prestimion discovered. His blinding speed was not matched by an equal stamina. The poison-taster had gambled everything on a terrifyingly intense all-out onslaught, but had expended himself without reaching his goal. His parries were less assured, now. His offensive thrusts were fewer and farther between. The malevolence of his gaze was tempered now by fatigue.

Sensing his advantage, Prestimion pressed forward, hoping to land a deciding stroke. For a moment he thought he had Mandralisca at his mercy. But then the battle line surged incoherently about him; he found himself swallowed up in the roaring madness of it and separated from the poison-taster by five or six shouting brawling men who passed between them. They swept him casually to one side as they hacked in a frenzy of blood-lust at each other, and moved on, all in a single group locked together by their fury; and when things cleared again there was no sight of his opponent.

Then Prestimion, as he paused to draw in deep breaths and looked around the field in the midst of this confusion, heard a great despairing cry suddenly go up, and a voice called out, "Prestimion is fallen! Prestimion is fallen!"

"Prestimion is fallen!" In an instant the cry was all over the field. "Prestimion is fallen!"

It was like a cold wind blowing across the battlefield. Its effect was felt everywhere. In an instant all the momentum of the battle, which had already been running toward Korsibar, shifted emphatically to his side. Hordes of his men now were moving downhill in triumph and those of Prestimion, disorganized and dispirited, were helplessly giving ground before them. What had merely been a retreat until now abruptly threatened to turn into a rout.

Gialaurys rode up from somewhere and leaned down toward Prestimion, who was watching in dismay, leaning on his sword, for he was not quite recovered yet from the exertions of his contest with Mandralisca. "Quick! Show yourself to them!" Gialaurys cried. And descended from his mount in a quick leap and thrust Prestimion up into its saddle as easily as if lifting a child.

Prestimion bared his head and stood high in his stirrups as he rode up and down along the ragged ranks of his men. "Here I am!" he shouted in a voice to split the sky, and found strength somewhere and drew his bow and sent a shaft uphill that brought one loyalist down, and then slew a second and a third, all three almost in a single instant. His arm trembled from the wound he had had at Mandralisca's hand, but the bow held steady.

Gialaurys, too, ran to and fro, shouting and pointing to show that Prestimion still lived. As the men caught sight of Prestimion's golden hair and saw him wielding his great bow, another cry went up: "Prestimion! Prestimion! Lord Prestimion lives!" They began to rally their courage. The disorderly retreat on the right was continuing; but elsewhere the rebel lines began to form again, and on the strong left flank Spalirises and Abrigant were beginning to move upward toward the massed ranks of the loyalist force.

But they would only be thrown back a second time, of that Prestimion was certain. He felt a moment of despair. His confidence had led him to overreach himself in planning this attack. There was no way to take the high ground from Korsibar. Some new strategy was needed on the spot.

And then Septach Melayn came riding by and said in Prestimion's ear, "Look you there, where our right flank's falling back. Can you believe it? Korsibar's infantrymen are following them down the hill!"

Prestimion stared, incredulous. It was like a gift from Providence.

"Why, then this is our moment," he said.

Indeed the whole side of Korsibar's shield-wall opposite the fleeing rebels had rashly broken its impenetrable rank and was giving pursuit down the slope, which forfeited them the great advantage of their position. A gift, yes, a gift of the Divine!

Prestimion sent word for the retreat to continue on the right and even to intensify, everyone without exception in that entire wing instructed to turn and flee, giving every sign of terror and panic. The feigned retreat drew the enemy, sensing victory, down the hill with them.

But at the same time Prestimion brought a host of fresh archers up on the left, ordering them to shoot their arrows high into the air so that they would come down behind the loyalists' shields. And at a signal Duke Miaule's cavalry-men came into the fray, riding swiftly uphill to surround those loyalists who had left their line, cutting them off from hope of escape.

The tide, which had run so strongly in Korsibar's favor only moments before, began quickly to turn back the other way.

In moments Korsibar's entire force was hovering on the brink of utter chaos as Miaule's men came at them unexpectedly from the side. That intimidating battery of energy-throwers had ceased its fire: in the frenzied melee the gunners no longer could distinguish friend from foe, and some had perished from the malfunctions of their own badly constructed instruments. And as the glare of their last few bolts died away, rebels on mountback came sweeping in over their fortification and fell upon them, slashing furiously with their swords. The loyalist ranks were broken and scattered in an instant. Everywhere on the field men were being trampled and cut down. Some, unable to rise, crawled toward safety. Others ran.

This was the time, Prestimion knew, to bring his ultimate weapon into play.

"The maguses!" he called. "Let them come forward!"

They came forward from the camp in a single group: old Gominik Halvor, whom Prestimion had summoned down from Triggoin for this, and his son Heszmon Gorse, and ten or a dozen other high wizards of the northern city, men famed throughout the world for their skill at the mystic arts. All of them were clad in their most solemn regalia and bore the implements of their trade in their arms. A great gasp of dismay went up from Korsibar's men higher on the hill as they saw this procession emerge from Prestimion's rear lines. Protected every step of the way by a phalanx of Prestimion's most trusted warriors, they advanced across the lowland plain. Then, to the accompaniment of trumpets and blaring kannivangitali, they gathered in a circle and set up a solemn droning chant and sent pyres of blue flame rising to the sky.

It was mid-morning now. The sun was bright overhead. But in a moment the sky began to grow thick with clouds and the sun seemed to dim, and then the blackness of a moonless midnight came over the field, and all those who fought there were wrapped so deep in that descending dark that they could barely see a dozen paces beyond their noses.

Prestimion's men had been warned of this. Korsibar's had not, and tumbled into a terrible confusion.

"Now!" Prestimion cried. "Now! Now! Up the hill again, and cut them to pieces!"

And from elsewhere on the battlefield, as the last shred of discipline among the bewildered loyalists was lost and they began to mill and churn in helpless disarray, came the roaring cry from Prestimion's captains: "Now! Now! Now! Now!"

Gialaurys, in the darkness, saw a place before him that was darker even than the rest; and as his eyes adjusted to the change that had come over the battlefield he realized that the darkness in front of him was a man who had the width of a wall, and he knew him to be his old nemesis the brutish Farholt.

"Would you wrestle again, my good lord, or shall we have it out with broadswords?" Gialaurys asked. "For now is your last moment at hand, one way or the other."

Farholt's answer was a harsh grunt and a great sweeping downward blow with his sword that Gialaurys barely managed to block as it emerged at him out of the dark; but Farholt struck again and again and yet again in devilish heat, three great clanging strokes that Gialaurys managed somehow to defend against, and then a fourth that rang against his helmet and knocked him staggering, as he had staggered that day when he wrestled with Farholt at the games in the Labyrinth. His mind was sent awhirl and he went wandering a few paces away, so that Farholt lost sight of him, and called out in the strange midday night, "Where are you, Gialaurys? Come: we have old business to finish here. For this is the final bout, and your carcass will feed the milufta-birds tonight."

"Business to finish indeed," said Gialaurys, still dizzied and awry, but inflamed now with red fury as never ever before. "Your corpse or mine, Farholt, meat for the miluftas in all truth. We will not both walk away from here." And went lurching back to the place where he thought Farholt to be, and grasped his sword with both hands and swung it around sideways through the air in the darkness with such force as can be mustered only once of a lifetime, for he was riven through and through with hatred and loathing and contempt for this man who had dogged his days so long. And felt his blade connect with the sword of Farholt that was trying to parry, and turn it. And went driving onward in that same single motion, and onward still, slicing through the armor about Farholt's waist as though it were mere paper, and cutting deep into Farholt's side and almost to his spine. Farholt made a single liquid sound and fell doubled up, and Gialaurys, standing over him, raised his sword up high again, but then even in the darkness came to understand there was no need to strike, for he had cut Farholt nearly in half with that one maddened swing.

In another part of the field Duke Svor, who had entered the battle because he saw no decent way to remain out of it, found himself jostling up against someone no taller than himself, and without pausing to think caught the man by his shoulder with one hand and pulled him up close against him, so that he could see into his face. And by the hard glint of his eyes he knew him to be none other than the icy-souled High Counsellor Farquanor, whom he had always detested more than any man in the world.

"I would not have thought to find you on this battlefield," Svor told him. "For you are no warrior, are you, Farquanor?"

"Nor you either, I would say. And yet we are here. Why is that, do you think?"

"I because I am loyal to my friend. And you, I suppose, because you hoped to win some further advantage from Korsibar by displaying your valor to him, such valor as there may be within you. Is that it, would you say?"

All this while Svor continued to hold the squirming Farquanor by the side of his collar, pressing down on the collarbone beneath.

"Let go of me, Svor. We have no quarrel, you and I. Let these great belching animals here slaughter each other; but why should we fight? We are natural allies of the spirit."

"Are we, now?" Svor laughed. "Tell me this, my dear beloved ally: was it you put Gonivaul up to pimping Thismet to me in the parley as the price of my defection? For that had the marks of your hand all over it."

"Let me go," said Farquanor again. "We can discuss these things some other time in some other place. Come, Svor, let's flee this field, and leave these madmen to their destruction."

"Ah, no. I will be a hero at last, I think. For the time has come for me to show that I can be valiant, at least when dealing with the likes of you."

With that he drew the sword that he had used so infrequently in his life until now, and took a step backward to run it through Farquanor; but just as Svor came lunging forward Farquanor produced a poniard that he had worn at his hip, and brought it upward at Svor's belly in a quick swift jab. It was only to be expected, Svor thought sadly, that Farquanor would have a little hidden weapon to call upon. But there was no avoiding it, and so he took the sharp point in his unguarded middle and felt the fire of it coursing like a river of molten metal through his vital organs. "Well done," Svor murmured. "You are yourself to the very last, Farquanor." And, saying that, drove his sword through Farquanor's gut so that its tip emerged on the far side, which drew them together in a close embrace. They fell to the ground together, still locked in that strange hug, and their bloods mingled on the battlefield.

★

Prestimion had lost his second mount, the one given him by Gialaurys, slain out from under him as he wheeled through the black noontime calling to his men. He continued on by foot, slinging his bow across his back and taking his sword in hand. Some light now had begun to come through once more as the spell of darkness weakened, and he saw all about him on the battlefield men dead and dying, and little battles going on here and there within the broader melee, and it seemed to him that his side had all the tide running with it. There was no sign any longer of that wall of men with shields Korsibar had stationed atop the hill, nor any fixed formations in back of them; the two armies had come together in mid-slope, muddled and chaotic, and the rebel forces appeared to be forming themselves in a circle around the shaken loyalists, pushing them ever tighter into a trap from which there was no escaping.

He sought for Septach Melayn, for Gialaurys, for Abrigant, for any familiar face. None of those could he find, but indeed shortly found someone familiar indeed, though not one to give him any joy. Coming up toward him out of the thinning darkness was Santirya Dambail, in splendid armor somewhat marred by mud and scratches. He carried a bare sword in one hand and some rough farmer's axe in the other. First the lackey and now the master, thought Prestimion. He was meeting with a surfeit of evil this day.

In the midst of that gory field Dantirya Sambail let forth a cheerful whoop.

"Well, cousin Prestimion, here we are! Shall we fight? Winner gets to be Coronal; for surely Korsibar has choked on his own bile by now, seeing his certain victory turned to ashes by your Triggoin sorcerers, and that leaves only you and me to contend for the crown. Sorcerers, Prestimion! Who would ever have thought it of you?"

And the Procurator laughed his most raucous laugh, and lifted the axe up on high, and swung it through the air.

The strong sweeping blow would have cut through Prestimion's arm at the shoulder, had it landed. But quickly Prestimion stepped forward and inward and put his sword up so that the hilt of it clanged against the handle of the descending axe and turned it aside; and then thrust his face up against that of Dantirya Sambail, with his eyes staring deep into the beautiful treacherous amethyst eyes of that ugly diabolic man.

In a low voice he said, "Put down the axe, cousin, and let there be an end to war between us. It is not in me to take your life; but I will if you force me to it."

"You are a generous man, Prestimion. Your soul is very large," said the Procurator with another boisterous guffaw, and his eyes became orbs of fierce purple fire. He leaned forward and downward with his shoulder against Prestimion, intending to throw him to the ground, for Dantirya Sambail was half a head taller than Prestimion and had perhaps twice the bulk. But Prestimion leaped swiftly back. His sword, a light rapier to the Procurator's heavy saber, had the same disadvantage of size that he himself did; but it was what he had, and he would use it.

*You are not Prestimion of Muldemar now,* he told himself. *You must be Septach Melayn, or else you are a dead man.*

For years Prestimion had studied Septach Melayn's swordsmanship with keen pleasure. It was a thing of utter beauty. It was poetry; it was music; it was mathematics. It was, also, a matter of quickness of wrist and keenness of eye and intelligent extension of arm. And Septach Melayn's natural grace and preternaturally elongated limbs gave him an innate advantage in all those aspects. Prestimion, short and compact and sturdy, was built to a different plan. But he would do what he could.

Before him stood the true author of all his grief—that much he understood now. Nothing unhappy had befallen him that Dantirya Sambail had not had had a hand in, somewhere. Prestimion felt himself grow hot with fury. Strike at him, he thought, and you are striking at all your misfortunes in a single thrust.

Dantirya Sambail came rushing at him with the axe again, and the saber held ready for the killing stroke after it. Prestimion stepped slightly to one side and pivoted, and then went darting boldly in under his ponderous opponent's onslaught, coming so close that the axe could not strike him. And even in those close quarters was able deftly to bring the tip of his sword straight upward into the pit of the Procurator's arm, piercing a path through nerve and muscle and tendon.

"Ha!" cried Dantirya Sambail in surprise and pain, and let the axe go clattering from his numbed hand. But there was enough presence of mind and sheer ferocity in him to bring the saber in his other hand around and strike Prestimion a terrible blow in the ribs with the flat of it, even jammed up against each other as they were. It knocked the breath from him and darkened his senses a moment, so that he went reeling back some five or six steps and came close to falling.

The Procurator ran heavily toward him and loomed over him, flushed and excited with the thrill of impending triumph, and jabbed at him with the saber. But it was a left-handed thrust poorly launched. Prestimion, though he was wincing from the pain in his battered side and the wound he had had earlier from Mandralisca, lifted his sword and brought it dancing through Dantirya Sambail's guard, probing for his heart and forcing him to move the saber aside to parry. And then with a quick reversal of direction that would have brought applause from Septach Melayn he drew the tip of the rapier along the inside of the Procurator's sword-arm, cutting a long bright red line down it from elbow to wrist.

Dantirya Sambail's sword fell clattering to the ground. Instantly Prestimion had the point of his own against the underside of Dantirya Sambail's outthrust jaw, where the soft flesh was.

"Go ahead," the Procurator said. "Shove it home, cousin!"

"What a pleasure that would be," said Prestimion. "But no. No, cousin, no." Not like this; not the slaughter of a prisoner, even this one. He could not. He *would* not. All his wrath had burned away. There had been enough killing for now. And Dantirya Sambail, evil though he was, was somehow much beloved in his own land of Zimroel. Prestimion would not want the hatred of the millions of people of Zimroel when he was Coronal.

He saw his brother Abrigant coming up out of the chaos of the field toward him, and Rufiel Kisimir of Muldemar, and four or five other men of his city with them. The poison-taster Mandralisca was with them, wounded and a prisoner, his wrists tied behind his back and one side of his face streaming red. He was glaring sullenly, as though he would gladly spit forth a tide of venom upon them all.

They observed Prestimion holding Dantirya Sambail at bay, and sped up beside him now, Abrigant seizing one of the Procurator's bloodied arms and Rufiel Kisimir the other and pulling them around hard behind his back.

"Strike, brother!" Abrigant cried. "What are you waiting for?"

"This is not the appointed hour of his death," said Prestimion quietly, putting down his sword. He drew breath, grimacing, and rubbed at his aching ribs. "Take him and bind him and put him under safe guard. He'll rest a time in the tunnels of Sangamor, and then the courts can have him. On some other day will he die, and not at my hands. Take the poison-taster, too. But see to it that they are kept in separate places far from one another." And walked away, leaving Dantirya Sambail astounded and gaping behind him.

★

Navigorn said, "We are lost, and no question of it. Our army is reduced to a rabble that can't even find the proper way to flee; Prestimion's men are everywhere around us and they know that victory is theirs. I see Farholt dead on the field, and Farquanor too, and many another. We should go to Prestimion and yield to him before more lives are lost, including our own."

Korsibar gave him an incredulous stare. "What? Surrender, is that what you advise, Navigorn?"

"I see no other path for us."

"This is not the first battle we've lost in this war."

"This is our worst defeat. And this time he'll take us both prisoner, and your whole Council as well."

"You no longer call me 'my lord,' I notice."

Navigorn made a sorrowful gesture. "What can I say? We have thrown our dice and the fall is against us. The game is over, Korsibar."

They were unbearable words. In his first hot rage Korsibar came close to raising his sword against him. But he held his hand and said simply, in the darkest and bleakest of voices, "I am still Coronal, Navigorn. There will be no surrender. And you are dismissed from my service."

"Yes," Navigorn said. "That I am."

He turned and walked swiftly away across the muddy bloodied field. Korsibar let his gaze follow after him for a long moment. He felt nothing. Nothing. He was moving into a place beyond all feeling, now. There was a cold numbness stealing over his body, traveling upward from his legs toward his heart, and from there to his brain.

*I never wanted to be king,* he thought. *It was put in my path, and I snatched it up as if in a dream.*

"What have you all done to me?" he said aloud. And then: "What have I done?"

It was a catastrophe beyond all prediction. Dead men lay

all around him. His maguses had told him that this would be a day of victory, that all the final reckonings would be made this day, that by nightfall Majipoor would have only one Coronal and the world would be at peace again. In his rashness he had allowed himself to draw a clear assurance of his triumph from those prophecies.

But now—look—look—

He moved numbly onward through the scene of the disaster, his face set like stone. Then the unmistakable form of Sanibak-Thastimoon rose up before him in the shadowy afterdawn of the muddy darkness that Prestimion's sorcerers had called down upon them.

"You," Korsibar said. Some heat returned to his soul. His voice was thick with rage. "You lied to me!"

"Never, my lord."

"A day of victory, you said. A day of final reckonings."

"And so it is," said the Su-Suheris coolly. "Were we not correct in our prognostication? For surely there has been a victory here today."

Korsibar's eyes widened. He saw now how Sanibak-Thastimoon had gulled him: or rather, how he had gulled himself by reading what he wished to hear into the mage's words.

He swept his arm across the field before them. "How did you allow this to befall us? Was there nothing you could have done to protect us? Look, Sanibak-Thastimoon, look! We are entirely put to rout!"

"He had the mightiest sorcerers of Majipoor arrayed among his troops. I am not invincible, my lord."

"You could have warned me that he'd somehow snuff out the sun at noon. We might have taken some steps to hold our line when the darkness came."

"May I remind you, my lord, that your line had already

broken of its own accord, before Prestimion's wizards had even brought the darkness down upon—"

It was too much. Korsibar felt all the woe of this dreadful day falling upon him like a crumbling mountain dropping from the sky, and pain and sorrow and guilt overflowed in him beyond control. They had all led him into this disaster, had seduced him into it step by step—this alien magus, first and foremost of all—and now they had left the monstrous shame of it to stain his name forever.

His sword sprang into his hand; he plunged wildly forward, slashing at the sorcerer, only to find nothing before him but a curtain of blackness, a zone of deeper darkness within the artificial dusk all about them. "Where are you?" he called. "Where did you go, Sanibak-Thastimoon!"

It seemed to him that he saw a movement at his side, and began to turn. But he was too late. The Su-Suheris, still half-concealed by his spell, had come around behind him: and now, as Korsibar flailed furiously at shadows with his sword, the sorcerer's dagger slipped into his back just below the cage of his ribs, gliding upward until it touched the tip of his heart.

All strength left him at that touch. Korsibar fell forward and knelt in the mud, choking and gasping, looking dazedly downward at the sight of his own blood cascading from his lips.

Through the thickening mists of his consciousness he heard a voice calling to him.

"Brother? *Brother!*"

It was Thismet, suddenly, swirling up out of nowhere like an apparition. Korsibar raised his head—it was a terrible effort—and stared at her with dimming eyes.

She knelt beside him.

"What are you—doing—here—?" he asked indistinctly.

"I came to urge you to yield to Prestimion while there was still a chance," she said.

He smiled and nodded, but said nothing.

Her arm was about his shoulder; but he was sagging heavily and she barely had the strength to hold him upright. Three harsh gusts of breath came from him, and then the death-rattle. Gently Thismet released him and he sprawled out before her. "Oh, Korsibar—Korsibar—so it was all for nothing, brother, all for nothing—"

She looked toward Sanibak-Thastimoon, who still stood to one side, arms folded, watching in silence.

"You!" she cried. "You're responsible for all this, with all your talk of how he was born for greatness, how he'd shake the world. Well, he shook it all right. But now look! Look!" She snatched up Korsibar's sword, that had fallen from his nerveless hand, and brandished it frenziedly at the sorcerer in a wild thrust. Sanibak-Thastimoon, towering far above her, swept it aside with his own as though it were a mere stick. And, stepping swiftly toward her, drove deep into her the dagger with which he had killed Korsibar, plunging it home between her breasts. She fell without a sound.

Then someone said nearby, "What, Sanibak-Thastimoon? Both of them dead, brother and sister too? And at your hand, is it?"

It was Septach Melayn. He came darting forward in an easy lope, sword in hand, long body already stretching into the posture of attack. The Su-Suheris retreated once more behind his spell of darkness; but Septach Melayn unhesitatingly swept his blade like a scythe through that zone of night before him, at the last moment imparting a twist to his wrist with the utmost of his dexterity and executing a horizontal cut into the dark nothingness. At once the black cloud vanished and Sanibak-Thastimoon stood revealed before him, with the eyes of his leftward head gaping wide in shock and the other fork of the long column of his two-pronged neck ending in nothing but a bloody stump.

Septach Melayn's sword flashed once more, and the job was done.

Pensively he looked down at the bodies of Korsibar and Thismet, lying side by side in the bloody mud of Beldak marsh. The starburst crown of Majipoor lay in the mud also, just next to Korsibar. Septach Melayn snatched it up, and wiped the mud from it as best he could with the cuff of his sleeve, and slung it around his left forearm as though it were a quoit. And went trudging across the field to look for Prestimion. There was much news he had to tell him, both good and sad.

# 10

All the remainder of that day and the next, and the one after that, the gathering of the dead went on, and the burials took place, one grave next to another all across the marsh of Beldak below Thegomar Edge. For there was no way to transport such a great host of corpses to their native cities for interment. It was best simply to let them rest here.

Prestimion felt little joy over his victory. They had brought him the lists of those who had been lost that day, and he studied them in sorrow. On his side the Count of Enkimod had fallen, and Earl Hospend, and Kanif of Kanifimot and Talauus of Naibilis, and some threescore more, at least, among his captains; and who knew how many soldiers of the line? And above all others there was Svor, whose body had been found entangled with that of dead Farquanor. That loss alone stung Prestimion more than all the rest together who had fallen in the battle that day, except for one.

He had heard from Septach Melayn how that one had died: as strangely as she had lived, encircled to the last by treason and betrayal. So he would never learn what his life with her might have been. He found a flower somewhere and laid it on her grave, and tried to seal away in some corner of his heart the pain that he knew he would always feel.

Korsibar he buried by Thismet's side, feeling as much regret for the one as for the other, though it was a different quality of regret for each: for one had been a great man wasted, and the other had been a woman he had learned unexpectedly and too late to love. But there had been greatness in her too, and it was gone now.

Farquanor—Farholt—well, who would miss them? But a whole host of Korsibar's other captains had fallen with them, such men as Mandrykarn and Venta, and Gapithain Duke of Korsz, and the good-hearted Kanteverel of Bailemoona and Sibellor of Banglecode; and also Count Iram, and good Earl Kamba of Mazadone who had taught the art of archery to him, and Vimnad Gezelstad, among many another. Prestimion would have had them all alive again, if he could, for they had each in their own way been ornaments to the world and he pitied them for the fatal decision they had made to cast in their lots with Korsibar.

A waste, a waste, a ghastly terrible waste. And all of it unnecessary, Prestimion thought.

If only it could all be undone—if only—

Of those of Korsibar's faction who had survived the battle, he pardoned all. The war was over: there were no more enemies and the world had but one Coronal. Navigorn of Hoikmar came before him first, and knelt and made the starburst with unfeigned sincerity. He had seen his error and repented of it, he said; and Prestimion believed him. After him came Oljebbin and Serithorn and Gonivaul, and Prestimion pardoned them too, though he had no illusions concerning those three. But he was determined that the bitterness of this war would be washed away. The faster these seething hatreds were put to rest, the better for all.

"And you," Prestimion said, looking down at the Vroon Thalnap Zelifor. "How many more shifts of allegiance can you make, now that there's only one allegiance to have?" And laughed, for there was no malice in his heart today. "You told me when we were in the west country that you were going back to the Castle, as I recall, only for the sake of fetching your mind-reading devices, and then would return with them to help me in my war."

"I cast the runes for you, and they said you were doomed," replied the Vroon. "And the report from Lake Mavestoi confirmed it: you had been lost in the flood. Why, then, should I go to the aid of a dead man? But my runes were wrong, and so were the reports."

"How glib you are, Thalnap Zelifor. You always have an answer. Well, I'll put you and your machines where they can do no more harm." He beckoned forth an evil-faced little thin-lipped man with shifty eyes, who had been in Duke Svor's service. Prestimion had never liked having him around, and there was no need to keep him now. "You," he said. "What's your name?"

"Barjazid, my lord."

"Barjazid. Very well, Barjazid. Escort this Vroon to the Castle, Barjazid, and clean out his entire workshop of mysterious mind-reading devices, and pack them and him up and take them both to Suvrael."

"To Suvrael, my lord?"

"To Suvrael. To distant torrid Suvrael. On pain of your life, Barjazid, get him to Suvrael, and let him play no tricks on you along the way. I'll punish nobody for what has happened in this war, but there are some I would not like to have about me any closer than Suvrael, and Thalnap Zelifor's one of them. He can't be trusted even in a world that has no enemies. Take him to Suvrael for me, Barjazid. And see that he stays there."

The little man gave Prestimion a starburst and a squinty-eyed look of devotion.

"It will be done, my lord."

He gathered Thalnap Zelifor up, and moved away.

Prestimion stood for a time in silence, looking out once more over the battlefield. A great weariness was on him, as though he had crossed the parched sun-smitten Valmambra two or three times this one day. He was Coronal of Majipoor now: the world had been given into his hand. Why was there no joy in that thought?

Well, the joy would come, he supposed. He would see vast Majipoor green and glowing, as he had in his vision when it was only a little ball he could hold in his hands; he would cherish it and nurture it and protect it and its people until the day of his death.

But just for now, this day of triumph and loss, there was only the weariness, and the sadness. He understood that he had been through a strange test these past few years, and he would be a while recovering from it. Had he expected to have the crown handed to him on a platter, as it had been to so many Coronals before him? That had not been his destiny, apparently. He had discovered that it was necessary to earn that crown a thousand times over, through all that he had suffered in the Labyrinth and in the desert and on the field of battle, and no doubt he must go on earning it and earning it all the days of his life to come.

A test, yes, all of it. Of his strength, of his will, of his patience, of his skill. Of his quality as a man. Of his right to be king. If he had suffered more than most of his predecessors to become Coronal, there must have been a reason for it. And out of his suffering would come something of value. He could not dare to believe otherwise. He would not. There had been a purpose to it all. It was unthinkable that there had not been.

Unthinkable.

And as Prestimion stood at the edge of the battlefield thinking these things, and reflecting on all he had experienced in this long harsh quest for the crown, and all he had learned, and all the ways he had changed, a strange idea came to him that sent a shiver of astonishment along his spine: a way to return the world, as much of it as could be returned, to what it had been before Korsibar had seized the throne.

Perhaps—perhaps—however difficult, however immense the task might be—

Surely it was worth the attempt, at any rate.

Turning to Septach Melayn and Gialaurys, he said, "Clear this place of everyone but you two, and bring Gominik Halvor and his son Heszmon Gorse before me. I have one last chore for them to do before we begin our march to Castle Mount."

It was night, now. The new star that had come into the heavens after the death of Prankipin stood high in the sky, bathing them in its eerie blue-white light. Lord Korsibar's star, men had called it, when it first appeared. But it was Lord Prestimion's star now.

The two mages took their places before him and waited, and Prestimion, when he had arranged his thoughts to suit himself, said, "I will ask a thing from you now that will be the greatest conjuration that has ever been worked in all the history of the world; and it is my hope that you will not refuse me."

"We already know what you want, my lord," said Heszmon Gorse.

"Yes. You would, I suppose. And can it be done?"

"It will be an even greater effort than you can suppose."

"Yes," said Prestimion. "Even now, I have no real knowledge of what's possible and what is not in your art, your science, whatever I must call it. But the thing has to be done. The world has suffered a terrible wound. We have never had such a war as this; and I want it expunged wholly from our history, which means from the minds of all who live today, and all those who follow after. I want the bloody stain of it to be wiped away as though it never had been."

"This will take our every skill," said Heszmon Gorse, "and even more, perhaps."

"You'll have the Lady Kunigarda of the Isle to assist you: her dream-machinery, all the personnel at her command at the Isle of Dreams, who have the means for reaching into many millions of minds at once. She is on our way toward us now with her special devices in her train, I am told, and will be with us soon. And also you will have the services of every magus you require: every last one of them will be at your command, if you desire it, the grandest convocation of the masters of your arts that has ever been brought together. You will see to it that when the task is done, what has happened will never have happened. No one will have memory of the existence of Korsibar and Thismet the children of Confalume and Roxivail: *no one*. This usurpation will have been unhappened. The world will believe that I have been Coronal from the day of Prankipin's death. And those who died in the battles of these civil wars will be deemed to have died in other ways, for other reasons, it matters not what they are, except that they must not have died on the field of battle. The world must forget this war. The world must come to believe it never occurred."

"A universal obliteration, that is what you require of us," said Gominik Halvor.

"Universal except for myself, and Gialaurys here, and Septach Melayn. We three must remember it to our last days, so that we can be sure that nothing like it will happen again. But we are to be the only ones."

"Even we, we are to forget, once the job is done?" the old magus asked.

Prestimion gave him a long steady look.

"Even you," he said.

And so it was done; and so the world was born clean and fresh again out of the blood and ashes of the war between the rival Coronals; and in the springtime of the new year Lord Prestimion made the journey once more down the River Glayge from the Castle to the Labyrinth to pay his respects to the Pontifex Confalume, whom insofar as anyone knew he had succeeded several years before as Coronal, in the hour of the death of the old Pontifex Prankipin.

He found Confalume robust and full of vigor, looking like a man only a little beyond the prime of his years, who might still be forceful enough to carry the responsibilities of a Coronal, if time had not moved him along to the senior throne. This was the strong vital Confalume that Prestimion remembered from the old days at the Castle, not the shattered one of the early hours of his reign that no one now recalled except a few.

Yes, this was a thriving Confalume, a Confalume rejuvenated. Most joyously did he embrace Prestimion, and they sat side by side on the thrones that were maintained for the two monarchs in the underground city, and spoke for a long while of such urgent matters of the realm as presently needed to be discussed between them.

"You will not be so long in coming the next time, will you?" Confalume asked, when those matters had been satisfactorily dealt with. He rose and put his hands on Prestimion's shoulders and looked squarely into Prestimion's eyes. "You know what pleasure it gives me whenever I see you, my son."

Prestimion smiled at that. And Confalume said, "Yes, 'my son,' is what I said. For I had always wanted a son, but the Divine would never send me one. But now I have one. For by law the Coronal is deemed the son by adoption of the Pontifex, is he not? And so you are my son, Prestimion. You are my son!" And then Confalume said, after a time, "You should marry, Prestimion. Surely there's a woman somewhere who'd be a fitting consort for you."

"Surely there is," said Prestimion, "and may it be that I

find her, some day. And let us say no more on that subject now, eh, father? In time there'll be a wife for me, that I know. But I am not quite ready just yet, I think, to set about searching for her." And the thought came to him of the woman that he and only two others in all the world knew had once existed. But of her he could say nothing, and never would again.

So it was that the great war of the usurpation had its end and vanished from the minds of the people of Majipoor, and the world's great age began anew. The reign of Confalume and Lord Prestimion together lasted many years, until Confalume in the immensity of his years was gathered to the Source, and Prestimion became Pontifex himself after a long and glorious time as Coronal, which the world would long remember and cherish. And the man Lord Prestimion chose to be Coronal when it was time for him to go to the Labyrinth was named Dekkeret, whose reign would be a glorious one also. But that is another story.

All Pan Books are available at your local bookshop or newsagent, or can be ordered direct from the publisher. Indicate the number of copies required and fill in the form below.

Send to:          Macmillan General Books C.S.
                  Book Service By Post
                  PO Box 29, Douglas I-O-M
                  IM99 1BQ

or phone:         01624 675137, quoting title, author and credit card number.

or fax:           01624 670923, quoting title, author, and credit card number.

or Internet:      http://www.bookpost.co.uk

Please enclose a remittance* to the value of the cover price plus 75 pence per book for post and packing. Overseas customers please allow £1.00 per copy for post and packing.

*Payment may be made in sterling by UK personal cheque, Eurocheque, postal order, sterling draft or international money order, made payable to Book Service By Post.

Alternatively by Access/Visa/MasterCard

Card No. | | | | | | | | | | | | | | | | | | | | |

Expiry Date | | | | | | | | | | | | | | | | | | | | |

Signature _____

Applicable only in the UK and BFPO addresses.

While every effort is made to keep prices low, it is sometimes necessary to increase prices at short notice. Pan Books reserve the right to show on covers and charge new retail prices which may differ from those advertised in the text or elsewhere.

NAME AND ADDRESS IN BLOCK CAPITAL LETTERS PLEASE

Name _____

Address _____

_____

_____

_____

                                                    8/95

Please allow 28 days for delivery.
Please tick box if you do not wish to receive any additional information. ☐